Caleb Carr was born in 1955 and lives in New York. This is his first novel.

Also by Caleb Carr

CASING THE PROMISED LAND
AMERICA INVULNERABLE (with James Chace)
THE DEVIL SOLDIER

The Alienist

CALEB CARR

WARNER BOOKS

A *Warner* Book

First published in the United States in 1994
by Random House, Inc.
First published in Great Britain in 1994
by Little, Brown and Company

This edition published by Warner Books in 1995
Reprinted 1995

A CIP catalogue record for this book
is available from the British Library.

ISBN 0 7515 1295 8

Printed in England by Clays Ltd, St Ives plc

Warner Books
A Division of
Little, Brown and Company (UK)
Brettenham House
Lancaster Place
London WC2E 7EN

Note

Prior to the twentieth century, persons suffering from mental illness were thought to be "alienated," not only from the rest of society but from their own true natures. Those experts who studied mental pathologies were therefore known as *alienists*.

PART I
Perception

Whilst part of what we perceive comes through our senses from the object before us, another part (and it may be the larger part) always comes out of our own mind.

> *William James,*
> The Principles of Psychology

> *These bloody thoughts,*
> *from what are they born?*

> *Piave,*
> *from Verdi's* Macbeth

Chapter 1

Theodore is in the ground.

The words as I write them make as little sense as did the sight of his coffin descending into a patch of sandy soil near Sagamore Hill, the place he loved more than any other on earth. As I stood there this afternoon, in the cold January wind that blew off Long Island Sound, I thought to myself: of course it's a joke. Of course he'll burst the lid open, blind us all with that ridiculous grin and split our ears with a high-pitched bark of laughter. Then he'll exclaim that there's work to do – 'action to get!' – and we'll all be martialed to the task of protecting some obscure species of newt from the ravages of a predatory industrial giant bent on planting a fetid factory on the little reptile's breeding ground. I was not alone in such fantasies; everyone at the funeral expected something of the kind, it was plain on their faces. All reports indicate that most of the country and much of the world feel the same way. The notion of Theodore Roosevelt being gone is that – unacceptable.

In truth, he'd been fading for longer than anyone wanted to admit, really since his son Quentin was killed in the last days of the Great Butchery. Cecil Spring-Rice once droned, in his best British blend of affection and needling, that Roosevelt was throughout his life 'about six'; and Herm Hagedorn noted that after Quentin was shot out of the sky in the summer of 1918 'the

5

boy in Theodore died.' I dined with Laszlo Kreizler at Delmonico's tonight, and mentioned Hagedorn's comment to him. For the remaining two courses of my meal I was treated to a long, typically passionate explanation of why Quentin's death was more than simply heartbreaking for Theodore: he had felt profound guilt, too, guilt at having so instilled his philosophy of 'the strenuous life' in all his children that they often placed themselves deliberately in harm's way, knowing it would delight their beloved father. Grief was almost unbearable to Theodore, I'd always known that; whenever he had to come to grips with the death of someone close it seemed he might not survive the struggle. But it wasn't until tonight, while listening to Kreizler, that I understood the extent to which moral uncertainty was also intolerable to the twenty-sixth president, who sometimes seemed to think himself Justice personified.

Laszlo Kreizler ... He didn't want to attend the funeral, though Edith Roosevelt would have liked him to. She has always been truly partial to the man she calls 'the enigma,' the brilliant doctor whose studies of the human mind have disturbed so many people so profoundly over the last forty years. Kreizler wrote Edith a note explaining that he did not much like the idea of a world without Theodore, and, being as he's now sixty-four and has spent his life staring ugly realities full in the face, he thinks he'll just indulge himself and ignore the fact of his friend's passing. Edith told me today that reading Kreizler's note moved her to tears, because she realized that Theodore's boundless affection and enthusiasm had been strong enough to touch a man whose removal from most of human society seemed to almost everyone else unbridgeable.

Some of the boys from the *Times* wanted me to come to a memorial dinner tonight, but a quiet evening with Kreizler seemed much the more appropriate thing. It wasn't out of nostalgia for any shared boyhood in New York that we raised our glasses, because Laszlo and Theodore didn't actually meet until Harvard. No, Kreizler and I were fixing our hearts on the spring of 1896 – nearly a quarter-century ago! – and on a series of events that still seems too bizarre to have occurred even in this city. By the end of our dessert and Madeira (and how poignant to have

Caleb Carr

a memorial meal in Delmonico's, good old Del's, now on its way out like the rest of us, but in those days the bustling scene of some of our most important encounters), the two of us were laughing and shaking our heads, amazed to this day that we were able to get through the ordeal with our skins; and still saddened, as I could see in Kreizler's face and feel in my own chest, by the thought of those who didn't.

There's no simple way to describe it. I could say that in retrospect it seems that all three of our lives, and those of many others, led inevitably and fatefully to that one experience; but then I'd be broaching the subject of psychological determinism and questioning man's free will – reopening, in other words, the philosophical conundrum that wove irrepressibly in and out of the nightmarish proceedings, like the only hummable tune in a difficult opera. Or I could say that during the course of those months, Roosevelt, Kreizler, and I, assisted by some of the best people I've ever known, set out on the trail of a murderous monster and ended up coming face to face with a frightened child. No, there's only one way to do it, and that's to tell the whole thing, going back to that first grisly night and that first butchered body; back even further, in fact, to our days with Professor James at Harvard. Yes, to dredge it all up and put it finally before the public – that's the way.

The public may not like it; in fact, it's been concern about public reaction that's forced us to keep our secret for so many years. Even the majority of Theodore's obituaries made no reference to the event. In listing his achievements as president of the Board of Commissioners of New York City's Police Department from 1895 to 1897, only the *Herald* – which goes virtually unread these days – tacked on uncomfortably, 'and of course, the solution to the ghastly murders of 1896, which so appalled the city.' Yet Theodore never claimed credit for that solution. True, he had been open-minded enough, despite his own qualms, to put the investigation in the hands of a man who *could* solve the puzzle. But privately he always acknowledged that man to be Kreizler.

He could scarcely have done so publicly. Theodore knew that the American people were not ready to believe him, or even to hear the details of the assertion. I wonder if they are now? Kreizler doubts it. I told him I intended to write the story, and he gave me one of his sardonic chuckles and said that it would only frighten and repel people, nothing more. The country, he declared tonight, really hasn't changed much since 1896, for all the work of people like Theodore, and Jake Riis and Lincoln Steffens, and the many other men and women of their ilk. We're all still running, according to Kreizler – in our private moments we Americans are running just as fast and fearfully as we were then, running away from the darkness we know to lie behind so many apparently tranquil household doors, away from the nightmares that continue to be injected into children's skulls by people whom Nature tells them they should love and trust, running ever faster and in ever greater numbers toward those potions, powders, priests, and philosophies that promise to obliterate such fears and nightmares, and ask in return only slavish devotion. Can he truly be right . . . ?

But I wax ambiguous. To the beginning, then!

Chapter 2

An ungodly pummeling on the door of my grandmother's house at 19 Washington Square North brought first the maid and then my grandmother herself to the doorways of their bedrooms at two o'clock on the morning of March 3, 1896. I lay in bed in that no-longer-drunk yet not-quite-sober state which is usually softened by sleep, knowing that whoever was at the door probably had business with me rather than my grandmother. I burrowed into my linen-cased pillows, hoping that he'd just give up and go away.

'Mrs. Moore!' I heard the maid call. 'It's a fearful racket – shall I answer it, then?'

'You shall not,' my grandmother replied, in her well-clipped, stern voice. 'Wake my grandson, Harriet. Doubtless he's forgotten a gambling debt!'

I then heard footsteps heading toward my room and decided I'd better get ready. Since the demise of my engagement to Miss Julia Pratt of Washington some two years earlier, I'd been staying with my grandmother, and during that time the old girl had become steadily more skeptical about the ways in which I spent my off-hours. I had repeatedly explained that, as a police reporter for the *New York Times*, I was required to visit many of the city's seamier districts and houses and consort with some less than savory characters; but she remembered my youth too well to accept that admittedly strained story. My homecoming

9

deportment on the average evening generally reinforced her suspicion that it was state of mind, not professional obligation, that drew me to the dance halls and gaming tables of the Tenderloin every night; and I realized, having caught the gambling remark just made to Harriet, that it was now crucial to project the image of a sober man with serious concerns. I shot into a black Chinese robe, forced my short hair down on my head, and opened the door loftily just as Harriet reached it.

'Ah, Harriet,' I said calmly, one hand inside the robe. 'No need for alarm. I was just reviewing some notes for a story, and found I needed some materials from the office. Doubtless that's the boy with them now.'

'John!' my grandmother blared as Harriet nodded in confusion. 'Is that you?'

'No, Grandmother,' I said, trotting down the thick Persian carpet on the stairs. 'It's Dr. Holmes.' Dr. H.H. Holmes was an unspeakably sadistic murderer and confidence man who was at that moment waiting to be hanged in Philadelphia. The possibility that he might escape before his appointment with the executioner and journey to New York to do my grandmother in was, for some inexplicable reason, her greatest nightmare. I arrived at the door of her room and gave her a kiss on the cheek, which she accepted without a smile, though it pleased her.

'Don't be insolent, John. It's your least attractive quality. And don't think your handsome charms will make me any less irritated.' The pounding on the door started again, followed by a boy's voice calling my name. My grandmother's frown deepened. 'Who in blazes is that and what in blazes does he want?'

'I believe it's a boy from the office,' I said, maintaining the lie but myself perturbed about the identity of the young man who was taking the front door to such stern task.

'The office?' my grandmother said, not believing a word of it. 'All right, then, answer it.'

I went quickly but cautiously to the bottom of the staircase, where I realized that in fact I knew the voice that was calling for me but couldn't identify it precisely. Nor was I reassured by the fact that it was a young voice – some of the most vicious thieves and killers I'd encountered in the New York of 1896 were mere striplings.

'Mr. Moore!' The young man pleaded again, adding a few healthy kicks to his knocks. 'I must talk to Mr. John Schuyler Moore!'

I stood on the black and white marble floor of the vestibule. 'Who's there?' I said, one hand on the lock of the door.

'It's me, sir! Stevie, sir!'

I breathed a slight sigh of relief and unlocked the heavy wooden portal. Outside, standing in the dim light of an overhead gas lamp – the only one in the house that my grandmother had refused to have replaced with an electric bulb – was Stevie Taggert, 'the Stevepipe,' as he was known. In his first eleven years Stevie had risen to become the bane of fifteen police precincts; but he'd then been reformed by, and was now a driver and general errand boy for, the eminent physician and alienist, my good friend Dr. Laszlo Kreizler. Stevie leaned against one of the white columns outside the door and tried to catch his breath – something had clearly terrified the lad.

'Stevie!' I said, seeing that his long sheet of straight brown hair was matted with sweat. 'What's happened?' Looking beyond him I saw Kreizler's small Canadian calash drawn by a black gelding called Frederick. The animal was, like Stevie, bathed in sweat, which steamed in the early March air. 'Is Dr. Kreizler with you?'

'The doctor says you're to come with me!' Stevie answered in a rush, his breath back. 'Right away!'

'But where? It's two in the morning—'

'Right away!' He was obviously in no condition to explain, so I told him to wait while I put on some clothes. As I did so, my grandmother shouted through my bedroom door that whatever 'that peculiar Dr. Kreizler' and I were up to at two in the morning she was sure it was not respectable. Ignoring her as best I could, I got back outside, pulling my tweed coat close as I jumped into the carriage.

I didn't even have time to sit before Stevie lashed at Frederick with a long whip. Falling back into the dark maroon leather of the seat, I thought to upbraid the boy, but again the look of fear in his face struck me. I braced myself as the carriage careened at a somewhat alarming pace over the cobblestones of Washington Square. The shaking and jostling eased only marginally as we turned onto the long, wide slabs of Russ pavement on Broadway. We were heading downtown, downtown and east, into that quarter of Manhattan where Laszlo Kreizler plied his trade and where life became, the further one progressed into the area, ever cheaper and more sordid: the Lower East Side.

For a moment I thought that perhaps something had happened to Laszlo. Certainly that would have accounted for the fretful way in which Stevie whipped and drove Frederick, an animal I knew him at most times to treat with complete kindness. Kreizler was the first human being who'd ever been able to get more than a bite or a punch out of Stevie, and he was certainly the only reason the young fellow wasn't still in that Randalls Island establishment so euphemistically known as the 'Boys' House of Refuge.' Besides being, as the Police Department had put it, 'a thief, pickpocket, drunkard, nicotine fiend, feeler' – the member of a banco team that lures dupes to the site of the game – 'and congenitally destructive menace,' all by the time he was ten, Stevie had attacked and badly maimed one of the guards on Randalls Island, who he claimed had tried to assault him. ('Assault,' in the newspaper language of a quarter-century ago, almost invariably meaning rape.) Because the guard had a wife and family, the boy's honesty, and finally his sanity, had been questioned – which was when Kreizler, as one of the foremost experts of the day in forensic psychiatry, had made his entrance. At Stevie's sanity hearing Kreizler painted a masterful picture of the boy's life on the streets since the age of three, when he had been abandoned by his mother, who put an opium habit above caring for her son. The judge had been impressed by Kreizler's speech, and skeptical of the injured guard's testimony; but he would only agree to release Stevie when Kreizler offered to take the boy in and vouched for his future conduct. I thought Laszlo quite crazy, at the time; but there was no doubting that in just over a year Stevie had become a very different youth. And, like almost everyone who worked for Laszlo, the boy was devoted to his patron, despite that peculiar quality of emotional distance that made Kreizler so perplexing to many who knew him.

Caleb Carr

'Stevie,' I called out over the din of the carriage wheels hitting the worn edges of the granite Russ slabs, 'where *is* Dr. Kreizler? Is he all right?'

'At the Institute!' Stevie answered, his blue eyes wide. Laszlo's work was based in the Kreizler Institute for Children, a combination of school and research center that he had founded during the eighties. I was about to ask what he was doing there at such an hour but swallowed the query when we charged headlong through the still-busy intersection of Broadway and Houston Street. Here, it was once sagely remarked, you could fire a shotgun in any direction without hitting an honest man.

'Then are we going to the Institute, too?' I shouted. But Stevie only reined the horse sharply left at Spring Street, where we disrupted business outside two or three concert saloons, houses of assignation where prostitutes who passed themselves off as dancers made arrangements for later meetings at cheap hotels with hapless fools who were generally from out of town. From Spring Stevie made his way to Delancey Street – which was in the midst of being widened to accommodate the expected traffic of the new Williamsburg Bridge, whose construction had only recently begun – and then we flew on past several darkened theaters. Echoing down from each passing side street I could hear the desperate, demented sounds of the dives: filthy holes that sold rotgut liquor laced with everything from benzine to camphor for a nickel a glass atop a dirty plank that passed for a bar. Stevie did not slacken the pace – we were headed, it seemed, for the very edge of the island.

I made one last attempt at communication: 'Aren't we going to the Institute?!'

Stevie shook his head in reply, then cracked the long horsewhip again. I shrugged, sitting back to hang on to the sides of the carriage and wonder what could have frightened this boy so very badly.

Delancey Street carried us past the shuttered stalls of fruit and clothing merchants and on into one of the worst of the Lower East Side, the neighborhood near the waterfront just above Corlears Hook. A vast, maudlin sea of small shacks and shoddy new tenements stretched away to either side of us. The area was a stewpot of different immigrant cultures and languages, the Irish predominating to the south of Delancey Street and the Hungarians farther north, near Houston. An occasional church of some denomination or other was visible among the rows upon rows of dismal residences, which even on this crisp morning were draped with lines of laundry. Some pieces of clothing and bedding, frozen almost solid, twisted in the wind stiffly at what might have seemed unnatural angles; but in truth, nothing in such a place could truly be called unnatural. We were in a neighborhood that knew little of laws, man-made or otherwise, a neighborhood that gave joy to visitors and residents only when they were allowed to view its recession in the distance after making their escape.

Near the end of Delancey Street the smells of sea and fresh water, along with the stench of refuse that was simply dumped off the edge of Manhattan every day, mingled to produce the distinctive aroma of that tidal pool we call the East River. A large structure soon slanted up before us: the ramp approach to the nascent Williamsburg Bridge. Without pausing, and much to my dismay, Stevie crashed onto the boarded roadway, the horse's hooves and carriage wheels clattering far more loudly against wood than they had against stone.

An elaborate maze of steel supports below the roadway bore us dozens of feet up into the night air. As I wondered what our destination could possibly be – for the towers of the bridge were nothing like completed, and the structure's opening was years away – I began to make out what looked like the walls of a large Chinese temple suddenly looming ahead. Composed of huge granite blocks and crowned by two squat watchtowers, each of which was ringed by a delicate steel walkway, this peculiar edifice was the Manhattan-side anchor of the bridge, the structure that would eventually hold one set of ends of the enormous steel suspension cables that would support the central span. In a way, though, my impression of it as a temple was not far off the mark: like the Brooklyn Bridge, whose Gothic arches I could see silhouetted against the night sky to the south, this new roadway over the East River was a place where many workers' lives had been sacrificed to the faith of Engineering, which in the past fifteen years had produced towering marvels all over Manhattan.

What I did not know was that the blood sacrifice that had been made atop the western anchor of the Williamsburg Bridge on that particular night was of a very different nature.

Near the entrance to the watchtowers, standing under the flimsy light of a few electric bulbs and bearing portable lanterns, were several patrolmen whose small brass insignia marked them as coming from the Thirteenth Precinct (we had passed the station house moments before on Delancey Street). With them was a sergeant from the Fifteenth, a fact that immediately struck me as odd – in two years of covering the criminal beat for the *Times*, not to mention a childhood in New York, I'd learned that each of the city's police precincts guarded its terrain jealously. For the Thirteenth to have summoned a man from the Fifteenth indicated that something significant was going on.

Stevie finally reined the gelding up near this group of blue greatcoats, then leapt from his seat and took the hard-breathing horse by the bit, leading him to the side of the roadway near an enormous pile of construction materials. The boy eyed the cops with familiar distrust. The sergeant from the Fifteenth Precinct, a tall Irishman whose pasty face was notable only because he did not sport the broad mustache so common to his profession, stepped forward and studied Stevie with a threatening smile.

'That's little Stevie Taggert, ain't it?' he said with a brogue. 'You don't suppose the commissioner's called me all this way to box your ears for ya, do ya, Stevie, ya little shit?'

I stepped down from the carriage and approached Stevie, who shot the sergeant a sullen glance. 'Pay no mind, Stevie,' I said, as sympathetically as possible. 'Stupidity goes with the leather helmet.' The boy smiled a bit. 'But I wouldn't mind your telling me what I'm doing here.'

Stevie nodded to the northern watchtower. 'Up there. The doctor says you're to go up.'

I started for the doorway in the granite wall, but Stevie stayed by the horse. 'You're not coming?'

The boy shuddered and turned away, pulling a battered cigarette out of his pocket. 'I seen it once. And if I never see such again I'll be done right.'

I felt increased apprehension as I turned and headed for the doorway, where I was stopped by the arm of the police sergeant. 'And who might you be, with the young Stevepipe driving you around past all respectable hours? This is a crime scene, y'know.' I gave the man my name and occupation, at which he grinned and showed me an impressive gold tooth. 'Ah, a gentleman of the press – and the *Times*, no less! Well, Mr. Moore, I've just arrived myself. Urgent call, apparently no other man they could trust. Spell it F-l-y-n-n, sir, if you will, and don't go labeling me no roundsman. Full sergeant. Come on, we'll head up together. Mind you behave, young Stevie, or I'll have you back on Randalls Island faster'n spit!'

Stevie turned back to the horse. 'Why don't you go chase yourself,' the boy mumbled, just loud enough for the sergeant to hear. Flynn spun with a look of lethal anger, but, remembering my presence, checked himself. 'Incorrigible, that one, Mr. Moore. Can't imagine what a man like you's doing in his presence. Need him as a contact with the underworld, no doubt. Up we go, sir, and mind, it's dark as the pit in here!'

So it was. I stumbled and tripped my way up a rough flight of stairs, at the top of which I could make out the form of another leatherhead. A roundsman from the Thirteenth Precinct turned on our approach and then called to someone else:

'It's Flynn, sir. He's here.'

We came out of the stairs into a small room littered with sawhorses, planks of wood, buckets of rivets and bits of metal and wiring. Wide windows gave a full view of the horizon in every direction – the city behind us, the river and the partially completed towers of the bridge before us. A doorway led out onto the walkway that ran around the tower. Near the doorway stood a slit-eyed, bearded sergeant of detectives named Patrick Connor, whom I recognized from my visits to Police Head-quarters on Mulberry Street. Next to him, looking out over the river with his hands clasped behind his back, rocking on the balls of his feet, was a much more familiar figure: Theodore.

'Sergeant Flynn,' Roosevelt said without turning. 'It's ghastly work that has prompted our call, I'm afraid. Ghastly.'

My discomfort suddenly heightened when Theodore spun to face us. There was nothing unusual in his appearance: an

Caleb Carr

expensive, slightly dandy checked suit of the kind that he fancied in those days; the spectacles that were, like the eyes behind them, too small for his tough, square head; the broad mustache bristling below the wide nose. Yet his visage was excessively odd, nonetheless. Then it occurred to me: his teeth. His numerous, usually snapping teeth – they were nowhere in sight. His jaws were clamped shut in what seemed passionate anger, or remorse. Something had shaken Roosevelt badly.

His dismay seemed to grow when he saw me. 'What – Moore! What in thunder are you doing here?'

'I'm glad to see you, too, Roosevelt,' I managed through my nervousness, extending a hand.

He accepted it, though for once he didn't loosen my arm from its socket. 'What – oh, I am sorry, Moore. I – delighted to see you, of course, delighted. But who told you—?'

'Told me what? I was abducted and brought here by Kreizler's boy. On his orders, without so much as a word of explanation.'

'Kreizler!' Theodore murmured in soft urgency, glancing out the window with a confounded and even fearful look that was not at all typical of him. 'Yes, Kreizler's been here.'

'Been? Do you mean he's gone?'

'Before I arrived. He left a note. And a report.' Theodore revealed a piece of paper clutched in his left hand. 'A preliminary one, at any rate. He was the first doctor they could find. Although it was quite hopeless . . .'

I took the man by the shoulder. 'Roosevelt. What is it?'

'To be sure, Commissioner, I wouldn't mind knowing meself,' Sergeant Flynn added, with quaint obsequiousness that was repellant. 'We get little enough sleep at the Fifteenth, and I'd just as soon—'

'Very well,' Theodore said, steeling himself. 'How are your stomachs, gentlemen?'

I said nothing, and Flynn made some absurd joke about the wide range of grisly sights he'd encountered in his life; but Theodore's eyes were all hard business. He indicated the door to the outer walkway. Detective Sergeant Connor stepped aside and then Flynn led the way out.

My first thought on emerging, despite my apprehension, was

that the view from the walkway was even more extraordinary than that from the tower windows. Across the water lay Williamsburg, once a peaceful country town but now rapidly becoming a bustling part of the metropolis that was destined, within months, to officially evolve into Greater New York. To the south, again, the Brooklyn Bridge; in the southwestern distance the new towers of Printing House Square, and below us the churning, black waters of the river—

And then I saw it.

Chapter 3

Odd, how long it took my mind to make any sense of the image. Or perhaps not; there was so much so very wrong, so very out of place, so ... distorted. How could I have expected myself to grasp it quickly?

On the walkway was the body of a young person. I say 'person' because, though the physical attributes were those of an adolescent boy, the clothes (little more than a chemise that was missing a sleeve) and facial paint were those of a girl. Or, rather, of a woman, and a woman of dubious repute at that. The unfortunate creature's wrists were trussed behind the back, and the legs were bent in a kneeling position that pressed the face to the steel of the walkway. There was no sign of any pants or shoes, just one sock hanging pathetically from a foot. But what had been done to the body ...

The face did not seem heavily beaten or bruised – the paint and powder were still intact – but where once there had been eyes there were now only bloody, cavernous sockets. A puzzling piece of flesh protruded from the mouth. A wide gash stretched across the throat, though there was little blood near the opening. Large cuts crisscrossed the abdomen, revealing the mass of the inner organs. The right hand had been chopped neatly off. At the groin there was another gaping wound, one that explained the mouth – the genitals had been cut away and stuffed between the jaws. The buttocks, too, had been shorn off, in what appeared large ...

19

one could only call them carving strokes.

In the minute or two that it took me to note all these details the vista around me faded into a sea of indistinguishable blackness, and what I thought was the churning progress of a ship turned out to be my own blood in my ears. With the sudden realization that I might be sick, I spun to grasp the railing of the walkway and hung my head out over the water.

'Commissioner!' Connor called, stepping out of the watchtower. But it was Theodore who got to me first, in a quick bound.

'Easy, now, John,' I heard him say, as he supported me with that wiry yet remarkably strong boxer's frame of his. 'Breathe deeply.'

As I followed his instructions I heard a long, trailing whistle from Flynn, who continued to stare at the body. 'Well, now,' he said, addressing the corpse without sounding particularly concerned. 'Somebody has done for you, young Georgio-called-Gloria, haven't they? You're a hell of a mess.'

'Then you do know the child, Flynn?' Theodore said, leaning me against the wall of the watchtower. Steadiness was returning to my head.

'That I do, Commissioner.' Flynn seemed in the dim light to be smiling. 'Though it was no child, this one, not if childhood be judged by behavior. Family name Santorelli. Must've been, oh, thirteen years old, or thereabouts. Georgio, it was called originally, and since it began working out of Paresis Hall, it called itself Gloria.'

'It?' I said, wiping cold sweat from my forehead with the cuff of my coat. 'Why do you call him "it"?'

Flynn's smile became a grin. 'Sure, and what would you call it, Mr. Moore? It warn't no male, not to judge by its antics – but God didn't create it female, teither. They're all its to me, that breed.'

Theodore's hands went forcefully to his hips, the fingers curling up into fists – he'd taken the measure of Flynn. 'I'm not interested in your philosophical analysis of the situation, Sergeant. Whatever else, the boy was a child and the child has been murdered.'

Flynn chuckled and glanced again at the body. 'No arguing *that*, sir!'

'Sergeant!' Theodore's voice scratched a little more than usual as he barked at Flynn, who stood up straight. 'Not another word out of you, sir, unless it's to answer my questions! Understood?'

Flynn nodded; but the cynical, amused resentment that all longtime officers in the department felt for the commissioner who in just one year had stood Police Headquarters and the whole chain of departmental command on its ear remained evident in the slightest curl of his upper lip. Theodore could not have missed it.

'Now then,' Roosevelt said, his teeth clicking in that peculiar way of theirs, cutting each word out of his mouth. 'You say the boy was called Georgio Santorelli, and that he worked out of Paresis Hall – that's Biff Ellison's establishment on Cooper Square, correct?'

'That'd be the one, Commissioner.'

'And where would you guess that Mr. Ellison is at this moment?'

'At this—? Why, in the Hall itself, sir.'

'Go there. Tell him I want him at Mulberry Street this morning.'

For the first time, Flynn looked concerned. 'Now, begging your pardon, Commissioner, but Mr. Ellison's not the sort of man to take that kind of a summons sweetly.'

'Then arrest him,' Theodore said, turning away and staring out at Williamsburg.

'Arrest him? Sure, Commissioner, if we arrested every owner of a bar or disorderly house that harbors boy-whores, just because one gets roughed up or even murdered, why, sir, we'd never—'

'Perhaps you would like to tell me the real reason for your resistance,' Theodore said, those busy fists of his starting to flex behind his back. He walked right up and put his spectacles in Flynn's face. 'Is Mr. Ellison not one of your primary sources of graft?'

Flynn's eyes widened, but he managed to draw himself up haughtily and affect wounded pride. 'Mr. Roosevelt, I've been on the force for fifteen years, sir, and I think I know how this city works. You don't go harassing a man like Mr. Ellison just because some little piece of immigrant trash finally gets what's coming to it!'

That was all, and I knew that was all – and it was fortunate for Roosevelt that I did, for had I not shot over at just that moment to grab his arms he would certainly have beaten Flynn into a bloody pulp. It was a struggle, though, to keep hold of those strong arms. 'No, Roosevelt, no!' I whispered in his ear. 'It's what his kind want, you know that! Attack a man in uniform and they'll have your head, there'll be nothing the mayor can do about it!'

Roosevelt was breathing hard, Flynn was once again smiling, and Detective Sergeant Connor and the roundsman were making no move toward physical intervention. They knew full well that they were precariously positioned at that moment between the powerful wave of municipal reform that had swept into New York with the findings of the Lexow Commission on police corruption a year earlier (of which Roosevelt was a strong exponent) and the perhaps greater power of that same corruption, which had existed for as long as the force and was now quietly biding its time, waiting until the public wearied of the passing fashion of reform and sank back into business as usual.

'A simple choice for you, Flynn,' Roosevelt managed, with dignity that was notably unimpaired for a man so full of rage. 'Ellison in my office or your badge on my desk. This morning.'

Flynn gave up the struggle sullenly. 'Sure. *Commissioner.*' He spun on his heel and headed back down the watchtower steps, mumbling something about a 'damned society boy playing at policeman.' One of the cops who had been positioned below the tower then appeared, to say that a coroner's wagon had arrived. Roosevelt told them to wait a few minutes and then dismissed Connor and the roundsman as well. We were now alone on the walkway, except for the ghoulish remains of what had once been, apparently, another of the many desperately troubled young people who every season were spat up by the dark, miserable tenement ocean that stretched away from us to the west. Forced to use whatever means they could – and Georgio Santorelli's had been the most basic – to survive on their own, such children were more *completely* on their own than anyone unfamiliar with the New York City ghettos of 1896 could possibly imagine.

'Kreizler estimates that the boy was killed earlier tonight,' Theodore said, glancing at the sheet of paper in his hand. 'Something about the temperature of the body. So the killer may still be in the area. I have men combing it. There are a few other medical details, and then this message.'

He handed the paper to me, and on it I saw scrawled in Kreizler's agitated block hand: 'ROOSEVELT: TERRIBLE ERRORS HAVE BEEN MADE. I WILL BE AVAILABLE IN THE MORNING, OR FOR LUNCH. WE SHOULD BEGIN – THERE IS A TIMETABLE.' I tried for a moment to make sense of it.

'It's fairly tiresome of him to be so cryptic' was the only conclusion I could reach.

Theodore managed a chuckle. 'Yes. I thought so, too. But I think I understand, now. It was examining the body that did it. Do you have any idea, Moore, how many people are murdered in New York every year?'

'Not really.' I gave the corpse another curious glance. 'If I were to guess I'd say hundreds. Perhaps one or two thousand.'

'So would I,' Roosevelt answered. 'But I, too, would only be guessing. Because we don't even pay attention to most of them. Oh, the force bends every effort if the victim is respectable and well-to-do. But a boy like this, an immigrant who turned to the flesh trade – I'm ashamed to say it, Moore, but there's no precedent for looking into such a case, as you could see in Flynn's attitude.' His hands went to his hips again. 'But I'm getting tired of it. In these vile neighborhoods husbands and wives kill each other, drunkards and dope fiends murder decent working people, prostitutes are slaughtered and commit suicide by the score, and at most it's seen as some sort of grimly amusing spectacle by outsiders. That's bad enough. But when the victims are children like this, and the general reaction is no different than Flynn's – by God, I get to feeling warlike with my own people! Why, already this year we've had three such cases, and not so much as a whisper from the precincts or the detectives.'

'Three?' I asked. 'I only know about the girl at Draper's.'

Shang Draper ran a notorious brothel at Sixth Avenue and Twenty-fourth Street, where customers could purchase the favors of children (mostly girls, but the occasional boy as well). In January a ten-year-old girl had been found beaten to death in one of the brothel's small paneled rooms.

'Yes, and you only know of *that* one because Draper had been slow with his graft payments,' Roosevelt said. The bitter battle against corruption waged by the current mayor, Colonel William L. Strong, and lieutenants such as Roosevelt had been courageous, but they had not succeeded in eradicating the oldest and most lucrative of police activities: the collection of graft from the operators of saloons, concert halls, disorderly houses, opium dens, and every other palace of vice. 'Someone in the Sixteenth Precinct, I still don't know who, made the most of that story to the press as a method of turning the screws. But the other two victims were boys like this, found in the streets and therefore useless in trying to pressure their panderers. So the stories went untold . . .'

His voice faded into the slap of the water below us and the steady rush of the river breeze. 'Were they both like this?' I asked.

'Virtually. Throats cut. And they'd both been gotten at by the rats and birds, like this one. It didn't make an easy sight.'

'Rats and birds?'

'The eyes,' Roosevelt answered. 'Detective Sergeant Connor puts that down to rats, or carrion pickers. But the rest of this . . .'

There hadn't been anything in the papers about these other two killings, although there was nothing surprising about that. I wondered for a moment what my own editors at the *Times* would have done if I'd suggested running a story about a young boy who made his living painting himself like a female whore and selling his body to grown men (many of them ostensibly respectable men), who was horribly butchered in a dark corner of the city. I would have been lucky to escape with a dismissal; forced internment at the Bloomingdale Asylum would have been the more likely result.

'I haven't spoken to Kreizler in years,' Roosevelt mused at length. 'Although he sent me a very decent note when' – for a moment his words became awkward – 'that is, at a very difficult time.'

I understood. Theodore was referring to the death of his first wife, Alice, who had passed away in 1884 after giving birth to their daughter, who bore the same name. His loss that day had been doubly staggering, for his mother had died within hours of his wife. Theodore had dealt with the tragedy typically, sealing off the sad, sacrosanct memory of his bride, and never mentioning her again.

He tried to rouse himself, and turned to me. 'Still, the good doctor must have called you here for a reason.'

'I'm deuced if I can see it,' I replied with a shrug.

'Yes,' Theodore said with another affectionate chuckle. 'As inscrutable as any Chinaman, our friend Kreizler. And perhaps, like him, I've been among the strange and awful too long, these past months. But I think I may be able to divine his purpose. You see, Moore, I've had to ignore all the other killings like this one, because there's no desire to investigate them in the department. Even if there were, none of our detectives is trained to make sense of such butchery. But this boy – justice can only be blind so long. I've a scheme, and I think Kreizler has a scheme – and I think *you're* the one to bring us together.'

'*Me?*'

'Why not? Just as you did at Harvard, when we all met.'

'But what am I supposed to do?'

'Bring Kreizler to my office. Late morning, as he says. We'll share thoughts and see what can be done. But mind you, be discreet – as far as anyone else is concerned, it's a social reunion of old friends.'

'Damn it, Roosevelt, *what* is a social reunion of old friends?'

But I'd lost him to the rapture of a plan. He ignored my plaintive question, took a deep breath, barreled his chest and appeared far more comfortable than he had to that point. 'Action, Moore – we shall respond with action!'

And then he grabbed me around the shoulders in a tight hug, his enthusiasm and moral certainty all back in full force. As for my own sense of certainty, any kind of certainty, I waited in vain for its arrival. All I knew was that I was being drawn into something that involved the two most passionately determined men I'd ever known – and that thought offered me no comfort as we went back downstairs to Kreizler's carriage, leaving the body of the pitiable Santorelli boy alone on that tower, high in the freezing sky that was still untouched by any trace of dawn.

Chapter 4

Cold, cutting March rain came with the morning. I rose early after too little sleep to find that Harriet had, mercifully, prepared me a breakfast of strong coffee, toast, and fruit (which she, drawing on the experience of a family full of inebriates, believed essential for anyone who imbibed often). I settled into my grandmother's glass-enclosed nook, overlooking her still-dormant rose garden in the rear yard, and decided to digest the morning edition of the *Times* before trying to telephone the Kreizler Institute. With the rain pattering on the copper roof and glass walls around me, I inhaled the fragrance of the few plants and flowers that my grandmother kept alive year-round and took in the paper, trying to reestablish contact with a world that, in light of the previous night's events, seemed suddenly and disturbingly removed.

SPAIN IS FULL OF WRATH, I learned; the question of American support for the nationalist rebels in Cuba was continuing to cause the vicious, crumbling regime in Madrid much worry. Boss Tom Platt, the town's cadaverous old Republican mastermind, was assailed by the editors of the *Times* for trying to prostitute the imminent reorganization of the city into a Greater New York – one that would include Brooklyn and Staten Island, as well as Queens, the Bronx, and Manhattan – to his own nefarious purposes. The approaching Democratic and Republican conventions both promised to center around the question of bimetallism, or whether or not America's solid old gold standard should be sullied by the introduction of silver-based currency. Three hundred and eleven black Americans had taken ship for Liberia; and the Italians were rioting because their troops had been badly defeated by Abyssinian tribesmen on the other side of that dark continent.

Momentous as all this no doubt was, it held little interest for a man in my mood. I turned to lighter matters. There were bicycling elephants at Proctor's Theatre; a troop of Hindu fakirs at Hubert's Fourteenth Street Museum; Max Alvary was a brilliant Tristan at the Academy of Music; and Lillian Russell was *The Goddess of Truth* at Abbey's. Eleanora Duse was 'no Bernhardt' in *Camille*, and Otis Skinner in *Hamlet* shared her penchant for weeping too easily and too often. *The Prisoner of Zenda* was in its fourth week at the Lyceum – I had seen it twice and thought for a moment about going again that night. It was a grand escape from the worries of the usual day (not to mention the grim sights of an extraordinary night): castles with watery moats, sword battles, a diverting mystery, and stunning, swooning women . . .

Yet even as I thought of the play, my eyes wandered to other items. A man on Ninth Street who had once cut his brother's throat while drunk, drank again and shot his mother; there were still no clues in the particularly vicious murder of artist Max Eglau at the Institution for the Improved Instruction of Deaf Mutes; a man named John Mackin, who had killed his wife and mother-in-law and then tried to end his own life by cutting his throat, had recovered from the wound but was now trying to starve himself. The authorities had convinced Mackin to eat by showing him the frightful force-feeding apparatus that would otherwise be used to keep him alive for the executioner . . .

I threw the paper aside. Taking in a last heavy gulp of sweet black coffee, and then a section of a peach shipped from Georgia, I redoubled my resolve to get to the Lyceum box office. I had just started back for my room to dress when the telephone let out with a loud clang, and I heard my grandmother in her morning room exclaim 'Oh, God!' in alarm and anger. The telephone bell did that to her, yet she never entertained any suggestion that it be removed, or at least muffled.

Harriet appeared from the kitchen, her soft, middle-aged features specked with soap bubbles. 'It's the telephone, sir,' she said, wiping her hands on her apron. 'Dr. Kreizler calling.'

Pulling my Chinese robe tighter, I headed for the little wooden box near the kitchen and took up the heavy black receiver, putting it to my ear as I placed my other hand on the anchored mouthpiece. 'Yes?' I said. 'Is that you, Laszlo?'

'Ah, so you're awake, Moore,' I heard him say. 'Good.' The sound was faint, but the manner was, as always, energetic. The words bore the lilt of a European accent: Kreizler had emigrated to the United States as a child, when his German father, a wealthy publisher and 1848 republican, and Hungarian mother had felt monarchist persecution to begin a somewhat celebrated life in New York as fashionable political exiles. 'What time does Roosevelt want us?' he asked, without any thought that Theodore might have refused his suggestion.

'Before lunch!' I said, raising my volume as if to overcome the faintness of his voice.

'Why the devil are you shouting?' Kreizler said. 'Before lunch, eh? Excellent. Then we've time. You've seen the paper? The bit on this man Wolff?'

'No.'

'Read it while you're dressing, then.'

I glanced at my robe. 'How did you know that I—'

'They have him at Bellevue. I'm supposed to assess him, anyway, and we can ask a few additional questions, to determine if he's connected to our business. Then on to Mulberry Street, a brief stop at the Institute, and lunch at Del's – squab, I should think, or the pigeon crepinettes. Ranhofer's poivrade sauce with truffles is superb.'

'But—'

'Cyrus and I will go directly from my house. You'll have to take a hansom. The appointment's for nine-thirty – try not to be late, will you, Moore? We mustn't waste a minute in this affair.'

And then he was gone. I walked back to the nook, picked up the *Times* again, and leafed through it. The article was on page eight:

Henry Wolff had been drinking in the tenement apartment of

his neighbor, Conrad Rudesheimer, the night before. The latter's five-year-old daughter had entered the room, and Wolff proceeded to make some comments that Rudesheimer found unsuitable for the ears of a young girl. The father objected; Wolff pulled a gun and shot the girl in the head, killing her, then fled. He had been captured, several hours later, wandering aimlessly – near the East River. I dropped the paper again, momentarily struck by a premonitory feeling that the events of the previous night atop the bridge tower had been only an overture.

Back in the hallway I ran headlong into my grandmother, her silver hair perfectly coiffed, her gray and black dress unimpeachably neat, and her gray eyes, which I had inherited, glaring. 'John!' she said in surprise, as if ten other men were staying in her house. 'Who in the world was on the telephone?'

'Dr. Kreizler, Grandmother,' I said, bounding up the stairs.

'Dr. Kreizler!' she called after me. 'Well, dear! I've had about enough of that Dr. Kreizler for one day!' As I closed the door of my bedroom and began to dress, I could still hear her: 'If you ask me, he's awfully peculiar! And I don't put much stock in his being a doctor, either. That Holmes man was a doctor, too!' She stayed in that vein while I washed, shaved, and scrubbed my teeth with Sozodont. It was her way; and for all that it was annoying, to a man who, within recent memory, had lost what he was sure was his only chance at domestic happiness, it was still better than a lonely apartment in a building full of other men who had resigned themselves to solitary lives.

Snatching a gray cap and a black umbrella as I dashed out the front door, I made for Sixth Avenue at a brisk pace. The rain was coming down much harder now, and a particularly stiff wind had begun to blow. When I reached the avenue the force of air suddenly changed directions as it swept under the tracks of the New York Elevated Railroad line, which ran above either side of the street just inside the sidewalks. The shift blasted my umbrella inside out, along with those of several other members of the throng that was hustling under the tracks; and the combined effect of the heightening wind, the rain, and the cold was to make the usually bustling rush hour seem absolute pandemonium. Making for a cab as I struggled with my cumbersome, useless umbrella, I was cut off by a merry young couple who maneuvered me out of their way with no great finesse and clambered quickly into my hansom. I swore loudly against their progeny and shook the dead umbrella at them, prompting the woman to scream in fright and the man to fix an anxious eye on me and tell me I was mad – all of which, considering my destination, gave me a good chuckle and made the wet wait for another hansom much easier. When one came around the corner of Washington Place I did not wait for it to stop, but leapt in, shut the doors around my legs, and hollered to the driver to get me to the Insane Pavilion at Bellevue: not the kind of order any cabbie wants to hear. The look of dismay on his face as we drove off gave me another little laugh, so that by the time we passed in front of the Italianate arcades and towers of Madison Square Garden I didn't even mind the feel of wet tweed against my legs. The square, solemn, red brick buildings of Bellevue appeared on the horizon, and in just a few more minutes we crossed First Avenue and pulled up behind a large black ambulance on the Twenty-sixth Street side of the hospital grounds, near the entrance to the Insane Pavilion. I paid my cabbie off and headed in.

The Pavilion was a simple building, long and rectangular. A small, uninviting vestibule greeted visitors and internees, and beyond this, through the first of many iron doors, was a wide corridor running down the center of the building. Twenty-four 'rooms' – really cells – opened off of the corridor, and separating these cells into two wards, female and male, were two more sliding, studded iron doors at the corridor's midway point. The Pavilion was used for observation and evaluation, primarily of persons who had committed violent acts. Once their sanity (or lack of it) had been determined and official reports were received, the internees were shipped out to other, even less inviting institutions.

As soon as I was inside the vestibule I heard the usual shouts and howls – some coherent protests, some simply wails of madness and despair – coming from the cells beyond. At the same instant I spotted Kreizler; odd, how strongly the sight of him has always been associated, in my mind, with such sounds. As usual, his suit and coat were black, and as often he was reading the music notices in the *Times*. His black eyes, so much like a large bird's, flitted about the paper as he shifted from one foot to the other in sudden, quick movements. He held the *Times* in his right hand, and his left arm, underdeveloped as the result of a childhood injury, was pulled in close to his body. The left hand occasionally rose to swipe at his neatly trimmed mustache and the small patch of beard under his lower lip. His dark hair, cut far too long to meet the fashion of the day, and swept back on his head, was moist, for he always went hatless; and this, along with the bobbing of his face at the pages before him, only increased the impression of some hungry, restless hawk determined to wring satisfaction from the worrisome world around him.

Standing next to Kreizler was the enormous Cyrus Montrose, Laszlo's valet, occasional driver, effective bodyguard, and alter ego. Like most of Kreizler's employees, Cyrus was a former patient, one who made me more than a little nervous, despite his apparently controlled manner and appearance. That morning he was dressed in gray pants and a tightly buttoned brown jacket, and his broad, black features did not seem even to register my approach. But as I came closer he tapped Kreizler on the arm and pointed my way.

'Ah, Moore,' Kreizler said, taking a chained watch from his vest with his left hand and extending his right with a smile. 'Splendid.'

'Laszlo,' I answered, shaking his hand. 'Cyrus,' I added, with a nod that was barely returned.

Kreizler indicated his newspaper as he checked the time. 'I'm somewhat irritated with your employers. Yesterday evening I saw a brilliant *Pagliacci* at the Metropolitan, with Melba and Ancona – and all the *Times* can talk about is Alvary's Tristan.' He paused to study my face. 'You look tired, John.'

'I can't imagine why. Tearing around in an uncovered carriage in the middle of the night is usually so restful. Would you mind telling me what I'm doing here?'

'A moment.' Kreizler turned to an attendant in a dark blue uniform and box cap who lounged in a straight-backed wooden chair nearby. 'Fuller? We're ready.'

'Yes sir, Doctor,' the man answered, taking an enormous ring

Caleb Carr

of large keys from his belt and starting for the doorway to the central corridor. Kreizler and I fell in to follow, Cyrus remaining behind like a waxwork.

'You *did* read the article, didn't you, Moore?' Kreizler asked, as the attendant unlocked and opened the doorway to the first ward. With the opening the howls and shouts from the cells became almost deafening and quite unnerving. There was little light in the windowless corridor, only that which a few over-worked electric bulbs could offer. Some of the small observation windows in the imposing iron doors of the cells were open.

'Yes,' I answered at length, very uneasily. 'I read it. And I understand the possible connection – but why do you need *me*?'

Before Kreizler could answer, a woman's face suddenly appeared in the first door to our right. Her hair, though pinned up, was unkempt, and the expression of her worn, broad features was one of violent outrage. That expression changed in an instant, however, when she saw who the visitor was. 'Dr. Kreizler!' she said in a hoarse but passionate gasp.

At that the train of reaction was propelled into high speed: Kreizler's name spread down the corridor from cell to cell, inmate to inmate, through the walls and iron doors of the women's ward and on into the men's. I'd seen this happen several times before, in different institutions, but it was no less remarkable on each occasion: the words were like the flow of water over coals, taking away crackling heat and leaving only a steaming whisper.

The cause of this singular phenomenon was simple. Kreizler was known throughout the patient, as well as the criminal, medical, and legal, communities in New York to be the man whose testimony in court or at a sanity hearing could determine, more than that of any other alienist of the day, whether a given person was sent to prison, to the somewhat less horrifying confines of a mental institution, or back out onto the streets.

Kreizler's reaction to the inmates' behavior was no less disconcerting, for one was left only to imagine what experiences in his life and career could have implanted in him the ability to walk through such a place and witness such desperate performances (all peppered by measured yet passionate pleas of 'Dr. Kreizler, I must talk with you!' 'Dr. Kreizler, please, I am not like these others!') without submitting to fear, revulsion, or despair. As he moved in measured strides down the long corridor, his brows drew together over his gleaming eyes, which shot quickly from side to side, cell to cell, with a look of sympathetic admonishment: as if these people were errant children. At no point did he allow himself to address any of the inmates, but this refusal was not cruel; quite the contrary, for to speak to any one would only have raised that unfortunate person's hopes, perhaps unrealistically, while dashing those of the other supplicants. Any patients present who had been in madhouses or prisons before, or who had been under observation for an extended period at Bellevue, knew that this was Kreizler's practice; and they made their most emphatic pleas with their eyes, aware that it was only with the organ of sight that Kreizler would acknowledge them.

We passed through the sliding iron doors and into the men's ward, and followed the attendant Fuller to the last cell on the left. He stood to the side and opened the small observation window in the heavily banded door. 'Wolff!' he called. 'Visitors for you. Official business, so behave.'

Kreizler stood before the window looking inward, and I watched over his shoulder. Inside the small, bare-walled cell a man sat on a rough cot, under which lay a dented steel chamber pot. Heavy bars covered the one small window, and ivy obscured the little external light that tried to enter. A metal pitcher of water and a tray bearing a bit of bread and an oatmeal-encrusted bowl lay on the floor near the man, whose head was in his hands. He wore only an undershirt and woolen pants without a belt or suspenders (suicide being the worry). Heavy shackles were clamped around his wrists and ankles. When he lifted his face, a few seconds after Fuller's call, he revealed a pair of reddened eyes that reminded me of some of my worst mornings; and his deeply lined, whiskered face bore an expression of detached resignation.

'Mr. Wolff,' Kreizler said, watching the man carefully. 'Are you sober?'

'Who wouldn't be?' the man answered slowly, his words indistinct, 'after a night in this place?'

Kreizler closed the small iron gate that covered the window and turned to Fuller. 'Has he been drugged?'

Fuller shrugged uncomfortably. 'He was raving when they brought him in, Dr. Kreizler. Seemed more than just drunk, the superintendent said, so they jabbed him full of chloral.'

Kreizler sighed in deep irritation. Chloral hydrate was one of the banes of his existence, a bitter-tasting, neutrally colored, somewhat caustic compound that slowed the rate of the heart and thus made the subject singularly calm – or, if used as it was in many saloons, almost comatose and an easy target for robbery or kidnapping. The body of the medical community, however, insisted that chloral did not cause addiction (Kreizler violently disagreed); and at twenty-five cents a dose, it was a cheap and convenient alternative to wrestling a patient into chains or a leather harness. It was therefore used with abandon, especially on mentally disturbed or simply violent subjects; but in the twenty-five years since its introduction, its use had spread to the general public, who were free, in those days, to buy not only chloral, but morphine, opium, cannabis, indica, or any other such substance at any drugstore. Many thousands of people had destroyed their lives by freely surrendering to chloral's power to 'release one from worry and care, and bring on healthful sleep' (as one manufacturer put it). Death by overdose had become common; more and more suicides were connected to chloral use; and yet the doctors of the day continued blithely to insist on its safety and utility.

'How many grains?' Kreizler asked, exchanging weariness for annoyance – he was aware that administration of the drug was neither Fuller's job nor his fault.

'They began with twenty,' the attendant answered sheepishly. 'I told them, sir, I told them you were scheduled for the evaluation and that you'd be angry, but – well, you know, sir.'

'Yes,' Kreizler answered quietly, 'I know.' Which made three of us – and what we knew was that on hearing of Kreizler's slated appearance and probable objections, the Pavilion's superintendent had almost certainly doubled the dose of chloral and significantly decreased Wolff's ability to participate in the kind of assessment Kreizler liked to make, which involved many probing questions and was ideally conducted on a subject free of the effects of drugs or alcohol. Such was the general feeling among his colleagues, particularly those of the older generation, toward Kreizler.

'Well,' Laszlo announced, 'there's nothing to do – we are here, Moore, and time presses.' I thought immediately about the strange reference to 'a timetable' in Kreizler's note to Roosevelt the night before; but I said nothing as he unbolted the door and pulled at its considerable weight. 'Mr. Wolff,' Kreizler announced, 'we must talk.'

For the next hour I sat through Kreizler's examination of this vague, disoriented man, who held as firmly as the chloral hydrate would allow to the notion that if he had truly erased most of young Louisa Rudesheimer's head with his pistol – and we assured him that he had – then he must be insane, and should of course be sent to an asylum rather than to prison or the gallows. Kreizler took careful note of this attitude but for the moment did not discuss the case itself. Instead he ran through a long list of seemingly unconnected questions about Wolff's past, his family, friends, and childhood. The questions were deeply personal and in any normal setting would have seemed presumptuous and even offensive; and the fact that Wolff's reactions to Kreizler's inquiries were less violent than most men's was almost certainly due to his being drugged. But the absence of anger also indicated a lack of precision and forthrightness in the responses, and the interview seemed destined for a premature end.

But not even Wolff's chemically induced calm could be maintained when Kreizler finally began to ask him about Louisa Rudesheimer. Had Wolff harbored any sexual feelings toward the girl? Laszlo inquired, with a bluntness not often heard in discussions of such subjects. Were there other children in his building or in his neighborhood toward whom he did harbor such feelings? Did he have a lady friend? Did he visit disorderly houses? Did he find himself sexually drawn to young boys? Why had he shot the girl and not stabbed her? Wolff was at first bewildered by all this, and appealed to the attendant, Fuller, asking whether or not he must answer. Fuller, with somewhat lascivious glee, made it plain that he must, and Wolff complied, for a time. But after half an hour of it he staggered to his feet, rattled his manacles and swore that no man could force him to

Caleb Carr

participate in such an obscene inquisition. He declared defiantly that he would rather face the hangman; at which point Kreizler stood and stared straight into Wolff's eyes.

'I fear that in New York State, the electrical chair is increasingly usurping the gallows, Mr. Wolff,' he said evenly. 'Although I suspect that, based on your answers to my questions, you will find that out for yourself. God have mercy on you, sir.'

Kreizler and I walked back down the Pavilion's main corridor as Fuller rebolted the door to Wolff's cell. The quiet pleas of the other patients began again, but we were soon through them. Once we were out and in the vestibule, the shouts and howls behind us gained in volume once more.

'I believe we can dismiss him, Moore,' Kreizler said, quietly and wearily, as he pulled on a pair of gloves that Cyrus handed him. 'Drugged though he may be, Wolff has revealed himself – violent, certainly, and resentful of children. A drunkard, as well. But he is not mad, nor do I think he is connected to our current business.'

'Ah,' I said, seizing the opportunity, 'now, about that—'

'They'll *want* him to be mad, of course,' Laszlo mused, not hearing me. 'The doctors here, the newspapers, the judges; they'd like to think that only a madman would shoot a five-year-old girl in the head. It creates certain ... *difficulties*, if we are forced to accept that our society can produce sane men who commit such acts.' He sighed once and took an umbrella from Cyrus. 'Yes, that will be a long day or two in court, I should think ...'

We exited the Pavilion, myself seeking refuge with Kreizler under his umbrella, and then climbed into the now-covered calash. I knew what was coming: a monologue that was a kind of catharsis for Kreizler, a restatement of some of his most basic professional principles, designed to relieve the enormous responsibility of helping send a man to his death. Kreizler was a confirmed opponent of the practice of executing criminals, even vicious murderers such as Wolff; but he did not allow this opposition to affect his judgment or his definition of true insanity, which was, by comparison with that of many of his colleagues, relatively narrow. As Cyrus jumped into the driver's seat of the calash and the carriage pulled away from Bellevue, Kreizler's diatribe began to cover subjects I'd heard him discuss many times before: how a broad definition of insanity might make society as a whole feel better but did nothing for mental science, and only lessened the chance that the truly mentally diseased would receive proper care and treatment. It was an insistent sort of speech – Kreizler seemed to be trying to push the image of Wolff in the electrical chair further and further away – and as it wound on, I realized that there was no hope of my gaining any hard information concerning just what in hell was going on and why I'd been called into whatever it was.

Glancing about at the passing buildings in some frustration, I let my eyes come to rest on Cyrus, momentarily thinking that, since he had to listen to this sort of thing more than anyone, I might get some sympathy out of the man. I should have known better. Like Stevie Taggert, Cyrus had had a hard life before coming to work for Laszlo and was now quite devoted to my friend. As a boy in New York Cyrus had seen his parents literally torn to pieces during the draft riots of 1863, when angry hordes of white men and women, many of them recently arrived immigrants, expressed their unwillingness to fight for the causes of the Union and slave emancipation by laying hold of any blacks they could find – including young children – and dismembering them, burning them alive, tarring them, whatever medieval tortures their Old World minds could conceive. A talented musician with a splendid bass-baritone voice, Cyrus had been taken in by a pandering uncle after his parents' death, and trained to be a 'professor,' a piano player in a brothel that proferred young black women to white men of means. But his youthful nightmare had left him rather reluctant to tolerate bigoted abuse from the house's customers. One night in 1887 he had come upon a drunken policeman taking his graft in trade, which the cop apparently thought included brutal blows from the back of his hand and taunts of 'nigger bitch.' Cyrus had calmly gone to the kitchen, fetched a large butcher knife, and dispatched the cop to that special Valhalla reserved for fallen members of the New York City Police Department.

Enter Kreizler once again. Expounding a theory he called

Caleb Carr

'explosive association,' he had revealed the genesis of Cyrus's actions to the judge in the case: during the few minutes involved in the killing, Laszlo said, Cyrus had returned in his mind to the night of his parents' death, and the well of anger that had been left untapped since that incident came gushing forth and engulfed the offending policeman. Cyrus was not insane, Kreizler announced; he had responded to the situation in the only way possible for a man with his background. The judge had been impressed by Kreizler's arguments, but given the public mood he could hardly release Cyrus. Internment in the New York City Lunatic Asylum on Blackwells Island was suggested; but Kreizler stated that employment at his Institute would be far more likely to effect rehabilitation. The judge, anxious to be rid of the case, agreed. The affair didn't do anything to mitigate Kreizler's public and professional reputation as a maverick, and it certainly didn't make the average visitor to Laszlo's home anxious to be alone in the kitchen with Cyrus. But it did ensure the man's loyalty.

There was no break in the pelting rain as we moved at a trot down the Bowery, the only major street in New York that, to my knowledge, has never known the presence of a church. Saloons, concert halls, and flophouses flashed by, and when we passed Cooper Square I spotted the large electric sign and shaded windows of Biff Ellison's Paresis Hall, where Georgio Santorelli had centered his pathetic operations. On we drove, through more tenement wastelands whose sidewalk mayhem was only slightly moderated by the rain. It was not until we had turned onto Bleecker Street and were nearing Police Headquarters that Kreizler said flatly:

'You saw the body.'

'Saw it?' I said in some annoyance, though I was relieved to finally discuss the subject. 'I still see it if I close my eyes for more than a minute. What the hell was the idea of getting my whole house up and forcing me to go down there, anyway? It's not as though I can report that kind of thing, you know that – all it did was agitate my grandmother, and that's not much of an achievement.'

'I'm sorry, John. But you needed to see just what it is we'll be dealing with.'

'*I* am not dealing with anything!' I protested again. 'I'm only a reporter, remember, a reporter with a gruesome story that I can't tell.'

'You do yourself no justice, Moore,' Kreizler said. 'You are a veritable cyclopedia of privileged information – though you may not realize it.'

My voice rose: 'Laszlo, what in *hell*—'

But once again, I could get no further. As we turned onto Mulberry Street I heard calling voices, and looked up to see Link Steffens and Jake Riis running toward the carriage.

Chapter 5

'The closer the church, the nearer to God,' was how one gangland wit had put his decision to base his criminal operations within a few blocks of Police Headquarters. The statement could have been made by any one of dozens of like characters, for the northern terminus of Mulberry Street at Bleecker (headquarters was located at Number 300) marked the heart of a jungle of tenements, brothels, concert halls, saloons, and gambling houses. The residents and customers of these combined to create a sort of carnival atmosphere around the place. Or perhaps one should rather say that it was a circus, and a brutal Roman one at that – for several times a day, bleeding victims of crime or wounded perpetrators of it would be dragged into the rather nondescript, hotel-like structure that was the busy brain of New York's law enforcement arm, leaving a sticky, grim reminder of the deadly nature of the building's business on the pavement outside.

Across Mulberry Street, at Number 303, was the unofficial headquarters of the police reporters: a simple stoop where I and my colleagues spent much of our time, waiting for word of a story. It was therefore not surprising that Riis and Steffens should have been awaiting my arrival. Riis's anxious manner and the gleeful grin that dominated Steffens's gaunt, handsome features indicated that something particularly tasty was up.

'Well, well!' Steffens said, raising his umbrella as he jumped onto the running board of Kreizler's carriage. 'The mystery guests arrive together! Good morning, Dr. Kreizler, a pleasure to see you, sir.'

'Steffens,' Kreizler answered with a nod that was not entirely congenial.

Riis came huffing up behind Steffens, his hulking Danish frame not so lithe as that of the much younger Steffens. 'Doctor,' he said, to which Kreizler only nodded. He had a positive dislike for Riis; the Dane's pioneering work in revealing the evils of tenement life – most notably through his collection of essays and pictures called *How the Other Half Lives* – did not change the fact that he was a strident moralist and something of a bigot, so far as Kreizler was concerned. And I have to admit, I often saw Laszlo's point. 'Moore,' Riis went on, 'Roosevelt has just thrown us out of his office, saying he is expecting the both of you for an important consultation – some very strange game is being played here, I think!'

'Don't listen to him,' Steffens said with another laugh. 'His pride's bruised. It seems that there's been another murder which, because of our friend Riis's personal beliefs, will never make the pages of the *Evening Sun* – we've all been riding him rather shamelessly, I'm afraid!'

'Steffens, by God, if you keep at me—' Riis balled up a healthy Scandinavian hand and waved the fist in Steffens's direction as he kept breathing hard and jogging along, trying to keep up with the still rolling carriage. As Cyrus reined the gelding to a halt outside headquarters, Steffens jumped down.

'Come now, Jake, no threats!' he said good-naturedly. 'This is all in fun!'

'What in hell are you two talking about?' I said, as Kreizler, trying to ignore the scene, stepped from the carriage.

'Now, don't play stupid,' Steffens answered. 'You've seen the body, and so has Dr. Kreizler – we know that much. But unfortunately, since Jake chooses to deny the reality of both boy-whores and the houses in which they work, he can't report the story!'

Riis huffed again, his big face getting redder. 'Steffens, I'll teach you—'

'And since we know *your* editors won't print such seamy stuff,

John,' Steffens went on, 'I'm afraid that leaves the *Post* – how about it, Dr. Kreizler? Care to give the details to the only paper in town that'll print them?'

Kreizler's mouth curled into a slight smile that was neither gentle nor amused, but somehow deprecating. 'The only, Steffens? What about the *World*, or the *Journal*?'

'Ah, I should have been more precise – the only *respectable* paper in town that will print them.'

Kreizler merely ran his eyes up and down Steffens's lanky figure. 'Respectable,' he echoed with a shake of his head, and then he was going up the stairs.

'Say what you like, Doctor,' Steffens called after him, still smiling, 'but you'll get a fairer shake from us than from Hearst or Pulitzer!' Kreizler did not acknowledge the comment. 'We understand you examined the killer this morning,' Steffens pressed. 'Would you at least talk about that?'

Pausing at the door, Kreizler turned. 'The man I examined was indeed a killer. But he has nothing to do with the Santorelli boy.'

'Really? Well, you might want to let Detective Sergeant Connor know that. He's been telling us all morning that Wolff got crazed for blood by shooting the little girl and went out looking for another victim.'

'What?' Genuine alarm was in Kreizler's face. 'No – no, he mustn't – it is absolutely vital that he not do that!'

Laszlo bolted inside. With his quarry now gone, my colleague from the *Evening Post* put his free hand to his hip, his smile shrinking just a bit. 'You know, John – that man's attitude doesn't win him many admirers.'

'It's not intended to,' I said, starting up the steps. Steffens grabbed my arm.

'Can't you tell us anything, John? It's not like Roosevelt to keep Jake and me out of police business – hell, we're more members of the Board of Commissioners than those fools who sit with him.'

That was true: Roosevelt had often consulted both Riis and Steffens on questions of policy. Nonetheless, I could only shrug. 'If I knew anything, I'd tell you, Link. They've kept me in the dark, too.'

'But the body, Moore,' Riis chimed in. 'We have heard ungodly rumors – surely they are false!'

Thinking for just a moment of the corpse on the bridge anchor, I sighed. 'However ungodly the rumors, boys, they can't begin to describe it.' With that I turned and strode up the steps.

Before I was inside the door Riis and Steffens were at it again, Steffens pelting his friend with sarcastic barbs and Riis angrily trying to shut him up. But Link was right, even if he expressed himself somewhat meanly: Riis's stubborn insistence that homosexual prostitution did not exist meant that another of the city's largest papers would never acknowledge the full details of a brutal murder. And how much more the report would have meant coming from Riis than from Steffens; for while most of Link's important work as an exponent of the Progressive movement lay in the future, Riis was long since an established voice of authority, the man whose angry declamations had caused the razing of Mulberry Bend (the very heart of New York's most notorious slum, Five Points) along with the destruction of many other pestilential pockets. Yet Jake could not bring himself to fully acknowledge the Santorelli murder; despite all the horrors he had witnessed, he could not accept the circumstances of such a crime; and as I entered the big green doors of headquarters I wondered, just as I had wondered a thousand times during staff meetings at the *Times*, how long many members of the press – not to mention politicians and the public – would be content to equate deliberate ignorance of evil with its nonexistence.

Inside I found Kreizler standing near the caged elevator, talking heatedly with Connor, the detective who had been at the murder scene the previous night. I was about to join them when my arm was taken and I was guided toward a staircase by one of the more pleasant sights available at headquarters: Sara Howard, an old friend of mine.

'Don't get involved in that, John,' she said, with a tone of sage wisdom that often marked her statements. 'Connor is taking a lashing from your friend, and he deserves the full treatment. Besides, the president wants you upstairs – *sans* Dr. Kreizler.'

'Sara!' I said happily. 'I am glad to see you. I've spent a night and a morning with maniacs. I need the sound of a sane voice.'

Caleb Carr

Sara's taste in dresses ran toward simple designs in shades of green that matched her eyes, and the one she wore that day, with only a minimal bustle and not much petticoat business, showed off her tall, athletic body to advantage. Her face was by no means striking but handsomely plain; it was the play of eyes and mouth, back and forth between mischievous and sad, that made it such a delight to watch her. Back in the early seventies, when I was in my teens, her family moved into a house near ours on Gramercy Park, and I'd subsequently watched her spend her single-digit years turning that decorous neighborhood into her private rumpus room. Time had not changed her much, except to make her as thoughtful (and occasionally brooding) as she was excitable; and following the demise of my engagement to Julia Pratt I had one night gotten more than a little drunk, decided that all women held by society to be beauties were in fact demons, and asked Sara to marry me. Her answer was to take me in a cab to the Hudson River and throw me in.

'You won't find many sane voices in this building today,' Sara said as we climbed the stairs. 'Teddy – that is, the president – isn't it strange to call him that, John?' And indeed it was; but when Roosevelt was at headquarters, which was ruled by a board of four commissioners of which he was chief, he was distinguished from the other three by the title 'president.' Very few of us guessed at the time that he would answer to an identical title in the none-too-distant future. 'Well, he's been in one of his whirlwinds over the Santorelli case. Every kind of person has been in and out—'

Just then Theodore's voice came booming down from the second-story hallway: 'And don't bother bringing your friends at Tammany into this, Kelly! Tammany is a monstrous Democrat creation, and this is a reform Republican administration – you've earned no favors here with your shoulder-hitting! I advise you to cooperate!' Deep chuckles from a pair of voices inside the staircase were the only reply to this, and the sounds were moving our way. Within seconds Sara and I were face-to-face with the foppishly dressed, cologne-drenched, enormous figure of Biff Ellison, as well as his smaller, more tastefully clad, and less aromatic criminal overseer, Paul Kelly.

The days when Lower Manhattan's underworld affairs were parceled out among dozens of freewheeling street gangs had for the most part come to an end by 1896, and dealings had been taken over and consolidated by larger groups that were just as deadly but far more businesslike in their approach. The Eastmans, named for their colorful chief, Monk Eastman, controlled all territory east of the Bowery between Fourteenth Street and Chatham Square; on the West Side, the Hudson Dusters, darlings of many New York intellectuals and artists (largely because they all shared a seemingly insatiable appetite for cocaine), ran affairs south of Thirteenth Street and west of Broadway; the area above Fourteenth Street on that side of town belonged to Mallet Murphy's Gophers, a group of cellar-dwelling Irish creatures whose evolution even Mr. Darwin would have been hard-pressed to explain; and between these three virtual armies, at the eye of the criminal hurricane and just blocks from Police Headquarters, were Paul Kelly and his Five Pointers, who ruled supreme between Broadway and the Bowery and from Fourteenth Street to City Hall.

Kelly's gang had been named after the city's toughest neighborhood in an attempt to inspire fear, though in reality they were far less anarchic in their dealings than the classic Five Points bands of an earlier generation (the Whyos, Plug Uglies, Dead Rabbits, and the rest), remnants of which still haunted their old neighborhood like violent, disaffected ghosts. Kelly himself was reflective of this change in style: his sartorial acumen was matched by polished speech and manners. He also possessed a thorough knowledge of art and politics, his taste in the former running toward modern and in the latter toward socialism. But Kelly knew his customers, too; and *tasteful* was not the word to describe the New Brighton Dance Hall, the Five Pointers' headquarters on Great Jones Street. Overseen by a singular giant known as Eat-'Em-Up Jack McManus, the New Brighton was a garish mass of mirrors, crystal chandeliers, brass railings, and scantily clad 'dancers,' a flash palace unequaled even in the Tenderloin, which, before Kelly's rise, had been the unquestioned center of outlaw opulence.

James T. 'Biff' Ellison, on the other hand, represented the

Caleb Carr

more traditional sort of New York thug. He had begun his career as a particularly unsavory saloon bouncer, and had first gained notoriety by beating and stomping a police officer nearly to death. Though he aspired to his boss's polish, on Ellison – ignorant, sexually depraved, and drug-ridden as he was – the attempt became grotesquely ostentatious. Kelly had murderous lieutenants whose doings were infamous and even daring, but none save Ellison would have dared to open Paresis Hall, one of the mere three or four saloons in New York that openly – indeed, exuberantly – catered to that segment of society which Jake Riis so assiduously refused to believe existed.

'Well, now,' Kelly said amiably, the stud in his cravat gleaming as he approached, 'it's Mr. Moore of the *Times* – along with one of the lovely new ladies of the Police Department.' Taking Sara's hand, Kelly lowered his chiseled, Black Irish features and kissed it. 'It certainly is more enjoyable getting summoned to head-quarters these days.' His smile as he stared at Sara was well-practiced and confident; none of which changed the fact that the air in the staircase had suddenly become charged with oppressive threat.

'Mr. Kelly,' Sara answered with a brave nod, though I could see that she was quite nervous. 'A pity your charm isn't matched by the company you choose to keep.'

Kelly laughed, but Ellison, who already towered over Sara and me, rose up even higher, his fleshy face and ferret's eyes darkening. 'It'd be best to watch your mouth, missy – it's a long walk from headquarters to Gramercy Park. A lot of unpleasant things could happen to a girl all alone.'

'You're a real rabbit, aren't you, Ellison?' I said, although the man could have broken me in half without much thought. 'What's the matter – run out of little boys to push around, you need to start on women?'

Ellison's face went positively red. 'Why, you miserable piece of scribbling shit – sure, Gloria was trouble, a whole bundle of trouble, but I wouldn't a cooked her for it, and I'll kill any man says I—'

'Now, now, Biff.' Kelly's tone was pleasant, but his meaning was unmistakable. 'There's no cause for any of that.' And then to me: 'Biff had nothing to do with the boy's murder, Moore. And I don't want to see my name connected with it, either.'

'Hell of a time to think of that, Kelly,' I answered. 'I saw his body – it was worthy of Biff, all right.' In fact, not even Ellison had ever done anything so horrendous, but there was no reason to acknowledge that to them. 'He was just a boy.'

Kelly chuckled as he took a few steps farther down the stairs. 'Yes, and a boy playing a dangerous game. Come on, Moore, boys like that die every day in this town – why the interest? Did he have a secret relative somewhere? A bastard kid of Morgan's or Frick's?'

'Do you think that's the only reason the case would be investigated?' Sara asked, somewhat offended – she hadn't been working at headquarters very long.

'My dear girl,' Kelly answered, 'both Mr. Moore and I *know* that's the only reason. But have it your way – Roosevelt is championing the benighted!' Kelly continued down the stairs, and Ellison pushed by me to follow. They paused a little farther down and then Kelly turned, his voice for the first time hinting at his occupation. 'But I warn you, Moore – I do *not* want to see my name connected with this.'

'Don't worry, Kelly. My editors would never run the story.'

He smiled again. 'Very sensible of them, too. There are momentous things going on in the world, Moore – why waste energy on a trifle?'

With that they were gone, and Sara and I collected ourselves. Kelly may have been a new breed of gangster, but he was a gangster all the same, and our encounter had been genuinely unsettling.

'Do you know,' Sara said thoughtfully as we started upstairs again, 'that my friend Emily Cort went slumming one night specifically to meet Paul Kelly – and that she found him the most entertaining man? But then, Emily always was an empty-headed little fool.' She took hold of my arm. 'By the way, John, why in the world did you call Mr. Ellison a rabbit? He's more like an ape.'

'In the language he speaks, a rabbit is a tough customer.'

'Oh. I must remember to write that down. I want my

knowledge of the criminal class to be as thorough as possible.'

I could only laugh. 'Sara – with all the professions open to women these days, why do you insist on this one? Smart as you are, you could be a scientist, a doctor even—'

'So could you, John,' she answered sharply. 'Except that you don't happen to want to. And neither do I. Honestly, sometimes you are the most idiotic man. You know perfectly well what I want.' And so did every other friend of Sara's: to be the city's first female police officer.

'But, Sara, are you any closer to your goal? You're only a secretary, after all.'

She smiled wisely, with a hint of that same tense sharpness behind the smile. 'Yes, John – but I'm in the building, aren't I? Ten years ago *that* would have been impossible.'

I nodded with a shrug, aware that it was useless to argue with her, and then looked around the second-floor hallway in an attempt to find a familiar face. But the detectives and officers that came from and went to the various rooms were all new to me. 'Hell's bells,' I said quietly, 'I don't recognize *anyone* up here today.'

'Yes, it's gotten worse. We lost a dozen more last month. They'd all rather resign or retire than face investigation.'

'But Theodore can't staff the whole force with goo-goos.' Which was the term for new officers.

'So everyone says. But if the choice is between corruption and inexperience, you know which way he'll go.' Sara gave me a firm push in the back. 'Oh, do stop dawdling, John, he wanted you right away.' We wove through uniformed leatherheads and 'fly cops' (officers dressed in civilian clothing) until we were at the end of the hall. 'And later,' Sara added, 'you must explain to me exactly why it is that cases like this one are not usually investigated.' Then, in a flurry, she rapped on the door of Theodore's office, opened it, and kept on shoving me till I was through. 'Mr. Moore, Commissioner,' she announced, closing the door and leaving me inside.

Voluminous reader and writer that he was, Theodore had a penchant for massive desks, and his office at headquarters was dominated by one. A few armchairs were crowded around it uncomfortably. A tall clock sat atop the white mantle of the fireplace, and there was a shiny brass telephone on a small side table; otherwise the only items in the room were stacks of books and papers, some resting on the floor and going halfway up to the ceiling. The shades on the windows, which faced out onto Mulberry Street, were drawn halfway down and Theodore stood before one of them, wearing a very conservative gray suit for the business day.

'Ah, John, excellent,' he said, hustling around the desk and then mangling my hand. 'Kreizler's downstairs?'

'Yes. You wanted to see me alone?'

Theodore paced about in a mix of serious yet merry anticipation. 'What's his mood? How will he respond, do you think? He's such a tempestuous fellow – I want to make sure I take the right tack with him.'

I shrugged. 'He's all right, I suppose. We were up at Bellevue seeing this Wolff character, the one who shot the little girl, and he was in a hell of a mood after that. But he worked it out during the ride down – on my ears. However, Roosevelt, since I have no idea what it is you want him for—'

Just then there was another quick, light knock on the door, and then Sara reappeared. She was followed by Kreizler: they had evidently been chatting, and as their conversation faded away I noticed that Laszlo was studying her intently. At the time this didn't seem particularly remarkable; it was how most people reacted to finding a woman employed at headquarters.

Theodore got between them in a flash. 'Kreizler!' he clicked loudly. 'Delighted, Doctor, delighted to see you!'

'Roosevelt,' Kreizler answered with a genuinely pleased smile. 'It's been a long while.'

'Too long, too long! Shall we sit and talk, or shall I have the office cleared so that we can enjoy a rematch?'

It was a reference to their first encounter at Harvard, which had involved a boxing match; and as we laughed and sat, the ice very nicely broken, my thoughts drifted back to those days.

Though I'd known Theodore for many years before his arrival at Harvard as a freshman in 1876, I'd never been very close to him. In addition to being sickly, he'd been a studious and generally well-behaved boy, whereas both I and my younger brother had spent our youths ensuring that anarchy reigned as much as possible on the streets of our Gramercy Park neighborhood. 'Ringleaders' was a label my brother and I were usually given by our parents' friends, and there was much talk about the remarkable misfortune of one family being afflicted with two black sheep. In reality there was nothing very evil or malicious in what we did; it was more that we chose to do it in the company of a small band of boys whose homes were the back alleys and doorways of the Gas House district to the east of us. Such were not considered acceptable playmates in our staid little corner of Knickerbocker society, where class counted for much and no adult was prepared to tolerate children with minds of their own. A few years away at preparatory school did nothing to discourage my tendencies; indeed, so great had the general alarm over my behavior grown by my seventeenth birthday that my application for admission to Harvard was almost rejected, a fate I would gladly have accepted. But my father's deep pockets swung the balance back in my supposed favor and off I went to the stultifying little village of Cambridge, where a year or two of college life did absolutely nothing to make me more inclined to accept a young scholar like Theodore when he arrived.

But in the fall of 1877, during my senior and Theodore's sophomore year, all this began to change. Laboring under the twin burdens of a difficult romance and a gravely ill father, Theodore began to develop from a rather narrow youth into a much more broad-minded and accessible young man. He never became anything like a man of the world, of course; but we nonetheless managed to discover philosophical dimensions in each other that allowed us to pass a good many evenings drinking and talking together. Soon we were conducting expeditions into Boston society, both high and low; and on that foundation a solid friendship began to grow.

Meanwhile, another childhood friend of mine, Laszlo Kreizler, having earlier completed an unprecedentedly quick course of study at the Columbia Medical College, had been drawn away from a job as a junior assistant at the Lunatic Asylum on Blackwells Island by a new graduate course in psychology offered at Harvard by Dr. William James. That gregarious, terrier-like professor, who would go on to fame as a philosopher, had recently established America's first psychological laboratory in a few small rooms in Lawrence Hall. He also taught comparative anatomy to undergraduates; and in the fall 1877 term, having heard that James was an amusing professor who was sympathetic when it came to grades, I signed up for his course. On the first day I found myself sitting next to Theodore, who was pursuing the interest in all things wild that had consumed him since early youth. Although Roosevelt often got into spirited discussions over some minor point of animal behavior with James, he, like all of us, quickly became charmed by the still-young professor, who had a habit of reclining on the floor when his students' participation was flagging and declaring that teaching was 'a mutual process.'

Kreizler's relationship with James was far more complex. Though he greatly respected James's work and grew to have enormous affection for the man himself (it really was impossible not to), Laszlo was nonetheless unable to accept James's famous theories on free will, which were the cornerstone of our teacher's philosophy. James had been a maudlin, unhealthy boy, and as a young man had more than once contemplated suicide; but he overcame this tendency as a result of reading the works of the French philosopher Renouvier, who taught that a man could, by force of will, overcome all psychic (and many physical) ailments. 'My first act of free will shall be to believe in free will!' had been James's early battle cry, an attitude that continued to dominate his thinking in 1877. Such a philosophy was bound to collide with Kreizler's developing belief in what he called 'context': the theory that every man's actions are to a very decisive extent influenced by his early experiences, and that no man's behavior can be analyzed or affected without knowledge of those experiences. In the laboratory rooms at Lawrence Hall, which were filled with devices for testing and dissecting animal nervous systems and human reactions, James and Kreizler battled over how the patterns of people's lives are formed and whether or not any of us is free to determine what kind of lives we will lead as adults. These encounters became steadily more heated – not to mention a subject of campus gossip – until finally, one night early in the second term, they debated in University Hall the question 'Is Free Will a Psychological Phenomenon?'

Most of the student body attended; and though Kreizler argued well, the crowd was predisposed to dismiss his statements. In addition, James's sense of humor was far more developed than Kreizler's at that time, and the boys at Harvard enjoyed their professor's many jokes at Kreizler's expense. On the other hand, Laszlo's references to philosophers of gloom, such as the German Schopenhauer, as well as his reliance on the evolutionist theories of Charles Darwin and Herbert Spencer in explaining that survival was the goal of man's mental as much as his physical development, provoked many and prolonged groans of undergraduate disapproval. I confess that even I was torn, between loyalty to a friend whose beliefs had always made me uneasy and enthusiasm for a man and a philosophy that seemed to offer the promise of limitless possibilities for not only my own but every man's future. Theodore – who did not yet know Kreizler, and who had, like James, survived many and severe childhood illnesses by dint of what he reasoned to be sheer willpower – was not troubled by any such qualms: he spiritedly cheered James's eventual and inevitable victory.

I dined with Kreizler after the debate in a tavern across the Charles that was frequented by Harvardians. In the middle of our meal Theodore entered with some friends and, seeing me with Kreizler, requested an introduction. He made some good-natured but pointed remarks about Laszlo's 'mystical mumbo jumbo concerning the human psyche' and how it was all the result of his European background; but he went too far when he spouted a jibe about 'gypsy blood,' for Laszlo's mother was Hungarian and he took great offense. Kreizler laid down the challenge for an affair of honor, and Theodore delightedly took him up, suggesting a boxing match. I knew that Laszlo would have preferred fencing foils – with his bad left arm he stood little chance in a ring – but he agreed, in keeping with the *code duello*, which gave Theodore, as the challenged party, the choice of weapons.

To Roosevelt's credit, when the two men had stripped to their waists in the Hemenway Gymnasium (entered, at that late hour, by way of a set of keys I had won from a custodian in a poker game earlier in the year) and saw Kreizler's arm, he offered to let him choose some weapon other than fists; but Kreizler was stubborn and proud, and though he was, for the second time in the same evening, predestined for defeat, he put up a far better fight than anyone had expected. His gameness impressed all present and, predictably, won him Roosevelt's heartfelt admiration. We all returned to the tavern and drank until the late hours; and though Theodore and Laszlo never became the most intimate of friends, a very special bond had been formed between them, one that opened Roosevelt's mind – if only a crack – to Kreizler's theories and opinions.

That opening was a good part of the reason we were now collected in Theodore's office; and as we talked of the old days in Cambridge, our immediate business receded for a time. The conversation soon spread to the more recent past, Roosevelt asking some genuinely interested questions about Kreizler's work with both the children at his Institute and the criminally insane, and Laszlo saying that he had followed Theodore's career as an assemblyman in Albany and a Civil Service Commissioner in Washington with great interest. It was pleasant talk among old friends who had a great deal of catching up to do, and for much of the time I was content to sit back and listen, enjoying the change of atmosphere from the previous night and morning.

But inevitably, the conversation turned to the Santorelli murder; and a sense of foreboding and sadness crept relentlessly into the room, dissipating pleasant memories as cruelly as some unknown savage had dispatched the boy on the bridge tower.

Chapter 6

'I have your report, Kreizler,' Roosevelt said, picking up the document from his desk. 'Along with the coroner's. It won't surprise you to learn that he gave us no additional insights.'

Kreizler nodded in distasteful familiarity. 'Any butcher or patent-medicine salesman can be appointed a coroner, Roosevelt. It's almost as easy as becoming an asylum superintendent.'

'Indeed. At any rate, your report seems to indicate—'

'It does not indicate *everything* I discovered,' Kreizler interrupted carefully. 'Indeed, it does not cover some of the most important points.'

'Eh?' Theodore looked up in surprise, the pince-nez that he wore in the office falling from his nose. 'I beg your pardon?'

'Many eyes see reports at headquarters, Commissioner.' Kreizler was doing his best to be diplomatic, which in his case was a genuine effort. 'I did not wish to take the chance of certain details becoming . . . public. Not yet.'

Theodore paused, his eyes narrowing pensively. 'You write,' he eventually said quietly, 'of terrible errors.'

Kreizler stood and walked to the window, pulling the shade aside just a crack. 'First of all, Roosevelt, you must promise me that persons such as' – he said the rank with true disgust – 'Detective Sergeant Connor will not be told any of this. The man has spent this morning propagating false information to the press – information that may well end up costing more lives.'

55

Theodore's ordinarily furrowed brow became positively creased. 'By thunder! If that's true, Doctor, I'll have the man's—'

Kreizler held up a hand. 'Just promise me that, Roosevelt.'

'You have my word. But at least tell me what Connor said.'

'He has given several reporters the impression,' Kreizler answered, beginning to walk the floor of the office, 'that this man Wolff was responsible for the Santorelli killing.'

'Then you think otherwise?'

'Unquestionably. Wolff's thoughts and actions are entirely too unpremeditated and unsystematic for this. Though he *is* utterly devoid of emotional restraint, and has no aversion to violence.'

'Would you consider him a . . .' For Roosevelt the language was somewhat unfamiliar. 'A psychopath?' Kreizler cocked an eyebrow. 'I have seen some of your recent writings,' Theodore went on, looking a bit self-conscious. 'Though I can't say how much I've truly understood.'

Kreizler nodded with a small, enigmatic smile. 'Is Wolff a psychopath, you ask. There is constitutional psychopathic inferiority, without question. But as to the *implications* of labeling him a psychopath – if you've read even some of the literature, Roosevelt, you know that that depends on whose opinions we accept.'

Roosevelt nodded in return and rubbed his chin with one of his tough hands. I did not then know, but would learn in the weeks to come, that one of the greatest single points of contention between Kreizler and many of his colleagues – a battle that had been fought primarily in the pages of the *American Journal of Insanity* – was the issue of what constituted a true homicidal lunatic. Men and women whose savagely violent acts betrayed peculiar patterns of moral thought, but whose intellectual capacities were acknowledged to be healthy, had recently been included within the broad classification of 'psychopathic personalities' by the German psychologist Emil Kraepelin. The classification had been generally accepted throughout the profession; the contested question was, were such psychopaths genuinely mentally diseased? Most doctors answered in the affirmative, and although they couldn't yet precisely identify the full nature and causes of the disease, they thought such discoveries only a matter of time. Kreizler, on the other hand, believed that psychopaths were produced by extreme childhood environments and experiences and were unafflicted by any true pathology. Judged in context, the actions of such patients could be understood and even predicted (unlike those of the truly mad). This was clearly the diagnosis he had reached with regard to Henry Wolff.

'Then you'll declare him competent to stand trial?' Roosevelt asked.

'I will.' Kreizler's face darkened perceptibly, and he stared at his hands as he folded them together. 'And, more importantly, I'll wager that long before that trial begins we will have proof that he is not connected to the Santorelli case. Grim proof.'

I was finding it hard to remain silent. 'That proof being . . .?' I asked.

Kreizler's hands fell to his sides as he returned to the window. 'More bodies, I fear. Especially if an attempt is made to tie Wolff to Santorelli. Yes.' Kreizler's voice became distracted. 'He'd be angered by having his thunder stolen that way . . .'

'*Who* would?'

But Laszlo didn't seem to hear me. 'Do either of you remember,' he continued, in the same distant tone, 'an interesting case of some three years ago, also involving murdered children? Roosevelt, I'm afraid it was at the height of your struggles in Washington, so you may not have heard. And Moore, I believe you were at the time involved in a rather heated battle with the *Washington Post*, which wanted Roosevelt's head on a platter.'

'The *Post*,' I sighed in disgust. 'The *Post* was in the muck up to its eyes with every illegal government appointee—'

'Yes, yes,' Kreizler answered, holding up the weakened left arm to head me off. 'There is no question that yours was the honorable position. The loyal one, too, although your editors seemed to be less enthusiastic in their support.'

'They came 'round in the end,' I said, puffing up the chest a bit. 'Not that it saved my job,' I added, slacking again.

'Now, now. No self-recrimination, Moore. But as I was saying, three years ago a water tower above a large tenement on Suffolk

Street was struck by lightning. The tower was the highest structure in the neighborhood, and the event was perfectly explicable, if slightly unusual. When the building's residents and the fire department reached the roof, however, some were inclined to view it as a providential event – for the tower contained the bodies of a pair of children. A brother and sister. Their throats had been cut. It so happened that I knew the family. They were Jews from Austria. The children were quite beautiful – delicate features, enormous brown eyes –, and also quite troublesome. An embarrassment to the family. They stole, lied, attacked other children – uncontrollable. In fact, there was very little remorse in the neighborhood over their deaths. The bodies were in an advanced state of decomposition when they were found. The boy's had fallen off an interior platform on which they were originally placed, and into the water. It was badly boated. The girl's was somewhat more intact for having stayed dry, but any clues that might have been gathered from it were destroyed by another incompetent coroner. I never saw anything more than the official reports, but I did note one curious detail from those.' He pointed with his left hand to his face. 'The eyes were gone.'

A strong quiver went through me as I remembered not only the Santorelli boy but the two other murders that Roosevelt had told me of the night before. Glancing at Roosevelt, I saw that he had made the same connection: while his body was quite still, his eyes were wide with apprehension. But we both tried to battle the feeling off, Roosevelt declaring, 'That's not uncommon. Particularly if the bodies were exposed for a long period of time. And if the throats were cut, there would have been plenty of blood to attract scavengers.'

'Perhaps,' Kreizler said with a judicious nod as he continued pacing. 'But the water tower was enclosed, with the exact purpose of keeping scavengers and vermin out.'

'I see.' Theodore puzzled with it. 'Were those facts reported?'

'They were,' Kreizler answered. 'In the *World*, I believe.'

'But,' I protested, 'the water tower or building doesn't exist that can keep certain animals out. Rats, for instance.'

'True, John,' Kreizler said. 'And in the absence of any further details, I was forced to accept that explanation. Why even New York City rats, on discovering a pair of bodies, should so carefully gnaw out only the eyes was a disturbing mystery that I tried to ignore and which remained unaddressed. Until last night.' Kreizler took to pacing the floor again. 'As soon as I saw the condition of the Santorelli boy, I made an examination of the ocular orbits of the skull. Working by torchlight was hardly ideal, but I found what I was looking for. On the malar bone as well as the supraorbital ridge were a series of narrow grooves, and on the greater wing of the sphenoid – at the base of the cavities – several small indentations. All consistent with the cutting edge and point of a knife, of the type most frequently used by hunters, I'd say. My guess would be that if we exhumed the bodies of the two 1893 victims – and I intend to request such action – we would find the same thing. In other words, gentlemen, the eyes were removed by the hand of man.'

My dread was increasing, and I fumbled for an argument: 'But what about what Sergeant Connor said—'

'Moore.' Kreizler's voice was definitive. 'If we are to continue this discussion we really must dispense with the opinions of men such as Sergeant Connor.'

Roosevelt shifted in his chair apprehensively; I could see in his face that he had run out of ways to avoid bringing Kreizler fully up to date. 'I feel I must tell you, Doctor,' he announced, gripping the arms of his chair, 'that we have had two more murders in the last three months that might also fit the . . . *pattern* you're describing.'

The statement stopped Laszlo dead in his tracks. 'What?' he said, urgently but quietly. 'Where – where were the bodies found?'

'I'm not precisely sure,' Theodore answered.

'And were they prostitutes?'

'I believe so, yes.'

'You *believe* so? Records, Roosevelt, I must have the records! Didn't anyone in this department ever think to make a connection? Didn't *you*?'

The records were sent for. From them we discovered that the bodies of the other two boys, both of whom had indeed been prostitutes, had also been found within what the coroners guessed were hours of their deaths. There was somewhat less mutilation involved than in the Santorelli murder; that seemed, however, a difference of quantity rather than quality, for the similarities among the cases far outweighed any slight differences. The first boy, a twelve-year-old African immigrant with no known name other than 'Millie,' had been chained to the stern of an Ellis Island ferry; and the second, a ten-year-old named Aaron Morton, had been found suspended by his feet from the Brooklyn Bridge. Both were nearly naked, according to the reports; both had their throats cut, along with various other bodily lacerations; and, again, both were missing their eyes. As Laszlo finished reading the accounts, he mumbled that last fact to himself several times, lost in cogitation.

'I believe I understand what you're suggesting, Kreizler,' Theodore figured aloud: he never liked to be left behind in any intellectual discussion, even one that took place on what was, for him, very alien territory. 'A murderer committed just this kind of an outrage three years ago. It was reported. And now another such man, who at some point read the story, has been inspired to imitation.' He was satisfied with his own extrapolation. 'Is that correct, Doctor? It wouldn't be the first time stories in certain of our newspapers have had that effect.'

Kreizler, however, just sat tapping a forefinger against his pursed lips, with a look that clearly stated that the whole affair was far more complicated than even he had guessed.

I searched for some way to reach a different conclusion. 'What about the rest of it?' I asked. 'The . . . the missing organs, and the cut-away flesh of the . . . well, the rest of it. There was none of that in the earlier cases.'

'No,' Kreizler answered slowly. 'But I believe there is an explanation for that difference, not that it need concern us now. The eyes are the link, the key, the way in – I would stake everything on that . . .' His voice faded again.

'All right,' I said, throwing up my hands. 'So someone murdered those two children three years ago, and now we've got a mimicking lunatic who also likes to mutilate dead bodies on our hands. What are we supposed to do about it?'

'Almost nothing in what you have just said, John,' Kreizler

Caleb Carr

replied evenly, 'is accurate. I am not at all certain he is a lunatic. Nor am I inclined to believe that he likes what he does, in the sense that you understand or intend that statement. But most importantly – and I'm afraid that here I must disappoint you, too, Roosevelt – I am as sure as I can be that this is not an imitator but the *same man*.'

And there it was – the statement that both Roosevelt and I had been dreading. I'd been a police reporter for quite a while, ever since my unceremonious removal from the Washington beat as a result of my previously mentioned defense of Roosevelt during his battle with the patronage system in the Civil Service. I'd even covered some celebrated murder cases abroad. I therefore knew that murderers like the one Kreizler was describing did exist; but that never made it any easier to hear that one was on the loose. And for Roosevelt – who, though a born fighter, understood few of the intimate details of criminal behavior – it was an even harder notion to swallow.

'But . . . three years!' Theodore said, aghast. 'Surely, Kreizler, if such a man did exist he could not have eluded the law for so long!'

'It's no great job to elude that which is not pursuing,' Kreizler answered. 'And even if the police had taken an interest, they would have been helpless. Because they could not have begun to understand what motivates the murderer.'

'Do you?' Roosevelt's words were almost hopeful.

'Not completely. I have the first few pieces – and we must find the rest. For it is only when we truly understand what drives him that we will have even a prayer of solving this case.'

'But what *could* drive a man to such things?' Roosevelt said in uncomfortable confusion. 'After all, the Santorelli boy had no money. We're investigating the family, but they all appear to have been in their home throughout the night. Unless it was a personal quarrel with someone else, then . . .'

'I doubt there was any quarrel involved,' Laszlo replied. 'In fact, the boy may never have seen his murderer before last night.'

'You're suggesting that whoever it is kills children he doesn't even *know*?'

'Possibly. It is not *knowing* them that is important to him – it is what they *represent*.'

The Alienist

'And that is?' I asked.

'*That* – is what we must determine.'

Roosevelt continued to test carefully: 'Do you have any evidence to support such a theory?'

'None, of the kind that you mean. I have only a lifetime of studying similar characters. And the intuition it has given me.'

'But . . .' As Roosevelt stood to take his turn pacing the floor, Kreizler grew more relaxed, the hard part of his work done. Theodore pounded one fist into an open hand insistently. 'Listen, Kreizler, it's true that I grew up, as we all did, in a privileged household. But I have made it my business since taking this job to acquaint myself with the underworld of this city, and I have seen many things. No one needs to tell me that depravity and inhumanity have taken on dimensions in New York unheard of anywhere in the world. But what unnameable nightmare, even *here*, could drive a man to this?'

'Do not,' Kreizler answered slowly, trying very hard to be clear, 'look for causes in this city. Nor in recent circumstances, nor in recent events. The creature you seek was created long ago. Perhaps in his infancy – certainly in childhood. And not necessarily here.'

Theodore was momentarily unable to answer, his face an open display of conflicting feelings. The conversation disturbed him deeply, in the same way that similar discussions had disturbed him ever since the first time he met Kreizler. Yet he had known the talk would come to this; known it, even counted on it, I began to see, since the moment he asked me to bring Laszlo to his office. For there was satisfaction in his aspect, too, the realization that what seemed a forbidding, unchartable ocean to every detective in his department was, to the experienced Kreizler, full of currents and courses. Laszlo's theories clearly offered a way of solving what Theodore had been assured was an unsolvable mystery, and thus extending justice to one (or, as it now seemed, more than one) whose death would never have been explored by anyone else in the Police Department. None of which explained why *I* was there.

'John,' Theodore said abruptly, without looking at me. 'Kelly and Ellison have been here.'

'I know. Sara and I ran into them in the staircase.'

'What?' Theodore fixed the pince-nez to his nose. 'Was there any trouble? Kelly is a devil, particularly when there's a woman about.'

'It wasn't what I'd call pleasant,' I answered. 'But Sara stood her ground like a trooper.'

Theodore breathed relief. 'Thank God. Though, confidentially, I still sometimes wonder if that was a wise choice.' He was referring to his decision to hire Sara, who, along with another departmental secretary, was one of the first two women ever to work for the New York City police force. Roosevelt had taken a lot of jibes and criticism for those hirings, both in and out of the press; but he had as little patience with the way women were treated in American society as any man I've ever known, and he was determined to give the two a chance.

'Kelly,' Theodore went on, 'has threatened to create great trouble among the immigrant communities if I try to connect Ellison or him to this case. He says he can whip up all sorts of agitation around the notion that the Police Department allows poor foreign children to be slaughtered with impunity.'

Kreizler nodded. 'It wouldn't be difficult. Since it's basically true.' Roosevelt looked sharply at Kreizler for a moment, but then softened, knowing he was right. 'Tell me, Moore,' Laszlo asked, 'what's your opinion of Ellison? Is there any chance he *is* involved?'

'Biff?' I sat back, stretched my legs out, and weighed it. 'He is, without question, one of the worst men in this city. Most of the gangsters who run things now have some kind of human spark in them somewhere, however hidden. Even Monk Eastman has his cats and birds. But Biff – for all I can tell, nothing touches him. Cruelty is really his only sport, the only thing that seems to give him any pleasure. And if I hadn't seen that body, if this were just a hypothetical question about a dead boy who worked out of Paresis Hall, I wouldn't hesitate to say he's a suspect. Motive? He would have had a few, the most likely being to keep the other boys in line, make sure they pay their full cut to him. But there's just one problem with it – style. Biff is a stiletto man, if you know what I mean. He kills quietly, neatly, and a lot of the people he's supposed to have killed have never been found. He's all flash in his clothes, but not in his work. So, much as I'd like to, I can't say as I see him involved in this. It's just not his – style.'

I glanced up to find Laszlo giving me a very puzzled look. 'John, that is the most intelligent thing I've ever heard you say,' he finally announced. 'And to think that you wondered why you'd been brought along.' He turned to Theodore. 'Roosevelt, I shall require Moore as my assistant. His knowledge of this city's criminal activities, and of the locales in which those activities take place, will make him invaluable.'

'Assistant?' I echoed. But they were back to ignoring me. Theodore's teeth and narrowing eyes showed that he was quite absorbed in, and pleased with, Kreizler's remark.

'Then you wish to take part in the investigation,' he said. 'I sensed you would.'

'Take part in the *investigation*?' I said, dumbfounded. 'Roosevelt, have you lost your Dutch mind? An alienist? A *psychologist*? You've already made an enemy of every senior officer on the force, and half the Board of Commissioners, to boot. They're taking odds in half the gambling hells in town that you'll be fired by Independence Day! If word gets out that you've brought someone like Kreizler in – why, you'd be better off hiring an African witch doctor!'

Laszlo chuckled. 'Which is approximately what most of our respectable citizens consider me. Moore's right, Roosevelt. The project would have to be undertaken in absolute secrecy.'

Roosevelt nodded. 'I'm aware of the realities of the situation, gentlemen, believe me. Secrecy it would be.'

'And there is,' Kreizler continued, making another careful attempt at diplomacy, 'the matter of *terms* . . .'

'If you mean salary,' Roosevelt said, 'since you will be acting in an advisory capacity, naturally—'

'I'm afraid that salary is not what I had in mind. Neither is an advisory capacity. Good lord, Roosevelt, the detectives on your force were not even able to divine the clue regarding the removal of the eyes – three murders in three months and the most vital aspect is attributed to rats! Who can say what other blunders they've committed. As for connecting this to the cases of three

Caleb Carr

years ago, assuming such a connection exists, I suspect we'd all die old men in our beds before they'd achieve it, whether they were 'advised' or not. No, it won't do to work with them. What I have in mind is an – *auxiliary* effort.'

Roosevelt, ever the pragmatist, was willing to listen. 'Go on,' he said.

'Give me two or three good young detectives with a sound appreciation of modern methods – men who have no stake in the old order of business in the department, who were never loyal to Byrnes.' (Thomas Byrnes was the much-revered creator and former head of the Division of Detectives, a shadowy man who had amassed a large fortune during his tenure – and who had retired, not coincidentally, when Roosevelt was appointed to the board.) 'We will set up an office outside of headquarters, though not too far away. Assign someone you trust as a liaison – again, someone new, someone young. Give us all the intelligence you can without revealing the operation.' Laszlo sat back, aware of the thoroughly unprecedented nature of his proposal. 'Give us all of this, and I believe we might even have a chance.'

Roosevelt braced himself against his desk and rocked quietly on his chair, watching Kreizler. 'It would mean my job,' he said, without what might have been called appropriate concern, 'if it were discovered. I wonder if you truly realize, Doctor, how very much your work frightens and angers the very people who run this city – both its politics and its business. Moore's comment about the African witch doctor is really no joke.'

'I assure you, I did not take it as one. But if you are sincere in your wish to stop what is happening' – Kreizler's plea was deeply in earnest – 'then you *must* agree.'

I was still somewhat amazed by what I was hearing and thought that this would certainly be the moment when Roosevelt would stop flirting with the idea and quash it. Instead he slammed another fist into an open hand. "By thunder, Doctor, I know of a pair of detectives that would suit your purpose down to the ground! But tell me – where would you begin?'

'For the answer to that,' Kreizler replied, pointing over to me, 'I must thank Moore. It was something he sent me long ago that sparked the idea.'

'Something *I* sent you?' For a moment egotism made me put aside my trepidation at this dangerous proposal.

Laszlo approached the window and raised the shade altogether so that he could look outside. 'You will remember, John, that some years ago you found yourself in London, during the Ripper killings.'

'Certainly I remember,' I answered with a grunt. It had not been one of my more successful holidays: three months in London in 1888, when a bloodthirsty ghoul had taken to accosting random prostitutes in the East End and disemboweling them.

'I asked you for information, and for local press reports. You very decently obliged and included in one pouch some statements made by the younger Forbes Winslow.'

I raked my memory of the time. Forbes Winslow, whose similarly named father had been an eminent British alienist and an early influence on Kreizler, had set himself up as an asylum superintendant during the 1880s by trading on his father's achievements. The younger Winslow was a conceited fool, for my money, but when the Jack the Ripper killings began he was sufficiently well known to be able to inject himself into the investigation; indeed, he'd claimed that his participation had caused the murders (still unsolved at the time of this writing) to come to an end.

'Don't tell me Winslow's pointed the way for you,' I said in astonishment.

'Only inadvertently. In one of his absurd treatises on the Ripper he discussed a particular suspect in the case, saying that if he had created an 'imaginary man' – that was his phrase, 'imaginary man' – to fit the known traits of the murderer, he could not have devised a better one. Well, of course the suspect he favored was proved innocent. But the expression lodged itself in my head.' Kreizler turned back to us. 'We know nothing of the person we seek, and are unlikely ever to find witnesses who know any more than we do. Circumstantial evidence will be sparse, at best – he has been at work for years, after all, and has had more than enough time to perfect his technique. What we must do – the only thing that *can* be done – is to paint an imaginary picture

Caleb Carr

of the sort of person that *might* commit such acts. If we had such a picture, the significance of what little evidence we collected would be dramatically magnified. We might reduce the haystack in which our needle hides to something more like a – a pile of straw, if you will.'

'I will *not*, thank you,' I said. My nervousness was only growing. This was precisely the kind of conversation that would fire Roosevelt's mind, and Kreizler knew it. Action, plans, a campaign – it almost wasn't fair to ask Theodore to make a sensible decision when faced with that kind of emotional entice-ment. I stood up and stretched my arms into what I hoped was a preemptive stance. 'Listen, you two,' I began, but Laszlo simply touched my arm, gave me one of those looks of his – so authoritative it was downright vexing – and said:

'Do sit down for a moment, Moore. There is one more thing you both should know. I have said that under the terms I am outlining we might have a chance of success – we would certainly have nothing more. Our quarry's years of practice have not been in vain. The bodies of the two children in the water tower were discovered, remember, only by the most fortunate of accidents. We know nothing about him – we do not even know that it *is* a "him." Cases of women murdering their own and other children – drastically extreme variants of puerperal mania, or what is now called postpartum psychosis – are not uncommon. We have one central cause for optimism.'

Theodore looked up brightly. 'The Santorelli boy?' He was learning fast.

Kreizler nodded. 'More precisely, the Santorelli boy's body. Its location, and those of these other two. The killer could have gone on hiding his victims forever – God only knows how many he's killed in the last three years. Yet now he's given us an open statement of his activities – not unlike the letters, Moore, that the Ripper wrote to various London officials during his killings. Some buried, atrophied, but not yet dead part of our murderer is growing weary of the bloodshed. And in these three bodies we may read, as clearly as if it were words, his warped cry that we find him. And find him quickly – for the timetable by which he kills is a strict one, I suspect. That timetable, too, we must learn to decipher.'

'Then you believe you *can* do it quickly, Doctor?' Theodore asked. 'An investigation like the one you're describing could not be carried on indefinitely, after all. We must have *results*!'

Kreizler shrugged, seemingly unaffected by Roosevelt's urgent tone. 'I have given you my honest opinion. We would have a fighting chance, nothing more – or less.' Kreizler put a hand on Theodore's desk. 'Well, Roosevelt?'

If it seems odd that I offered no further protest, I can only say this: Kreizler's explanation that his present course of action had been inspired by a document I had sent him years ago, coming as it did on the heels of our shared reminiscences about Harvard and Theodore's mounting enthusiasm for this plan, had suddenly made it plain to me that what was happening in that office was only partly a result of Georgio Santorelli's death. Its full range of causes seemed to stretch much farther back, to our childhoods and subsequent lives, both individual and shared. Rarely have I felt so strongly the truth of Kreizler's belief that the answers one gives to life's crucial questions are never truly spontaneous; they are the embodiment of years of contextual experience, of the building of patterns in each of our lives that eventually grow to dominate our behavior. Was Theodore – whose credo of active response to all challenges had guided him through physical sickness in youth and political and personal trials in adulthood – truly free to refuse Kreizler's offer? And if he accepted it, was I then free to say no to these two friends, with whom I had lived through many escapades and who were now telling me that my extracurricular activities and knowledge – so often dismissed as useless by almost everyone I knew – would prove vital in catching a brutal killer? Professor James would have said that, yes, any human being is free, at any time, to pursue or decline anything; and perhaps, objectively, that is true. But as Kreizler loved to say, you cannot objectify the subjective, you cannot generalize the specific. What *man*, or *a* man, might have chosen was arguable; Theodore and I were the men who were there.

So – on that dismal March morning Kreizler and I became detectives, as all three of us knew we must. That certainty was based, as I say, on thorough awareness of each other's characters

Caleb Carr

and pasts; yet there was one person in New York at that threshold moment who had correctly guessed at our deliberations and their conclusion without ever having been so much as introduced to us. Only in retrospect can I see that that person had taken a careful interest in our activities that morning; and that he chose the moment of Kreizler's and my departure from Police Headquarters to deliver an ambiguous yet unsettling message.

Hustling through a new onslaught of heavy rain delivered by an increasingly forbidding sky, Laszlo and I got back into his calash, where I became immediately aware of a peculiar stench, one very unlike the usual odors of horse waste and garbage that predominated on the streets of the city.

'Kreizler,' I said, wrinkling my nose as he sat beside me, 'has someone been—'

I stopped when I turned to see Laszlo's black eyes fixed on a remote corner of the carriage floor. Following his gaze I caught sight of a balled-up, heavily stained white rag, which I poked at with my umbrella.

'Quite a distinct blend of aromas,' Kreizler murmured. 'Human blood and excrement, unless I'm mistaken.'

I groaned and grabbed my nose with my left hand as I realized he was right. 'Some local boy's idea of funny,' I said, picking up the rag with the point of my umbrella. 'Carriages, like top hats, make good targets.' As I flung the rag out of the window it disgorged a ball of equally stained printed paper that fell to the carriage floor. I moaned again and tried unsuccessfully to spear the document with my umbrella. As I did the thing began to come unbunched and I was able to make out a bit of the printing on it.

'Well,' I grunted, perplexed. 'This sounds like something in *your* department, Kreizler. "The Relationship of Hygiene and Diet to the Formation of Infantile Neural—"'

With shocking abruptness Kreizler grabbed my umbrella from my hand, stabbed its tip through the bit of paper, and then flung both items out the window.

'What in – Kreizler!' I jumped out of the carriage, retrieved the umbrella, separated it from the offensive piece of paper, and then got back into the calash.

As I glanced at Kreizler I saw a trace of real apprehension in his features; but then he seemed to force the trace away, and when he spoke it was in a determinedly casual tone. 'I am sorry, Moore. But I happen to be familiar with that author. As poor a stylist as he is a thinker. And this is no time to be sidetracked – we've much to do.' He leaned forward and called out Cyrus's name, at which the big man's head appeared under the canopy of the carriage. 'The Institute, and then on to lunch,' Laszlo said. 'And pick up some speed, if you can, Cyrus – we could use a bit of fresh air in here.'

It was obvious, at that point, that the person who had left the befouled rag in the calash was not a child; for, based on the brief passage that I'd been able to read as well as on Kreizler's reaction, the monograph from which the sheet of paper had been torn was almost certainly one of Laszlo's own works. Thinking that one of Kreizler's many critics was responsible for the act, I didn't delve any deeper into it; but in the weeks to come, the full significance of the incident would become harrowingly clear.

Chapter 7

We were anxious to begin marshalling our forces for the investigation, and the delays we experienced, though brief, were frustrating. When Theodore got wind of the speculative interest in Kreizler's visit to headquarters displayed by reporters and police officers, he realized that he'd made a mistake by holding the meeting there, and told us he needed a couple of days to get things calmed down. Kreizler and I used the time to make arrangements regarding our 'civilian' occupations. I had to convince my editors to grant me a leave of absence, a goal made somewhat easier by a timely telephone call from Roosevelt, who explained that I was wanted on vital police business. Nonetheless, I was only allowed out of the editorial offices of the *Times* at Thirty-second and Broadway when I pledged that if the investigation resulted in a story that was fit to print, I would not take it to another paper or magazine, regardless of how much money I was offered. I assured my sour-faced taskmasters that they wouldn't want the story anyway, and then breezed down Broadway on a typical March morning in New York: twenty-nine degrees at eleven A.M., with winds of fifty miles an hour cutting through the streets. I was scheduled to meet Kreizler at his Institute, and I had thought to walk, so great was my sense of release at not being answerable to my editors for an indefinite period. But real New York cold – the kind that freezes horse urine in little rivulets on the surface of the streets – will conquer the best of spirits eventually. Outside the Fifth Avenue Hotel I decided to get a cab, pausing only to watch Boss Platt emerge from a carriage and vanish inside, his stiff, unnatural movements doing nothing to reassure the onlooker that he was, in fact, alive.

Kreizler's leave of absence, I speculated inside the cab, would not be so simple a matter as mine. The two dozen or so children at his Institute depended on his presence and his counsel. Indeed, I had not initially seen how he proposed to take up another vocation, even temporarily, so great was the need for his steadying hand at the Institute; but then he told me that he still planned to spend two mornings and one night per week there, at which times he would leave our investigation in my hands. It was not the kind of responsibility I'd anticipated, and I was surprised when the notion left me feeling eager rather than anxious.

Shortly after my cab passed through Chatham Square and turned onto East Broadway, I disembarked at Numbers 185–187: the Kreizler Institute. Stepping onto the sidewalk, I saw that Laszlo's calash was also at the curb, and I glanced up at the windows of the Institute, half-expecting to see him looking out for me but finding no face.

Kreizler had bought the Institute's two four-story, red-brick and black-trim buildings with his own money in 1885, and then had their interiors remodeled so that they became one unit. The subsequent upkeep of the place was covered by the fee he charged his wealthier clients, as well as by the considerable income he took in from his work as an expert legal witness. The children's rooms were on the top floor of the Institute, and class and recreational halls occupied the third. On the second floor were Kreizler's consulting and examination rooms, as well as his psychological laboratory, where he performed tests on the children's powers of perception, reaction, association, memory, and all the other psychic functions that so fascinated the alienist community. The ground floor was reserved for his rather forbidding operational theater, where he performed the occasional brain dissection and postmortem. My cab had pulled up near the black iron stairs that led to the main entrance, at Number 185, and Cyrus Montrose was at the top of them, his head housed in a bowler, his huge frame enveloped in an even more sizable greatcoat, and his wide nostrils breathing cool fire.

'Afternoon, Cyrus,' I said with a difficult smile as I climbed the stairs, vainly hoping that I didn't sound as uneasy as I always felt when caught in his shark's stare. 'Is Dr. Kreizler here?'

'That's his carriage, Mr. Moore,' Cyrus answered, in a pleasant enough voice that still managed to make me sound like one of the bigger idiots in the city. But I just grinned resolutely on.

'I expect you've heard that the doctor and I will be working together for a while?'

Cyrus nodded with what, if I hadn't known better, I would have sworn was a wry smile. 'I've heard, sir.'

'Well!' I brushed my jacket back and slapped at my vest. 'I guess I'll go find him. Afternoon, Cyrus!'

I got no answer from the man as I entered, not that I deserved one; there was no reason for both of us to behave like morons.

The Institute's small vestibule and front hall – white with dark wood wainscoting – were full of the usual fathers, mothers, and children, all crowded onto two long, low benches and waiting to see Kreizler. Almost every morning in the late winter and early spring, Laszlo personally conducted interviews to determine who would be admitted to the Institute the following fall. The applicants ranged from the wealthiest northeastern families to the poorest of immigrants and rural laborers, but they all had one thing in common: a troubled or troublesome child whose behavior was in some way extreme and inexplicable. This was all very serious, of course, but that didn't change the fact that the Institute was, on such mornings, a bit of a zoo. As you walked down that hallway you were likely to be tripped, spat at, cursed, and otherwise maltreated, particularly by those children whose only mental deficiency was that they'd been overindulged, and whose parents clearly could and should have saved themselves the trip to Kreizler's office.

As I moved to the door of Kreizler's consulting room, I locked gazes with one such prospective troublemaker, a fat little boy with malevolent eyes. A dark, heavily lined woman of about fifty, wrapped in a shawl and mumbling something that I suspected was Hungarian, was pacing back and forth in front of the consulting room door; I had to dodge both her and the boy's kicking legs in order to get close enough to knock. Having done so I heard Kreizler shout 'Yes!' and then I entered, the pacing woman watching me with apparent concern.

After the fairly innocuous vestibule, Laszlo's consulting room was the first place that his prospective patients (whom he always referred to as 'students,' insisting that his staff do the same in order to avoid making the children conscious of their situations and conditions) saw on entering the space and experience that were the Kreizler Institute. He had therefore taken care that its furnishings were not intimidating. There were paintings of animals that, while reflecting Laszlo's good taste, nonetheless amused and reassured the children, as did the presence of toys – ball-and-cup, simple building blocks, dolls, and lead soldiers – which Laszlo actually used in making preliminary tests of agility, reaction time, and emotional disposition. The presence of medical instruments was minimal, most being kept in the examination room beyond. It was there that Kreizler would perform his first series of physical investigations, should a given case interest him. These tests were designed to determine whether the child's difficulties stemmed from secondary causes (that is, bodily malfunctions that affected mood and behavior) or primary abnormalities, meaning mental or emotional disorders. If a child showed no evidence of secondary distress, and Kreizler thought he could do some good in the case (in other words, if there were no signs of hopeless brain disease or damage), the child would be 'enrolled': he or she would live at the Institute nearly full-time, going home only for holidays, and then only if Kreizler thought such contact safe. Laszlo very much agreed with the theories of his friend and colleague Dr. Adolf Meyer, and often quoted one of Meyer's dictums: 'The degenerative processes in children have their chief encouragement in the equally defective home surroundings.' Allowing troubled children a new environmental context was the most important goal of the Institute; and beyond that, it was the cornerstone of Laszlo's passionate effort to discover whether or not what he called the 'original mold' of the human psyche could be recast and the fate to which the accidents of birth consign each of us thereby redetermined.

Kreizler was sitting at his rather ornate secretary, writing by the light of a small Tiffany desk lamp of muted green and gold glass. Waiting for him to look up, I approached a small bookshelf near the secretary and took down one of my favorite volumes: *The Career and Death of the Mad Thief and Murderer, Samuel Green.* The case, dating from 1822, was one that Laszlo often cited to the parents of his 'students,' for the infamous Green had been, in Kreizler's words, 'a product of the whip' – beaten throughout his childhood – and at the time of his capture had openly acknowledged that his crimes against society were a form of revenge. My own attraction to the book was prompted by its frontispiece, which depicted 'The Madman Green's End' on a Boston gallows. I had always enjoyed Green's crazed stare in the picture, and was amusedly reacquainting myself with it when Kreizler, without turning from his desk, thrust out a few sheets of paper and said:

'Look at these, Moore. Our first success, small though it is.'

Putting the book aside and taking the papers from him, I found that they were a series of forms and releases that seemed to refer to a graveyard, and to two graves in particular; there was a note concerning exhumation of bodies, and a nearly illegible document signed by one Abraham Zweig—

I was distracted by the unmistakable feeling of being watched. Turning, I saw a young girl of about twelve, with a round, pretty face that bore a somewhat frightened and slightly persecuted expression. She had taken up the book I'd laid down, and was glancing from me to the frontispiece as she fixed the top few buttons of a simple but clean dress. She read the small legend that explained the engraving, and apparently leapt to some unpleasant conclusions – her face grew fearful and she looked to Kreizler, while shying away from me.

Laszlo turned to her. 'Ah, Berthe. Ready to leave?'

The girl pointed at the book uncertainly, then spoke in a tremor as she turned her finger on me: 'Then . . . am *I* mad, too, Dr. Kreizler? And is this man going to put me in one of those places?'

'What?' Kreizler answered, taking the book away and giving me an admonishing look. 'Mad? Ridiculous! We have only good news.' Laszlo spoke to her as to any adult – directly, bluntly – but with a tone that he reserved for children: patient, kind, occasionally indulgent. 'Come right over here.' The girl approached him, and Kreizler helped her jump onto his knee. 'You are a very healthy, very *intelligent* young lady.' The girl blushed and laughed, quietly and happily. 'Your difficulty stems from a series of small growths that are living in your nose and ears. These growths, unlike you, enjoy the fact that your house is *too blasted cold*.' He tapped her head in time with these last words. 'You shall have to see a doctor, who is a friend of mine, and have these growths removed. All of which can be done while you're having a very pleasant sleep. And as for this man' – he put Berthe back on the floor – 'he is my friend, Mr. Moore. Say hello.'

The girl curtsied ever so slightly, but did not speak. I bowed back. 'Very pleased to meet you, Berthe.'

She only laughed again, at which Laszlo made a ticking noise. 'Enough of your giggling. Go and fetch your mother and we'll arrange everything.'

The girl ran to the door and Kreizler tapped the papers in my hand with some excitement. 'Fast work, eh, Moore? They arrived here not an hour ago.'

'Who did?' I asked in bewilderment. 'What did?'

'The Zweig children!' he answered quietly. 'The ones in the water tower – I have their remains downstairs!'

It was so ghoulish a notion that I couldn't help but shudder. Before I could ask why in the world he should have done such a thing, however, the girl Berthe had brought her mother – the woman with the shawl – into the office. The woman exchanged a few words in Hungarian with Kreizler, but his knowledge of that language was limited (his German father had not wished his children to speak their mother's tongue) and the conversation soon shifted back to English.

'Mrs. Rajk, you really must listen to me!' Laszlo said, exasperated.

'But, Doctor,' the woman protested, wringing her hands, 'sometimes, you see, she understands good, and then I know she is being like a demon, tormenting us—'

'Mrs. Rajk, I'm not certain how many different ways I can explain this to you,' Kreizler said, making one more attempt at

Caleb Carr

evenhandedness as he pulled his silver watch from his vest pocket and quickly looked at it. 'Or in how many languages. The swelling is occasionally less marked, you see?' He pointed at his own ear, nose, and throat. 'At such times she is in no pain, and can not only hear and speak but breathe easily. So she is alert and attentive. But most of the time the vegetations in the pharynx and the posterior nasal cavity – the throat, the nose – cover the eustachian tubes, connected to her ears, and generally make such an effort difficult, if not impossible. The fact that your flat is full of cold drafts aggravates the condition.' Kreizler put his hands on the young girl's shoulders, and she smiled happily again. 'In short, she is not doing any of this deliberately to torment either you or her instructor. Do you understand?' He leaned down into the mother's face, giving her a close examination with the hawk's eyes. 'No. Obviously you do not. Well, then, you must simply accept my statement – there is nothing wrong with her mind *or* her soul. Take her to St. Luke's. Dr. Osborne performs these procedures quite regularly, and I believe I can persuade him to lower his fee. By next fall' – he tousled the girl's hair, and she looked up at him gratefully – 'Berthe will be more than recovered and quite ready to excel at school. Correct, young lady?'

The girl didn't answer, but let out another little laugh. The mother tried one more 'But—' before Kreizler took her by the arm and hustled her out through the vestibule to the front door. 'Really, Mrs. Rajk, that is enough. The fact that you cannot understand it does not mean that it doesn't exist. Take her to Dr. Osborne! I shall consult with him, and if I find you have not obeyed me I shall be extremely angry.' He closed the front door on them, turned back into the vestibule, and was immediately besieged by the remaining families. Shouting an announcement that there would be a short break in the interviewing, Kreizler retreated into the consulting room again and slammed the door.

'The great difficulty,' he mumbled, as he returned to his secretary and began straightening papers, 'of convincing people that the mental health of children must be better attended to is that more and more of them believe that their child's every little trouble betrays a momentous condition. Ah, well . . .' He closed the secretary and locked it, then turned. 'Now, Moore. Down we go. Roosevelt's men should already be here. I asked Cyrus to bring them in directly through the ground-floor door.'

'You're going to interview them *here*?' I asked, as we went through the examination room and escaped the families out front by way of a back door to the Institute's courtyard.

'In fact, I am not going to interview them at all,' Kreizler answered, as the cold air hit us. 'I will allow the Zweig children to do that. I will only study the results. And remember, Moore – not a word about what we're doing, until I'm sure these men are acceptable.'

It had begun to snow lightly, and several of Kreizler's young patients – dressed in the Institute's simple gray and blue uniform – had come out into the courtyard to play among the flakes. When they saw Kreizler they ran over to cheerfully but very respectfully greet him. Laszlo smiled back at them, and asked a few questions about their teachers and their schoolwork. A couple of the bolder students gave some frank answers about this or that teacher's appearance and bodily aromas, at which Laszlo admonished them, though not harshly. As we turned away and entered the ground-floor doorway, I heard joyful shouts start to echo off the courtyard walls once more, and thought of how recently many of these children had been on the streets and just a few short steps from Georgio Santorelli's fate. More and more, my mind was seeing all things in relation to the case.

A dark, dank hallway led us to the operating theater, a very long room that was kept dry and warm by a gas space heater that hissed in one corner. The walls were smooth and whitewashed, and white cabinets with glass doors ran along each wall, holding a collection of gruesome, glistening instruments. On white shelves above these were a collection of chilling models: realistically painted plaster casts of human and simian heads, with their skulls partly removed to reveal brain positioning and their faces still expressive of their death throes. Sharing the shelf space with these was a large collection of actual brains from a wide variety of creatures, housed in specimen jars full of formaldehyde. The remainder of the wall space was occupied by charts of human and animal nervous systems. In the center of the room were two steel operating tables, with channels for draining bodily fluids running

Caleb Carr

down the center of their beds to the foot, where they emptied into steel receptacles on the floor. There were forms of roughly human dimensions on each of these tables, covered with sterile sheets. A pronounced aroma of animal decay and earth emanated from them.

Standing by the tables were two men, both wearing three-piece wool suits, the taller man's a subdued but fashionably checked pattern, the shorter's simple black. Their faces were almost totally obscured by the harsh glare of the electric operating lamps that were positioned above the tables and between us.

'Gentlemen,' Laszlo said, moving directly toward them. 'I am Dr. Kreizler. I hope you haven't been waiting long.'

'Not at all, Doctor,' said the taller man, shaking Kreizler's hand. As he leaned into the bright light around the table I could see that his Semitic features were quite handsome – strong nose, steady brown eyes, and a good head of curling hair. The shorter man, by contrast, had small eyes, a fleshy face that was beaded with sweat, and thinning hair. They both looked to be in their early thirties. 'I'm Sergeant Marcus Isaacson,' the taller man went on, 'and this is my brother, Lucius.'

The shorter man looked annoyed as he extended a hand. '*Detective Sergeant* Lucius Isaacson, Doctor,' he said. Then, leaning back and speaking out of the side of his mouth, he murmured, 'Don't do that again. You said you wouldn't.'

Marcus Isaacson rolled his eyes, then tried to smile at us as he, too, spoke out of the side of his mouth. 'What? What did I do?'

'Don't introduce me as your brother,' Lucius Isaacson whispered urgently.

'Gentlemen,' Kreizler said, a little perplexed by this spat. 'Allow me to introduce a friend of mine, John Schuyler Moore.' I shook hands with them both as Kreizler continued: 'Commissioner Roosevelt speaks quite highly of your talents, and thinks you may be able to give me some assistance with a bit of research I'm doing. You have two areas of speciality that particularly interest me—'

'Yes,' Marcus said, 'criminal science and forensic medicine.'

Kreizler went on: 'First of all, I'd like to know—'

'If you're wondering about our names,' Marcus interrupted,

'our mother and father were very concerned, when they arrived in America, that their children not be subjected to anti-Jewish feeling in school.'

'We were relatively lucky,' Lucius added. 'Our sister's name is Cordelia.'

'You see,' Marcus continued, 'they were learning English by studying Shakespeare. When I was born they'd just started, with *Julius Caesar*. A year later, they were still on it, and my brother came. But by the time our sister arrived, two years after that, they were making progress, and had gotten to *King Lear*—'

'I've no doubt, gentlemen,' Kreizler finished for him, ever more concerned and treating them fully to the arched eyebrows and the predatory gaze. 'Interesting though that may be, what I had intended to ask was how you arrived at your areas of specialization, and what led you to the police force.'

Lucius sighed, looking up. 'Nobody wants to hear how we got our names, Marcus,' he mumbled. 'I've told you that.'

Marcus's face went a little red and then he addressed Kreizler with deliberate seriousness, sensing the meeting wasn't going well. 'Well, you see, Doctor, it was our parents again, though I do understand that it may not be a particularly interesting explanation. My mother wanted me to be a lawyer, and my brother – the *detective sergeant* here – he was supposed to be a doctor. It didn't work out. We'd started reading Wilkie Collins when we were boys, and had pretty well decided by the time we went to college that we wanted to be detectives.'

'Law and medical training were useful, at first,' Lucius continued, 'but then we moved on and did some work for the Pinkertons. It wasn't until Commissioner Roosevelt took over the department that we actually got a chance to join the police. I suppose you've heard that his hiring practices are a bit ... unorthodox.'

I knew what he was referring to, and later explained it to Laszlo. Besides investigating nearly every officer and detective in the Police Department, and thus prompting many to resign, Roosevelt had made a point of hiring unlikely new recruits, in an effort to break the hold that the clique headed by Thomas Byrnes and such precinct heads as 'Clubber' Williams and 'Big Bill'

Devery had on the force. Theodore was especially fond of bringing in Jews, whom he considered exceptionally honest and brave, referring to them as 'Maccabean warriors for justice.' The Isaacson brothers were apparently representative of this effort, though 'warriors' was not the first word that came to mind on meeting them.

'I take it,' Lucius ventured hopefully, wanting to get off the subject of their backgrounds, 'that you want some help with this exhumation?' He indicated the two tables.

Kreizler studied him. 'How did you know it's an exhumation?'

'The smell, Doctor. It's very distinct. And the positions of the bodies indicate a formal burial, not a random interment.'

Kreizler liked that, and brightened a bit. 'Yes, Detective Sergeant, you have presumed correctly.' He moved over and whipped the sheets off the tables, at which point the stench was complemented by the rather disturbing sight of two small skeletons, one draped in a decaying black suit and the other in an equally decrepit white dress. Some bones were still connected, but many had come free of one another, and there were bits of hair and nails, along with spatterings of dirt, all over them. I tightened up and tried not to look away: this sort of thing was going to be my fate for a while, and I figured that I'd better get used to it.

The Isaacson brothers' faces displayed nothing but fascination as they approached the tables and listened to Laszlo: 'Brother and sister, Benjamin and Sofia Zweig. Murdered. Their bodies found—'

'In a water tower,' Marcus said. 'Three years ago. The case is still officially open.'

This, too, pleased Kreizler. 'Over here,' he continued, indicating a small white table in the corner that was piled with clippings and documents, 'you'll find all the information concerning the case that I've been able to assemble. I should like the two of you to review it, and study the bodies. There is some urgency about the matter, so I can only offer you the afternoon and evening. I will be at Delmonico's at eleven-thirty tonight. Meet me there, and in exchange for your information

The Alienist   81

I shall be happy to offer you an excellent dinner.'

Marcus Isaacson's enthusiasm broke for a moment of curiosity. 'Dinner isn't necessary, Doctor, if this is official business. Though we appreciate the offer.'

Laszlo nodded with a slight smile, amused at Marcus's attempt to draw him out. 'We'll see you at eleven-thirty, then.'

At that the Isaacsons started in on the materials before them, barely conscious of Kreizler's and my farewells. We went upstairs, and as I fetched my coat from the consultation room, Laszlo continued to look intrigued.

'There's no doubting they're idiosyncratic,' he said as he walked me to the front door. 'But I've a feeling they know their work. We shall see. Oh, by the way, Moore – do you have a clean set of clothes for tonight?'

'Tonight?' I asked, pulling my cap and gloves on.

'The opera,' he replied. 'Roosevelt's candidate for liaison between our investigation and his office is due to meet us at my house at seven.'

'Who is he?'

'No idea,' Laszlo said with a shrug. 'But whoever it is, the liaison's role will be crucial. I thought we'd take him to the opera, and see how he reacts. It's as good a test of character as any. We'll use my box at the Metropolitan. Maurel is singing Rigoletto. It should suit our purpose.'

'It certainly should,' I said happily. 'And speaking of purposes, who's singing the hunchback's daughter?'

Kreizler turned away with an expression of mild disgust. 'My God, Moore, I should like to get the particulars of your infancy someday. This irrepressible sexual mania—'

'I only asked who's singing the hunchback's daughter!'

'All right, all right! Yes, Frances Saville, she of the legs, as you put it!'

'In that case,' I said, bouncing down the steps and toward the carriage, 'I definitely have clothes.' As far as I was concerned, you could take Nellie Melba, Lillian Nordica and all the rest of the half-attractive, four-star voices at the Metropolitan and, as Stevie Taggert would have put it, go chase yourself. Give me a really beautiful girl with a decent voice and I was a docile audience

Caleb Carr

member. 'I'll be at your place at seven.'

'Splendid,' Kreizler answered with a frown. 'I can scarcely wait. Cyrus! Take Mr. Moore to Washington Square!'

'I spent the quick trip back up and across town pondering what an unusual – but nonetheless enjoyable – way to open a murder investigation the opera and dinner at Delmonico's would be. Unfortunately, such entertainments did not turn out to be said opening; for when I arrived home, I found a very agitated Sara Howard on my doorstep.

Chapter 8

Sara paid no attention to my greeting. 'This is Dr. Kreizler's carriage, isn't it?' she asked. 'And his man. Can we take them?'

'Take them where?' I answered, looking up to see my grandmother peering anxiously out the window of her parlor. 'Sara, what's going on?'

'Sergeant Connor and another man, Casey, went down to talk to the Santorelli boy's parents this morning. They returned and said they'd found nothing – but there was blood on the cuff of Connor's shirt. Something's happened, I know it, and I want to find out what.' She wasn't looking at me, perhaps because she knew what my reaction was likely to be.

'A little off the beaten trail for a secretary, isn't it?' I asked. Sara didn't answer, but a look of bitter disappointment filled her face, a frustration so severe that all I could do was open the calash door. 'What about it, Cyrus?' I said. 'Any objection to taking Miss Howard and myself on a little errand?'

Cyrus shrugged. 'No, sir. Not so long as I'm back at the Institute by the end of interviewing hours.'

'And so you shall be. Climb aboard, Sara, and meet Mr. Cyrus Montrose.'

In an instant Sara's aspect went from ferocious to exuberant – not an uncommon transformation for her. 'There are moments, John,' she said, jumping up onto the calash, 'when I think I may have been wrong about you all these years.' She shook Cyrus's hand eagerly and then sat down, throwing a blanket over my legs and hers when I got in. Directing Cyrus to an address on Mott Street, she clapped her hands once excitedly as the calash began moving.

There aren't many women who would have ventured into one of the worst parts of the Lower East Side with such relish. But Sara's adventurous spirit had never been much tempered by prudence. Furthermore, she had experience with the area: right after Sara's graduation from college, her father had gotten the idea that her education might be fully balanced by some firsthand experience of life in places other than Rhinecliff (where the Howards' country estate was located) and Gramercy Park. So she put on a starched white blouse, a dreary black skirt, and a rather ridiculous boater and spent the summer assisting a visiting nurse in the Tenth Ward. During those months she saw a great deal – most, indeed, of what the Lower East Side could throw at a person. None of it, however, was any worse than what we were bound for that day.

The Santorellis lived in a rear tenement a few blocks below Canal Street. Rear tenements had been outlawed in 1894, but there had been a grandfather clause in the bill, so that those that already existed were allowed to remain standing with minimal improvement. Suffice it to say that if a tenement building that fronted the street was dark, disease-ridden, and threatening, the smaller buildings that often stood behind them were exponentially more so. By the look of the particular front tenement we pulled up before that day, we were in for a typical experience: huge barrels of ash and waste stood by the urine-soaked stoop of the structure, on which was gathered a group of filthy, rag-clad men, each indistinguishable from the next. They were drinking and laughing among themselves, but they stopped abruptly at the sight of the calash and Cyrus. Sara and I stepped out and onto the curb.

'Don't wander too far, Cyrus,' I said, trying not to betray my jitters.

'No, sir,' he answered, gripping the pommel of his horsewhip tightly. With his other hand he reached into the pocket of his greatcoat. 'Perhaps you should take these, Mr. Moore.' He produced a set of brass knuckles.

'Hmm,' I noised, studying the weapon. 'I don't think that'll be necessary.' Then I dropped the sham. 'Besides, I wouldn't know how to use them.'

'Hurry up, John,' Sara said, and then we mounted the stoop.

'Here!' One of the loitering men grabbed my arm. 'D'you know there's a coon driving your rig?'

'Is there?' I answered, guiding Sara through the almost visible stench that hovered around the men.

'Black as the ace of spades!' another of the men asserted, seemingly astonished.

'Remarkable,' I replied, as Sara got inside. Before I could follow, the first man grabbed me again.

'You're not another cop, are you?' he asked menacingly.

'Absolutely not,' I answered. 'I despise cops.'

The man nodded once but said nothing, from which I divined that I was allowed to pass.

To get to the rear building it was necessary to navigate the pitch-black hallway of the front structure: always an unsettling experience. With Sara in the lead we felt our way along the filthy walls, trying but failing to adjust to the lack of light. I started when Sara stumbled on something; and I started even more violently when that something began to wail.

'Good lord, John,' Sara said after a moment. 'It's a baby.'

I still couldn't see a thing, but as I got closer the smell gave it away – a baby, all right, and the poor creature must have been covered in its own excrement.

'We've got to get it help,' Sara said, and I thought of the men on the stoop. When I looked back toward the front door, however, I saw them silhouetted against the snowfall outside, swinging sticks as they watched us, and occasionally laughing in a very unpleasant way. There would be no help from that quarter, so I began to try doors inside the hall. Finally finding one that would open, I pulled Sara toward and through it.

Inside were an old man and woman, ragpickers, who would only accept the baby after I offered them a half-dollar. They told us that the infant belonged to a couple across the hall who were out, as they were every day and night, jabbing morphine and drinking in a dive around the corner. The old man assured us that they would get the baby something to eat and clean it up, at which Sara gave them another dollar. Neither of us was under any illusions as to how much good a cleaning and feeding would do the child in the long run, but it was one of those all-too-common moments in New York when one is faced with a damnable set of options.

Finally, we reached the back door. The alleyway between the front and rear buildings was overflowing with more barrels and buckets, and the smell was indescribable. Sara placed a handkerchief over her nose and mouth and told me to do the same. Then we ran across to the ground-floor hallway of the rear building. There were four apartments with what seemed like a thousand people living in them on the first floor. I tried to identify all the languages being spoken, but lost count at about eight. A smelly collection of Germans with growlers of beer was camped on the staircase, and they parted grudgingly as we went up. It was evident, even in the half-light, that the stairs were coated with almost an inch of something extremely sticky that I didn't want to investigate. It didn't seem to bother the Germans.

The Santorelli flat was on the second floor in the back: the darkest spot in the whole building. When we knocked, a small, horribly thin woman with sunken eyes answered the door, speaking the Sicilian dialect. I knew only enough Italian for the opera, but Sara was better off – again because of her nursing days – and communicated quite easily. Mrs. Santorelli was not at all alarmed to see Sara (in fact she seemed to have been expecting her); but she expressed much concern over my presence, fearfully demanding to know if I was either a policeman or a journalist. Sara had to think fast, and I said I was her assistant. Mrs. Santorelli looked puzzled at that, but finally let us in.

'Sara,' I said as we entered, 'do you know this woman?'

'No,' she answered, 'but she seems to know me. Strange.'

The flat was composed of two rooms without any real windows, just small slits that had recently been cut in the walls to comply with new tenement regulations concerning ventilation. The Santorellis had rented one of the rooms to another family of Sicilians, which meant that six of them – the parents and Georgio's four brothers and sisters – lived in a space about nine feet by sixteen. There was nothing hanging on the bare, soot-encrusted walls, and two big buckets in the corners took care of sanitation. The family also had a kerosene stove, of the inexpensive type that so often used to put an end to such buildings.

Lying on an old, stained mattress in one corner wrapped in what blankets they had was the cause of Mrs. Santorelli's great agitation: her husband. His face was cut, bruised, and swollen, and his forehead was drenched in sweat. There was a bloody rag lying next to him, and, incongruously, a bound wad of money, which must have amounted to several hundred dollars. Mrs. Santorelli took up the wad, shoved it at Sara, and then urged her at the husband, tears starting to stream down her face.

We soon discovered that Mrs. Santorelli believed Sara to be a nurse. She had dispatched her four children to find one only an hour earlier. Again thinking quickly, Sara sat and began to examine Santorelli, quickly discovering that one of his arms was fractured. In addition, most of his torso was covered in bruises.

'John,' Sara said firmly, 'send Cyrus for bandages, disinfectant, and some morphine. Tell him we'll want a good clean piece of wood to use as a splint, as well.'

In what seemed one movement I was out the door, through the Germans and the alleyway, and down the stoop to the curb. I shouted the order to Cyrus, who sped off in the calash, and as I went back through the men on the stoop one of them held a hand to my chest.

'Just a minute,' he said. 'What's all that for?'

'Mr. Santorelli,' I answered. 'He's badly hurt.'

The man spat hard at the street. 'Damned cops. I hate those damned guineas, but I'll tell you, I hate cops more!'

This recurring theme seemed once again to be the signal for me to proceed. Back upstairs, Sara had gotten hold of some hot water and was busy washing Santorelli's wounds. The wife was still chattering, waving her hands and occasionally bursting into tears.

'There were six men, John,' Sara said to me, after listening for a few minutes.

Caleb Carr

'Six?' I echoed. 'I thought you said two.'

Sara indicated the bed with a jerk of her head. 'Come over here and help me – she'll be suspicious, otherwise.' Sitting down, I found that it was difficult to say which smelled worse, the mattress or Santorelli. But none of it seemed to bother Sara. 'Connor and Casey were definitely here,' she said. 'Along with two other men and two priests.'

'Priests?' I said, taking up a hot compress. 'What in hell—'

'One Catholic, apparently, and one not. She can't be more specific about the second. The priests had the money. They told the Santorellis to use some of it to pay for a decent burial for Georgio. The rest was a – consideration, apparently for silence. They told her not to allow anyone to exhume Georgio's body, even the police, and not to talk to anyone about the matter – especially any journalists.'

'*Priests?*' I said again, wiping at one of Santorelli's welts with no great enthusiasm. 'What did they look like.'

Sara put the question, then translated the answer: 'One short, with large white sideburns – that was the Catholic – and one thin with spectacles.'

'Why in the world would two priests have any interest in this?' I wondered. 'And why would they want to keep the police out of it? You say Connor and Casey were here for that conversation?'

'Apparently.'

'So whatever's going on, they're involved. Well, Theodore will be happy to hear that. Two more vacancies in the Division of Detectives, I'll wager. But who were the other two men?'

Again, Sara put the question to Mrs. Santorelli, who rattled off an answer that Sara didn't seem to comprehend. She asked again, but got the same reply.

'I may not understand this dialect as well as I thought,' Sara said. 'She says the other two *weren't* policemen, but then she says that they *were* policemen. I don't—'

Sara stopped and we all turned when a loud knock came at the door. Mrs. Santorelli shied away from it, and I was in no hurry to thrust myself into the breach; but Sara said, 'Oh, go on, John, don't be foolish. It's probably Cyrus.'

I stepped to the door and opened it. Outside in the hall was one of the men from the stoop. He held up a package. 'Your medicines,' he said with a grin. 'We don't allow no coons in this building.'

'Ah,' I said, accepting the package. 'I see. Thank you.'

Giving the goods to Sara, I sat back down on the bed. Santorelli was by this time semiconscious and Sara administered some of the morphine: she intended to set his arm. The break was not bad, she said, but it nonetheless made a somewhat nauseating cracking sound as she got it back into place. Between his grogginess and the drug, however, Santorelli didn't seem to feel a thing, though his wife let out a nice little howl and some kind of a prayer. I began wiping disinfectant on the other wounds while Sara continued her conversation with Mrs. Santorelli.

'It seems,' Sara said at length, 'that Santorelli got very indignant. Threw the money in the priests' faces, and said he demanded that the police find the murderer of his son. At that point the priests left, and ...'

'Yes,' I said. '*And.*' I was well aware of how Irish cops generally dealt with a lack of cooperation from the non-English-speaking population. A good example of the technique was lying next to me.

Sara shook her head. 'It's all so strange,' she sighed, starting to apply gauze to some of the worst cuts and bruises. 'Santorelli nearly got himself killed – yet he hasn't seen Georgio for four years. The boy's been living on the streets.'

Mrs. Santorelli's trust had been inspired by Sara's care for her husband, and once she began to tell us the story of her son Georgio, it would have been difficult to stop her.

Georgio was a shy boy in his early years, but smart and determined enough to attend the public school on Hester Street and get good marks. Starting at about age seven, however, there was a problem with some other boys at school. The older ones were apparently able to persuade Georgio to perform sexual acts, ones that Mrs. Santorelli didn't much want to define. Sara pressed her on the issue, however, sensing that such information would be important, and we found that it involved sodomy of both the anal and oral varieties. The behavior was discovered and reported to the parents by a teacher. The Latin concept of

Caleb Carr

masculinity being as broad and forgiving as it is, Georgio's father nearly lost his mind, and took to beating the boy at regular intervals. Mrs. Santorelli demonstrated for us how her husband would bind Georgio by his wrists to the front door, then whip him across the backside with a wide belt, which she also showed us. It was a cruel implement, and in Santorelli's hands it apparently inflicted such damage that Georgio sometimes avoided school altogether, simply because he couldn't sit down.

The odd thing, however, was that instead of becoming compliant, Georgio only grew more willful every time he got a whipping. After months of such punishment, he began to stay away from the family's flat for nights at a time, and gave up school altogether. Then one day the parents spotted him on a street west of Washington Square, wearing ladies' cosmetics and hawking himself like any street cruiser. Santorelli confronted the boy, and said that if he ever returned home he'd kill him. Georgio screamed angry insults in return, and the father was getting ready to attack him right then and there when another man – probably Georgio's panderer – stepped in and advised the Santorellis to disappear. That was the last they ever saw of their son, until they viewed his mangled body at the morgue.

The tale roused many questions in my mind, and I could see that Sara felt the same. We would never get to ask them. Just as we were wrapping Santorelli back up in the worn, dirty blankets in which we'd found him, a booming came at the door; and I, thinking it was the men from the stoop, opened it. In an instant, two large, mustachioed thugs in suits and bowlers had forced their way into the flat. The mere sight of them sent Mrs. Santorelli into hysterics.

'Who the hell're you people?' one of the thugs demanded.

Sara made a brave show of saying that she was a nurse; but the explanation that I was her assistant, which had worked so admirably on a desperate woman who didn't speak English, went nowhere with these two.

'Assistant, eh?' the thug said, as they both moved on me. Sara and I carefully edged our way to the door of the flat. 'That's a hell of a rig out there, for a nurse and her assistant!'

'Well, I do value your opinion,' I said with a smile; then I grabbed Sara and we flew down the stairs. Never have I been so grateful that the girl was of an athletic disposition, for even in her skirt she was faster than our pursuers. Such did not help, however, when we reached the hall of the front building and saw the men on the stoop blocking our exit. They began moving our way, slapping their sticks in the palms of their hands ominously.

'John,' Sara said, 'are they really trying to trap us?' Her voice was, I remember thinking, damned steady – which I found extremely irritating.

'Of *course* they're trying to trap us, woman!' I said, breathing hard. 'You and your detective games, we're going to be beaten to death! Cyrus!' I cupped my hands and bellowed at the front door as the men began to move our way. 'Cyrus!' I let my hands fall, despondent. 'Where in hell *is* the man?'

Sara only clutched her bag tightly without a word; and when the two thugs in the bowlers appeared at the rear end of the hall, apparently sealing our fates, she reached into it. 'Don't worry, John,' she said confidently. 'I won't let anything happen to you.' And with that she withdrew a .45-caliber Army Model Colt revolver, with a four-and-a-half-inch barrel and pearl grips. Sara was what you might call a firearms enthusiast.

'Oh, my God,' I said, ever more alarmed. 'Sara, you can't just blast away in a dark hallway, you don't know what you'll hit—'

'Can you suggest a better idea?' she said, looking around, realizing that I was right and feeling alarm for the first time.

'Well, I—'

But it was too late: the men from the stoop were upon us in a screaming rush. I grabbed Sara and covered her with my body, hoping she wouldn't shoot me in the gut during the ensuing attack.

You can imagine my shock when that attack failed to materialize. We were momentarily buffeted by the men with sticks, but that was only as they passed. Still screaming, they fell on the two thugs behind us with rare ferocity. Given the odds, it wasn't much of a contest: we heard a few seconds of shouting, grunting, and wrestling, and then the hall was filled with heavy breathing and a few moans. Sarah and I got out onto the stoop and then raced to the calash, where Cyrus stood waiting.

'Cyrus!' I said. 'Are you aware that we could've been killed in there?'

'It didn't seem very likely, Mr. Moore,' he answered calmly. 'Not given what those men were saying before they went in.'

'And what was that, pray tell?' I asked, still not satisfied with his attitude.

Before he could answer the bodies of the two thugs came flying out the door of the tenement, hitting the snowy pavement hard. Their bowlers followed. The men were unconscious, and in a general condition that made Mr. Santorelli look a picture of health. Our friends with the sticks followed triumphantly, even though a few of them had taken some hard knocks, too. The one who'd spoken to me earlier looked over at us, producing huge frosty clouds as he breathed hard.

'I may hate coons,' he said with a grin. 'But, damnation, I do hate cops more!'

'*That*,' Cyrus murmured, 'was what they were saying.'

I looked at the thugs on the ground. 'Cops?' I said to the man by the stoop.

'*Ex*-cops,' he answered, walking toward me. 'Used to be roundsmen in this neighborhood. They've got a hell of a nerve, coming back to a building like this.' I nodded, looking at the unconscious bodies on the sidewalk before me, and then signaled thanks to the man. 'Your honor,' he said, indicating his mouth, 'that was thirsty work.' I pulled out some coins and threw them to him. He tried but failed to catch the money, at which his mates fell grabbing to the ground. They were soon at each other's throats. Sara and I got into the calash, and in a few minutes Cyrus had us on Broadway, heading uptown.

Sara was full of good cheer, now that we were safe, and she fairly leapt around the carriage, recalling each dangerous moment of our expedition rapturously. I smiled and nodded, glad that she'd been able to have a moment of positive action; but my mind was on something else. I was going over what Mrs. Santorelli had said, and trying to examine it as Kreizler would have. There was something in the tale of young Georgio that reminded me of Laszlo's account of the children in the water tower; something very important, though I couldn't quite put my finger – and then I had it. The behavior. Kreizler had described two troublesome children, embarrassments to their family – and I had just been told about another such youth. All three, in Kreizler's hypothesis, had met their ends at the hands of the same man. Was this apparent similarity of character a factor in their deaths, or simply a coincidence? It might have been the latter. But somehow I didn't think Kreizler would find it so . . .

Lost in these thoughts, I didn't quite hear Sara asking me a rather stunning question; but when she repeated it, the out-landishness of the notion became clear even to my distracted mind. We'd been through a great deal, however, that day, and I could not find it in me to disappoint her.

Chapter 9

I got to Kreizler's house, at 283 East Seventeenth Street, a few minutes early, white-tied and caped and not at all sure of the conspiracy I'd entered into with Sara – a conspiracy that for better or worse would now play out. The snow had deepened to several inches, forming a quiet, pleasant layer over the bare shrubs and iron fences of Stuyvesant Park, across the street from Laszlo's house. Opening the small gate to his similarly small front yard, I walked to the door and gently rapped the brass knocker. The French windows of the parlor, one story up, were slightly ajar, and I could hear Cyrus at the piano, giving forth with 'Pari siamo' from *Rigoletto* – Kreizler was warming his ears up for the evening.

The door opened, bringing me face to face with the skittish, uniformed figure of Mary Palmer, Laszlo's maid and house-keeper. Mary rounded out the list of former patients who had entered Kreizler's service, and she was yet another who made the visitor who knew her full story a bit uneasy. Beautifully built, with a bewitching face and sky-blue eyes, Mary had been considered idiotic by her family since birth. She could not speak coherently, putting words and syllables together in unintelligible jumbles, and so was never taught to read or write. Her mother and father, the latter a respected schoolmaster in Brooklyn, had trained her to perform menial household functions, and seemed to care for her adequately; but one day in 1884, when she was seventeen,

Mary chained her father to his brass bed while the rest of the family was out, and then set fire to the house. The father died a horrible death; and since there was no apparent reason for the attack, Mary was involuntarily committed to the lunatic asylum on Blackwells Island.

There she was discovered by Kreizler, who was struck by the fact that Mary lacked most, if not all, of the symptoms of dementia praecox, the only condition that, in his opinion, constituted true insanity. (The term is currently being supplanted, Laszlo says quite rightly, by Dr. Eugene Bleuler's label 'schizophrenia'; as I understand it, the word denotes a pathological inability to either recognize or interact with the reality around one.) Kreizler began to try to communicate with the girl, and soon discovered that in fact she suffered from classic motor aphasia, complicated by agraphia: she could understand words and think in clear sentences, but those parts of her mind that controlled speech and writing were badly damaged. Like most such unfortunates, Mary was bitterly aware of her difficulty, but lacked the ability to explain it (or anything else) to others. Kreizler was able to communicate by asking questions that Mary could answer with the simplest of statements – often just 'yes' or 'no' – and he taught her as much of rudimentary writing as her condition would permit. Weeks of work brought him to a new and shocking understanding of her history: apparently, her own father had been sexually violating her for years before the killing, but she, of course, had been unable to relate this fact to anyone.

Kreizler had demanded a legal review of the case, and Mary was eventually freed. Afterwards, she managed to convey to Laszlo the idea that she would make an ideal houseservant. Knowing that the girl's chances of an independent life were otherwise slim, Kreizler had taken her on, and now she not only maintained but jealously guarded his home. The effect of her presence, combined with those of Cyrus Montrose and Stevie Taggert, was to temper my mood whenever I visited that elegant house. Despite the place's collection of contemporary and classic art and splendid French furniture, as well as the grand piano out of which Cyrus perpetually coaxed fine music, I had never been able when there to fully elude the awareness that I was surrounded by thieves and killers, each of whom had a very good explanation for his or her acts but none of whom gave the impression of being willing to put up with questionable behavior from anyone else ever again.

'Hello, Mary,' I said, handing her my cape. She gave me a small dip on one knee in reply, looking at the floor. 'I'm early. Is Dr. Kreizler dressed?'

'No, sir,' she said with deliberate effort. Her face filled with the simultaneous relief and frustration that were characteristic when her words came out correctly: relief at having succeeded, frustration at not being able to say more. She opened an arm sheathed in billowy blue linen toward the stairs, and then moved to hang my cape on a nearby rack.

'Well, then, I guess I'll have a drink and enjoy Cyrus's exceptional singing,' I said.

I took the stairs two at a time, feeling a bit confined in my evening clothes, then entered the parlor. Cyrus nodded to me and kept singing, while I anxiously fetched a silver cigarette box off the marble mantle over the very warm fireplace. Removing one of the tasty blends of Virginia and Russian black tobacco, I drew a match from a smaller silver case on the mantle and lit it.

Kreizler came trotting down the stairs from above, in a set of white tie and tails that were impeccably cut. 'No sign of Roosevelt's man?' he said, just as Mary appeared with a silver tray. On it were four ounces of Sevruga caviar, some thin slices of toast, a bottle of ice-cold vodka, and several small, frosted glasses: a thoroughly admirable habit Kreizler had picked up during a trip to St. Petersburg.

'None,' I answered, stubbing out my cigarette and eagerly attacking the tray.

'Well, I'll want punctuality from everyone involved,' he pronounced, checking the time. 'And if he doesn't . . .'

At that the door knocker downstairs clicked several times, and the sounds of entrance filtered up the stairs. Kreizler nodded. 'That, at least, is a good sign. Cyrus – something a little less grim, I think. "Di provenza il mar."'

Cyrus followed the instruction, launching softly into the gentle Verdi tune. I swallowed my caviar in an anxious gulp, and then Mary entered again. Her aspect was somewhat uncertain, even mildly agitated, and she tried but failed to announce our guest. As she hustled away to the back of the house with another small bend of her knee, a figure strode out of the dark stairway and into the parlor: Sara.

'Good evening, Dr. Kreizler,' she said, the folds of her emerald-green and peacock-blue evening dress making small whispering sounds as she came into the room.

Kreizler was somewhat taken aback. 'Miss Howard,' he said, his eyes clearly delighted but his voice perplexed. 'This is a pleasant surprise. Have you brought our liaison?' There was a long pause. Kreizler looked from Sara to me and then back at Sara. His expression did not change as he began to nod. 'Ah. *You* are our liaison – correct?'

For a moment Sara looked unsure of herself. 'I don't want you to think that I simply badgered the commissioner into this. We discussed it thoroughly.'

'I was there, too,' I said quickly, though a bit unsteadily. 'And when you hear the story of our afternoon, Kreizler, you'll have no doubt that Sara's the right person for the job.'

'It does make practical sense, Doctor,' Sara added. 'No one will notice my activities when I'm at Mulberry Street, and my absences will be even less of a cause for curiosity. There aren't many other people at headquarters who could say the same. I have a decent background in criminology, and I have access to places and people you and John might not – as we saw today.'

'It seems I missed a great deal today,' Kreizler said, in an ambiguous tone.

'Finally,' Sara continued, hesitant in the face of Laszlo's coolness, 'in the event of trouble . . .' She quickly pulled a small Colt Number One Derringer from a large muff she wore on her left hand and pointed it at the fireplace. 'You'll find that I'm a better shot than John.'

I took a quick step away from the gun, prompting Kreizler to chuckle once abruptly; Sara apparently thought he was laughing at her, and bridled a bit.

'I assure you, I'm quite serious, Doctor. My father was an expert marksman. My mother, however, was an invalid, and I had no siblings. I therefore became my father's hunting and trap-

shooting partner.' All of which was perfectly true. Stephen
Hamilton Howard had lived the life of a true country squire on
his estate near Rhinebeck, and had trained his only child to ride,
shoot, gamble, and drink with any Hudson Valley gentleman –
which meant that Sara could do all those things well, and in
volume. She indicated the small, delicately engraved pistol in her
hand. 'Most people consider the derringer a weak weapon; but
this one holds a forty-one-caliber bullet, and could knock your
man at the piano through the window behind him.'

Kreizler turned toward Cyrus, as if expecting the man to
register some sort of alarm – but there was no break in his gentle
rendition of 'Di provenza il mar.' Laszlo took note of that.

'Not that I prefer this kind of gun,' Sara finished, putting it
back in the muff. 'But ...' She took a deep breath, swelling the
pale, bare flesh above the low neckline of her dress. 'We *are* going
to the opera.' She touched the lovely emerald necklace she was
wearing and smiled for the first time. Vintage Sara, I thought, and
then I swallowed an entire glass of vodka.

There was another long pause, during which Kreizler's and
Sara's eyes stayed locked. Then Laszlo looked away, becoming his
usual frenetic self. 'Indeed we are,' he said, picking up a bit of
caviar and a glass and handing them to Sara. 'And if we don't
hurry, we shall miss the "Questa o quella." Cyrus, will you see if
Stevie has the barouche ready?' At that, Cyrus was up and making
for the stairs, but Kreizler caught him. 'And, Cyrus – this is Miss
Howard.'

'Yes, sir, Doctor,' Cyrus answered. 'We've met.'

'Ah,' Kreizler said. 'Then it will come as no surprise to learn
that she will be working with us?'

'No, sir.' Cyrus gave Sara a slight bow. 'Miss Howard,' he said.
She nodded and smiled back, and then Cyrus continued his
progress to the stairs.

'So Cyrus was involved, as well,' Kreizler said, as Sara drank her
vodka quickly yet gracefully. 'I confess my interest is piqued. On
our way uptown you two must tell me all about this mysterious
expedition to – where *did* you go?'

'The Santorellis',' I answered, taking a last mouthful of caviar.
'And we have come away loaded with useful information.'

'The Santo—' Kreizler was genuinely impressed, and suddenly much more serious. 'But ... where? How? You must tell me everything, *everything* – the keys will be in the details!'

Sara and Laszlo walked in front of me down the staircase, chatting as if this development had been expected all along. I breathed deeply in relief, for I hadn't known how Kreizler would react to Sara's proposal, and then put another cigarette to my mouth. Before I could light it, however, I was momentarily unnerved again, this time by the unexpected sight of Mary Palmer's face, which appeared through a crack in the dining room door as I passed. Her wide, pretty eyes were locked on Sara apprehensively, and she seemed to be trembling.

'Things,' I whispered to the girl reassuringly, 'are likely to be a little unusual around here, Mary. For the foreseeable future.' She didn't seem to hear me, but made a small sound and then ran away from the door.

Outside the snow was still falling. The larger of Kreizler's two carriages, a burgundy barouche with black trim, was waiting. Stevie Taggert had hitched up Frederick and another, matching gelding. Sara, pulling the hood of her cowl up, moved through the front yard and accepted Cyrus's help getting into the vehicle. Kreizler held me back at the front door.

'An extraordinary woman, Moore,' he whispered matter-of-factly.

I nodded. 'Just don't cross her,' I murmured back. 'Her nerves are strung like piano wire.'

'Yes, that's apparent,' he said. 'The father she speaks of – he's dead?'

'Hunting accident. Three years ago. They were very close – in fact, she spent some time in a sanatorium afterwards.' I didn't know whether I should divulge all, but given our situation it seemed advisable. 'Some people said it was suicide, but she denies it. Hotly. So that's a subject you might want to stay away from.'

Kreizler nodded and pulled on his gloves, watching Sara all the while. 'Women of such temperament,' he said as we moved to the carriage, 'do not seem fated for happiness in our society. But her capabilities are obvious.'

We got inside the barouche, and Sara began to eagerly relate the details of our interview with Mrs. Santorelli. As we made our way through the snow-quieted streets south of Gramercy Park toward Broadway, Kreizler listened without comment, his fidgeting hands the only evidence of his excitement; but by the time we reached Herald Square, where the sounds of human bustling became much louder around the elevated train station, he was full of detailed questions that rested our memories to the utmost. Laszlo's curiosity was roused by the strange tale of the two ex-cops and the two priests who had accompanied Roosevelt's detectives, but he had far more interest (as I had suspected he would) in young Georgio's sexual behavior and in the boy's character more generally. 'One of the first ways in which we can know our quarry is to know his victims,' Kreizler said, and as we pulled up under the large electric globes that lit the porte-cochere awning of the Metropolitan Opera House he asked Sara and me what sense of the boy we had formed. Each of us needed to think about that one for a bit, and we grew quiet and pensive as Stevie drove off with the barouche and Cyrus accompanied us through the doors.

To the old guard of New York society, the Metropolitan Opera was 'that yellow brewery uptown.' This terse dismissal was prompted, on the most obvious level, by the boxiness of the building's Early Renaissance architecture and the color of the bricks used in its construction; but the attitude behind the comment was sparked by the Metropolitan's upstart history. Occupying the block bounded by Broadway, Seventh Avenue, and Thirty-ninth and Fortieth streets, the Metropolitan, which opened in 1883, had been paid for by seventy-five of New York's most famous (and infamous) nouveaux riches: men with names like Morgan, Gould, Whitney, and Vanderbilt, none of whom were deemed by the old Knickerbocker clans to be socially acceptable enough to warrant selling them boxes at the venerable Academy of Music on Fourteenth Street. In reply to this unstated yet very apparent assessment of their worth, the founders of the Metropolitan had ordered not one or two tiers of boxes for their new house, but three; and the social wars that were waged in them before, during, and after performances were as vicious as anything that occurred downtown. In spite of all this backbiting, however, the impresarios who managed the Metropolitan, Henry Abbey and Maurice Grau, had brought together some of the best operatic talents in the world; and an evening at the 'yellow brewery' was, by 1896, fast becoming a musical experience that no other house or company in the world could surpass.

As we entered the relatively small main vestibule, which had none of the opulence of its various European counterparts, we got the usual stares from several broadminded souls who were not happy to see Kreizler accompanied by a black man. Most, however, had seen Cyrus before and endured his presence with weary familiarity. We moved up the tight, angular main staircase at a quick pace, and were among the last people to enter the auditorium. Kreizler's box was on the left-hand side of the second tier of the 'Diamond Horseshoe' (as the boxes were known), and we rushed through the red velvet saloon to get to our seats. As we settled in, the houselights began to fade. I pulled out a small set of foldable glasses, and just had time to check the boxes around and across from us for familiar faces. I got a quick glimpse of Theodore and Mayor Strong having what seemed a very grave conversation in the Roosevelt box, and then I cast my eyes on the dead center of the horseshoe, box 35, where that formidable financial octopus with the malignant nose – J. Pierpont Morgan – sat amid shadows. There were several ladies with him, but before I could ascertain who they were, the house went black.

Victor Maurel, the great Gascon baritone and actor for whom Verdi had written some of his most memorable parts, was in rare form that night, though I fear that we in Kreizler's box – with the possible exception of Cyrus – were too preoccupied with other matters to fully appreciate the performance. During the first intermission our conversation turned quickly from music back to the Santorelli case. Sara wondered at the fact that the beatings Georgio received from his father actually seemed to increase the boy's desire to pursue his sexual irregularities. Kreizler, too, remarked on this irony, saying that if Santorelli had only been able to talk to his son and explore the roots of his peculiar behavior, he might have been able to change it. But by employing violence he turned the affair into a battle, one in which Georgio's very psychic survival became associated, in the boy's mind, with the actions his father objected to. Sara and I puzzled with *that* concept all the way through Act II; but by the second intermission we were beginning to get it, to understand that a boy who made his living allowing himself to be used in the worst possible ways was, in his own view, asserting himself by doing so.

The same thing could in all probability have been said of the Zweig children, Kreizler remarked, vindicating my assumption that he would not write off to coincidence the similarity between those two victims and Georgio Santorelli. Laszlo went on to say that we could not overemphasize the importance of this new information: we now had the beginnings of a pattern, something on which to build a general picture of what qualities inspired violence in our killer. We owed that knowledge to Sara's determination to visit the Santorellis, as well as to her ability to make Mrs. Santorelli trust her. Laszlo expressed his indebtedness somewhat awkwardly, but nonetheless genuinely; and the look of fulfillment on Sara's face was worth all the trials of the day.

Things were fairly chummy, in other words, when Theodore entered our box with Mayor Strong during that same intermission. In an instant, the atmosphere in the little enclosure was transformed. For all his use of the rank 'colonel' and his reputation as a reformer, William L. Strong was much like any other well-to-do, middle-aged New York businessman – meaning that he had no use for Kreizler. His Honor said nothing in reply to our greetings, just sat in one of the free seats in the box and waited for the lights to go down. It was left to Theodore to awkwardly explain that Strong had something important he wished to say. Talking during a performance at the Metropolitan was not generally considered a barbarity – indeed, some of the city's most noteworthy personal and business affairs were conducted at such times – but neither Kreizler nor I shared this disrespect for the efforts of those onstage. We did not, in other words, provide a friendly audience when Strong began his lecture during the ominous opening of Act III.

'Doctor,' the mayor said without looking at him, 'Commissioner Roosevelt assures me that your recent visit to police headquarters was entirely social. I trust that is true.' Kreizler didn't answer, which irked Strong a bit. 'I am surprised, however, to see you attending the opera with an employee of the Police Department.' He nodded rather rudely in Sara's direction.

'If you'd like to see my *entire* social calendar, Mayor Strong,' Sara said bravely, 'I can arrange that.'

Theodore clutched his forehead quietly but vigorously, and Strong's anger grew, though he did not acknowledge Sara's remark. 'Doctor, you are perhaps unaware that we are engaged in a great crusade to root out corruption and degeneracy in our city.' Again, Kreizler would not reply, but kept his eyes on Victor Maurel and Frances Saville as they sang together. 'In this battle we have many enemies,' Strong continued. 'If they can find any way to embarrass or discredit us, they will use it. Am I clear, sir?'

'Clear, sir?' Kreizler finally answered, still not looking at Strong. 'Certainly you are ill mannered, but as to clear ...' He shrugged.

Strong stood up. 'Then let me be plain. If you were to associate yourself with the Police Department in any capacity, Doctor, it would constitute just such a way for our enemies to discredit us. Decent people have no use for your work, sir, for your abominable opinions of the American family, or for your obscene probing into the minds of American children. Such matters are the province of parents and their spiritual advisors. If I were you, I should limit my work to the lunatic asylums, where it belongs. At any rate, no one associated with this administration has any use for such filth. Kindly remember that.' The mayor stood up and made for the exit, pausing to turn briefly on Sara. 'And you, young lady, would do well to remember that hiring women to work at headquarters was an *experiment* – and that experiments often fail!'

With that, Strong disappeared. Theodore lingered behind just long enough to whisper that future public appearances by the three of us might not be wise, and then he took off after the mayor. It was an outrageous but nonetheless typical incident: there were undoubtedly many people in the audience that night who would have said very similar things to Kreizler, given the chance. Laszlo, Cyrus, and I, having heard it all before, didn't take it as hard as Sara, who was a newcomer to this kind of intolerance. For much of the remaining performance, she looked as though she might be preparing to blow Strong's brains out with her derringer; but Maurel and Saville's final duet was so superbly heartrending that even angry Sara put the real world aside. When the lights went up for the last time we all stood and bellowed bravos and bravas, getting a small wave from Maurel in return. As soon as Sara caught a glimpse of Theodore and Strong in their box, however, her indignation was back in force.

'Honestly, Doctor, how can you tolerate it?' she said, as we made our way out. 'The man is an idiot!'

'As you will soon discover, Sara,' Kreizler said calmly, 'one cannot afford to pay the slightest attention to such statements. Although there is one aspect of the mayor's interest in this matter that does concern me.'

I didn't even have to think about it – the idea had occurred to me while Strong was talking: 'The two priests,' I said.

Laszlo nodded to me. 'Indeed, Moore. Those two troublesome priests – one wonders who arranged for such "spiritual advisors" to accompany the detectives today. For the moment, however, that must remain a mystery.' He checked his silver watch. 'Good. We should arrive exactly on time. I hope our guests will do the same.'

'Guests?' Sara said. 'But where are we going?'

'To dinner,' Kreizler answered simply. 'And to what I hope will be a most illuminating conference.'

Chapter 10

It is often difficult, I find, for people today to grasp the notion that one family, working through several restaurants, could change the eating habits of an entire country. But such was the achievement of the Delmonicos in the United States of the last century. Before they opened their first small café on William Street in 1823, catering to the business and financial communities of Lower Manhattan, American food could generally be described as things boiled or fried whose purpose was to sustain hard work and hold down alcohol – usually bad alcohol. The Delmonicos, though Swiss, had brought the French method to America, and each generation of their family refined and expanded the experience. Their menu, from the first, contained dozens of dishes both delectable and healthy, all offered at what, considering the preparation that went into them, were reasonable prices. Their wine cellar was as expansive and as excellent as any in Paris. So great was their success that within decades they had two downtown restaurants, and one uptown; and by the time of the Civil War, travelers from all over the country who had eaten at Delmonico's had taken news of the experience home with them were demanding that the owners of restaurants everywhere give them not only pleasant surroundings, but food that was nutritious and expertly prepared. The craving for first-rate dining became a kind of national fever in the latter decades of the century – and Delmonico's was responsible.

But fine food and wine were only part of the reason for the Delmonicos' prosperity: the family's professed egalitarianism also drew customers in. On any given night at the uptown restaurant on Twenty-sixth Street and Fifth Avenue, one was just as likely to run into Diamond Jim Brady and Lillian Russell as Mrs. Vanderbilt and the other matrons of New York's high society. Even the likes of Paul Kelly were not turned away. Perhaps more amazing than the fact that anyone could get in was the fact that everyone was forced to wait an equal amount of time for a table – reservations were not taken (save for parties in the private dining rooms), and no favoritism was ever exhibited. The wait was sometimes annoying; but to find yourself on line behind someone like Mrs. Vanderbilt, who would squawk and stamp about 'such treatment!' could be very entertaining.

On the particular night of our conference with the Isaacson brothers, Laszlo had taken the precaution of engaging a private room, knowing that our conversation would be deeply upsetting to anyone around us in the main dining room. We approached the block-long restaurant from the Broadway side, then turned left at Twenty-sixth Street and pulled up to the main entrance. Cyrus and Stevie were dismissed for the evening; the rest of us would get cabs home after dinner. We stepped up to the door and then inside, and were immediately greeted by young Charlie Delmonico.

The family's older generation had almost completely died off by 1896, and Charlie had given up a career on Wall Street to take over the business. He couldn't have been better suited to the task: suave, dapper, and eternally tactful, he attended to every detail without a look of care ever narrowing his enormous eyes or ruffling a hair of his natty beard.

'Dr. Kreizler,' he said as we approached, taking our hands and smiling delicately. 'And Mr. Moore. Always a pleasure, gentlemen, especially when you are together. And Miss Howard as well – it's been some time since you've been in. I'm grateful that you are able to return.' That was Charlie's way of saying he understood Sara had been through a lot since her father died. 'Your other guests, Doctor, have already arrived, and are waiting upstairs.' He kept talking as we checked our outer garments. 'I remembered you saying that you found neither olive nor crimson conducive to digestion, so I have placed you in the blue room – will that be satisfactory?'

'Considerate, as ever, Charles,' Kreizler answered. 'Thank you.'

'You're welcome to go right up,' Charlie said. 'Ranhoffer is, as always, ready.'

'Ah-ha!' I said, at the mention of Delmonico's brilliant chef. 'I trust he's girding himself for our stern judgment?'

Charlie smiled again, that same gentle curve of the mouth. 'I believe he has something quite remarkable planned. Come, gentlemen.'

We followed Charlie through the mirrored walls, mahogany furniture, and frescoed ceiling of the main dining room and then up to the private blue room on the second floor. The Isaacson brothers were already seated at a small but elegant table, looking a bit bewildered. Their confusion mounted when they saw Sara, whom they knew from headquarters; but she very cagily side-stepped their questions, saying that someone had to take notes for Commissioner Roosevelt, who was taking a personal interest in the case.

'He is?' Marcus Isaacson answered, the dark eyes to either side of the pronounced nose going wide with apprehension. 'This isn't – well, this isn't some sort of test, is it? I know that everyone in the department is up for review, but – well, a case that's three years old, it doesn't really seem fair to judge us ...'

'Not that we don't appreciate that the case is still open,' Lucius said hurriedly, mopping a few beads of sweat from his brow with a handkerchief as waiters arrived with platters of oysters and glasses of sherry and bitters.

'Calm yourselves, Detective Sergeants,' Kreizler said. 'This is no review. You are here precisely because you are known to be unassociated with those elements of the force that have brought on the current controversies.' At that, both Isaacsons let out considerable amounts of air and attacked the sherry. 'You were not,' Kreizler continued, 'particular favorites of Inspector Byrnes, I understand?'

The two brothers eyed each other, and Lucius nodded to

Caleb Carr

Marcus, who spoke: 'No, sir. Byrnes believed in methods that were – well, outdated, let's say. My brother – that is, Detective Sergeant Isaacson – and I have both studied abroad, which made the inspector extremely suspicious. That, and our – background.'

Kreizler nodded; it was no secret how the department's old guard felt about Jews. 'Well, then, gentlemen,' Laszlo said. 'Suppose you tell us what you were able to discover today.'

After arguing for a moment about who would report first, the Isaacsons decided it would be Lucius:

'As you know, Doctor, there is a limited amount one can tell from bodies that are in such an advanced state of decomposition. Still, I believe we uncovered a few facts that slipped by the coroner and the investigating detectives. To begin with, the cause of death – excuse me, Miss Howard, but aren't you going to take notes?'

She smiled at him. 'Mentally. I'll transfer them to paper later.'

This answer did nothing for Lucius, who eyed Sara nervously before going on: 'Yes, uh – the cause of death.' The waiters reappeared to remove our oyster trays and substitute some green turtle soap *au clair*. Lucius wiped his broad brow again and took a taste while the waiters opened a bottle of amontillado. 'Mmm – delicious!' he decided, the food easing his mind. 'But as I was saying – the police and coroner's reports indicated that death was caused by the throat wounds. Severing of the common carotid arteries, et cetera. It's the obvious interpretation, if you've got a body with a cut throat. But I noticed almost immediately that there was extensive damage to the laryngeal structures, especially the hyoid bone, which in both cases was fractured. That, of course, indicates strangulation.'

'I don't understand,' I said. 'Why would the murderer cut their throats if he'd already strangled them?'

'Blood lust,' Marcus answered, very matter-of-factly, as he ate his soup.

'Yes, blood lust,' Lucius agreed. 'He was probably concerned with keeping his clothes clean, so that he wouldn't attract any attention during his escape. But he needed to see the blood – or maybe smell it. Some murderers have said it's the smell rather than the sight that satisfies them.'

Fortunately, I'd already finished my soup. I looked over to Sara, who was absorbing it all with great poise. Kreizler was studying Lucius with immense fascination.

'So,' Laszlo said, 'you hypothesize strangulation. Excellent. What else?'

'There's the business about the eyes,' Lucius answered, leaning back so that his soup bowl could be removed by the waiters. 'I had some trouble with the reports on that one.' We were now presented with *aiguillettes* of bass done in a creamy Mornay sauce – quite tasty. The amontillado was exchanged for Hochheimer.

'Excuse me, Doctor,' Marcus said quietly. 'But I did want to say – remarkable food. I've never had anything quite like it.'

'I'm delighted, Detective Sergeant,' Kreizler answered. 'There is much more to come. Now, then – as to the eyes?'

'Right,' Lucius said. 'The police report made some mention of birds or rats having gotten at the eyes. And the coroner was apparently willing to stand by that, which is fairly extraordinary. Even if the bodies had been out in the open rather than in an enclosed water tower, why would scavengers feed only on the eyes? What puzzled me most, though, about such a theory was that the knife marks were quite distinct.'

Kreizler, Sara, and I all stopped in mid-chew and looked at each other. 'Knife marks?' Kreizler said quietly. 'There was no mention of knife marks in any of the reports.'

'Yes, I know!' Lucius said jovially. The conversation, though gruesome, seemed to be relaxing him; the wine didn't hurt, either. 'It really was strange. But there they were – some very narrow grooves on the malar bone and supraorbital ridge, along with some additional cuts on the sphenoid.'

They were virtually the same words Kreizler had used in describing Georgio Santorelli's body.

'At first glance,' Lucius continued, 'one might've been led to believe that the various cuts were unconnected, indications of separate jabs of a blade. But they seemed to me to bear a relation to each other, so I tried an experiment. There's a fairly good cutlery store in the neighborhood of your Institute, Doctor, which also sells hunting knives. I went there and bought the kind of blade I thought was probably used, in three different lengths

– nine-inch, ten-inch, and eleven.' He fumbled in the inside pocket of his jacket. 'The largest proved the best fit.'

At that he dropped a gleaming knife of what seemed gigantic proportions onto the center of the table. Its handle was made of deer antler, the hilt was brass, and the steel of the blade was engraved with a picture of a stag in some brush.

'The Arkansas toothpick,' Marcus said. 'It's unclear whether Jim Bowie or his brother originally designed the thing, back in the early thirties, but we do know that most of them are now manufactured by one of the Sheffield firms, in England, for export to our western states. It can be used for hunting, but it's basically a fighting knife. For hand-to-hand combat.'

'Could it be used,' I said, again remembering Georgio Santorelli, 'as a – well, as a carving and chopping instrument? I mean, would it be heavy enough, and hold a fine edge?'

'Absolutely,' Marcus answered. 'The edge depends on the quality of the steel, and in a knife this size, especially if it's manufactured in Sheffield, you tend to get high-quality, hard steel.' He caught himself, and looked at me with the same suspicious puzzlement he had shown that afternoon. 'Why do you ask?'

'It looks expensive,' Sara said, deliberately changing the subject. 'Is it?'

'Sure,' Marcus said. 'Durable, though. One of these would last you years.'

Kreizler was staring at the knife: this, his gaze seemed to say, is what *he* uses.

'The marks on the sphenoid,' Lucius resumed, 'were created at the same time that the cutting edge dug into the malar bone and the supraorbital ridge. It's perfectly natural, since he was working in such a small area – the eye socket of a child's skull – with such a large instrument. Still, for all that, it was probably a skillful job. The damage could have been much greater. Now . . .' He took a large sip of wine. 'If you want to know *what* he was doing, or *why*, there we can only speculate. Possibly he was selling body parts to anatomists and medical colleges. Although he would probably have taken more than just the eyes, in that case. It's somewhat confusing.'

None of us could say anything to that. We stared at the knife, myself at least afraid to touch it, as the waiters appeared again with plates of saddle of lamb *à la Colbert* and bottles of Château Lagrange.

'Admirable,' Kreizler said. He finally looked up at Lucius, whose fat face was starting to turn red with the wine. 'A truly splendid job, Detective Sergeant.'

'Oh, that's not all of it,' Lucius answered, digging into his lamb.

'Eat slowly,' Marcus whispered. 'Remember your stomach.'

Lucius paid no heed. 'That's not all,' he repeated. 'There were some very interesting fractures of the frontal and parietal bones, at the top of the skull. But I'll let my brother – I'll let Detective Sergeant Isaacson explain those.' Lucius looked up at us with a grin. 'I'm enjoying my food too much to talk anymore.'

Marcus watched him, shaking his head. 'You're going to be sick tomorrow,' he mumbled. 'And you're going to blame me – but I warned you.'

'Detective Sergeant?' Kreizler said, leaning back with a glass of Lagrange. 'You will have to possess some remarkable information indeed, if you hope to outdo your – *colleague*, here.'

'Well, it *is* interesting,' Marcus answered, 'and it may well tell us something substantive. The fracture lines that my brother found were inflicted from above – from *directly* above. Now, in an assault, which this obviously was, you'd expect angles of attack, either from similarity of height or difficulty of approach due to the struggle. The nature of the wounds indicates, however, that not only did the assailant have complete physical control over his victims, but he was also tall enough to strike directly downward very forcefully with a blunt instrument of some kind – possibly even his fists, though we doubt that.'

We allowed Marcus a few moments to eat; but when succulent Maryland terrapin arrived to replace the lamb, from which Lucius had to be almost forcefully separated, we urged him to go on:

'Let me see. I'll try to make this as accessible as I can – if we take the respective heights of the two children, and then add the aspects of the skull fractures that I've just described to the equation, we can start to speculate about the height of the attacker.' He turned to Lucius. 'What did we guess, roughly six-foot-two?' Lucius nodded and Marcus continued. 'I don't know how much any of you know about anthropometry – the Bertillon system of identification and classification—'

'Oh, are you trained in it?' Sara said. 'I've been anxious to meet someone who is.'

Marcus looked surprised. 'You know Bertillon's work, Miss Howard?'

As Sara nodded eagerly Kreizler cut in: 'I must confess ignorance, Detective Sergeant. I've heard the name, but little more.'

And so while disposing of the terrapin we also reviewed the achievements of Alphonse Bertillon, a misanthropic, pedantic Frenchman who had revolutionized the science of criminal identification during the eighties. As a lowly clerk assigned the task of going through the files that the Paris police department kept on known criminals, Bertillon had discovered that if one took fourteen measurements of any human body – not only height, but foot, hand, nose, and ear size, and so on – the odds were over 286 million to one that any two people would share the same results. Despite enormous resistance from his superiors, Bertillon had begun to record the body-part sizes of known criminals and then to categorize his results, training a staff of assistant measurers and photographers in the process; and when he used the information thus collected to solve several infamous cases that had stumped the Paris detectives, he became an international celebrity.

Bertillon's system had been adopted quickly throughout Europe, later in London, and only recently in New York. Throughout his tenure as head of the Division of Detectives, Thomas Byrnes had rejected anthropometry, with its exact measurements and careful photographs, as too intellectually demanding for most of his men – undoubtedly an accurate assumption. Then, too, Byrnes had created the Rogues' Gallery, a room full of photographs of most known criminals in the United States: he was jealous of his creation, and considered it sufficient for the purposes of identification. Finally, Brynes had established his own principles of detection and would not have them overthrown by any Frenchman. But with Byrnes's departure from the force, anthropometry had picked up more advocates, one of whom was evidently sitting at our table that night.

'The main shortcoming of Bertillon's system,' Marcus said, 'besides the fact that it depends on skilled measurers, is that it can only match a suspected or convicted criminal to his record and aliases.' Having eaten a small bowl of sorbet Elsinore, Marcus started to take a cigarette from his pocket, evidently thinking that the meal was over. He was very pleasantly surprised when a plate of canvasback duck, prepared with hominy and a currant *gelée*, was placed before him, along with a glass of splendid Chambertin.

'Excuse my asking, Doctor,' Lucius said in continuing confusion, 'but . . . is there actually a conclusion to this meal, or do we just work our way into breakfast?'

'So long as you are full of useful information, Detective Sergeants, the food will continue coming.'

'Well, then . . .' Marcus took a big bite of duck, closing his eyes in appreciation. 'We'd better stay interesting. Now, as I was about to say, the Bertillon system offers no physical evidence of criminal commission. It can't put a man *at* the scene of the crime. But it can help us shorten the list of known criminals who may be responsible. We're betting that the man who killed the Zweig children was somewhere in the neighborhood of six-foot-two. That'll produce relatively few candidates, even from the files of the New York police. It's an advantageous starting point. And the better news is that, with so many cities now adopting the system, we can make our check nationwide – even to Europe, if we want to.'

'And if the man has no prior criminal record?' Kreizler asked.

'Then, as I say,' Marcus answered with a shrug, 'we're out of luck.' Kreizler looked disappointed at this, and Marcus – eyeing, it seemed to me, his plate, and wondering if the food would really stop coming when we reached a dead end – cleared his throat. 'That is, Doctor, out of luck so far as official departmental methods go. However, I'm a student of some other techniques that might prove useful in that eventuality.'

Lucius looked worried. 'Marcus,' he mumbled. 'I'm still not sure, it's not accepted, yet—'

Marcus answered quietly but quickly: 'Not in *court*. But it would still make sense in an investigation. We *discussed* this.'

'Gentlemen?' Kreizler said. 'Will you share your secret?'

Lucius gulped his Chambertin nervously. 'It's still theoretical, Doctor, and is not accepted anywhere in the world as legal evidence, but ...' He looked to Marcus, seemingly worried that his brother had cost him dessert. 'Oh, all right. Go ahead.'

Marcus spoke confidentially. 'It's called dactyloscopy.'

'Oh,' I said. 'You mean fingerprinting.'

'Yes,' Marcus replied, 'that's the colloquial term.'

'But—' Sara broke in. 'I mean no offense, Detective Sergeant, but dactyloscopy has been rejected by every police department in the world. Its scientific basis hasn't even been proven, and no actual case has ever been solved by using it.'

'I take no offense at that, Miss Howard,' Marcus answered. 'And I hope *you* won't take any when I say that you're mistaken. The scientific basis has been proven, and several cases have been solved using the technique – though not in a part of the world that you're likely to have heard much about.'

'Moore,' Kreizler interrupted, his voice snapping a bit, 'I'm beginning to understand how you must often feel – once again, gentlemen and lady, I'm lost.'

Sara started to explain the subject to Laszlo, but after that last little quip of his I had to jump in and take over. Dactyloscopy, or fingerprinting (I explained in what I hoped was a very condescending voice), had been argued for decades as a method of identifying all human beings. The scientific premise was that fingerprints do not change throughout a person's lifetime – but there were a great many anthropologists and physicians who didn't yet accept that fact, despite overwhelming supporting evidence and occasional practical demonstrations. In Argentina, for example – a place that, as Marcus Isaacson said, not many people in America or Europe thought much about (or of) – fingerprinting had gotten its first practical test when a provincial police officer in Buenos Aires named Vucetich used the method to solve a murder case that involved the brutal bludgeoning of two small children.

'And so,' Kreizler said, as our waiters appeared yet again, bearing *petits aspics de foie gras*, 'I take it there is a general shift away from Bertillon's system.'

'Not yet,' Marcus answered. 'It's an ongoing fight. Even though the reliability of prints has been demonstrated, there's a great deal of resistance.'

'The important thing to remember,' Sara added – and how very satisfying, to see *her* now lecturing Kreizler! – 'is that fingerprints can show who has been in a given place. It's ideal for our—' She caught herself, and calmed. 'It has great potential.'

'And how are the prints taken?' Kreizler asked.

'There are three basic methods,' Marcus answered. 'First, obviously, are visible prints – a hand that's been dipped in paint, blood, ink, anything like that, and has then touched something else. Then there are plastic prints, left when someone touches putty, clay, wet plaster, and so on. Last, and the most difficult, are latent prints. If you pick up that glass in front of you, Doctor, your fingers will leave a residue of perspiration and body oil in the pattern of your fingerprint. If I suspect that you might have done so' – Marcus removed two small vials from his pockets, one containing a gray-white powder and one a black substance of similar consistency – 'I will dust with either aluminum powder' – he held up the gray-white vial – 'or with finely ground carbon' – he held up the black. 'The choice depends on the color of the background object. White shows up against dark objects, black against light; either would be suitable for your glass. The powders are absorbed by the oils and perspiration, leaving a perfect image of your print.'

'Remarkable,' Kreizler said. 'But if it is now scientifically accepted that a human being's fingerprints never vary, *how* can this not be admitted as legal evidence in court?'

'Change isn't something most people enjoy, even if it's progressive change.' Marcus put the vials down on the table and smiled. 'But I'm sure you're aware of that, Dr. Kreizler.'

Kreizler nodded once in acknowledgment of this comment, then pushed his plate away and sat back again. 'Grateful as I am for all of your very instructive words,' he said, 'I get the feeling,

Caleb Carr

Detective Sergeant, that they have some more specific purpose.'

Marcus turned to Lucius yet again, but his brother only shrugged in resignation. With that, Marcus pulled something flat from the inner pocket of his jacket.

'Chances are,' he said, 'no coroner would notice or care if they happened on something like this today, much less three years ago.' He dropped the sheet – actually a photograph – on the table in front of us, and our three heads went close together to view it. It was a detail of something, several white objects – bones, I soon determined, but I couldn't be more specific.

'Fingers?' Sara wondered aloud.

'Fingers,' Kreizler answered.

'Specifically,' Marcus said, 'the fingers of Sofia Zweig's left hand. Note the nail on the tip of the thumb, the one you can see fully.' He took a magnifying lens from his pocket and handed it to us, then sat back to nibble *foie gras*.

'It seems,' Kreizler mused as Sara picked up the lens, 'bruised. At least, there is discoloration of some kind.'

Marcus looked at Sara. 'Miss Howard?'

She put the lens before her face, and brought the photograph closer. Her eyes struggled to focus, and then went wide in discovery. 'I see . . .'

'See what?' I said, squirming like a four-year-old.

As Laszlo looked over Sara's shoulder, his expression became even more astounded and impressed than hers. 'Good lord, you don't mean—'

'What, what, what?' I said, and Sara finally handed me the glass and the picture. I followed instructions and examined the nail at the tip of the thumb. Without the glass it looked, as Kreizler had said, discolored: Magnified, it clearly bore the mark of what I knew to be a fingerprint, left in some kind of dark substance. I was dumb with surprise.

'It's a very lucky chance,' Marcus said. 'Though partial, it's sufficient for identification. Somehow, it managed to survive both the coroner and the mortician. The substance is blood, by the way. Probably the girl's own, or her brother's. The print, however, is too large to be either of theirs. The coffin has preserved the stain extremely well – and now we have a permanent record of it.'

The Alienist

Kreizler looked up, as close to beaming as he was likely to get. 'My dear Detective Sergeant, this is almost as impressive as it is unexpected!'

Marcus looked away, smiling self-consciously, as Lucius piped up in the same worried tone. 'Please remember, Doctor, that it has no legal or forensic significance. It's a clue, and could be used for investigative purposes, nothing else.'

'And nothing else, Detective Sergeant, is needed. Except, possibly' – Laszlo clapped his hands twice and the waiters reappeared – 'dessert. Which you gentlemen have thoroughly earned.' The waiters took away our last dinner dishes and returned with Alliance pears; steeped in wine, deep fried, powdered with sugar, and smothered in apricot sauce. I thought Lucius would have an attack when he saw them. Kreizler kept his eyes on the two brothers. 'This is truly commendable work. But I'm afraid, gentlemen, that you have undertaken it under slightly . . . false premises. For which I apologize.'

We then explained our activities fully to the Isaacsons, as we consumed the pears and some delicious *petits fours* that followed. Nothing was left out of our account: the condition of Georgio Santorelli's body, the troubles with Flynn and Connor, our meeting with Roosevelt, and Sara's conversation with Mrs. Santorelli were all discussed in detail. Nor did any of us try to sugar-coat the issue – the person we were hunting, Kreizler said, might be unconsciously urging us to find him, but his conscious thoughts were fixed on violence, and if we got too close that violence might easily spill over onto us. This warning did give Marcus and Lucius some little pause, as did the thought that our business would be undertaken in secret and disavowed by all city officials if discovered. But both men's overarching reaction to the prospect was excitement. Any good detective would have felt the same, for it was the chance of a lifetime: to try new techniques, to operate outside the stifling pressures of departmental bureau-cracy, and to make one's name if the affair were concluded successfully.

And, I must confess, after the meal we'd just eaten and the wine that had accompanied it, such a conclusion seemed some-what inevitable. Whatever reservations Kreizler, Sara, and I had

had about the Isaacsons', their work far outweighed such considerations: in the space of a day, we'd been given a general idea of our murder's physical stature and weapon of choice, as well as a permanent image of one physical attribute that might ultimately prove his undoing. Add to all this the fruit of Sara's initiative – an initial impression of what the killer's victims had in common – and success seemed, to a man in my drunken state, well within our grasp.

Yet it also seemed to me that my own part in this stage of the work had been too minor. I had made no inauguratory contribution, except to escort Sara earlier that day; and as we fairly well carried Lucius Isaacson to a cab, the clock in Del's having long since tolled two, I combed my rather fuzzy mind for a way to right that situation. What I came up with was equally fuzzy: after getting Sara and Kreizler a hansom and saying goodnight to them (he would drop her off at Gramercy Park), I turned south and made for Paresis Hall.

Chapter 11

Knowing that I would need to be on my toes once I reached the hall, I decided to walk the mile or so to Cooper Square and let the cold air sober me up a bit. Broadway was nearly deserted, except for the occasional group of young men in white uniforms who were shoveling snow into large wagons. This was the private army of Colonel Waring, the street-cleaning genius who had tidied up Providence, Rhode Island, and then been imported to work the same magic in New York. Waring's boys were unquestionably efficient – the amount of snow, horse manure, and general garbage on the streets had declined sharply since their advent – but their uniforms apparently made them think that they had some sort of enforcement status. Every so often a kid of about fourteen, dressed in one of Waring's white tunics and helmets, would catch a less than stellar citizen throwing refuse carelessly onto the street and try to make an arrest. It was impossible to convince these zealots that they had no such authority, and the incidents continued. Sometimes they ended in violence, a record of which the boys were proud – and one which made me cautious as I passed them that night.

By the time I reached Cooper Square I was feeling fairly alert and mighty cold. As I passed the big, brown mass of Cooper Union I began to think of the large glass of brandy I intended to order at Paresis Hall; I was thus caught thoroughly off guard when a workmen's truck, bearing the legend GENOVESE & SONS –

– IRONWORKS – BKLYN., N.Y., came careening around the north end of Cooper Square Park behind a huffing gray horse that looked like he'd rather be anywhere than out on such a night. The truck ground to a halt, and four toughs in miner's caps got out of the back, rushing into the park. They soon reappeared, dragging two expensively dressed men.

'Filthy fags!' one of the toughs shouted, catching the first man a nice blow across the face with what appeared to be a piece of pipe. Blood came instantly from the man's nose and mouth, spattering across his clothes and onto the snow. 'Get off the streets, if you want to bugger each other!'

Two of the other ambassadors from Brooklyn held the second man, who appeared older than the first, while a third put his face close. 'Like to fuck boys, do you?'

'I'm sorry, but you're really not my sort,' the man answered, with a composure that made me think this had happened to him before. 'I like young men who bathe.' That one cost him three solid blows to the stomach, after which he doubled over and retched onto the frozen ground.

It was one of those moments for fast thinking: I could jump in and get *my* head cracked, or I could—

'Hey!' I shouted at the toughs, and they turned their cold-blooded stares on me. 'You boys'd better watch it – there's half a dozen cops on their way, saying no guineas from Brooklyn better start anything in the Fifteenth Precinct!'

'Oh, there are, eh?' said the tough who seemed to be the leader, as he moved back to the truck. 'And which way're they coming from?'

'Right down Broadway!' I said, jerking a thumb behind me.

'Come on, boys!' said the tough. 'Let's settle some mick hash!' That brought shouts and cheers from the other three as they piled into the truck, asking if I wanted to come along but not waiting for an answer.

I moved over to the two injured men, but could only say 'Do you need—' before they ran off in full flight, the older man clutching his ribs and moving with difficulty. I realized that when the toughs failed to find the cops, they'd probably return for me, and I therefore moved quickly across the Bowery under the tracks of the Third Avenue Elevated to Biff Ellison's place.

Paresis Hall's electric sign was still burning bright at close to three in the morning. The joint had taken its name from a patent medicine that advertised in dive toilets, promising protection and relief from the more serious social diseases. The windows of the Hall were shaded, and honest citizens of the neighborhood were grateful for that fact. Inside the busy doorway – around which stood a wide range of effeminate men and boys, all of them attempting to drum up business with entering and departing customers – was a long, brass-railed bar, along with a large number of round wooden tables and simple chairs of the sort that were easily broken in fights and easily replaced afterwards. A rough stage had been built at the far end of the long, high-ceilinged room, on which more boys and men in various stages of female dress cavorted to lively yet discordant music provided by a piano, clarinet, and violin.

The essential purpose of Paresis Hall was to arrange affairs between customers and the various types of prostitutes who worked there. This second group included everything from youths like Georgio Santorelli to homosexuals who did not favor women's clothes to the occasional bona fide female, who hung about in the hope that some one of the souls who wandered in would rediscover his heterosexuality to her profit. Most of the assignations worked out in the Hall took place at cheap hotels in the neighborhood, though the second floor had a dozen or so rooms out of which young boys who particularly pleased Ellison were allowed to conduct their business.

But what was most distinctive about the Hall, along with only a few other such places in town, was a near total lack of the secretiveness that usually marked homosexual dealings in the city. Released from the need to be in any way careful, Ellison's patrons cavorted raucously and spent freely, and the Hall did enormous business. In the end, however, neither the scale nor the unusualness of its operations could keep it from being at heart like any other dive: sordid, smoky, and thoroughly disheartening.

I hadn't been inside the door thirty seconds before there was a small but strong arm around my torso and a cold piece of metal at my throat. The sudden aroma of lilac alerted me to Ellison's

Caleb Carr

presence in the general area behind me; and I assumed that the metal I felt was the signature weapon of one of Biff's cronies, Razor Riley. Riley was a skinny, dangerous little miscreant from Hell's Kitchen who, though a Gopher, occasionally ran with and worked for Ellison, whose sexual preferences he shared.

'I thought Kelly and me made ourselves pretty clear the other day, Moore,' Ellison boomed. I still couldn't see him. 'You ain't tying me to the Santorelli business. You gutsy or just crazy coming in here like this?'

'Neither, Biff,' I said, as clearly as extreme fear would allow: Riley was notoriously fond of cutting people up. 'I just wanted you to know that I did you a good turn.'

Ellison laughed. '*You*, scribbler? What could you do for me?' At that he came around to face me, his ridiculous checked suit and gray bowler all reeking of cologne. He held a long, thin cigar in one beefy hand.

'I told the commissioner you didn't have anything to do with it,' I gasped.

He came close, his thick lips parting to release the stench of bad whiskey. 'Yeah?' he said, his little eyes gleaming. 'And did you convince him?'

'Sure,' I said.

'Oh? How?'

'Simple. I told him it wasn't your style.'

Ellison had to pause as the mass of cells that, in his case, passed for a brain mulled this over. Then he smiled. 'Say – you're right, Moore. It *ain't* my style! Well, whattaya know – let 'im go, Razor.'

At that the several employees and customers who had gathered to see if there would be bloodshed dispersed in disappointment. I turned to the wiry figure of Razor Riley and watched as he folded his favorite weapon, pocketed it, and then smoothed his waxed mustache. He put his hands on hips, ready to fight – but I just straightened my white tie and neatened my cuffs.

'Try milk, Riley,' I said. 'I hear it helps the bones grow.'

Riley went for his pocket again, but Ellison laughed and restrained him with an effusive hug. 'Aw, that's all right, Razor, let the guy crack wise, it ain't gonna hurt you.' Then he turned to me and put an arm around my neck. 'Come on, Moore, I'll buy you a drink. And you can tell me how come it is you turned into my pal all of a sudden.'

We stood at the bar, and I could see all the sad business of the Hall reflected in a large mirror that ran along the wall behind the endless bottles of bad liquor. Remembering exactly who and what I was dealing with, I abandoned the cherished idea of a brandy (besides being of shockingly poor quality, it was likely to be laced with any combination of camphor, benzine, cocaine shavings, and chloral hydrate) and ordered a beer. The swill I was given may even have *been* beer, too, at some point in its existence. As I took a sip, one of the chanteuses on the stage at the other end of the Hall began to whine:

> *There's a name that's never spoken,*
> *And a mother's heart half broken,*
> *There is just another missing from the old home,*
>   *that's all . . .*

Ellison took a glass of whiskey, then turned when a boy-whore patted his rump. Biff tweaked the youth's cheek roughly.

'Well, Moore?' he said, staring into the boy's painted eyes. 'Why the good turn? Don't tell me you'd like to sample the wares down here.'

'No, not tonight, Biff,' I said. 'What I thought was that maybe since I helped you out with the cops, you might be willing to share some information – you know, give me a hand with the story, that kind of thing.'

He eyed me up and down as the boy-whore disappeared into the noisy throng. 'Since when does the God-almighty *New York Times* run stories like that? And where the hell you been tonight, anyway, a funeral?'

'The opera,' I answered. 'And the *Times* isn't the only paper in town.'

'Yeah?' He didn't sound convinced. 'Well, I don't know nothing about it, Moore. Gloria, she used to be okay. Really. Hell, I let her use one of the rooms upstairs, even. But she got – troublesome. Starts asking for a bigger cut, starts telling the

Caleb Carr

other girls they ought to ask for one, too. So, a couple a nights ago, I says – Gloria, keep it up and you're out on your pretty little ass. Then she plays like she'll make nice, but I don't trust her no more. I was gonna get rid of her – not in any permanent meaning of the word, right? – but just kick her out, let her work the streets a couple of weeks and see how she liked it. And then – this.' He gulped whiskey and blew cigar smoke. 'The little guttersnipe had it coming, Moore.'

I waited a moment for him to go on; but his attention was distracted by two young men in stockings and garters who were shouting threats at each other out on the dance floor. Knives soon appeared. Ellison chuckled at the sight, and then offered his assessment:

'You two bitches cut each other up you won't be no good to nobody!'

'Biff?' I said eventually. 'So that's all you can tell me?'

'That's all,' he answered with a nod. 'Now how about you get outta here before there's trouble?'

'Why? You hiding something? Upstairs, maybe?'

'No, I ain't hiding anything,' he answered, annoyed. 'I just don't like reporters in my place. And my customers don't like it, neither. Some of 'em are respectable boys, you know – got families and positions to consider.'

'Then maybe you'll let me take a look at the room Geor – *Gloria* used. Just to convince me you're square.'

Ellison sighed, leaning back on the bar. 'Don't push it, Moore.'

'Five minutes,' I answered.

He considered it and nodded. 'Five minutes. But don't talk to nobody. Third door on your left, when you get up the stairs.' I started to move away. 'Hey.' As I turned back, he handed me my beer. 'Don't abuse my hospitality, pal.'

I nodded and took the beer, then pushed through the crowd to a staircase at the back of the Hall. Several boys and men approached me, seeing the evening suit and smelling money. They propositioned me with every conceivable line, some running their hands along my chest and thighs. But I put a good grip on my billfold and stayed on course to the staircase, trying to keep the physically repellant suggestions with which I was peppered from registering in my mind. As I passed the stage, the droning singer – a fat, middle-aged man wearing heavy facial powder, lip rouge, and a top hat – repeated the refrain:

> *Yes, there is still a mem'ry living,*
> *There's a father unforgiving,*
> *And a picture that is turn-ed to the wall!*

The inside of the staircase was unlit, but the glow of the hall crept in enough to let me see where I was going. The old, colorless paint on the walls was peeling badly, and as I mounted the first step I heard a grunting sound coming from behind me. Looking into a dark recess on the other side of the doorway, I saw the faint outlines of a youth, his face shoved up against the wall, and another, an older man, who was pressing against the youth's naked backside. With a shudder that made me trip I turned away and hurried up the stairs, pausing once I was in the bare second-floor hall to take a big belt of beer.

Calming a bit, but beginning to wonder about the wisdom of my initiative, I found the third door on the left: a thin, simple wooden job, just like all the others in the hallway. I grabbed the knob, but then thought to knock. I was surprised when a boy's voice said:

'Who is it?'

I opened the door slowly. There was nothing in the room but an old bed and a night table next to it. The paint on the walls was a red that had turned brown, and it was peeling in the corners. There was a small window that looked out on the blank brick wall of the building next door, across about ten feet of alley space.

On the bed sat a flaxen-haired kid, maybe fifteen, his face painted much as Georgio Santorelli's had been. He wore a sheer linen shirt with lace cuffs and collar, and some theatrical tights. The makeup around his eyes was smudged – he'd been crying.

'I'm not working right now,' he said, straining to reach a falsetto pitch. 'Maybe you could come back in an hour or so.'

'That's all right,' I said, 'I'm not—'

'I said I'm not working!' the young man shouted, losing the

falsetto altogether. 'Oh, God, get out, can't you see I'm upset?'

He broke down in tears, clutching at his face, and I stood by the door, suddenly noticing that it felt very warm in the room. I watched the boy for a few minutes, and then something occurred to me:

'You knew Gloria,' I said.

The boy sniffed and wiped carefully at his eyes. 'Yes. I knew her. Oh, my face – please go away.'

'No, you don't understand. I'm trying to find out who killed him – her.'

The boy looked up at me plaintively. 'Are you a cop?'

'No, a reporter.'

'A reporter?' He looked back at the floor, wiped his eyes again, and chuckled humorlessly. 'Well, I've got a hell of a story for you.' He stared out the window forlornly. 'Whoever it was that they found down on that bridge – it couldn't have been Gloria.'

'Wasn't Gloria?' The rising temperature in the room was making me thirsty, and I took another big swig of beer. 'What makes you think so?'

'Because Gloria never left this room.'

'Never—' It occurred to me that I'd been up too long and had too much to drink: I was having trouble following the kid. 'What do you mean?'

'I'll tell you what I mean. That night, I was in the hallway, outside my room, with a customer. I saw Gloria come in here, alone. I was out there for a good hour, and her door never opened. I figured she was asleep. My customer left after buying me a couple of drinks – the guy didn't want to pay the price for Sally. That's me. Sally's expensive, and he didn't have what it takes. So I stood there another half an hour, waiting for somebody else to wander up. I didn't feel like working the floor. And then one of the girls comes screaming in, saying that a cop just told her they found Gloria dead downtown. I ran right in here, and sure enough, she was gone. But she never left.'

'Well ...' I tried hard to figure it. 'The window, then.' As I crossed to it, I stumbled a bit; I really did need some sleep. The window groaned as I opened it, and when I put my head out, the air wasn't as cold as it should have been.

'The window?' I heard Sally say. 'How? Did she fly? It's a straight drop down, and Gloria didn't have a ladder, or rope, or anything. Besides, I asked one of the girls working the front of the alley if she saw Gloria come out that way. She said no.'

The drop from the window to the alley was indeed a precipitous one; it seemed an unlikely escape route. As for the roof, it was another two stories up, along a brick wall that offered no apparent purchases, and was without a fire escape of any kind. I came back inside and closed the window. 'Then—' I said. 'Then . . .'

Suddenly I collapsed onto the bed. Sally let out one little shriek at that, and then another when she looked toward the door. Following her glance with difficulty, I saw Ellison, Razor Riley, and a couple of their favorites in the doorway. Riley had his trademark out, and was wiping it back and forth across the palm of one hand. Despite the condition of my mind, I knew instantly that they'd slipped chloral into my beer. A lot of chloral.

'I told you not to talk to anybody, Moore,' Ellison said. And then to the youths: 'Well, girls – he's a pretty one to look at, ain't he? Who wants to have some fun with the reporter?'

Two of the young painted men leapt onto the bed and began to tug at my clothes. I was able to get halfway up and onto my elbows before Riley raced over and laid a shot on my jaw. Going back down, I recall hearing the singer downstairs launch into 'You Made Me What I Am Today – I Hope You're Satisfied'; then the two youths were fighting over my billfold and tearing at my pants as Riley began to bind my hands.

Unconsciousness was coming fast – but just before it arrived, I thought I caught a glimpse of Stevie Taggert jumping into the room like a wild wolf cub, brandishing a long piece of wood studded with rusty nails . . .

Chapter 12

The drug-induced dream that followed was peopled by bizarre creatures, half-human and half-animal, that flew, climbed, and slithered down the sides of a high stone wall while I watched in despair, unable to get to the ground. At one point, the primeval landscape around the wall was shaken by an earthquake that seemed to speak with Kreizler's voice, after which the creatures in my dream became more numerous and my need to get to the ground more desperate. Consciousness, when it finally came, brought little relief, for I had no idea where I was. My head felt remarkably clear, from which I took it that I'd been asleep for many hours; but the airy, expansive room around me was completely strange. Spottily furnished with a combination of clerical desks and elegant Italian appointments, it seemed a nonsensical chamber, well suited to another dream. Arched windows in the style of the Gothic Revival ringed the space, and gave it the feel of a monastery; but the spacious dimensions were more like those of a Broadway sweatshop. Anxious to inspect the place more closely, I tried to get up, but fell back in a slight swoon; and since there seemed to be no one about to call to for assistance, I was forced to content myself with studying my strange surroundings while flat on my back.

I was lying on some sort of a divan, which I would have dated as early nineteenth century. Its green and silver covering matched several chairs, as well as a sofa and love seat, that were nearby. On one long, inlaid mahogany dining table stood a silver candelabra, next to which was a Remington typewriter. This incongruity was echoed in the room's wall hangings: Across from my divan, an ostentatiously framed oil view of Florence hung next to an enormous map of Manhattan that was encrusted with several pins. The pins bore small red flags. On the opposite wall was a large chalkboard, notably blank, and beneath this black patch sat the most substantial of the five clerical desks, which together formed a ring at the outer perimeter of the room. Large fans hung from the ceiling, and two enormous Persian carpets, with elaborate designs against a deep green background, covered the center of the floor.

It wasn't any sane person's living quarters, and it certainly wasn't an office. Hallucination, I began to think – but then I looked out the window directly in front of me and saw two familiar sights: the top of McCreery's department store, with its elegant mansard roof and cast-iron arched windows, and, to the left, a similar top section of the St. Denis Hotel. The two institutions, I knew, occupied opposite corners of Eleventh Street, on the west side of Broadway.

'Then I must be – across the street,' I mumbled, just as sounds began to reach my ears from outside: the rhythmic clicking of horses' hooves, and the drag of metal trolley car wheels against track. Then, suddenly, a loud bell tolled. I spun to my left as fast as my condition would allow, and out another arched window I saw what I knew to be the spire of Grace Church, on Tenth Street. It seemed close enough to touch.

Finally, I heard human voices, and used all my strength to sit up on the divan. I had questions at the ready, but was struck silent by the image of half a dozen workmen, none of whom I recognized, rolling first a very ornately carved billiard table and then a baby grand piano into the room atop small, wheeled sleds. As they huffed and cursed at each other, one of them noticed that I was sitting up.

'Hey!' he said with a grin. 'Will ya lookit that – Mr. Moore's awake! How are ya, Mr. Moore?' The other men all smiled and tipped their caps, not seeming to expect an answer.

Talking was more difficult than I'd anticipated, and I could only manage 'Where am I? Who are you?'

'Fools is what we are,' the same man said. 'Been riding on top of the lift with that damned billiard table – only way to get it up here. A damned crazy stunt, but the doc's paying, and he says it goes up.'

'Kreizler?' I said.

'The same,' the man answered.

I became distracted by a slight discomfort in my stomach. 'I'm hungry,' I said.

'And so you should be,' said a female voice in reply, from somewhere in the back recesses of the enormous room. 'Two nights and a day without food will have that effect, John.' From out of the shadows came Sara, dressed in a simple navy dress that did not encumber her movements. She carried a tray, on which sat a steaming bowl. 'Try some broth and bread, it'll give you strength.'

'Sara!' I said with difficulty, as she sat on the divan and placed the tray on my lap. 'Where am I?'

But her attention was distracted when the workmen, having seen her sit next to me, began to whisper among themselves and then laughed conspiratorially. Sara spoke quietly without looking at them:

'Mr. Jonas and his men, being unaware of our undertaking and knowing that I'm not a servant, seem to think my status here is something on the order of group mistress.' She began pouring the salty, delicious chicken broth into me. 'The amazing thing is that they all have wives . . .'

I interrupted my happy slurping long enough to say, 'But Sara – where *are* we?'

'We're home, John. At least, it'll have to pass for home for as long as this investigation takes.'

'Next to Grace Church and across the street from McCreery's – that's home?'

'Our headquarters,' she answered, and I could see that she very much enjoyed the word. Then her aspect grew concerned. 'Speaking of which, I've got to get back to Mulberry Street and report to Theodore. The telephone line has been installed, he's been anxious about that.' She turned toward the back of the room 'Cyrus! Can you come out and help Mr. Moore?'

Cyrus soon joined us, the sleeves of his blue and white striped shirt rolled up and a pair of suspenders strapped over his broad chest. He looked at me with more concern than sympathy, clearly not wanting to assume the task of spoon-feeding.

'That's all right,' I said, taking the utensil from Sara. 'I'm feeling much better, I can manage. But, Sara, you haven't told me—'

'Cyrus knows everything,' she answered, grabbing a simple coat from an elaborately detailed oak stand that stood by the door. 'And I'm late. Finish the broth, John. Mr. Jonas!' She disappeared out the door. 'I'll need the elevator!'

Seeing that I was, in fact, able to feed myself, Cyrus seemed to relax considerably, and pulled up one of the delicate, straight-backed chairs with the silver and green upholstery. 'You're looking much better, sir,' he said.

'I'm alive,' I answered. 'And even more remarkably, I'm in New York. I was sure I'd wake up in South America, or on a privateering ship. Tell me, Cyrus – my last memory is of Stevie. Did he . . .?'

'Yes, sir,' Cyrus answered evenly. 'Confidentially, he's had his share of trouble sleeping since he saw the body on the bridge. He was out roaming the neighborhood that night, when he saw you walking down Broadway. He said you looked – kind of unsteady on your feet, sir, so he followed you. Just to be sure you'd be all right. When he saw you go into Paresis Hall, he figured he'd wait outside. Understandably. But then a policeman caught sight of him, and accused him of the usual activity for that spot. Stevie denied it, and told the cop he was waiting for you. The officer didn't believe him, and so Stevie bolted into the Hall. He wasn't trying to rescue you, he was just trying to escape – but the way things worked out, the one was the other. The cop didn't arrest anybody, of course, but he made sure you got out with your skin.'

'I see. And how did I get to – say, where in hell *are* we, Cyrus?'

'Number 808 Broadway, Mr. Moore. Top floor, which would be the sixth. The doctor engaged it as a base of operations for the investigation. Not so close to Mulberry Street as'll be noticed, but a carriage can have you there in just a few minutes. Or, if traffic's heavy, the trolley will do the same.'

'And what about all these – furnishings, or whatever they are?'

'The doctor and Miss Howard went looking for furniture yesterday, over in Brooklyn. At an office supplier's. But the doctor said he couldn't live with that sort of stuff for a day, much less an extended period of time. So they bought just the desks, and then went to an auction on Fifth Avenue. The furniture of the Marchese Luigi Carcano of Italy was being sold off. They bought quite a bit of it.'

'They certainly did,' I said, as two of the workmen reappeared bearing a large clock, two Chinese vases, and some green draperies.

'As soon as we had most of it in, the doctor figured he'd move you from his house to here.'

'That would be the earthquake,' I said.

'Sir?'

'A dream I had. Why here?'

'Said we couldn't waste any more time nursing you. He gave you a little more chloral, so you'd come out of it easy. Wanted you ready for work when you woke up.'

Then there were more noises outside the door. I heard Kreizler say, 'Ah, is he. Good!' and then he burst in, trailed by Stevie Taggert and Lucius Isaacson. 'Moore!' he called. 'You're awake at last, eh?' He strode over and grabbed my wrist, checking the pulse. 'How do you feel?'

'Not as bad as I expected to.' Stevie had taken a seat on one of the windowsills and was playing with a fairly sizable jackknife. 'I understand I've got you to thank for that, Stevie,' I called. He just smiled and looked out the window, his hair falling in front of his face. 'That's a debt I won't forget.' The boy laughed a bit; he never seemed to know what to make of being appreciated.

'It's a miracle that he happened to follow you, Moore,' Kreizler said, pulling at my eyelids and examining the orbs underneath. 'By all rights you should be dead.'

'Thank you, Kreizler,' I said. 'In that case I don't suppose you'd like to know what I discovered.'

'And what might that be?' he answered, probing my mouth

with some kind of instrument. 'That the Santorelli boy was never seen leaving Paresis Hall? That he was believed still in his chamber, from which there is no secondary exit?'

The thought that I'd endured my ordeal for nothing was truly depressing. 'How do you know that?'

'We thought it was delirious rambling at first,' Lucius Isaacson said, going to one of the desks and emptying the contents of a paper sack onto it. 'But you kept repeating it, so Marcus and I went down to check the story out with your friend Sally. Very interesting – Marcus is out working on some possible explanations right now.'

Cyrus crossed the room to hand Lucius an envelope. 'Commissioner Roosevelt sent this by runner, Detective Sergeant.'

Lucius quickly opened and perused the message. 'Well, it's official,' he said uncertainly. 'My brother and I have been "temporarily detached from the Division of Detectives, for personal reasons." I only hope my mother doesn't hear about it.'

'Excellent,' Kreizler said to him. 'You'll have access to the resources of headquarters without being required to appear there regularly – an admirable solution. Perhaps now you can spend a little time teaching John here some slightly more sophisticated methods of detection.' Laszlo laughed once, then lowered his voice as he checked my heart. 'I don't mean to belittle your effort, Moore. It was an important bit of work. But do try to remember that this affair is no joke, especially to many of the people we shall be interviewing. Traveling in pairs on such occasions will be more prudent.'

'You're preaching to the converted,' I answered.

Kreizler poked and prodded me a bit more, then stood away. 'How's your jaw?'

I hadn't thought of it, but when I put my hand to my mouth there was some tenderness. 'That dwarf,' I said. 'He hasn't got much without the razor.'

'Good man!' Kreizler laughed, slapping my back lightly. 'Now finish your broth and get dressed. We've got an assessment to do at Bellevue, and I want Jonas's men to finish this place. Our first staff meeting will be at five o'clock.'

'Assessment?' I said, getting to my feet and expecting to swoon again. But the broth really had restored me. 'Who?' I asked, noticing that I was wearing a nightshirt.

'Harris Markowitz, of 75 Forsyth Street,' Lucius answered, walking (I'm reluctant to say waddling, though it had that aspect) over to me with a few sheets of typewritten paper. 'A haberdasher. A couple of days ago his wife came in to the Tenth Precinct claiming her husband had poisoned their two grandchildren – Samuel and Sophie Rieter, ages twelve and sixteen – by putting what she called 'a powder' in their milk.'

'Poison?' I said. 'But our man's not a poisoner.'

'Not that we know of,' Kreizler answered. 'But his activities may be more varied than we think – although I don't actually believe this man Markowitz is any more connected to our case than Henry Wolff was.'

'The children do, however, fit the apparent pattern among the victims,' Lucius said, tactfully but pointedly. And then to me: 'The Rieter children were recent immigrants – their father and mother sent them over from Bohemia to stay with Mrs. Rieter's parents and try to find domestic work.'

'Immigrants, true,' Kreizler answered. 'And if this were three years ago I might be more impressed. But our quarry's recent taste for prostitutes seems too significant, as do the current mutilations, to allow us to concentrate solely on the immigrant connection. However, even if this Markowitz isn't involved with our business, there are other reasons to investigate such cases. By eliminating them, we can gain a clearer picture of what the person we seek is *not* – a negative image, if you will, that we can eventually print into a positive.'

Cyrus had brought me some clothes, and I began to put them on. 'But aren't we going to raise suspicions by doing so many assessments of child-murderers?'

'We must rely on the Police Department's lack of imagination,' Laszlo answered. 'It's not unusual for me to be seen doing such work. The explanation for your presence, Moore, will of course be reporting. By the time anyone at headquarters thinks to connect it all to the current string of murders, our work will, I hope, be done.' He turned to Lucius. 'Now, then, Detective Sergeant, you might just review the details of the

The Alienist

case for our adventurous friend, here.'

'Well, Markowitz was clever enough,' Lucius answered, almost as if he admired the man. 'He used a large amount of opium, all residual bodily traces of which, as you may know, vanish within hours of death. He put it in two glasses of milk, which were fed to the grandchildren at bedtime. When they'd slipped into a comatose state, Markowitz turned on the gas jet in their room. The police arrived the next morning, the place stank of gas, and the detective in charge drew the obvious conclusion. His hypothesis seemed confirmed when the coroner – actually a fairly capable man, in this case – had the contents of the stomachs checked and nothing out of the ordinary turned up. But when the wife kept insisting that the poisoning had in fact taken place, an idea occurred to me. I went down to the flat and located the bedclothes that the children had slept on. It was likely that at least one of the victims had vomited sometime during unconsciousness or the death throes. If the sheets and blankets hadn't been washed yet, there would be stains. Sure enough, I found them. We ran the standard Stas and reagent tests, and that was where we found the opium traces. In the vomit. Faced with that, Markowitz confessed.'

'And he doesn't drink?' Kreizler asked. 'No drug addictions?'

'Apparently not,' Lucius answered with a shrug.

'Nor did he stand to gain materially from the children's deaths?'

'In no way.'

'Good! Then we have several elements we need – extensive premeditation, a lack of intoxication, and no obvious motive. All would characterize our killer. But if we discover that Markowitz is not in fact our man – as I suspect we will – then our task becomes to determine *why* he isn't.' Laszlo picked up a piece of chalk and began to rap on the large blackboard, as if trying to coax information out of it. 'What makes him different from Santorelli's murderer? Why *didn't* he mutilate the bodies? When we know that, we can focus our imaginary picture just a bit more. Then, as we build our killer's list of attributes, more and more candidates can be eliminated at first glance. For the moment, however – we have a wide field.' He pulled on his gloves. 'Stevie!

Caleb Carr

You'll be driving. I want Cyrus to oversee the installation of the piano. Don't let them butcher it, Cyrus. Detective Sergeant, you will be at the Institute?'

Lucius nodded. 'The bodies should arrive by noon.'

'Bodies?' I said.

'The two boys killed earlier this year,' Laszlo answered, moving to the door. 'Hurry, Moore, we'll be late!'

Chapter 13

True to Kreizler's prediction, Harris Markowitz proved thoroughly unsuitable as a suspect in our case. Aside from being short, stout, and well into his sixties – and thus wholly unlike the physical specimen described by the Isaacsons at Delmonico's – he was obviously quite out of his mind. He'd killed his grandchildren, he claimed, in order to save them from what he perceived to be a monstrously evil world, whose salient aspects he described in a series of rambling, highly confused outbursts. Such poor systemization of unreasonably fearful thoughts and beliefs, as well as the apparently complete lack of concern for his own fate that Markowitz exhibited, often characterized cases of dementia praecox, Kreizler told me as we left Bellevue. But while Markowitz clearly had nothing to do with our business, the visit was still valuable, as Laszlo had hoped it would be, in helping us determine aspects of our killer's personality by way of comparison. Obviously, our man was not murdering children out of any perverse desire to attend to their spiritual well-being. The furious mutilation of the bodies after death made that much plain. Nor, clearly, was he unconcerned with what would happen to him as a result of his acts. But most of all, it was apparent from his open display of his handiwork, that the killings did disturb some part of him. In other words, there was evidence in the bodies *not of the murderer's derangement but of his sanity.*

I puzzled with that concept all the way back to Number 808

Broadway, but on arrival my attention was distracted by my first really clear-headed perusal of the place that, as Sara had said, would be our home for the foreseeable future. It was a handsome yellow-brick building, which Kreizler told me had been designed by James Renwick, the architect responsible for the Gothic edifice of Grace Church next door, as well as for the more subdued St. Denis Hotel across the street. The southern windows of our headquarters looked directly out onto the churchyard, which lay in a dark shadow cast by Grace's enormous tapering spire. There was quite a parochial, serene feel about this little stretch of Broadway, despite the fact that we were smack in the center of one of the city's busiest shopping strips: besides McCreery, there were stores selling everything from dry goods to boots to photographs within steps of Number 808. The single greatest monument to all this commerce was an enormous cast-iron building across Tenth Street from the church, formerly A.T. Stewart's department store, currently operated by Hilton, Hughes and Company, and eventually to gain its greatest fame as Wanamaker's.

The elevator at Number 808 was a large, caged affair, quite new, and it took us quietly back up to the sixth floor. Here we discovered that great progress had been made during our absence. Things were now so arranged that it actually looked like human affairs were being conducted out of the place, though one would still have been hard-pressed to say precisely what kind. At five o'clock sharp each of us sat at one of the five desks, from which vantage points we could clearly see and discuss matters with one another. There was nervous but pleasant chatter as we settled in, and real camaraderie when we began to discuss the events of our various days. As the evening sun dipped above the Hudson, sending rich golden light over the rooftops of western Manhattan and through our Gothic front windows, I realized that we had become, with remarkable speed, a working unit.

We had enemies, to be sure: Lucius Isaacson reported that at the conclusion of his examination of the other two murdered boys, a pair of men claiming to be representatives of the cemetery from which the bodies had been taken had appeared at the Institute, demanding an end to the proceedings. Lucius had gathered all the information he needed, by then, and decided not to put up a fight – but the physical description of the two men that he gave, right down to the bruises on their faces, matched the two thugs that had chased Sara and me out of the Santorellis' flat. Fortunately, the two ex-cops had not recognized Lucius as a detective (they had probably been fired before his arrival on the force); but it was nonetheless apparent that, as we had no idea who was commanding these men or what their object was, the Institute was no longer a safe place to conduct business.

As for Lucius's examination itself, the results were just what we'd hoped for: both bodies bore the same knife marks that had been found on Georgio Santorelli and the Zweig children. With that confirmation, Marcus Isaacson took two more pins with red flags and stuck them into the large map of Manhattan, one at the Brooklyn Bridge, and one at the Ellis Island ferry station. Kreizler posted the dates of those killings – January first and February second – on the right-hand side of the large chalkboard, along with March third, the day Georgio had died. Somewhere in those months and days, we all knew, was one of the many patterns we needed to identify. (That pattern would ultimately prove far more complex, Kreizler believed from the start, than the apparent similarity of the number of the month and the number of the day.)

Marcus Isaacson told of his efforts, still unrewarded, to establish a method by which 'Gloria' could have gotten out of his room at Paresis Hall without being seen. Sara informed us that she and Roosevelt had worked out a scheme whereby our group would be able to visit the sites of any future murders that were obviously the work of the same killer before they were disturbed by other detectives or by the heavy hands of coroners. The plan represented another risk for Theodore, but he was by now fully committed to Kreizler's agenda. For my part, I related the story of our trip to see Harris Markowitz. When all this business was concluded, Kreizler stood at his desk and indicated the large chalkboard, on which, he said, we would create our imaginary man: physical and psychological clues would be listed, cross-referenced, revised, and combined until the work was done. Accordingly, he next posted those facts and theories that we had so far discovered and hypothesized.

When he had finished, it seemed that there were precious few white marks on that enormous black space – and at least some of the few, Kreizler warned, would not remain. The use of chalk, he said, was an indication of how many mistakes he expected himself and the rest of us to make along the way. We were in uncharted country and must not become discouraged by setbacks and difficulties, or by the amount of material we would have to master along the way. The rest of us were a little confused by that statement; Kreizler then produced four separate but identical piles of books and papers.

Articles by Laszlo's friend Adolf Meyer and other alienists; the works of philosophers and evolutionists from Hume and Locke to Spencer and Schopenhauer; monographs by the elder Forbes Winslow, whose theories had originally inspired Kreizler's theory of context; and finally, in all its weighty, two-volume splendor, our old professor William James's *The Principles of Psychology* – these and more were dropped on our desks, producing loud, ponderous booms. The Isaacsons, Sara, and I all exchanged worried glances, looking and feeling like beleaguered students on the first day of class – which, obviously, is just what we were. Kreizler spelled out the purpose of our going through such an ordeal:

From that moment on, he said, we must make every possible effort to rid ourselves of preconceptions about human behavior. We must try not to see the world through our own eyes, nor to judge it by our own values, but through and by those of our killer. *His* experience, the context of *his* life, was all that mattered. Any aspect of his behavior that puzzled us, from the most trivial to the most horrendous, we must try to explain by postulating child-hood events that could lead to such eventualities. This process of cause and effect – what we would soon learn was called 'psychological determinism' – might not always seem entirely logical to us, but it would be consistent.

Kreizler emphasized that no good would come of conceiving of this person as a monster, because he was most assuredly a man (or a woman); and that man or woman had once been a child. First and foremost, we must get to know that child, and to know his parents, his siblings, his complete world. It was pointless to talk about evil and barbarity and madness; none of these concepts would lead us any closer to him. But if we could capture the human child in our imaginations – then we could capture the man in fact.

'And if that is not reward enough,' Kreizler concluded, glancing from one of our gaping faces to another, 'there is always food.'

Food, we learned during the next few days, was quite a major reason why Laszlo had selected Number 808 Broadway: we were within easy walking distance of some of Manhattan's best restaurants. Ninth Street and University Place offered exceptional French dining at traditional Parisian *banquettes* in both the Café Lafayette and the small dining room of the proportionally small hotel run by Louis Martin. Should the mood run to German fare, we could trot up Broadway to Union Square and turn in to that huge, darkly paneled Mecca of gourmands, Lüchow's. Tenth Street and Second Avenue offered hearty Hungarian meals at the Café Boulevard, while there was no better Italian cooking to be had than that served in the dining room of the Hotel Gonfarone, on Eighth and MacDougal streets. And, of course, there was always Del's, a bit further away but assuredly worth the trip. All these centers of culinary brilliance would become our informal conference rooms during legions of lunches and dinners, although there would be many occasions on which the grim work with which we were preoccupied made it difficult indeed to concentrate on gustatory satisfaction.

That was especially true during those first days, when it became increasingly hard to escape the knowledge that, although we were cutting a new path on this job and needed to take the time to study and understand all the psychological as well as criminological elements that would necessarily form the basis of a successful conclusion, we were also working against a clock. Out in the streets below our arched windows were dozens of children like Georgio Santorelli, plying the ever-dangerous flesh trade without knowing that a new and especially violent danger was loose among them. It was an odd feeling, to go to an assessment with Kreizler or to study notes at Number 808 Broadway or to stay up until the small hours reading at my grandmother's, trying to force my mind to absorb information at a speed it was (to say the least) unaccustomed to, all the while a voice whispering in the back of my head: 'Hurry up or a child will die!' The first few days of it almost drove me mad – studying and restudying the condition of the various bodies, as well as the sites at which they were discovered, trying to find patterns in both groups while simultaneously wrestling with passages like this one from Herbert Spencer:

'Can the oscillation of a molecule be represented in consciousness side by side with a nervous shock, and the two be recognized as one? No effort enables us to assimilate them. That a unit of feeling has nothing in common with a unit of motion, becomes more than ever manifest when we bring the two into juxtaposition.'

'Give me your derringer, Sara,' I remember calling out when I first ran across that statement. 'I'm going to shoot myself.' Why in the world should I have to understand such things, I wondered during that first week or so, when what I wanted to know was where, *where* was our murderer? Yet in time I came to see the point of such efforts. Take that particular Spencer quote, for example – I eventually grasped that the attempts of people like Spencer to interpret the activities of the mind as the complex effects of material motion within the human organism had failed. This failure had reinforced the inclination of younger alienists and psychologists like Kreizler and Adolf Meyer to view the origins of consciousness primarily in terms of formative childhood experience, and only secondarily in terms of pure physical function. That had real relevance, in terms of understanding that our killer's path from birth to savagery had not been the random result of physical processes that we would have been powerless to chart but rather the product of conceivable events.

It was up to us to theorize what terrible series of experiences had confirmed the killer's methods, in his mind, as the most reliable reaction to the challenges of his life.

Yes, it soon became clear that we needed to know all this and more, much more, if we were going to have any hope of fully fleshing out our imaginary man. And as that truth sank in, we all began to study and read with greater determination and speed, trading thoughts and ideas at all hours of the day and night. Sara and I would often shout heady philosophy over crackling telephone lines at two in the morning, much to my grandmother's despair, as we first groped and then more competently reached for greater knowledge. The rather remarkable fact that we were getting an extremely rapid education (the bulk of it was chewed and swallowed, if not completely digested, in the first ten days) was obscured by the practical task at hand, and by the attention we had to pay to whatever physical clues and methodical theories Marcus and Lucius Isaacson detected and devised. Not that there were many of these, in the beginning; we hadn't had enough access to any of the crime scenes for that. The knowledge that we needed more than what we had to build a detailed picture of the killer's method only increased the morbidly expectant air in our headquarters. Though buried in our work, we were all aware that we were waiting for something to happen.

As March turned to April, it did. At 1:45 A.M. on a Saturday, I was dozing in my room at my grandmother's house with my copy of the second volume of Professor James's *Principles* resting rather uncomfortably across my face. That afternoon I'd begun a noble effort to tackle James's thoughts on 'Necessary Truths and the Effects of Experience' at Number 808 Broadway but had been distracted by the entrance of Stevie Taggert, who'd torn a list of the following day's entries at the new Acqueduct racing park on Long Island from a late city edition of the *Herald* and wanted some advice on handicapping from me. I'd lately been employing Stevie as a runner to my betting agent (unbeknownst to Kreizler, of course) and the boy had quite taken to the sport of kings. I'd encouraged him not to bet his own money unless and until he really knew what he was doing; but with his background that hadn't taken long. At any rate, when the telephone rang that night, I was in the midst of a deep sleep brought on by hours of thick reading. I bolted directly upright at the sound of the bell and sent the volume of James slamming against the opposite wall. The telephone clanged again as I got into my robe, and once more before I dashed through the hallway clumsily and picked the receiver up.

'Blank slate,' I mumbled in a sleepy rush, assuming that the caller was Sara.

It was. 'Excuse me?' she answered.

'What we were talking about this afternoon,' I said, rubbing my eyes. 'Is the mind a blank slate at birth, or do we have innate knowledge of certain things? My money's on the blank slate.'

'John, be quiet for a moment.' Her voice was tinged with anxiety. 'It's happened.'

That roused me. 'Where?'

'Castle Garden. The Battery. The Isaacsons are getting their camera and other equipment ready. They have to arrive before the rest of us, so that the officer who was first on the scene can be dismissed. Theodore's there now, making sure it goes smoothly. I've already called Dr. Kreizler.'

'Right.'

'John—'

'Yes?'

'I've never – I'm the only one who's never – how bad will it be?'

What could I say? There were only practicalities to consider. 'You'll want ammonia salts. But try not to worry too much. We'll all be there. Pick me up in a cab, we'll go together.'

I heard her breathe deeply once. 'All right, John.'

The same outer object may suggest either of many realities formerly associated with it – for in the vicissitudes of our outer experience we are constantly liable to meet the same thing in the midst of differing companions.

> *William James,*
> The Principles of Psychology

Whatever I thought right seemed bad to others;
whatever seemed wrong to me,
others approved of.
I ran into feuds wherever I found myself,
I met disfavor wherever I went;
if I longed for happiness, I only stirred up misery;
so I had to be called 'Woeful':
Woe is all I possess.

> *Wagner,*
> Die Walküre

Chapter 14

By the time Sara reached Washington Square in a hansom, she'd dispatched many of her fears and replaced them with tough determination. Seemingly oblivious of several trivial questions I asked as we charged down the granite slab pavement of Broadway, she sat staring straight ahead, impassively focused on – what? She would not say, and it was impossible to assume with any certainty. My suspicion, however, was that she was preoccupied with that great guiding goal of her life, to prove that a woman could be a capable, effective police officer. And so she gazed at the back of our laboring horse and said barely a word, using every mental power she possessed to ensure that when the time came she would conduct herself as well as any seasoned detective.

All of which stood in some contrast to my own attempts to ease apprehension with idle chatter. By the time we reached Prince Street I'd gotten pretty tired of my own nervous voice; and by Broome I was just about ready to give up all attempts at communication in favor of watching the whores and their marks come out of the concert halls. On one corner a Norwegian sailor, so drunk he was drooling a river of spit down onto the front of his uniform, was being propped up by two dancers while a third slowly and brazenly went through his pockets. It wasn't an uncommon sort of sight; but on this night it planted a thought in my head.

'Sara,' I said, as we crossed Canal Street and clattered on

toward City Hall. 'Have you ever been to Shang Draper's?'

'No,' she answered quickly, her breath condensing in the frigid air. April, as always in New York, had brought precious little respite from the biting cold of March.

It wasn't much of an opening for conversation, but I took it. 'Well, it's just that the average whore who works a disorderly house knows more ways to shake down a mark than I could probably list – and the children who work in a place like Draper's, or Paresis Hall, for that matter, are as sharp as any adults. What if our man's one of those marks? Suppose he was cheated one time too many and now he's out to settle the score? It was always a theory in the Ripper killings.'

Sara shifted the heavy blanket that covered our laps, still not exactly what I'd call interested. 'I suppose it might be possible, John. What makes you think of it now?'

I turned to her. 'Those three years, between the Zweigs and our first murder this past January – what if our theory, that there were other bodies and that they're well hidden, is wrong? What if he didn't commit any other murders in New York – because he wasn't here?'

'Wasn't here?' Sara's tone became more animated. 'You mean, he took a trip? Left town?'

'What if he had to? A sailor, for instance. Half the marks in places like Draper's or Ellison's are seamen. It might make sense. If he were a regular customer, he wouldn't have aroused any suspicion – he might even have known the boys.'

Sara thought it over, then nodded. 'It's not bad, John. It would certainly allow him to come and go without being noticed. Let's see what the others think when we ...' Her speech hitched up a bit, and then she turned back toward the street, anxious again. 'When we get there.'

Things grew quiet inside the hansom once more.

Castle Garden sits in the heart of Battery Park, and to get to it we had to travel to the base of Broadway and beyond. That meant a fast trip through the pastiche of architectural styles that made up the publishing and financial districts of Manhattan in those days. On first glance, it was always a bit odd to see structures like the *World* Building and the dozen-storied

National Shoe and Leather Bank looming (or at least, in those days before the Woolworth and Singer towers, they *seemed* to be looming) over such squat, ornate Victorian monuments as the Old Post Office and the headquarters of the Equitable Life Assurance Society. But the longer one was exposed to the neighborhood, the more one detected a common quality among all these buildings that overrode any stylistic variance: wealth. I had spent much of my childhood in this part of Manhattan (my father ran a moderately sized investment house) and from an early age I'd been struck by the fantastic activity that surrounded the getting and keeping of money. This activity could be alternately seductive and repellant; but by 1896 it was unarguably New York's strongest reason for being.

I felt this undercurrent of enormous power again that night, even though the district was dark and dormant at two-thirty in the morning; and as we passed the graveyard at Trinity Church – where the father of the American economic system, Alexander Hamilton, lay buried – I found myself smiling bemusedly and thinking: He's audacious, all right. Whoever our quarry was, and whatever the personal turmoil that was propelling him, he was no longer confining his activities to the less respectable parts of town. He had ventured into this preserve of the wealthy elite and dared to leave a body in Battery Park, within easy sight of the offices of many of the city's most influential financial elders. Yes, if our man was in fact sane, then this latest act was not only barbarous but audacious, in that peculiar way that has always produced a mixture of horror and grudging acknowledgment in natives of this city.

Our hansom released us at Bowling Green, and we crossed over to enter Battery Park. Kreizler's calash stood at the curb on Battery Place, with Stevie Taggert aboard and huddled in a large blanket.

'Stevie,' I said. 'Keeping an eye out for the precinct boys?'

He nodded and shivered. 'And staying away from that,' he said, nodding toward the interior of the park. 'It's an awful business, Mr. Moore.'

Inside the park, a very few arc lights directed us along a straight path toward the prodigious stone walls of Castle Garden.

Formerly a heavily armed fort called Castle Clinton, the structure had been built to guard New York during the War of 1812, after which it was turned over to the city and converted into a covered pavilion that saw years of use as an opera house. In 1855 it was transformed again, into New York's immigration station; and before Ellis Island usurped that role in 1892, no fewer than seven million transplanted souls had passed through the old stone fort in Battery Park. City officials had recently been casting around for some new use to make of the thing, and had decided on housing the New York Aquarium inside its round walls. That remodeling was now under way, and the telltale signs of construction greeted Sara and me even before we could clearly make out the fort's walls against the night sky.

Under those walls we found Marcus Isaacson and Cyrus Montrose standing over a man who wore a long greatcoat and had a wide-brimmed hat clutched tightly in his hands. There was a badge pinned to the man's coat, but at the moment he looked anything but authoritative: he was seated on a pile of cut boards, holding his pale face over a bucket and breathing hard. Marcus was trying to ask him some questions, but the fellow was clearly in some kind of shock. We approached, and both Cyrus and Marcus nodded our way.

'The watchman?' I asked.

'Yes,' Marcus answered. His voice was energized but tightly controlled. 'He found the body at about one o'clock, on the roof. Apparently he makes his rounds every hour or so.' Marcus leaned over the man. 'Mr. Miller? I'm going back upstairs. Take your time, come back up when you're ready. But under no circumstances are you to leave. All right?' The man looked up, his dark, grizzled features full of horror, and nodded blankly. Then he quickly bent over the bucket again, though he didn't retch. Marcus turned to Cyrus. 'Make sure he stays put, will you, Cyrus? We need a lot more answers than we've gotten.'

'All right, Detective Sergeant,' Cyrus answered, and then Marcus, Sara, and I went through the mammoth black gates of Castle Garden.

'The man's a wreck,' Marcus said, jerking his head back toward the watchman. 'All I've gotten out of him is a passionately sworn statement that at twelve-fifteen the body was not where it is now, and that these front doors were bolted. The rear doors were chained, I've checked them – no sign of tampering with the locks. I'm afraid it's all very reminiscent of the Paresis Hall situation, John. No way in or out, but someone managed it all the same.'

The renovation of the interior walls of Castle Garden was only half finished. On the floor space between all the lathing, plaster, and paint sat a series of huge glass water tanks, some under construction, some finished but unfilled, and some already housing their designated occupants: various species of exotic fish, whose wide eyes and skittish movements seemed all too appropriate, given what had occurred in their new home that night. Flashes of silver and brilliantly colored scales caught the light of a few dim worklamps that were on, increasing the eerie impression that the fish were a terrified audience searching for a way out of this place of death and back to those deep, dark regions where men and their brutal ways were unknown.

We climbed an old staircase in one wall of the fort, eventually emerging above the shell that had been built over the old ramparts to cover the formerly open central yard. A decagonal turret with two windows in each face stood at the center of the roof, which offered a commanding view of New York Harbor and Bartholdi's still-new statue of Lady Liberty out on Bedloe's Island.

Near the edge of the roof closest to the waterfront were Roosevelt, Kreizler, and Lucius Isaacson. Next to them stood a large, boxy camera on a wooden tripod, and lying in front of the camera, bathed in the light of another worklamp, was the cause of our coming together. The blood was visible even from a distance.

Lucius's attention was fixed on the body, but Kreizler and Roosevelt were facing away and talking very heatedly. When Kreizler saw us emerge from the staircase he came directly over, Roosevelt following behind and shaking his head. Marcus moved to the camera as Laszlo addressed Sara and me.

'Based on the condition of the body,' Kreizler said, 'there would seem to be little doubt. It's our man's work.'

'A roundsman from the Twenty-seventh Precinct was first on

the scene,' Theodore added. 'He says he can remember seeing the boy regularly at the Golden Rule, though he doesn't recall any name.' (The Golden Rule Pleasure Club was a disorderly house on West Fourth Street that specialized in boy-whores.)

Kreizler put his hands on Sara's shoulders. 'It's not an easy sight, Sara.'

She nodded. 'I didn't expect it to be.'

Laszlo studied her reactions carefully. 'I'd like you to assist the detective sergeant with his postmortem – he's aware of your training as a nurse. It won't be long before the precinct investigators arrive, and there's much for each of us to do before then.'

Sara nodded again, breathed once deeply, and moved toward Lucius and the body. Kreizler began to speak to me, but I put him off for a moment and trailed a few steps behind Sara as she moved toward the glowing hemisphere of electric light in the corner of the rooftop.

The body was that of an olive-skinned boy, with delicate Semitic features and thick black hair on the right side of his head. On the left side, a large section of scalp had been torn away, revealing the slick surface of the skull. Other than that, the mutilations seemed to be identical to those that had marked Georgio Santorelli (except that the injuries to the buttocks had not been repeated): the eyes were missing, the genitals had been cut off and stuffed in the mouth, the torso was crisscrossed by deep lacerations, the wrists were bound, and the right hand had been severed and apparently removed from the scene. As Kreizler had said, there seemed little doubt about who was responsible. It was all as distinctive as a signature. That same terrible sense of pathos that I'd felt on the Williamsburg Bridge anchor returned to steal my breath and rattle what seemed every bone in my body.

I watched Sara carefully without moving closer, ready to assist if she should be overcome, but not wishing her to think that I expected her to be. Her eyes, as they took in the sight, went wide and her head shook, quickly and quite visibly. She clasped her hands together tightly, took another deep breath, and then stood by Lucius.

'Detective Sergeant?' she said. 'Dr. Kreizler says I'm to assist you.'

Lucius looked up, impressed at Sara's composure, and then wiped his forehead with a handkerchief. 'Yes. Thank you, Miss Howard. We'll begin with the injury to the scalp . . .'

I headed back to Kreizler and Roosevelt. 'That's one gutsy girl,' I said with a shake of my head, but neither of them acknowledged the remark.

Kreizler slapped a newspaper on my chest and spoke bitterly. 'Your friend Steffens has written quite an article for the morning edition of the *Post*, John. How, *how* could anyone be so stupid?'

'There's no excuse,' Roosevelt said glumly. 'I can only think that Steffens considered the story fair game, so long as he didn't reveal your involvement in the case, Doctor. But I'll have him in my office first thing this morning and, by thunder, I'll make the situation clear to him!'

Prominently displayed on the *Post*'s front page was an article announcing that the Zweig killings and the Santorelli murder were now believed by 'high police officials' to be the work of the same man. The article made less out of the apparently unusual nature of the killer than out of the fact that the link to the Zweigs demonstrated that the 'ghoulish fiend' was not drawn exclusively to child prostitutes: It was now clear, Steffens declared in his best rabble-rousing style, that 'No children are safe.' There were other sensational details, as well: Santorelli, it was stated, had been 'assaulted' before his death (in fact, Kreizler had found no evidence of sexual violation), and in some quarters of the city the murders were being talked of as the work of a supernatural creature – though 'the infamous Ellison and his cohorts' made 'far more promising suspects.'

I folded the paper and tapped it slowly against my leg. 'This is very bad.'

'Bad,' Kreizler said, controlling his anger, 'but done. And we must try to undo it. Moore, is there any chance that you can persuade your editors to run a piece in the *Times* denouncing all this as speculation?'

'It's possible,' I answered. 'But it would tip them off to my involvement in the investigation. And they'd probably have someone dig deeper once they knew that much – the connection to the Zweigs is going to make a lot of people a lot more interested in this.'

'Yes, if we attempt to counteract this, I suspect we'll only make things worse,' Theodore pronounced. 'Steffens must be told to keep quiet, and we must hope that the article is ignored.'

'How can it be?!' Laszlo erupted. 'Even if every other person in this city fails to pay attention, there is *one* who will see it – and I fear, I truly *fear*, his reaction!'

'And do you imagine that I don't, Doctor?' Theodore countered. 'I knew the press would interfere eventually – that's why I urged you to hurry your efforts. You can hardly expect to go for weeks without *someone* mentioning the matter!'

Theodore put his hands to his hips, and Kreizler turned away, unable to say anything in reply. After a few moments Laszlo spoke again, more calmly, this time. 'You're right, Commissioner. Instead of arguing we should be making use of the opportunity we have now. But for God's sake, Roosevelt – if you must share official business with Riis and Steffens, make this an exception.'

'There's no need to worry on that account, Doctor,' Roosevelt answered, in a conciliatory tone. 'This isn't the first time Steffens has annoyed me with his speculations – but it will be the last.'

Kreizler shook his head in disgust once more, then shrugged. 'Well, then. To work.'

We joined the Isaacsons and Sara. Marcus was busy taking detailed photographs of the body as Lucius continued his postmortem, calling out the injuries in a flurry of medical and anatomical jargon, his voice steady and full of purpose. Indeed, it was remarkable how little either detective displayed those quirks of behavior that were usually a cause of laughter or consternation in observers: they moved around the rooftop in a flurry of cerebral inspiration, locking onto apparently insignificant details like trained dogs and taking charge of business as if they, not Roosevelt or Kreizler, were directing the investigation. As their efforts continued, all of us, even Theodore, lent them every possible assistance, taking notes, holding pieces of equipment and lights, and generally making sure that there was no need for either of them to break their concentration even for a moment.

Once he had finished photographing the body, Marcus left Lucius and Sara to complete their grim work and began to 'dust' the rooftop for fingerprints. Roosevelt, Kreizler, and I, meanwhile, went to work finding surfaces that might be smooth and hard enough to 'hold' such prints: door handles, windows, even an apparently new ceramic chimney that ran along the side of the decagonal tower just a few feet from where the body lay. This last site was the one that bore fruit, primarily because, Marcus told us, the watchman had rather lazily allowed the fire downstairs to go out hours earlier. By a particularly clean section of the glazed ceramic, at about the point where a man of the height Marcus and Lucius had posited for our killer would have rested his hand were he leaning against the chimney for support, Marcus put his face close and grew agitated. He told Theodore and me to hold up a small tarpaulin that would block the wind that blew in off the harbor. Then he spread the carbon powder on the chimney with a delicate camel's hair brush and produced, one can only say magically, a set of smudgelike prints. Their position was exactly consistent with the hypothetical lean of the killer.

Taking the photograph of Sofia Zweig's bloodstained thumb from his coat pocket, Marcus held it up against the chimney, Laszlo moved close and watched the whole process carefully. Marcus's dark eyes went very wide as he studied the prints, and they were positively afire when he turned to Kreizler and said, in a notably controlled voice, 'It looks like a match.' At that, he and Kreizler went for the big camera, while Theodore and I continued to hold the tarp. Marcus took several close shots of the prints, the burst of the flash powder illuminating the whole roof area but quickly dissipating in the blackness out over the harbor.

Next Marcus had us inspect the ledges of the roof for, as he put it, 'Any signs of disturbance or activity – even the smallest chips, cracks, or holes in the masonry.' Now, a building that faces New York harbor is going to have a lot of chips, cracks, and holes in its masonry; but we dutifully set about the task, Roosevelt, Kreizler, and myself each shouting when we located something that seemed to conform to our vague instructions. Marcus, whose attention was focused on a sturdy railing that surmounted the front of the roof, ran over to inspect each of these finds. Most of the sightings proved false; but on the very back of the roof, in the darkest, most hidden corner of the structure, Roosevelt found some marks that Marcus evidently thought bore immense potential.

His next request was rather odd: having taken a rope and tied one end around his waist, he wrapped the bulk of the coil around a section of the roof's front railing and then handed it to Roosevelt and me. We were instructed to let the rope out as Marcus descended along the rear wall of the fort. When we asked the purpose behind this, Marcus only said that he was working on a theory about the killer's method of reaching apparently inaccessible spots. So great was the detective sergeant's fixation on his work, along with our own desire not to distract him, that we asked for no further explanation.

As we lowered him down the wall, Marcus occasionally made noises of discovery and satisfaction, then told us to lower him further. Roosevelt and I would then grunt and struggle again with the rope. In the midst of all this, I took the opportunity to acquaint Kreizler (who, with his bad arm, had elected not to assist us) with the thoughts concerning the occupation and habits of our killer that had occurred to me on the way downtown. His reaction was thoughtful, though mixed:

'You may have something with the notion of his being a regular customer at the houses where these boys work, Moore. But as for the man's being a transient of some kind . . .' Laszlo strolled over to watch Lucius Isaacson work. 'Consider what he's done – deposited six bodies, six that we know of, in increasingly public places.'

'It does,' Theodore said with a small roar as we let out more rope, 'suggest a man familiar with the city.'

'Intimately familiar,' Lucius threw in, having heard our comments. 'There's no sense of haste about these injuries. The cuts aren't jagged or ripped. So he probably wasn't in any particular hurry. My guess would be that, in this and every other case, he's known exactly how long he has to do his work. He probably selects his sites accordingly. That would match our previous assumption that he's a capable planner. And the work with the

　　　　　　　　　　　　　　　　Caleb Carr

eyes, again, reveals a very careful, steady hand – as well as a fair knowledge of anatomy.'

Kreizler considered that for a moment. 'How many men would be capable of it, Detective Sergeant?'

Lucius shrugged. 'We've got several options as I see it. A doctor, of course, or at least someone with more than cursory medical training. A skilled butcher, possibly – or perhaps a very practiced hunter. Someone accustomed to making full use of a carcass, who would know not only how to dress the principal meat sections but the secondary sources of food, as well – the eyes, innards, feet, and the rest.'

'But if he's so careful,' Theodore asked, 'why commit these atrocities in the open? Why not go to a more hidden place?'

'The display,' Kreizler answered, walking back to us. 'The thought that he's in a publicly accessible spot seems to mean a great deal to him.'

I said, 'The desire to be caught?'

Kreizler nodded. 'So it would appear. Dueling with the desire to escape.' He turned to look out over the harbor. 'And there are other aspects that these sites have in common . . .'

Just then we got a loud shout from Marcus telling us to pull him up. On Theodore's count we gave out with several long, laborious heaves, bringing Marcus quickly back to the rooftop. To Kreizler's questions about what he'd found, Marcus replied that he didn't wish to speculate until he was fairly certain of his theory; he then moved off to make a few notes, as Lucius called out:

'Dr. Kreizler? I'd like you to look at this.'

Kreizler went immediately over to the body, but Theodore and I moved more trepidatiously – there was only so much of it the untrained eye could take. Even Sara, who had started out so bravely, was now averting her eyes whenever possible, the prolonged exposure apparently exacting quite an emotional toll.

'When you examined Georgio Santorelli, Doctor,' Lucius said, as he removed the short length of twine that bound the dead boy's wrists, 'do you remember finding any abrasions or lacerations in this area?' He held up the victim's left hand, indicating its base.

'No,' Kreizler answered simply. 'Other than the severing of the right hand there was nothing appreciable.'

'And no lacerations or bruising of the forearm?' Lucius inquired.

'None.'

'Yes. It would support what we've already hypothesized.' Lucius let the dead arm drop, then mopped his brow. 'That's fairly coarse twine,' he continued, pointing first at the bit of cord on the rooftop, and then at the boy's wrist again. 'Even during a brief struggle it should have left significant marks.'

Sara looked from the twine to Lucius. 'Then – there was no struggle?' And in the way she said it there was real sadness, sadness that reverberated heavily in my chest – for the implication was obvious. Lucius went on to state it:

'It's my suspicion that the boy allowed himself to be tied, and that even during strangulation, he made very little attempt to fight against the murderer. He may not have been fully aware of what was happening. You see, if there'd been an attack and actual resistance, we'd also find cuts or at least bruises on the forearms, made when the boy tried to fend the assault off. But again, there's nothing. So ...' Lucius glanced up at us. 'I'd say the boy knew the killer. They may even have engaged in this kind of binding on other occasions. For ... sexual purposes, in all likelihood.'

Theodore sucked air sharply. 'Good lord ...'

Watching Sara's face again, I saw a glint in the corners of her eyes: welling tears that she blinked away quickly.

'That last part's just a theory, of course,' Lucius added. 'But I feel very confident in saying the boy knew him.'

Kreizler nodded slowly, his eyes narrowing and his voice going soft: 'Knew him – and trusted him.'

Lucius finally stood and turned away from the body. 'Yes,' he said, switching the worklamp off.

At that, Sara got to her feet in a sudden movement and rushed to the edge of the roof farthest from where we were standing. The rest of us glanced at each other questioningly, and then I went after her. Approaching slowly, I saw that she was looking out at Lady Liberty, and I confess to some surprise at not finding her heaving with sobs. Instead her body was quite still, even rigid. Without turning she said:

'Please don't come any closer, John.' Her tone, far from hysterical, was icily even. 'I'd rather not have any men around me. Just for a moment.'

I stood awkwardly still. 'I'm – sorry, Sara. I only wanted to help. You've seen a lot tonight.'

She let out a bitter little chuckle. 'Yes. But there's nothing you can do to help.' She paused, but I didn't leave. 'And to think,' she continued at length, 'that we actually thought it might have been a woman . . .'

'*Thought*?' I said. 'So far as I know, we still haven't ruled it out.'

'Perhaps the rest of you haven't. I don't suppose you could be expected to. You're working at a disadvantage, in that area.'

I turned when I felt a presence at my side and found Kreizler carefully moving closer. He indicated silence to me as Sara spoke on:

'But I can tell you, John – that's a man's work, back there. Any woman who would have killed the boy wouldn't have . . .' She groped for words. 'All that stabbing, binding, and poking . . . I'll never understand it. But there's no mistaking it, once you've . . . had the experience.' She chuckled once grimly. 'And it always seems to begin with trust . . .' There was another very awkward pause, during which Kreizler touched my arm and with a movement of his head told me to return to the other side of the roof. 'Just leave me for a few minutes, John,' Sara finally finished. 'I'll be fine.'

Kreizler and I moved away quietly, and when we were out of Sara's hearing Laszlo murmured, 'She's right, of course. I've never come across any feminine mania – puerperal or otherwise – that could compare to this. Though it probably would have taken me a ridiculously long time to realize it. We must find more ways to take advantage of Sara's perspective, John.' He glanced around quickly. 'But first we must get out of here.'

While Sara remained at the edge of the roof, the rest of us set to work gathering up the Isaacsons' equipment and removing all traces of our presence, primarily the little splotches of aluminum and carbon powder that dotted the area. As we did so, Marcus initiated a conversation concerning the fact that half of the six murders we now felt confident assigning to our killer had occurred on rooftops: a significant fact, for rooftops in the New York of 1896 were secondary but nonetheless well-worn routes of urban travel, lofty counterparts to the sidewalks below that were full of their own distinctive types of traffic. Particularly in the tenement slums, a broad but definable range of people sometimes did a full day's business without ever descending to the street – not only creditors seeking payment, but settlement and church workers, salesmen, visiting nurses, and others. Rents in the tenements were generally scaled in proportion to the amount of exertion required to reach a given flat, and thus the most unfortunate residents occupied the top floors of buildings. Those who had business with these poorest of the poor, rather than braving the steep and often dangerous staircases repeatedly, would simply move from one high floor to another by way of the rooftops. True, we still didn't know just how our man was getting *to* those rooftops; but it was clear that once there he made his way around with great skill. The possibility that he had once held, or currently did hold, one of those roof-traveling jobs was therefore worth exploring.

'Whatever his occupation,' Theodore announced, coiling the rope we'd used to lower Marcus down the wall, 'it would take a cool mind to plan this kind of violence so precisely and then carry it out so thoroughly, when he knows that the possibility of apprehension is never very far off.'

'Yes,' Kreizler answered. 'It almost suggests a martial spirit, doesn't it, Roosevelt?'

'What's that?' Theodore turned to Kreizler with an almost injured look. 'Martial? That was not my meaning, Doctor – not my meaning at all! I would be loathe indeed to call this the work of a soldier.'

Laszlo smiled a bit, devilishly aware that Theodore (who was still years away from his exploits on San Juan Hill) viewed the military arts with the same boyish reverence he had since childhood. 'Perhaps,' Kreizler needled further. 'But a cool head for carefully planned violence? Isn't that what we endeavor to instill in soldiers?' Theodore cleared his throat loudly and stomped away from Kreizler, whose smile only broadened. 'Make a note of it, Detective Sergeant Isaacson,' Laszlo called out. 'A military background of some kind is definitely indicated!'

Theodore spun around once more, eyes wide; but he only managed to bellow 'By thunder, sir!' before Cyrus burst out of the staircase.

'Doctor!' he shouted. 'I think we'd better get moving!' Cyrus raised one of his big arms to point north, and all our eyes followed the indication.

At the edges of Battery Park, near the several points of entry, crowds were gathering: not the kind of well-dressed, politely behaved throngs that occupied the area during the day, but milling pockets of shabbily dressed men and women on whom the mark of poverty was plain even from a distance. Some carried torches and several were accompanied by children, who seemed to be thoroughly enjoying this unusual early morning foray. As yet there were no overt signs of threat, but it had all the makings of a mob.

Chapter 15

Sara came and stood by me. 'John – who are they?'

'Offhand,' I answered, feeling a different and a more vital sense of concern than I had at any point during that night, 'I'd say that the morning edition of the *Post* has reached the streets.'

'What do you suppose they want?' Lucius asked, his head sweating more than ever despite the cold.

'They want an explanation, I expect,' Kreizler answered. 'But how did they know to come *here*?'

'There was a cop from the Twenty-seventh Precinct,' Cyrus said, still very anxious, for it had been a mob much like the one we now faced that had tortured and killed his parents. 'He was down there with two other men, explaining something to them. Then those two fellas went into the crowd and started talking it up pretty good, about how it's only poor foreign kids that're getting killed. Seems most of those people out there come from over on the East Side.'

'The officer was, no doubt, Roundsman Barclay,' Theodore said, his face full of that particular anger that was inspired by treacherous subordinates. 'He's the man who was here earlier.'

'There goes Miller!' Marcus said suddenly, at which I looked down to see the watchman fleeing without his hat toward the Bedloe's Island ferry station. 'Fortunately I kept his keys,' Marcus added. 'He didn't look like a man who'd be around long.'

Just then the noise of the largest group of people, who were straight ahead of us and quite visible through the branches of the park's still-bare trees, began to grow louder, reaching a crescendo with a couple of venomous yells. We heard a clatter of horses' hooves and carriage wheels, and then Kreizler's calash appeared, barreling down the main path of the park toward the castle. Stevie held his horsewhip high and drove Frederick hard, around the front walls of the fort to the pair of large doors in the rear.

'Good man, Stevie,' I murmured, turning to the others. 'That'll be our best way out – through the back doors and up the river side of the park!'

'I suggest we get to it,' Marcus said. 'They're moving.'

With another series of shouts, the crowd at the main entrance came into the park, at which the groups to their right and left also began to surge forward. It now became clear that there were still more people streaming into the area from surrounding streets – the mob would soon number in the many hundreds. Someone had done an expert job of inflammation.

'The devil!' Theodore grunted ferociously. 'Where is the night watch from the Twenty-seventh? I'll have them over hot coals!'

'An ideal plan for the morning,' Kreizler said, making for the staircase. 'At the moment, however, escape seems imperative.'

'But this is a crime scene!' Theodore continued indignantly. 'I will not have it disturbed by any mob, whatever their complaint!' He glanced about the roof, then picked up a stout section of cut wood. 'Doctor, none of you can be found here – take Miss Howard and go. The detective sergeants and I will face these people at the front gate.'

'We will?' It had gotten out of Lucius's mouth before he quite knew what he was saying.

'Steel yourself,' Roosevelt answered with a grin, grabbing Lucius's shoulder heartily and then taking a few good cuts at the night air with his piece of wood. 'After all, this fort defended us from the British empire – it can certainly withstand a mob from the Lower East Side!' It was one of those moments when you wanted to slap the man, even if there was sense in his blustering.

In order to conceal completely the nature of our work, it was necessary for the rest of us to take the Isaacsons' equipment away in the calash. Having made our way back down and through the tanks of fish, we stowed the various boxes on board the carriage, and then I turned to wish the Isaacsons good luck. Marcus seemed to be searching the ground for something, while Lucius was checking a police-issue revolver uncomfortably.

'You may not be able to avoid a fight,' I said to them, with a smile that I hoped was reassuring, 'but don't let Roosevelt force you into one.'

Lucius only groaned a bit, but Marcus smiled bravely and shook my hand. 'We'll meet you at Number 808,' he said.

With that they closed the fort's rear doors and replaced the chains and locks. I jumped up and grasped the side of the calash – Kreizler and Sara were already in the two seats, and Cyrus was up top with Stevie – and we started with a jolt down a path that took us to the harbor's edge and then northward along the river. The noise of the crowd outside Castle Garden had continued to grow, but as we passed within sight of the fort's front gates the angry shouts suddenly subsided. I strained my head around to see Theodore outside the structure's heavy black portal, calmly holding his club with one hand and pointing toward the edge of the park with the other. The action-crazed fool simply couldn't stay safely inside. The Isaacsons were in the doorway behind him, ready to rebolt the doors at a moment's notice. But that didn't look to be necessary – the crowd actually seemed to be listening to Theodore.

As we approached the northern edge of the park, Stevie picked up speed, and nearly ran us headlong into a phalanx of about twenty cops as they trotted toward Castle Garden. We took a hard left at Battery Place in order to keep to the deserted waterfront, and as we did I got a brief but clear glimpse of an expensive brougham that was parked at a corner which enjoyed a full view of the events at the fort. A hand – well manicured, with a tasteful silver ring on the little finger – appeared at the brougham's door, followed by the upper part of a man's body. Even in the dim light of the arc lamps I could see the gleam of an elegant tie stud, and soon a set of handsome Black Irish features: Paul Kelly. I yelled to Kreizler and told him to look, but we were moving too fast for him to catch a glimpse. When I

Caleb Carr

related what I'd seen, however, his face showed that he'd drawn the obvious conclusion.

The crowd, then, had been Kelly's work, probably in response to Steffens's remarks about Biff Ellison in the *Post*. It all fit – Kelly was not known for making idle threats, and whipping up a fury over the murders among a deeply and perpetually disgruntled segment of the populace would have been child's play for so devious a man. Nevertheless, the move had almost cost our team dearly, indeed I feared it might still do so; and as I continued to cling to the side of the speeding calash, I vowed that, should anything happen to Theodore and the Isaacsons, I would hold the chief of the Five Pointers personally responsible.

Stevie didn't ease up on Frederick at any point during our ride home, and no one asked him to. There were pools of rainwater in many of the roughly paved streets on the West Side, and by the time we reached Number 808 Broadway I was splattered with mud, cold as the tomb, and ready to call it a night (or a morning, since dawn was not far off). But the job of dragging the equipment upstairs and recording our thoughts on the murder while they were still fresh remained, and we set about it dutifully. When the elevator reached the sixth floor, Kreizler discovered that he had misplaced his key, and I gave him mine, which was caked with mud. Overall, it was a bedraggled, exhausted little group that filed into headquarters at 5:15 A.M. that Saturday.

My surprise and joy were all the greater, therefore, when the first thing that greeted my senses was the smells of steak and eggs frying and strong coffee brewing. A light was on in the small kitchen at the rear of our floor, and I could see Mary Palmer – dressed not in her blue linen uniform but in a pretty white blouse, a plaid skirt, and an apron – moving about in quick, capable motions. I dropped the cases I was lugging.

'God has sent me an angel,' I said, stumbling toward the kitchen. Mary started a bit when she saw my muddy frame coming out of the shadows, but her blue eyes soon settled down and she showed me a little smile, offering a bit of hot, sizzling steak on the end of a long fork and then a cup of coffee. I started to say, 'Mary, how did you ...,' but quickly abandoned the attempt and concentrated on the delicious food and drink. She had quite a production going: a legion of eggs and what looked like sides of lean beef in deep iron skillets that she must have brought from Kreizler's house. I could have stayed in there for quite a while, bathing in the warmth and the aromas; but as I turned back around, I found Laszlo standing behind me, his arms folded and a sour scowl on his face.

'Well,' he said. 'I suppose I know now what happened to my key.'

I assumed his admonishment was in jest. 'Laszlo,' I said through a mouthful of steak, 'I believe I may actually revive—'

'Will you excuse Mary and me for a moment, Moore?' Kreizler said, in the same hard tone; and from the look on the girl's face, I could see that she knew he was quite serious, even if I didn't. Instead of questioning him, however, I scooped some eggs and a bit more steak onto a plate, grabbed my mug of coffee, and headed for my desk.

As soon as I was out of the kitchen I heard Kreizler start to lecture Mary in no uncertain terms. The poor girl was unable to offer any reply other than an occasional no and a small, quiet sob. It didn't make sense to me; for my money she'd done yeoman service, and Kreizler was being inexplicably mean. My thoughts were soon distracted, however, by Cyrus and Stevie, who hovered over my plate in drop-jawed hunger.

'Now, now, boys,' I said, covering my food with my arms. 'No need to get physical. There's plenty more in the kitchen.'

They both bolted energetically toward the back, straightening up only slightly when they encountered Kreizler. 'Get something to eat,' Laszlo told them brusquely, 'and then take Mary back to Seventeenth Street. Quickly.'

Stevie and Cyrus each mumbled assent, and then descended on the unsuspecting steak and eggs. Kreizler pulled one of the Marchese Carcano's green chairs between Sara's and my desks and fell into it wearily.

'You don't want anything to eat, Sara?' Laszlo asked quietly.

She had her head on her arms on top of her desk, but raised it just long enough to smile and say, 'No. Thank you, Doctor, I couldn't. And I don't think Mary would appreciate my presence in the kitchen.' Kreizler nodded.

Caleb Carr

'A little hard on the girl, weren't you, Kreizler?' I said, as sternly as I could manage through more mouthfuls of food.

He sighed once and closed his eyes. 'I'll have to ask you not to interfere, John. It may seem severe – but I don't want Mary to know anything about this case.' He opened his eyes and looked toward the kitchen. 'For a variety of reasons.'

There are moments in life where one feels as though one's walked into the wrong theater during the middle of a performance. I was suddenly aware of some very odd chemistry at work among Laszlo, Mary, and Sara. I couldn't have put a label on it, not if I'd been paid; but as I pulled a bottle of good French cognac from the bottom drawer of my desk and added some of it to my still-steaming coffee, I became increasingly aware that the air in the large room had suddenly become charged. This instinctive feeling was confirmed when Mary, Stevie, and Cyrus came out of the kitchen and Kreizler asked for his key back. Mary returned it reluctantly, and then I caught her shooting Sara a quick, angry scowl as she went out the door with the other two. No doubt about it – there was a subtext to all this activity.

But there were more important issues at hand, and with Mary, Stevie, and Cyrus gone, the rest of us were free to begin trading thoughts on them. Kreizler went to the chalkboard, which he had divided into three general areas: CHILDHOOD on the left-hand side, INTERVAL in the center, and ASPECTS OF THE CRIMES to the right. In their proper areas Laszlo began to jot down the theories that we had come up with on the roof of Castle Garden, leaving a small space for any salient insights that the Isaacsons might have had since we left them. Kreizler then stood back to review the list of details; and though it offered, to my way of thinking, evidence of a good night's work, Laszlo seemed to find it wanting. He tossed his bit of chalk up and down, shifting from one foot to the other, and finally announced that there was one more significant factor we must make note of: in the top right-hand corner of the board, under the heading ASPECTS OF THE CRIMES, he chalked the word WATER.

That baffled me; but Sara, after giving it some thought, pointed out that every one of the murders since January had taken place within sight of a large amount of water – and the

Zweigs had actually been deposited *in* a water tower. When I asked if that wasn't just a coincidence, Kreizler said that he doubted so careful a schemer as our killer left very much to coincidence. Laszlo then walked to his desk and pulled an old leather-bound volume from one stack of books. As he switched on a small desk lamp I braced myself, expecting some lengthy technical quote from the likes of Professor Mosso of Turin (who, I'd recently learned, was doing groundbreaking research in measuring the physical manifestations of emotional states). But what Laszlo read, in a quiet, tired voice, was something quite different:

' "Who can understand his errors? Cleanse thou me from secret faults." '

Kreizler switched off the desk lamp and sat back down. I took a blind stab and guessed that the quote was from the Bible, to which Laszlo nodded, remarking that he never ceased to be amazed at the number of references to cleansing that could be found in religious works. He was quick to add that he did not necessarily believe that our man suffered from a religious mania or dementia; rather, he was citing the quote to indicate, somewhat poetically, the extent to which the killer was oppressed by feelings of sin and guilt, for which water was the usual metaphorical antidote.

That remark stuck in Sara's craw. In a troubled, somewhat impatient voice she noted that Kreizler persistently returned to the notion that our killer was aware of the nature of his actions, and desired apprehension – yet at the same time the man continued to go out and slaughter young boys. If we accepted the supposition of his sanity, then we were left with the nagging question of what possible satisfaction or benefit he could be deriving from the butchery. Before replying to this pointed observation, Laszlo paused, considering his words carefully. He knew, as did I, that it had been a long and bewildering night for Sara. I also knew that after viewing one of those bodies the last thing one wanted to hear was a descriptive analysis of the mental context of the man responsible; the sadness, anger, and horror were all too great. But the fact remained that such an analysis was imperative, especially at that vivid moment. Sara must be coaxed back to the task immediately before us, a goal that Laszlo approached obliquely by asking her some gentle, seemingly unconnected questions:

Imagine, he said, that you enter a large, somewhat crumbling hall that echoes with the sounds of people mumbling and talking repetitively to themselves. All around you these people fall into prostrate positions, some of them weeping. Where are you? Sara's answer was immediate: in an asylum. Perhaps, Kreizler answered, but you could also be in a church. In the one place the behavior would be considered mad; in the other, not only sane, but as respectable as any human activity can be. Kreizler went on to try some other examples: If a woman and her children were threatened with every kind of violence by a group of attackers, and the only weapon at the mother's disposal was something along the lines of a meat cleaver, would Sara consider the woman's necessarily gruesome efforts to dispatch the men the work of a mad savage? Or if another mother were to learn that her husband was beating and having sexual relations with their children, and she cut his throat in the middle of the night, would that qualify as unacceptable brutality? Sara said that, while she would answer no to those questions, she also considered such cases very different from the one we were presently dealing with. That brought a quick rejoinder from Laszlo: The only difference, he declared, was among Sara's perceptions of the various examples. An adult protecting a child, or a child protecting itself, was apparently a context in which Sara could justify even fearsome violence; but what if our murderer viewed his current work as just that sort of protection? Could Sara shift her point of view enough to grasp that every victim and situation leading up to a murder resonated within the killer to a distant experience of threat and violence and led him for reasons that we had not yet fully defined to take angry measures in his own defense?

Sara remained more reluctant than unable to follow all this; I, on the other hand, was surprised to find my own thoughts falling right into line with Kreizler's. Perhaps the brandy was pushing my mind past its usual limits; whatever the case, I piped up to say that each dead body seemed, in the light Laszlo was casting, to be a kind of mirror. Kreizler lifted a satisfied fist and said, Precisely

– the bodies were a mirror image of some savage set of experiences that were central to the evolution of our man's mind. Whether we took the biological approach, and concentrated on the formation of what Professor James called 'neural pathways,' or the philosophical route, which would lead into a discussion of the development of the soul, we would arrive at the same conclusion: the idea of a man for whom violence was not only deeply ingrained behavior but the starting point of his meaningful experiences. What he saw when he looked at those dead children was only a representation of what he felt had been done to him at some point deep in his past. Certainly, when *we* looked at the bodies our first thoughts were of vengeance for the dead and protection of future victims. Yet the profound irony was that our killer believed he was providing himself with just those things: vengeance for the child he had been, protection for the tortured soul he had become.

Despite the care Kreizler took in explaining all this to Sara, the effort brought no change in her attitude. It was simply too soon to expect her to put the experience of Castle Garden away and get back to business. She shifted and writhed in her chair, shaking her head and protesting that everything Kreizler said sounded like a somewhat absurd rationalization: Laszlo was comparing the emotional and physical trials of childhood with the worst kind of adult blood lust, she stated defiantly, whereas no such correlation existed – the two phenomena were out of all proportion to each other. Kreizler answered that such might seem to be the case, but only because Sara was deciding the proportions herself, based on the context of *her* experience. Anger and destructiveness were not the guiding instincts of her life – but what if they had been, since long before she'd become capable of conscious thought? What mere physical action could satisfy such deep-seated rage? In the case of our man, not even the brutal killings could achieve it; had they been able to, he would still have been quietly going about his business, hiding the bodies and never courting discovery.

Seeing that all these sound points were continuing to have little effect on our intransigent partner, I took the opportunity to suggest that we all try to get some sleep. The sun had begun to creep up over the city during our talk, bringing with it that

Caleb Carr

state of extreme disorientation that accompanies most all-night vigils. I'm sure that Kreizler also knew that rest would put many things right; all the same, he made one last request, as Sara left with me, that she not allow horror and anger to lead her too far from the course of our undertaking. Her role had, that night, been revealed as even more important than he'd originally thought it: Our murderer had spent his childhood among men *and* women, and whatever else the rest of us could suppose about the women involved in those experiences, our theories would never amount to more than a badly flawed set of assumptions. It would be up to Sara to provide us with a different perspective, to create for us a woman (or series of women) who might have helped foster such rage. We could not succeed without that.

Sara nodded wearily at the thought of this new responsibility, and I knew I'd better get her away from Kreizler, who was exhausting enough even on a full night's sleep. I opened the front door and guided her out into the elevator, and as we descended to the ground the only audible sound was the quiet, strangely comforting hum of the device's engine echoing in the dark shaftway.

On the first floor we ran into the Isaacsons, whose return had been delayed not by the mob at Castle Garden (which had dissipated fairly soon after our departure) but by Theodore, who had insisted that they accompany him to one of his favorite Bowery haunts for a victory breakfast of steak and beer. The two detective sergeants looked just as exhausted as Sara and I, and since they had to go up and report before they'd be allowed any sleep, we didn't talk much. Marcus and I made a quick plan to meet the following afternoon and venture over to the Golden Rule Pleasure Club, and then it was into the elevator for them and out to find a cab on largely deserted Broadway for Sara and myself.

There weren't many hacks braving the early morning cold, though what few there were had mercifully congregated outside the St. Denis Hotel across the street. I helped Sara into a hansom, but before giving the driver her destination she looked up at the still-lit windows of the sixth floor of Number 808.

'He never seems to stop,' she said quietly. 'It's almost as if – as if he has a personal stake in it.'

'Well,' I answered, yawning broadly, 'a lot of his professional ideas could be validated by the result.'

'No,' Sara said, still quietly. 'Something else – something more . . .'

Following her gaze up to our headquarters, I decided to express a concern of my own: 'I wish I knew what was going on with Mary.'

Sara smiled. 'You never were the most romantically perceptive man, John.'

'Meaning?' I asked, genuinely baffled.

'Meaning,' Sara answered, somewhat indulgently, 'that she's in love with him.' As I stood there agape, she tapped on the roof of the hansom. 'Gramercy Park, driver.'

Sara was still smiling as the cab pulled around and headed up Broadway. A couple of the other hacks asked me if I also needed a rig, but after that last bit of intelligence I could only shake my head blankly. Maybe the walk – or, as it was, stumble – home would help me make some sense of it, I thought; but I couldn't have been more wrong. The implications of Sara's statement, and the look on her face as she delivered it, were all too bizarre to be made sense of in a few weary minutes. All the walk did was exhaust me further, and by the time I hit the sheets in my grandmother's house I was far too weak in body and disturbed in spirit to even remove my muddy clothes.

Caleb Carr

Chapter 16

An altogether unpleasant mood took hold of me during my sleep, and I woke at noon to find that my temper had shortened to a lamentable extent. This black outlook deepened when a messenger boy appeared with a note from Laszlo. Apparently a Mrs. Edward Hulse of Long Island had been arrested during the night after trying to kill her own children with a carving knife. Though the woman had been released into her husband's custody, Kreizler had been asked to assess her mental condition, and had invited Sara along. There was no thought of establishing a connection between Mrs. Hulse and our case, Laszlo explained; rather, Sara's interest (which, sure enough, had been revitalized by several hours' sleep) was in assembling details of character for the imaginary women that Laszlo had asked her to create as a way of further understanding our imaginary man. None of this was cause for annoyance on my part; it was more the way Kreizler phrased it all, as if he and Sara were off for a pleasant, stimulating day in the country together. As I crumpled the note up, I acidly wished them a lovely time; and I believe I spat in a sink afterwards.

A telephone call from Marcus Isaacson set our meeting for five o'clock, at the El station at Third Avenue and Fourth Street. I then dressed and surveyed the possibilities for my own afternoon – they appeared few and bleak. Emerging from my room, I discovered that my grandmother was giving a luncheon; the party consisted of one of her dim-witted nieces, the niece's equally engaging husband (who was a partner in my father's investment firm), and one of my second cousins. All three guests were full of questions about my father, questions that I, having been out of touch with him for many months, had no way of answering. They also made a few polite inquiries about my mother (who I did know was at that moment traveling in Europe with a companion), and politely dodged the subject of my former fiancée, Julia Pratt, who they were acquainted with socially. The entire conversation was punctuated by insincere smiles and chuckles, and its general effect was to make me thoroughly morose.

The truth is, it had been many years since I'd been able to speak pleasantly with most members of my family, for reasons that, while powerful, were not difficult to explain. Right after I got out of Harvard, my younger brother – whose passage into adulthood had been even more troubled than my own – had fallen off a Boston boat and drowned. A lengthy autopsy revealed what I could have told anyone if they'd asked: that my brother had been a habitual user of alcohol and morphine. (During his last years he'd become a regular drinking companion of Roosevelt's younger brother, Elliot, whose life was also ended by dipsomania some years later.) The funeral that followed was full of respectful but perfectly nonsensical tributes, all of which avoided the subject of my brother's adult battle with terrible bouts of melancholy. There were many causes of his unhappiness, but at heart I believe now, as I believed then, that it was essentially the result of growing up in a household, and a world, where emotional expression of any kind was at best frowned on and at worst strangled. Unfortunately, I'd stated this opinion during the funeral, and was nearly forced into an asylum as a result. Relations between myself and my family had never quite recovered. Only my grandmother, who had doted on my brother, displayed any understanding of my behavior or any willingness to allow me into her home and her life. The rest of them regarded me as at least mentally impaired, and perhaps downright dangerous.

For all these reasons, the arrival of my relatives on Washington Square that day was a sort of crowning blow, and my disposition could not have been worse as I walked out the front door of the

Caleb Carr

house into the chilly day. Realizing that I had absolutely no idea where I was going, I sat down on the steps, suddenly aware that I was jealous. The realization was so surprising that my tired eyes popped fully open. Somehow my unconscious mind had drawn some unpleasant conclusions from the pieces of information that I had received the night before: if Mary Palmer was in fact in love with Kreizler, and she saw Sara as a threat, and both Kreizler and Sara were aware of it, and Kreizler didn't want Mary around as a result, but had no trouble spending swimming little spring afternoons with Sara – well, it was all fairly clear. Not that it was a romantic sort of jealousy that had crept into me; I had only considered an amorous link with Sara once, years ago, and then just for a few drunken hours. No, I was more injured at the thought of being excluded. On such a day a jaunt to Long Island with friends would definitely have been beneficial.

I spent several minutes debating whether or not I should call on an actress with whom I'd passed many days (and still more nights) since the end of the Julia Pratt business; and then, for no reason that I could divine, my thoughts turned to Mary Palmer. Bad as I felt, she must have been feeling worse, if what Sara had said to me was true. Why not make a quick trip up to Stuyvesant Park, I mused, and give the girl an afternoon out? Kreizler might not approve; but Kreizler was off having a pleasant day with a splendid girl, and his complaints were therefore invalid. (Thus did spite work its inevitable way into my thoughts.) Yes, as I walked by the new arch at the north end of Washington Square Park, the idea only grew more appealing – but where exactly to take the girl?

On Broadway I corralled several paper boys, and relieved them of some of their wares. The previous night's events at Castle Garden received much attention on the front pages. Apparently there was growing concern over the mood in the immigrant neighborhoods. A citizens' committee was being formed to go to City Hall and express concern about both the murders and, more emphatically, the possible effect of those crimes on civic order. All of which meant little or nothing to me at that particular moment – I quickly turned to the entertainment pages. The pickings seemed slim, until I caught a notice for Koster and Bial's Theater on Twenty-third Street. In addition to singers, gymnastic come-dians, and a Russian clown, Koster and Bial were offering a program of short projected films, the first ever in New York, according to the notice. It seemed the right fare, and the theater was certainly convenient to Kreizler's house. I grabbed the first cab I saw.

Mary was alone in the house when I arrived, and in as depressed a mood as I'd expected to find her. She was also, at first, very resistant to the idea of venturing out. She looked away from me and shook her head vigorously, pointing around the rooms as if to indicate that her housekeeping chores were too extensive for her to even consider such an idea. But I had been inspired by the notion of cheering someone up: I described the bill at Koster and Bial's with rare zest and to her wary glances replied that the outing would be nothing more than an expres-sion of thanks for the excellent early morning breakfast. Reas-sured and obviously excited, she soon gave in and fetched her coat, as well as a small black hat. Not a sound escaped her as we went out of the house, but she smiled in a very pleased and grateful way.

For an idea that had grown out of such questionable feelings, this turned out to be a remarkably good one. We got into our seats at Koster and Bial's, a very average theater of only moderate capacity, just as a music hall comedy team from London were winding up their performance. We were in time for the Russian clowns, whose silent antics Mary quite enjoyed. The comedic gymnasts, who threw barbs and jokes at each other while executing some truly remarkable physical feats, were also good, though I could have lived without the French singers and a rather strange dancer who followed them. The audience was large but good-natured, and Mary seemed to enjoy watching them almost as much as the acts.

There were no wandering eyes, however, when a glittering white screen descended across the proscenium and the house went completely black. Light flashed from somewhere behind us, and then there was near-panic in the first few rows when we were all faced with the image of a wall of blue sea water seemingly crashing into the theater. Naturally, none of us was familiar with

Caleb Carr

the phenomenon of projected images, an experience that in this case had been heightened by the hand-tinting of the black-and-white film. After order had been restored in the theater and the first offering, 'Sea Waves,' had come to an end, we were treated to eleven other brief subjects, including a pair of 'Burlesque Boxers,' and some less amusing pictures of the German kaiser reviewing his troops. Sitting there one hardly had the sense that one was witnessing the advent of a new form of communication and entertainment that would, in the hands of such modern masters as D. W. Griffith, drastically change not only New York City but the world; I was far more concerned with the fact that those flickering, tinted images brought Mary Palmer and me closer together for a brief time, relieving the loneliness that was for me transitory and for her a permanent aspect of existence.

It wasn't until we were back out on the street that my mental repose was turned to restless inquisitiveness by the training I'd struggled through during the last several weeks. As I watched my very pleased, very attractive companion enjoying the cold, bright afternoon, I wondered: How could this girl have killed her father? I fully appreciated that there were few things so reprehensible as a man violating his own daughter; but there were other girls who'd endured the experience without chaining the guilty party to a bed and roasting him alive. What had pushed Mary to the act? The beginnings of an explanation, I soon realized, were quite easy to detect even years after the fact. As Mary watched the dogs and pigeons in Madison Square Park, or when her blue eyes were captured by such glittering treasures as the enormous golden statue of naked Diana atop the square spire of Madison Square Garden, her lips moved as if to give expression to her pleasure – and then her jaws clamped closed, her face displaying a fear of what incoherent, humiliating noises might emerge should she try to speak. I remembered that Mary had been considered idiotic; and most children are anything but kind to idiots. In addition, her mother had considered her fit for nothing more than charwork. Thus by the time her father's sexual advances began, Mary must already have been so frustrated and tormented that she was near ready to explode. Removal of any one of these disadvantages and wretched experiences might have changed the outcome of her life; together, they wove a fatal pattern.

Perhaps life had been very similar for our killer, I posited as Mary and I entered Madison Square Garden in order to have a cup of tea in the arcade restaurant on the roof. By now I had realized that a companion's extensive chatter only made Mary feel more keenly her inability to participate verbally, so I began to communicate through smiles and gestures, privately pursuing what seemed a fertile line of psychological reasoning as I did so. With Mary sipping her tea and craning her neck in order to gather all the sights that were available from the excellent vantage point of the Garden's roof arcade, I remembered what Kreizler had said the night before: that violence, for our murderer, had been the childhood starting point. In all likelihood that meant beatings administered by adults – such would fit with Laszlo's theory that there were both self-protective and vengeful instincts at work in the man. But thousands of young boys suffered such torment. What had pushed this one, like Mary, over a seemingly indefinable but very real line into violence? Had he, too, suffered from some crippling impairment or deformity that during his youth made him an object of derision and scorn? And, having endured this, had he gone on to suffer some sort of outrageous, degrading sexual assault?

It still seems odd that so lovely a girl as Mary Palmer should have inspired me to such grim cogitations; but odd or no, I felt I was onto something, and wanted to get Mary back to Kreizler's place so that I could meet Marcus Isaacson on time and share my thoughts with him. I felt a bit bad about ending an outing that had brought Mary such apparent joy – by the time we reached Stuyvesant Park she was absolutely radiant – but she also had duties to attend to; and her mind was brought back to them in a rush, I could see, when she spotted Kreizler's calash sitting outside the house on Seventeenth Street.

Stevie was brushing the horse Frederick down, while Kreizler was standing and smoking a cigarette on the small iron balcony that ran outside the French windows of the parlor on the second floor. Both Mary and I braced for trouble as we entered the small front yard; and we were both surprised when a very genuine smile came into Kreizler's face. He took out his silver watch, checked the time, and spoke in a cheerful voice:

'You two must have had quite an afternoon – was Mr. Moore a satisfactory host, Mary?'

Mary smiled and nodded, then rushed to the front door. There she turned and, after removing the small black hat, said 'Thank you' with a big smile and only a trace of difficulty. Then she disappeared inside, and I looked up at Kreizler.

'I believe we may yet get spring, John,' he said, indicating Stuyvesant Park with a wave of his cigarette. 'Despite the cold, the trees are budding.'

'I thought you'd still be on Long Island,' I answered.

He shrugged. 'There's little for me to learn there. Sara, on the other hand, seemed quite fascinated by Mrs. Hulse's attitude toward her children, so I left her.' That seemed a bit strange, given the theories I'd cooked up earlier that day; but Kreizler's manner was quite normal. 'Will you come up for a drink, John?'

'I've got to meet Marcus at five – we're going to explore the Golden Rule. Any interest?'

'A great deal of interest,' he answered. 'But it will be better if I'm not seen in too many places associated with the case. I trust the pair of you to take copious mental notes. Remember – the keys will be in the details.'

'Speaking of that,' I said, 'I've had some ideas that I think may be useful.'

'Excellent. We'll discuss them at dinner. Telephone me at the Institute when you've finished. I've a few things to see to there.'

I nodded and turned to depart; but my perplexity was too strong to leave matters so unresolved.

'Laszlo?' I said uncertainly. 'You're not angry that I took Mary out this afternoon?'

He shrugged simply again. 'You didn't discuss the case with her?'

'No.'

'Then, on the contrary, I'm grateful. Mary isn't exposed to enough people and new experiences. I'm sure it will have an excellent effect on her disposition.'

And that was that. I turned back around and headed through the gate, leaving behind the slight inkling into the behavior of my friends that I thought I'd achieved that morning. I got onto the Third Avenue El at Eighteenth Street and headed downtown, trying to keep my thoughts away from other people's personal business and on the case. By the time we passed Cooper Square, I was actually succeeding; and when I met Marcus at Fourth Street, I was ready to pay close attention to his most recent theories on our murderer's method, a recitation that took up most of our time during the march across town to the Golden Rule Pleasure Club.

Chapter 17

The notion of our killer's being an experienced mountain and rock climber had first occurred to Marcus, he explained, when I brought the boy Sally's story back from Paresis Hall. But when he'd tried to find evidence of such activity at the Williamsburg Bridge anchor, and then at the Hall, he'd come up with almost nothing, and thought of abandoning the idea. His mind kept being brought back to the idea, however, by the speed with which the man had negotiated some pretty tricky spots, as well as by the absence of any ladders or other, more conventional climbing apparatus. There could be no other explanation, to Marcus's way of thinking: the murderer had to be using advanced mountaineering techniques to get in and out of the windows of his intended victims' rooms. That the man was especially expert was indicated by the fact that he must have been carrying the boys when he left the buildings, since they almost certainly knew nothing about climbing. All of this was consistent with the Isaacsons' idea that the killer was a big, powerful man. Faced with all these considerations, Marcus had done some more detailed research into climbing techniques, and returned to the bridge anchor and Paresis Hall.

This time, his better-trained eye had indeed found marks on the exterior walls of Ellison's joint that could have been left by a climber's nail-studded boots, as well as by pitons. The marks were hardly conclusive, so he hadn't mentioned them at any of our meetings. But at Castle Garden Marcus had discovered distinctive rope fibers along the rear edge of the rooftop: a further suggestion that the killer was a climber. The fibers seemed to lead to the front railing of the roof, which turned out to be very solidly anchored. That had been the point at which Marcus had told us to lower him down the rear wall of the fort, where he found more marks that matched those he'd discovered at the Hall. Marcus had then begun to work out a probable sequence of events for the Castle Garden killing:

The murderer, with his latest victim on his back, had climbed to the roof of the fort using pitons. (The watchman hadn't noticed the sound of the hammering because, Marcus had learned, he actually spent most of his time sleeping, a fact of which Marcus was sure the killer was aware.) Once on the roof, our man had committed the murder, then wrapped a rope around the front railing and rappelled back to the ground. This last was a European term for the technique of descending a sheer mountainside by way of a rope that had been looped around a secure anchor point above. Both strands of the rope were then dropped, so that the whole could be pulled down by the climber when he reached the bottom. As our killer lowered himself along the wall, he'd been able to remove the pitons he'd used for support earlier.

Satisfied with his reasoning, Marcus had first attempted to find specific evidence to support it at Paresis Hall, since the Santorelli murder was long past and there weren't likely to be any policemen around. But then he'd realized that at the Hall the killer would have been descending from the roof, not coming up from the ground, and probably wouldn't have used pitons at all (the marks Marcus had originally thought to be left by pitons at that site were therefore made by something else, probably something altogether unconnected to our case). So Marcus had returned to Castle Garden just before meeting me, and continued a search of the grounds that he'd barely begun the night before – I'd been right when I thought he was looking for something just before our hasty departure from that place. The few cops who were positioned at Castle Garden that afternoon were nowhere near the rear entrance of the fort, and so Marcus had been free to scour that area.

At this point in his tale, my companion reached into his coat pocket and pulled out a rather innocuous steel spike that he'd discovered lying in some grass. The thing had an eye at one end: for securing ropes, Marcus told me. He'd dusted the piton for prints once he'd gotten it home, and found a set that exactly matched those we'd taken from the ceramic chimney the night before. I had to give the man a firm, admiring slap on the back, at that: Marcus was as dogged as any detective I'd met during the years I'd been covering the police beat, and considerably more intelligent. It was small wonder he hadn't gotten along with the old guard at the Division of Detectives.

For the remainder of our walk Marcus went on to explain the larger implications of his discovery. Though mountaineering hadn't really caught on as a form of recreation in North America as of 1896, in Europe the sport was well established. Throughout the last century, expert teams on that continent had knocked off peaks in the Alps and the Caucasus, and one intrepid German had even ventured to East Africa and conquered Mount Kilimanjaro. Nearly all these groups, Marcus told me, had been either English, Swiss, or German; and in those countries mountain and rock climbing of a less ambitious nature had become a very popular form of recreation. Given that our killer displayed what could only be called expertise, it was likely that he'd been exposed to the sport quite a long time ago, perhaps even in his youth; and it was therefore very possible that his family had emigrated to America from one of those three European nations in the not too distant past. That might not mean much just at the moment; but it was easy to see that, when added to other crucial factors further down the road, it could become highly illuminating. In such knowledge there was real cause for hope.

We would need an abundant reservoir of that particular emotion during our visit to the Golden Rule Pleasure Club, a pestilential little hole that could not have had a more sadly ironic name. Paresis Hall at least had the advantages of being above-ground and fairly roomy; the Golden Rule was housed in a dank, cramped basement that had been divided into small 'rooms' by shoddy partitions, where any one client's activities were made known to everyone in the place by sound if not by sight. Run by a large, repulsive woman called Scotch Ann, the Golden Rule offered only effeminate young boys who painted themselves, spoke in falsetto voices, and called each other by women's names, leaving the other variations on male homosexual behavior to joints like Ellison's. In 1892 the Golden Rule had gained notoriety when the Reverend Charles Parkhurst, a Presbyterian pastor and head of the Society for the Prevention of Crime, had visited the place during his campaign to bare the links between New York's criminal underworld and various agencies of the city government, particularly the Police Department.

Parkhurst's revelations about how very degenerate life in much of New York had become led to a New York State Senate committee's investigation of official corruption in the city. Headed by Clarence Lexow, the committee ended up calling for 'an indictment against the Police Department of New York City as a whole,' and many members of the old police guard felt the sting of reform. As I've said before, however, degeneracy and corruption are not passing aspects but permanent features of life in New York; and walking into a place like the Golden Rule never fails to bring one hard up against the fact that the drives and desires that spawn such joints – drives that would bring ostracism and even prosecution in any other part of the United States – have at least as many disciples and defenders as does 'decent society.'

Of course, the defenders of decent society and the disciples of degeneracy are often the same people, as became clear to Marcus when we entered the nondescript front door of the Golden Rule on that Saturday evening. Almost immediately, we came face-to-face with a round-bellied, middle-aged man in expensive evening clothes, who shielded his face as he exited the place and then hurried into a very expensive carriage that was waiting for him at the curb. Behind him came a boy of fifteen or sixteen, typically dolled up for a night's work and counting money with great satisfaction. The boy called something after the man in the usual grating falsetto register that was, for the uninitiated, so strange and disturbing; and then he walked by us very playfully, promising a full evening's entertainment should we choose him from among his mates. Marcus turned immediately away and stared at the ceiling, but I answered the boy, telling him we were not customers and that we wanted to see Scotch Ann.

'Oh,' the boy droned languorously in his natural voice. 'More cops, I guess. Ann!' He moved toward a large room farther inside the basement, from which emanated raucous laughter.

We followed the boy for a few steps, stopping at the entrance to the large room. Inside it were a few pieces of once ostentatious but now decrepit furniture, and over the cold, moldy floor was thrown a well-worn Persian carpet. On the carpet was a squatting, half-naked man in his thirties, who crawled about and laughed as several even more scantily dressed boys vaulted over him.

'Leapfrog,' Marcus mumbled, taking it in with a nervous glance. 'Didn't they lure Parkhurst into something like that when he came here?'

'That was at Hattie Adams's, up in the Tenderloin,' I answered. 'Parkhurst didn't last long in the Golden Rule – when he found out what actually went on here he bolted.'

Sauntering out from the area of the back rooms came Scotch Ann, heavily painted, obviously drunk, and well past her prime, if indeed she had ever had one. A flimsy pink dress clung to her powdered body (rising so high on her chest that one could not say if she was, in fact, a woman at all), and her face bore the harassed, weary scowl common to disorderly house owners when presented with an unexpected visit from the law.

'I don't know what you want, boys,' she said, in a gruff voice that'd been destroyed by alcohol and smoking, 'but I already pay two precinct captains five hundred bucks a month each to let me stay open. Which means there's nothing left over for fly cops. And everything I know about the murder I already told one detective—'

'That's lucky,' Marcus said, showing his badge and taking Ann by the arm toward the front door. 'Then it's all fresh in your mind. But don't worry, information is all we want.'

Somewhat relieved that her recitation would cost her nothing, Scotch Ann gave forth with the story of Fatima, originally Ali ibn-Ghazi, a fourteen-year-old Syrian boy who had been in America just over a year. Ali's mother had died within weeks of the family's arrival in New York, after picking up a lethal disease down in the Syrian ghetto near Washington Market. The boy's father, an unskilled laborer, had subsequently been unable to find any work at all, and took to begging. He put his children on display in order to spur the generosity of passers-by, and it was while Ali was serving in this capacity, on a corner near the Golden Rule, that Scotch Ann first caught sight of him. The boy's delicate Near Eastern features made him, as Ann put it, 'a natural for my place.' She quickly 'came to terms' with the father, terms that closely resembled indenture or perhaps even slavery. Thus was born 'Fatima,' at the mention of which absurd appellation I discovered that I was rapidly losing patience with the practice of renaming young boys so that they could be proferred to adult men who either had inane scruples about who they molested or were aroused by particularly ridiculous perversions. 'She was a real moneymaker,' Scotch Ann told us. I felt like belting the woman, but Marcus pursued the investigation calmly and professionally. Ann could provide us with few other particulars about Ali, and became concerned when we said we wanted to both see the room out of which he'd worked and interview any boys who were particularly friendly with him.

'I suppose there weren't many,' Marcus said casually. 'He was probably a difficult young man.'

'Fatima?' Ann said, pulling her head back. 'If she was, I never knew about it. Oh, she could play the hellcat with the customers – you'd be surprised how many of them like that kind of thing – but she never complained, and the other girls seemed to dote on her.'

Marcus and I exchanged a quick, puzzled look. The statement didn't match the pattern we'd come to expect concerning the victims. As we followed Ann down a dirty little corridor that ran among the partitioned rooms in the back, Marcus puzzled with this apparent inconsistency, then nodded and murmured to me, 'Wouldn't *you* mind your manners around someone you'd been sold in bondage to? Let's wait and see what the rest of the girls say. *Boys*, I mean.' He shook his head. 'Damn it, now they've got *me* doing it.'

The other boys who worked in the Golden Rule, however,

provided no information that substantially contradicted their whoremistress. Standing in the narrow corridor and individually interviewing over a dozen painted youths as they exited from their partitioned rooms (forced, all the while, to listen to the obscene grunts, groans, and declarations of lust that emerged from those confines), Marcus and I were consistently presented with a portrait of Ali ibn-Ghazi that lacked any angry or obstreperous details. It was disturbing, but we had no time to dwell on it, for the last rays of daylight were fading and we needed to examine the outside of the building. As soon as the room Ali had regularly used, which faced an alleyway behind the club, had been vacated by a furtive pair of men and an exhausted-looking boy, we entered it, braving the warm, humid atmosphere and the smell of sweat in order to check Marcus's theory about the killer's method of movement.

Here, at least, we found what we were looking for: a filthy window that could be opened, above which were four stories of sheer, unencumbered brick wall leading to the roof of the building. We would need to get a look at that roof before the sun set fully; nevertheless, as we left the little chamber, I paused long enough to ask one momentarily idle boy in a neighboring room what time Ali had left the Golden Rule on the night of his death. The young man frowned and struggled with the question a bit as he stared into a decaying mirror.

'Damn me – that's peculiar, ain't it?' he said, in a tone that seemed too jaded to be coming from so young a mouth. 'Now that you mention it, I don't remember ever seeing him go.' He threw up a hand and went on with his work. 'But I was probably engaged. It was the weekend, after all. One of the other girls must've seen her leave.'

But the same question, put a few more times to various painted faces as we walked out of the club, brought similar answers. Ali's departure, then, had almost certainly been effected through the window in his room, and then up the rear wall of the building. Marcus and I ran outside, up to the first-floor entrance and the small vestibule, then into a vermin-infested staircase that wound up to a pitch-black doorway splattered with tar that opened onto the roof. Our quick movements were inspired by more than the dying sunlight: we both knew that we were tracing our killer's steps more precisely than we'd been able to do before, and the effect was both chilling and exhilarating.

The roof was like any other in New York, spotted with chimneys, bird droppings, ramshackle utility sheds, and the odd bottle or cigarette end that indicated the occasional presence of people. (Because it was early in the spring and still chilly, there were none of the signs of regular habitation – chairs, tables, hammocks – that would appear during the summer months.) Like a hunting dog, Marcus strode directly to the back of the slightly sloped rooftop and, with no thought to the height, peered over and into the alley. Then he removed his coat, spread it below him, and lay down on his stomach so that his head hung out over the edge of the building.

'The same marks,' he said without turning, but there was a broad smile in his voice. 'All consistent. And here—' He picked something that was invisible to me out of one of the many patches of tar. 'Rope fibers,' he said. 'He must've anchored it to that chimney.' Following Marcus's pointing finger, I glanced at a squat brick structure toward the front of the roof. 'That's a lot of rope. Plus the other pieces of equipment. He'd need a bag of some kind to carry it all in. We ought to mention that when we're asking around.'

Studying the monotonous expanse of the other roofs on the block I said, 'He probably wouldn't have come up through this building's staircase – he's smarter than that.'

'And he's familiar with getting around on rooftops,' Marcus answered, as he got to his feet, pocketed some of the rope fibers, and picked up his coat. 'I think we can be pretty sure, now, that he's spent a lot of time on them – probably in some kind of professional capacity.'

I nodded. 'So it wouldn't be tricky for him to size up every building on the block, find the one with the least activity, and use its staircase.'

'Or ignore the staircases altogether,' Marcus said. 'Remember, it's late at night – he could scale the walls without anybody seeing him.'

Looking to the west, I saw that the reflective expanse of the

Caleb Carr

Hudson River was quickly turning from bright red to black. I turned fully around twice in the near-darkness, seeing the entire area in a new way.

'Control,' I mumbled.

Marcus stayed right with me: 'Yes,' he said. 'This is his world, up here. Whatever mental turmoil Dr. Kreizler sees in the bodies, this is very different. On these rooftops he's acting with complete confidence.'

I sighed and shook as a river breeze hit us. 'The confidence of the devil himself,' I mumbled, and was surprised when I got an answer:

'Not the devil, sir,' said a small, frightened voice from somewhere back by the door to the stairs. 'A saint.'

Chapter 18

'Who's there?' Marcus said sharply, moving toward the voice cautiously. 'Come out, or I'll have you up for interfering with police business!'

'No, please!' the voice answered, and then one of the painted youths from the Golden Rule, one I didn't recall having seen downstairs, stepped out from behind the stairway door. The makeup on his face was badly smudged, and he had a blanket pulled around his shoulders. 'I only want to help,' he said in a pathetic voice, his brown eyes blinking nervously. With a sinking feeling I realized that he could not have been more than ten years old.

Taking hold of Marcus's arm and pulling him back, I urged the boy forward. 'That's all right, we know you do,' I said. 'Just come out into the open.' Even in the increasingly dim light of the rooftop I could see that the boy's face, as well as the blanket he was huddled in, were smudged with soot and tar. 'Have you been here all night?' I guessed.

The boy nodded. 'Ever since they told us.' He was starting to weep. 'This wasn't supposed to happen!'

'What?' I asked urgently. 'What wasn't? The murder?'

At the mention of the word the boy clamped his small hands over his ears and shook his head insistently. 'He was supposed to be good, Fatima said so, everything was supposed to turn out all right!'

I went over, put an arm around the boy, and guided him to a low wall that separated the roof we were on from that of the building next door. 'All right,' I said. 'It's all right, nothing more's going to happen.'

'But he could come back!' the boy protested.

'Who?'

'*Him* – Fatima's saint, the one that was supposed to take him away!'

Marcus and I glanced at each other quickly: *Him*. 'Look,' I said to the boy quietly, 'suppose you start by telling me your name.'

'Well,' the boy sniffed, 'downstairs they—'

'Just forget what they call you downstairs, for a minute.' I rocked his shoulders a bit with my arm. 'You just tell me what name you were born with.'

The boy paused, his big eyes taking our measure warily. I must admit the situation was quite confusing for me, too; all I could think to do was pull out a handkerchief and begin wiping the paint from the boy's face.

It did the trick. 'Joseph,' the boy murmured.

'Well, Joseph,' I said chummily. 'My name's Moore. And this man is Detective Sergeant Isaacson. Now – suppose you come clean about this saint of yours.'

'Oh, he wasn't mine,' Joseph answered quickly. 'He was Fatima's.'

'You mean Ali ibn-Ghazi's?'

He nodded rapidly. 'She – he – Fatima had been saying for I guess about two weeks that she'd found a saint. Not like a patron saint, in church, not like that – just a person who was kind, and was going to take her away from Scotch Ann to live with him.'

'I see. I guess you knew Ali pretty well, then?'

Another nod. 'He was my best friend in the club. All the girls liked her, of course, but we were special friends.'

I had pretty well cleaned up Joseph's face, and he turned out to be quite a handsome, appealing boy. 'It seems Ali got along with everyone,' I remarked. 'Customers, too, I guess.'

'Where'd you hear *that*?' Joseph answered, his words coming faster and faster. 'Fatima hated working here. He always made it seem to Scotch Ann like he liked it, because he didn't want to go back to his father. But he hated it, and when he was alone with a customer, well – he could get pretty angry. But some customers—' The boy turned away, very clearly perplexed.

'Go on, Joseph,' Marcus said. 'It's all right.'

'Well . . .' Joseph turned from one to the other of us. 'Some customers, they *like* it when you don't like it.' His eyes turned down to gaze at his feet. 'Some even pay more for it. Scotch Ann always thought Fatima was pretending, to make more money. But she really did hate it.'

A sharp jab of both physical revulsion and deep sympathy hit me somewhere in the abdomen, and Marcus's face betrayed a similar reaction; but we did have an answer to our earlier question.

'There it is,' Marcus whispered to me. 'Hidden, but real – resentment and resistance.' He spoke aloud to Joseph: 'Did any of the customers ever get mad at Fatima?'

'Once or twice,' the boy said. 'But mostly, like I say, they liked it.'

There was a lull in the talk, and then the sound of an elevated train on Third Street jarred me back to business. 'And this saint of his,' I said. 'This is very important, Joseph – did you ever see him?'

'No, sir.'

'Did Fatima ever meet a man on the roof?' Marcus asked. 'Or did you ever notice someone carrying a large bag of some kind?'

'No, sir,' Joseph said, a bit bewildered. Then he brightened, trying to please us: 'The man came in more than once after Fatima met him, though. I do know that. But he told her never to say who he was.'

Marcus smiled just a bit. 'A customer, then.'

'And you never guessed which one it was?' I asked.

'No, sir,' Joseph answered. 'Fatima said that if I kept it all secret and was good, then maybe the man would take me away, too, someday.'

I put my arm back around his shoulders tightly, looking out over the rooftops once more. 'You must hope that doesn't ever happen, Joseph,' I said, and then his brown eyes began to shed tears again.

The Golden Rule didn't yield any more significant information that evening, or did the other residents of the building or the block that we questioned. Before departing the scene, however, I felt I ought to ask the boy Joseph if he wanted to leave Scotch Ann's employ – he seemed entirely too young for such business, even by disorderly house standards, and I thought there was a good chance that I could get Kreizler to take him on as a charity case at the Institute. But Joseph, orphaned since age three, had already had his fill of institutes, orphanages, and foster homes (not to mention alleyways and empty railroad cars), and nothing I said about Kreizler's place being 'different' had any effect on him. The Golden Rule had been the only home he'd ever known where he hadn't been ill fed and beaten – repulsive as she might be, Scotch Ann had an interest in keeping her boys relatively healthy and scar-free. That fact counted for more with Joseph than anything I might say about the place's evils and dangers. In addition, his suspicions about men who promised a better life somewhere else had only been heightened by the saga of Ali ibn-Ghazi and his 'saint.'

And so there seemed to be nothing for me to do but say goodbye to that frightened little ten-year-old, but then, just as I was leaving the place, an idea occurred to me, one that I thought might both help keep Joseph safe and advance our investigation.

'Joseph,' I said, kneeling down to speak to him in the entranceway to the club, 'do you have many friends who work in other places like this?'

'Many?' he answered, putting a finger to his mouth pensively. 'Let's see – I guess I do know *some*. Why?'

'I want you to tell them what I'm going to tell you. The man who killed Fatima has killed other children who do this kind of work – mostly boys, though maybe not only boys. The main thing to remember is that for some reason that we don't understand yet they all come from houses like yours. So I want you to tell your friends that from now on they've got to be very, very careful about their customers.'

Joseph reacted to this rather urgent statement by drawing back a bit and looking up and down the street fearfully. But he didn't run away. 'Why only places like this?' he asked.

'Like I say, we don't know. But he'll probably be back, so tell everyone you know to keep their eyes open. Look for someone who gets angry when any of you are' – I strained for a word – 'difficult.'

'You mean uppity?' Joseph asked. 'That's what Scotch Ann calls it – uppity.'

'Right. He may have picked Fatima because of it. Don't ask me why, because I don't know. But watch for it. And, most important of all – don't go anywhere with anyone. Never leave the club, no matter how nice the man seems or how much money he offers you. The same goes for your friends. All right?'

'Well – okay, Mr. Moore,' Joseph answered slowly. 'But maybe – maybe you and Detective Sergeant Isaacson can come back and check on us, sometime. Those other cops, the ones that were here this morning, they didn't seem to care much. They just told everybody to keep quiet about Fatima.'

'We'll try to do that,' I answered, taking a pen and a piece of paper from my coat pocket. 'And if you ever have anything you want to tell someone, anything at all that you think is important, you come straight to this address during the day, and to this one at night.' I gave him not only our headquarters location but also the number of my grandmother's house on Washington Square, wondering for an instant what the old girl would make of this boy if he ever did show up. Then I had him write down the telephone number of the Golden Rule. 'Don't go to any other cops – tell us everything first. And don't tell any other cops that we were here.'

'Don't worry,' the boy answered quickly. 'You're the first two cops I ever met that I'd talk to, anyway.'

'That's probably because I'm not a cop,' I said with a smile.

The grin was returned, and with a start I realized that I was seeing someone else's face echoed in Joseph's features. 'You didn't seem like one,' the boy said. Then his brows knotted up with another question: 'So why are you trying to find out who killed Fatima?'

I put a hand on the boy's head. 'Because we want to stop him.' Just then the harsh sound of Scotch Ann's gravelly voice came bursting out of the Golden Rule's front hall, and I nodded in its direction. 'You'd better go. Remember what I said.'

At a quick, youthful pace Joseph disappeared back into the club, and I stood up to find Marcus smiling at me.

'You handled that pretty well,' he said. 'Spent much time around kids?'

'Some,' I answered, without elaborating. I had no desire to reveal how much young Joseph's eyes and smile had reminded me of my own dead brother's at the same age.

As we walked back across town, Marcus and I discussed the new lay of things. Sure now that the man we sought was well acquainted with places like the Golden Rule and Paresis Hall, we tried to identify who other than customers would regularly investigate such haunts. The idea of a reporter or social essayist like Jake Riis – a man out to reveal the evils of the city and perhaps driven to mad extremities by overexposure to vice – occurred to us, but just as quickly we realized that no one had yet made much of a print crusade out of child prostitution, and certainly not out of homosexual child prostitution. That left us with missionaries and other church workers, a category that seemed more promising: remembering what Kreizler had said about the connection between religious manias and mass murder, I wondered if indeed we were dealing with someone determined to be the hand of a wrathful god on this earth. Kreizler had said he didn't consider a religious motivation likely, but Kreizler could be wrong about that – after all, missionaries and church workers were known to travel frequently by rooftops when doing their tenement work. Marcus and I were ultimately led away from such a hypothesis, however, by what Joseph had told us. The man who had killed Ali ibn-Ghazi had come to the Golden Rule regularly, and his visits had gone unnoticed. Any reforming crusader worth his salt would have worked hard to be the center of attention.

'Whoever or whatever he is,' Marcus announced, as we closed back in on Number 808 Broadway, 'we know one thing – that he *can* come and go unnoticed. He looks completely as if he belongs in those houses.'

'Right,' I said. 'Which brings us back to customers, which means it could be almost anyone.'

'Your theory about an angry customer might still work. Even

if he's not a transient, he still might've been fleeced one too many times.'

'I'm not so sure. I've seen men who've been robbed by whores. They might beat the living daylights out of one of them, but the kind of mutilation we've seen? He'd *have* to be mad.'

'Then maybe we're back to another one of the Ripper theories,' Marcus said. 'Maybe his brain's deteriorating from disease – a disease he picked up in a place like Ellison's or the Golden Rule.'

'No,' I answered, flattening my hands out in front of me and trying to make it all clearer in my mind. 'The one constant we've been able to hold on to is that he's not crazy. We can't question that now.'

Marcus paused, and then spoke carefully: 'John – you've asked yourself, I suppose, what'll happen if some of Kreizler's basic assumptions are wrong?'

Taking a deep, weary breath I said, 'I've asked myself.'

'And your answer?'

'If they're wrong, then we'll fail.'

'And you're satisfied with that?'

We'd reached the southwest corner of Eleventh Street and Broadway, where trolley cars and carriages were lugging all manner of weekend revelers up- and downtown. Marcus's question hung in the air over this scene for a moment, causing me to feel very detached from the normal rhythms of city life and very uneasy about the immediate future. What, indeed, would all this terrible learning we were doing amount to if our basic assumptions were wrong?

'It's a dark road, Marcus,' I finally said quietly. 'But it's the only road we've got.'

Chapter 19

There were snow flurries that night, and Easter morning saw the city covered by a light white powder. At nine A.M. the thermometer still had not climbed above forty degrees and I really was tempted to stay at home and in bed. But Lucius Isaacson had important news for us all, or so he said in a telephone call; and so, with the bells of Grace Church clanging and scores of bonneted worshipers crowding around and through its doors, I trudged back into the headquarters that I'd left only half a dozen hours earlier.

Lucius had spent the previous evening interviewing Ali ibn-Ghazi's father, from whom he had learned almost nothing. The elder Ghazi had been determinedly reticent, especially after Lucius had shown him his badge. Initially, Lucius had thought this uncooperative behavior nothing more than the usual slum-dweller's method of dealing with the police; but then Ghazi's landlord had told Lucius, as the latter left the building, that Ghazi had received a visit that afternoon from a small group of men – including two priests. His general description of them had matched that given by Mrs. Santorelli; but the landlord had further noticed that one of the priests wore the distinctive signet ring of the Episcopal Church. This meant that, however improbable it might have seemed, Catholics and Protestants were working together toward some end. The landlord was of no help in determining that end, for he was unable to say what the two priests had spoken to Ghazi about; but immediately after their departure Ghazi had settled a sizable back rent debt, in full and in large notes. Lucius would have given us this news the night before, but after leaving the Syrian ghetto he had made what he thought would be a brief stop at the morgue. Thinking to find out whether Ali's body had been inspected by a coroner, and, if it had, what official judgment had been passed on the matter, Lucius had been kept waiting for nearly three hours. He'd finally been informed that Ali's body had already been removed for burial; and the only copy of the coroner's report, which the night officer at the morgue assured Lucius had been unusually brief, had been dispatched to Mayor Strong's office.

It was impossible to say precisely what the two priests, the coroner, the mayor, or anyone else involved in these activities was up to; but obfuscation and the suppression of facts seemed the very least of it. The feeling that we faced a greater challenge than simply catching our killer – a feeling that had taken seed after Georgio Santorelli's murder – now began to grow and chafe at each of us.

Spurred on by that sinister irritant, our team assumed and maintained a quickened pace over the next week or so. Murder sites and disorderly houses were visited and revisited by the Isaacsons, who spent hours trying to discover new clues and days trying to coax new information out of anyone who might have seen or heard anything of importance. But they generally ran up against the same wall of interference that had silenced Ali ibn-Ghazi's father. Marcus, for example, was anxious to put the watchman from Castle Garden to a much more severe test than he'd been able to do on the night of Ali's death – but when he returned to the old fort he was told that the watchman had quit his job and departed from the city, leaving no indication as to his destination. It was safe to assume, we all agreed, that wherever the man had disappeared to, he had taken with him one of the impressive wads of money that the two unidentified priests were dispensing around town.

Kreizler, Sara and I, meanwhile, pressed on with the job of fleshing out our imaginary man by using persons apprehended for similar crimes as points of reference. Sadly, there continued to be no shortage of these; if anything, their number only increased as the weather improved. At least one incident, bizarrely enough, was actually inspired by the weather: Kreizler and I investigated the case of one William Scarlet, who was apprehended in his home while attempting to kill his eight-year-old daughter with a hatchet, and his only explanation was that he'd been driven mad by a powerful thunderstorm that had swept through the city that night. Surprisingly enough, Kreizler could find very little to dispute this, and thus the case was of little use to us.

On the very next day, Kreizler took Sara along to investigate the case of Nicolo Garolo, an immigrant living on Park Row, who had severely stabbed his sister-in-law and the woman's three-year-old daughter after the little girl allegedly claimed that Garolo was trying to 'hurt' her. 'Hurt' in this case clearly indicated sexual assault, to Laszlo, and the fact that all the participants were immigrants was also intriguing. The familial connection, however, ultimately limited the relevance of the crime to our work, although Garolo's sister-in-law did provide Sara with some interesting material for the construction of her imaginary women.

In addition to all this, there were the papers to go through, twice a day, in order to cull bits of useful information. This was a fairly indirect process, however, being as the New York papers had begun one by one to stop covering the boy-whore murders in the days following the Castle Garden affair. In addition, the citizens' group that was supposed to have been organizing for an information-gathering visit to City Hall never materialized. In short, the brief flicker of interest in the case that had been displayed outside the immigrant ghettos following the ibn-Ghazi murder had been very effectively snuffed out, leaving the daily papers with nothing to offer us but reports of other killings from around the country. These we patiently studied in an effort to gain more elements that could be used in the elaboration of theories.

It was not uplifting work; for while New York might have been America's leading center of violent crime, particularly of those varieties directed toward children, the rest of the United States was doing its part to keep national statistics high. There was, for example, the vagabond in Indiana (once interned in an asylum but recently released as sane) who killed the children of a woman who had hired him to do menial work; or the thirteen-year-old girl in Washington whose throat had been cut in Rock Creek Park for absolutely no reason that anyone could divine; and the reverend in Salt Lake City who murdered as many as seven girls and burned their remains in a furnace. We studied all these cases and many more – indeed, every day presented us with at least one incident or criminal to hold up against our developing portrait for comparison.

Even Kreizler's servants were contributing to the quest for a solution, either through example or direct participation. I have already described my own speculations concerning Mary Palmer and the possible parallel between her case and ours. Those thoughts were duly weighed and their salient aspects recorded on the big chalkboard, although Mary herself was never consulted about them, as Laszlo continued to insist that she be told as little as possible about the case. Cyrus, on the other hand, had managed to get hold of much of the reading material that Kreizler had assigned to the rest of us, and he devoured it eagerly. He made no comments during meetings save when asked, but at those moments he often proved quite insightful. At one midnight conference, for instance, when we were speculating on the mental and physical condition of our murderer immediately after he'd committed his crimes, we suddenly came hard up against the fact that none of us had ever taken the life of another human being. We all knew, of course, that there was someone in the room who had, but none of us felt much like asking Cyrus for an experienced opinion – none of us, that is, except Kreizler, who had no trouble posing the question in simple, straightforward language. Cyrus answered in much the same way, confirming that after his act of violence he would have been capable of neither elaborate planning nor extensive physical exertion; but we were all surprised when he punctuated this statement with some interesting thoughts on Cesare Lombroso, the Italian sometimes supposed to be the father of modern criminology.

Lombroso had postulated the existence of a criminal 'type' of human being (in essence a throwback to early, savage man), but

Cyrus stated that he found such a theory implausible, given the wide range of motivations and behaviors he'd recently learned could be involved in criminal actions – including his own. Interestingly enough, Dr. H. H. Holmes had stated during the course of his trial that he believed himself to be representative of Lombroso's criminal type. Mental, moral, and physical degeneracy had accounted for his actions, Holmes claimed, and so his legal responsibility should of course be considered as diminished. The argument had gotten him nowhere in court; and after discussing his and other cases, we concluded that our killer's work could no more be ascribed to evolutionary retrogression than could Holmes's. In both subjects, the intellectual capacity demonstrated was simply too significant.

And then there was the day that young Stevie Taggert drove me across town and he put a question to me:

'Mr. Moore, sir – about the man you're looking for. I heard Dr. Kreizler say the other day that none of the dead boys had been – well, you know, sir, "assaulted." Is that right?'

'Yes, that's been true so far, Stevie. Why?'

'It's just that it makes me wonder, sir. Does that mean he ain't a fag?'

I sat up at the frankness of the query – sometimes you had to work very hard to remember that Stevie was only twelve. 'No, that doesn't mean that he's not a – a fag, Stevie. But the fact that his victims do the work they do doesn't mean that he *is* one, either.'

'You figure maybe he just hates fags?'

'That may have something to do with it.'

'What I'm thinking, Mr. Moore, is that maybe he *is* a fag, and maybe he *hates* fags, too. Kinda like that guard who gimme such a hard time out on Randalls Island.'

'I'm afraid I don't get you,' I said.

'Well, you know, in court, when I was up for cracking that guy's skull, they tried to make me out for crazy, saying the guy had a wife and kids and all, so how could he be a fag? And in the Refuge House, if he caught two boys going at each other like that, brother, would he lay into 'em. But all the same, I wasn't the first kid he tried it with. No, sir. So I figure maybe that's why he had such a mean disposition – he never really knew, deep down, just what he was. Know what I mean, Mr. Moore?'

Remarkably enough, I did know what he meant. We'd had many long discussions at our headquarters concerning the sexual proclivities of our killer, and we would have many more before our work was done; yet Stevie had come close to crystallizing all our conclusions in that one statement.

There really wasn't one of us whose brain wasn't working overtime to come up with ideas and theories that would propel our investigation forward; but, as might be expected, no one was working harder than Kreizler. I remembered Sara's statement that Kreizler seemed to have some sort of personal stake in the work we were doing; and though I wanted to ask her for elaboration, I feared that such a conversation would only revive my tendency to speculate about their personal relationship.

But a discussion became inevitable one morning, when Kreizler – fresh from a long night at his Institute – set off without a break to do a mental competency assessment of a man who'd dismembered his wife on a homemade altar. Laszlo had lately been gathering evidence to support the theory that our murders were being conducted as bizarre rituals, during which the killer – much like a Mohammedan whirling dervish – used extreme yet fairly formalized physical action to bring about psychic relief. Kreizler based this idea on several facts: the boys were all strangled before they were mutilated, thus giving the killer complete control over the scene as he played it out; furthermore, the mutilations followed an extremely consistent pattern, centering on the removal of the eyes; and finally, every killing had occurred near water, and on a structure whose function arose from that same water. Other murderers were known to have viewed their grim deeds as personal rites, and Kreizler believed that if he could talk to enough of them he'd begin to understand how to read any messages that might be contained in the mutilations themselves.

On the morning in question, Sara and I happened to be just coming into 808 Broadway as Laszlo tried to enter his calash and very nearly fainted. He shook the spell off with ammonia salts and a laugh, but Cyrus told us that this time it had been two days since he'd had anything like real sleep.

'He'll kill himself if he doesn't slow down,' Sara said, as the calash rolled off and we got into the elevator. 'He's trying to make up for the lack of clues and facts with effort. As if he can force an answer to this thing.'

'He's always been that way,' I replied, shaking my head. 'Even when we were boys, he was always *at* something, and always so deadly serious. It was somewhat amusing, in those days.'

'Well, he's not a child now, and he ought to learn to take care of himself.' That was Sara's tough side talking; it was a different tone that came through when she asked, with what seemed affected casualness and without looking at me, 'Have there never been any women in his life, John?'

'There was his sister,' I answered, knowing that it wasn't what she was driving at. 'They used to be very close, but she's married now. To an Englishman, a baronet or some such.'

With what I thought was effort, Sara remained dispassionate. 'But no women – romantically, I mean?'

'Oh. Yes, well, there was Frances Blake. He met her at Harvard and for a couple of years it looked as though they might get married. I never saw it, myself – for my money she was something of a shrew. He seemed to find her charming, though.'

Sara's most mischievous smile, that tiny curl of her upper lip, appeared. 'Perhaps she reminded him of someone.'

'She reminded *me* of a shrew. Look, Sara, what do you mean when you say Kreizler seems as though he's got some personal stake in this thing? Personal how?'

'I'm not quite sure, John,' she answered, as we walked into our headquarters and found the Isaacsons engaged in a vehement squabble over some evidential details. 'But I can say this—' Sara lowered her voice, indicating that she didn't wish to pursue the conversation in front of any of the others. 'It's more than just his reputation, and more than just scientific curiosity. It's something old and deep. He's a very deep man, your friend Dr. Kreizler.'

With that Sara drifted off to the kitchen to make herself some tea, and I was dragged into the Isaacsons' argument.

Thus did we pass most of April, with the weather warming up, small pieces of information slowly but steadily falling into place, and questions about each other opening wider without being openly addressed. There would be time to explore such matters later, I kept telling myself – for now the work was what mattered, the job at hand, on which depended who knew how many lives. Focus was the key – focus and preparation, readiness to meet whatever could be hatched from the mind of the man we sought. I took this attitude confidently, feeling, after viewing two of his victims, that I'd seen the worst he had to offer.

But an incident that occurred at the end of the month presented my teammates and me with a new kind of horror, one born not of blood but of words – one that, in its own way, was as terrible as anything we'd yet encountered.

Chapter 20

On a particularly pleasant Thursday evening, I was sitting at my desk reading a story in the *Times* about one Henry B. Bastian of Rock Island, Illinois, who several days earlier had killed three boys who worked on his farm, cut up their bodies, and fed the pieces to his hogs. (The citizens of the town had been unable to think of a cause for the dastardly crime; and when local law enforcement officers had closed in to arrest Bastian, he killed himself, thus eliminating any chance that the world would ever discover or study his motives.) Sara was putting in an increasingly rare appearance at Mulberry Street, and Marcus Isaacson was there, too. He frequently visited headquarters at off-hours, in order to rummage undisturbed through the anthropometry files: Marcus still held out hope that our killer might have a prior criminal record. Lucius and Kreizler, meanwhile, were wrapping up a long afternoon at the Ward's Island Lunatic Asylum, where they had been studying the phenomena of secondary personalities and brain hemisphere dysfunction, in order to determine if either pathology might characterize our killer.

Kreizler considered such possibilities remote, to say the very least, essentially because patients afflicted with dual consciousnesses (arising from either psychic or physical trauma) did not generally exhibit the capacity for extensive planning that our killer had shown. But Laszlo was determined to chase down even the most improbable theories. Then, too, he genuinely liked such outings with Lucius, which allowed him to trade bits of his unique medical knowledge for invaluable lessons in criminal science. Thus when Kreizler telephoned at about six o'clock to say that he and the detective sergeant had finished their research, I was not entirely surprised to hear more vigor in Laszlo's voice than had been the case in recent days; and I replied with equal energy when he suggested that we meet for a drink at Brübacher's Wine Garden on Union Square, where we could compare notes on the day's activities.

I spent another half an hour on the evening papers, then wrote a note for Sara and Marcus, telling them to come along to Brübacher's and join us. After pinning the note to the front door, I snatched a walking stick out of the Marchese Carcano's elegant ceramic stand and headed out into the warm evening, as merrily, I'll wager, as any man who's spent the day immersed in blood, mutilation, and murder has ever done.

The mood on Broadway was a festive one, the stores being open late for Thursday evening shopping. It was not yet dusk, but McCreery's was apparently still on its winter lighting schedule: the windows were bright beacons, offering what seemed certain customer satisfaction to the passing throngs. Evening services had concluded at Grace Church, but there were still a few worshipers gathered outside, their light dress a testament to spring's long-awaited but irreversible arrival. With a rap of my stick against the pavement I turned north, ready to spend at least a few minutes back among the world of the living, and on my way to one of the best places to do so.

'Papa' Brübacher, a truly *gemütlich* restaurateur who was always glad to see a regular customer, had assembled one of the best wine and beer cellars in New York, and the terrace of his establishment, across the street from the east side of Union Square, was an ideal place from which to watch people stroll in the park as the sun descended beyond the western terminus of Fourteenth Street. Such, however, were not the principal reasons why sporting gentlemen like myself frequented the place. When streetcars had first made their appearance on Broadway, some unknown conductor had gotten it into his head that if the snake-like bends that the tracks made around

Caleb Carr

Union Square weren't taken at full speed the car would lose its cable. The other conductors on the line had bought into this never-proven theory, and before long the stretch of Broadway along the park had been dubbed 'Dead Man's Curve,' because of the frequency with which unsuspecting pedestrians and carriage riders lost life or limb to the hurtling streetcars. Brübacher's terrace provided a commanding view of all this action; and throughout warm afternoons and evenings it was customary, when one of the engines of injury was heard or seen approaching, for bets to be laid among the wine garden's customers as to the likelihood of an accident occurring. These bets could, on occasion, be sizable, and the guilt that the winners felt when a collision did take place never managed to drive the game out of existence. Indeed, the frequency of accidents, and thus the volume of gaming, had risen to such proportions that Brübacher's had earned the sobriquet 'Monument House,' and was now a required stop for any visitor to New York who aspired to the title of gamesman.

As I crossed Fourteenth Street to the small curbed island east of Union Square that was home to Henry K. Brown's splendid equestrian statue of General Washington, I began to hear the usual shouts – 'Twenty bucks the old lady doesn't make it!'; 'The guy's only got one leg, he doesn't have a prayer!' – emanating from Papa Brübacher's. The call of the game sped my steps, and when I arrived I jumped the ivy-laden iron railing that ringed the terrace and nestled in with a couple of old pals of mine. After ordering a liter of smooth, dark Würzburger that had a head as thick as whipped cream, I rose just long enough to embrace old Brübacher, then finally began to lay bets with a fury.

By the time Kreizler and Lucius Isaacson showed up, at just past seven, my friends and I had witnessed two near-misses on nannies with perambulators and one brush of a streetcar against a very expensive landau. An intense debate as to whether this latter contact constituted a collision ensued, one that I was just as glad to get away from by retreating to a relatively remote corner of the terrace with Lucius and Kreizler, who ordered a bottle of Didesheimer. The debate that I found *them* engaged in, however, steeped as it was in references to brain parts and functions, proved no more entertaining. The distant sound of an approaching streetcar at last signaled a new round of betting, and I had just wagered the full contents of my billfold on the agility of a fruit peddler when I looked up to find myself face-to-face with Marcus and Sara.

I was going to suggest that they get in on the action, as the fruit peddler's pushcart was particularly heavy-laden and the encounter looked to be an exciting even-money affair; but when I paused long enough to study their respective faces and attitudes – Marcus's wild-eyed and agitated, Sara's pallid and stunned – I realized that something extraordinary had occurred, and put my money away.

'What in hell's happened to you two?' I said, setting my beer stein on a table. 'Sara, are you all right?'

She nodded rather weakly, and Marcus began to scan the terrace fervently, while fidgeting with his hands uncontrollably. 'A telephone,' he said. 'John, where's a telephone?'

'Just inside the door, there. Tell Brübacher you're a friend of mine, he'll let you—'

But Marcus was already shooting away from me into the restaurant, while Kreizler and Lucius, who had broken off their conversation, stood and watched in confusion.

'Detective Sergeant,' Kreizler said, as Marcus passed. 'Has there been some—'

'Excuse me, Doctor,' Marcus said. 'I've got to – Sara has something you ought to see.' Marcus took two steps inside the open terrace doorway and grabbed the telephone, putting the little conical receiver to his ear and clicking the armrest rapidly. Brübacher looked on in surprise, but at a nod from me he let Marcus continue. 'Operator? Hello, operator?' Marcus began to stamp his right foot hard. 'Operator! I need to get a line through to Toronto. Yes, that's right, Canada.'

'Canada?' Lucius echoed, his own eyes going wide. 'Oh, God – Alexander Macleod! Then that means—' Lucius glanced at Sara, looking as if he suddenly understood what she'd been through, and then joined his brother at the 'phone. I guided Sara

Caleb Carr

over to Kreizler's table, and then she very slowly drew an envelope out of her bag.

'This arrived at the Santorellis' flat yesterday,' she said, in a dry, pained voice. 'Mrs. Santorelli brought it to Police Headquarters this morning. She couldn't read it and was asking for help. No one would give her any, but she refused to go home. Eventually I found her sitting out by the front steps. I translated it. At least, I translated most of it.' She shoved the note into Laszlo's hand and her head dropped lower. 'She didn't want to keep it, and since there's nothing anyone at headquarters can do with it, Theodore asked me to bring it along and see what you make of it, Doctor.'

Lucius came back over to join us, and he and I watched anxiously as Kreizler opened the envelope. When Laszlo had glanced over its contents he drew in breath quickly though quietly, and nodded his head. 'So,' he noised, in a voice that seemed to say he'd been expecting something like this. Then we all sat down, and without any introduction Kreizler read the following in a very quiet voice (I have preserved the author's original spelling in this transcription):

My dear Mrs. Santorelli,
   I don't know as it is you what is the source of the vile LIES I read in the newspapers, or if the police are behind it and the reporters are part of their scheme, but as I figger it might be you I take this occashun to straten you out:
In some parts of this world such as where dirty immigrants like yourself come from it is often found that human flesh is eaten regular, as other food is so scarce and people would starve without it. I have personally read this and know it to be true. Of course it is usuly children what is eaten as they are tenderest and best tasting, especially the ass of a small child.
Then these people that eat it come here to America and shit their little children shit all around, which is dirty, dirtier than a Red Injun.
On February 18 I seen your boy parading himself, with ashes and paint on his face. I decided to wait, and saw him several times before one night I took him away from THAT PLACE.

Saucy boy, I already knew I must eat him. So we went straight to the bridge and I trussed him and did him quick. I collected his eyes and took his ass and it fed me for a week, roasted with onions and carrots.

But I never fucked him, though I could have and he would have liked me to. He died unsoiled by me, and the papers ought to say so.

'There is no closing and no signature,' Kreizler finished, in a voice that was little more than a whisper. 'Understandably.' He sat back and stared at the note on the table.

'Good Christ,' I breathed, falling a few steps back and then into a chair.

'It's him, all right,' Lucius said, picking up the note and scanning it. 'That business about the – the buttocks, that was never reported in any of the papers.' He put the letter down and returned to Marcus, who was still bellowing the name Alexander Macleod into the telephone.

Staring blankly, Sara began to feel into the air behind her for a chair, at which Laszlo snatched one and slipped it under her. 'I couldn't translate the entire thing for the poor woman,' Sara said, her voice still almost inaudible. 'But I did give her the gist of it.'

'You did well, Sara,' Kreizler said reassuringly, crouching by her, and being careful that he wasn't overheard by anyone else on the terrace. 'If the killer is aware of her, it's best that she be aware of him, and of what he's thinking. But she hardly needs the details.' Returning to his chair, Laszlo tapped one finger on the note. 'Well, it appears that opportunity has placed a treasure trove into our hands. I suggest we make use of it.'

'Make *use* of it?' I said, still in some shock. 'Laszlo, how can you—'

Laszlo ignored me, and turned to Lucius. 'Detective Sergeant? May I ask who your brother is attempting to contact?'

'Alexander Macleod,' Lucius answered. 'The best handwriting man in North America. Marcus studied with him.'

'Excellent,' Kreizler said. 'The ideal place to begin. From such an analysis we can proceed into a more generalized discussion.'

'Wait a minute.' I stood up, trying both to keep my voice down and to prevent all the horror and revulsion I felt at the note from rushing out; nevertheless, I was somewhat astounded by their attitude. 'We have just found out that this – this *person* not only killed that boy but *ate* him, or at least part of him. Now what exactly do you expect to find out from some goddamned handwriting expert?'

Sara looked up, forcing herself to get a grip on it all. 'No. No, they're right, John. I know it's horrible, but give yourself a minute to think.'

'Indeed, Moore,' Kreizler added. 'The nightmare may have deepened for us, but imagine how much more it has done so for the man we seek. This note shows that his desperation has reached a new height. He may, in fact, be entering a terminal phase of self-destructive emotions—'

'What? Excuse me, Kreizler, but *what*?' My heart was continuing to beat fast, and my voice trembled as I strained to keep it at a whisper. 'You're still going to insist that he's sane, that he wants us to catch him? He's *eating* his victims, for God's sake!'

'We don't know that,' Marcus said, quietly but firmly, as he leaned out the terrace doorway and covered the telephone's mouthpiece with two fingers.

'Precisely,' Kreizler declared, standing and coming round to me as Marcus began to talk into the 'phone again. 'He may or may not be eating parts of his victims, John. What he most certainly is doing is *telling* us that he is eating them, knowing that such a statement can only shock us and cause us to work all the harder to find him. That is a sane action. Remember all we've learned: if he were mad he'd kill, cook the flesh, eat it, and God knows what else, without ever telling anyone – at least, not anyone he knew would go directly to the authorities with the information.' Kreizler gripped my arms hard. 'Just think what he's given us – not only handwriting but information, a vast amount of information to be interpreted!'

Just then Marcus yelled 'Alexander!' again, but with more satisfaction this time. He smiled as he went on. 'Yes, it's Marcus Isaacson, in New York. I have a rather urgent matter, and I just need to clear up one or two details . . .' At that Marcus lowered his voice and leaned into a corner by the doorway, his brother staying with him and straining to listen.

Marcus's telephone conversation lasted another fifteen minutes. In the meantime the note sat on the table, as gruesome and unapproachable in its own way as had been the dead bodies that the killer had left lying all over Manhattan. Indeed, in one respect it was even more frightening: for the killer, despite the ghoulish reality of his work, had thus far been little more than an imaginary patchwork of traits so far as we were concerned. But to hear his particular and bona fide voice changed everything at a shot. No longer could he be *anyone* out there – *he* was *him*, the only person whose mind could plan these acts, the only person capable of speaking these words. Looking around at the shouting bettors on the terrace and then out at the passersby on the street, I suddenly felt that I'd be much more likely now to know him if I met him. It was a new and haunting sensation, one that I had difficulty absorbing; yet even as I grappled with it, I could already sense that Kreizler was right. Whatever terrible and troubling thoughts dominated the murderer, this note could not be dismissed as a series of mad ravings – it was undeniably coherent, though just how coherent I was only on the verge of learning.

As soon as Marcus returned from the 'phone he picked up the letter, sat at the table, and studied the thing intensely for some five minutes. Then he began to make affirmative little humming noises, at which we all drew around him expectantly. Kreizler produced a notepad and a pen, ready to write down anything of value. The calls of the bettors continued to burst out every few minutes, and I shouted over to ask them to keep it down. It was a request that, ordinarily, would have produced howls of outrage and derision; but my voice must have betrayed some of the urgency of the moment, for my friends did comply. Then, in the dwindling light of that beautifully balmy spring evening, Marcus began to expound, quickly but clearly.

'There are two general areas involved in the study of handwriting,' he said, his voice dry with excitement. 'First, there's document examination, in the traditional legal sense – meaning strictly scientific analysis with a view toward comparison and establishing authorship; and second, a group of techniques that are more – well, *speculative*. This second group isn't considered

Caleb Carr

scientific, by most people, and it doesn't carry much weight in court. But we've found it very useful in several investigations.' Marcus glanced at Lucius, who nodded without speaking. 'So – let's start with the basics.'

Marcus paused long enough to order a tall glass of Pilsener to keep his throat from drying up, then continued.

'The man – and the attack of the pen in this case is undoubtedly masculine – who wrote this note had at least several years of schooling that entailed penmanship. This schooling occurred in the United States, no more recently than fifteen years ago.' I could not help a befuddled look, to which Marcus explained, 'There are clear signs that he was trained, hard and regularly, in the Palmer system of penmanship. Now, the Palmer system was introduced in 1880, and was quickly taken up by schools all over the country. It remained what you might call dominant until just last year, when it began to be replaced in the East and in some big western cities by the Zaner-Blosser method. Assuming that our killer's primary education ended at no later than age fifteen, he can't now be any older than thirty-one.'

It seemed a sound line of reasoning; and with small scratching sounds, Kreizler put these points on his pad.

'All right, then,' Marcus went on. 'If we assume that our man's about thirty now, and that he finished school at fifteen or younger, then he's had another fifteen years to evolve both his writing and his personality. It doesn't look like that's been a particularly pleasant time. To begin with, and as we've already guessed, he's an inveterate liar and schemer – he actually knows his grammar and his spelling, but he's gone pretty far out of his way to try to make us think that he doesn't. See, up here, at the top of the note, he's written "straten," along with "figger" and "occashun." He's had the idea that maybe he can get us to believe that he's ignorant, but he's slipped up – at the bottom, he writes that after he snatched Georgio he took him "straight to the bridge," and he has no trouble spelling it.'

'One can only assume,' Kreizler mused, 'that by the end of the letter he's concerned with making his point, rather than with playing games.'

'Exactly, Doctor,' Marcus said. 'So his writing is extremely natural. The fact that the misspellings are intentional is also indicated by his script – the false passages are much more hesitating and less certain. The *t*'s in particular lack the hard, slashing definition that they have in the rest of the writing. His grammar reveals the same point: in some spots he tries to mimic the talk of an uneducated farmhand – "I *seen* your boy," and whatnot – but then he can let off a sentence like, "He died unsoiled by me, and the papers ought to say so." It's completely inconsistent – but, assuming he checked back over the thing after writing it, he failed to spot the inconsistency. That indicates that, while he's unquestionably a capable planner, he may have an exaggerated opinion of his own cleverness.'

After another sip of Pilsener Marcus lit a cigarette and continued, his words finally starting to emerge at a relaxed pace: 'Up to this point, we're on pretty solid ground. All this is good science, and would stand up in a court of law. Age about thirty, several years of decent schooling, a deliberate attempt at deception – no judge would reject it. Now, however, things become less clear-cut. Are any traits of character betrayed by the script itself? A lot of handwriting analysts believe that all people, not just criminals, reveal their basic attitudes during the physical act of writing, regardless of what words are actually written. Macleod's done a lot of work in this area, and I think it may be useful to apply his principles here.'

A sudden shout of 'Jesus Christ, I never seen a fat man move like that in my *life*!' came from across the terrace, and I was about to make another request for quiet when I saw my friends already attending to the job. Marcus was then free to proceed:

'First of all, the slashing downstrokes and the extreme angularity of a lot of the characters suggest a man who's pretty tormented – he's under enormous inner tension of some kind, and it can't find any vent other than anger. In fact, the thrusting, snapping motion of the hand – you see it, here? – is so pronounced that a tendency toward physical violence, and maybe even sadism, is pretty safe to assume. But it gets more complicated than that, because there are other, contrasting elements. In the high register, what's called the "upper zone" of the writing, you can see these florid little wanderings of the pen. They usually

Caleb Carr

indicate a writer with imagination. In the lower zones, on the other hand, there's a fair amount of confusion – it's most apparent in the tendency to place the loops of letters like g and f on the wrong side of the stem. It doesn't happen every time, but the fact that it keeps happening is important, given that he's been trained in penmanship and is at all other times very deliberate and very calculating.'

'Excellent,' Kreizler judged; yet I noticed his pen wasn't moving. 'But I wonder, Detective Sergeant, if these last elements could not have been divined from the contents of the note, as well as from your initial and somewhat more scientific analysis of the handwriting?'

Marcus smiled and nodded. 'Probably. And that shows why the so-called art of reading personality into handwriting hasn't been accepted as a science yet. But I thought it'd be useful to include the observations, because they at least show no marked inconsistency between the content and the script of the note. If it were a fake, you'd almost certainly find that kind of a gap.' Kreizler accepted the statement with a nod, though he still didn't write any of it down. 'Well, that about does it for the handwriting,' Marcus concluded, as he pulled out his vial of carbon powder. 'I'm just going to dust the edges of the paper itself for fingerprints and make sure we get a match.'

As he did so, Lucius, who'd been scrutinizing the envelope, spoke up: 'There's nothing particularly revealing about the postmark. The thing was sent from the Old Post Office by City Hall, but our man probably traveled to get there. He's careful enough to expect that the postmark will be examined. But we can't rule out the possibility that he lives in the City Hall area.'

Marcus had pulled a set of photographed prints from his pocket, and was holding them against the now smudged letter.

'Um-hmm,' he noised. 'A match.' And as he said it the unrealistic but flickering hope that the note was a forgery was snuffed out.

'Which leaves us,' Kreizler said, 'with the considerable task of interpreting the contents.' He pulled out his watch and checked the time – nearly nine. 'It might be better if our minds were fresh, but . . .'

'Yes,' Sara said, her balance finally restored, '*but*.'

We all knew what the 'but' was – our killer wasn't factoring rest periods for his pursuers into his schedule. With that pressing thought in mind, we got up to depart for Number 808 Broadway, where coffee would be brewed. Whatever engagements any of us had been foolish enough to make for later in the evening were implicitly canceled.

As we left the terrace, Laszlo touched my arm, indicating that he wanted a private word. 'I had hoped that I was wrong, John,' he said, as the others went ahead. 'And I still may be, but – I've suspected from the beginning that our man has been observing our efforts. If I'm right he probably followed Mrs. Santorelli to Mulberry Street and kept careful track of whom she spoke to. Sara says she translated the note for the unfortunate woman near the front steps of the building – the killer, if he was there, could not have missed their discussion. He may have followed Sara here; he may be watching us right now.' I spun to look at Union Square and the blocks around us, but Kreizler pulled me back in a jerk. 'Don't – he won't be visible, and I don't want any of the others to suspect this. Especially Sara. It may affect their work. But you and I should heighten all precautions.'

'But – *watching* us? Why?'

'Vanity, perhaps,' Laszlo answered. 'Desperation, as well.'

I was dumbfounded. 'You say you've suspected all along?'

Kreizler nodded as we began to follow the others. 'Since we found that bloodstained rag in the calash on the very first day. The torn page that was wrapped up in it was—'

'Was an article of yours,' I said quickly. 'Or so I guessed.'

'Yes,' Laszlo answered. 'The killer must have been observing the bridge anchor at the time I was called to the scene. I suspect that the page was his way of *acknowledging* me, somehow. And mocking me, too.'

'But how can you be sure it was definitely the killer who left it?' I asked, looking for a way to avoid the harrowing conclusion that we had been, at least intermittently, under the scrutiny of a murderer.

'The rag,' Kreizler explained. 'Though bloodied and soiled, the material bore a striking resemblance to that of the Santorelli

Caleb Carr

boy's chemise – which, if you recall, was missing a sleeve.'

Ahead of us, Sara had begun to look over her shoulder inquisitively, prompting Laszlo to pick up his pace. 'Remember, Moore,' he said. 'Not a word to the rest of them.'

Kreizler rushed up to Sara, leaving me to steal one more very nervous glance at the dark expanse of Union Square Park across Fourth Avenue.

The stakes, as they say, were rising.

Chapter 21

'First of all,' Kreizler announced, as we came into our head-quarters that night and began to settle ourselves at our desks, 'I think we can finally dispense with one lingering uncertainty.' At the top right-hand corner of the chalkboard, under the ASPECTS OF THE CRIMES heading, sat the word ALONE, with a question mark after it – a question mark that Laszlo now removed. We were already relatively certain that our killer had no accomplices: no pair or team of confederates, we'd reasoned, could have engaged in such behavior for a period of years without some one of them revealing it. During the initial phase of the investigation the only catch to this theory had been the question of how one man on his own could have negotiated the walls and rooftops of the various disorderly houses and murder sites; Marcus, however, had taken care of that problem. Thus, while the use of the pronoun 'I' in the letter was not conclusive in and of itself, it seemed, when taken in conjunction with these other facts, definitive evidence that a solitary man was at work.

We all nodded assent to this reasoning, and Kreizler went on: 'Now, then – to the salutation. Why "*My dear* Mrs. Santorelli"?'

'Could be habit of form,' Marcus answered. 'It would be consistent with his schooling.'

'"*My* dear"?' Sara queried. 'Wouldn't schoolchildren learn just "dear"?'

'Sara's right,' said Lucius. 'It's overly affectionate and informal.

He knows his letter is going to devastate the woman, and he's enjoying it. He's playing with her, sadistically.'

'Agreed,' Kreizler said, underlining the word SADISM, which was already written on the right-hand side of the board.

'And I'd like to point out, Doctor,' Lucius added with conviction, 'that this further demonstrates the nature of his hunting.' (Lucius had lately become firmly convinced that our killer's apparent anatomical knowledge arose from his being an accomplished hunter, because of the stalking nature of many of his activities.) 'We've already dealt with the blood-lust aspect – but the toying confirms something else, something beyond even blood-crazed hunting. It's a sporting mentality.'

Laszlo weighed it. 'Your argument is sound, Detective Sergeant,' he said, writing SPORTSMAN so that it bridged the CHILDHOOD and INTERVAL areas. 'But I'll need a bit more convincing' – he chalked on a question mark after the word – 'given the prerequisite and its implications.'

The prerequisite for the killer's being a sportsman, put simply, was a certain amount of leisure time in his youth, when he could have engaged in hunting not only for survival, but for pleasure, as well. This, in turn, implied either that he had an upper-class urban background (the upper being the only real leisure class in the city in those days before child labor laws, when even middle-class parents tended to work their offspring long hours), or that he had been brought up in a rural area. Each assumption would have narrowed our search significantly, and Laszlo needed to be completely certain of our reasoning before he would accept either of them.

'As for his opening statement,' Kreizler went on. 'Aside from the pronounced emphasis on "lies"—'

'That word has been retraced several times,' Marcus cut in. 'There's a lot of feeling behind it.'

'Then lies are not a new phenomenon for him,' Sara extrapolated. 'You get the feeling he's all too familiar with dishonesty and hypocrisy.'

'And yet is still outraged by them,' Kreizler said. 'Any theories?'

'It ties in with the boys,' I offered. 'In the first place, they're dressed up as girls – a kind of deceit. Also, they're whores, and they're supposed to be compliant – but we know that the ones he killed could be troublesome.'

'Good,' Kreizler said with a nod. 'So he doesn't like misrepresentation. Yet he's a liar himself – we need an explanation for that.'

'He's learned,' Sara said simply. 'He's been exposed to dishonesty, surrounded by it perhaps, and he does hate it – but he's picked it up as a method of getting by.'

'And you only do that kind of learning once,' I added. 'It's the same thing as the violence: he saw it, he didn't like it, but he learned it. The law of habit and interest, just like Professor James says – our minds work on the basis of self-interest, the survival of the organism, and our habitual ways of pursuing that interest become defined when we're children and adolescents.'

Lucius had grabbed volume one of James's *Principles* and leafed to a page: '"The character has set like plaster,"' he quoted, holding a finger up, '"never to soften again."'

'Even if . . .?' Kreizler asked, drawing him out.

'Even if,' Lucius answered quickly, flipping a page and scanning it with his finger, 'those habits become counter productive in adulthood. Here: "Habit dooms us all to fight out the battle of life upon the lines of our nurture or our early choice, and to make the best of a pursuit that disagrees, because there is no other for which we are fitted, and it is too late to begin again."'

'A spirited reading, Detective Sergeant,' Kreizler observed, 'but we need examples. We have postulated an original violent experience or experiences, perhaps sexual in nature' – Laszlo indicated a small blank square in the CHILDHOOD section of the board that was boxed off and subheaded THE MOLDING VIOLENCE AND/OR MOLESTATION – 'which we suspect form the basis of his understanding and practice of such behavior. But what of the very strong emotions centered on dishonesty? Can we do the same?'

I shrugged. 'Obviously, he might himself have been accused of it. Unjustly, in all likelihood. Perhaps frequently.'

'Sound,' Kreizler answered, chalking the word DISHONESTY, and then beneath it, BRANDED A LIAR, on the left-hand side of the board.

Caleb Carr

'And then there's the family situation,' Sara added. 'There's a lot of lying that goes on in a family. Adultery is probably the first thing we think of, but—'

'But it doesn't tie in to the violence,' Kreizler finished. 'And I suspect that it must. Could the dishonesty apply *to* the violence – to violent incidents that were deliberately concealed and remained unacknowledged both inside and outside the family?'

'Certainly,' Lucius said. 'And it would be all the worse if the *image* of the family was something very different.'

Kreizler smiled with real satisfaction. 'Precisely. Then if we have an outwardly respectable father who at the very least beats his wife and children . . .'

Lucius's face screwed up a bit. 'I didn't necessarily mean a father. It could have been anyone in the family.'

Laszlo waved him off. 'The father would be the greatest betrayal.'

'Not the mother?' Sara said carefully. And there was more in the question than just the subject at hand: at that moment it seemed that she was trying to read Laszlo as much as the killer.

'There's no literature to suggest it,' Kreizler answered. 'The recent findings of Breuer and Freud on hysteria point to prepubertal sexual abuse by the *father* in nearly every case.'

'With all due respect, Dr. Kreizler,' Sara protested, 'Breuer and Freud seem fairly confused about the meaning of their findings. Freud began by assuming sexual abuse as the basis for all hysteria, but recently he seems to have altered that view, and decided that *fantasies* concerning abuse may be the actual cause.'

'Indeed,' Kreizler acknowledged. 'There is much that remains unclear in their work. I myself cannot accept the single-minded emphasis on sex – to the exclusion even of violence. But look at it from an empirical standpoint, Sara – how many households have you known that were ruled by dominating, violent mothers?'

Sara shrugged. 'There is more than one kind of violence, Doctor – but I shall have more to say about that when we reach the end of the letter.'

Kreizler had already written VIOLENT BUT OUTWARDLY RESPECTABLE FATHER on the left-hand side of the board, and seemed ready, even anxious, to move on. 'The entire first paragraph,' he said, slapping at the note. 'Despite its deliberate misspellings, it has a consistent tone.'

'You get that immediately,' Marcus answered. 'He's already decided in his mind that there are a lot of people after him.'

'I think I know what you're driving at, Doctor,' Lucius said, again rifling through the stack of books and papers on his desk. 'One of the articles you gave us to read, the one you translated yourself . . . ah!' He yanked one set of papers free. 'Here – Dr. Krafft-Ebing. He discusses "intellectual monomania," as well as what the Germans call *"primäre Verrücktheit,"* and argues for replacing both terms with the word "paranoia."'

Kreizler nodded as he wrote the word PARANOID on the INTERVAL section of the board: 'Feelings, perhaps even delusions, of persecution that have taken root after some traumatic emotional experience or set of experiences, but which do not result in dementia – Krafft-Ebing's admirably succinct definition, and it does seem to fit. I very much doubt that our man is in a deluded state as yet, but his behavior is probably quite antisocial, nevertheless. Which does not mean that we seek a misanthrope – that would be too simple.'

'Couldn't the murders themselves satisfy the antisocial drive?' Sara asked. 'Leaving him, the rest of the time, outwardly normal and – well, participatory, functional?'

'Perhaps even *overly* functional,' Kreizler agreed. 'This will not be a man who, in the opinion of his neighbors, could slaughter children and claim to have eaten them.' Kreizler jotted these ideas down and then faced us again. 'And so – we arrive at the second and even more extraordinary paragraph.'

'One thing it tells us right away,' Marcus pronounced. 'He hasn't traveled much abroad. I don't know what he's been reading, but widespread cannibalism hasn't been seen in Europe lately. They'll eat just about anything else, but not each other. Although you can never be quite sure about the Germans . . .' Marcus caught himself and glanced at Kreizler. 'Oh. No offense intended, Doctor,' he said.

Lucius clapped a hand to his forehead, but Kreizler only smiled wryly. The Isaacsons' idiosyncracies no longer perplexed him in any way. 'No offense taken, Detective Sergeant – you can, indeed, never be certain about the Germans. But if we accept that his travel has been limited to the United States, what are we to make of your theory that his mountaineering skills indicate a European heritage?'

Marcus shrugged. 'First-generation American. The parents were immigrants.'

Sara drew a quick breath. '"Dirty immigrants"!'

Kreizler's face filled with gratification again. 'Indeed,' he said, writing IMMIGRANT PARENTS on the left side of the chalkboard. 'The phrase resounds with loathing, doesn't it? It's the kind of hatred that generally has a specific root, obscure though it may be. In this case, he probably had a troubled relationship with one or both parents early on, and eventually grew to despise everything about them – including their heritage.'

'Yet it's his own heritage, too,' I said. 'That might account for some of the savagery toward the children. It's self-loathing, as if he's trying to clean the dirt out of himself.'

'An interesting phrase, John,' Kreizler answered. 'And one we shall return to. But there is one more practical question to be answered here. Given the hunting and the mountaineering, and now the supposition that he has not been abroad, can we say anything about the geographical background?'

'Same thing as before,' Lucius replied. 'Either a rich city family, or the countryside.'

'Detective Sergeant?' Laszlo said to Marcus. 'Would any one region be better than another for this training?'

Marcus shook his head. 'You could learn it anywhere that had appreciable rock formations – which means a lot of places in the United States.'

'Hmmm,' Laszlo agreed, with some disappointment. 'Not much help there. Let's let it lie for now and go back to that second paragraph. The language itself would seem to support your theory concerning the "upper-zone flourishes" of the handwriting, Marcus. This is indeed an imaginative tale.'

'That's a hell of an imagination,' I said.

'True, John,' Kreizler answered. 'Without doubt, excessive and morbid.'

Lucius snapped his fingers at that. 'Wait,' he said, again going for his books. 'I'm remembering something—'

'Sorry, Lucius,' Sara called, with one of her curling little smiles. 'I've beaten you to it.' She held up an open medical journal. 'This fits in with the dishonesty discussion, Doctor,' she went on. 'In his article "A Schedule for the Study of Mental Abnormalities in Children," Dr. Meyer lists some of the warning signs for predicting future dangerous behavior – excessive imagination is one of them.' She read from the article, which had appeared in the *Handbook of the Illinois Society for Child-Study* in February of 1895: '"Normally children can reproduce voluntarily all sorts of mental pictures in the dark. This becomes abnormal when the mental pictures become an obsession, i.e., cannot be suppressed. Especially pictures that create fear and unpleasant feelings are apt to become excessively strong."' Sara emphasized the final sentence of the quotation: '"Excessive imagination may lead to the construction of lies and the irresistible impulse to play them on others."'

'Thank you, Sara,' Kreizler said. MORBID IMAGINATION then went up on both the CHILDHOOD and ASPECTS section of the chalkboard, which puzzled me. To my request for an explanation Laszlo replied, 'He may be writing this letter in his adulthood, John, but so distinctive an imagination does not spring to life in maturity. It's been with him always – Meyer is borne out here, incidentally, for this child did indeed become dangerous.'

Marcus was tapping a pencil into one hand thoughtfully. 'Any chance this cannibalism business was a childhood nightmare? He says he's read it. Any chance he read it *then*? The effect would have been greater.'

'Ask yourself a more basic question,' Laszlo answered. 'What is the strongest force behind imagination? Normal imagination, but also and particularly the morbid?'

Sara had no trouble with that: 'Fear.'

'Fear of what you see,' Laszlo pressed, 'or of what you hear?'

'Both,' Sara answered. 'But mostly what you hear – "nothing is as terrible in reality," et cetera.'

'Isn't reading a form of hearing?' Marcus asked.

'Yes, but even well-to-do children don't learn to read until many years into childhood,' Kreizler answered. 'I offer this only as a theory, but suppose the cannibalism story was then what it is now – a tale designed to terrify. Only now, rather than the terrorized party, our man is the terrorizer. As we've constructed him thus far, wouldn't he find that immensely satisfying, even amusing?'

'But who told it to him?' Lucius asked.

Kreizler shrugged. 'Who generally terrifies children with stories?'

'Adults who want them to behave,' I answered quickly. 'My father had a story about the Japanese emperor's torture chamber that had me up for nights, picturing every detail—'

'Excellent, Moore! My very point.'

'But what about—' Lucius's words became a bit halting. 'What about the – I'm sorry, but I'm afraid I still don't know how to discuss certain things with a lady present.'

'Then pretend one isn't,' Sara said, a bit impatiently.

'Well,' Lucius went on, no more comfortably, 'what about the focus on the – buttocks?'

'Ah, yes,' Kreizler answered. 'Part of the original story, do we think? Or a twist of our man's invention?'

'Uhhh—' I droned, having thought of something but, like Lucius, unsure of how to phrase it in front of a woman. 'The, uh – the – references, not only to dirt, but to – fecal matter—'

'The word he uses is "*shit*,"' Sara said bluntly, and everyone in the room, including Kreizler, seemed to spring a few inches off the floor for a second or two. 'Honestly, gentlemen,' Sara commented with some disdain. 'If I'd known you were all so modest I'd have stuck to secretarial work.'

'Who's modest?' I demanded – not one of my stronger retorts.

Sara frowned at me, '*You*, John Schuyler Moore. I happen to know that you have, on occasion, paid members of the female sex to spend intimate moments with you – I suppose *they* were strangers to that kind of language?'

'No,' I protested, aware that my face was a bright red beacon. 'But they weren't – weren't—'

'Weren't?' Sara asked sternly.

'Weren't – well, ladies!'

At that Sara stood up, put one hand to a hip and with the other produced her derringer from some nether region of her dress. 'I would like to warn you all right now,' she said tightly, 'that the next man who uses the word "lady," in that context and in my presence, will be *shitting* from a new and artificially manufactured hole in his gut.' She put the gun away and sat back down.

The room was as quiet as the grave for half a minute, and then Kreizler spoke softly: 'I believe you were discussing the references to shit, Moore?'

I gave Sara a rather injured and indignant glance – which she thoroughly ignored, the wretch – and then resumed my thought: 'They seem connected – all the scatological references and the preoccupation with that part of the anato—' I could feel Sara's eyes burning a hole in the side of my head. 'And the preoccupation with the *ass*,' I finished, as defiantly as I could manage.

'Indeed they do,' Kreizler said. 'Connected metaphorically as well as anatomically. It's puzzling – and there's not a great deal of literature on such subjects. Meyer has speculated on the possible causes and implications of nocturnal urinary incontinence, and anyone who works with children finds the occasional subject who is abnormally fixated on feces. Most alienists and psychologists, however, consider this a form of mysophobia – the morbid fear of dirt and contamination, which our man certainly seems to have.' Kreizler chalked the word MYSOPHOBIA up in the center of the board, but then stood away from it, looking dissatisfied. 'There seems, however, more to it than just that . . .'

'Doctor,' Sara said, 'I've got to urge you again to broaden your concepts of the mother and father in this case. I know your experience with children past a certain age is as extensive as anyone's, but have you ever been closely involved with the care of an infant?'

'Only as a physician,' Kreizler answered. 'And then rarely. Why, Sara?'

'It's not a time of childhood that men figure greatly in, as a rule. Do any of you know men who have played a large part in raising children younger than, say, three or four?' We all shook our heads. I suspect that even if one of us *had* known such a man he would have denied it, just to keep the derringer out of sight.

Sara turned back to Laszlo. 'And when you find children with an abnormal fixation on defecation, Doctor, what form does it generally take?'

'Either an excessive urge or morbid reluctance. Generally.'

'Urge or reluctance to what?'

'To go to the toilet.'

'And how have they learned to go to the toilet?' Sara asked, keeping right after Kreizler.

'They've been taught.'

'By men, generally?'

Kreizler had to pause, at that. The line of questioning had seemed obscure at first, but now we could all see where Sara was going: if our killer's rather obsessive concern with feces, buttocks, and the more generalized 'dirt' (no subjects were, after all, mentioned more in the note) had been implanted in childhood, it was likely that contact with a woman or women – mother, nurse, governess, or what have you – had been involved in the process.

'I see,' Kreizler finally said. 'I take it, then, that you have yourself observed the process, Sara?'

'Occasionally,' she replied. 'And I've heard stories. A girl does. It's always assumed that you'll need the knowledge. The whole affair can be surprisingly difficult – embarrassing, frustrating, sometimes even violent. I wouldn't bring it up, except that the references are so insistent. Doesn't it suggest something out of the ordinary?'

Laszlo cocked his head. 'Perhaps. I'm afraid I can't consider such observations conclusive, however.'

'Won't you at least consider the possibility that a woman – perhaps the mother, though not necessarily – has played a darker role than you've yet allowed?'

'I hope that I am not deaf to *any* possibilities,' Kreizler said, turning to the board but writing nothing. 'However, I fear we have strayed too far into the realm of the barely plausible.'

Sara sat back, again disappointed at the result of her attempts to make Kreizler see another dimension in the imaginary tale of our killer. And I must confess, I was somewhat confused myself; after all, it had been Kreizler who had asked Sara to come up with such theories, knowing that none of us could. To dismiss her thoughts in such a manner seemed arbitrary at best, especially when those thoughts sounded (to the semi-trained ear, at any rate) as well reasoned as his own hypotheses.

'The resentment of immigrants is repeated in the third paragraph,' Kreizler said, plowing on. 'And then there is the reference to a "Red Injun." Other than another attempt to make us think him an ignoramus, what do we make of it?'

'The whole phrase seems important,' Lucius answered. '"Dirtier than a Red Injun." He was looking for a superlative, and that's what he came up with.'

Marcus pondered the question: 'If we assume that the immigrant resentment is family-based, then he himself isn't an Indian. But he must've had some kind of contact with them.'

'Why?' Kreizler asked. 'Race hatred doesn't require familiarity.'

'No, but the two usually do accompany each other,' Marcus insisted. 'And look at the phrase itself – it's fairly casual, as if he naturally associates filth with Indians and assumes everyone else does, too.'

I nodded, seeing his point. 'That'd be out West. You don't usually hear that kind of talk in the East – it's not that we're more enlightened, by any means, but too few people share the point of reference. What I mean is, if he'd said "dirtier than a nigger," you might guess the South, right?'

'Or Mulberry Street,' Lucius suggested quietly.

'True,' I acknowledged. 'I'm not saying the attitude's confined. After all, this could just be somebody who's read too many Wild West stories—'

'Or someone with excessive imagination,' Sara added.

'But,' I went on, 'it might work as a general indication.'

'Well, it's the obvious implication,' Kreizler sighed, piquing me a bit. 'But someone somewhere said that we must never overlook the obvious. What about it, Marcus – does the idea of a frontier upbringing appeal?'

Marcus thought it over. 'It has attractions. First of all, it explains the knife, which is a frontier weapon. It also gives us the hunting, recreational and otherwise, without the need for a wealthy background. And while there's plenty of terrain for mountaineering in the West, it's concentrated in specific areas, which might help. There are whole communities of German and Swiss immigrants out there, too.'

'Then we shall mark it as a favored possibility,' Kreizler said, doing so on the board, 'though we can go no farther for the time being. That takes us to the next paragraph, at which point our man finally gets down to specifics.' Kreizler picked up the note again, and then began to rub the back of his neck slowly. 'On February eighteenth he spots the Santorelli boy. Having spent more time than I'd care to admit going over calendars and almanacs, I can tell you right away that February eighteenth was Ash Wednesday this year.'

'He mentions ashes on the face,' Lucius added. 'That would mean that the boy went to church.'

'The Santorellis are Catholic,' Marcus added. 'There aren't many churches near Paresis Hall, Catholic or otherwise, but we could try checking a broader area. It's possible someone will remember seeing Georgio. He would have been fairly distinctive, especially in a church setting.'

'And it's always possible that the killer got his first glimpse of him near the church,' I said. 'Or even in it. If we get very lucky, someone may have witnessed the meeting.'

'You two seem to have planned your weekend quite thoroughly,' Kreizler answered, at which Marcus and I, realizing that we'd proposed long days of footwork, frowned at each other. 'Although,' Laszlo went on, 'the use of the word "parading" makes me doubt that they met very near a house of worship – particularly one in which Georgio had just attended services.'

'It does suggest that the boy was hawking his wares' I said.

'It suggests many things.' Laszlo thought for a moment, sounding the word: '"Parading . . ." It might fit with your idea that the man suffers from a disability or deformity of some kind, Moore. There's a trace of envy in the word, as if he himself is excluded from such behavior.'

'I don't quite see that,' Sara answered. 'It sounds more – disdainful, to me. That could simply be due to Georgio's occupation, of course, but I don't think so. There's no pity or sympathy in the tone, only harshness. And a certain sense of familiarity, as with the lying.'

'Right,' I said. 'It's that lecturing tone you'd get from a schoolmaster who knows just what you're up to because he was a boy once himself.'

'Then you're saying he disdains an open display of sexual behavior, not because he was prevented from engaging in such activities himself, but precisely because he *did* engage in them?' Laszlo cocked his head and puzzled with the notion. 'Perhaps. But wouldn't the adults in his life have stifled such antics? And doesn't that lead us back to the idea of envy, even if there's no physical deformity?'

'But the issue must still have caused a scene, at least once,' Sara volleyed, 'in order for such restrictions to have been laid down.'

Laszlo paused and then nodded. 'Yes. Yes, you have a point, Sara.' That brought a small but satisfied smile to her face. 'And then,' Kreizler continued, 'whether he defied or submitted to the ban, the seed of future difficulty would have been planted. Good.' Kreizler made a few quick scribbles to this effect on the left-hand side of the board. 'On, then, to the ashes and paint.'

'He puts the two together very easily,' Lucius said, 'whereas, to the average observer, there'd appear to be some inconsistency – I'll bet the priest at the service thought so.'

'It's as if the one isn't any better than the other,' Marcus added. 'The tone remains pretty deprecating.'

'And that presents a problem.' Kreizler went to his desk and fetched a bound calender, one that bore a cross on its cover. 'On February eighteenth he saw Georgio Santorelli for the first time, and I very much doubt that the encounter was accidental. The specificity suggests that he was out looking for just that type of boy on that day in particular. We have to assume, therefore, that the fact of its being Ash Wednesday is significant. In addition, the ashes, in tandem with the paint, seem to have heightened his reaction, which was essentially one of anger. That might suggest that he resented a boy-whore's presuming to participate in a Christian rite – yet as the detective sergeants have noted, there is no sense of reverence for that rite in his language. Quite the contrary. I have not, to this point, believed that we are dealing with a man who suffers from a religious mania. The evangelical and messianic qualities that tend to mark such pathologies are not displayed, even in this note. And though my conviction in this regard has, admittedly, been a bit weakened by the schedule of the killings, the indications remain contradictory.' Kreizler studied the calendar hard. 'If there were only some significance to the day Georgio was killed . . .'

We knew what he was referring to. Laszlo's recent investigation of the timings of the murders had revealed that all save one could be tied to the Christian calendar: January 1st marked the circumcision of Jesus and the Feast of Fools; February 2nd was the Purification of the Virgin Mary, or Candlemas Day; and Ali-ibn-Ghazi had died on Good Friday. There had been holy days when no murders had taken place, of course – Epiphany, for instance, has passed without incident, as had the Five Wounds of Christ on February 20th. But if March 3rd, the date of the Santorelli killing, had possessed a Christian connotation, we could have been relatively certain that some kind of religious element was involved in our man's timing. No such connotation existed, however.

'Then maybe we're back to the theory of the lunar cycle,' Marcus said, bringing up a very old bit of folk wisdom that we'd spent a fair amount of time debating, which ran to the effect that behavior such as our killer's was somehow connected to the waxing and waning of the moon, making it true 'lunacy.'

'I still don't like it,' Kreizler said with a wave of his hand, eyes ever on his calendar.

'The moon *has* been linked to other physical and behavioral shifts,' Sara said. 'You'll find a lot of women, for instance, who believe it controls the menstrual cycle.'

'And our man's urges do seem to run according to a cycle of some kind,' Lucius agreed.

'So they do,' Kreizler replied. 'But the suggestion of such an unprovable astrological influence on psychobiology draws us away from the ritualistic nature of the murders. The claimed cannibalism is a new and apparently distinct element of those rituals, I'll admit. But the savagery has been consistently rising, and it was almost predictable that we should reach some such crescendo – although the absence of that particular feature in the ibn-Ghazi murder suggests he may have ventured into an area that, whatever his shocking statements in the note, was not truly to his liking.'

The conversation ground to a halt for a moment, and as it did an idea began to form in my mind. 'Kreizler,' I said, carefully weighing my words, 'let's assume for a moment that we're right about all this. You've said yourself that it seems to further reinforce the notion that there's a religious element to the murders.'

Kreizler turned to me, weariness starting to show in his eyes. 'It can be taken that way,' he said.

'Well, what about our two priests, then? We've already figured that their behavior could easily be seen as an attempt to protect someone. Suppose it's one of their own?'

'Ahh,' Lucius said quietly. 'You're thinking of someone like that reverend in Salt Lake City, John?'

'Exactly,' I answered. 'A holy man gone very wrong. One with a second, and secret, life. Suppose his superiors have gotten wind of what he's doing, but they can't locate him for some reason – maybe he's gone into hiding. The potential for scandal would be enormous. And given the role that the Catholic and Episcopal churches play in the life of this city, the leaders of either group could easily get not only the mayor's office but the richest men in town to help them conceal it. Until they can deal with it privately, I mean.' I sat back, rather proud of this bit of work, but waiting for Kreizler's reaction. His continued silence didn't seem a good sign; so I added, a bit uncomfortably, 'It's just a thought.'

'It's a damned good thought,' Marcus judged, with an enthusiastic knock of his pencil against his desk.

'It might tie a lot of things together,' Sara agreed.

Kreizler finally began to react: a slow nod. 'It might, indeed,' he said, as he scrawled INCOGNITO PRIEST? in the center of the board. 'The traits of background and character that we have described could fit a man of the cloth as well as any other – and the fact of his being a priest offers an attractive alternative to a religious mania. These could be personal conflicts playing out according to a schedule that happens to be natural, even convenient, for him. A more vigorous investigation of those other two priests will doubtless shed further light on the subject.' Kreizler turned. 'And that—'

'I know, I know,' I said, holding up a hand. 'The detective sergeants and myself.'

'How splendid to be correctly anticipated,' Kreizler answered with a chuckle.

As Marcus and I briefly discussed our growing investigative chores for the next few days, Lucius glanced over the note again. 'The next line,' he announced, 'seems to get back to the notion of sadism. He decides to wait, and to see the boy several times before the murder – again, he's toying with him, while all the time he knows what he's going to do. It's the sporting, sadistic hunter.'

'Yes, I fear there's nothing new in that sentence – not until we reach the end.' Kreizler tapped his chalk on the board. '"That place" – the only expression, other than "lies," which receives the upper case.'

'Hatred again,' Sara said. 'Of Paresis Hall specifically, or of the general type of behavior practiced there?'

'Maybe both,' Marcus said. 'After all, Paresis Hall caters to a very specific clientele – men who want boys who dress up like women.'

Kreizler kept tapping at the box marked THE MOLDING VIOLENCE AND/OR MOLESTATION 'We have returned to the core of the matter. This is not a man who hates all children, nor a man who hates all homosexuals – nor, for that matter, a man who hates all boy-whores who dress up like women. This is a man of very particular tastes.'

'But you still do consider him homosexual, don't you, Doctor?' Sara asked.

'Only in the sense that the London Ripper could be called heterosexual,' Kreizler answered, 'because his victims happened to be women. The issue is almost irrelevant – this note proves as much. He may be homosexual, and he may be a pedophile, but sadism is the predominant perversion, and violence seems far more characteristic of his intimate contacts than do sexual or amorous feelings. He may not even be able to distinguish between violence and sex. Certainly, any sense of arousal seems to translate quickly into violence. And that, I am sure, is a pattern that was established during these initial molding experiences. The antagonists in those episodes were without question male – that fact comes into play far more than any true homosexual orientation, when he's selecting his victims.'

'Was it a man that committed those early acts, then?' Lucius asked. 'Or maybe another boy?'

Kreizler shrugged. 'A difficult question. But we know this – certain boys inspire in the killer a rage so deep he's constructed his entire existence around its expression. Which boys? As Moore has pointed out, those who are – either in the killer's eyes or in fact – deceitful, as well as insolent.'

Sara indicated the note with a nod of her head. ' "Saucy." '

'Yes,' Kreizler answered. 'We have been correct in that assumption. We have further postulated that he chooses violence as a form for expressing that rage because he learned to do so in some sort of domestic setting, quite probably from a violent father whose actions went unacknowledged and unpunished. What was the cause of that original violence, insofar as our killer understood it? We have speculated on that, too.'

'Wait,' Sara said, in a moment of realization. She looked up at Kreizler. 'We've come full circle, haven't we, Doctor?'

'We have indeed,' Kreizler replied, drawing a line from one side of the chalkboard to the other: from the killer's traits to those of his victims. 'Whether our man, in his youth, was a liar, sexually precocious, or generally so ill behaved that he required terrorizing in addition to beatings, he was in some fundamental way *very much like the boys he is now killing*.'

That, as they say, was a thought. If, by committing these murders, our killer was not only trying to destroy intolerable elements of the world around him, but also and more fundamentally parts of himself that he simply could not abide, then Kreizler might well be right about his entering a new and markedly more self-destructive phase; indeed, eventual self-destruction seemed, in this light, almost a certainty. But why, I asked Kreizler, should the man see those aspects of himself as so intolerable? And, if he did, why not simply change them?

'You said it yourself, Moore,' Laszlo replied. 'We only do that sort of learning once. Or, to paraphrase our former teacher, this killer makes the best of a pursuit that disagrees, because there is no other for which he is fitted, and it is too late for him to begin again. In the remainder of this fourth paragraph he describes abducting the boy, using a highly imperative tone. Does he mention desire? No – he tells us that he "must." He must because those are the laws by which his world, disagreeable as it may be, has always functioned. He has become what Professor James calls a "mere walking bundle of habits," and to abandon those habits would, he fears, mean abandoning himself. You remember what we once said about Georgio Santorelli – that he came to associate his psychic survival with the activities that caused his father to beat him? Our man is not so very different. He no doubt enjoys his murders as much or as little as Georgio enjoyed his work. But for both of them those activities were, and are, vital, despite the deep self-loathing they may create – and which you have already detected in this note, Moore.'

Now, I'll confess that I hadn't been fully aware of just how many incisive statements I'd made that evening; but I was now having no trouble keeping up with Laszlo's elaboration of them. 'He gets back to that toward the end of the letter,' I said. 'The remark about Georgio being "unsoiled" by him – the filth he despises is actually in him, a part of him.'

'And would be transmitted through the act of sex,' Marcus added. 'So you're right, Doctor – sex is not something he values or enjoys. It's the violence that's his goal.'

'Isn't it possible that he isn't even capable of sex?' Sara asked. 'Given the kind of background we're supposing, that is. In one of the treatises you gave us, Doctor, there's a discussion of sexual stimulation and anxiety reactions—'

'Dr. Peyer, at the University of Zurich,' Kreizler said. 'The observations grew out of his larger study of *coitus interruptus*.'

'That's right,' Sara continued. 'The implications seemed strongest for men who had emerged from difficult home lives. Persistent anxiety could result in a pronounced suppression of the libido, creating impotence.'

The Alienist

'Our boy's pretty tender on that subject,' Marcus said, going to the note and reading from it. 'I never fucked him, though I could have.'

'Indeed,' Kreizler said, writing IMPOTENCE in the center of the board without hesitation. 'The effect would only be to magnify his frustration and rage, producing ever more carnage. And that carnage emerges now as our most difficult puzzle. If these mutilations are indeed personal rituals, unconnected to any definite religious theme other than dates, then regardless of whether he's a priest or a plumber it becomes all the more important to understand the details, for they will be specific to him.' Kreizler went over to the note. 'This document, I fear, gives us very little help along such lines.' Laszlo rubbed his eyes as he checked his silver watch. 'And it's quite late. I suggest we conclude.'

'Before we do that, Doctor,' Sara said, quietly but firmly, 'I'd like to get back to one point concerning the adults in this man's past.'

Kreizler nodded, with little or no enthusiasm. 'The women involved,' he sighed.

'Yes.' Sara stood up and walked to the chalkboard, pointing to its various divisions. 'We've theorized that we have a man who, while still a child, was harassed, embarrassed, blamed, and finally beaten. I can't contest the theory that the beatings were administered by a male hand. But the intimate nature of so many of the other aspects seems to me to suggest very strongly a woman's rather sinister presence. Listen to his tone throughout the note, which, after all, is addressed to *Mrs.* Santorelli *specifically* – it's defensive, badgered, even whining at moments, and obsessed with scatological and anatomical details. It's the voice of a boy who's been scrutinized, and humiliated regularly, who's been made to feel that he himself is filth, without ever experiencing a place or person of refuge. If his character truly did form in his childhood, Dr. Kreizler, then I must repeat that the mother would be the far more likely culprit, in this regard.'

Kreizler's face betrayed irritation. 'If that were so, Sara, then wouldn't massive resentment have been bred? And wouldn't the victims be women, like the Ripper's?'

'I don't argue your reasoning with regard to the victims,' Sara answered. 'I'm asking for a deeper look in another direction.'

'You seem to think,' Laszlo replied, a bit snappishly, 'that I suffer from blinkered vision. I remind you that I do have *some* experience with these things.'

Sara studied him for a moment, and then quietly asked, 'Why do you resist so strongly the notion of a woman's active involvement in the formation?'

Laszlo suddenly rose, slammed a hand down on his desk, and shouted, 'Because her role cannot have *been* active, damn it!'

Marcus, Lucius and I froze for a moment, then exchanged uneasy glances. The rather shocking outburst, quite apart from being unwarranted, didn't even seem to make sense, given Laszlo's professional opinions. And yet it went on: 'Had a woman been *actively* involved in this man's life, at any point, we would not even be here – the crimes would never have *happened*!' Kreizler tried to regain an even keel, but only half-succeeded. 'The whole notion is absurd, there is *nothing* in the literature to suggest it! And so I really must insist, Sara – we shall presume a record of feminine passivity in the formation and proceed to the issue of the mutilations! *Tomorrow!*'

As has hopefully become clear by now, Sara Howard was not the kind of woman to take such talk from any man, even one she admired and perhaps (in my opinion, at any rate) had still deeper feelings for. Her eyes went very thin at this last shot from Laszlo, and her voice was ice itself when she said:

'Since you appear to have decided this issue long ago, Doctor, it seems pointless to have asked me to research the subject.' I was a little worried that she'd go for the derringer, but she opted for her coat instead. 'Perhaps you thought it would be an amusing way to keep me occupied,' she stormed on. 'But I'll tell you right now that I don't need to be amused, cajoled, or otherwise mollycoddled – by any of you!'

And with that she was out the door. The Isaacsons and I traded more perturbed looks, but there was no need to say anything. We all knew that Sara had been right and Kreizler inexplicably, pigheadedly wrong. As Laszlo sighed and collapsed into his chair, it seemed for an instant that he might realize as much himself; but he did nothing more than ask us all to leave, claiming weariness. Then he fixed his eyes on the letter before him. The rest of us fetched our things and filed out, saying good-night to Kreizler but receiving no reply.

Had the incident sparked no repercussions, I would hardly mention it here. True, it was the first real moment of discord we'd experienced at Number 808 Broadway, but it was inevitable that there should be a few, and no doubt we all would have gotten over it soon. But this sharp exchange between Kreizler and Sara did have repercussions: illuminating repercussions that not only revealed much that was unknown, even to me, about Kreizler's past, but also lit our way toward a face-to-face encounter with one of the most disturbing criminals in the recent history of the United States.

Chapter 22

We saw very little of Kreizler during the next week or so, and I later learned that he spent nearly all of that time interviewing men who'd been arrested for domestic violence as well as the wives and children who'd suffered at their hands. He came into our headquarters only once or twice, saying next to nothing but collecting notes and data with great, almost desperate determination. He never managed to apologize to Sara; but, even though the few words that passed between them were awkward and stilted, she did find it in herself to forgive his harsh statements, which she attributed to a combination of Kreizler's increasingly emotional involvement in the case and the nervousness that we'd all begun to feel with the changing of the month. Whatever calendar our killer was using, if he followed his established pattern he would strike again soon. At the time, anticipation of that event did seem a more than adequate explanation for Kreizler's uncharacteristic behavior; but such anticipation, it turned out, was only part of what was driving my friend so hard.

For our part, Marcus and I decided during those first few days of May to divide the tasks we'd outlined on the night the killer's note arrived. Marcus canvassed every Catholic church on the Lower East Side (as well as some outside that neighborhood) in an attempt to find anyone who might have noticed Georgio Santorelli, while I took on the job of learning more about the two priests. After a weekend spent trying to get new details out of the man who owned the building where Ali ibn-Ghazi's father lived, however, as well as from Mrs. Santorelli and her fellow tenants (Sara once again did the interpreting), it became clear that more money had been spread around to ensure more people's silence. I was therefore forced to shift my activities to the two church organizations involved. We figured that my status as a reporter for the *Times* would gain me the easiest and quickest access, and I decided to start my inquiries at the top: with visits to the Roman Catholic archbishop of New York, Michael Corrigan, as well as the Episcopal bishop of New York, Henry Codman Potter. Both men lived in very pleasant town houses in the fifties near Madison Avenue, and I figured I could cover both interviews in one day.

Potter came first. Although New York's Episcopal's only numbered in the tens of thousands in those days, some of those tens of thousands were among the wealthiest of the city's families; and the parish reflected that fact in its luxuriously appointed churches and chapels, its extensive real estate holdings, and its heavy involvement in city affairs. Bishop Potter – often referred to as New York's 'first citizen' – personally preferred the quaint villages and churches of his upstate parishes to the bustle, noise, and dirt of New York; but he knew where the Church made its money, and he did his part to expand the flock in the city. All of which is to say that Potter was a man with big things on his mind; and although I waited in his very luxurious sitting room for longer than it would've taken him to say mass, when he finally did appear he found that he could spare me only some ten minutes of his time.

I asked if he was aware that a man dressed as a priest and wearing a signet ring that bore the large red and smaller white crosses of the Episcopal Church had been going around to people who had information concerning the recent child murders and paying them large sums of money to keep quiet. If the question shocked Potter, he didn't show it: cool as a cucumber he told me that the man was undoubtedly an imposter or a lunatic or both – the Episcopal Church had no interest in interfering with any police business, certainly not a murder case. Then I inquired as to whether a signet ring like the one that had been spotted would be a particularly easy item to get hold of. He shrugged and sat back comfortably, the flesh of his neck falling down over his stiff white and black collar, and said that he had no idea how easy it would be to lay hands on such a thing. He supposed any capable jeweler could manufacture one. Obviously, I wasn't going to get anywhere with the man; but just for the hell of it I decided to ask if he was aware of Paul Kelly's partially realized threat to stir up trouble among the immigrant communities over the issue of the murders. Potter said he was barely aware of Mr. Kelly at all, much less of any threats he might have made; being as the Episcopal Church had very few members among what Potter called the 'recently arrived citizens of the city,' little attention would have been paid to such matters by either himself or his subordinates. Potter concluded by suggesting that I visit Archbishop Corrigan, who had much more contact with such groups and neighborhoods. I told him that Corrigan's residence was my next stop, and was on my way.

I'll admit that I'd been in a suspicious mood even before I encountered Potter; but his very *un*-churchmanlike lack of interest only made me more so. Where was any sense of concern for the victims of the crimes? Where was the pledge that if there was anything he could do, I had only to ask? Where was the head-shaking wish that the fiendish murderer be captured, and the fervent pressing of the flesh on that wish?

All these, I soon learned, were at Archbishop Corrigan's residence, behind the almost-completed magnificence of the new St. Patrick's Cathedral on Fifth Avenue between Fiftieth and Fifty-first streets. The new St. Pat's was unarguable evidence that the architect James Renwick had only been warming up when he'd designed our downtown neighbor, Grace Church. The enormous spires, archways, stained glass windows, and brass doors of St. Patrick's were on a scale, and had been executed with a speed, unheard of even in New York.

Archbishop Corrigan was far more animated and engaging than Potter had been. He took me on a short tour of the cathedral, and outlined all the work that was still to be done: the Stations of the Cross needed to be installed, the Ladies' Chapel was as yet unbuilt, the chimes had to be paid for, and the spires required crowning. I began to think that he was going to ask me for a contribution; but I soon discovered that all this was just a buildup to a visit to the Catholic Orphan Society, where I was to be shown that the Church had another side. The Society was located across Fifty-first Street, in a four-story building with a pleasant front yard and plenty of well-behaved children wandering about. Corrigan took me there, he said, because he wanted me to understand the depth of the Church's commitment to lost and abandoned children in New York; they were avowedly just as important to him as the great cathedral in whose shadow the Orphan society stood.

All of which was fine – except that I suddenly realized I hadn't *asked* him anything yet. This very pleasant, welcoming, deep-feeling fellow *knew* why I was there, a fact that became especially apparent after I started putting the same questions I'd asked Potter to him. Corrigan answered as if he'd been carefully rehearsed: Oh, yes, it was a terrible shame about those murdered boys; horrible; he couldn't imagine why anyone purporting to be a Catholic priest would be interfering (though he didn't seem very shocked by the suggestion); certainly, he would make inquiries, but he could assure me ... On and on. I finally spared him any further effort by pleading a pressing engagement downtown.

I was now sure that in recent days I hadn't developed what Dr. Krafft-Ebing called 'paranoia': we were faced with some sort of a conspiracy, a deliberate effort to conceal the facts of these murders. And what reason could these distinguished gentlemen have for such an effort, I thought with mounting excitement, other than to protect themselves from scandal – the kind of scandal that would have arisen if the murderer were revealed to be one of their own?

Marcus agreed with my reasoning; and over the next couple of days we began playing devil's advocate in an effort to find flaws in the theory of a renegade priest. Nothing we could come up with, however, ruled out the core hypothesis. Perhaps it was unlikely, for example, that a priest would be an accomplished mountaineer, but it was not impossible; and as for his remark about a 'Red Injun,' that could have grown out of missionary experience in the West. The hunting skills might have presented

Caleb Carr

a problem, insofar as Lucius had already postulated that the man had spent a *lifetime* hunting – but our imagined priest could easily have developed the expertise in childhood. Priests, after all, are not born such. They have parents, families, and pasts like everyone else. And *that*, finally, meant that all of Kreizler's psychological speculations could be made to fit Marcus's and my picture as well as any other.

During the rest of the week Marcus and I looked for more details to support our work. A priest who possessed the kind of intimate knowledge of rooftops that our killer displayed would almost certainly be associated with mission work, we reasoned, and we therefore investigated those Catholic and Episcopal agencies that dealt with the poor. Much resistance was encountered, during this pursuit, and little hard information was gleaned. But our enthusiasm was not dampened; in fact, by Friday we were feeling so confident about our theory that we decided to explain it to Sara and Lucius. They expressed some appreciation for our efforts, but also insisted on highlighting little inconsistencies that Marcus and I had played down. What about the theory of a military background, Lucius asked. Where would a priest have gained such a capacity to treat danger so coolly? Perhaps, we answered, he had served as a chaplain in some part of the Army of the West. That would give us not only the military experience, but the Indian and frontier connections, as well. Sara queried how if our man had served many years on the frontier, had he found the time to become so intimately familiar with New York City? In childhood, we answered. If that were true, Sara continued, then we would have to accept that he did indeed come from a wealthy family, in order to explain his mountaineering and sporting expertise. All right, we said, – so he was wealthy. Then there was the fact that Catholics and Protestants were working together: Wouldn't either group, Sara asked, be just as happy if the other had a murderous priest on its hands? We couldn't answer that one with anything more effective than a claim that Sara and Lucius were merely jealous of our work.

Kreizler appeared at about five o'clock, but did not participate in the debate; instead, he pulled me rather urgently aside and told me that I was to accompany him immediately to the Grand

Central Depot. The fact that I hadn't had much contact with Laszlo for a number of days hadn't kept me from worrying about him, and this sudden, secretive announcement that we were going to board a train didn't ease my mind. I asked him if I needed to pack a bag, but he said no, that we were only taking a brief ride on the Hudson River Line for the purpose of conducting an interview at an institution that was not far upstate. He'd decided to schedule the meeting for the evening, he said, because most of the institution's senior staff would be gone, and we could come and go fairly unnoticed. That was all the detail he was prepared to provide, a fact that struck me at the time as very mysterious; knowing what I do now, however, it makes perfect sense, for had he told me exactly where we were bound and who we were scheduled to meet, I almost certainly would have refused to go.

It's less than an hour by train from the middle of Manhattan to the small town on the Hudson River named by an early Dutch trader for the Chinese city of Tsing-sing; but for visitors and prisoners alike, the trip to Sing Sing is usually divorced from real time, seeming at once the shortest and longest journey imaginable. Situated hard by the water and offering a commanding view of the Tappan Zee bluffs opposite, Sing Sing Prison (originally known as 'Mt. Pleasant') was opened in 1827 amid claims that it embodied the most advanced ideas in penology. And indeed, in those days when prisons were, in effect, small factories where inmates manufactured everything from combs to furniture to cut stone, prisoners did seem in many ways better off (or at least better occupied) than they were seventy years later. But prison manufacture died with the advent of organized labor, which would not tolerate wages being driven down by cheap convict workers; and for this reason more than any other, Sing Sing had degenerated, by 1896, into a horribly pointless place, where prisoners still wore their striped costumes, still obeyed the rule of silence, and still marched in lockstep, even though the jobs they'd once marched to had all but vanished.

Forbidding as the prospect of a visit to such a brutal, hopeless place was, it was overshadowed by the real apprehension I experienced when Kreizler finally told me who we were going to see.

With his black eyes fixed unwaveringly on mine he said, 'Jesse Pomeroy.'

At the mention of the name we both sat in silent apprehension, as if it alone might bring horror and mayhem into our near-empty train car; and when we spoke again, to review the case, it was in hushed tones. For while there'd been murderers more prolific than Jesse Pomeroy in our lifetimes, none was ever quite so unsettling. In 1872, Pomeroy had enticed a series of small children to remote spots near the small suburban village where he lived, then stripped and bound them and tortured them with knives and whips. He'd eventually been caught and locked up; but his behavior during incarceration was so exemplary that when his mother – long since abandoned by her husband – made an emotional appeal for parole just sixteen months after Jesse's sentence began, it was granted. Almost immediately after the release a new and even more horrifying crime occurred near the Pomeroy home: a four-year-old boy was found dead on a beach, his throat cut and the rest of his body terribly mutilated. Jesse was suspected, but evidence was lacking; several weeks later, however, the body of a missing ten-year-old girl was discovered in the basement of the Pomeroy house. The girl had also been tortured and mutilated. Jesse was arrested, and in the weeks that followed, every unsolved case in the vicinity that involved a missing child was reopened. None of them was ever tied directly to Pomeroy, but the case against him for the murder of the little girl was solid. Jesse's lawyers quite understandably decided to plead insanity for their client. The attempt, however, was doomed from the start. Pomeroy was originally condemned to hang, but the sentence was commuted to life in solitary confinement because of the villain's age:

Jesse Pomeroy, you see, had been but twelve years old at the start of his terrible career; and when he was shut away forever in a lonely prison cell – one that he still inhabits as I write these words – he was only fourteen.

Kreizler had crossed paths with what the press took to calling 'the boy-fiend' soon after Pomeroy's lawyers entered the plea of not guilty by reason of insanity in the summer of 1874. At the time, such pleas were judged, as they are today, according to the

'McNaghten Rule,' named after an unfortunate Englishman who, in 1843, fell under the delusion that Prime Minister Robert Peel wanted to kill him. McNaghten had tried to circumvent this fate by himself killing Peel; and though he failed to achieve that object, he did manage to murder the prime minister's secretary. He was subsequently acquitted, however, when his lawyers successfully argued that he did not understand the nature or wrongness of his act. In such manner were the floodgates of insanity opened onto the courtrooms of the world; and thirty years later, Jesse Pomeroy's defenders hired a battery of mental experts to assess their client and, hopefully, pronounce him as mad as McNaghten. One of these experts was a very young Dr. Laszlo Kreizler, who, along with several other alienists, found Pomeroy quite sane. The judge in the case ultimately agreed with this group, but he took special pains to say that he had found Dr. Kreizler's particular explanation of the boy-fiend's behavior arcane and quite possibly obscene.

Such a statement was not surprising, given Laszlo's heavy emphasis on Pomeroy's family life. But it was another part of Kreizler's twenty-year-old investigation, I suddenly realized as we neared Sing Sing, that was of particular significance with regard to our present purposes: Pomeroy had been born with a harelip, and during infancy had contracted a fever that left his face pockmarked and one of his eyes, even more portentously, ulcerated and lifeless. Even at the time it hadn't seemed coincidental that Pomeroy had taken special care to mutilate the eyes of his victims during his vicious outings; but at the time of his trial he'd always refused to discuss that aspect of his behavior and thus prevented any solid conclusions from being drawn.

'I don't understand, Kreizler,' I said, as our train lurched to a stop at the Sing Sing station. 'Why are we here?'

'You can thank Adolf Meyer,' Kreizler answered, as we stepped to the station platform and were approached by an old man in a moth-eaten cap who had a rig for hire. 'I was on the telephone with him for several hours today.'

'Dr. Meyer?' I asked. 'How much did you tell him?'

'Everything,' Kreizler answered simply. 'My trust in Meyer is absolute. Even though, in certain matters, he believes I'm off course. He quite agrees with Sara, for instance, about the role of a woman in the childhood formation of our killer. In fact, that was what brought Pomeroy to mind, along with the eyes.'

'The role of a woman?' We had gotten into the old man's rig and were rolling away from the station toward the prison. 'Kreizler, what do you mean?'

'Never mind, John,' he answered, looking out for the prison walls as the light around us began to diminish rapidly. 'You'll find out soon enough, and there are things you need to know before we go inside. First of all, the warden agreed to this visit only after I offered a fairly sizable bribe, and he will not greet us personally when we arrive. Only one other man, a guard called Lasky, knows who we are and what our purpose is. He will take the money and then guide us in and out, hopefully unnoticed. Say as little as possible, and nothing to Pomeroy.'

'Why not to Pomeroy? He's not an official of the prison.'

'True,' Laszlo answered, as the monotonous edifice of Sing Sing's thousand-cell main block appeared just ahead of us. 'But although I believe Jesse can help us with the question of the mutilations, he's entirely too perverse to do so if he knows what we're up to. So, for a variety of reasons, make no mention of your name or our work at any point. I hardly need remind you' – Kreizler lowered his voice as we reached the prison's front gate – 'how very many dangers inhabit this place.'

Chapter 23

Sing sing's main block ran parallel to the Hudson, with several outbuildings, shops, and the two-hundred-cell women's jail running perpendicular to it and toward the riverfront. A series of tall chimneys rose out of various buildings on the grounds and completed the image of a very dreary factory, one whose principal product, by that point in its history, was human misery. Convicts shared cells originally designed for individual prisoners, and the little maintenance work that was done in the place was not enough to counteract the powerful forces of decrepitude: the sights and smells of decay were everywhere. Even before we passed through the main gate, Kreizler and I could hear the monotonous sound of marching feet echoing out of the yard, and while this unhappy tramp was no longer punctuated by the crack of the cat – lashings had been outlawed in 1847 – the ominous wooden clubs worn by the guards left no doubt about the primary method of maintaining discipline in the place.

The guard Lasky, an enormous, ill-shaved man of appropriately black temperament, eventually appeared, and after following him through the stone pathways and patchy grass borders of the yard we entered the main cell block. In one corner near the door several prisoners wearing iron and wood yokes that held their arms up and away from their bodies were being angrily berated by a group of guards, whose dark uniforms were no more tidy than our man Lasky's and whose dispositions seemed, if anything, worse. As we entered the cell block proper, a sudden shout of pain shook Kreizler and me: inside one of the little four-by-eight-foot chambers more guards were going at one prisoner with a 'humming-bird,' an electrical device that administered painful shocks. Both Kreizler and I had seen all this before, but familiarity did not breed acceptance. As we kept moving, I glanced at Laszlo once and saw my own reaction reflected in his face: given such a penal system, the high rate of recidivism in our society was really no mystery at all.

Jesse Pomeroy was being held all the way at the other end of the block, making it necessary for us to walk past dozens more cells full of faces that displayed an enormous range of emotions, from the deepest anguish and sorrow to the most sullen rage. As the rule of silence was enforced at all times we heard no distinct human voices, only an occasional whisper; and the echo of our own steps throughout the cell block, combined with the unceasing scrutiny of the prisoners, soon became almost maddening. When we reached the end of the building we entered a small, dank hallway that led into a tiny room with no real windows, just small chinks in the stone walls near the ceiling. Jesse Pomeroy was sitting in a strange sort of wooden stall inside this room. The stall had water pipes coming out of its top, but its interior was, so far as I could tell, bone dry. After a few seconds of puzzling with it, I realized what the thing was: an infamous 'ice water bath,' in which particularly ill-behaved prisoners had formerly been doused with pressurized freezing water. The treatment had resulted in so many deaths from shock that it had been outlawed decades earlier. Apparently, though, no one had ever bothered to dismantle the contraption; no doubt the guards still found even the threat of such torment effective.

Pomeroy was wearing a heavy set of shackles on his wrists, and an iron 'collar cap' rested on his shoulders and surrounded his head. This latter device, a grotesque punishment for particularly unruly prisoners, was a two-foot-high barred cage, and its weight, equal to that of the prisoner's head, offered unending discomfort that drove many victims to the verge of madness. Despite both the shackles and the collar cap, however, Jesse had a book in his hand and was quietly reading. When he looked up at us I took careful note of the pocked skin of his face, the ugly disfigurement of his upper lip (which was barely covered by a stringy, weak mustache), and finally his milky, repulsive left eye. It was quite apparent why we'd come.

'Well!' he said quietly, getting to his feet. Even though Jesse was in his thirties and wearing the tall cage around his head, he was short enough to be able to stand inside the old stall. A smile came onto his ugly mouth, one that displayed the peculiar blend of suspicion, surprise, and satisfaction common to convicts who receive unexpected visitors. 'Dr. Kreizler, if I'm not very much mistaken.'

Kreizler managed a smile that seemed quite genuine. 'Jesse. It's been a long time, I'm surprised you remember me.'

'Oh, I remember you, all right,' Pomeroy answered, in a boyish tone that was nonetheless laced with threat. 'I remember all of you.' He studied Laszlo for another second, then turned suddenly to me. 'But I've never seen *you* before.'

'No,' Kreizler said, before I could answer. 'You haven't.' Laszlo turned to our guide, who was looking very put upon. 'All right, Lasky. You can wait outside.' Kreizler handed him a large wad of money.

Lasky's face achieved something like a pleased look, though he only said 'Yes, sir,' before turning to Pomeroy. 'You watch yourself, Jesse. Bad as you've had it today, it could still get worse.'

Pomeroy didn't acknowledge that statement, but kept on watching Kreizler as Lasky departed. 'Pretty hard to get an education in this place,' Jesse said, after the door had closed. 'But I'm trying. I figure maybe that's where I went wrong – no education. I taught myself Spanish, you know.' He continued to sound very much like the young man he'd been twenty years ago.

Laszlo nodded. 'Admirable. I see you're wearing a collar cap.'

Jesse laughed. 'Ahh – they *claim* I burned a guy's face with a cigarette while he was sleeping. They say I stayed up all night, making an arm out of wire just so's I could reach him with the butt through the bars. But I ask you—' He turned my way, the milky eye floating aimlessly in his head. 'Does that sound like

Caleb Carr

me?' A small laugh escaped him, pleased and mischievous – again just like a young boy's.

'I gather, then, that you've grown tired of skinning rats alive,' Kreizler said. 'When I was here several years ago, I heard that you'd been asking other prisoners to catch them for you.'

Still another chuckle, this one almost embarrassed. 'Rats. They do squirm and squeal. Bite you pretty good, too, if you're not careful.' He displayed several small but nasty scars on his hands.

Kreizler nodded. 'As angry as you were twenty years ago, eh, Jesse?'

'I wasn't angry twenty years ago,' Pomeroy answered, without losing his grin. 'I was *crazy*. You people were just too stupid to figure that out, is all. What the hell are you doing here, anyway, Doc?'

'Call it a reassessment,' Kreizler answered cagily. 'I sometimes like to drop in on old cases, to measure their progress. And since I had business in the prison, anyway—'

For the first time Pomeroy's voice became deadly serious. 'Don't play games with me, Doc. Even with these cuffs on I could have your eyes out before Lasky gets through that door.'

Kreizler's face lit up a bit at that, but his tone remained cool. 'I suppose you'd consider that another demonstration of your insanity?'

Jesse chuckled. 'Wouldn't you?'

'I didn't twenty years ago,' Kreizler answered with a shrug. 'You mutilated the eyes of both the children you killed, as well as those of several you tortured. But I saw no madness in it – it was quite understandable, actually.'

'Oh?' Pomeroy turned playful again. 'How's that?'

Kreizler paused a moment, then leaned forward. 'I've yet to see a man driven truly insane by simple envy, Jesse.'

Pomeroy's expression went blank, and he shot a hand toward his face so quickly that it banged against the bars of the collar cap painfully. Tightening both hands into fists he seemed on the verge of springing up, and I got ready for trouble; but then he just laughed it off. 'Let me tell you something, Doc – if you paid for that education of yours, you got took. You figger just because I got a bum eye I'd go around fixing people with two good ones?

Not likely. Look at me – I'm a *catalogue* of Mother Nature's mistakes. How come I never cut anybody's mouth up, or carved the skin off their faces?' It was Jesse's turn to lean closer. 'And if it's just envy, Doc, how come you ain't out chopping off people's arms?'

I turned quickly to Kreizler, and could see that he hadn't been ready for such a remark. But he'd long ago learned to control his reactions to anything a subject might say, and he only blinked once or twice without taking his eyes from Pomeroy. Jesse, however, was able to read into those blinks, and he sat back with a satisfied grin.

'Yeah, you're smart, all right,' he chuckled.

'Then the mutilation of the eyes meant nothing,' Kreizler said; and looking back I can see that he was maneuvering carefully. 'Simply random acts of violence.'

'Don't put words in my mouth, Doc.' Pomeroy's voice took on a warning edge again. 'We been through that, a long time ago. All I'm saying is I didn't have a sane reason to do it.'

Kreizler cocked his head judiciously. 'Perhaps. But, since you're unwilling to state what reason you did have, the argument is pointless.' Laszlo got up. 'And, as I've a train to catch back to New York—'

'*Sit down.*' The violence embodied in the command was almost palpable; but Kreizler nonetheless made a pointed show of being unimpressed. Pomeroy grew uneasy at that. 'I'll only tell you this once,' Jesse went on urgently. 'I was crazy then, but I ain't crazy anymore – which means that, when I think back to it now, I can see everything pretty clear. There wasn't any sane reason for me to do what I did to them kids. I just – it was just more than I could stand, that's all, and I had to stop it.'

Laszlo knew that he was close. As a further inducement he sat back down, and then spoke very softly. 'Had to stop what, Jesse?'

Pomeroy looked up at the small chink in the top of the blank stone wall, through which a few stars were now visible. 'The staring,' he mumbled, in an altogether new and detached tone of voice. 'The watching. All the time, the watching. That had to stop.' He turned our way again, and it seemed to me there were tears in his good eye; his mouth, however, had curled into a smile

Caleb Carr

again. 'You know, I used to go to the menagerie – in town? This was when I was real small. And it used to occur to me that everything those animals did, people were watching them. Just staring at them, with those dumb, blank faces, bug-eyed and hang-jawed – especially the kids, because they were too stupid to know any better. And those goddamn animals would look back, and you could see they was mad, God damn me, ferocious was the word, all right. All they wanted was to rip those people apart, just to get them to knock it off. Pacing back and forth, back and forth, thinking that if they could get out for just one minute they'd show 'em what you get when you never leave a thing alone. Well, I might not've been in a cage, Doc, but those dumb damned eyes was everywhere around me, all the same, ever since I could remember. Staring, watching, all the time, everywhere. You tell me, Doc, you tell me if that ain't enough to drive somebody crazy. And when I got big enough, and I'd see one of those dumb little bastards standing there, licking a piece of candy with his eyes popping out of his head – well, Doc, the fact is, I *wasn't* in no cage back then, so there wasn't nothing to stop me from doing what needed to be done.'

Pomeroy made no move after he'd stopped talking, but sat stone still and waited for a reaction from Kreizler.

'You say it was always that way, Jesse,' Laszlo said. 'For as long as you can remember? With everyone you knew?'

'Everyone but my dad,' Pomeroy answered, with a humorless, almost pitiable laugh. 'He must've got so tired of looking at me he ran off. Not that I know – I don't remember him at all. But it's what I figured, based on how my mama used to act.'

Again, Kreizler's face danced with anticipation for the briefest of instants. 'And how was that?'

'That was like – *this*!' In a flash Jesse was up and holding his caged head just a couple of feet away from Laszlo's face. I got to my feet, but Jesse made no further move forward. 'Tell your bodyguard he can set down, Doc,' he said, his good eye locked on Kreizler. 'I'm just giving you a demonstration. Always like this, was how it seemed to me. Every minute, watching me, what for I couldn't tell you. For my own good, she used to say, but she didn't act like it.' The collar cap was weighing heavy on Jesse's outstretched neck, and he finally turned away. 'Yeah, she sure took an interest in this old face of mine.' The dead laugh came back. 'Never wanted to kiss it, though, I can tell you!' Something seemed to strike him, and he paused quietly, again looking up at the chink in the wall. 'That first boy I went after, I made him kiss it. He didn't want to, but after I – well. He did it.'

Laszlo waited a few seconds before asking: 'And the man whose face you burned today?'

Jesse spat at the floor through the bars of the collar cap. 'That idiot – the same damned thing! Just couldn't keep his eyes to himself, I musta told him twenty goddamn times to—' Catching himself, Pomeroy suddenly spun on Kreizler, with real fear in his face; then the fear quickly vanished, and that lethal smile came back. 'Whup. Looks like I shot it to hell, didn't I? Fine piece of work, Doc.'

Laszlo stood up. 'It was none of my doing, Jesse.'

'Yeah,' Pomeroy laughed. 'Maybe you're right. As long as I live I'll never know how you get me to talking that way. If I had a hat, I'd tip it. But, since I don't—'

In one fast move Pomeroy bent over, grabbed a gleaming object out of one of his boots, and held it out toward us menacingly. Tightening his body he stood on his toes, ready to spring forward. I backed up instinctively against the wall behind me, and Kreizler did likewise, though more slowly. As a series of wet chortles came out of Pomeroy's mouth, I looked closer to see that his weapon was a long shard of thick glass, wrapped at one end with a bloodstained rag.

Chapter 24

More swiftly than most men could have managed it even without being shackled, Pomeroy kicked the stool he'd been sitting on across the room and jammed it under the knob of the door, preventing entry from the hall outside.

'Don't worry,' he said, still grinning. 'I got no desire to cut you two up – I just want to have a little fun with that big idiot outside!' He turned away from us, laughed again, and called out: 'Hey, Lasky! You ready to lose your job? When the warden sees what I done to these boys, he won't let you guard the shithouse!'

Lasky cursed in reply and began pounding on the door. Pomeroy kept the shard of glass leveled in the general direction of our throats but made no more threatening move, just laughed harder and harder as the guard's rage mounted. It wasn't long before the door began to loosen on its hinges, and soon after that the stool fell away from the knob. In a noisy burst Lasky hurtled into the room, the door crashing to the floor as he did. After struggling to his feet he saw first that Kreizler and I were all right and next that Pomeroy was armed. Grabbing the wooden stool from where it lay, Lasky went after Jesse, who made only a half hearted attempt to resist.

Throughout this encounter Kreizler displayed no apparent fear for our safety, but kept shaking his head slowly as if he knew exactly what was happening. Lasky soon had the shard of glass out of Pomeroy's hands, after which be began to pummel the prisoner mercilessly with his fat fists. The fact that he couldn't get at Jesse's face seemed only to outrage him further, and the shots that he landed to the prisoner's body became all the more savage. Yet even as Pomeroy cried out in pain, he continued to laugh – a wild kind of laughter, full of abandon and even, in some awful way, delight. I was utterly mystified and paralyzed; but Kreizler, after several minutes of this display, stepped forward and began to pull at Lasky's shoulders.

'Stop it!' he shouted to the guard. 'Lasky, for God's sake, stop, you fool!' He kept yanking and tugging, but the huge Lasky was oblivious to his efforts. 'Lasky! Stop, man, don't you see, you're doing what he wants! *He's enjoying it!*'

The guard continued to pound away, and finally Kreizler, himself consumed by what seemed a sort of desperation, used the full weight of his body to shove Lasky away from Pomeroy. Surprised and enraged, Lasky got to his feet and took a hefty swing at Kreizler's head, which Laszlo easily eluded. Seeing that the guard intended to keep coming after him, Kreizler balled his right hand into a fist and gave Lasky several quick shots that were vividly reminiscent of his very creditable stand against Roosevelt almost twenty years earlier. As Lasky reeled and fell back, Kreizler caught his breath and stood over him.

'It's got to stop, Lasky!' he declared, in a voice so passionate that it made me rush over and stand between him and the prostrate guard, in order to prevent my friend from continuing his attack. Pomeroy lay on the floor, writhing in agony, trying to clutch his ribs with his shackled hands and still laughing grotesquely. Kreizler turned to him, breathing hard, and softly repeated:

'It's got to stop.'

As Lasky's head cleared, his eyes focused on Kreizler. 'You son of a bitch!' He tried to get to his feet, but it was a struggle. 'Help,' he gasped, spitting a little blood onto the floor. 'Help! Guard in trouble!' His voice echoed out into the hall. 'The old shower room! Help me, dammit!'

I could hear running feet coming toward us from what sounded like the far end of the building. 'Laszlo, we've got to move,' I said quickly.

Caleb Carr

We passed four more guards in the cell block hallway, and I quickly told them that there'd been trouble between Lasky and Pomeroy and that the guard had been hurt. Seeing that Kreizler and I were uninjured, the guards sped on their way, while I forced Laszlo to make a dash past another group of uniformed men who stood in a confused huddle at the front gate. It didn't take long for the guards inside to learn the truth of the situation, and soon they were howling threats as they chased after us. Fortunately, the old man we'd hired was still outside the prison gate with his rig, and by the time the pursuing guards appeared we were several hundred yards away from the place, making for the train station and – in my case, at least – praying that we wouldn't have to wait long once we got there.

The first train to appear belonged to a small local line and was scheduled to make a dozen stops before it reached Grand Central; our predicament being what it was, however, we accepted the lengthy protraction of our trip and hopped on board. Kreizler and I went to the last of the train's cars and stood outside its rear door on the observation platform. Watching the walls and chimneys of Sing Sing disappear into the black woods of the Hudson Valley as we sped away, I produced a small flask of whiskey, from which we both took deep pulls. When at last we could no longer see any part of the prison, we began to breathe easily again.

'You've got one hell of a lot of explaining to do,' I said to Laszlo, as we stood in the warm rush of air that blew back from the engine of the train. My feeling of relief was so pronounced that I could not suppress a smile, though I was quite serious about wanting answers. 'You can start with why we came here.'

Kreizler took another pull from my flask, then studied it. 'This is a particularly barbaric blend, Moore,' he said, avoiding my demand for information. 'I'm a bit shocked.'

I drew myself up. '*Kreizler . . .*'

'Yes, yes, I know, John,' he replied, waving me to silence. 'You're entitled to some answers. But just where to begin?' Sighing once, Laszlo took another drink. 'As I told you before, I spoke to Meyer earlier today. I gave him a complete outline of our work to date. I then told him about my – my exchange of words with Sara.' Grunting once shamefacedly, Laszlo kicked at the railing of the deck. 'I really must apologize to her for that.'

'Yes,' I replied, 'you must. What did Meyer say?'

'That he found Sara's points concerning the role of a woman in the formation quite sound,' Kreizler answered, still a bit contrite. 'I suddenly found myself arguing with him as I'd argued with Sara.' Taking another pull from the flask, Kreizler grunted again and murmured, 'The fallacy, damn it all . . .'

'The what?' I asked, bewildered.

'Nothing,' Kreizler answered, with a shake of his head. 'It's of no importance now. What *is* important is that as I thought the whole issue over this afternoon I found that both Meyer and Sara were right – there was powerful evidence that a woman had played an ominous role in the formation of our killer. His obsessive furtiveness, the particular breed of sadism, all such factors pointed toward the sort of conclusions that Sara had outlined. As I say, I tried to argue with Meyer, just as I'd argued with Sara, but then he brought up Jesse Pomeroy, and used my own twenty-year-old words to contradict what I was now saying. Pomeroy, after all, never even knew his own father, nor did he ever, so far as I have been able to tell, suffer excessive physical punishment as a child. Yet his was – and is – a personality in many ways similar to that of the man we seek. As you know, Pomeroy was steadfast in his unwillingness to discuss his mutilative activities at the time of his capture. I could only hope that time and solitary confinement has loosened his resolve. We were lucky there.'

I nodded, thinking back to Pomeroy's statements. 'What he said about his mother, and other children, and the scrutiny he was always under – do you think that's really crucial?'

'I do, indeed,' Laszlo answered, his words starting to move at a characteristically quicker clip. 'And so is his pronounced emphasis on the unwillingness of the people who inhabited his world to touch him. Quite probably the only physical contact with others that he ever knew was taunting or tormenting in nature. And from there we can draw a direct line to his violence.'

'How so?'

'Well, Moore, I'll offer you yet another statement from

Professor James. It's a concept that he often brought up in class in the old days, and one which struck me like a thunderbolt the first time I read it in the *Principles*.' Laszlo turned to the sky and tried hard to remember the exact wording: '"If all cold things were wet and all wet things cold, if all hard things pricked our skin, and no other things did so; is it likely that we should discriminate between coldness and wetness, and hardness and pungency respectively?" As always, James wouldn't see this idea through to its logical conclusion, in the dynamic realm of behavior. He discussed only functions, such as taste and touch – but everything I have ever seen indicates that it works dynamically, as well. Imagine it, Moore. Imagine that you had – because of disfigurement, cruelty, or some other misfortune – never known any human touch that was not stern or even harsh. How should you feel about it?'

I shrugged and lit a cigarette. 'Rotten, I guess.'

'Perhaps. But in all likelihood you would *not* feel that it was extraordinary. Put it this way – if I say the word "mother" to you, your mind will immediately run through a set of unconscious but entirely familiar associations based on experience. So will mine. And both of our sets of associations will doubtless be a mixture of the good and the bad, as will almost any person's. But how many people will have a set of associations as uniformly negative as we know Jesse Pomeroy's to be? Indeed, in Jesse's case we can go beyond the limited concept of mother to the notion of humanity generally. Say the word "people" to him and his mind leaps only to images of humiliation and pain, as routinely as if I were to say "train" to you and you were to answer "movement."'

'Is that what you meant when you told Lasky that Pomeroy was enjoying the beating he was getting?'

'It was. You may have noticed that Jesse deliberately constructed that entire event. It's not hard to see why. Throughout his childhood he was surrounded by tormentors, and for the last twenty years virtually the only people he's come into contact with have been men like Lasky. His experiences, both in prison and out, cause him to believe that interaction with his own species can only be adversarial and violent – he even compares himself empathetically to an animal in a menagerie. Such is his reality. All he can do is attempt to manipulate the participants into their actions as he once manipulated the children he tortured and killed. It's the only kind of power or satisfaction – the only method of ensuring his psychic survival – he's ever known, and he therefore employs it.'

As I smoked and struggled with this idea, I began to pace the deck. 'But isn't there something – well, something inside of him, inside of any person that would object to that kind of a situation? I mean, wouldn't there be sadness or despair, even about his own *mother*? The *desire* to be loved, at least? Isn't every child born with—'

'Be careful, Moore,' Kreizler warned as he lit a cigarette of his own. 'You're about to suggest that we're born with specific *a priori* concepts of need and desire – an understandable thought, perhaps, were there any evidence to support it. The organism knows one drive from the beginning – survival. And yes, for most of us, that drive is somehow intimately bound up with the notion of a mother. But were our experiences terribly different – if the concept of mother suggested frustration and finally danger, rather than sustenance and nurturing – the instinct for survival would cause us to structure our outlook differently. Jesse Pomeroy experienced this. I now believe *our* killer did, too.' Laszlo drew heavily on his cigarette. 'I can now thank Pomeroy, for that. Meyer, as well. But most of all, I must thank Sara. And I intend to do so.'

Kreizler was true to that declaration. At one of the small towns we passed through on our way back to Grand Central he asked the station attendant if it would be possible to send what he assured the man was an urgent wire ahead to New York. The attendant agreed and Kreizler wrote out the message, which ordered Sara to meet us at Delmonico's at eleven o'clock. Laszlo and I had no time to change for dinner once we reached the city, but Charlie Delmonico had seen us in far worse shape in our time, and when we arrived at Madison Square he made us feel as welcome as ever.

Sara was waiting at a table in the main dining room, one that looked out onto the park across Fifth Avenue and was as far from

Caleb Carr

the other parties in the restaurant as possible. She expressed both concern for our safety – the wire had made her anxious – and then, once she saw that we were unharmed, great curiosity about our trip. Her manner with Kreizler, even before he offered her the promised set of apologies, was quite pleasant, and therefore odd: I wouldn't say that Sara was the sort of person to hold a grudge, exactly, but once stung she was usually very wary of the guilty party. I tried hard, however, to ignore the strange chemistry between them, and kept my attention on the business before us.

Sara said that given what we'd learned from the Pomeroy visit we could now safely assume that our man was, like Jesse, extremely sensitive about his physical appearance. Such sensitivity, she said, more than explained the profundity of the anger toward children. Kreizler also tended toward the theory that our man was in some way physically deformed. I, however, having several weeks earlier been the first to advance such a theory, now warned both of them to be very careful about accepting it. We already knew that the man we were pursuing stood over six feet tall and could get up and down the sides of buildings by way of a simple rope while carrying an adolescent boy: if he was deformed, it could not be in his arms or his legs, or anywhere, really, save his face – and that would narrow our search down quite a bit. Kreizler said that, given this consideration, he was prepared to narrow things down still further by declaring that it was the killer's eyes that were the location of his deformity. The man was concentrating on his victims' ocular organs more carefully and consistently than even Pomeroy had done, a fact that Kreizler considered more than significant: it was, he said, decisive.

Throughout our meal Kreizler encouraged Sara to at last fully explain what sort of a woman she thought might have played the kind of sinister role in our killer's life that she'd postulated a week earlier. Jumping right in, Sara said she believed that only a mother could have had the kind of profound impact that was evident in this case. An abusive governess or female relative might be harrowing for a child, but if that child had recourse to his natural mother for protection and consolation the effect would have been dramatically reduced. It was apparent to Sara that the man we were after had never known such recourse, a circumstance that could be explained in a number of ways; but Sara's preferred theory was that the woman had not wished to bear children in the first place. She'd only done so, Sara speculated, because she'd either become pregnant or had been offered no other socially acceptable role to play by the particular world in which she lived. The end result of all this was that the woman had deeply resented the children she did bear, and for this reason Sara thought there was an excellent chance that the killer was either an only child or had very few siblings. Any physical deformity in one of the children she did have would, of course, have heightened the mother's already negative feelings toward that child, but Sara did not believe that deformity alone was enough to explain such a relationship. Kreizler agreed with her on this point, saying that while Jesse Pomeroy attributed all his difficulties with his mother to his appearance, there were certainly additional and deeper factors involved as well.

One conclusion was becoming increasingly clear from all this: it was unlikely that we were dealing with people who enjoyed the advantages of wealth. In the first place, wealthy parents are seldom obliged to cope with their children if they find them troublesome or undesirable. Then, too, a young woman of means in the 1860s could have devoted her life to pursuits other than motherhood, though such a choice would admittedly have prompted more criticism and comment at that time than it would have some thirty years later. Of course, an accidental pregnancy could happen to anyone, rich or poor; but the extreme sexual and scatological fixations displayed by our killer had suggested to Sara close scrutiny and frequent humiliation, and these in turn spoke of a life lived at very close quarters – the kind of life that poverty breeds.

Kreizler produced his small notebook and reminded us that there were just five short days till the Feast of the Ascension, the next significant date on the Christian calendar. It was now time, he said, for our investigation to dispense with an attitude of pure research and analysis and move toward a posture of engagement. We had gained a good general idea of what our killer looked like, as well as how, where, and when he would strike. We were ready at last to try to anticipate and prevent that next move. I felt a sudden flood of anxiety in the pit of my very full stomach at that statement, and Sara looked to be experiencing much the same sort of reaction. But we both knew that this development was inevitable; was, indeed, what we'd been actively working toward since the beginning. And so we stiffened our resolve as we left the restaurant and gave no voice to any sort of apprehension.

Once outside I felt a very meaningful tug on my arm from Sara. I turned to find her looking away from me, but in a way that clearly indicated that she wanted to talk. When Kreizler offered to share a hansom with her as far as Gramercy Park she declined, and as soon as he was gone she ushered me into Madison Square Park and under a gas lamp.

'Well?' I said, noticing that her aspect had become somewhat agitated. 'This had better be important, Sara. It's been a hell of an evening, and I'm—'

'It *is* important,' Sara answered quickly, producing a folded sheet of paper from her bag. 'That is, I *think* it is.' Her brows came together and she seemed to be weighing something carefully before showing me the paper. 'John, how much do you actually know about Dr. Kreizler's past? His family, I mean.'

I was surprised by the topic. 'His family? As much as anyone, I suppose. I visited them quite a bit when I was a boy.'

'Were they – were they, well, happy?'

I shrugged. 'Always seemed to be. With good reason, too. His parents were about the most socially sought-after couple in town. You wouldn't know it to see them now, of course. Laszlo's father had a stroke a couple of years ago, and they stay pretty shut up. They have a house on Fourteenth Street and Fifth Avenue.'

'Yes,' Sara said quickly, surprising me again. 'I know.'

'Well,' I went on, 'back then they were always throwing big parties and introducing luminaries from all over Europe into New York society. It was quite a scene – we all loved going there. But why do you ask, Sara? What's this all about?'

She paused, sighed, and then held the piece of paper out to me. 'I've been trying all week to understand why he was sticking so stubbornly to the idea that a violent father and passive mother raised our killer. I developed a theory, and went through the records of the Fifteenth Precinct to test it. This is what I found.'

The document was a report filed by one Roundsman O'Bannion, who, on a September night in 1862 – when Laszlo was a boy of only six – had investigated a domestic disturbance at the Kreizler home. The yellowing report contained just a few details: it spoke of Laszlo's father, apparently drunk, spending the night in the precinct house under a charge of assault (the charge was later dropped), and then of a local surgeon being brought to the Kreizler home to treat a young boy whose left arm had been badly shattered.

Conclusions weren't hard to draw; given my lifelong acquaintance with Laszlo, however, as well as the image I'd always had of his family, my mind resisted them. 'But,' I said, refolding the document absentmindedly, 'but we were told that he fell . . .'

Sara let out a deep breath. 'Apparently not.'

During a long pause I looked around at the park, somewhat stunned. Familiar conceptions die hard, and their passage can be damned disorienting; for a few moments the trees and buildings of Madison Square looked strangely different. Then an image of Laszlo as a boy suddenly flashed through my head, followed by another of his big, outwardly gregarious father and his vivacious mother. As I saw these faces and forms I simultaneously remembered the comment that Jesse Pomeroy had made during our visit to Sing Sing about chopping off people's arms; and from there my mind leapt to a seemingly meaningless remark that Laszlo himself had made on the train ride home:

'"The fallacy, damn it all,"' I whispered.

'What did you say, John?' Sara asked quietly.

I shook my head hard, trying to clear it. 'Something Kreizler mentioned tonight. About how much time he's wasted in the last few days. He spoke of "the fallacy," but I didn't get the reference. Now, though . . .'

Sara gasped a little as she, too realized the answer. 'The psychologist's fallacy,' she said. 'In James's *Principles*.'

I nodded. 'The business about a psychologist getting his own point of view mixed up with his subject's. That's what's had him in its grip.' A few more silent moments passed, and then I looked down at the report, feeling a sudden sense of practical urgency that made me put off the nearly impossible task of absorbing the full implications of the document. 'Sara,' I said. 'Have you discussed this with anyone else?' She shook her head slowly. 'And do they know at headquarters that you took the report?' Another shake of the head. 'But you've realized what it suggests?' She nodded this time and I reciprocated; then, slowly and deliberately, I tore the report into pieces, and set them on a patch of grass.

Pulling a box of matches from my pocket and striking one, I started to light the bits of paper, saying firmly, 'No one is to know anything about this. Your own curiosity's been satisfied, and if his behavior becomes erratic again, we'll know why. But beyond that, no good can ever come of its getting out. Do you agree?'

Sara crouched by me and nodded once more. 'I'd already decided the same thing.'

We watched the burning pieces of paper turn into flakes of smoking ash, both of us silently hoping that this would be the last we'd ever need to speak of the matter, that Laszlo's behavior would never again warrant investigation into his past. But as it turned out, the unhappy tale so sketchily referred to in the now-incinerated report did surface again at a later point in our investigation, to cause a very real – indeed an almost fatal – crisis.

Chapter 25

The idea of placing New York's chief boy-pandering venues under careful scrutiny on those days when we thought our killer might strike originated with Lucius Isaacson. There was no denying that it would be a delicate piece of work. Every one of those bars and brothels could expect to lose a significant number of patrons if it became known that they were being watched. Cooperation from the proprietors was therefore highly unlikely: we'd have to position ourselves so as to elude both their notice and our killer's. Lucius readily admitted that he didn't have enough experience with such operations to chart a prudent course, so we summoned the one member of our band who we thought could provide expert advice: Stevie Taggert. Stevie had spent a good part of his criminal career robbing houses and flats, and the ways of surreptitious surveillance were known to him. I think the young man suspected he was in some kind of trouble when he walked into our headquarters that Saturday afternoon and found the rest of us seated in a semicircle and staring at him eagerly. And since Kreizler had often told Stevie that he should try to forget his criminal ways, it was doubly difficult to convince the suspicious boy to talk about such things. Once satisfied that we really did need his help, however, Stevie pursued the conversation with what seemed real enjoyment.

We had originally thought to place one member of our team outside each of the houses most likely to be visited: Paresis Hall, the Golden Rule, Shang Draper's in the Tenderloin, the Slide on Bleecker Street, and Frank Stephenson's Black and Tan, also on Bleecker, a dive that offered white women and children to black and Oriental men. But this plan, Stevie assured us as he chewed noisily on a thick piece of licorice, was badly flawed. First of all, we knew that the killer was traveling via rooftops: We would be more assured of success, and less likely to raise suspicions, if we attempted to intercept him on one of those high arenas. Furthermore, even discounting the quite physical opposition that we might run into from the house managers in the course of our efforts, there was the fact that the man we were hoping to catch was large and powerful: he could easily turn the tables and get the drop on *us*, given his familiarity with rooftop navigation. Stevie recommended placing two operatives at each site, which meant that we would not only have to enlist three more participants (Cyrus, Roosevelt, and Stevie himself eventually filled out the list) but also eliminate one location. According to Stevie, this last problem was easily solved; he found it extremely unlikely that our killer would venture into the Tenderloin, a noisy, crowded, brightly lit area that offered too many chances of being seen or apprehended. Nonchalantly taking a cigarette from a box on my desk and lighting it, Stevie said that we could therefore dispense with Shang Draper's; and as he blew little rings of smoke, he went on to recommend that we gain access to the various rooftops involved by entering adjacent buildings under false pretenses. This would help to ensure that things seemed thoroughly natural to the killer when and if he showed up. Kreizler nodded in agreement, then plucked Stevie's cigarette out of his mouth and crushed it on the floor. Disappointed, the boy went back to his licorice.

When to begin and end our surveillance was the next issue addressed. Would the murderer visit the chosen disorderly house on the eve of Ascension Day, and actually kill his victim during the small hours of the feast itself, or would he wait until the next night? His pattern suggested the latter, and so it was decided that we would position ourselves on Thursday night.

With the plan complete I grabbed my jacket and headed for the door. Marcus inquired as to my destination and I told him I was going down to the Golden Rule to see the boy Joseph and provide him with details of the killer's appearance and method.

'Is that wise?' Lucius asked in a worried tone, as he stacked some papers on his desk. 'We're only five days away from putting this plan in motion, John. We don't want to do anything that would complicate matters by changing the normal routines of those places.'

Sara looked puzzled. 'Surely there's nothing wrong with giving the boys every chance to avoid danger.'

'Of course,' Lucius answered quickly. 'I'm not suggesting we put anybody in any more danger than we can avoid. It's just that – well, we've got to set this trap carefully.'

'As always, the detective sergeant has a point,' Kreizler said, taking my arm and walking to the door with me. 'Be careful how much you tell your young friend, Moore.'

After walking to the Golden Rule I arranged to meet Joseph in a small billiard parlor around the corner. When he arrived I noticed that his face was quite rosy after being scrubbed free of the usual paint, a fact that touched me. I remembered that our first interaction had involved a similar cleaning of Joseph's face; and I was struck by the thought that he hadn't wanted me to see him all made up this time, either. Indeed, his entire manner did not seem that of a boy-whore, when he was dealing with me, but rather that of a young man who desperately needed an older male friend; or was *I* now suffering from Professor James's famous fallacy, and allowing the way in which Joseph reminded me of my brother to influence my reading of the boy's behavior.

Joseph ordered himself a short beer in a manner that suggested he'd done so many times before (and which ruled out my presuming to lecture him about the perils of alcohol). As we started to knock some ivory balls around a table casually, I told Joseph I had some new information about the man who'd killed Ali ibn-Ghazi, and I asked him to pay very close attention, so that he'd be able to pass the news on to his friends. Then I launched into a physical description:

The man was tall, I said, about six-foot-two, and very strong. He was capable of lifting a boy like Joseph, or someone even larger, without difficulty. Yet despite his size and strength, there

Caleb Carr

was something wrong with him, something that he was very sensitive about. It was probably some part of his face; maybe his eyes. They might be injured, scarred, deformed in some way. Whatever the problem, he didn't like it when people mentioned it or looked at it. Joseph said that he'd never noticed such a man, but that a lot of the Golden Rule's customers hid their faces when they came in. I told him to watch for it in future, and went on to the subject of what the man might wear. Nothing fancy, I said, because he didn't want to attract attention to himself. Also, he probably didn't have much money, which meant that he couldn't afford expensive clothes. It was likely, as Marcus had told Joseph during our last visit, that he would be carrying a large bag; inside the bag were tools he used to climb up and down walls, in order to reach the rooms of the boys he was after without being detected.

Then came the hard part: I told Joseph that the man was especially careful about not being seen because he'd been in all the houses like the Golden Rule before and might be very easy for some (maybe most) of the boys to identify. He might even be someone they knew and trusted, someone who'd helped them out, who'd tried to show them how to make new lives for themselves. A settlement or charity worker, perhaps – maybe even a priest. The main thing was that he didn't look or sound like someone who could do the things he'd been doing.

Joseph kept track of all these details by ticking them off on his fingers, and when I'd finished he nodded and said, 'Okay, okay, I've got it. But do you mind if I ask you something, Mr. Moore?'

'Fire away,' I answered.

'Well, then – how is it you know all these things about the guy, anyway?'

'Sometimes,' I said with a small laugh, 'I'm a little confused about that, myself. Why?'

Joseph smiled, but also began to kick his legs nervously. 'It's only because – well, a lot of my friends, they didn't believe me when I told them what you said last time. They didn't see how anybody could know. Thought maybe I was making it up. And then, a lot of people are going around saying it isn't even a person that's doing it. Some kind of – ghost, or something. That's what some people say.'

'Yes, I've heard. But you'll be doing yourself a favor if you ignore that kind of talk. There's a man behind it, all right. I can guarantee that, Joseph.' I rubbed my hands together. 'Now, then – how about a game?'

Over the years I've heard people say that the game of billiards (three-cushion, pocket, or what have you) is nothing more or less than a fast way for a young man to go to the devil. But the way I saw it, a career as a professional gambler – that nightmare of so many mothers and fathers in this city – would've been nothing but a step up for this boy; and so for the next hour or so I taught him most of the tricks of the table that I knew. It was a pleasant time, jarred only by the occasional recollection of where Joseph would be heading when we parted company. There was nothing, however, for me to do about that: such boys were their own men.

It was nearly dark by the time I got back to our headquarters, which was still alive with activity. Sara was on the telephone with Roosevelt, attempting to explain that there was no one else we could trust to fill the eighth surveillance spot on Thursday night and that he would therefore have to come along. Normally, Theodore would have required no urging; but recently his troubles at Mulberry Street had multiplied. Two of the men who sat on the Board of Commissioners with him, along with the chief of police, had decided to side with Boss Platt and the antireform forces. Roosevelt was being scrutinized more closely than ever by his enemies, in the hope that he would commit some indiscretion that would justify his dismissal. He did agree to be part of the surveillance effort, ultimately; but he had real misgivings.

Kreizler and the Isaacsons, meanwhile, were engaged in another spirited discussion of our killer's timing. Lucius had postulated that the one inconsistency in the man's schedule – the killing of Georgio Santorelli on March 3rd – could be accounted for by the deceptively mundane phrase 'I decided to wait' in the note to Mrs. Santorelli. It was distinctly possible, the younger Isaacson elaborated, that the sighting and selection of a victim were as crucial in their own way to the murderer's psychic satisfaction as the act of killing itself. Kreizler quite approved of this theory, and added that so long as the man experienced no interference with his intended goal – to murder the boy – he might even derive sadistic pleasure from the delay. This meant that the Santorelli killing could be made to fit the overall timing pattern, because the critical mental event had occurred on Ash Wednesday.

Laszlo and the Isaacsons parted company, however, over the question of whether the man struck on some holidays but not others because he was only angered by certain religious stories and events. Marcus and Lucius protested that there had to be *some* reason why only certain holidays were selected, and Kreizler did agree; but he said that we simply hadn't found the contextual key to that particular part of the puzzle yet.

There being no guarantee that our Ascension Day surveillance plan would produce any results, we all pursued alternate lines of inquiry during the days leading up to it. Marcus and I kept diligently after our priest theory, while Kreizler, Lucius, and Sara engaged in a new and promising activity: canvassing asylums throughout our own and various other parts of the country, by cable and in person, to see if any of them had treated a patient who matched our emerging portrait within the last fifteen years. Despite his firm conviction that our killer was sane, Kreizler hoped that the man's idiosyncrasies had caused his commitment at some earlier point in his life, and checking the asylums seemed a prudent investment of time and energy.

On Ascension Eve we apportioned our responsibilities for the next night: Marcus and Sara, the latter carrying both her firearms, would take up watch on the roof of the Golden Rule; Kreizler and Roosevelt would man Paresis Hall, where Theodore's authority would be sufficient to keep Biff Ellison in line if there was trouble; Lucius and Cyrus would cover the Black and Tan, Cyrus's color offering a convenient explanation for their presence should such prove necessary; and Stevie and I would be just down Bleecker Street, atop the Slide. Positioned outside each of these houses would be several street arabs of Stevie's acquaintance, who, without being told any details of the operation, could be dispatched to bring assistance from the other locations in the event something did happen at any one of them. Roosevelt thought that this task might be better served by policemen, but Kreizler vehemently opposed such an idea. Privately, Laszlo told me he suspected that any contact between officers of the law and the killer would result in the latter's quick death, Theodore's prohibitive orders notwithstanding. We had now experienced enough mysterious interference to know that there were forces far more powerful than Roosevelt at work, and those forces unquestionably had as their goal the complete suppression of the case. It was obvious that such a result could best be achieved through a quick dispatch of the apprehended suspect.

As it turned out, all our anxious anticipation of what might happen on Ascension Day was in vain, for the night passed without incident. We took up our various surveillance positions and spent the long, slow hours until six A.M. battling no greater enemy than boredom. As a result, the days that followed were full of more useless arguments over why the killer should have elected to strike on Good Friday but not on Ascension Day. There was a growing feeling, voiced first by Sara, that the coincidence of the holidays and the murders might be nothing more than that; but Marcus and I remained firmly committed to the idea that our killer's calendar and that of the Christian faith were somehow connected, since this theory only helped our hypothesis about a rogue or defrocked priest being the killer. We urged that our interceptive sights be set on the next significant holiday – Pentecost, just eleven days after the Feast of the Ascension – and that we try to use the intervening time as productively as possible. Sad to say, though, Marcus and I ran into a brick wall with our priest research; and it began to seem that our entire theory might not be very much more than a well-reasoned waste of time.

Our teammates, on the other hand, did achieve some progress during the week before Pentecost: answers to the cables and letters that Sara, Lucius, and Kreizler had sent out to almost every reputable asylum in the country began to trickle in. Most of these were firmly negative, but a few offered hope, reporting that a man or men of the general physical stature that Kreizler had described, and characterized by at least some of the mental symptoms he'd noted, had been committed within their walls at some point during the past fifteen years. A few institutions even sent copies of case files along; and while none of these ultimately proved of any value, a brief note postmarked Washington, D.C., did create quite a stir one afternoon.

On that day I happened to be watching as Lucius strolled through the room, carrying a batch of the asylum letters and case files. He caught sight of something, then suddenly spun on his heels, dropped the pile of papers, and stared at Kreizler's desk. His eyes went quite wide for a moment, and his forehead almost instantly began to perspire; but as he took out a handkerchief and began to mop the sweat away, his voice remained steady.

'Doctor—' he said to Laszlo, who was standing by the door talking with Sara. 'This note from the superintendent of St. Elizabeth's – have you looked at it?'

'Only once,' Kreizler answered, crossing over to where Lucius stood. 'It didn't seem to offer very much.'

'Yes, that was what I thought.' Lucius picked up the letter. 'The descriptions awfully vague – the reference to "some sort of facial tic," for instance, might cover a lot of ground.'

Kreizler studied Lucius, '*But*, Detective Sergeant . . .?'

'But—' Lucius grappled with his thought. 'Well, it's the postmark, Doctor: Washington. St. Elizabeth's is the federal government's principal asylum for the insane, isn't it?'

Kreizler paused for a moment and then his black eyes jumped in their quick, electric way. 'That's right,' he said, quietly yet urgently. 'But since they never mentioned the man's background, I didn't—' He knocked a fist against his forehead. 'Fool!'

Laszlo made a dash for the telephone, and Lucius followed. 'Given the legal situation in the capital,' Lucius said, 'it would hardly represent an unusual case.'

'You've a mastery of understatement, Detective Sergeant,' Kreizler said. 'There are several such cases, every *year*, in the capital!'

Sara was walking toward them, drawn by the excitement. 'Lucius? What is it, what's struck you?'

'The postmark,' Lucius said again, slapping at the letter. 'There's a very troublesome little codicil to the Washington laws that deal with insanity and the involuntary commitment of patients to asylums. If the patient hasn't actually been adjudicated insane in the District of Columbia but is confined to a Washington institution, he can apply for a writ of *habeas corpus* – and he stands an almost one hundred percent chance of being released.'

'Why's that so troublesome?' I asked.

'Because,' Lucius said, as Kreizler attempted to get a telephone line through to Washington, 'so many mental patients in that city, especially at St. Elizabeth's, have been sent there from other parts of the country.'

'Oh?' Now it was Marcus's turn to draw near. 'Why's that?'

Lucius took a deep breath, his own excitement mounting. 'Because St. Elizabeth's is the receiving hospital for soldiers and sailors who've been judged unfit for military duty. Unfit – because of mental illness.'

The slow, drifting way in which Sara, Marcus, and I had been approaching Lucius and Kreizler now became something of a stampede. 'It didn't occur to us at first,' Lucius explained, shying away from our advance, 'because there's no mention of the man's background in the letter. Only descriptions of his appearance and his symptoms – delusions of persecution and persistent cruelty. But if he did, in fact, see military service and was sent to St. Elizabeth's – well, there's a chance, a slim but real chance that it's—' Lucius paused, seemingly afraid to say the word: 'him.'

The idea seemed a sound one; but our mood of hopefulness was fairly well dashed by Kreizler's 'phone call. After being kept waiting for quite a while, he did finally manage to get the superintendent of St. Elizabeth's on the line, but the man treated Laszlo's request for further information with the utmost contempt. Apparently, he knew all about the notorious Dr. Kreizler and felt the way many asylum superintendents did about my friend. Kreizler asked if there wasn't some other member of the hospital staff who could look into the matter, to which the superintendent replied that his staff were severely overworked and had already lent 'extraordinary' assistance in this matter. If Kreizler wanted to rummage through the hospital's records, he could damned well come down to Washington and do so himself.

The difficulty was that Kreizler couldn't just drop everything

Caleb Carr

and shoot off to the capital – none of us could, for we were just a couple of days away from Pentecost. There was nothing to do but put the trip to Washington at the top of the list of things to be attended to after our next all-night vigil, then swallow our excitement and patiently focus on the immediate job to be done. Given the poor results that had attended our Ascension Day efforts, however, I couldn't help feeling that such focus was going to prove somewhat difficult to achieve.

Nonetheless, when Pentecost Sunday arrived we all returned to our various nocturnal aeries and waited again for the appearance of our killer. I cannot say what the mood on the other three rooftops was; but for Stevie and myself, up above the Slide, boredom struck early. It being Sunday night fairly little noise echoed up from Bleecker Street, while the occasional grunt and hiss of the Sixth Avenue Elevated nearby evolved in quality from monotonous to somewhat lulling. Before long it was all I could do to stay awake.

At about twelve-thirty I glanced over to see Stevie quietly laying out a deck of cards in thirteen piles on the tar in front of him. 'Solitaire?' I whispered.

'Jewish faro,' he answered, giving the criminal class's name for the game of stuss, a particularly shady and complicated method of bilking suckers that I'd never been able to comprehend. Seeing a chance to fill this void in my gambling education, I crept over to sit by Stevie, and he quietly tried for the better part of an hour to explain the game to me. I absorbed none of it; and finally, frustrated as well as bored, I stood up and looked out at the city around us.

'This is useless,' I decided quietly. 'He's never going to show up.' I turned to look across Cornelia Street. 'I wonder how the others are doing.'

The building that housed the Black and Tan – where Cyrus and Lucius had been posted – was just across the way, and looking beyond its cornice I could see the back of Lucius's balding pate reflected in the moonlight. I laughed quietly and called it to Stevie's attention.

'He oughtta wear a hat,' Stevie laughed. 'If we can see it, so can other people.'

'True,' I answered; and then, as the balding head moved to another spot on the roof and finally disappeared, my face screwed up in puzzlement. 'Has Lucius *grown* since we started this investigation?'

'Must've been standing on the dividing wall,' Stevie answered, going back to his cards.

In such innocuous ways are disasters presaged. It was another fifteen minutes before a series of urgent shouts that I recognized to be Lucius's started to blare across Cornelia Street; and when I looked over, the urgency and fear in the detective sergeant's face were enough to make me immediately grab Stevie by the collar and head for the staircase. It was apparent even to my tired, bored brain that we'd had our first contact with the killer.

Chapter 26

Once on the sidewalk, Stevie and I dispatched our waiting contingent of street arabs to fetch Kreizler, Roosevelt, Sara, and Marcus, then sped across Cornelia Street to the Black and Tan. Making straight for the front door, we ran headlong into Frank Stephenson, who had been drawn out of his infamous brothel by Lucius's shouts for assistance. Like most men of his profession, Stephenson employed plenty of muscle, and several of these thugs were standing on the stoop with him, blocking our entrance. I was in no mood, however, to go through the usual game of threat and counterthreat with them: I simply said that we were on police business, that there was a police officer on the roof, and that the president of the Board of Police Commissioners would be arriving soon. That litany was enough to get Stephenson and his boys out of the way, and in seconds Stevie and I were on the roof.

We found Lucius crouching over Cyrus, who had suffered a nasty blow to the skull. A small pool of blood glittered on the tar beneath Cyrus's head, while his half-open eyes were rolled frightfully up into their sockets and his mouth was producing strained wheezing sounds. Ever cautious, Lucius had brought some gauze bandages along with him, and was now carefully wrapping them around the top of Cyrus's head, in an effort to stabilize what was at the very least a bad concussion.

'It's my fault,' Lucius said, before Stevie and I had even asked any questions. Despite his firm concentration on what he was doing, there was deep remorse in Lucius's voice. 'I was having trouble staying awake, and went for coffee. I forgot that it was Sunday – it took longer to find some than I'd anticipated. I must've been gone for more than fifteen minutes.'

'Fifteen minutes?' I said, running to the back of the roof. 'Could that have been enough time?' Looking down into the rear alleyway, I saw no signs of activity.

'I don't know,' Lucius answered. 'We'll have to see what Marcus thinks.'

Marcus and Sara arrived a few minutes later, followed soon by Kreizler and Theodore. Pausing just long enough to check on Cyrus's condition, Marcus produced a magnification lens and a small lantern, then quickly began searching various parts of the rooftop. Explaining that fifteen minutes would indeed have been enough time for a capable climber to get down and up the side of the building, Marcus kept rummaging around until he found some rope fibers that might or might not have been evidence of our killer's presence. The only way to be sure was to find out from Frank Stephenson if any of his 'workers' were missing. Backed up by Theodore, Marcus headed downstairs, while the rest of us stood around Lucius and Kreizler, who were both now at work on Cyrus's head. Kreizler sent Stevie to tell the street arabs to fetch an ambulance from nearby St. Vincent's Hospital, although there was some question as to whether it was safe to move a man in Cyrus's condition. After bringing him round with ammonia salts, however, Kreizler was able to learn that Cyrus still had feeling and movement in all his limbs, and Laszlo therefore felt certain that the bumpy ride up Seventh Avenue to the hospital, while uncomfortable, would do no further damage.

Kreizler's concern for Cyrus's safety was pronounced; before letting him slip back into semiconsciousness, however, Laszlo wafted more of the ammonia salts under his nose and urgently asked if he'd been able to see who'd struck him. Cyrus only shook his head and moaned pitiably, at which Lucius said that it was useless for Kreizler to press the issue: the wound on Cyrus's head indicated that he'd been struck from behind, and had therefore probably never realized what was happening.

Caleb Carr

It took another half an hour for the ambulance from St. Vincent's to arrive, enough time for us to learn that, in fact, a fourteen-year-old boy from the Black and Tan was not in his assigned room. The details were of a sort that was by now grimly familiar to all of us: the missing youth was a recently arrived German immigrant named Ernst Lohmann, who had not been seen leaving the premises and who had been working out of a chamber that had a window which opened onto the rear alley. According to Stephenson, the boy had requested the room especially that day; so in all likelihood the killer had planned the exodus in advance with his unwitting victim, though how long ago – hours or days – it was impossible to say. I'd told Marcus before he went downstairs that the Black and Tan was not particularly known for offering male whores who dressed up like women, and he'd questioned Stephenson on this point. Sure enough, the one boy in the house who handled such requests was Ernst Lohmann.

Finally, two uniformed ambulance attendants from St. Vincent's appeared on the roof, carrying a folding stretcher. As they bore Cyrus carefully downstairs and then loaded him into the solemn black ambulance, which was pulled by an equally forbidding horse with blood-red eyes, I realized that a terrible death watch was now beginning: not for Cyrus, who though badly hurt would almost certainly recover fully, but for young Ernst Lohmann. After the ambulance had driven off, with Kreizler and Sara accompanying Cyrus to the hospital, Roosevelt turned to me, and I could see he'd reached the same conclusion.

'I don't care what Kreizler says, John,' Theodore announced, setting his jaw and balling his fists. 'This is a race against time and savagery now, and I'm going to use the force under my command.' I followed him as he rushed to Sixth Avenue to find a hansom. 'The Ninth Precinct is closest. I shall make all arrangements from there.' He caught sight of an empty rig, and approached it. 'We know the basic pattern – he'll be making for the waterfront. I'll have detachments search every foot of—'

'Roosevelt – wait.' I managed to grab his arm and pull him to a halt just as he was getting into the cab. 'I understand your feelings. But for heaven's sake, don't reveal any details to your men.'

'Not reveal – good God, John!' His teeth started to click louder and his eyes danced with rage behind the spectacles. 'Do you understand what's happening? Why, at this very moment—'

'I know, Roosevelt. But it won't help things to let the whole force in on it. Just say that there's been a kidnapping, and that you have reason to suspect the criminals are trying to leave the city by boat or by bridge. It's the best way to handle it, please believe me.'

Theodore took a big, strong breath into his broad chest, then nodded once. 'Perhaps you're right.' He slammed one fist into the other hand. 'Blast all this damned interference! But I'll do as you say, John – provided you'll stand aside and let me get to it!'

With a sharp crack of his horsewhip Roosevelt's cabbie commenced a fast trip up Sixth Avenue, and I returned to the front of the Black and Tan. There a small and already surly crowd had gathered and was being told the details of the evening's activities by Frank Stephenson. Technically speaking, the Black and Tan was in the territory of the Hudson Dusters, and Stephenson owed no allegiance to Paul Kelly; but the two men did know each other, and the job Stephenson did exciting that little crowd outside his house that night made me very suspicious that Kelly had foreseen the possibility that one of Stephenson's boys might be snatched or killed, and had paid him handsomely to make the most of such an event. Stephenson let off a lot of angry statements to the effect that the police had been on the scene and had exercised neither caution nor diligence. The victim was too poor, he said, and entirely too foreign to warrant police interest; if people in such neighborhoods as their own wanted to prevent these kinds of things, they'd have to take matters into their own hands. Marcus, of course, had already identified himself to Stephenson as a police officer; and as the crowd's mood grew uglier and an increasing number of threatening glances were thrown our way, the Isaacsons, Stevie, and I decided to retreat to our headquarters, where we would try to stay abreast of events through the rest of the night by telephone.

Such proved a lot trickier than it sounded. There was no one

Caleb Carr

for us to ring up – Theodore would never take a call from us while he was in the company of regular police officers – and no one was likely to get in touch with us. At about four we did have word from Kreizler, who said that he and Sara had gotten Cyrus comfortably settled in a private room at St. Vincent's and would be returning to our headquarters soon. Other than that, however, there was profound silence. Lucius, though very much relieved by Kreizler's call, nonetheless felt profoundly guilty about all that had happened, and paced the floor rather frantically. Indeed, had it not been for Marcus I think we might all have slowly gone mad sitting there with nothing to do. But the taller Isaacson decided that if we couldn't lend our bodies to the search we could at least use our minds, and, pointing to the large map of Manhattan, he suggested that we try to anticipate where the killer would go this time to perform his vicious ritual.

Yet even if we hadn't been distracted by the thought that events were proceeding without our being able to affect them, I doubt that we would have gotten very far in this endeavor. But how could we extrapolate from these surmises sufficiently to guess what site he would choose next? One suggestion was that he'd return to another bridge; and, if we assumed that he wouldn't repeat himself in this regard, we were left with either the old High Bridge over the East River at the northern end of Manhattan (an aqueduct that carried Croton Reservoir water into the city) or the nearby Washington Bridge, which had opened a few years earlier. Marcus, however, realized that the killer probably knew that his pursuers were gaining ground on him. Based on the timing of his attack on Cyrus, for example, it seemed certain that it had been *he* who had put *us* under surveillance earlier in the evening rather than vice versa. A man who was paying that kind of attention to his antagonists' activities would likely guess that we were anticipating his return to a favored type of locale and go elsewhere. For Marcus's money, it was the killer's hatred of immigrants that offered the best chance of revealing the probable next murder site; and, following this line of reasoning, the detective sergeant argued that the man would head for someplace like the docks belonging to those steamship lines that packed huge numbers of desperate foreigners into the lower decks of their vessels and brought them to America.

When we finally did get an answer to this deadly conundrum, it was so obvious as to make all of us feel quite ashamed. At about four-thirty, just as Kreizler was walking into our headquarters, Sara telephoned from Mulberry Street, where she'd gone to find out what was happening.

'They've had a message from Bedloe's Island,' she said, as soon as I'd picked up the earpiece. 'One of the night guards at the Liberty Statue – he's found a body.' My heart sank, and I said nothing. 'Hello?' Sara said. 'Are you on the line, John?'

'Yes, Sara, I'm here.'

'Then listen carefully, I can't talk long. There's already a pack of senior officers getting ready to head out there. The commissioner's going with them, but he's told me we mustn't show ourselves. He says all he can do is try to prevent any coroners from examining the body before it's sent to the morgue. He'll try to get us in to see it there.'

'But the crime scene, Sara—'

'John, please don't be thickheaded. There's nothing anyone can do. We had our chance tonight and we botched it. Now we've got to get what we can, when we can, at the morgue. In the meantime—' Suddenly I heard loud voices in the background on the other end of the line: one of them I recognized as Theodore, another was unquestionably Link Steffens, and then there were several others I couldn't place. 'I've got to ring off, John. I'll be there as soon as I've had word from the island.' With a click she was gone.

I gave the others the details, after which it took several minutes for everyone to absorb the fact that despite our weeks of research and days of preparation we'd been unable to prevent another murder. Lucius, of course, took it especially hard, believing himself responsible now not only for a friend's cracked skull but for a boy's death. Marcus and I tried to be sympathetic, but nothing we could say would console him. Kreizler, on the other hand, took a very unemotional line, and told Lucius that since the killer had been observing our efforts there was little doubt that he would eventually have found some way to stage a successful attack, if not on that night then on another. We were lucky, Laszlo declared, that Cyrus's concussion had been the full extent of our casualties – Lucius could also have been laid out on that rooftop, the victim of more than just a nasty knock on the head. There was no time for self-recrimination, Kreizler concluded; Lucius's keen mind and expertise, undiluted by guilt, were sorely needed. This little speech seemed to mean a great deal to Lucius, as much for its author as for its content, and he was soon composed enough to join our efforts to tabulate what if anything we'd learned that night.

Every move the killer had made confirmed our theories concerning his nature and methods – but the most important aspect of his behavior, so far as Kreizler was concerned, was his attention to our efforts and his attack on Cyrus. Why had he chosen to steal Ernst Lohmann away when he knew that we were watching? And, once committed to such a dangerous course of action, why had he only knocked Cyrus unconscious instead of killing him? The man was, after all, already certain to go to the gallows, if caught, and he could only hang once. Why take the chance that Cyrus might put up a fight, get a glimpse of his attacker during it, and then live to tell us about it? Kreizler wasn't at all sure that we could answer these questions definitely; but it was at least clear that the man had enjoyed the evening's sense of heightened risk. And since he knew that we were getting closer to him, perhaps letting Cyrus live was his way of urging us on: a defiant challenge, as well as a desperate plea.

Important as all this no doubt was, I could not keep my mind from wandering, as Kreizler spoke, to thoughts of what had occurred on Bedloe's Island that night. Beneath Bartholdi's great statue – which symbolized freedom to so many but was now, in my mind, an ironic emblem of our killer's slavery to a murderous obsession – another boy had met a terrible and undeserved end. I tried to stifle the vague but powerful image of a youth I'd never seen, bound and on his knees beneath Lady Liberty, trusting fully in the man who was about to wring his neck, and then feeling sudden, brief, all-consuming horror at the realization that he had given his trust unwisely and was going to pay the fullest possible price for his mistake. Then, in rapid succession, other pictures flashed across my mind: first the knife, that fearsome instrument created to meet the dangers of a world very unlike New York; then the long, slow, careful movements of that blade through flesh, and the sharp, mean chops at the limbs; the blood, no longer propelled by the heart, flowing out onto the grass and rocks in leisurely, thick streams; and the sickening grind and squeak of sharp steel against the ocular orbits of the skull ... There was nothing that resembled justice or humanity in it. Whatever Ernst Lohmann's way of making a living, whatever his error in trusting a stranger, the penalty was too severe, the price too abominably high.

When my attention returned to the ongoing conversation, I heard Kreizler hissing in frustrated urgency:

'Something – there's got to be *something* new that we've learned tonight.'

Neither Marcus, Lucius, nor I spoke; but Stevie, who was glancing at each of us uncertainly, seemed to have something to say, and finally piped up with: 'Well, there is one thing, Doctor.' Kreizler turned to him expectantly. 'He's losing his hair.'

And then I remembered the head that we'd thought belonged to Lucius but which had sat atop a body far too tall to be the detective sergeant's. 'That's right,' I said. 'We saw him – good Christ, Stevie, for that one moment we were *looking* at him!'

'Well? *Well?*' Kreizler demanded. 'Surely you noticed something else!'

I looked to Stevie, who only shrugged. Tearing my own memory of that one instant apart like a demon, I sought a forgotten detail, one overlooked moment when I'd clearly seen ... nothing. The back of a balding head. That was all that had been visible.

Kreizler sighed in great disappointment. 'Balding, eh?' he said, as he scratched the word on the chalkboard. 'Well, I suppose it's more than we knew yesterday.'

'It doesn't seem much,' Lucius said. 'Measured against a boy's life.'

A few minutes later Sara finally telephoned again. The body of Ernst Lohmann was on its way to the morgue at Bellevue. The guard who'd found it, naturally, had witnessed no part of the killing, but had heard a sound just before he spotted the dead boy that could have been a steam launch drawing away from the island. Roosevelt had told Sara that he needed some time to get rid of the police officers that were with him; he thought that if we were to meet him at Bellevue at six-thirty he could make sure that we would be allowed to examine the body without interference. That left just over an hour; I decided to go home, bathe, and change my clothes before joining the others at the morgue.

I arrived at Washington Square to find my grandmother, thankfully and remarkably, still asleep. Harriet was up and about, though, and she offered to draw my bath. As she scurried up the stairs, I remarked on my grandmother's sound slumber.

'Yes, sir,' Harriet said. 'Ever since the news came she's been much easier in her mind.'

'The news?' I said, in tired confusion.

'Sure you've heard, sir? About that horrible Dr. Holmes – it was in all the papers yesterday. I believe we still have the *Times* in the nook, if you'd like me to—'

'No, no,' I said, stopping her as she came back down the stairs. 'I'll get it. If you'll just draw the bath, Harriet, I'll be your servant for a lifetime.'

'Hardly necessary, Mr. John,' she answered, going up again.

I found the previous day's *Times* in the copper and glass nook next to my grandmother's favorite chair. The story was blazoned across the front page: HOLMES COOL TO THE END. The infamous 'torture doctor' had been dispatched on a Philadelphia gallows, after confessing without remorse to the murder of twenty-seven additional people, mostly women he'd romanced and robbed. The drop had fallen at 10:12 A.M., and twenty minutes later he'd been pronounced dead. As added precautions – against what, the paper did not say – Holmes's coffin had been filled with cement after he'd been laid in it, and then, when the box had been deposited in a ten-foot hole in an unnamed cemetery, another ton of cement had been poured in over it.

My grandmother still had not stirred when I left the house again for Bellevue; in fact, I later learned from Harriet that she slept until well past ten.

Chapter 27

As it turned out, the greatest difficulty with our trip to the morgue early Monday morning did not result from a confrontation with any member of that institution's staff. They were all quite new on the job (having recently replaced a group who'd been fired for selling bodies to anatomists at $150 a head) and too unsure of their authority to go up against Roosevelt. No, our problem was simply getting into the building, for by the time we arrived, another angry mob of Lower East Side residents had formed to demand an explanation as to why their children were still being slaughtered without so much as one suspect being taken into custody. The general air among this crowd was not only angrier than that of the group that'd assembled at Castle Garden, it was also far more indignant. Absent was any mention of Ernst Lohmann's profession or living arrangements (he turned out to have no family that we could ever locate); the youth was pictured as an abandoned innocent left to the mercy of a police department, a city government, and an upper class that did not care how he lived – or, if he died, who was responsible. This much more systematic, not to mention political, representation of Lohmann's plight – and that of the immigrant communities generally – may have been due to the fact that there were a good number of Germans in the crowd; but I suspected that it had far more to do with the ongoing influence of Paul Kelly, although I did not see either him or his brougham anywhere near the morgue as we moved through the crowd around it.

We entered the dreary red-brick building through a black iron door in the back, Sara, the Isaacsons, and I crowding around Laszlo so that no one could see his face. Roosevelt met us just inside the doorway and, after brushing off a pair of attendants who wanted to know our business, led us directly to an examination room. The stench of formaldehyde and decay in this sickening chamber was so strong that it seemed to be pulling the yellowing paint off the walls. There were tables bearing draped bodies shoved into each corner, and aging, chipped specimen jars full of various pieces of human bodies sat gruesomely on a series of sagging shelves. A large electrical lamp was suspended from the center of the ceiling, and under it was a dented and rusted operating table, which at some point in the distant past must have looked like those Laszlo kept in the basement theater of his Institute. Atop the table was a body covered by a dirty, wet sheet.

Lucius and Kreizler went immediately to the table, and Lucius tore the sheet away – wanting, it seemed to me, to face as quickly as possible the boy for whose death he felt such heavy responsibility. Marcus followed behind them, but Sara and I remained by the door, not wanting to approach the body if we could avoid it. Kreizler produced his little notebook and then the usual recitation began, Lucius listing the injuries that the boy had suffered in a voice that was monotonous yet, paradoxically, passionate:

'Severing of the complete genitalia at their base. . . . Severing of the right hand just above the wrist joint – both the ulna and radius cleanly cut. . . . Lateral lacerations of the abdominal cavity, with attendant damage to the small intestine. . . . Massive damage to the entire arterial system within the thorax, and apparent removal of the heart. . . . Removal of the left eye, attendant damage to the malar bone and supraorbital ridge on that side. . . . Removal of those sections of the scalp covering the occipital and parietal bones of the skull. . . .'

It was a grim roster, all right, and I tried not to listen; but one of the latter items caught my notice. 'Excuse me, Lucius,' I interrupted, 'but did you say removal of the left eye?'

'Yes,' came his quick reply.

'The left eye *only*?'

'Yes,' Kreizler answered. 'The right eye is still intact.'

Marcus looked excited. 'He must've been interrupted.'

'It does seem the most plausible explanation,' Kreizler replied. 'Probably he detected the guard's approach.' Laszlo then pointed at the center of the body. 'This business with the heart is new, Detective Sergeant.'

Marcus rushed over to the door. 'Commissioner Roosevelt,' he said, 'can you give us another forty-five minutes in here?'

Roosevelt checked his watch. 'It would be close. The new warden and his staff usually come in at eight. Why, Isaacson?'

'I need some of my equipment – for an experiment.'

'Experiment? Just what sort of an experiment?' For Theodore, distinguished naturalist that he was, the word 'experiment' held almost as much power as 'action.'

'There are some experts,' Marcus explained, 'who think that, at the moment of death, the human eye permanently records the last image it sees. It's thought that the image can be photographed, using the eye itself as a sort of lens. I'd like to give it a try.'

Theodore considered the proposition for a moment. 'You think the boy may have died looking at his murderer?'

'There's a chance.'

'And will the next examiner be able to tell you've made the attempt?'

'No, sir.'

'Mmm. Quite an idea. All right.' Theodore nodded once definitively. 'Fetch your equipment. But I warn you, Detective Sergeant – we are going to be out of here by seven forty-five.'

Marcus bolted off toward the rear door of the building. After his exit Lucius and Kreizler continued to prod and pick at the body, and I eventually sank to the floor, exhausted and disheartened past the point where my legs could support me. Looking up at Sara and hoping to find some sympathy in her face, I saw instead that she was staring at the end of the examination table.

'Doctor,' she finally said quietly, 'what's the matter with his foot?'

Laszlo turned, glanced at Sara, and then followed her gaze to the dead boy's right foot, which was hanging out over the end of the table. It appeared swollen, and was set on the leg at an odd angle; but as this was nothing compared to the rest of the injuries to the body, it seemed scant wonder that Lucius had missed it.

Kreizler took hold of the foot and examined it carefully. '*Talipes varus*,' he eventually announced. 'The boy was club-footed.'

That caught my interest. 'Clubfooted?'

'Yes,' Kreizler answered, letting the extremity drop again.

It was a measure, I suppose, of just how rigorously our minds had been trained in recent weeks that, exhausted as we might have been, we were still able to extrapolate an important set of implications from a fairly common physical deformity that had afflicted this latest victim. We began to discuss these implications at some length, continuing to do so as Marcus returned with his photographic equipment and got ready to take his experimental pictures. Subsequent questioning of those who had known the Lohmann boy at the Black and Tan bore our speculations out, and they are therefore worth mentioning.

Sara suggested that the killer might originally have been drawn to Lohmann because of a kind of identification with the boy's physical plight. But if Lohmann had been resentful of any mention of his deformity – a strong possibility in a boy of his age and occupation – he would have reacted adversely to such charitable expressions. This reaction would, in turn, have sparked the killer's usual rage with difficult young men. Kreizler agreed with all this and further explained that the betrayal inherent in Lohmann's refusal of the killer's empathy would have stirred a new and even deeper anger in our man. This could well account for the fact that the boy's heart was missing: the killer had apparently meant to take his mutilations to a new extreme but had been interrupted by the guard. We all knew that this spelled trouble – we were not dealing with a man who would react well to having his intimate moments cut short.

At this point in our discussion Marcus announced that he was ready to begin his experiment, at which Kreizler took a few steps back from the operating table to allow the several pieces of equipment Marcus had brought along to be moved next to the body. After requesting that the overhead electrical bulb be switched off, Marcus asked his brother to slowly lift Ernst Lohmann's remaining eye out of its socket. When Lucius had complied, Marcus took a very small incandescent lamp and placed it behind the eye, onto which he focused his camera. After exposing two plates to this image, he then activated two small wires, whose ends were bared. He ran these wires into the nerves of the eye, activating the latter, and exposed several more plates. As a final step, he shut off the incandescent lamp and took two images of the unlit but still electrically activated eye. The whole thing seemed quite bizarre (indeed, I later learned that the French novelist Jules Verne had written of the procedure in one of his outlandish stories); but Marcus was quite hopeful, and as he turned the overhead lamp back on, he expressed his determination to return to his darkroom immediately.

We had packed all of Marcus's equipment up and were nearly ready to depart when I caught sight of Kreizler staring at the Lohmann boy's face, with far less detachment than he'd displayed during his examination of the body. Without myself looking at the mangled corpse, I stood by Laszlo and silently put a hand on his shoulder.

'A mirror image,' Kreizler mumbled. At first I thought he was referring to some part of Marcus's procedure; but then I remembered the conversation we'd had weeks ago when we'd said that the condition of the victims' bodies was in a real way a reflection of the psychic devastation that perpetually gnawed at our killer.

Roosevelt moved up beside me, his eyes also fixed on the body. 'It's an even worse sight, in this place,' he said quietly. 'Clinical. Utterly dehumanized . . .'

'But why this?' Kreizler asked, of no one in particular. 'Why just exactly *this*?' He held out a hand to the body, and I knew he was speaking of the mutilations.

'The devil himself only knows,' Theodore answered. 'I've never seen anything like it, short of a red Indian.'

Laszlo and I both froze, and then spun silently on the man. Our stares must have been fairly intense, for Theodore looked momentarily unnerved. 'And what's gotten into you two?' he asked, a bit indignantly. 'If I may make so bold?'

'Roosevelt,' Laszlo said evenly, taking a step forward. 'Would you mind repeating what you just said?'

'I've been accused of many things when I speak,' Theodore answered, 'but never mumbling. I believe I was clear.'

'Yes. Yes, you were.' The Isaacsons and Sara had drawn close, reading something big in the fire that had swept into Laszlo's previously downcast features. 'But what exactly did you mean?'

'I was simply thinking,' Roosevelt explained, still a little defensively, 'of the only other violence like this that I've ever come across. It was when I was ranching, in the Dakota Badlands. I saw several bodies of white men who'd been killed by Indians, as a warning to other settlers. The corpses were cut up terribly, much like this one – in an effort, I suppose, to terrify the rest of us.'

'Yes,' Laszlo said, as much to himself as to Theodore. 'That's what you naturally would suppose. But was that, in fact, the purpose of it?' Kreizler began to pace around the operating table, rubbing his left arm slowly and nodding. 'A model, he needs a model. . . . It's too consistent, too considered, too – structured. He's modeling it after something . . .' Checking his silver watch, Laszlo turned back to Theodore. 'Would you happen to know offhand, Roosevelt, what time the Museum of Natural History opens its doors?'

'I should hope I would,' Theodore answered proudly, 'as my father was a founder and I myself am quite involved in—'

'What *time*, Roosevelt?'

'Nine o'clock.'

Kreizler nodded. 'Excellent. Moore, you'll come with me. As for the rest of you – Marcus, get to your darkroom and let's see if this experiment of yours has produced anything. Sara, you and Lucius go back to Number 808 and get in touch with the War Department in Washington. Find out if they keep any records of soldiers dismissed for mental illness. Tell them we are only interested in soldiers who have served in the Army of the West. If you can't get a telephone line through, send a cable.'

'I know a few people at War,' Roosevelt added. 'If it would be any help.'

'It would indeed,' Laszlo answered. 'Sara, take the names. Go, go, on your way, all of you!' As Sara and the Isaacsons left, taking with them Marcus's equipment, Kreizler came back to Roosevelt and me. 'You've realized what we're looking for, Moore?'

'Yes,' I said. 'But why the museum, exactly?'

'An old friend of mine. Franz Boas. If mutilations such as these do have some kind of cultural significance among Indian tribes, he'll be able to tell us. And should such prove the case, Roosevelt, resounding congratulations will be due you.' Kreizler laid the dirty old sheet back over Ernst Lohmann's body. 'Unfortunately, I let Stevie take the calash home, which means we'll have to get a cab. Can we drop you anywhere, Roosevelt?'

'No,' Theodore answered, 'I'd better stay and cover our tracks. There may be a lot of questions, considering that crowd. But I wish you good hunting, gentlemen!'

The number of disgruntled people outside the morgue had only grown during the time we'd spent examining the Lohmann boy's remains. Sara and the Isaacsons had apparently gotten through the throng without incident, for we saw no sign of them. Kreizler and I were not so lucky, however. We'd only made it halfway to the main gate of the hospital grounds, with the crowd suspiciously scrutinizing us every step of the way, when our path was blocked by a thickset, square-headed man who carried an old ax handle. The man fixed a cold stare of recognition on Kreizler, and when I turned I saw that Laszlo seemed to know him as well.

'Ah!' the man exclaimed, from deep in the pit of his considerable belly. 'So they've brought in the famous Herr Doctor Kreizler!' The accent indicated a lower-class German.

'Herr Höpner,' Laszlo answered, in a firm but wary tone that indicated the man might know how to use the ax handle he was carrying. 'I'm afraid my colleague and I have urgent business elsewhere. Kindly stand aside.'

'And what, then, of the Lohmann boy, Herr Doctor?' The man Höpner did not move. 'Have you something to do with this matter?' A few of the people standing near him muttered echoes to the demand.

'I have no idea what you're talking about, Höpner,' Kreizler answered coolly. 'Please move.'

Caleb Carr

'No idea, eh?' Höpner began to slap the piece of wood against one palm. 'I must doubt that. Do you know the good doctor, *meine Freunde?*' he said to the crowd. 'He is the famous alienist who destroys families – who steals children from their homes!' Professions of shock sprang from all sides. 'I demand to know what part you have in this matter, Herr Doctor! Did you snatch the Lohmann boy from his parents, just as you snatched my daughter from me?'

'I've told you once,' Laszlo said, his teeth starting to grind. 'I know nothing about any Lohmann boy. And as for your daughter, Herr Höpner, she *asked* to be removed from your home, because you could not refrain from beating her with a stick – a stick not unlike the one you now hold.'

The crowd drew breath as one, and Höpner's eyes went wide. 'What a man does in his own home with his own family is his own business!' he protested.

'Your daughter felt differently about that,' Kreizler said. 'Now, for the last time – *raus mit dir!*'

It was a command to move, such as one might give to a servant or some other underling. Höpner looked like he'd been spat on. Raising the ax handle he made a move toward Kreizler, but suddenly stopped when one hell of a commotion rose from somewhere behind Kreizler and me. Turning to look over the crowd, I could see a horse's head and the roof of a carriage plowing our way. And along with them I spied a face that I knew: Eat-'Em-Up Jack McManus. He was hanging on to the side of the vehicle, swinging the gargantuan right arm that had made him a formidable force in the prize ring for nearly a decade before he'd quit the fight game to work as a bouncer – for Paul Kelly.

Kelly's elegant black brougham, brass lanterns shining on either side, made its way to where we were standing. The small, sinewy man in the driver's seat cracked his whip in general warning, and the crowd, knowing who was inside the carriage, moved aside and said nothing. Jack McManus jumped down once the wheels had stopped rolling, then looked at the crowd threateningly and straightened his miner's cap. Finally he opened the door of the brougham.

'I suggest you get in, gentlemen!' said an amused voice from within the carriage. Kelly's handsome face soon appeared at the door. 'You know how mobs can be.'

Chapter 28

'Ha! Will you look at them!' Kelly was full of glee as he stared back at the crowd during our bumpy flight out of the Bellevue grounds. 'The pigs have actually gotten off their knees for once! This ought to make for a few sleepless nights on Mansion Mile, eh, Moore?' I was sitting next to Kreizler across from Kelly in the front half of the brougham. As the gangster turned back around to face us, he pounded his gold-headed stick on the floor and laughed again. 'It won't last, of course – they'll be back to packing their kids into sweatshops for a dollar a week before the Lohmann boy's even been boxed. It'll take more than just another dead boy-whore to keep them going. But for now, it does make a glorious picture!' Kelly extended his heavily ringed right hand to Kreizler. 'How do you do, Doctor? It's a genuine privilege.'

Laszlo took the hand very tentatively. 'Mr. Kelly. At least *someone* finds this situation amusing.'

'Oh, I do, Doctor, I do – that's why I arranged it!' Neither Kreizler nor I said anything in acknowledgment. 'Well, come on, gentlemen, you don't think people like that would stand up for themselves without some urging, do you? A little money in the right places doesn't hurt, either. And I must say, I never expected to run into the eminent Dr. Kreizler in such a situation!' His surprise was transparently false. 'Can I drop you gentlemen somewhere?'

I turned to Kreizler. 'Saves us the cab fare,' I said, to which Laszlo nodded. Then I spoke to Kelly: 'The Museum of Natural History. Seventy-seventh and—'

'I know where it is, Moore.' Kelly slammed his stick on the roof of the brougham and spoke with harsh authority: 'Jack! Tell Harry to take us to Seventy-seventh and Central Park West. In a hurry!' The sinister charm then returned: 'I'm a little surprised to see you here, too, Moore. I thought that after your run-in with Biff you'd lose interest in these murders.'

'It'll take more than Ellison to make me lose interest,' I declared, hoping it sounded more defiant than I felt.

'Oh, I can give you more,' Kelly volleyed, jerking his head in Jack McManus's direction. The twinge of apprehension I felt in my gut must have shown in my face, because Kelly laughed out loud. 'Relax. I said you wouldn't get hurt as long as you kept my name out of it, and you've played straight. I wish your friend Steffens had your sense. Come to think of it, Moore, you haven't been writing much of *any*thing lately, have you?' Kelly grinned slyly.

'I'm collecting all the facts before I publish,' I said.

'Of course you are. And your friend the doctor's just out stretching his legs, is that it?'

Laszlo shifted in his seat uneasily, but spoke calmly. 'Mr. Kelly, as long as you've offered us this remarkably timely ride, I wonder if I might ask you a question.'

'Of course, Doctor. It may be hard for you to believe, but I've got a lot of respect for you – why, I even read a monograph you wrote once.' Kelly laughed. '*Most* of it, at any rate.'

'I'm gratified,' Kreizler answered. 'But tell me – knowing as little as I do about the murders you speak of, I am, nevertheless, curious as to what possible reason you can have for inflaming, and perhaps endangering, people who have nothing to do with the matter?'

'*Am* I endangering them, Doctor?'

'Surely you realize that such behavior as yours can only lead to wider civil unrest and violence. A great many innocent people are likely to be hurt, and still more jailed.'

'That's right, Kelly,' I added. 'In a town like this what you're

Caleb Carr

starting could get out of hand pretty damned quickly.'

Kelly thought about that for a few moments, without ever losing his smile. 'Let me ask *you* something, Moore – horse races go off every day, but the average guy only takes an interest in the ones he's betting on. Why's that?'

'Why?' I said, a bit confused. 'Well, because if you've got no stake in it . . .'

'There you are, then,' Kelly interjected, chuckling thoughtfully. 'You two gentlemen sit here talking about this city and civil unrest and all of that – but what stake do *I* have in it? What do I care if New York burns to the ground? Whoever's still standing when it's over is going to want a drink and someone to spend a lonely hour with – and I'll be here to supply those items.'

'In that case,' Kreizler said, 'why concern yourself with the matter at all?'

'Because it *riles* me.' For the first time, Kelly's face went straight. 'That's right, Doctor – it riles me. Those pigs back there get fed all that slop about society by the boys on Fifth Avenue just as soon as they're off the boat, and what do they do? They knock themselves out trying to eat every bit of it. It's a sucker bet, a crooked game, whatever you want to call it, and there's a part of me that just wouldn't mind seeing it go the other way for a little while.' His amiable grin suddenly returned. 'Or maybe there are deeper reasons for my attitude, Doctor. Maybe you could find something in the – the *context* of my life that would explain it, if you had access to that kind of information.' The remark surprised me considerably, and I could see that Kreizler, too, hadn't expected it. There was something very intimidating about Kelly's rough-hewn intellectual agility: a sense that here was a man who could pose a serious threat on any number of levels. 'But whatever the reasons,' our host went on brightly, glancing out of the carriage, 'I'm enjoying this entire affair *immensely.*'

'Enough,' Kreizler pressed, 'to complicate a solution?'

'Doctor!' Kelly feigned shock. 'I've got half a mind to be insulted.' The gangster flipped open a lid on the head of his cane, revealing a small compartment full of a fine crystalline powder. 'Gentlemen?' he said, offering it our way. Laszlo and I both declined. 'Gets the system moving at this ungodly hour of the day.' Kelly placed some of the cocaine on his wrist and snorted it hard. 'I don't like to give the appearance of some cheap burny blower, but I'm not much for the morning. Anyway, Doctor' – he wiped at his nose with a fine silk handkerchief and closed the lid of the cane – 'I wasn't aware that there'd *been* any serious attempt to solve this case.' He stared straight at Kreizler. 'Do you know something I don't know?'

Neither Kreizler nor I answered the question, which prompted Kelly to go on, sarcastically but at length, about the appalling lack of any serious official effort to solve the murders. Finally, the brougham lurched to a fortuitous halt on the west side of Central Park. Laszlo and I stepped out onto the intersection of Seventy-seventh Street, hoping that Kelly would now let the matter drop; but as we got to the curb the gangster poked his head out behind us.

'Well, it's been my honor, Doctor Kreizler,' he called. 'You too, scribbler. One final question, though – you don't imagine that the big boys are actually going to let you *finish* this little investigation of yours, do you?'

I was taken too off guard to reply; but Kreizler had evidently adjusted to the situation and replied, 'I can only answer that question with another, Kelly – do *you* intend to let us finish?'

Kelly cocked his head and looked at the morning sky. 'To tell you the truth, I hadn't thought about that. I didn't think I'd have to. These murders really have been very useful to me, as I say. If you were actually to jeopardize that usefulness – ah, but what am I saying? With what you're up against, you'll be lucky to stay out of jail yourselves.' He held his stick up. 'Good morning, gentlemen. Harry! Back to the New Brighton!'

We watched the brougham pull away, Eat-'Em-Up Jack McManus still hanging off of it like some kind of overgrown, malevolent monkey, and then turned to head into the Early Renaissance walls and turrets of the Museum of Natural History.

Though not yet three decades old, the museum already housed a first-rate collection of experts and an enormous, bizarre assortment of bones, rocks, stuffed animals, and pinned insects. But of all the prestigious departments that called the castle-like structure home, none was more renowned, or more iconoclastic, than that of anthropology; and I later learned that the man we were on our way to see that day, Franz Boas, was primarily responsible for this.

He was about Kreizler's age, and had been born in Germany, where he'd originally been trained as an experimental psychologist before moving on to ethnology. Thus there were obvious circumstantial reasons why Boas and Kreizler should have become acquainted; but none of these was as important to their friendship as was a pronounced similarity of professional ideas. Kreizler had staked his reputation on his theory of context, the idea that no adult's personality can be truly understood without first comprehending the facts of his individual experience. Boas's anthropological work represented, in many ways, the application of this theory on a larger scale: to entire cultures. While doing groundbreaking research with the Indian tribes of the American Northwest, Boas had reached the conclusion that history is the principal force that shapes cultures, rather than race or geographical environment, as had been previously assumed. All cultures are equally valid, when seen in this light; and to his many critics who said that certain cultures had obviously made more progress than others, and could thus be considered superior, Boas replied that 'progress' was an entirely relative concept.

Boas had thoroughly energized Natural History's Department of Anthropology with his new ideas since his appointment in 1895; and when you strolled through the department's exhibition rooms, as we did that morning, a sense of intellectual vitality and excitement raced through you. Of course, this reaction might have been prompted as much by the sight of the ferocious faces carved into the dozen enormous totem poles that lined the walls; or the large canoe full of plaster Indians – cast from life – who paddled wildly through some imaginary body of water in the center of the main hall; or the case after case of weapons, ritual masks, costumes, and other artifacts that occupied the remaining floor space. Whatever the cause, upon entering those rooms one felt very much like one had stepped out of fashionable Manhattan and into some corner of the globe that those of us who knew no better would immediately have labeled savage.

Kreizler and I found Boas in a cluttered office in one of the museum's turrets overlooking Seventy-seventh Street. He was a small man, with a large, roundish nose, an ample mustache, and thinning hair. In his brown eyes was that same fire of the crusader that marked Kreizler's gaze; and the two men shook hands with a warmth and vigor that is only shared by truly kindred spirits. Boas was in a somewhat harassed state: he was preparing a massive expedition to the Pacific Northwest, to be paid for by the financier Morris K. Jesup. Kreizler and I therefore had to state our case quickly. I was somewhat shocked by the complete candor with which Kreizler revealed our work; and the story gave Boas a shock of his own, to judge by the way he stood up, looked sternly at the two of us, and then firmly closed the door to his office.

'Kreizler,' he said, in an accented voice that was as definitive as Laszlo's, if slightly gentler, 'do you have any idea of what you're exposing yourself to? Should this become known, and should you fail – the risk is atrocious!' Boas threw his arms up and went for a small cigar.

'Yes, yes, I know, Franz,' Kreizler answered, 'but what would you have me do? These are children, after all, however outcast and unfortunate, and the killings will go on. Besides – there are enormous possibilities, should we *not* fail.'

'I can understand a *journalist* getting involved,' Boas railed on, nodding at me as he lit his cigar. 'But your work, Kreizler, is important. You are already distrusted by the public as well as by many of your colleagues – should this go badly you will be utterly ridiculed and dismissed by them!'

'As always you are not listening to me,' Kreizler answered indulgently. 'You might assume that I've been over such considerations many times in my own mind. And the fact of the matter is that Mr. Moore and I are pressed for time, as are you. Therefore, I must ask bluntly – can you help us or not?'

Boas puffed away and scrutinized us both carefully, shaking his head. 'You want information on the Plains tribes?' Laszlo nodded. 'All right. But one thing is *streng verboten*—' Boas pointed a finger at Kreizler. 'I will not have you saying that the tribal customs of such people are responsible for the behavior of a murderer in this city.'

Laszlo sighed. 'Franz, please—'

'Oh, about you I have little doubt. But I know nothing of these people you are working with.' Boas eyed me again, more than a little suspiciously. 'We already have enough trouble changing the public view of the Indians. So you must pledge that to me, Laszlo.'

'I pledge it for my colleagues as well as for myself.'

Boas grunted once disdainfully. 'Colleagues. I'm certain.' He began shuffling papers on his desk in annoyance. 'My own knowledge of the tribes in question is insufficient. But I have just hired a young man who will be able to help you.' Rising and crossing to the door quickly, Boas pulled it open and shouted at a secretary: 'Miss Jenkins! Where is Dr. Wissler, please?'

'Downstairs, Dr. Boas,' came a reply. 'They're installing the Blackfoot exhibit.'

'Ah.' Boas returned to his desk. 'Good. That exhibit's already late getting in place. You'll have to talk to him down there. Don't be deceived by his youth, Kreizler. He's come a long way in just a few years, and seen a great deal.' Boas's tone softened as he came around to Laszlo and extended his hand again. 'Much like some other distinguished experts I've known.'

The two men smiled at each other briefly, but Boas's face went straight with suspicion once more as he shook my hand and then showed us out of his office.

After trotting quickly downstairs, we passed back through the hall that contained the large canoe, then asked a guard for directions. He indicated another exhibition room, the door of which was locked. Kreizler rapped on it a few times, but there was no response. We could hear banging and voices within, and then a series of wild, rather chilling whoops and cries such as one might indeed have heard on the western frontier.

'Good God,' I said, 'they're not going to put live Indians on display, are they?'

'Don't be ridiculous, Moore.' Kreizler pounded on the door again, and finally it opened.

Facing us was a curly-haired young man of about twenty-five with a small mustache, a cherub's face, and dancing blue eyes. He wore a vest and tie, and a very professorial pipe was sticking out of his mouth; but on his head was an enormous and rather frightening war bonnet, composed of what I assumed were eagle's feathers.

'Yes?' the young man said, with a very engaging grin. 'Can I help you?'

'Dr. Wissler?' Kreizler said.

'Clark Wissler, that's right.' The man suddenly realized he was wearing the war bonnet. 'Oh, I beg your pardon,' he said, removing it. 'We're installing an exhibit, and I'm particularly concerned about this piece. You're—'

'My name is Laszlo Kreizler, and this is—'

'*Doctor* Kreizler?' Wissler said hopefully, opening the door further.

'That's right. And this—'

'This is a real pleasure, is what this is!' Wissler held out his hand and shook Kreizler's energetically. 'An honor! I believe I've read everything you've written, Doctor – although you really ought to write more. Psychology needs more work like yours!'

As we entered the large room, which was in near total disarray, Wissler went on in this vein, pausing only briefly to shake my hand. It seemed that he, too, had originally trained in psychology before moving on to anthropology; and even in his current work, he focused on the psychological aspects of different cultures' value systems, as expressed through their mythologies, artwork, social structures, and the like. This was a fortunate circumstance, for after we drew away from a group of workmen and into a deserted corner of the large room to tell Wissler in confidence of our work, he expressed even stronger concern than had Boas about the potential effects of tying such abominable acts as our killer's to any Indian culture. When Kreizler gave him the same assurances he'd given Boas, however, Wissler's unbridled admiration for Laszlo allowed trust to flourish. The fellow reacted to our thorough description of the mutilations involved in the murders with quick and penetrating analysis, of a kind I've rarely heard from one so young.

'Yes, I can see why you've come to us,' he said. Still carrying the war bonnet, he looked around for a place to lay it, but saw only construction rubble. 'I'm sorry, gentlemen, but—' He slipped the bonnet back on his head. 'I really must keep this clean until the display is ready. So – the mutilations you're describing, or at least some of them, do bear a resemblance to acts that have been committed on the bodies of dead enemies by various tribes on the Great Plains – most notably the Dakota, or Sioux. There are important differences, however.'

'And we shall get to those,' Kreizler said. 'But what of the similarities – why are such things done? And are they done only to dead bodies?'

'Generally,' Wissler answered. 'Despite what you may have read, the Sioux don't show a marked propensity for torture. There are some mutilation rituals, certainly, that involve the living – a man who can prove that his wife has been unfaithful, for example, can cut her nose off to mark her as an adulteress – but such behavior is very strictly regulated. No, most of the terrible things you'll come across happen to enemies of the tribe who are already dead.'

'And why to them?'

Wissler relit his pipe, being careful to keep the match away from the eagle's feathers. 'The Sioux have a very complex set of myths concerning death and the spirit world. We're still collecting data and examples and trying to comprehend the entire fabric of their beliefs. But basically, each man's *nagi*, or spirit, is gravely affected not only by the way in which the man dies, but by what happens to his body immediately after death. You see, the *nagi*, before embarking on its long journey to the spirit land, lingers near the body, for a time – preparing for the trip, as it were. The *nagi* is allowed to take whatever useful implements the man possessed in life, in order to help him on the journey, and to enrich his afterlife. But the *nagi* also assumes whatever form the body was in at the time of death. Now, if a warrior killed an enemy he admired, he wouldn't necessarily mutilate his body, because, according to another part of the myth, that dead enemy must serve the warrior in the spirit land – and who wants a mutilated servant? But if the warrior truly hated his enemy, and didn't want him to enjoy all the pleasures of the spirit land, then he might do some of the things you're talking about. Castration, for instance – because male spirits can copulate with female spirits in the Sioux vision of the afterlife without the female spirits becoming pregnant. Cutting off the dead man's genitals, obviously, means he won't be able to take advantage of that very appealing aspect of the spirit land. There are also games and contests of strength – a *nagi* without a hand, or without a vital organ, can't expect to do well in them. We've seen many examples of mutilations like that on battlefields.'

'And what about the eyes?' I asked. 'The same thinking, in that area?'

'The eyes are somewhat different. You see, the *nagi*'s journey to the spirit world involves a very perilous test: he must cross a great mythical river on a very narrow log. If the *nagi* is afraid of this test, or fails it, he must return to our world and wander forever as a lost and forlorn ghost. Of course, a spirit who can't see stands no chance of making the great trip, and his fate is preordained. The Sioux don't take this lightly. There are few things they fear more than being lost in this world in the afterlife.'

Kreizler was recording all this in his little notebook, and began to nod as he got this last concept down. 'And the differences between the Sioux mutilations and what we've described?'

'Well . . .' Wissler smoked and puzzled. 'There are some larger issues, as well as some details, that set the examples you're giving me apart from Sioux customs. Most importantly, there's the injury to the buttocks, and the claim to cannibalism. The Sioux, like most Indian tribes, are horrified by cannibalism – it's one of the things they disdain most about whites.'

'Whites?' I said. 'But we're not – well, let's be fair, we're not cannibals.'

'Not usually,' Wissler answered. 'But there have been a few notable exceptions that the Indians know about. Remember the Donner party of settlers, in 1847? They got trapped for months without food in a snowbound mountain pass – and some of them ate each other. Made for good stories among the western tribes.'

'But' – I felt the need to protest further – 'well, hang it, you can't base your judgment of an entire culture on what a few people do.'

'Of course you can, Moore,' Kreizler said. 'Remember the

principle we've established for our killer: because of his past experience, his early encounters with a relatively small number of people, he has grown to view the entire world in a distinctive fashion. We may call it a mistaken fashion, but, given his past, he cannot do otherwise. It's the same principle here.'

'The western tribes haven't had contact with a very flattering cross section of white society, Mr. Moore,' Wissler agreed. 'And then there are miscommunications that back up those original impressions. When the Sioux leader Sitting Bull was dining with some white men several years back, for example, he was served pork – which he, never having seen such meat, but having heard the story of the Donner party, immediately assumed was white human flesh. That's the unfortunate way in which cultures get to know each other, generally.'

'What of the other differences?' Kreizler asked.

'Well, there's the stuffing of the genitals into the mouth – that's gratuitous, in a way that wouldn't make sense to the Sioux. You've emasculated the man's spirit already. Stuffing the genitals into his mouth isn't going to serve any practical purpose. But most of all, there's the fact that these victims are children. Kids.'

'Now, wait a minute,' I said. 'Indian tribes have massacred children, we know that.'

'True,' Wissler agreed. 'But they wouldn't commit this kind of ritual mutilation against them. At least, no self-respecting Sioux would. These mutilations are carried out against enemies that they want to make sure never find the spirit land, or can't enjoy it when they get there. To do this to a child – well, it would be admitting that you considered the child a threat. An equal. It'd be cowardly, and the Sioux are very touchy about cowardice.'

'Let me ask you this, Dr. Wissler,' Kreizler said, having glanced over his notes. 'Would the behavior we've described to you be consistent with someone who had witnessed Indian mutilations but was too ignorant of their cultural meaning to interpret them as anything more than savagery? And who, in imitating them, might think that *more* savagery will make his actions look *more* like an Indian's?'

Wissler weighed the idea and nodded, knocking burnt tobacco

from his pipe. 'Yes. Yes, that'd be about how I'd see it, Dr. Kreizler.'

And then Laszlo got that look in his eyes, the one that said we had to get out, get into a cab, and get back to our headquarters. He pled pressing business to Wissler, who very much wanted to talk further, and promised to return for another visit soon. Then he bolted for the door, leaving me to apologize more fully for the abrupt departure – which, not surprisingly, Wissler didn't seem to mind at all. Scientists' minds may jump around like amorous toads, but they do seem to accept such behavior in one another.

By the time I caught up to Kreizler on the street, he'd already flagged down a hansom and gotten into it. Thinking there was a good chance he'd leave me behind if I didn't hurry, I dashed to the curb and leapt in, closing the doors on our legs.

'Number 808 Broadway, driver!' Laszlo shouted, and then he began to wave his fist. 'Do you see, Moore? Do you see? He's been out there, our man, he's witnessed it! He defines such behavior as horrible and dirty – "dirty as a Red Indian" – yet he also considers himself full of filth. He combats those feelings with anger and violence – but when he kills, he only sinks further down, down to a level he despises even more, down to the lowest, most animal behavior he can imagine – modeled on that of Indians, but, in his mind, even more Indian *than* an Indian.'

'He's been on the frontier, then,' was what it all meant to me.

'He *must* have been,' Laszlo answered. 'Either as a child or as a soldier – hopefully we can clear that up through our Washington inquiries. I tell you, John, we may have blundered last night, but today we're closer!'

310   Caleb Carr

Chapter 29

Closer we may have been, but we were not, sadly, as close as Laszlo hoped. Sara and Lucius, we learned on returning to our headquarters, had been unable to get anywhere with the War Department, despite Theodore's contacts. All information relating to soldiers hospitalized or dismissed from service for reasons of mental distress was confidential and could not be discussed by telephone. A trip to Washington now loomed as doubly important; indeed, all clues seemed, for the moment, to be leading us away from New York, for if our killer had, in fact, either grown up on the western frontier or served in one of the military units that patrolled that region, then someone would have to head out there to see whether or not an evidential trail of any kind existed.

We spent the remainder of the morning researching possible points, both in time and on the map, at which we might begin to look for such a trail. Eventually we came up with two overall areas: Either the killer had, as a child, witnessed the brutal campaigns against the Sioux that had led up to and followed General Custer's death at the Little Big Horn in 1876, or he had participated as a soldier in the brutal repression of dissatisfied Sioux tribesmen that had culminated in the battle of Wounded Knee Creek in 1890. Either way, Kreizler was anxious to have someone make the trip out west immediately: for, as he told us, he now suspected that the murder of the Zweig children had not been the killer's first taste of blood. And if the man had in fact

311

committed murder in the West there would have to be some record of the case somewhere. True, such a crime would quite probably have been written off as the work of marauding Indians. But there would still be documents relating to it, either in Washington or in some western administrative office. And even if no such killing had taken place, we would nonetheless need to have operatives out there ready to follow up whatever leads were uncovered in the capital. Only by visiting the actual localities involved could we discover exactly what had happened to our man, and thus be able to predict his future moves accurately.

Kreizler planned to make the trip to Washington himself; and when I told him that I still knew a good number of journalists and government workers in that city – including one especially good contact at the Department of the Interior's Bureau of Indian Affairs – he deemed it advisable for me to come along. That left Sara and the Isaacsons, all of whom were eager to make the western trip. Someone, however, had to remain in New York to coordinate our various efforts. After much discussion, it was decided that Sara was the logical choice for this job, since she was still making – and was expected to make – occasional appearances at Police Headquarters on Mulberry Street. Though bitterly disappointed about missing the western journey, Sara had a firm grasp of the overall picture and accepted her assignment with as much grace as possible.

Roosevelt, meanwhile, was the obvious person to put the Isaacsons in touch with guides in the western states, and when we telephoned him about the project he became wildly enthusiastic, threatening to accompany the two detectives himself. We pointed out, however, that the press followed him wherever he went, and especially when he went out west. Tales of his hunting trips and photographs of him wearing his fringed buckskin suit were guaranteed to sell copies of whatever papers and magazines they appeared in, and questions concerning who he was traveling with and why would naturally be asked. We couldn't afford that kind of publicity. Besides, with the power struggle on Mulberry Street about to enter a new and perhaps decisive phase, the Police Department's main exponent of reform could hardly up and disappear into the wilderness.

The Isaacsons would go on their own, then; and we reasoned that if they left immediately, they could be in place by the time Laszlo and I dug up any useful information to wire them from Washington. It was with some shock, therefore, that Marcus arrived at Number 808 Broadway after developing his eyeball photographs (which turned out to be a resounding failure, Monsieur Jules Verne notwithstanding) and learned that he would be leaving the next morning for Deadwood, South Dakota. From there he and his brother would proceed south to the Pine Ridge Sioux Reservation and Agency, where they would begin to investigate any and all mutilative murders from the last ten to fifteen years that had not been solved. Meanwhile, I would use my contact at the Bureau of Indian Affairs to pursue the same line of research in Washington. Kreizler, for his part, would press the War Department and St. Elizabeth's hospital for information concerning western soldiers dismissed for reasons of mental instability, while doing further research on the individual that St. Elizabeth's had written to us about.

By the time we'd finished hammering all this out it was late afternoon, and the weight of a sleepless night was beginning to bear down on all of us quite heavily. In addition, there were domestic arrangements to make, and of course all our packing needed to be done. We decided to cut our day somewhat short. As we left Sara announced that she intended to pick Kreizler and me up the next day in a cab and take us to the station, the near-dead look on each of our faces having caused her to doubt that we could be relied on to rise at all, much less catch a train.

Just as Kreizler and I were walking out the door of Number 808, Stevie appeared, his own strength reconstituted by several hours' sleep. Reminding us that Cyrus had been alone in a hospital room all day, Stevie said that he'd brought the calash and was prepared to drive us to St. Vincent's Hospital to pay our wounded comrade a visit. Weary though we were, neither Laszlo nor I could refuse; and, remembering the appalling quality of food in the average New York hospital, we decided to call Charlie Delmonico and have him order his staff to prepare a really first-rate meal that we could transport to St. Vincent's.

We found Cyrus heavily bandaged and nearly asleep at about

six-thirty. He was delighted with the meal, and complained about nothing, even the fact that the nurses in the hospital objected to caring for a black man. Kreizler lit into a couple of hospital administrators about that, but otherwise we passed a very pleasant hour in Cyrus's room, the window of which offered an excellent view of Seventh Avenue, Jackson Square, and the sunset beyond.

It was nearly dark when we stepped back out onto Tenth Street. I told Stevie that we'd mind the calash for a few minutes so that he could go up and say hello to Cyrus, at which the boy eagerly ran into the hospital. Kreizler and I were about to deposit our creaking bones in the soft leather upholstery of the carriage when an ambulance clattered up at considerable speed and came to a halt next to us. Had I been less exhausted I might have noticed that the ambulance driver's face was not altogether strange to me; as it was, I focused the little attention I could muster on the vehicle's doors, which burst open and spewed forth a second man. I recognized this individual – who looked like anything but a hospital attendant – with an immediate, throbbing pulse of dread.

'What in hell?' I mumbled, as the man stared at me and grinned.

'Connor!' Laszlo said in shock.

The former detective sergeant's toothy gash widened, and then he took a few threatening steps forward. 'So you remember me, then? All the better.' From under his somewhat ragged jacket he produced a revolver. 'Get in the ambulance. Both of you.'

'Don't be absurd,' Laszlo answered sharply, despite the gun.

I tried to take a different tack, having a far better idea than did Kreizler of who we were dealing with: 'Connor, put the gun away. This is crazy, you can't just—'

'Crazy, is it?' the man replied angrily. 'Hardly. I'm just doing my new job. I lost my old one, you might remember. Anyway, I've been told to fetch you two – though I'd just as soon leave you dead on the sidewalk. So *move.*'

Odd how fear can cure exhaustion. I was suddenly aware of a new burst of energy, all of it directed at my feet. But flight was out of the question – Connor was quite serious, I knew, about his willingness to shoot us. So I pulled Kreizler, who struggled and objected all the way, to the rear of the ambulance. As we got in I looked up just long enough to see that the driver of the vehicle was one of the men who'd tried to waylay Sara and me at the Santorellis' flat. Loose ends were beginning to come together.

Connor locked the ambulance door from the outside, then climbed up top with the other man. We careened off at the same hell-bent speed that'd marked their arrival, although it was impossible to tell through the small caged windows in the vehicle's rear door exactly where we were heading.

'Feels like uptown,' I said, as we were jostled around the dark compartment.

'*Kidnapped*?' Kreizler said, maintaining that irritatingly detached tone that he assumed at times of danger. 'Is this someone's very bizarre idea of humor?'

'It's no joke,' I said, trying the door but finding it quite solid. 'Most cops are only about three steps away from being criminals, anyway. I'd say Connor's taken those steps.'

Laszlo was utterly astounded. 'One doesn't really know what to say in such a situation. Do you have any particularly gruesome confessions you'd like to make, Moore? I'm not a cleric, of course, but—'

'Kreizler, did you hear what I just said? This is not a joke!' Just then, we whipped around a corner and were thrown with a crash to one side of the ambulance.

'Hmmm,' Kreizler noised, pulling himself up and checking for damage. 'I begin to see your point.'

In another fifteen minutes our wild ride finally came to an end. Whatever neighborhood we were in was very quiet, the stillness broken only by the grunts and curses of our drivers. Connor finally opened the door again, and we spilled out onto what I recognized to be Madison Avenue, in the Murray Hill district. A nearby lamppost bore a marker that read '36th Street,' and in front of us stood a very large but tasteful brownstone with two columns on each side of its front door and large bay windows bulging out toward the street.

Kreizler and I looked at each other, instant recognition in our faces. 'Well, well,' Kreizler said, intrigued and perhaps even a little awed.

I, on the other hand, was nearly flattened. 'What in hell?' I whispered. 'Why would—'

'Move,' Connor said, indicating the front door but staying by the ambulance.

Kreizler glanced at me again, shrugged, and began to climb the front steps. 'I suggest we enter, Moore. He's not a man accustomed to waiting.'

A very English butler admitted us to Number 219 Madison Avenue, the interior of which reflected the same rare combination – extreme wealth and very fine taste – that marked the outside of the brownstone. Marble flooring met our feet, and a simple yet spacious white stairway wound away into the house's upper floors. Our destination, however, lay directly ahead. We passed splendid European paintings, sculpture, and ceramics – all elegantly and simply displayed, with none of that piling-on effect that families like the Vanderbilts were so appallingly entranced by – and kept moving toward the back of the house. There the butler opened a paneled door that led into a cavernous room that was dimly lit. Laszlo and I stepped inside.

The high walls of the room were paneled with Santo Domingo mahogany that was nearly black; indeed, the room was known, to the staff of the house as well as in New York legend, as 'the Black Library.' Luxurious carpets covered the floor, and a large fireplace was set into one wall. More European canvases, framed in rich, ornate gold, hung from the walls, and tall bookshelves were crammed with splendid leatherbound rarities gathered during dozens of trips across the Atlantic. Some of the most important meetings in the history of New York – indeed, of the United States – had taken place in this room; and while that fact might have caused Kreizler and me to wonder all the more what we were doing there, the collection of faces that stared at us on our entrance soon made matters clearer.

Sitting on a settee on one side of the fireplace was Bishop Henry Potter, and in a matching piece of furniture on the fireplace's other flank was Archbishop Michael Corrigan. Behind each man stood a priest: Potter's man tall and thin, with spectacles, and Corrigan's short, rotund, and sporting large white sideburns. Before the fireplace stood a man I recognized as

Anthony Comstock, the notorious censor of the U.S. Post Office. Comstock had spent twenty years using his congressionally mandated (and constitutionally quite questionable) powers to persecute zealously anyone who dealt in contraceptive devices, pregnancy abortions, ribald literature and photographs, and anything else that met his rather expansive definition of 'obscene.' Comstock's was a hard, mean face, not surprisingly; yet it wasn't as disconcerting as that of the man who stood next to him. Ex-Inspector Thomas Byrnes had a pair of high, bushy eyebrows that arched over penetrating, all-encompassing eyes; yet at the same time, his enormous, drooping mustache made an accurate reading of his mood and thoughts disturbingly difficult. As we came further into the chamber Byrnes turned to us, and the eyebrows arched enigmatically; then he tilted his head toward an enormous walnut desk that sat in the center of the room. My eyes followed his indication.

Sitting at the desk, going over a few papers and scribbling an occasional note, was a man whose power was greater than that of any financier the world has ever known; a man whose otherwise handsome features were counterbalanced by a nose that had been cracked, swollen and deformed by *acne rosacea*. You had to be very careful, however, not to stare at that nose openly – you were likely to pay for your morbid fascination in more ways than you could imagine.

'Ah,' said Mr. John Pierpont Morgan, looking up from his papers and then standing. 'Come in, gentlemen, and let's get this business settled.'

PART III
Will

The fons et origo *of all reality, whether from the absolute or the practical point of view, is thus subjective, is ourselves. As bare logical thinkers, without emotional reaction, we give reality to whatever objects we think of, for they are really phenomena, or objects of our passing thought, if nothing more. But, as thinkers with emotional reaction, we give what seems to us a still higher degree of reality to whatever things we select and emphasize and turn to WITH A WILL.*

> *William James,*
> The Principles of Psychology

Don Giovanni, you invited me to sup with you: I have come.

> *Da Ponte,*
> *from Mozart's* Don Giovanni

Chapter 30

I stepped trepidatiously toward a pair of luxuriantly upholstered easy chairs that sat near Morgan's desk and across from the fireplace. Kreizler, however, stood rigidly still, answering the financier's hard stare with one of his own.

'Before I sit in your house, Mr. Morgan,' Laszlo said, 'may I ask if it is your general custom to compel attendance with firearms?'

Morgan's large head snapped around to scowl at Byrnes, who only shrugged in a very unconcerned way. The ex-cop's gray eyes twinkled a bit, as if to say: When you lie down with dogs, Mr. Morgan . . .

Morgan's head began a slow, slightly disgusted shake. 'Neither my custom nor my instructions, Dr. Kreizler,' he said, holding out an arm to the easy chairs. 'I hope you will accept my apologies. This affair seems to have brought out strong emotions in all who have knowledge of it.'

Kreizler grunted quietly, only partially satisfied, and then we both sat down. Morgan also returned to his seat, and brief introductions were made (save of the two priests behind the settees, whose names I never did learn). After that Morgan gave the slightest of nods to Anthony Comstock, who moved his unimposing little figure into the center of the room. The voice that emerged from that frame proved as thoroughly unpleasant as was the face.

'Doctor. Mr. Moore. Let us be frank. We know of your investigation, and for a variety of reasons we want it stopped. If you do not agree, there are certain matters you will be pressed on.'

'Pressed on?' I said, my immediate dislike for the postal censor giving me confidence. 'This isn't a morals case, Mr. Comstock.'

'Assault,' Inspector Byrnes said quietly, looking at the crowded bookshelves, 'is a *criminal* charge, Moore. We've got a guard at Sing Sing who's missing a couple of teeth. Then there's the matter of consorting with known gangland leaders—'

'Come on, Byrnes,' I said quickly. The inspector and I'd had many run-ins during my years at the *Times*, and though he made me very nervous I knew it would be foolish to show it. 'Even you can't call a carriage ride "consorting."'

Byrnes didn't acknowledge the comment. 'Finally,' he went on, 'there's your misuse of the staff and resources of the Police Department . . .'

'Ours is not an official investigation,' Kreizler replied evenly.

A smile seemed to grow under Byrnes's mustache. 'Cagy, Doctor. But we know all about your arrangement with Commissioner Roosevelt.'

Kreizler showed no emotion. 'You have proof, Inspector?'

Byrnes pulled a slender volume from a shelf. 'Soon.'

'Now, now, gentlemen,' said Archbishop Corrigan in his affable way. 'There's no reason to leap to adversarial positions.'

'Yes,' Bishop Potter agreed, without much enthusiasm. 'I'm sure that an amenable solution can be reached, once we understand one another's – points of view?'

Pierpont Morgan said nothing.

'What I understand,' Laszlo announced, primarily to our silent host, 'is that we have been abducted at gunpoint and threatened with criminal indictment, simply because we have attempted to solve an abominable murder case which has so far baffled the police.' Kreizler pulled out his cigarette case and, removing one of the number within, began to knock it noisily and angrily against the arm of his chair. 'But perhaps there are subtler elements of this escapade to which I am blind.'

'Blind you are, Doctor,' Anthony Comstock said, with the

annoying grate of a zealot. 'But there is nothing subtle about the matter. For many years I have attempted to suppress the written work of men such as yourself. An absurdly broad interpretation of our First Amendment by so-called public servants has made that impossible. But if you believe for one moment that I will stand by and watch you become actively involved in civic affairs—'

A flash of irritation passed over Morgan's face, and I could see that Bishop Potter caught it. Like a dutiful lackey – for Morgan was one of the Episcopal Church's chief benefactors – the bishop stepped in to cut Comstock off:

'Mr. Comstock has the energy and brusqueness of the righteous, Doctor Kreizler. Yet I fear that your work does unsettle the spiritual repose of many of our city's citizens, and undermines the strength of our societal fabric. After all, the sanctity and integrity of the family, along with each individual's responsibility before God and the law for his own behavior, are twin pillars of our civilization.'

'I grieve for our citizens' lack of repose,' Kreizler answered curtly, lighting his cigarette. 'But seven children that we know of, and perhaps many more, have been butchered.'

'But that is a matter for the police, surely,' Archbishop Corrigan said. 'Why involve such questionable work as your own in it?'

'Because the police can't solve it,' I threw in, before Laszlo could answer. These were all fairly standard criticisms of my friend's work, but they were making me a bit hot, nonetheless. 'And, using Dr. Kreizler's ideas, we can.'

Byrnes let out a barely audible chuckle, while Comstock's face grew red. 'I do not believe that is your true motivation, Doctor. I believe you intend, with the help of Mr. Paul Kelly and whatever other atheistic socialists you can find, to spread unrest by discrediting the values of the American family and society!'

If it seems surprising that Kreizler and I neither laughed at this grotesque little man's statements nor rose to physically thrash him, it must be remembered that Anthony Comstock, however harmless his title of 'Postal Censor' might sound, wielded enormous political and regulatory power. Before the end of his forty-year career, he would boast of having driven more than a dozen of his enemies to suicide; and many more than that had their lives and reputations ruined by his persecutory obsessions. Both Laszlo and I knew that while we were a current target, we had not yet entered the ranks of Comstock's permanent fixations; but if we now pushed him to pay such unbalanced attention to us, we might one day arrive back at our usual places of employment to discover ourselves under federal indictment for some trumped-up violation of public morals. For these reasons I said nothing in reply to his outbursts, while Kreizler only breathed smoke wearily.

'And why,' Laszlo finally asked, 'should I wish to spread such unrest, sir?'

'Vanity, sir!' Comstock shot back. 'To advance your nefarious theories, and gain the attention of an ill-educated and sorely confused public!'

'It seems to me,' Morgan said, quietly but firmly, 'that Dr. Kreizler already receives more attention from the public than he might prefer, Mr. Comstock.' None of the others even attempted to agree or disagree with this statement. Morgan rested his head on one large hand and spoke to Laszlo. 'But these are serious charges, Doctor. If they were not, I would hardly have asked that you be brought to this meeting. I take it you are not in league with Mr. Kelly?'

'Mr. Kelly has a few ideas that are not altogether unsound,' Kreizler answered, knowing that the comment would further pique the group around us. 'But he is essentially a criminal, and I have no use for him.'

'I am glad to hear it.' Morgan seemed genuinely satisfied with the answer. 'And what of these other questions, about the social implications of your work? I must admit that I am not well acquainted with such matters. But as you may know, I am senior warden of St. George's Church, across Stuyvesant Park from your own house.' One of Morgan's coal-black eyebrows went up. 'I have never seen you among the congregation, Doctor.'

'My religious opinions are a private matter, Mr. Morgan,' Laszlo replied.

'But surely you realize, Dr. Kreizler,' Archbishop Corrigan

interrupted cautiously, 'that our city's various church organizations are vital to the maintenance of civic order?'

As these words were coming out of Corrigan's mouth, I found myself glancing at the two priests, who continued to stand like statues behind their respective bishops – and suddenly, I got an inkling as to just why we were in that library and talking to that collection of men. This germ of understanding began to grow as soon as it flashed across my brain, but I said nothing, for comment would only have sparked further disagreement. No, I simply sat back and let my thoughts run on, becoming more comfortable as I recognized that Laszlo and I were in less danger than I'd originally thought.

'"Order,"' Kreizler replied to Corrigan's query, 'is a word rather open to interpretation, Archbishop. As to *your* concerns, Mr. Morgan – if what you required was an introduction to my work, I believe I could have suggested an easier route than abduction.'

'No doubt,' Morgan answered uneasily. 'But as we are here, Doctor, perhaps you will favor me with an answer. These men have come to solicit my aid in putting an end to your investigation. I would like to hear both sides of the issue before deciding on a course of action.'

Kreizler sighed heavily, but did go on: 'The theory of individual psychological context that I have developed—'

'Rank determinism!' Comstock declared, unable to contain himself. 'The idea that every man's behavior is decisively patterned in infancy and youth – it speaks against freedom, against responsibility! Yes, I say it is un-American!'

At another annoyed glance from Morgan, Bishop Potter laid a calming hand on Comstock's arm, and the postal censor relapsed into disgruntled silence.

'I have never,' Kreizler went on, keeping his eyes on Morgan, 'argued against the idea that every man is responsible before the law for his actions, save in cases involving the truly mentally diseased. And if you consult my colleagues, Mr. Morgan, I believe you will discover that my definition of mental disease is rather more conservative than most. As for what Mr. Comstock somewhat blithely calls freedom, I have no argument with it as a political or legal concept. The psychological debate surrounding the concept of *free will*, however, is a far more complex issue.'

'And what of your views on the family as an institution, Doctor?' Morgan asked, firmly but without any trace of censure. 'I have heard these and many other good men speak of them with great alarm.'

Kreizler shrugged, stubbing out his cigarette. 'I have very few views on the family as a social institution, Mr. Morgan. My studies have focused on the multitude of sins that can often be concealed by the family structure. I have attempted to expose those sins, and to deal with their effects on children. I will not apologize for that.'

'But why single out families in *this* society?' Comstock whined. 'Surely there are regions of the world where far worse crimes—'

Morgan stood suddenly. 'Thank you, gentlemen,' he said to the postal censor and the churchmen, in a voice that promised hard measures if there was further argument. 'Inspector Byrnes will show you out.'

Comstock looked a bit nonplussed, but Potter and Corrigan had evidently experienced such dismissal before: they departed the library with remarkable speed. Alone with Morgan, I felt much relieved, and it seemed that Kreizler did, too. For all the man's great and mysterious power (he had, after all, single-handedly arranged the United States government's rescue from financial ruin just one year earlier) there was something comforting in his obvious cultivation and breadth of vision.

'Mr. Comstock,' Morgan said as he sat back down, 'is a God-fearing man, but there is no talking to him. *You*, on the other hand, Doctor ... Though I understand very little of what you have told me, I get the feeling that you are a man with whom I can do business.' He straightened his frock coat, dabbed at his mustache, and sat back. 'The mood in the city is volatile, gentlemen. More volatile, I suspect, than you realize.'

The moment had come, I decided, to share my realizations: 'And that's why the bishops were here,' I announced. 'There's been more trouble in the slums and ghettos. A lot more. And they're worried about their money.'

'Their money?' Kreizler echoed in confusion.

I turned to him. 'They weren't covering for the murderer. They were never concerned with the murderer. It was the reaction among the immigrants that had them spooked. Corrigan's afraid that they'll get angry enough to listen to Kelly and his socialist friends – angry enough to stop showing up on Sunday and coughing up what little money they have. Basically, the man's afraid he won't get to finish his damned cathedral, and all the other little holy projects he's probably got planned.'

'But what about Potter?' Kreizler asked. 'You told me yourself that the Episcopals don't have many adherents among the immigrants.'

'That's right,' I said, smiling a bit. 'They don't. But they have something even more profitable, and I'm an ass for not remembering it. Perhaps Mr. Morgan would be willing to tell you' – I turned toward the big walnut desk and found Morgan staring back at me uncomfortably – 'who the largest slum landlord in New York is?'

Kreizler took in breath sharply. 'I see. The Episcopal Church.'

'There is nothing illegal in any of the church's operations,' Morgan said quickly.

'No,' I replied. 'But they'd be in a tight spot if those tenement dwellers were to rise up in a mass and demand better housing, wouldn't they, Mr. Morgan?' The financier turned away silently.

'But I still don't understand,' Kreizler puzzled. 'If Corrigan and Potter are so afraid of the effects of these crimes, why obstruct a solution?'

'We have been told that a solution is impossible,' Morgan answered.

'But why try to frustrate an *attempt*?' Kreizler pressed.

'Because, gentlemen,' said a quiet voice from behind us, 'as long as the case is thought to be unsolvable, no one can be blamed for not solving it.'

It was Byrnes again, back in the room without our having heard his approach. The man really was unnerving. 'The great unwashed,' he went on, taking a cigar from a case on Morgan's desk, 'will be made to understand that these things happen. It's no one's fault. Boys engage in criminal conduct. Boys die. Who kills them? Why? Impossible to determine. And there's no need to. Instead, you fix the public's attention on the more basic lesson—' Byrnes struck a match on his shoe and lit his cigar, the tip of which flamed high. 'Obey the law in the first place and none of the rest occurs.'

'But damn it, Byrnes,' I said, 'we *can* solve it, if you'll just get out of the way. Why, just last night I myself—'

Kreizler stopped me by grabbing my wrist tightly. Byrnes slowly came over to my chair, leaned down, and let me have a big dose of cigar smoke. 'Last night you what, Moore?'

It was impossible not to remember at such a moment that you were dealing with a man who'd personally beaten dozens of suspected and *de facto* criminals senseless, a style of interrogation that had become known throughout New York and the rest of the country by the name Byrnes himself had given it: 'the third degree.' All the same, I attempted defiance. 'Don't try that strong-arm stuff with me, Byrnes. You've got no authority anymore. You haven't even got your thugs to back you up.'

I glimpsed teeth behind the mustache. 'You'd like me to call Connor in?' I said nothing, and Byrnes chuckled. 'You always had a big mouth, Moore. Reporters. But let's play it your way. Tell Mr. Morgan here how you'll solve the case. Your principles of detection. Explain them.'

I turned to Morgan. 'Well, it won't make sense to men like Inspector Byrnes, sir, and it may not to you, but – we've adopted what you might call a reverse investigative procedure.'

Byrnes laughed out loud. 'What you might call ass-backwards!'

Realizing my mistake, I went for another approach: 'That is, we start with the prominent features of the killings themselves, as well as the personality traits of the victims, and from those we determine what kind of a man *might* be at work. Then, using evidence that would otherwise have seemed meaningless, we begin to close in.'

I knew I was on shaky ground, and was relieved to hear Kreizler chime in at this point:

'There is some precedent, Mr. Morgan. Similar efforts, though far more rudimentary, were made during the Ripper murders in London eight years ago. And the French police are currently seeking a Ripper of their own – they've used some techniques that are not unlike ours.'

'The London Ripper,' Byrnes called out, 'was not apprehended without my hearing about it, was he, Doctor?'

Kreizler frowned. 'No.'

'And the French police, using their anthropo-hodge-podge – have they made any progress in their case?'

Laszlo's scowl deepened. 'Very little.'

Byrnes finally did us the decency of looking up from his book. 'Quite a pair of examples, gentlemen.'

There was a moment of silence, during which I felt our cause to be weakening. Putting new determination into my words, I said, 'The fact remains—'

'The fact remains,' Byrnes interrupted, coming back over to us but speaking to Morgan, 'that this is an intellectual exercise which offers no hope of solving the case. All these people are doing is giving every person they interview the idea that a solution is possible. As I say, that's not just useless, it's dangerous. The only thing the immigrants ought to be told is that they *and* their children had better obey the laws of this city. If they don't, nobody else can be held responsible for what happens. Maybe they'll find that point hard to swallow. But this idiot Strong and his cowboy police commissioner will be out before long. And then we'll be able to bring back the old *force-feeding* techniques. Quickly.'

Morgan nodded slowly, then glanced from Byrnes to Kreizler. 'You've made your point, Inspector. I wonder if now you'll excuse us?'

In contrast to Comstock and the churchmen, Byrnes seemed almost amused by Morgan's curt dismissal: as he left the library he began to whistle lowly. When the paneled door had closed again, Morgan stood up and looked out a window. It almost seemed as though he was making sure Byrnes left his house.

'Can I offer you gentlemen anything to drink?' Morgan said at length. After Kreizler and I both declined, our host took one of the cigars from the case on his desk and lit it, then began slowly to pace the thickly carpeted floor. 'I agreed to see the delegation that has just left us,' he announced, 'out of deference to Bishop

Potter, and because I have no desire to see the recent outbreaks of civil unrest go on.'

'Excuse me, Mr. Morgan,' I said, a bit amazed by his tone. 'But have you, or any of the gentlemen who were here, even *discussed* this matter with Mayor Strong?'

Morgan passed a hand before him quickly. 'Inspector Byrnes's point about Colonel Strong is well taken. I have no interest in dealing with a man whose power is limited by elections. Besides, Strong doesn't have the mind to deal with a matter of this nature.' Morgan's heavy, deliberate pacing went on, and Kreizler and I remained silent. The library slowly filled up with thick cigar smoke, and when Morgan finally stood still and spoke again, I could barely see him through the brownish haze.

'As I see it, gentlemen, there really are only two advisable courses – yours, and that advocated by Byrnes. We must have order. Particularly now.'

'Why now?' Kreizler asked.

'You are probably not in a position to know, Doctor,' Morgan answered carefully, 'that we are at a crossroads, both in New York and in the country as a whole. This city is changing. Dramatically. Oh, I don't simply mean the population, with the influx of immigrants. I mean the city itself. Twenty years ago, New York was still primarily a port – the harbor was our chief source of business. Today, with other ports challenging our preeminence, shipping and receiving have been eclipsed by both manufacture and banking. Manufacture, as you know, requires workers, and other, less fortunate, nations in the world have provided them. The leaders of organized labor claim that such workers are treated unfairly here. But fairly or no, they continue to come, because it is better than what they have left behind. I mark from your speech that you are of foreign extraction yourself, Doctor. Have you spent much time in Europe?'

'Enough,' Kreizler answered, 'to take your point.'

'We are not obligated to provide everyone who comes to this country with a good life,' Morgan went on. 'We are obligated to provide them with a chance to attain that life, through discipline and hard work. That chance is more than they have anywhere else. That is why they keep coming.'

Caleb Carr

'Assuredly,' Laszlo answered, impatience beginning to show in his voice.

'We shall not be able to offer such a chance, in future, should our national economic development – which is currently in a state of deep crisis – be retarded by foolish political ideas born in the ghettos of Europe.' Morgan put his cigar down in a tray, went to a sideboard, and poured out three glasses of what turned out to be excellent whiskey. Without asking a second time if Laszlo and I wanted any, he handed two of the glasses to us. 'Any events which can be prostituted to serve the purposes of those ideas must be suppressed. That is why Mr. Comstock was here. He believes that ideas such as yours, Doctor, can be so prostituted. Were you to succeed in your investigation, Mr. Comstock believes that your ideas might gain greater credence. Thus you see—' Morgan took up his cigar again, and drew in an enormous volume of smoke. 'You have made yourselves a wide variety of powerful enemies.'

Kreizler stood up slowly. 'Need we count you among those enemies, as well, Mr. Morgan?'

The pause that followed seemed interminable, for on Morgan's answer hung any hope of our success. Should he decide that Potter, Corrigan, Comstock, and Byrnes were right, and that our investigation represented a range of threats to the status quo in our city that simply could not be tolerated, we might just as well fold our tents and head for home. Morgan could arrange the purchase or sale of anyone and anything in New York, and the interference we'd already experienced would be nothing compared to what we'd meet if he decided to oppose us. Conversely, should he signal to the rest of the city's rich and powerful that our effort was to be, if not actively encouraged, at least tolerated, we could hope to proceed without any more severe interference than that which our opponents had already attempted.

Morgan finally let out a deep breath. 'You need not, sir,' he said, stamping out his cigar. 'As I say, I do not understand all of what you gentlemen have explained to me, about either psychology or criminal detection. But I make it my business to know men. And neither of you strikes me as having the worst interests of society at heart.' Kreizler and I each nodded once calmly, belying the enormous relief that was coursing through our veins. 'You will still face many obstacles,' Morgan went on, in an easier tone than he'd used before. 'The churchmen who were here can, I believe, be persuaded to stand aside – but Byrnes will continue to harass you, in an effort to preserve the methods and organization he has spent so many years establishing. And he will have Comstock's support.'

'We have prevailed against them so far,' Kreizler answered. 'I believe we can continue to do so.'

'Of course, I can offer you no public support,' Morgan added, indicating the library door and walking with us to it. 'That would be entirely too – complicated.' Meaning that, for all his superior intellectual acumen and personal erudition, Morgan was at heart a true Wall Street hypocrite, one who spoke publicly about God and the family but privately kept his yacht stocked with mistresses and enjoyed the esteem of men who lived by similar rules. He would certainly lose some of that esteem, if he were thought to be in league with Kreizler. 'However,' he went on, as he walked us to his front door, 'since a quick conclusion to the affair is in everyone's best interest, if you should find yourselves in need of resources . . .'

'Thank you, but no,' Kreizler said, as we went out. 'It would be best not to have even a cash connection between us, Mr. Morgan. You must consider your position.'

Morgan bridled at the acidity of the comment, and, murmuring a fast 'Good evening,' closed the door without shaking hands.

'That was a little gratuitous, don't you think, Laszlo?' I said as we went down the stairs. 'The man was only trying to help.'

'Don't be so gullible, Moore,' Kreizler snapped. 'Men like that are only capable of doing what they perceive to be in their best interests. Morgan's betting that we're more likely to find the killer than Byrnes and company are to keep the immigrant population's anger indefinitely suppressed. And he's right. I tell you, John, it would be almost worthwhile to fail, simply to observe the consequences to such men.'

I was entirely too exhausted to listen to one of Laszlo's tirades, and scanned Madison Avenue quickly. 'We can catch a cab at the

Caleb Carr

Waldorf,' I decided, seeing none close by.

There was very little activity on the avenue during our descent of Murray Hill, and Laszlo eventually stopped decrying the evils of the group we'd just left. As we walked on, both silence and weariness deepened, and our entire encounter in the Black Library began to take on a rather unreal quality.

'I don't think I've ever been so tired,' I yawned as we reached Thirty-fourth Street. 'Do you know, Kreizler, that for just a second when we first met Morgan I thought *he* might actually be the killer?'

Laszlo laughed loud. 'As did I! Deformity in the face, Moore – and that nose, that nose! One of the only possible locations for such deformity that we never discussed!'

'Imagine if it had been him. Things are dangerous enough as it is.' We found a hansom outside the ornately elegant Waldorf Hotel, whose sister structure, the Astoria, was just being built at the time. 'And they'll only get more so – Morgan's right about that. Byrnes is a bad enemy to have, and Comstock strikes me as being flat out of his mind.'

'They can threaten all they like,' Kreizler answered happily as we climbed into a cab. 'We know who they are, now, and defense should be an easier matter. Besides, their attacks will grow increasingly difficult. For in the days to come our opponents shall find us mysteriously' – Laszlo splayed his fingers out into the air before him – '*gone*.'

Chapter 31

Sara was at the door of my grandmother's house at nine-thirty the next morning, and though I'd gotten better than ten hours of sleep I still felt disoriented and thoroughly worn out. A copy of the *Times* Sara had tucked under her arm informed me that it was May 26th, and the bright glare of the sun that assaulted me as I went out to Sara's cab stated unarguably that spring was continuing its march toward summer; but I might as well have been on the planet Mars (which, I learned from a semiconscious reading of the front page of the paper, was the object of study for a newly formed group of eminent Boston astronomers, who believed that what they called the 'red star of war' was 'inhabited by human beings'). Sara got a few good laughs out of my slightly ridiculous condition during the first leg of our cab ride to Kreizler's; but when I started to relate details of Laszlo's and my unexpected trip to Pierpont Morgan's, she became all seriousness.

We found Kreizler sitting in his calash on Seventeenth Street, with Stevie in the driver's seat. I transferred my small bag from the cab to the carriage and then climbed aboard with Sara. Just as we pulled away I looked up to catch sight of Mary Palmer standing on the small balcony outside Kreizler's parlor. She was watching us anxiously, and what looked from a distance like tearstains were glistening on her cheeks. Turning to Laszlo, I saw that he was also looking back at her; and when he turned forward again, a smile came into his face. It seemed an odd reaction to the girl's distress, to say the least. I thought perhaps Sara had something to do with it all, but when I glanced at her I found that she was deliberately staring across the street and into Stuyvesant Park. Irritated by all these new hints of personal complexities among my friends, and incapable at that moment of making any sense of them, I did nothing more than lean back and let the spring sun bake my face as we clattered east.

Our ride to the Grand Central Depot had not been designed with relaxation in mind, however. On Eighteenth Street and Irving Place Stevie drew to a halt outside a tavern, and Kreizler, taking my bag as well as his own, told Sara and me to accompany him inside. We obeyed, myself with a few grumbles. Moments after we'd entered the dark, smoky place I looked outside to see two other men and a woman, their faces obscured by hats, getting into the calash and driving off with Stevie. Once they'd gotten out of sight Kreizler rushed back out onto the street and flagged down a cab, then waved Sara and me into it. This annoying little exercise, Laszlo explained as we headed uptown again, was designed to frustrate the agents he believed Inspector Byrnes had assigned to shadow us. It was a very clever provision, no doubt, but it only made me impatient to get on our train, where, I hoped, I'd be allowed to go back to sleep.

One more mystery stood between me and sweet repose, however. Sara accompanied us into Grand Central when we arrived, and then to the platform where the Washington train stood in steaming readiness. Kreizler kept peppering her with last minute instructions about communications and whatnot, as well as with tips on how to handle Stevie while we were gone and what to do with Cyrus once he emerged from the hospital. Then the loud whistle on the train's engine screamed and a conductor's smaller pipe began to wail, signaling us to get on board. I turned away from my companions, expecting some slightly embarrassing farewell scene to take place; all Kreizler and Sara did, however, was shake hands collegially, after which Laszlo dashed past me onto the train. I stood there for a moment with my jaw hanging open, prompting a chuckle from Sara.

'Poor John,' she said, giving me a warm hug. 'Still trying to

The Alienist

sort things out. Don't worry – it'll all be clear, someday. And you mustn't fret too much about your priest theory being wrong. You'll have another idea soon.'

With that she shoved me into the train, just as it began to grunt and wheeze out of the station.

Kreizler had engaged a first-class compartment, and after we'd settled into it I immediately stretched out on one seat with my face toward the small window, determined to strangle any curiosity I had about the behavior of my friends with sleep. For his part, Laszlo pulled out a copy of Wilkie Collins's *The Moonstone* that Lucius Isaacson had lent him and began very contentedly reading. Further annoyed, I rolled over, pulled my cap down over my face, and began deliberately snoring even before I'd fallen asleep.

I was unconscious for over two hours, and woke to see rich, green New Jersey pastures shooting by the window. Stretching fully, I noted that my evil mood of the morning had at last departed: I was hungry, but otherwise quite pleased with life. A small note from Kreizler on the seat opposite me stated that he had gone to the dining car to secure a table for lunch, and I quickly neatened my appearance and made for that destination, ready to break bread with a vengeance.

The rest of our trip was first-rate. The farmlands of the northeast are never more picturesque than in late May, and they formed a splendid backdrop for one of the better meals I've ever had on a train. Kreizler's spirits were still quite high, and for once he proved willing to discuss subjects other than the case. We talked of the upcoming national political conventions (the Republicans were set to gather in St. Louis in June, and the Democrats would follow suit in Chicago later in the summer), and then about a piece in the *Times* that stated that there had been a riot in Harvard Square following a victory posted by our alma mater's baseball team over Princeton. During dessert Kreizler nearly choked to death when he came across a report that Henry Abbey and Maurice Grau, managers of the Metropolitan Opera, had announced the failure of their company and debts of some $400,000. Laszlo's composure was partially restored by the additional news that a group of 'private backers' (undoubtedly headed by our host of the previous evening) were organizing to put the company back on a solid footing. The first step in this process was to be a high-priced benefit performance of *Don Giovanni* on June 21st. Kreizler and I determined that this was an event we must attend, no matter what state our investigation might be in at the time.

We arrived in Washington's handsome Union Station late in the afternoon, and by dinnertime we were ensconced in a pair of very comfortable rooms at that imposing Victorian edifice on Pennsylvania Avenue and Fourteenth Street known as the Willard Hotel. All around us and quite visible from our fourth-story windows were the houses of our nation's government. In a very few minutes I could have strolled over to the White House and asked Grover Cleveland how it would feel to relinquish that residence twice in one lifetime. I had not seen the capital since the simultaneous terminations of my career as a political reporter and my engagement to Julia Pratt; and it was only as I stood in my room at the Willard and stared at the beautiful panorama of Washington on a spring evening that I fully recognized how very far away from that former life I had grown. It was a melancholic sort of realization, and not to my liking; to counteract it, I quickly sought out a telephone and put in a call to Hobart Weaver, the old carousing partner of mine who was now a fairly high-level functionary at the Bureau of Indian Affairs. I found him still at his desk, and we made plans to meet that evening in the hotel dining room.

Kreizler joined us. Hobart was a portly, addlebrained, bespectacled fellow, who loved nothing more than free food and drink. By providing both commodities in abundance I was able to ensure that he would be not only discreet but uninquisitive about what Laszlo and I were up to. He informed us that the Bureau did, in fact, keep records of murders that were either known or presumed to have been committed by Indians. We told him that we were interested only in unsolved cases, though when he asked what parts of the country we were concerned with Kreizler could only reply, 'frontier regions during the last fifteen years.' Covering such a broad spectrum would, Hobart assured us, involve a lot of sifting through records, a task that he and I would have to undertake surreptitiously: Hobart's boss, Interior Secretary Michael Hoke Smith, shared President Cleveland's dislike of reporters, especially prying reporters. But as Hobart packed steadily more fowl and wine into his short round body, he became ever more convinced that we could do the job (although he remained completely oblivious of our purpose); and just to fully crystallize his resolve, I took him after dinner to a saloon that I knew of in the southeast section of the city where the entertainment was of what might be called the immodest variety.

Kreizler and I breakfasted together early the next morning. It was our hope that, making hard stages, the Isaacsons would be in Deadwood, South Dakota, by Thursday evening. They had been instructed to check the Western Union Telegraph office in that town for communications from us as soon as they arrived, and Kreizler sent the first such cable just after Wednesday morning's breakfast. In it he told the brothers that, for reasons that would be explained later, priesthood had been eliminated as a likely profession for our quarry. New possibilities would be forwarded as soon as we had formulated them. Then it was off to St. Elizabeth's Hospital for Laszlo, while I took a cheerful stroll up to F Street and over to the Patent Office building, which housed most of the staff and records of the Interior Department.

The enormous Greek Revival Patent Office had been completed in 1867 and was of a general layout that was fast becoming the rule for official buildings in the capital: rectangular, hollow, and as monotonous on the inside as it was without. All of the two blocks between Seventh and Ninth streets were taken up by the thing, and it was no small job, once I'd gotten inside, to find Hobart's office. This vastness ultimately proved a blessing, however, for my presence provoked no comment: there were hundreds of federal employees wandering the hallways of the building's four wings, most of them ignorant of one another's identities and functions. Hobart, none the worse for the previous evening's activities, had already located a small desk for my use in a corner of one basement records room and had also laid hands on the first batch of files that I would have to investigate: reports from various frontier forts and administrative centers going back to 1881 and relating to violent incidents between settlers and the various Sioux tribes.

During the next two days I saw very little of Washington, outside of my little corner of that dusty records room. As will happen during extended periods of windowless research, reality soon began to lose its hold on my mind and the horrifying descriptions I pored over, of massacres, murders, and reprisals, took on a vividness that they would not have had if I'd been reading them, say, in one of the city's parks. Inevitably, I became distracted by tales that I knew held no promise for us, but which were so morbidly fascinating on their own merits that I had to see how they turned out. Most of the accounts were of acts of vengeance on the part of the Sioux which, while severe, seemed at least understandable when measured against the abominable treachery of the white soldiers, Indian agents (the Bureau of Indian Affairs was the most corrupt agency in a notoriously corrupt department), and traders in firearms and whiskey against whom they were committed. Reading the stories brought back to me vividly the concern with which Franz Boas and Clark Wissler had approached our investigation: the average white citizen of the United States, deeply distrustful of the Indian tribes, was also utterly ignorant of such records as I was exploring, and thus of the true state of white-Indian affairs.

Late Wednesday, after the conclusion of my first long day in the Interior basement, Kreizler and I met to compare notes in his room at the Willard. The superintendent of St. Elizabeth's had proved as troublesome in person as he had been over the telephone wire, and Kreizler had been forced to resort to Roosevelt – who, in turn, had asked a friend of his in the attorney general's office to place a call to the man – in order to gain access to the hospital records. The process had taken up most of Kreizler's day, and while he'd had time to amass a list of names of soldiers who'd served with the Army of the West and subsequently been sent to St. Elizabeth's because of questionable mental stability, his overall mood when we met was one of severe disappointment: for while the man who'd been the subject of the original letter we'd received from St. Elizabeth's had indeed been a soldier, he'd apparently also been born and raised in the East, and never served anywhere west of Chicago.

'No roving bands of marauding Indians in Chicago anymore, I suppose?' I asked as Laszlo stared at a sheet detailing particulars of the man's background and service.

'No,' Kreizler answered quietly. 'It's a true pity. There are many other details that would recommend the fellow.'

'Best not to dwell on them,' I said. 'We've got plenty of other candidates. So far Hobart and I have picked out four cases of mutilative murders in the Dakotas and Wyoming – all committed when both Sioux groups and army units were close by.'

Kreizler put aside his piece of paper with great effort and looked up. 'Did any involve children?'

'Two of the four,' I answered. 'In the first, two girls were killed with their parents, and in the second an orphaned girl and boy died with their grandfather, who was their guardian. The problem is that in both cases only the adult males were mutilated.'

'Were any theories formulated?'

'Both were assumed to have been reprisal raids by war parties. But there's an interesting detail in the case involving the grandfather. It happened in the late fall of '89 near Fort Keough, during the period when the last great reservation was broken up. There were a lot of disgruntled Sioux around, mostly followers of Sitting Bull and another chief called' – I scanned my notes quickly with one finger – 'Red Cloud. Anyway, a small cavalry detail stumbled onto the murdered family, and the lieutenant in command initially laid the crime off to some of Red Cloud's more bellicose subordinates. But one of the older soldiers in the company said that Red Cloud's band hadn't launched any murder raids lately, and that the dead grandfather'd had a history of run-ins with Bureau agents and army men at another fort – Robinson, I think it was. Apparently the man had accused a cavalry sergeant at Robinson of trying to sexually assault his grandson. As it turned out, the sergeant's unit was in the Fort Keough area when the family was killed.'

Kreizler hadn't been paying much attention up to that point, but these last facts brought him around. 'Do we know the soldier's name?'

'Wasn't included in the file. Hobart's going to do a little

digging at the War Department tomorrow.'

'Good. But make sure you cable the information we have now to the detective sergeants in the morning. The details can follow.'

We then went over the rest of the cases I'd culled, though for various reasons we eventually ruled them all out. After that, we dove into the stack of names that Kreizler had gathered at St. Elizabeth's, and succeeded in eliminating all but a few of them over the next several hours. Finally, at well past one o'clock in the morning, I retired to my room and poured out a healthy whiskey and soda, which I only managed to get halfway through before I fell asleep in my clothes.

Thursday morning found me back at my desk at the Interior Department, lost in more stories of unsolved deaths on the frontier. Along toward noon Hobart returned from his brief trip to the War Department, where he'd discovered a disappointing fact: The cavalry sergeant who'd figured in the story about the murdered grandfather had been forty-five years old at the time of the incident. That made him fifty-two in 1896: too old to fit the portrait we'd painted of our killer. Still, it seemed worthwhile to make a note of the man's name and last known whereabouts (he'd opened a dry goods store in Cincinnati after retiring from the army), just in case the age portion of our hypothesis turned out to be wrong.

'Sorry I couldn't have brought better news,' Hobart said, as I jotted down the particulars. 'Any interest in lunch?'

'Plenty,' I answered. 'Pick me up in an hour, I should make it through the 1892 cases by then.'

'Fine.' He started to move away from the desk, then touched his jacket pocket and seemed to remember something. 'Oh, John. I meant to ask you – this search of yours is definitely confined to the frontier states and territories, is that right?' He pulled a folded paper from his pocket.

'That's right. Why?'

'Nothing. Just an odd story. I found it after you left last night.' He tossed the piece of paper on my desk. 'But it won't work – happened in New York State. Chops?'

I picked up the paper and began reading it. 'What?'

'For lunch. Chops? There's a splendid new place on the Hill. Good beer, too.'

'Fine.'

Hobart sped away to catch a pretty young archivist who'd just passed my desk. From the direction of a nearby staircase I heard the woman squeal, and then there was a slapping sound and a little yelp of pain from Hobart. Chuckling quietly at the fellow's hopelessness, I leaned back in my chair to study the document he'd left me.

It related the curious story of a minister named Victor Dury and his wife, who in 1880 had been found murdered in their very modest home outside New Paltz, New York. The bodies had been what the document called 'most foully and savagely torn to bits.' Reverend Dury had formerly been a missionary in South Dakota, where he'd apparently made enemies among the Indian tribes; in fact, the constabulary in New Paltz had decided that the murders were an act of revenge on the part of several embittered Indians who'd been sent east by their chief for that very purpose. This bit of 'detective' work had been the result of a note from the assassins found on the scene that explained the killings and stated that the dead couple's teenaged son was being taken back to live among the Indians as one of their own. It was quite a grim little tale, one that would have been of obvious use to us had its setting been further west. I put the paper aside, but in a few minutes picked it up again, wondering if there wasn't at least a chance that we were wrong about our killer's geographic background. Finally deciding to discuss the matter with Kreizler, I tucked the document away in my pocket.

The rest of the day offered only two cases that held out any hope of advancing our investigation. The first involved a group of children and their teacher who'd been slaughtered during their studies in an isolated schoolhouse; and the second, yet another prairie family who'd been massacred after a treaty violation. Realizing that the two accounts were meager reward for a long day's work, I set my sights on the Willard Hotel, hoping that Kreizler had had better luck during his second day of research. But Laszlo had discovered only a few additional names of soldiers who'd served in the Army of the West during the fifteen-year span we were investigating, then been institutionalized in the capital because of violent, unstable behavior, and finally suffered from some sort of facial disfigurement. Of these few, only one fell within the general age range that we were looking for (about thirty). As we sat down to dinner in the hotel dining room Kreizler handed me the case file on this man, and I offered him the document that told the tale of the Dury murders.

'Born and raised in Ohio,' was my first comment on Laszlo's find. 'He'd have to've spent a lot of time in New York after his discharge.'

'True,' Kreizler said, unfolding the paper I'd given him as he set to work halfheartedly on a bowl of crab bisque. 'Which presents a problem – he didn't leave St. Elizabeth's until the spring of '91.'

'A fast study,' I commented with a nod. 'But it's possible.'

'I'm also not encouraged by the disfigurement – a long scar across the right cheek and the lips.'

'What's the matter with that? Sounds fairly revolting.'

'But it suggests a war injury, Moore, and that rules out childhood distress over the—'

Kreizler's eyes suddenly went very wide and he set his spoon down slowly as he finished reading the document I'd given him. Looking slowly from it to me, he then spoke in a tone of suppressed excitement. 'Where did you get this?'

'Hobart,' I answered simply, putting the file on the soldier from Ohio aside. 'He found it last night. Why?'

His hands moving quickly, Kreizler snatched some more folded papers from his inside pocket. Quickly flattening them on the table, he then thrust the pile across to me. 'Notice anything?'

It took one or two seconds, but I did. At the top of the first sheet of paper, which was yet another form from St. Elizabeth's Hospital, there was a space marked PLACE OF BIRTH.

In that space had been scribbled the words 'New Paltz, New York.'

Chapter 32

'This is the man they originally wrote to us about?' I asked.

Kreizler nodded eagerly. 'I've kept the file with me. I dislike hunches generally, but I couldn't get away from this one. There are so many particulars that match – the poor upbringing in a strictly religious household, and the one sibling, a brother. Remember Sara's idea about his being from a small family, because the mother disliked childbearing?'

'Kreizler . . .' I said, trying to slow him down.

'And that tantalizing reference to "a facial tic," which even in his hospital record is never explained in any greater detail than "an intermittent and violent contraction of the ocular and facial muscles." No explanation as to why.'

'Kreizler—'

'And then there's the pronounced emphasis on sadism in the admitting alienist's report, along with the particulars of the incident that caused his commitment—'

'Kreizler! Will you please shut up and let me look at this?'

He rose suddenly, all excitement. 'Yes – yes, of course. And while you do, I'll check the cable office for messages from the detective sergeants.' He put the document I'd given him back down. 'I've a powerful feeling about this, Moore!'

As Kreizler dashed out of the dining room I began to carefully go over the first page of the hospital file:

Corporal John Beecham, admitted to St. Elizabeth's Hospital

in May of 1886, had at that time stated that he'd been born in New Paltz, the small town just west of the Hudson River and some sixty-five miles north of New York that had been the scene of the Dury murders. The specific date of birth cited was November 19, 1865. His parents were identified only as 'deceased,' and he had one brother, eight years older than himself.

I reached over and grabbed the Interior Department document that told of the murdered minister and his wife. Those crimes had been committed in 1880, and the victims were listed as having a teenaged son who'd been kidnapped by Indians. A second and older son, Adam Dury, was apparently at his home just outside Newton, Massachusetts, at the time of the murders.

I grabbed another sheet of the hospital file and scanned the notes penned by John Beecham's admitting alienist, in an effort to find the specific cause of the corporal's confinement. Despite the sloppiness of the doctor's handwriting, I soon had it:

'Patient was part of force requested by governor of Illinois to quell disturbances arising from strikes in Chicago area beginning May 1st (Haymarket riots, etc.). During May 5th action against strikers North Chicago, soldiers ordered to open fire; patient subsequently found stabbing corpse of one dead striker. Lieutenant M—— discovered patient *in flagrante*; patient claims M—— always "had it in for him," etc., and was constantly "watching" him; M—— ordered patient relieved of duty, regimental surgeon pronounced him unfit for service.'

Then followed the comments on sadism and delusions of persecution that Kreizler had already told me about. In the rest of the file I found more reports written by other alienists during Beecham's four-month stay at St. Elizabeth's, and I scanned them for further references to the man's parents. There was no mention anywhere of his mother, and very little talk of his childhood generally; but one of the final assessments, written just before Beecham's release, contained the following paragraph:

'Patient has applied for writ h.c. [*habeas corpus*] and continues to claim nothing wrong or criminal in behavior; says society must have laws and men to enforce them; father was evidently a very godly man, who emphasized importance of rules and punishment of violators. Recommend increased dosage c. hydrate.'

Just then Kreizler came speeding back to the table, shaking his head. 'Nothing. Their arrival must have been delayed.' He indicated the various papers I was holding. 'Well, Moore, what do you make of it all?'

'The timing matches,' I answered slowly. 'Along with the location.'

Kreizler clapped his hands together and sat back down. 'I never would have *dreamed* of such a possibility. Who could have? Kidnapped by Indians? It's almost absurd.'

'It may *be* absurd,' I replied. 'I haven't gotten the impression in the last couple of days that Indians take many male children captive – and certainly not if they're as old as sixteen.'

'Can you be certain of that?'

'No. But Clark Wissler probably could. I'll put in a call tomorrow morning.'

'Do that,' Kreizler answered with a nod, taking the Interior document back from me and again studying it. 'We need more particulars.'

'That occurred to me, too. I can telephone Sara, and put her onto a friend of mine at the *Times* who'll let her into the morgue.'

'The morgue?'

'Where back issues are kept. She could find the story, it must have made the New York papers.'

'Yes – yes, it would have.'

'In the meantime, Hobart and I'll see if we can find out who this "Lieutenant M——" is, and whether or not he's still in the army. He might be able to supply more details.'

'And I'll return to St. Elizabeth's, and talk to anyone who had any personal knowledge of Corporal John Beecham.' Kreizler lifted his wineglass with a smile. 'Well, Moore – new hope!'

Anticipation and curiosity made sleep difficult that night, but morning brought the welcome news that the Isaacsons had finally arrived in Deadwood. Kreizler instructed them by wire to stay put until they heard from us that afternoon or evening, while I went to the lobby to place my telephone calls to New York. It took some doing to get through to the Museum of Natural

History, and locating Clark Wissler was an even greater challenge; but when his voice finally did come through the line he was not only helpful but quite enthusiastic – largely, I think, because he was able to say confidently that the story described in the Interior Department document was almost certainly a fabrication. The idea that any Indian chieftain would dispatch assassins all the way to New Paltz – and that they would reach that destination without incident – was outlandish enough; but the further assertions that, having committed the murders, they would then leave behind an explanatory note, kidnap rather than kill the victims' adolescent son, and make their way back across the country without ever being noticed was too farfetched even to be considered. Someone, Wissler was sure, had put a none-too-clever bit of trickery over on the obviously dull-witted authorities in New Paltz. I thanked him heartily for his help, then rang off and 'phoned Number 808 Broadway.

Sara answered in a very edgy voice: Apparently there'd been a lot of interest displayed in our headquarters during the previous forty-eight hours by a variety of unsavory characters. Sara herself had been followed fairly constantly, she was certain of that; and even though she never went out unarmed, such close scrutiny was nerve-racking. Boredom only worsened things: Because Sara had had little to do since our departure, her mind was free to focus all the more on her spectral stalkers. For this reason the thought of activity, even if it was only research at the *Times*, acted as a tonic on her spirits, and she devoured the details of our latest theory with relish. I then asked her how long she thought it would be before Cyrus would be able to accompany her around town, to which she answered that although the big fellow had been released from the hospital, he was still too weak to leave his bed at Kreizler's house.

'I'll be all right, John,' she insisted to me, though her words lacked some of their usual conviction.

'Of course you will,' I answered. 'I doubt if half the criminals in New York are as well armed. Or cops, for that matter. All the same, get Stevie to stick with you. He's quite the item in a brawl, even at his size.'

'Yes,' Sara answered, with a calming laugh. 'He's already been very helpful – sees me home every night. We smoke cigarettes together, though you needn't tell Dr. Kreizler that.' I wondered for a moment why she persisted in calling him 'Dr. Kreizler,' but there was more pressing business at hand.

'I've got to go, Sara. Telephone as soon as you have anything.'

'All right. Watch out for yourselves, John.'

I rang off and went to find Kreizler.

He was still in the cable office, putting the last words to a wire that he proceeded to send to Roosevelt. Phrasing his sentences vaguely (and putting no signature to the message), Laszlo asked Theodore to contact first the office of the mayor of New Paltz, in an attempt to ascertain whether a family or person named Beecham had lived in that town at any point during the last twenty years, and second the authorities in Newton, Massachusetts, to see if one Adam Dury still resided there. Anxious as we both were to get replies to these questions, we knew that they would take time, and that we still had plenty of work to do at St. Elizabeth's and the Interior Department. Somewhat reluctantly, we left the cable office and went out into another magnificent spring morning.

Even though there were many details to be attended to that day, it was impossible for me to keep my mind from wandering back to the larger mysteries surrounding John Beecham and Victor Dury, and I'm sure Kreizler experienced much the same thing. Several questions became particularly persistent: If the story about Indian assassins was, in fact, false, who had concocted it? Who had actually committed the murder, and what had happened to the younger Dury boy? Why was there so little discussion, in the hospital records, of John Beecham's early life, and no mention at all of his mother? And where was that obviously troubled man now?

The day's work brought no answers to these questions: neither the Interior nor the War Department could supply further details of either the Dury murder or John Beecham's life before his commitment to St. Elizabeth's. Kreizler fared no better at said hospital, which, he told me that evening, was neither required nor empowered to find out where a patient was going once he had secured his release through a writ of *habeas corpus*. In

Caleb Carr

addition, none of the few members of the nonmedical staff who had been at the hospital at the time of Beecham's commitment could remember anything about the man other than his facial spasms. He was apparently utterly unremarkable in his outward manner, a fact that, while frustrating in terms of our present purposes, did fit in nicely with the proposition that our killer was not a man who would attract any notice save at the time of his violent acts.

The only useful bit of information that did emerge on that Friday was brought to the Willard in the evening by Hobart Weaver. According to War Department records, the lieutenant who'd had John Beecham relieved of duty in 1886 was one Frederick Miller, since promoted to captain and currently serving at Fort Yates, North Dakota. Laszlo and I knew that an interview with this man might prove invaluable; yet a trip to Yates would take the Isaacson brothers in the opposite direction from their original destination, the Pine Ridge Agency. Still, it was the most solid lead we'd been able to develop, and on balance seemed worth the detour. And so, at six o'clock that evening, Kreizler and I sent a wire to Deadwood, telling the detective sergeants to secure passage north immediately.

As for incoming messages, the cable office had received a wire from Roosevelt, saying that there was, in fact, a man living in Newton, Massachusetts, named Adam Dury. Theodore still hadn't heard from New Paltz regarding our question about a man or family named Beecham, but he was pursuing the matter. Kreizler and I were left with little to do but wait and hope that we'd hear more from either Roosevelt or Sara later in the evening. After telling the desk clerk that we would be in the bar, Laszlo and I retired to that dark, richly paneled room, then sought out a secluded spot along the lengthy brass rail and ordered a pair of cocktails.

'While we wait, Moore,' Kreizler said, sipping his sherry and bitters, 'you can edify me about this labor disturbance that led to John Beecham's commitment. I have a vague recollection but nothing more.'

I shrugged. 'Not much to explain. In '86 the Knights of Labor organized strikes in every major city in the country for May 1st.

The situation in Chicago got out of hand very quickly – strikers fought breakers, police busted up strikers, breakers went at it with cops – a mess. On the fourth day a big crowd of strikers got together in Haymarket Square, and the cops arrived in force to keep things orderly. Somebody – nobody knows who – threw a bomb into the police ranks. Killed a few. It could've been a striker, or an anarchist trying to start trouble, or even an agent of the factory owners, looking to discredit the strikers. The point was, the governor had a good excuse to call out the militia and some federal troops. The day after the bomb blast, there was a strikers' rally at a mill in one of the northern suburbs. The troops showed up, and their commander later claimed he ordered the strikers to disperse. The strike leaders said they never heard any such order. Whatever the case, the troops opened fire. It was an ugly scene.'

Kreizler nodded, going over the thing in his mind. 'Chicago . . . the city has a fairly large immigrant population, does it not?'

'Sure. Germans, Scandinavians, Poles – you name it.'

'There would have been a good number of them among the strikers, don't you think?'

I held up a hand. 'I know where you're headed with this, Kreizler, but it doesn't necessarily mean anything. There were immigrants involved in every strike in the country at that time.'

Laszlo frowned a bit. 'Yes, I suppose so. Still—'

Just then a young bellboy in a brass-buttoned red uniform entered the bar, calling out my name. Jumping up, I went to the lad, who told me that I was wanted by the desk clerk. Kreizler followed as I dashed out front. The clerk handed me his telephone, and as soon as I took it up I heard Sara's very excited voice:

'John? Are you there?'

'Yes, Sara. Go ahead.'

'Sit down. We may be onto something.'

'I don't want to sit down. What is it?'

'I found the story of the Dury murder in the *Times*. There were featured articles for about a week, and smaller notices after that. Just about anything you'd want to know about the family was in them.'

'Wait,' I said. 'Tell it to Kreizler so he can take notes.'

Laszlo put his small notebook on the registration desk, annoying the clerk, and then lifted the telephone's earpiece. This is the story he heard, which I followed from his scribblings:

The Reverend Victor Dury's father had been a Huguenot who'd left France in the early part of the last century to avoid religious persecution (the Huguenots being Protestants, and most of their countrymen Catholics). He'd gone to Switzerland, but the family's fortunes had not flourished there. His oldest son, Victor, a Reformed Church minister, had decided to try his luck in America. Arriving at mid-century, Dury had made his way to New Paltz, a town founded by Dutch Protestants in the eighteenth century that had later become home to scores of French Huguenot immigrants. Here Dury had started a small evangelical movement, funded by the citizens of the town, and within a year he'd moved with his wife and young son to Minnesota, with the intention of spreading the Protestant faith among the Sioux there (said Indians not yet having been pushed west to the Dakotas). Dury didn't make much of a missionary: he was harsh and overbearing, and his vivid descriptions of the wrath that God would bring down on unbelievers and transgressors did little to impress the Sioux with the advantages of a Christian life. The group in New Paltz that had been financing his work had been on the verge of recalling him when the great Sioux uprising of 1862 – one of the most savage Indian–white conflicts in history – broke out.

During that event the Dury family only narrowly escaped the grisly fate that befell many of their fellow whites in Minnesota. But the experience nonetheless provided the reverend with an idea that he thought would ensure continued backing for his mission. Laying his hands on a daguerreotype camera, he went around taking photographs of massacred whites; and when he returned to New Paltz in 1864, he became famous – indeed infamous – for showing these pictures to large collections of the town's better-off citizens. It was a blatant attempt to frighten those staid, fat people into providing more funds, but it back-fired: the pictures of slain and mutilated corpses were so horrifying, and Dury's behavior during the presentations so feverish, that the reverend's sanity began to be questioned. He became something of a social pariah, unable to find a religious posting. Ultimately, he was reduced to working as a caretaker in a Dutch Reformed church. The unexpected arrival of a second son in 1865 only made financial matters worse, and the family was eventually forced to move into a tiny house outside town.

Knowing Dury's troubled history and behavior as well as they did, and no more informed about Indian habits than the average white community in the eastern United States, most of the citizens of New Paltz had never questioned the idea that Dury's murder in 1880 was prompted by the bitterness he'd engendered among the Sioux in Minnesota during his stay among them nearly two decades earlier. All the same, there was some scattered talk (its originators anonymous, of course) of bad relations between the Durys and their oldest son, Adam, who'd moved away to become a farmer in Massachusetts many years before the killings. Rumors that Adam might have snuck west into New York State and done his parents in – for what precise reason no one would publicly say – began to spread, but were never treated as anything other than gossip by the police; and while no trace of the younger Dury boy, Japheth, had ever been found, the idea of his being kidnapped to become an Indian brave fitted in thoroughly with what New Paltz's citizens had been taught to expect from the savages who inhabited the western territories.

So ended the tale of the Dury family; Sara's research, however, had not been limited to that story. Recalling that she'd known a few people in New Paltz during her youth (even though the town was, as she put it, 'on quite the wrong side of the river'), she'd made some social calls after leaving the *Times*, just to see if any of those old acquaintances knew anything about the murders. The one such person she found at home did not. But Sara had gone on to ask for a general description of everyday life in New Paltz, and in so doing had stumbled on a rather electrifying fact: that New Paltz sits at the foot of the Shawangunk Mountains, a range well known for its large, forbidding rock formations. Almost afraid of the answer she might get, Sara'd next asked whether or not any citizens of the town enjoyed climbing those formations as a pastime. Oh, yes, she'd been told, it was quite a popular sport

– especially among those residents who had most recently arrived from Europe.

Both Kreizler and I were fairly stunned by this last item and needed time to absorb both it and the rest of the tale. Telling Sara that we would telephone again later in the evening, Laszlo rang off, following which we returned to the hotel bar to mull things over.

'Well?' Kreizler said in a somewhat awed tone, as we ordered a fresh round of iced cocktails. 'What do you make of it?'

I took in a deep breath. 'Let's start with facts. The older Dury boy witnessed some of the most horrendous atrocities imaginable before he was old enough to make any sense of them.'

'Yes. And his father was a priest, or at least a minister – the religious calendar, Moore. Their home would have been regulated by it.'

'The father also seems to have been a very hard, not to mention a rather peculiar, man – though outwardly respectable, at least in the beginning.'

Kreizler mapped his thoughts on the bar with a finger. 'So . . . we can assume a pattern of domestic violence, one beginning early and continuing unabated for years. It plants an urge for revenge that steadily mounts.'

'Yes,' I agreed. 'We've got no shortage of motive. But Adam's older than we've posited.'

Kreizler nodded. 'While the younger boy, Japheth, would have been the same age as Beecham. Now, if *he* committed the murders, then fabricated the note, disappeared, and took a different name—'

'But he's not the one who witnessed the massacres and mutilations,' I said. 'He wasn't even born yet.'

Kreizler knocked a fist against the bar. 'True. He would have had no frontier experience.'

Letting the facts recombine in a number of ways in my head, I tried but failed to come up with a new interpretation. All I could say after several minutes was, 'We still don't know anything about the mother.'

'No.' Kreizler kept rapping his knuckles on the bar. 'But they were a poor family, living at close quarters. That would have been especially true during the Minnesota period, which would have been the most vivid time in the eldest son's life.'

'Right. If only he were younger . . .'

Laszlo sighed and shook his head. 'A host of questions – and the answers to be found, I suspect, only in Newton, Massachusetts.'

'So – do we go up there and find out?'

'Who knows?' Kreizler sipped his cocktail nervously. 'I confess to feeling at a loss, Moore. I'm no professional detective. What do we do? Stay here and try to uncover more information about Beecham, at the same time pursuing any new leads we may uncover? Or go to Newton? How does one know when it's time to stop looking at all possibilities and pursue one course?'

I thought about that for a moment. 'We *can't* know,' I finally decided. 'We don't have the experience. But—' I got up and headed for the cable office.

'Moore?' Kreizler called after me. 'Where the devil are you going?'

It took me just five minutes to condense the key aspects of Sara's research into a cable, which I dispatched to the telegraph office in Fort Yates, North Dakota. The message concluded with a simple request: ADVISE COURSE.

Kreizler and I spent the rest of the evening in the Willard's dining room, fixed in place until the staff informed us that they were going home. At that point, with sleep utterly out of the question, we went for a walk around the White House grounds, smoking and putting every conceivable twist on the story we'd heard that night, while simultaneously searching for a way to connect it to Corporal John Beecham. Pursuing the Dury lead would take time, that much was becoming very apparent; and while nether of us said as much, we both knew that should such time be wasted we would likely find ourselves, at the moment of the killer's next attempt, no better prepared than we had been on Pentecost to stop him. Two courses of action, both full of risks, awaited our decision. Wandering about aimlessly in the Washington night, Kreizler and I were effectively paralyzed.

It was fortunate indeed, therefore, that when we returned to the Willard the clerk had a wire in hand for us. It had originated in Fort Yates, and must have been sent only moments after the Isaacsons got to that destination. Though brief, it was unhesitating in tone: THE LEAD IS SOLID. FOLLOW IT.

Chapter 33

The approach of dawn found us on a train and headed back to New York, where we planned to look in at Number 808 Broadway before going on to Newton, Massachusetts. It would have been impossible to do anything constructive in Washington – even sleep – once we'd had our inclination to pursue the Dury lead confirmed; the train ride north, on the other hand, would at least satisfy the craving for action and thereby allow us to rest easily for several hours. Such, at any rate, was my hope when we got on board; but I hadn't been dozing in our darkened compartment for long when a feeling of deep uneasiness caused me to stir. Striking a match to try to determine if there was any rational basis for my fear, I saw Kreizler, sitting across from me, staring out the compartment window at the blackened landscape as it sped by.

'Laszlo,' I said quietly, studying his wide eyes by the orange light of the match. 'What is it, what's happened?'

The knuckle of his left forefinger was rubbing against his mouth. 'The morbid imagination,' he mumbled.

I hissed suddenly as the match burned down to my fingers. Letting the flame fall to the floor and go out, I mumbled into the resurgent darkness, 'What imagination? What are you talking about?'

'"I myself have personally read this and know it to be true,"' he said, quoting our killer's letter. 'The cannibalism business.

We've postulated a morbid, impressionable imagination as an explanation.'

'And?'

'The pictures, John,' Laszlo answered, and though I couldn't see his face (or anything else in the compartment), his voice remained tense. 'The photographs of massacred settlers. We've been assuming that our man must have been on the frontier at some point in his life, that only personal experience could have provided a model for his current abominations.'

'You're saying Victor Dury's pictures could've served that purpose?'

'Not for anyone. But for this man, given the impressionability created by a childhood of violence and fear. Remember what we said about the cannibalism – it was something he read, or perhaps heard, probably as a child. A frightening story that left a lasting impression. Wouldn't photographs produce a far more extreme result, in a person characterized by such an obsessive and morbid imagination?'

'It's possible, I suppose. You're thinking about the missing brother?'

'Yes. Japheth Dury.'

'But why would anyone show such things to a child?'

Kreizler answered in a distracted tone: '"Dirtier than a Red Injun . . ."'

'I beg your pardon?'

'I'm not certain, John. Perhaps he stumbled on them. Or perhaps they were used as a disciplinary tool. More answers to be found in Newton, I hope.'

I thought the matter over for a moment, then felt my head bobbing back down toward the seat that I was lying on. 'Well,' I finally said, giving in to the bob, 'if you don't get some rest you won't be fit to talk to anyone, in Newton or anywhere else.'

'I know,' Kreizler answered. Then I could hear him shifting on his seat. 'But the thought struck me . . .'

The next thing I knew we were in the Grand Central Depot, being rudely awakened by the slams of compartment doors and the bumps of bags against the wall of our compartment. Looking none the better for our eventful night, Kreizler and I stumbled

The Alienist

off the train and out of the station into an overcast, gloomy morning. Since Sara would not yet be at our headquarters, we decided to make stops at our respective homes, then rendezvous at Number 808 when we were feeling (and hopefully looking) a bit more human. I got another two hours' sleep and a splendid bath at Washington Square, then breakfasted with my grandmother. The mental ease that had so thankfully settled on her following the execution of Dr. H.H. Holmes was, I noticed during the meal, beginning to wear thin: she scanned the back pages of the *Times* nervously, looking for the next deadly threat with which to preoccupy her evening hours. I took the liberty of pointing out the futility of such a course to her, only to be told rather curtly that it was not her intention to take advice from someone who found it appropriate to commit social suicide in not one but two cities by being seen in public with 'that Dr. Kreizler.'

Harriet packed me a fresh overnight bag for the trip to Newton, and by nine o'clock I was in the caged elevator at Number 808 Broadway, full of coffee and feeling remarkably game. It seemed as though I'd been away from our headquarters far longer than four days, and I looked forward to seeing Sara again with unabashed enthusiasm. When I reached the sixth floor I found her in close conversation with Kreizler, but, determined now to utterly ignore whatever it was that was going on between them, I dashed over and gave her a big, spinning hug.

'John, you ass!' she said with a smile. 'I don't care if it *is* spring – you know what happened the last time you were fresh with me!'

'Oh, no,' I said, dropping her quickly. 'Once in that river is enough for any lifetime. Well? Has Laszlo brought you up to date?'

'Yes,' Sara answered, tightening the bun on the back of her head and flashing defiance in her green eyes. 'You two have had all the fun, and I've just told Dr. Kreizler that if you think I'm going to sit around here for one more minute while you barrel off to yet another adventure, you're very much mistaken.'

I brightened up a bit. 'You're coming to Newton?'

'I said I wanted adventure,' she answered, swiping at my nose with a sheet of paper. 'And being locked up on a train with you two does not, I'm afraid, fill that bill. No, Dr. Kreizler says someone's got to go to New Paltz.'

'Roosevelt telephoned a few minutes ago,' Laszlo said to me. 'Apparently the name Beecham does appear in various records in that town.'

'Ah,' I said. 'Then it would appear that Japheth Dury did *not* become John Beecham.'

Kreizler shrugged. 'It's a further complication, that's all we can be sure of, and it requires investigation. You and I, however, must get to Newton as soon as possible. And with the detective sergeants still gone, that leaves Sara. It's her territory, after all – she grew up in the region and doubtless knows how to ingratiate herself with the local officials.'

'Oh, doubtless,' I said. 'What about coordinating things here?'

'An overrated job, if ever there was one,' Sara answered. 'Let Stevie do it, until Cyrus is out of bed. Besides, I shouldn't be gone more than a day.'

I turned a lecherous glance on the girl. 'And how valuable is my support in this scheme?'

Sara spun away. 'John, you really are a pig. Dr. Kreizler's already agreed.'

'I see,' I answered. 'Well, then – that's that, I suppose. My opinion not being worth the air it takes to express it.'

And in such fashion was Stevie Taggert set loose to ransack our headquarters for cigarettes. As of high noon that day the youth was left in charge of the place, his face as we departed giving me the impression that he'd smoke the upholstery from the Marchese Carcano's chairs if he couldn't find anything better. Stevie paid careful attention to Laszlo's instructions about how to contact us while we were gone, but when those instructions led into a warning speech concerning the evils of nicotine addiction, the boy seemed suddenly to go deaf. Laszlo, Sara, and I had barely started downstairs in the elevator when the sounds of drawers and cupboards opening and closing became audible from above. Kreizler only sighed, aware that for the moment we had bigger fish to fry; but I knew that once our case was settled there would be many long lectures on clean living to be heard at the house on Seventeenth Street.

The three of us stopped briefly at Gramercy Park so that Sara could pick up a few things, following which we engaged in another bit of subterfuge with the same set of decoys that Laszlo had hired prior to our trip to Washington. Then it was back to the Grand Central Depot. Sara split off to buy a ticket for the Hudson Line, while Kreizler and I made purchases at the New Haven Line windows. Goodbyes were, as they had been on Monday, brief and unrevealing of any connection between Sara and Kreizler; I was beginning to think I was as wrong about them as I'd been about a rogue priest being responsible for the murders. Our Boston train departed on time, and before long we'd passed through the eastern portions of Westchester County and into Connecticut.

The difference between Laszlo's and my trip to Washington earlier in the week and our present journey to Boston, on Saturday afternoon, was roughly the difference between the two respective landscapes surrounding us, as well as that between the kinds of people who inhabited the regions. Gone, on Saturday, were the verdant, rolling fields of New Jersey and Maryland: all around us the scraggly countryside of Connecticut and Massachusetts crept awkwardly down to Long Island Sound and the sea beyond, bringing to mind the hard life that had made such mean, contentious people out of the farmers and merchants of New England. Not that one needed such an indirect indication of what life in that quarter of the country was like; human exemplars were sitting all around us. Kreizler hadn't purchased first-class seats, a mistake whose gravity only became fully evident when the train reached top speed and our fellow travelers raised their grating, complaining drawls to overcome the rattle of the cars. For hours Kreizler and I endured loud conversations about fishing, local politics, and the shameful economic condition of the United States. Despite the din, however, we did manage to formulate a sound plan for dealing with Adam Dury if and when we found him.

We detrained at Boston's Back Bay Station, outside of which were collected a group of drivers who had rigs for hire. One man in the group, a tall, gaunt fellow with vicious little eyes, stepped toward us as we approached with our bags.

'Newton?' Laszlo said to him.

The man cocked his head and stuck out his lower lip. 'Good ten miles,' he judged. 'I won't be back 'fore midnight.'

'Then double your price,' Laszlo answered peremptorily, throwing his bag into the front seat of the man's rather battered old surrey. Although the driver looked a bit disappointed at losing the chance to quibble over the cost of the trip, he responded to Laszlo's offer with alacrity, jumping up onto the rig and grabbing his whip. I rushed to climb aboard, and then we drove off to the sound of the other rig drivers groaning about what kind of interloping fool would offer double the going rate for a ride to Newton. After that, all was silence for quite a while.

A troubled sunset that seemed to promise rain reached out over eastern Massachusetts, as the fringes of Boston slowly gave way to mile after mile of monotonous, rocky farmland. We didn't reach Newton until well past dark, whereupon our driver offered to take us to an inn that he said was the best in town. Both Kreizler and I knew that this probably meant the place was operated by some member of the man's family, but we were tired, hungry and on terra incognita: there was little to do but acquiesce. Rolling through the impossibly quaint streets of Newton, as picturesque and monotonous a community as one could hope to find even in New England, I began to get the disturbingly familiar feeling of being trapped by narrow lanes and narrow minds, a kind of anxiety that had often consumed me during my time at Harvard. The 'best inn in Newton' did nothing to relieve this uneasiness: sure enough, it was a loosely clapboarded building, with spare furnishings and a menu that ran to things boiled. The only bright moment occurred during supper, when the innkeeper (our driver's second cousin) said that he could provide directions to the farm of Adam Dury; and, hearing that Kreizler and I would need a ride in the morning, the man who'd brought us offered to spend the night and perform the service. Such details taken care of, we retired to our low, dark rooms and hard little beds to allow our stomachs to do their best with the boiled mutton and potatoes we'd dined on.

Rising early the next day, Laszlo and I tried but failed to avoid the innkeeper's breakfast offering of thick, tough flapjacks and coffee. The sky had cleared, evidently without shedding any rain, and outside the inn stood the old surrey, with our driver aboard and ready to depart. Traveling north, we saw little sign of any human activity for nearly half an hour; then a herd of dairy cattle came into view, grazing in a pitted, rock-strewn pasture, beyond which a small group of buildings stood amid a stand of oaks. As we approached these structures – a farmhouse and two barns – I made out the figure of a man standing ankle deep in barnyard manure and trying with difficulty to shoe a tired old horse.

The man, I noted quickly, had thinning hair, and his scalp glistened in the morning sun.

Chapter 34

To judge by the dilapidated state of his barns, fences, and wagons, as well as the absence of any assistants or particularly healthy-looking animals, Adam Dury had not made much of a go of his little dairy cattle enterprise. Few people live in closer proximity to life's grimmer realities than do poor farmers, and the atmosphere of such places is inevitably sobering: Kreizler's and my excitement at actually laying eyes on the man we'd traveled a fairly long way to find was immediately tempered by appreciation of his circumstances, and after getting down from the surrey and telling our driver to wait, we approached him slowly and carefully.

'Excuse me – Mr. Dury?' I said, as the fellow continued to struggle with the old horse's left foreleg. The fly-ridden brown beast, its hide bare in several spots where a yolk would have rested, appeared to have absolutely no interest in making its master's task any easier.

'Yes,' the man answered sharply, still showing us nothing more than the back of his balding head.

'Mr. Adam Dury?' I inquired further, trying to induce him to turn around.

'You must know that, if you've come to see me,' Dury answered, finally dropping the horse's leg with a grunt. He stood up, rising to a height of well over six feet and then slapped the horse's neck, half in anger and half affectionately. 'This one thinks he'll die before me, anyway,' he mumbled, still facing the horse, 'so why should he be cooperative? But we've both got many more years of this to go, you old ...' Dury finally turned round, revealing a head whose skin was so tightly drawn that it appeared little more than a flesh-colored skull. Large yellow teeth filled the mouth, and the almond-shaped eyes were of a lifeless blue tint. His arms were powerfully developed, and the fingers of his hands as he wiped them on his worn overalls seemed remarkably long and thick. He took our measures with a squinting grimace that was neither friendly nor hostile. 'Well? What can I do for you two gentlemen?'

I moved directly – and, if I may say so, gracefully – into the bit of subterfuge that Laszlo and I had worked out on the Boston train. 'This is Dr. Laszlo Kreizler,' I said, 'and my name is John Schuyler Moore. I'm a reporter for the *New York Times*.' I found my billfold and revealed some professional identification. 'A police reporter, actually. My editors have assigned me to investigate some of the more – well, to come to the point, some of the more outstanding unsolved cases of recent decades.'

Dury nodded, a bit suspiciously. 'You've come to ask about my parents.'

'Indeed,' I answered. 'You've no doubt heard, Mr. Dury, of the recent investigations into the conduct of the New York City Police Department.'

Dury's thin eyes went even thinner. 'The case was none of their affair.'

'True. But my editors are concerned with the fact that so many noteworthy cases are never pursued or solved by law enforcement agencies *throughout* the state of New York. We've decided to review several and see what's happened in the years since their occurrence. I wonder if you'd mind just going over the basic facts of your parents' deaths with us?'

All the features of Dury's face seemed to shift and resettle in a kind of wave, as if a shudder of pain had rippled through him quickly. When he spoke again, the tone of distrust had vanished from his voice, to be replaced only by resignation and sorrow. 'Who could have any interest now? It's been more than fifteen years.'

I attempted sympathy, as well as moral indignation: 'Does time justify the lack of a solution, Mr. Dury? And you are not alone, remember – others have seen murderous acts go unsolved and unavenged, and they'd like to know why.'

Dury weighed the matter for another moment, then shook his head. 'That's their business. I've got no desire to talk about it.'

He began to move away; knowing New Englanders as well as I did, however, I'd anticipated this reaction. 'There would, of course,' I announced calmly, 'be a fee.'

That got him: he paused, turned, and eyed me again. 'Fee?'

I gave him a friendly smile. 'A consulting fee,' I said. 'Nothing excessive, mind you – say, one hundred dollars?'

Aware that such a sum would, in fact, mean a great deal to a man in his straits, I was not surprised to see Dury's almond eyes jump. 'One hundred dollars?' he echoed in quiet disbelief. 'For *talking*?'

'That's right, sir,' I answered, producing the sum from my billfold.

Thinking it all over just a bit more, Dury finally took the money. Then he turned to his horse, swatted its rump, and sent it off to graze on a few patches of grass that grew near the edge of the yard. 'We'll talk in the barn,' he said. 'I've got work to do, and I can't ignore it for the sake of' – he took heavy steps away from us through the sea of manure – 'ghost stories.'

Kreizler and I followed, much relieved at the apparent success of the bribe. Concern returned, however, when Dury spun round at the barn door.

'Just a minute,' he said. 'You say this man's a doctor? What's his interest?'

'I make a study of criminal behavior, Mr. Dury,' Laszlo answered smoothly, 'as well as of police methods. Mr. Moore has asked me to provide expert advice for his article.'

Dury accepted that, though it seemed that he didn't much like Kreizler's accent. 'You're German,' he said. 'Or maybe Swiss.'

'My father was German,' Kreizler answered. 'But I was raised in this country.'

Dury seemed ill satisfied by Kreizler's explanation, and silently walked on into the barn.

Inside that creaky structure the stench of manure grew stronger, softened only by the sweet aroma of hay, a store of which was visible in the loft above us. The bare plank walls of the building had once been whitewashed, but most of the paint had fallen away to reveal roughly grained wood. A chicken coop was visible through one four-foot doorway, the gurgles and clucks of its occupants floating out toward us. Harnesses, scythes, shovels, picks, mauls, and buckets were everywhere, hanging from the walls and the low roof or lying on the earthen floor. Dury went directly over to a very old manure spreader, the axle of which was propped up on a pile of rocks. Taking up a mallet and slamming away at the wheel that faced us, our host eventually forced it from its mount. Dury then hissed in disgust and began to fuss with the end of the axle.

'All right,' he said, grabbing a bucket of heavy grease and never looking our way. 'Ask your questions.'

Kreizler nodded to me, indicating that it might be best if I took the lead in the questioning. 'We've read the newspaper accounts that appeared at the time,' I said. 'I wonder if you might tell us—'

'Newspaper accounts!' Dury grunted. 'I suppose you've also read, then, that the fools suspected *me* for a time.'

'We've read that there was gossip,' I answered. 'But the police said that they never—'

'Believed it? Not much, they didn't. Only enough to send two of their men all the way over here to harass my wife and myself for three days!'

'You're married, Mr. Dury?' Kreizler asked quietly.

For just a second or two, Dury eyed Laszlo, again resentfully. 'I am. Nineteen years, not that it's any business of yours.'

'Children?' Kreizler asked, in the same cautious tone.

'No,' came the hard answer. 'We – that is, my wife – I – no. We have no children.'

'But I take it,' I said, 'that your wife was able to attest to your being here when the – the terrible incident occurred?'

'That didn't mean much to those idiots,' Dury answered. 'A wife's testimony counts for little or nothing in a court of law. I had to ask a neighbor of mine, a man who lives nearly ten miles away, to come and verify that we were pulling a stump together on the very day my parents were murdered.'

'Do you know why the police should have been so hard to convince?' Kreizler asked.

Dury slammed his mallet down on the ground. 'I'm sure you read about *that* too. *Doctor*. It was no secret. There'd been bad blood between my parents and myself for many years.'

I held a hand up to Kreizler. 'Yes, we saw some mention of such,' I said, trying to coax more details out of Dury. 'But the police accounts were very vague and confused, and it was difficult to draw any conclusions. Which seems remarkable, given that the question was vital to the investigation. Maybe you could make it a little clearer for us?'

Lifting the manure spreader's wheel onto a workbench, Dury began to pound at it again. 'My parents were hard people, Mr. Moore. They had to be, to make the trip to this country and survive the life they chose for themselves. But while I can say that now, such explanations are quite beyond a small boy who—' A blast of passionate language seemed about to escape the man, but he held it down with obvious effort. 'Who only hears a cold voice. And only feels a thick strap.'

'Then you *were* beaten,' I said, thinking back to Kreizler's and my original speculations after first reading of the Dury murders in Washington.

'I wasn't referring to myself, Mr. Moore,' Dury answered. 'Though God knows neither my father nor my mother ever shrank from punishing me when I misbehaved. But that was not what caused our – estrangement.' He looked out a small, filthy window for a moment, then pounded at the wheel again. 'I had a brother. Japheth.'

Kreizler nodded as I said, 'Yes, we read about him. Tragic. You have our sympathy.'

'Sympathy? I suppose. But I'll tell you this, Mr. Moore – whatever those savages did to him was no more tragic than what he endured at the hands of his own parents.'

'He suffered cruelties?'

Dury shrugged. 'Some might not call them such. But I did, and do still. Oh, he was a strange lad, in some respects, and the ways in which my parents reacted to his behavior might have seemed – natural, to an outsider. But it wasn't. No, sir, there was the devil in it all, somewhere . . .' Dury's attention wandered for a moment, but then he shook it off. 'I'm sorry. You wanted to know about the case.'

I spent the next half hour asking Dury some obvious questions about what had happened on that day in 1880, requesting clarification of details that we were not, in fact, confused about, as a method of concealing our true interests. Then I managed, by asking him why any Indians should have wanted to kill his parents, to lead him into a more detailed discussion of what life in his home during the Minnesota years had been like. From there, it was no great job to expand the discussion to a history of the family's private dealings more generally. As Dury related these, Laszlo stealthily withdrew his small notebook and began to silently scribble a record of the account:

Though born in New Paltz in 1856, Adam Dury's earliest memories dated back only as far as his fourth year, when his family had relocated to Fort Ridgely, Minnesota, a military post inside that state's Lower Sioux Agency. The Durys lived in a one-room log house about a mile outside the fort, the kind of residence that afforded young Adam an excellent vantage point from which to study his parents and their relationship. His father, as Kreizler and I already knew, was a strictly religious man, who made no attempt to sugar-coat the sermons he delivered to those curious Sioux who came to hear him speak. Yet Laszlo and I were both surprised to learn that, despite this vocational rigidity, the Reverend Victor Dury had not been especially cruel or violent to his older son; rather, Adam said that his earliest memories of his father were happy ones. True, the reverend could deliver painful punishments when required; but it was usually Mrs. Dury who called for such action.

As he spoke of his mother, Adam Dury's aspect grew darker and his voice became far more hesitant, as if even her memory held some tremendous threatening power over him. Cold and strict, Mrs. Dury had apparently not offered her son much in the way of comfort or nurturing during his youth; indeed, as I listened to his description of the woman, I couldn't help but think back to Jesse Pomeroy.

'Much as it pained me to be shunned by her,' Dury said, as he attempted to fit the now repaired wheel back onto the manure spreader, 'I believe her remote spirit hurt my father even more – for she was no real wife to him. Oh, she performed all the menial domestic duties, and kept a very tidy home, despite our meager circumstances. But when your family lives in one small room, gentlemen, you cannot help but be aware of the – the more intimate dimension of your parents' marriage. Or the lack thereof.'

'You're saying they weren't close?' I asked.

'I'm saying that I don't know why she married him,' Dury answered gruffly, making the axle and wheel before him bear the brunt of his sadness and anger. 'She could scarcely abide his slightest touch, much less his – his attempts to build a family. My father, you see, wanted children. He had ideas – dreams, really – of sending his sons and daughters out into the western wilderness to expand and carry on his work. But my mother . . . Their every attempt was an ordeal for her. Some of these she suffered through, and some she – resisted. I honestly do not know why she ever took the vow. Except – when he preached . . . My father was quite an orator, in his way, and my mother attended nearly every service he ever held. She did seem to enjoy that part of his life, strangely enough.'

'And after you returned from Minnesota?'

Dury shook his head bitterly. 'After we returned from Minnesota things deteriorated completely. When my father lost his post he lost the only human connection he had to my mother. They rarely spoke in the years after that, and never touched, not that I can recall.' He looked up at the filthy window. 'Except once . . .'

He paused for several seconds, and to urge him on I murmured: 'Japheth?'

Dury nodded, slowly rousing himself from his sad reverie. 'I'd taken to sleeping outdoors when it was warm enough. Near the mountains – the Shawangunks. My father had learned the sport of mountaineering in Switzerland from his own father, and the

Shawangunks were an ideal spot to keep his hand in, as well as to pass the techniques on to me. Though I was never very good at it, I always went along with him, because they were happier times – away from the house and that woman.'

If the words had been explosives I don't think their concussion could have hit Kreizler and me any harder. Laszlo's weak left arm shot out, and his hand grabbed my shoulder with surprising force. Dury saw none of it and, unaware of the effect his words were having on us, continued:

'But during the coldest months there was no avoiding the indoors, not unless I wanted to die of exposure. And I remember one February night when my father ... he may have been drinking, though he rarely did. But, sober or no, he began to finally rebel against my mother's inhuman behavior. He spoke of the duties of a wife, and the needs of a husband, and he began to grab at her. Well ... My mother screamed in protest, of course, and told him he was acting like the savages we'd left behind in Minnesota. But my father wouldn't be stopped that night – and despite the cold I fled the house through a window, and slept in an old barn that belonged to a neighbor of ours. Even from that distance I could hear my mother's cries and sobs.' Once again, Dury seemed to lose all awareness of his present surroundings and spoke in a detached, almost lifeless voice: 'And I wish I could say that those sounds horrified me. But they didn't. In fact, I distinctly remember urging my father on ...' His presence of mind returned, and, somewhat embarrassed, he picked up his hammer and began pounding at the wheel once more. 'No doubt I've shocked you, gentlemen. If so, I apologize.'

'No, no,' I answered quickly. 'You're only giving us a better understanding of the background, we quite understand that.'

Dury shot Laszlo another quick, skeptical look. 'And you, Doctor? Do you quite understand, too? You haven't had much to say.'

Kreizler kept very cool under Dury's scrutiny. There was, I knew, little chance that this man of the earth was going to make so seasoned a madhouse campaigner as Kreizler uneasy. 'I have been too absorbed to comment,' Laszlo said. 'If you'll allow me to say so, Mr. Dury, you are very well spoken.'

Dury laughed once humorlessly. 'For a farmer, you mean? Yes, that was my mother's doing. She made us work at our school lessons for hours every night. I could both read and write before the age of five.'

Kreizler cocked his head in appreciation. 'Laudable.'

'My knuckles didn't think so,' Dury answered. 'She used to come across them with a stick like – but once again, I'm off the subject. You wanted to know what became of my brother.'

'Yes,' I answered. 'But before that, tell us – what sort of a boy was he? You've said odd – odd in what way?'

'Japheth?' Having secured the wheel to the manure spreader's axle, Dury stood and laid hold of a large pole. 'In what way was he not? ... I suppose you couldn't expect much more, from a child born out of anger and unwanted by both his parents. To my mother he was a symbol of my father's savagery and lust, and to my father – to my father, much as he wanted more children, Japheth was always a symbol of his degradation, of that terrible night when desire made an animal of him.' Using the long pole, Dury knocked the piled rocks out from under the spreader's axle, at which the machine fell to the earthen floor of the barn and rolled a few feet forward. Satisfied with his work, Dury took up a shovel and kept talking. 'The world is full of pitfalls for a boy left on his own. I tried to give Japheth what help I could, but by the time he was old enough for us to be real friends I had been sent to work on a nearby farm and saw little of him. I knew that he was suffering all that I'd endured in that house, and even more. And I wished that I could have been more help.'

'Did he ever tell you,' I asked, 'just what was happening?'

'No. But I saw some of it,' Dury said as he began to shovel manure from the floor of several livestock stalls into the spreader. 'And on Sundays I'd try to spend time with him, and show him that there was much he could still enjoy about life, whatever happened at home. I taught him how to climb the mountains, and we spent whole days and nights up there. But in the end ... In the end, I don't believe that anyone could have counteracted my mother's influence.'

'Was she – violent?'

Dury shook his head, and spoke in a voice that seemed

judicious and honest. 'I don't think Japheth suffered in that way any more than I had. The occasional strap to the backside from my father, and nothing more. No, I believed then, and I still believe now, that my mother's ways were far more – devious.' Dury laid his shovel aside, sat down on one of the large rocks that had supported the spreader, and took out a pouch of tobacco and a pipe. 'I suppose, in a way, that I was luckier than Japheth, only because my mother's feelings toward me had always taken the form of thorough indifference. But Japheth – it didn't seem enough for her to merely deprive him of love. She took issue with his every action, his every move, however insignificant. Even when he was an infant, even before he had any awareness or control over himself – she'd badger him about everything he did.'

Kreizler leaned forward, offering a match that Dury took only reluctantly. 'What do you mean by "everything," Mr. Dury?' Laszlo asked.

'You're a medical man, Doctor,' Dury answered. 'I think you can guess.' Smoking for a few seconds to get a good coal going in his pipe, Dury finally shook his head and grunted angrily. 'The cruel bitch! Hard words, I know, for a man to assign to his own dead mother. But if you could have seen her, gentlemen – *at* him, always at him. And when he complained, or cried, or went into a rage over it, she'd say things so despicable that I would've thought them beyond even her.' Dury stood up and continued shoveling. 'That he wasn't her son. That he was the child of red Indians – dirty, man-eating savages who'd left him in a bundle at our door. The poor little fellow half-believed it, too.'

Pieces were falling into place with every passing minute; and as they did, it became steadily more difficult for me to control a profound, swelling sense of discovery and triumph. I almost wished that Dury would end his account, just so I could run outside and scream to the heavens that, all opposition be damned, Kreizler and I were going to catch our man. But I knew that self-control was more important now than it had ever been, and I tried to follow Kreizler's self-composed example.

'And what happened,' Laszlo asked, 'when your brother got a bit older? Old enough, that is, to—'

Caleb Carr

With savage, terrifying suddenness, Adam Dury screamed incomprehensibly and threw his shovel against the rear wall of the barn. The chickens in the adjacent coop sent up a flurry of frightened clucks and feathers, and, hearing them, Dury wrenched his pipe from his mouth and attempted to regain control over himself. Kreizler and I made no move, though I know my own eyes had gone quite wide with shock.

'I think,' Dury seethed, 'that we had all best be honest with each other. *Gentlemen.*'

Kreizler said nothing, and my own voice quavered badly as I asked, 'Honest, Mr. Dury? But I assure you—'

'Damn it!' Dury shouted, slamming a foot to the earth. Then he waited a few more seconds, until he could speak more calmly again. 'Don't you think there was talk of it at the time? Do you imagine that simply because I'm a farmer I'm also an idiot? I know what it is you're here to find out!'

I was about to offer further protests, but Kreizler touched my arm. 'Mr. Dury has been exceptionally forthright with us, Moore. I believe we owe him the same courtesy.' Dury nodded, and his breathing became something like regular as Kreizler went on: 'Yes, Mr. Dury. We believe there is every chance that your brother murdered your parents.'

A pitiable sound, half-sob and half-gasp, got out of our host. 'And is alive?' he said, almost all traces of anger gone from his voice.

Kreizler nodded slowly, and Dury held his arms up helplessly. 'But why should it matter now? So long ago – it's over, done. If my brother is alive, he's never contacted me. Why should it matter?'

'Then you suspected it yourself?' Kreizler said, avoiding the question as he produced a flask of whiskey and held it out to Dury.

Dury nodded again and took a drink, no longer displaying the resentment toward Laszlo that he'd shown earlier. I had thought that attitude the result of Kreizler's accent; I could see now that it had been spawned by Dury's suspicion that this visit – from what he must have thought a very strange sort of doctor – might reach just such a pass.

'Yes,' Dury said at length. 'You must remember, Doctor, that I'd lived among the Sioux, as a boy. I had several friends, in their villages. And I'd witnessed the uprising in '62. I knew that the explanation the police finally accepted of my parents' death was almost certainly a lie. And more than that, I knew – my brother.'

'You knew that he was capable of such an act,' Kreizler said softly. He was maneuvering very carefully, now, just as he'd done with Jesse Pomeroy. His voice remained calm, but his questions became steadily more pointed. 'How, Mr. Dury? How did you know?'

I felt a twinge of real sympathy when a tear appeared on Dury's cheek. 'When Japheth was – oh, nine or ten,' he said softly, after taking another deep pull from the flask, 'we spent a few days up in the Shawangunks. Hunting and trapping small game – squirrel, possum, coons, and such. I'd taught him to shoot, but he wasn't much for it. A born trapper, Japheth was. He'd spend a whole day searching out an animal's lair or nest and then wait for hours, alone in the dark, to spring his scheme. It was a talent. But one day we were hunting separately – I'd gone to trail some bobcat tracks I'd spotted – and as I came back to camp I heard a strange, terrible scream. A wail. High-pitched and faint, but awful. As I came into the camp I caught a glimpse of Japheth. He'd trapped himself a possum, and he was – he was cutting the thing to pieces while it was still alive. I ran up and put a bullet in the poor creature's brain, and took my brother aside. He had an evil sort of light in his eyes, but after I'd hollered at him for a while, he began to cry and seemed truly sorry. I thought it was a lone incident – the kind of thing a boy might do if he knew no better, and wouldn't do again once he'd been told.' Dury began to poke at his pipe, which had gone out.

Kreizler offered another match. 'But it wasn't,' he said.

'No,' Dury answered. 'It happened several times over the next few years – several times that I knew of, that is. He never bothered the big animals, the cattle or horses on the farms around us. It was always – always the small creatures that seemed to bring it out in him. I kept trying to put a stop to it; and then . . .'

His voice trailing off, Dury sat and stared at the ground, seemingly unwilling to go on. Kreizler, however, kept after him gently: 'And then something worse happened?'

Dury smoked and nodded. 'But I didn't hold him responsible, Doctor. And I think you'll agree that I was right not to.' One of his hands became a fist and he slammed it into his thigh. 'But my mother, damn her, just took it as another example of Japheth's devilish behavior. Claimed he brought it on himself, as if any boy would!'

'I'm afraid you'll have to explain, Mr. Dury,' I said.

He nodded quickly, then took a final sip of whiskey before handing the flask back to Kreizler. 'Yes, yes. I'm sorry. Let me see – this would have been during the summer of – hell, it was just before I moved away, the summer of '75 it must've been. Japheth was eleven. At the farm where I'd been working they'd recently hired a new man; he was just a few years older than me. A charming character, to all appearances. Seemed to have quite a way with children. We got to be friendly, and eventually I invited him along on a hunting trip. He took a great interest in Japheth, and my brother took a real liking to him – so much so that the fellow came along on a few more outings. Japheth and he would go off trapping together, while I hunted larger game. I'd explained to this – this *thing* that I thought was a man that Japheth was to be discouraged from tormenting any animals they might catch. The fellow seemed to understand the situation thoroughly. I trusted him, you see, to look after my brother.' A dull knocking sound came from the outer wall of the barn. 'And he betrayed that trust,' Dury said, getting to his feet. 'In the worst way a man can.' Opening the filthy window and sticking his head out of it, Dury called: 'Now, you! Go on away from there, I've told you – go on!' He came back inside, scratching at the few hairs on his head. 'Fool horse. Covers himself in burrs to get at a little patch of clover that grows behind the barn, and I don't seem to ... I'm sorry, gentlemen. At any rate, I found Japheth in our camp one evening, half-naked and weeping, bleeding from the – well, bleeding. The fiend I'd left him with was gone. We never saw him again.'

From the exterior of the barn came the same muffled pounding, prompting Dury to grab a long, thin switch and head for the door. 'If you'll just give me a moment, gentlemen.'

'Mr. Dury?' Kreizler called. Our host stopped and turned at the barn doorway. 'This fellow, the farmhand – can you recall his name?'

'Indeed I can, Doctor,' Dury answered. 'Guilt has burned it into my memory. Beecham – George Beecham. Excuse me.'

The name struck me harder than had any piece of information that had been revealed thus far, and turned much of the triumphant exhilaration that I'd been feeling back into confusion. '*George* Beecham?' I whispered. 'But, Kreizler, if Japheth Dury is, in fact—'

Kreizler held up an urgent, silencing finger. 'Save your questions, Moore, and remember one thing – if we can avoid it, let's keep our true object from this man. We know almost everything we need to know. Now – make an excuse, and let's depart.'

'Everything we need – well, you may know everything you need to know, but I've still got a thousand questions! And why should we keep it from him, he's got a right—'

'What good can it do him?' Kreizler whispered harshly. 'The man has suffered and agonized over this affair for years. What purpose can it serve, of his *or* ours, to tell him that we believe his brother responsible not only for his parents' murders, but for the deaths of half a dozen children?'

That gave me pause; for if, in fact, Japheth Dury was alive, but had never tried to contact his brother, Adam, then there was no way in which this tormented farmer could further assist our investigation. And to tell him of our suspicions, even before they were substantiated, did indeed seem the very height of mental cruelty. For all these reasons, when Dury returned from disciplining his horse, I followed Kreizler's instructions and concocted a tale about a train back to New York and deadlines that had to be met, using all the standard excuses I'd employed a thousand times in my journalistic career to get out of similarly difficult situations.

'But you've got to tell me something honestly, before you go,' Dury said, as he walked us back to the surrey. 'This business about writing an article on cases that have gone unsolved – is there any truth in that? Or are you going to reopen this case alone and speculate about my brother's involvement by using the information I've given you?'

'I can assure you, Mr. Dury,' I answered, the truth enabling me to speak with conviction, 'there will be no newspaper articles about your brother. What you've told us allows us to see how the police investigating the case went wrong – nothing more. It shall be treated just as you've told it to us – in the strictest confidence.'

That brought a firm shake of my hand by Dury. 'Thank you, sir.'

'Your brother suffered a great deal,' Kreizler answered, also shaking Dury's hand. 'And I suspect that his suffering has gone on, in the years since your parents were killed – if indeed he is still alive. It is not our place to judge him, or to profit from his misery.' The tight skin of Dury's face grew tighter as he strained to hold back strong emotions. 'I have just one or two more questions,' Laszlo went on, 'if you wouldn't mind.'

'If I have the answers, they're yours, Doctor,' Dury said.

Kreizler inclined his head appreciatively. 'Your father. Many Reformed ministers place little emphasis on church holidays – but I get the feeling he did otherwise?'

'Indeed,' Dury answered. 'Holidays were among the only pleasant occasions in our house. My mother objected, of course. She'd get out her Bible and explain why such celebrations amounted to papistry and what punishments those who cele-brated them could expect. But my father persisted – in fact, he gave some of his finest sermons on holidays. But I can't see how—'

Kreizler's black eyes were positively alight as he held up a hand. 'It's a small point, I know, but I was curious.' Climbing up onto the surrey, Laszlo appeared to remember something. 'Oh, and another detail.' Dury looked up expectantly as I joined Kreizler in the carriage. 'Your brother, Japheth,' Laszlo went on. 'At what point did he develop the – the difficulty in his face?'

'His spasms?' Dury answered, again puzzled by the question. 'He always had them, to the best of my recollection. Perhaps not when he was an infant, but soon after that and for the rest of his

'– well, for as long as I knew him, at any rate.'

'They were constant?'

'Yes,' Dury said searching his memory. Then he smiled. 'Except, of course, in the mountains. When he was trapping. Those eyes of his were as calm as a pond then.'

I wasn't at all sure how many more revelations I could hear without bursting, but Kreizler took it all in stride. 'A sad but in many ways remarkable boy,' he pronounced. 'You wouldn't have a photograph of him, I suppose?'

'He always refused to be photographed, Doctor – understandably.'

'Yes. Yes, I suppose so. Well, goodbye, Mr. Dury.'

We finally pulled away from the little farm. I turned to watch Adam Dury tread heavily back into the barn, his long, powerful legs and large, booted feet still sinking deep into the mire and refuse that surrounded the building. And then, just before he went inside, he stopped suddenly and turned quickly toward the road.

'Kreizler,' I said. 'Did Sara mention there being anything about Japheth Dury's tic in the newspaper stories about the family?'

'Not that I recall,' Kreizler answered, without turning around. 'Why?'

'Because based on Adam Dury's present expression, I'd say it *wasn't* ever mentioned – and he's just realized it. He's going to have a tough time figuring out how we could've known.' Though my enthusiasm was still mounting, I tried hard to get it under control as I turned back around and declared, 'Good God! Tell me, Kreizler – tell me we've got him! A lot of what that man said confuses the hell out of me, but please, *please* tell me that we've got a solution!'

Kreizler allowed himself to smile, and held up his right fist passionately. 'We've got the pieces of one, John – that much I'm sure of. Perhaps not *all* the pieces, yet, and perhaps not correctly arranged – but yes, we have most of it! Driver! You may take us directly to the Back Bay Station! There is a 6:05 train to New York, as I remember – we must be on it!'

For what must have been miles we were full of scarcely

Caleb Carr

coherent expressions of triumph and relief; and if I'd known how brief this feeling would be, I might have savored it more than I did. But an hour or so past the halfway point of our return trip to the Back Bay Station, a sound not unlike the short, sharp crack of a broken tree limb rang out in the distance, signaling the end of all exultation. I can distinctly remember the crack's being immediately followed by a very short, hissing sort of sound; and then something slammed into the horse that was drawing our surrey, bringing a fountain of blood from the beast's neck and knocking it stone-dead to the ground. Before the driver, Kreizler, or I could react there was another sharp crack and hiss, and then an inch or so of flesh was torn out of Laszlo's upper right arm.

Chapter 35

With a short cry and a long curse Kreizler spun to the floor of the surrey. Knowing that we were still badly exposed, I forced him to jump out of the carriage and then crawl underneath it, where we both pressed ourselves close to the ground. Our driver, by contrast, walked out and into the open, for the apparent purpose of studying his dead horse. I urged the man to get down; but the evident loss of future revenue had made him blind to his present safety, and he continued to make a tempting target out of himself – until, that is, another report sounded and a bullet whined into the ground near his feet. Looking up and suddenly comprehending the danger he was in, the driver took to his heels and made for some thick woods fifty yards behind us, on the opposite side of the road from a stand of trees that seemed to be harboring our assailant.

As he continued to seethe and swear oaths, Kreizler also managed to get his jacket off, following which he instructed me on how to minister to his wound. It didn't appear as serious as it was messy – the bullet had just nicked the muscles of his upper arm – and the most important thing was to stop the bleeding. After removing my belt I fashioned it into a tourniquet just above the bleeding gash, and then drew it tight. Tearing Laszlo's shirtsleeve, I made it into a bandage, and soon the crimson flow had ebbed. When a bullet crashed into a wheel of the surrey, however, shattering one of the thick spokes, I was reminded of how soon we might have other injuries to address.

'Where is he?' Kreizler said, scanning the trees in front of us.

'I saw some smoke, just left of that white birch,' I answered, pointing. '*Who* is he, is what I want to know.'

'I fear we have entirely too many possibilities to choose from,' Kreizler replied, tightening his bandage a bit and groaning as he did. 'Our adversaries from New York would be the most obvious choice. Comstock's authority and influence are quite *national*.'

'Long-range assassins don't really seem like Comstock's style, though. Or Byrnes's, for that matter. What about Dury?'

'Dury?'

'Maybe that realization about the twitch changed his attitude – he may think we're crossing him.'

'But did he really seem a murderer,' Kreizler asked, folding his arm and cradling it, 'for all his violent talk? Besides, he made it sound as though he's a decent shot – unlike this fellow.'

That gave me a thought: 'What about . . . *him*? Our killer? He could've followed us from New York. And if it *is* Japheth Dury, remember that Adam said he never really took to shooting.'

Kreizler considered the idea as he continued to scan the woods, then shook his head. 'You're being fanciful, Moore. Why follow us here?'

'Because he knew where we were going. He knows where his brother lives, and that talking to Adam could help us track him down.'

Laszlo's head kept shaking. 'It's too fantastic. It's Comstock, I tell you—'

Another gunshot suddenly cut through the air, and then a bullet tore large shards of wood out of the side of the surrey.

'Point well taken,' I said, in answer to the bullet. 'We can argue about all this later.' I turned to study the woods behind us. 'Looks like the driver made it to those trees all right. Do you think you can run with that arm?'

Kreizler groaned once sharply. 'As easily as I can lie here, damn it!'

I grabbed Laszlo's jacket. 'When you get into the open,' I said, 'try not to run in a straight line.' We both turned and crawled to the other side of the carriage. 'Keep your movements irregular.

Go on ahead, and I'll follow in case you have trouble.'

'I've a rather unsettling feeling,' Kreizler said, scanning the fifty yards of open space, 'that such trouble is likely to be permanent, in this case.' That thought seemed to strike Laszlo hard. Just as he was about to take flight, he stopped and fingered his silver watch, then handed it to me. 'Listen, John – on the chance that – well, I want you to give this to—'

I smiled and pushed the watch back at him. 'A rank sentimentalist, just as I always suspected. Go on, you can give it to her yourself – move!'

Fifty yards of supposedly open northeastern terrain can seem a lot more difficult to cover than you might imagine when the stakes of the run are mortal. Every little rodent hole, ditch, puddle, root, and stone between the carriage and the woods became an almost insurmountable obstacle, my pounding heart having robbed my legs and feet of their usual agility. I suppose it took Kreizler and me somewhere under a minute to run the fifty yards to safety; and though we were apparently menaced by only a single gunman who didn't have anything like expert aim, it felt as though we were in a full-scale battle. The air around my head seemed alive with bullets, though I don't think more than three or four shots were actually taken at us; and by the time I completed the escape, with branches lashing at my face as I propelled myself further and further into the wooded darkness, I was as close to incontinent as I hope ever to be.

I found Kreizler propped up against an enormous fir tree. His bandage and tourniquet had loosened, allowing a new flow of blood to stream down his arm. After retightening both dressings I draped his jacket around his shoulders, for it seemed that he was growing cold and losing color.

'We'll stay parallel to the road,' I said quietly, 'until we catch sight of some traffic. We're not far from Brookline, and we can get a lift to the station from there.'

I got Laszlo up and helped him start through the thick woods, keeping one eye on the road so that we never lost track of it. When we came within sight of the buildings of Brookline I figured it was safe to come out of the woods and move at a faster clip. Soon after we had, an ice van came by and drew to a halt, its

Caleb Carr

driver jumping down to ask what had befallen us. I made up a story about a carriage accident, prompting the man to offer us a ride as far as the Back Bay Station. This proved a doubly fortunate stroke, for several large pieces of ice from the van driver's stock eased the pain in Kreizler's arm.

By the time the Back Bay Station came into view it was almost five-thirty, and the afternoon sunlight had begun to take on an amber, hazy quality. I asked our driver to let us off near a small stand of scraggly pines some two hundred yards from the station itself, and after we'd gotten off the van and thanked the man for his help and his ice, which had almost completely checked the flow of blood from Kreizler's arm, I hustled Laszlo into the shadowy darkness beneath the deep green boughs.

'I'm as enamored of nature as the next man, Moore,' Kreizler said in confusion. 'But this hardly seems the time. Why didn't we drive to the station?'

'If that was one of Comstock and Byrnes's men back there,' I answered, picking a spot among the pine needles that offered a good view of the station house, 'he'll probably guess that this is our next move. He may be waiting for us.'

'Ah,' Laszlo noised. 'I see your point.' He crouched down on the pine needles, then began rearranging his bandage. 'So we wait here, and then board the train unseen when it arrives.'

'Right,' I answered.

Kreizler drew out his silver watch. 'Almost half an hour.'

I glanced over at him pointedly and smiled a bit. 'Just enough time for you to explain that schoolboy gesture with your watch back there.'

Kreizler looked away quickly, and I was surprised by the extent to which the comment seemed to embarrass him. 'There is,' he said, returning my smile despite himself, 'no chance that you'll forget that incident, I suppose?'

'None.'

He nodded. 'I thought not.'

I sat down near him. 'Well?' I said. 'Are you going to marry the girl or not?'

Laszlo shrugged a bit. 'I have – considered it.'

I let my head fall with a quiet laugh. 'My God . . . marriage.

Have you – well, you know – asked her?' Laszlo shook his head. 'You might want to wait until the investigation's over,' I said. 'She'll be more likely to agree.'

Kreizler looked puzzled at that. 'Why?'

'Well,' I answered simply, 'she'll have proved her point, if you know what I mean. And be more amenable to tying herself down.'

'Point?' Kreizler said. 'What point?'

'Laszlo,' I answered, lecturing him a bit, 'in case you haven't noticed, this whole affair means rather a lot to Sara.'

'*Sara*?' he repeated in bewilderment – and by the way he said the name I realized just exactly how wrong I'd been since the very beginning.

'Oh, no,' I sighed. 'It's *not* Sara . . .'

Kreizler stared at me for a few more seconds, then leaned back, opened his mouth, and let out a deeper laugh than any I'd ever heard from him; deep, and irritatingly long.

'Kreizler,' I said contritely, after a full minute of this treatment. 'Please, I hope you'll—' He didn't stop, however, at which annoyance began to come through in my voice. 'Kreizler. Kreizler! All right, I've made a jackass out of myself. Now will you have the decency to shut up?'

But he didn't. After another half-minute the laugh finally did begin to calm, but only because it was now causing some pain in his right arm. Holding that wounded limb, Laszlo continued to chuckle, tears appearing in his eyes. 'I am sorry, Moore,' he finally said. 'But what you must have been thinking—' And then another round of painful laughter.

'Well, what in hell was I *supposed* to think?' I demanded. 'You've had enough time alone with her. And you said yourself—'

'But Sara has no interest in marriage,' Kreizler answered, finally getting himself under control. 'She's little enough interest in men at all – she's constructed her entire life around the idea that a woman can live an independent, fulfilling existence. You ought to know that.'

'Well, it did cross my mind,' I lied, trying to salvage some vestige of dignity. 'But the way that you were acting, it seemed as though – well, I don't know how it seemed!'

'That was one of the first conversations I had with her,' Kreizler explained further. 'There were to be no complications, she said – everything would be strictly professional.' Laszlo studied me as I pouted. 'It must have been very trying for you,' he said, with another chuckle.

'It was,' I answered petulantly.

'You might've simply *asked*.'

'Well, Sara wasn't the only one trying to be professional!' I protested, stamping a foot. 'Though I can see now that I shouldn't have bothered with any—' I suddenly stopped, my volume falling again. 'Wait a minute. Just one minute. If it's not Sara, then who in hell—' I turned slowly to Laszlo, and then he turned equally slowly to the ground: the explanation was all over his face. 'Oh, my God,' I breathed. 'It's Mary, isn't it?'

Kreizler looked toward the station, and then into the distance in the direction from which the train would approach us, as if searching for salvation from this inquisition. None came. 'It's a complicated situation, John,' he finally said. 'I must ask you to understand and respect that.'

Too shocked to offer any commentary, I proceeded to sit mutely through Laszlo's subsequent explanation of this 'complicated situation.' Clearly there were aspects of the thing that disturbed him deeply: Mary had originally been a patient of his, after all, and there was always the danger that what she believed was affection for him was in reality a kind of gratitude and, worse still, respect. For this reason, Laszlo explained to me carefully, he'd tried very hard not to encourage her or to permit himself any reciprocal emotions when it had first become clear to him, almost a year earlier, how she felt. At the same time, he was anxious that I should understand how very much his and Mary's mutual attraction had grown from beginnings that in many ways were perfectly natural.

When Kreizler first started to work with the illiterate and supposedly uncomprehending Mary, he quickly realized that he would not be able to communicate with her until he could establish a bond of trust. And he forged that bond by revealing to her what he now referred to ambiguously as his own 'personal history.' Unaware that I currently knew more about his personal history than he'd ever told me, Kreizler didn't realize how fully I understood his words. Mary had probably been, I speculated, the first person who ever heard the tale of Laszlo's apparently violent relationship with his own father, and such a difficult disclosure would indeed have bred trust, and more: while Laszlo had only intended to encourage Mary to tell her own tale by telling his, he had, in fact, planted the seeds of an unusual sort of intimacy. That intimacy had survived into the period when Mary came to work for him, making life on Seventeenth Street far more interesting, not to mention perplexing, than it had ever been before. When it eventually became impossible for Kreizler to deny first that Mary's feelings for him went beyond mere gratitude, and, second, that he was experiencing a similar attraction to her, he entered on a long period of self-examination, trying to determine if what he felt was not at heart a kind of pity for the unfortunate, lonely creature whom he'd taken under his roof. He only fully satisfied himself that it was not several days before our investigation burst in on his life. The case forced him to put off a resolution of his personal predicament; yet it also helped him clarify what form that resolution might take. For when it became clear that not only were the members of our team in physical danger, but his servants, as well, Kreizler experienced a desire to protect Mary that went far beyond the usual duties of a benefactor. At that point he decided that she should be told as little as possible about the case, and play no part in its prosecution: knowing that his enemies might come at him through the people he cared about, Laszlo hoped to safeguard Mary by making sure that, on the off chance some outsider found a way to communicate with her, she had no useful information to divulge. It hadn't been until the morning of our departure for Washington that Kreizler had decided it might be time for his and Mary's relationship to, as he rather awkwardly put it, 'evolve.' He informed her immediately of this decision; and she watched him depart with tears in her eyes, fearful that something would happen to him while he was away and thus prevent their ever becoming more than master and servant.

As Kreizler finished his story, I heard the first whistle of the

Caleb Carr

New York train in the eastern distance. Still stunned, I nonetheless began going over the events of recent weeks in my mind, trying to determine where it was that I had gone so wrong in my interpretation.

'It was Sara,' I finally said. 'Since the beginning she's been behaving like – well, I don't know just what she's been behaving like, but it's been damned peculiar. Does she know?'

'I'm sure of it,' Kreizler answered, 'though I've never told her. Sara seems to view everything around her as a test case on which to sharpen her detecting skills. I believe this little puzzle has been most entertaining for her.'

'Entertaining,' I said with a grunt. 'And I thought it was love. I'll bet she knew I was off on the wrong track. It's just the kind of thing she'd do, let me go around thinking – well, you wait till we get back. I'll show her what happens when you play that kind of game with John Schuyler—'

I stopped as the New York train appeared a mile or so down the tracks to our left, still moving at high speed toward the station.

'We can continue this on board,' I said, helping Kreizler up. 'And rest assured we *will* continue it!'

After waiting for the train to come to a full, grunting halt outside the station, Kreizler and I began a quick trot across another rock- and ditch-riddled field toward the vehicle's last car. We climbed onto the observation deck and then moved stealthily on inside, where I got Laszlo comfortably positioned in a rear seat. There was as yet no sign of the conductor, and we used the few minutes before our departure to neaten Kreizler's bandage, and our general appearances, as well. I glanced out at the station platform every few seconds, trying to spot anyone whose demeanor might betray him for an assassin, but the only other people entraining were an elderly, well-to-do woman with a walking stick and her large, rather harried nurse.

'Looks as though we may have gotten a break,' I said, standing in the aisle. 'I'll just have a quick look up ahead and—'

My voice froze as my eyes turned to the rear door of the car. Two large forms had appeared, seemingly out of nowhere, on the observation deck; and although their attention was directed away from the train – they were arguing with a station official – I could see enough of them to recognize the two thugs who had chased Sara and me from the Santorellis' flat.

'What is it, Moore?' Kreizler asked, eyeing me. 'What's happened?'

Knowing that in his current condition Laszlo wasn't going to be much good in a confrontation of any kind, I tried to smile, and then shook my head. 'Nothing,' I said quickly. 'Nothing at all. Don't be so jumpy, Kreizler.'

We both turned at the sound of the elderly woman and her nurse entering the front door of our car. Though my stomach was alive with sudden dread, my mind was working reliably: 'I'll be right back,' I told Laszlo, and then I approached the newcomers.

'Excuse me,' I said, smiling and doing my best to be engaging. 'May I be of some assistance in getting you settled, madam?'

'You may,' the old woman answered, in a tone that indicated she was very familiar with being waited on hand and foot. 'This wretched nurse of mine is utterly useless!'

'Oh, surely not,' I answered, eyeing the walking stick that the woman was leaning on: it had a fine head of heavy silver, which was fashioned into the likeness of a swan. I seized the woman's arm and guided her into a seat. 'But there are limits,' I said, surprised at the old woman's weight and ungainliness, 'to even the best nurse's capabilities.' The nurse gave me a smile, at that, and I took the opportunity to lay hold of the old woman's stick. 'If you'll allow me to hold this, madam, I think we can – there!' With a loud groan the seat received its occupant, who let out a rush of air.

'Oh!' the woman exclaimed. 'Oh, yes, that's better. Thank you, sir. You are a gentleman.'

I smiled again. 'A pleasure,' I said, walking away.

As I passed Kreizler he gave me a dumbfounded look. 'Moore, what the devil—'

I indicated silence to him, then approached the rear door of the car, keeping my face to one side so that I couldn't be seen from without. The two men were still arguing with the station attendant on the platform, about what I couldn't tell; but when I looked down I saw that one of them held a rifle case. 'He'll have to go first,' I mumbled to myself; but before making any move

Caleb Carr

I waited for the train to start rolling out of the station.

When that moment finally came I heard the two men outside yell some final, and fairly raw, insults at the stationman: in seconds they would turn and be inside. I took a deep breath, then opened the door quickly and quietly.

Not for nothing had I spent many seasons following the trials and tribulations of New York's baseball Giants. During afternoons in Central Park I'd developed a healthy batting swing of my own, which I now exercised with the old woman's cane across the neck and skull of the thug who held the rifle case. The man cried out, but before he could even clutch at the injury I'd put a hand between his shoulder blades and shoved him over the railing of the observation deck. Although the train was still moving fairly slowly, there was no chance of the man getting back on board – but I was still faced with the second thug, who screamed 'What in hell?' as he spun on me.

Suspecting that his first instinct would be to go for my throat, I crouched down low and let him have the silver swan in the groin. The man doubled over for just an instant, and when he rose again he looked more infuriated than disabled by the blow. He threw a fist that glanced off my skull as I leaned out over the railroad tracks to avoid it. The train, I divined from a brief, somewhat dizzy glance downward, was picking up speed. Clumsy even for a man his size, the thug had stumbled when his blow failed to land securely, and as he tried to regain his balance I laid the swan across his cheek, although the move was cramped and didn't prevent him from coming for me again. I held the stick up with both hands, but my opponent, anticipating another swing, raised his beefy arms to protect either side of his head. Then he grinned maliciously and moved forward.

'Now, you shit,' he grunted, and then he suddenly lunged. I had only one avenue of attack: leveling the stick at his throat, I shot its end into his Adam's apple sharply, producing a sudden, choked cry and momentarily paralyzing the man. I quickly dropped the stick, grabbed hold of the roof of the deck, pulled myself up and let the thug have a full kick with both feet. The blow sent him, too, over the railing, and into an embankment by the tracks. There he rolled to a halt, still clutching his throat.

Lowering myself back down I took a few deep, gasping breaths, then looked up to see Kreizler coming through the door.

'Moore!' he said, crouching by me. 'Are you all right?' I nodded, still breathing hard, as Laszlo looked into the distance behind us. 'Your condition certainly seems preferable to the state *those* two are in. However, if you're able to walk I suggest you get back inside – that woman's gone into hysterics. She thinks you've stolen her walking stick, and she's threatening to send for the authorities when we reach our next stop.'

With my pulse finally beginning to calm, I straightened out my clothes, then picked up the walking stick and headed into the car. Stumbling a bit as I walked down the aisle, I approached the old woman.

'Here you are, madam,' I said, cordially if still a bit breathlessly. She drew back in fear. 'I only wanted to admire it in the sunlight.'

The woman accepted the stick without saying anything; but as I walked back to my seat I heard her shriek and exclaim: 'No – get it away! There's *blood* on it, I tell you!'

Collapsing with a groan, I was joined by Kreizler, who offered me his flask. 'I can only suppose that those were *not* men to whom you owe a gambling debt,' he said.

I shook my head and had a drink. 'No,' I breathed. 'Connor's boys. More than that I can't tell you.'

'Did they really intend to *kill* us, do you think?' Laszlo wondered. 'Or simply to frighten us?'

I shrugged. 'I doubt we'll ever know. And frankly, I'd rather not talk about it just at the moment. Besides, we were in the midst of a very important discussion, before they butted in ...'

The conductor soon appeared, and as we bought two tickets to New York from him, I began to cross-examine Laszlo about the whole Mary Palmer business, not because I had any trouble believing it – no one who'd ever met the girl would have had any trouble believing it – but because, on the one hand, it soothed my nerves, and, on the other, it disarmed Kreizler so thoroughly and refreshingly. All the dangers we'd faced that day, indeed all the grimness of our investigation generally, somehow shrank in

Caleb Carr

significance as Laszlo very tenuously revealed his personal hopes for the future. It was an unfamiliar sort of conversation for him, and difficult in many ways; but never had I seen the man look or sound so completely human as he did on that train ride.

And never would I see him so again.

Chapter 36

Our train, a local to begin with, made abominably poor time, so that when we stumbled out of the Grand Central Depot the first hints of dawn were beginning to show in the eastern sky. After agreeing that the long job of interpreting the information we'd gotten from Adam Dury could wait until that afternoon, Kreizler and I got into separate cabs and headed for our respective homes to get some sleep. All seemed quiet at my grandmother's house when I reached Washington Square, and it was my hope that I'd be able to slip into bed before the morning's activities began. I almost made it, too; but just as I was preparing to undress, having successfully navigated the stairs without making a sound, a light knocking came at my bedroom door. Before I'd given any reply, Harriet's head poked into the room.

'Oh, Mr. John, sir,' she said, clearly very upset. 'Thank heavens.' She came fully into the room, pulling her robe tighter around herself. 'It's Miss Howard, sir – she was calling all yesterday evening, and last night, as well.'

'Sara?' I said, alarmed at the look on Harriet's usually cheerful face. 'Where is she?'

'At Dr. Kreizler's – she said you'd find her there. There's been some sort of – well, I don't know, sir, she didn't explain much of anything, but something terrible's happened, I could tell it from her voice.'

I jammed my feet back into my shoes in a rush. 'Dr. Kreizler's?'

I said, my heart beginning to race. 'What in the world's she doing there?'

Harriet wrung her hands vigorously. 'Like I say, sir, she didn't tell me – but please hurry, she's called more than a dozen times!'

Like a shot I was back out onto the street. Knowing that I wouldn't find a cab any closer than Sixth Avenue at that hour, I bolted west at the fastest pace I could manage and didn't come to a halt till I'd jumped into a hansom that was parked underneath the El tracks. I gave the driver Kreizler's address and told him the matter was urgent, at which he grabbed his whip and put it to work. As we charged uptown – myself in a kind of fearful daze, too tired and mystified to make sense out of Harriet's statement – I began to feel an occasional splash against my face and leaned out of the cab to look at the sky: heavy clouds had rolled in over the city, staving off the light of daybreak and moistening the streets with a steady rain.

My driver didn't let up for a moment during the trip to Stuyvesant Square, and in a remarkably short time I was standing on the sidewalk in front of Kreizler's house. I gave the cabbie a generous amount of money without asking for change, to which he announced that he would wait for me at the curb, suspecting that I would need another ride soon and not wanting to lose so openhanded a fare at such a slow hour of the morning. I moved cautiously but quickly to the front door of the house, which was pulled open by Sara.

She looked uninjured, for which I was grateful enough to give her a big embrace. 'Thank God,' I said. 'From the way Harriet sounded I was afraid that—' I suddenly pulled back when I caught sight of a man standing behind Sara: white-haired, distinguished, wearing a frock coat and carrying a Gladstone bag. I glanced at Sara again, and noticed that her face was full of an exhausted sadness.

'This is Dr. Osborne, John,' Sara said quietly. 'An associate of Dr. Kreizler's. He lives nearby.'

'How do you do?' Dr. Osborne said to me, without waiting for a reply. 'Now, then, Miss Howard, I hope I've been clear – the boy is not to be moved or disturbed in any way. The next twenty-four hours will be crucial.'

Sara nodded wearily. 'Yes, Doctor. And thank you for being so attentive. If you hadn't been here—'

'I only wish that there was more I could have done,' Osborne answered quietly. Then he put his tall hat on his head, nodded to me, and set off. Sara pulled me inside.

'What in hell's happened?' I said, as I followed her up the stairs. 'Where's Kreizler? And what's this about a boy? Has Stevie been hurt?'

'Shush, John,' Sara answered, quietly but urgently. 'We've got to keep things quiet in this house.' She resumed the climb to the parlor. 'Dr. Kreizler's – gone.'

'Gone?' I echoed. 'Gone where?'

Walking into the dark parlor, Sara made a move toward a lamp, but then decided with a wave of her hand to leave it alone. She collapsed onto a sofa, and took a cigarette out of a case on a nearby table.

'Sit down, John,' she said; and something about the range of emotions contained in those few words – resignation, sorrow, anger – made me comply instantly. I held out a match for her cigarette and waited for her to go on. 'Dr. Kreizler's at the morgue,' she finally said, in a smoky breath.

I took in air quickly. 'The *morgue*? Sara, what is it, what's happened? Is Stevie all right?'

She nodded. 'He will be. He's upstairs, along with Cyrus. We've got two cracked skulls to care for now.'

'Cracked skulls?' I parroted again. 'How in—' A sudden, sickening rush swept through my gut, as I glanced around the parlor and the adjacent hallway. 'Wait a minute. Why are you here? And why are you letting people in and out? Where's Mary?'

Sara didn't answer, at first, just rubbed her eyes slowly and then drew in some more smoke. Her voice, when it reemerged, was curiously faint. 'Connor was here. Saturday night, with two of his thugs.' The twisting in my stomach became more extreme. 'Apparently they'd lost track of you and Dr. Kreizler – and they must have been taking a lot of heat from their superiors, based on the way they were acting.' Standing up slowly, Sara strode to the French windows and opened one just a crack. 'They forced their way into the house, and shut Mary in the kitchen. Cyrus was in

Caleb Carr

bed, which left Stevie. They asked him where you and Dr. Kreizler were, but – well, you know Stevie. He wouldn't say.'

I nodded, and mumbled, '"Go chase yourselves,"' softly.

'Yes,' Sara answered. 'So – they started in on him. Along with his skull he's got a few broken ribs, and his face is a mess. But it's the head that – well, he'll live, but we don't know yet just what sort of shape he'll live *in*. Things ought to be clearer by tomorrow. Cyrus tried to get out of bed to help, but he only collapsed in the hallway upstairs and bumped his head again.'

Though afraid to ask, I did: 'And Mary?'

Sara's arms went up in resignation. 'She must've heard Stevie screaming. I can't imagine what else would have made her act so – rashly. She got hold of a knife, and managed to get out of the kitchen. I don't know what she thought she was going to do, but . . . The knife ended up in Connor's side. Mary ended up at the bottom of the stairs. Her neck was . . .' Sara's voice trailed off.

'Broken,' I finished for her, in a horrified whisper. 'She was dead?'

Sara nodded, and then cleared her throat to speak again. 'Stevie got to the telephone, and called Dr. Osborne. I came by when I got back from New Paltz last night, and everything was – well, taken care of. Stevie did manage to say that it was an accident. That Connor didn't mean to do it. But when Mary stabbed him he spun around and . . .'

For long seconds my vision faded, everything around me blending into a kind of vague grayness; then I heard a sound that I'd last detected on the Williamsburg Bridge anchor the night Georgio Santorelli was killed – the powerful churning of my own blood. My head began to shake, and when I put my hands up to hold it still I noticed that my cheeks were moist. The kinds of memories that usually accompany news of such a tragedy – quick, out of sequence, and in some cases silly – flashed through my mind, and when I heard my own voice again I didn't really know where it was coming from.

'It's not possible,' I was saying. 'It isn't. The coincidence, it doesn't make – Sara, Laszlo was just telling me—'

'Yes,' she said. 'He told me, too.'

I got up, feeling awfully unsteady on my feet, and went to stand by the window with Sara. The dark clouds in the dawn sky were continuing to prevent daybreak from really taking hold of the city. 'The sons of bitches,' I whispered. 'The lousy sons of . . . Have they got Connor?'

Sara threw the stub of her cigarette out the window, shaking her head. 'Theodore's out now, with some detectives. They're searching the hospitals, and all of Connor's known haunts. I'm guessing they won't find him, though. How Connor's men found out you were in Boston is still a bit of a mystery, though it's probably safe to say they checked the ticket sellers at the depot.' Sara touched my shoulder as she continued to stare out the window. 'You know,' she murmured, 'from the very first time I walked into this house, Mary was afraid that something would happen to take him away from her. I tried to help her understand that that something wouldn't be me. But she never seemed to lose the fear.' Sara turned and went back across the room to sit down. 'Perhaps she was smarter than the rest of us.'

I put a hand to my forehead. 'It *can't* be . . .' I breathed again; but on a deeper level I knew that, in fact, it could easily be, given who we were dealing with, and that I'd better start adjusting to the reality of this nightmare. 'Kreizler,' I said, forcing some kind of strength into my voice. 'Kreizler's at the morgue?'

'Yes,' Sara answered, taking out another cigarette. 'I couldn't tell him what happened – Dr. Osborne did it. He said he's had practice.'

I gnashed a new surge of remorse away with my teeth, tightened my fist, and headed for the stairs. 'I've got to get over there.'

Sara caught my arm. 'John. Be careful.'

I nodded quickly. 'I will.'

'No. I mean *really* careful. With him. If I'm right, the effects of this are going to be a lot worse than you may be expecting. Cut him a wide path.'

I tried to smile, and put a hand on hers; then I kept on moving, down the stairs and out the door.

My cabbie was still waiting at the curb, and when I appeared he jumped back up onto his hansom smartly. I told him to get me to Bellevue in a hurry, and we sped off at the same lively pace. The

Caleb Carr

rain was beginning to pick up, blown by a strong, warm, westerly wind, and as we bounced up First Avenue I pulled off my cap and tried to use it to shield my face from the water that was spraying off the roof of the cab. I don't remember having any thoughts, as such, during that ride; there were just more quick images of Mary Palmer, the quiet, pretty girl with the remarkable blue eyes who, in the space of just a few hours, had evolved in my mind from housemaid to future wife of a dear friend to no more. There was no sense in what had happened, no sense at all, and even less in trying to create any; I just sat there and let the images fly by.

When I reached the morgue I found Laszlo outside the large iron door in the back that we'd used to enter the building when we'd examined Ernst Lohmann's body. He was leaning against the building, his eyes as wide, vacant, and black as the gaping holes our killer had left in the heads of his victims. Rain was cascading down off a gutter on the edge of the roof above and drenching him, and I tried to pull him away from it. But his body was stiff and intractable.

'Laszlo,' I said quietly. 'Come on. Get in the cab.' I tugged at him a few more times without achieving anything, and then he finally spoke, in a hoarse monotone:

'I will not leave her.'

I nodded. 'All right. Then let's just stand in the doorway here, you're getting soaked.'

His eyes alone moved as he glanced at his clothes; then he nodded once, and stumbled with me into the minimal shelter of the doorway. We stood there for quite some time until, finally, he spoke in the same lifeless voice:

'Did you know – my father—'

I looked at him, my own heart ready to burst at the pain that was in his face, and then nodded. 'Yes. I knew him, Laszlo.'

Kreizler shook his head in a stiff jerk. 'No. Do you know *what* my – father always said to me, when I was – a boy?'

'No. What?'

'That—' The voice was still scraping terribly, as if it were a labor to produce it, but the words began to come faster. 'That I didn't know as much as I thought I did. That I thought I knew how people should behave, that I thought I was a better person than he was. But one day – one day, he said, I would know that I wasn't. Until then, I'd be nothing more than an – imposter . . .'

Once again, I couldn't find a way to tell Laszlo how fully I understood, in light of Sara's discovery, what he was saying; so I simply put a hand to his uninjured shoulder as he began to straighten his clothes absentmindedly. 'I have – made arrangements. The mortician will be here soon. Then I've got to get home. Stevie and Cyrus . . .'

'Sara's looking after them.'

His voice became suddenly strong, even somewhat violent: '*I've* got to look after them, John!' He shook a fist before him. '*I've* got to. *I* brought these people into my house. *I* was responsible for their safety. Look at them now – look! Two near dead, and one – one . . .' He gasped and looked at the iron door, as if he could see right through it to the rusted metal table on which now lay the girl who had embodied his hope of a new life.

Gripping him tighter, I said, 'Theodore's out looking—'

'I'm no longer interested in what the commissioner of police is doing,' Kreizler answered, quickly and sharply. 'Nor in the activities of anyone else in that department.' He paused, and then, wincing as he moved his right arm, took my hand from his shoulder and looked away from me. 'It's over, John. This wretched, bloody business, this . . . *investigation*. Over.'

I was at something of a loss for words. He seemed perfectly serious. 'Kreizler,' I finally said, 'give yourself a couple of days before you—'

'Before I what?' he answered quickly. 'Before I get one of you killed, too?'

'You're not responsible for—'

'Don't *tell* me I'm not responsible for it!' he raged. 'Who, then, if not me? It's my own vanity, just as Comstock said. I've been in a blind fury, trying to prove my precious points, oblivious of any danger it might pose. And what have they wanted? Comstock? Connor? Byrnes, those men on the train? They've wanted to stop me. But *I* thought that what I was doing was too important for me to take any note – I thought I knew better! We've been hunting a killer, John, but the killer isn't the real danger – *I* am!' He hissed suddenly and clenched his teeth. 'Well, I've seen enough. If I'm the danger then I shall remove myself. Let this man keep killing. It's what they want. He's a part of their order, their precious social order – without such creatures they've no scapegoats for their own wretched brutality! Who am I to interfere?'

'Kreizler,' I said, ever more worried, for there was no question now that he meant what he was saying. 'Listen to yourself, you're going against everything—'

'No!' he answered. 'I'm going *along*! I'll go back to my Institute and my dead, empty house, and *forget* this case. I'll see to it that Stevie and Cyrus heal and never again face unknown attackers because of my vain schemes. And this bloody society that they've built for themselves can go down the path they have planned for it, and *rot*!'

I stood back a couple of steps, knowing in some part of myself that it was useless to argue with him, but stung by his attitude nonetheless. 'All right, then. If self-pity's going to be your solution—'

He swung at me hard with his left arm, but missed badly. 'Damn you, Moore!' he seethed, breathing in short, quick contractions. 'Damn you, and damn them!' He grabbed the iron door and drew it open, then paused to get his breathing under control. Eyes again wide with horror, he stared into the dark, miserable hallway before him. 'And damn me, too,' he added quietly. The heaving in his chest finally began to subside. 'I'm going to wait inside. I would appreciate it if you'd go. I'll arrange to have my things removed from Number 808. I – I'm sorry, John.' He entered the morgue, the iron door swinging shut with a crash as he went.

I stood there for a moment, my sodden clothes now starting to cling to my body and limbs. I looked up at the square, feelingless brick buildings around me, and then at the sky. More clouds were being blown in by the westerly wind, which was only picking up pace. In a sudden movement I reached down, tore a bit of grass and earth from the ground beneath me, and then threw it at the black door.

'Damn you *all*, then!' I shouted, holding up my muddy fist;

but there was no relief in the exclamation. I let the hand fall slowly, then wiped rainwater from my face and stumbled back to my cab.

Chapter 37

Not wanting to see or talk to anyone after I left the morgue, I ordered my cabbie to take me to Number 808 Broadway. The building was fairly deserted, and when I stumbled into our headquarters the only sound I could hear was the blast of rain against the ring of Gothic windows around me. I collapsed onto the Marchese Carcano's divan and stared at the large, note-covered chalkboard, my spirits sinking ever lower. Grief and hopelessness were finally and mercifully overwhelmed by exhaustion, and I fell asleep for most of the dark, gloomy day. But at about five o'clock I shot up to the sound of loud knocking at the front door. Staggering over and opening the thing, I found myself facing a dripping Western Union boy who had a sodden envelope in his hand. I took the message from him and peeled it apart, my lips moving rather idiotically as I read it:

CAPTAIN MILLER, FORT YATES, CONFIRMS CPL JOHN BEECHAM HAD FACIAL SPASM. CARRIED SIMILAR KNIFE. KNOWN TO CLIMB MOUNTAINS WHEN OFF DUTY. ADVISE.

As I finished reading the wire for a third time, I became aware that the delivery boy was saying something, and I looked up blankly. 'What's that?'

'Reply, sir,' the boy said impatiently. 'Do you want to send a reply?'

'Oh.' I thought about it for a moment, trying to decide what the best course would be in light of the morning's developments. 'Oh . . . yes.'

'You'll have to write it down on something dry,' the boy said. 'My forms are soaked.'

I walked over to my desk, pulled out a slip of paper, and scribbled a short note: RETURN BY FASTEST TRAIN. EARLIEST OPPORTUNITY. The delivery boy read the thing and gave me a price for its transmission, to which I pulled some money out of my pocket and handed it to him uncounted. The boy's attitude immediately improved, from which I divined that I'd given him a sizable tip, and then he was back in the elevator and on his way.

There seemed little point in the Isaacsons staying in North Dakota if our investigation was about to come to an abrupt conclusion. Indeed, if Kreizler was serious about dealing himself out of the game there seemed little point in any of us doing anything except cashing in our chips and heading back to our ordinary walks of life. Whatever understanding Sara, the Isaacsons, and I had of our killer was due to Laszlo's tutelage, and as I looked out over rainswept Broadway, where furtive shoppers were doing their best to avoid rushing carriages and delivery wagons as they tried to get in out of the downpour, I could imagine no way in which we could succeed without his continued leadership.

I'd just reconciled myself to this conclusion when I heard a key turning in the front door. Sara came bustling in, umbrella and grocery parcels in hand, her movements and air nothing like they'd been that morning. She was stepping and talking quickly, even lightly, as if nothing at all had happened.

'It's a flood, John!' she announced, shaking her umbrella and depositing it in the ceramic stand. She took off her wrap, then lugged her parcels back toward the little kitchen. 'You can barely get across Fourteenth Street on foot, and it's worth your life to try to find a cab.'

I looked back out the window. 'Cleans the streets, though,' I said.

'Do you want something to eat?' Sara called. 'I'll get some coffee going, and I brought food – sandwiches will have to do, I'm afraid.'

'Sandwiches?' I answered, not very enthusiastically. 'Couldn't we just go out somewhere?'

'Out?' Sara said, reemerging from the kitchen and coming over to me. 'We can't go out, we've got—' She stopped as she caught sight of the Isaacsons' telegram, then picked it up carefully. 'What's this?'

'Marcus and Lucius,' I answered. 'They got confirmation on John Beecham.'

'But that's wonderful, John!' Sara said in a rush. 'Then we—'

'I've already sent a reply,' I interrupted, disturbed by her manner. 'Told them to get back as soon as they can.'

'Even better,' Sara said. 'I doubt if there's much more for them to discover out there, and we'll need them here.'

'Need them?'

'We've got work to do,' Sara answered simply.

My shoulders drooped with the realization that my worries about her attitude had been well founded. 'Sara, Kreizler told me this morning that—'

'I know,' she answered. 'He told me, as well. What of it?'

'What of it? It's over, that's what of it. How are we supposed to go on without him?'

She shrugged. 'As we went on with him. Listen to me, John.' Grabbing hold of my shoulders, Sara led me over to my desk and sat me on it. 'I know what you're thinking – but you're wrong. We're good enough now without him. We can finish this.'

My head had started shaking even before she finished this statement. 'Sara, be serious – we don't have the training, we don't have the background—'

'We don't need any more than we have, John,' she answered firmly. 'Remember what Kreizler himself taught us – context. We don't need to know everything about psychology, or alienism, or the history of all similar cases to finish this job. All we need to know is *this* man, his *particular* case – and we do, now. In fact, when we put together what we've gathered during the last week, I'll bet that we know him as well as he knows himself – perhaps even better. Dr. Kreizler was important, but he's gone now, and we don't need him. You can't quit. You mustn't.'

There were undeniable bits of truth in what she was saying, and

I took a minute to digest them; but then my head began to shake again. 'Look, I know how much this opportunity means to you. I know how much it could have helped you convince the department—'

I shut up instantly as she took a good cut at my shoulder with her right fist. 'Damn it, John, don't insult me! Do you honestly think I'm doing this just for the opportunity? I'm doing it because I want to sleep soundly again someday – or have your little trips up and down the eastern seaboard made you forget?' She dashed over and grabbed some photographs off of Marcus's desk. 'Remember these, John?' I glanced down only briefly, knowing what she held: pictures of the various crime scenes. 'Do you really think *you're* going to spend many easy hours if you stop now? And what happens when the next boy is killed? How will you feel then?'

'Sara,' I protested, my voice rising to match hers, 'I'm not talking about what I'd *prefer* here! I'm talking about what's *practical.*'

'How practical is it to walk away?' she shouted back. 'Kreizler's only doing it because he *has* to – he's been hurt, hurt as badly as anyone can be, and this is the only way he can find to respond. But that's *him*, John. *We* can go on! We've *got* to go on!'

Letting her arms fall to her sides, Sara took several deep breaths, then smoothed her dress, walked across the room, and pointed to the right side of the chalkboard. 'The way I see it,' she said evenly, 'we've got three weeks to get ready. We can't waste a minute.'

'Three weeks?' I said. 'Why?'

She went over to Kreizler's desk and picked up the thin volume with the cross on its cover. 'The Christian calendar,' she said, holding it up. 'I assume you found out why he's following it?'

I shrugged. 'Well, we may have. Victor Dury was a reverend. So the – the—' I tried to find an expression, and finally latched onto one that sounded like something Kreizler would have said: 'The rhythms of the Dury house, the cycle of the family's life, would naturally have coincided with it.'

Sara's mouth curled up. 'You see, John? You weren't entirely wrong about a priest being involved.'

'And there was something else,' I said, thinking back to the questions that Kreizler had put to Adam Dury just as we were leaving the latter's farm. 'The reverend was fond of holidays – gave some rattling good sermons, apparently. But his wife . . .' I tapped a finger slowly on my desk, considering the idea; then, realizing its importance, I looked up. 'It was his wife who was Japheth's chief tormentor, according to his brother – and she gave the boys hellfire and brimstone over holidays.'

Sara looked very gratified. 'Remember what we said about the killer hating dishonesty and hypocrisy? Well, if his father's preaching one thing in his sermons, while at the same time, at home . . .'

'Yes,' I mumbled, 'I do see it.'

Sara returned to the chalkboard slowly, and then did something that rather struck me: She picked up a piece of chalk and, without hesitation, jotted down the information I'd given her on the left-hand side of the board. Her handwriting, at that angle, was not quite as neat and practiced as Kreizler's, but it looked like it belonged there, just the same. 'He's reacting to a cycle of emotional crisis that's existed all his life,' Sara said confidently, setting the chalk back down. 'Sometimes the crises are so severe that he kills – and the one he'll reach in three weeks may be the worst of all.'

'So you've said,' I answered. 'But I don't remember there being any significant holy days in late June.'

'Not significant for everyone,' Sara said, opening the calendar. 'But for him . . .'

She held the book out to me, pointing to one page in particular. I looked down to see the notation for Sunday, June 21st: The Feast of Saint John the Baptist. My eyes jumped open.

'Most churches don't make much of a to-do about it anymore,' Sara said quietly. 'But—'

'Saint John the Baptist,' I said quietly. 'Water!'

Sara nodded. 'Water.'

'Beecham,' I whispered, making a connection that, though perhaps a long shot, was nonetheless apparent: '*John Beecham* . . .'

'What do you mean?' Sara asked. 'The only Beecham I found

any mention of in New Paltz was a George.'

It was my turn to go to the board and pick up the chalk. Tapping it on the boxed-off area marked THE MOLDING VIOLENCE AND/OR MOLESTATION, I explained at high speed: 'When Japheth Dury was eleven, he was attacked – raped – by a man his brother worked with. A man who'd befriended him, a man he trusted. That man's name was *George* Beecham.' A small, urgent sound came out of Sara, and one of her hands went to her mouth. 'Now, *if* Japheth Dury, in fact, took the name Beecham after the killings, in order to begin a new life—'

'Of course,' Sara said. 'He *became* the tormentor!'

I nodded eagerly. 'And why the name John?'

'The Baptist,' Sara answered. 'The purifier!'

I laughed once and wrote these thoughts down in the appropriate segments of the board. 'It's just speculation, but—'

'John,' Sara said, admonishing me good-humoredly. 'That entire *board* is just speculation. But it *works*.' I set the chalk down and turned back around to find Sara absolutely beaming. 'You see now, don't you?' she said. 'We've got to do it, John – we've *got* to keep going!'

And of course we did.

So began twenty of the most extraordinary and difficult days of my life. Knowing that the Isaacsons would not get back to New York any earlier than Wednesday night, Sara and I set ourselves the task of sharing, interpreting, and recording all the information we'd gathered during the previous week, in order to have it ready for the detective sergeants to quickly assimilate on their return. We spent most of the next few days together at Number 808, going over facts and – on a less obvious, unacknowledged level – reshaping the atmosphere and spirit of our headquarters so as to ensure that Kreizler's would not become a crippling absence. All obvious signs and reminders of Laszlo's presence were quietly put aside or removed, and we pushed his desk into a corner, so that the other four could be re-formed into a smaller (or rather, as I chose to view it, tighter) ring. Neither Sara nor I were particularly happy about doing any of this, but we tried not to be sad or maudlin, either. As always, focus was the key: so long as we kept our vision steadily fixed on the twin goals of preventing

Caleb Carr

another murder and capturing our killer, we found we could get through even the most painful and disorienting moments of transition.

Not that we simply wiped Kreizler out of our minds; on the contrary, Sara and I spoke of him several times, in an effort to fully comprehend just what twists and turns his mind had taken after Mary's death. Naturally, these conversations involved some discussion of Laszlo's past; and thinking about the unfortunate reality of Kreizler's upbringing as I talked with Sara dispelled the last of the anger I felt over Laszlo's abandonment of the investigation, to the extent that on Tuesday morning I actually went, without telling Sara, back to Kreizler's house.

I made the trip in part to see how Stevie and Cyrus were doing, but primarily to smooth over the bumps and cracks that had been left by Laszlo's and my parting at Bellevue. Thankfully, I found that my old friend was also anxious to put things right in this regard, though he was still quite determined not to return to our investigation. He spoke of Mary's death quietly, making it easy for me to appreciate how thoroughly his spirit had been savaged by the incident. But more than that, I think it was the shattering of his confidence that prevented him from coming back to the hunt. For only the second time in his life that I could recall (the first having occurred during the week before we visited Jesse Pomeroy), Laszlo seemed to truly doubt his own judgment. And while I didn't agree with his self-indictment, I certainly couldn't blame him. Every human being must find his own way to cope with such severe loss, and the only job of a true friend is to facilitate whatever method he chooses. And so I finally shook Laszlo's hand and accepted his determination to bow out of our work, even though it pained me deeply. We said goodbye, and I wondered again how we would ever get along without him; yet before I'd even gotten clear of his front yard, my thoughts had turned back to the case.

Sara's trip to New Paltz, I learned during those three days before the Isaacsons returned, had confirmed many of our hypotheses concerning our killer's childhood years. She'd been able to locate several of Japheth Dury's contemporaries, and they acknowledged – rather ruefully, to give them their due – that the boy had suffered much mockery because of his violent facial spasms. Throughout his years at school (and as Marcus had speculated, the New Paltz school had taught the Palmer system of handwriting at that time), as well as on those occasions when he accompanied his parents into town, Japheth would often be set on by gangs of children who made a great game out of competing to see who could most accurately imitate the boy's tic. This last was no ordinary twitch, the now-grown citizens of New Paltz had assured Sara: it was a contraction so severe that Japheth's eyes and mouth would be pulled around almost to the side of his head, as if he were in terrible pain and were about to break into violent tears. Apparently – and strangely – he never struck back when attacked by the children of New Paltz, and never turned a spiteful tongue on anyone who teased him; rather, he always went silently about his business, so that after a few years the children in town grew bored of tormenting him. Those few years, however, had apparently been enough to poison Japheth's spirit, coming as they did on top of a lifetime's coexistence with someone who never tired of hounding him: his own mother.

Sara didn't crow excessively about the extent to which she'd been able to predict the character of that mother, though God knows she would've been justified in doing so. Her interviews in New Paltz had supplied her with only a general description of Mrs. Dury, but she'd read enough into those generalities to be very encouraged. Japheth's mother was well remembered in the town, partly for her zealous advocacy of her husband's missionary work, but even more vividly for her harsh, cold manner. Indeed, it was widely held among New Paltz's other matrons that Japheth Dury's facial spasms had been the result of his mother's relentless badgering (thus demonstrating that folk wisdom can sometimes attain the status of psychological insight). Encouraging as all this was, it gave Sara only a fraction of the satisfaction offered by Adam Dury's account. Almost every one of Sara's hypotheses had been borne out by what Laszlo and I had heard in Dury's barn; Adam had even told us that his mother often told Japheth he was a 'dirty red Indian.' A woman had indeed played a 'sinister role' in our killer's life; and while the reverend's may have been the hand that actually administered beatings in the Dury household,

Caleb Carr

Mrs. Dury's behavior appeared to have represented another sort of punishment to both her sons, one that was just as powerful. Indeed, both Sara and I felt confident in saying that if one of Japheth's parents had been the 'primary' or 'intended' victim of his murderous rage, it was almost certainly his mother.

In sum, it now seemed certain that we were dealing with a man whose fantastic bitterness toward the most influential woman in his life had led him to shun the company of women generally. This left us with the question of why he should have chosen to kill boys who dressed up and behaved like females, rather than *de facto* women. In coming up with an answer to this riddle, Sara and I were led back to our earlier theory that the victims all possessed character traits not unlike the killer's own. The hateful relationship between Japheth Dury and his mother must, we reasoned, have spilled over into self-hatred, as well – for how could any boy despised by his mother fail to question his own worth? Thus Japheth's anger had crossed sexual lines, becoming a sort of hybrid, or mongrel; and it had found its only release in destroying boys who embodied, in their behavior, similar ambiguity.

The final step in Sara's and my process of assembling our recently collected clues was the fleshing out of our killer's transformation from Japheth Dury into John Beecham. Sara had learned little about George Beecham in New Paltz – he'd lived in the town for just a year, and only appeared in local records because he'd voted in the 1874 congressional election – but we were fairly sure that we understood the selection of the name, nonetheless. Since the beginning of our investigation, it had been clear to all of us that we were dealing with a sadistic personality, one whose every action betrayed an obsessive desire to change his role in life from that of the victim to that of the tormentor. It was perversely logical that, as a way of initiating and symbolizing this transformation, he should alter his name to that of a man who had once betrayed and violated him; and it was just as logical that he should keep that name when he began to murder children who apparently trusted him in just the way that he had once trusted George Beecham. There was a clear sense that, careful as the killer doubtless was to cultivate that trust, he despised his victims for being foolish enough to give it. Again, he hoped to eradicate an intolerable element of his own personality by eradicating mirror reflections of the child he'd once been.

And so Japheth Dury had become John Beecham, who, according to the assessments of his doctors at St. Elizabeth's Hospital, was highly sensitive to scrutiny of any kind, and also harbored at least strong feelings (if not outright delusions) of persecution. It was unlikely that these traits of personality had been much ameliorated after his release from St. Elizabeth's in the late summer of 1886, since that release had been secured through the exploitation of a legal technicality and against the doctors' wishes; and if indeed John Beecham was our killer, then, in fact, his suspicion, hostility, and violence had only worsened over the years. Sara and I determined that in order for Beecham to have gained the thorough familiarity with New York that he evidently had, he must have come to the city very soon after his release from St. Elizabeth's, and stayed in it ever since. There was cause for hope in this supposition, because he'd probably had contact with a good many people over the course of ten years, and become, in some neighborhood or walk of life, a familiar character. Of course, we didn't know precisely what he looked like; but, starting with the physical characteristics that we'd theorized early on, and then refining them by using Adam Dury as a physical model, we believed we could concoct a description that, in conjunction with the name John Beecham, would make identification a fairly easy matter. Of course, there was no guarantee that he was still using the name John Beecham; but both Sara and I believed that, given what the name meant to him, he had continued and would continue to do so, until forced to stop.

That was about all the hypothesizing we could do, pending the Isaacsons' return. Wednesday evening arrived, however, without our having had any word from the detective sergeants, and so Sara and I decided to attend to another unpleasant task: that of convincing Theodore to allow us to go on with the investigation in spite of Kreizler's departure. We both suspected that this wasn't going to be easy. Having spent the beginning of the week searching for Connor, as well as attending to the ongoing battle

between the forces of reform and corruption at Police Headquarters, Roosevelt remained unapprised of developments within
our investigation as of Wednesday evening; but, knowing that he
would learn the truth from either Kreizler or the Isaacsons
eventually, Sara and I decided to take the bear by the ears and tell
him ourselves.

Anxious to avoid stirring up a potentially dangerous new
round of speculation among the journalists and detectives at
headquarters, we elected to visit Theodore at his home. He and
his wife, Edith, had recently rented a town house at 689 Madison
Avenue that belonged to Theodore's sister, Bamie, a comfortable, well-furnished home that was nonetheless inadequate to the
task of containing the antics of the five Roosevelt children. (It
must be remembered, in fairness, that the White House itself
would soon prove similarly inadequate.) Knowing that Theodore
generally made sure to be home for dinner with his brood, Sara
and I took a hansom up Madison Avenue to Sixty-third Street at
about six o'clock, mounting the steps of Number 689 at sunset.

Before I'd even rapped on the door the sounds of youthful
mayhem became audible from within. The front portal was
eventually opened by Theodore's second son, Kermit, who at the
time was six years old. He wore the traditional white shirt,
knickers, and longish hair of a boy of his age during that era; but
in his right fist he rather ominously held what I supposed to be
the horn of an African rhinoceros, mounted on a heavy stand. His
face was all defiance.

'Hello, Kermit,' I said with a grin. 'Is your father at home?'

'*No one shall pass!*' the boy shouted grimly, staring me in the
eye.

I lost my grin. 'I beg your pardon?'

'No one shall pass!' he repeated. 'I, Horatio, will guard this
bridge!'

Sara let out a small laugh and I nodded in acknowledgment.
'Ah. Yes, Horatio at the bridge. Well, Horatio, if it's all the same
to you . . .'

I took a step or two into the house, to which Kermit raised
the rhino horn and banged it down with surprising force on the
toes of my right foot. I let out a sharp cry of pain, prompting

Sara to laugh harder, as Kermit again declared, '*No one shall pass*!'

Just then Edith Roosevelt's pleasant but firm voice echoed in from somewhere to the rear of the house: 'Kermit! What's going on out there?'

Kermit's eyes suddenly went round with apprehension, and then he spun and made for the nearby staircase, hollering 'Retreat! Retreat!' as he went. With the pain in my toes beginning to subside I marked the approach of a rather serious-looking young girl of four or so: Theodore's younger daughter, Ethel. She was carrying a large picture book full of vivid zoological illustrations and walking with evident purpose; but when she caught sight first of Sara and me and then of Kermit vanishing up the stairs, she paused, flicking a thumb in her brother's direction.

'Horatio at the bridge,' she droned, rolling her eyes and shaking her head. Then she put her face back in the book and continued her progress down the hall.

Suddenly a doorway to our right burst open, producing a rotund, uniformed, and clearly terrified maid. (There were very few servants in the Roosevelt household: Theodore's father, a prodigious philanthropist, had given away much of the family fortune, and Theodore supported his family primarily through his writing and his meager salary.) The maid seemed oblivious of Sara's and my presence as she dashed over to take refuge behind the open front door.

'No!' she screamed, to no one that I could see. 'No, Master Ted, I will not do it!'

The hall doorway through which the maid had appeared thereupon disgorged an eight-year-old boy who wore a solemn gray suit and spectacles much like Theodore's. This was Ted, the oldest son, whose status as scion of the family was amply demonstrated not only by his appearance, but by a rather intimidating young barred owl that sat perched on his shoulder, as well as by a dead rat that he held by its tail in one gloved hand.

'Patsy, you really are being ridiculous,' Ted said to the maid. 'If we don't teach him what his natural prey is, we'll never be able to send him back into the wild. Just hold the rat above his beak—' Ted stopped as he finally became aware that there were two callers standing in the doorway. 'Oh,' he said, his eyes brightening behind the spectacles. 'Good evening, Mr. Moore.'

'Evening, Ted,' I answered, shying away from the owl.

The boy turned to Sara. 'And you're Miss Howard, aren't you? I met you at my father's office.'

'Well done, Master Roosevelt,' Sara said. 'It seems you have a good memory for detail – a scientist needs one.'

Ted smiled very self-consciously at that, then remembered the rat in his hand. 'Mr. Moore,' he said quickly, with renewed enthusiasm. 'Do you think you could take this rat – here, by the tail – and just hold it about an inch above Pompey's beak? He's not used to the sight of prey, and it sometimes scares him – he's been living on strips of raw beefsteak. I've got to have a free hand to make sure he doesn't fly off.'

One less accustomed to life in the Roosevelt household might've balked at this request; I, however, having been present for many such scenes, simply sighed, took the rat by the tail, and positioned it as Ted had requested. The owl spun his head around once or twice rather bizarrely, then lifted his large wings and flapped them in apparent confusion. Ted, however, had a good hold of the talons with his gloved hand, and proceeded to make some hooting, squealing sounds that seemed to calm the bird. Eventually Pompey turned his remarkably flexible neck so that his beak was pointing directly at the ceiling, grabbed the rat by the head, and proceeded to swallow the thing, tail and all, in a half-dozen gruesome gulps.

Ted grinned wide. 'Good boy, Pompey! That's better than boring old steak, isn't it? Now all you've got to do is learn to catch them for yourself, and then you can go off and be with your friends!' Ted turned to me. 'We found him in a hollow tree in Central Park – his mother'd been shot, and the other hatchlings were already dead. He's come along fine, though.'

'*Look out, below!*' came a sudden cry from the top of the stairs, at which Ted's face grew very anxious and he hustled back out of the hall with his owl. The maid tried to follow him, but became transfixed by the sight of a large white mass that was bulleting down from the second floor atop the staircase bannister. Unable to decide which way to run, the maid finally crumpled to the floor and covered her head with a shriek, narrowly avoiding what might have been a very grim collision with Miss Alice Roosevelt, twelve years old. Slamming from the bannister to a carpet on the floor with well-practiced skill and a howling laugh, Alice proceeded to jump up, straighten her rather busy white dress, and hold a taunting finger out to the maid.

'Patsy, you great goose!' she laughed. 'I've told you, never stay still, you've *got* to pick a direction and run!' Turning the delicate, pretty face that would, in several years, cut a swath through Washington's most eligible bachelors like a scythe through so much wheat, Alice faced Sara and me, smiling and curtsying ever so slightly. 'Hello, Mr. Moore,' she said, with the confidence of a girl who knows, even at twelve, the power of her own charms. 'And is this *really* Miss Howard?' she went on, more excitedly and ingenuously. 'One of the women who works at headquarters?'

'It is, indeed,' I replied. 'Sara, meet Alice Lee Roosevelt.'

'How do you do, Alice?' Sara said, extending a hand.

Alice was all mature confidentiality as she took Sara's hand and replied, 'I know that a lot of people think it's scandalous that women are working at headquarters, Miss Howard, but *I* think it's *bully!*' She held up a small satchel, the drawstring of which was wrapped around her wrist. 'Would you like to see my snake?' she asked, and before the somewhat startled Sara could answer Alice had produced a wriggling, two-foot garter snake.

'Alice!' It was Edith's voice again, and this time I turned to see her lithely moving down the hallway toward us. 'Alice,' she repeated, in the careful but authoritative voice she used with this, the only child in the house that was not her own. 'I *do* think, dear, that we might let newcomers in the house get their things off and sit down before we introduce them to the reptiles. Hello, Miss Howard. John.' Edith touched Alice's forehead gently. '*You're* the one I depend on for civilized behavior, you know.'

Alice smiled up at Edith and then turned to Sara again, putting the snake back in the satchel. 'I'm sorry, Miss Howard. Won't

Caleb Carr

you come into the parlor and sit down? I've so many questions I want to ask you!'

'And I'd love to answer them sometime,' Sara said amiably. 'But I'm afraid we need to talk to your father for a few minutes—'

'I can't imagine why, Sara,' Theodore boomed, as he emerged from his study and into the hallway. 'You'll find that the children are the real authorities in this house. You'd be better off talking to them.'

At the sound of their father's voice the other Roosevelt children we'd encountered reappeared and mobbed him, each shouting out the events of his or her day in an effort to gain his counsel and approval. Sara and I watched this scene along with Edith, who simply shook her head and sighed, unable to quite comprehend (as was anyone acquainted with the family) the miracle of her husband's relationship to his children.

'Well,' Edith finally said to us quietly, still watching her family, 'you'd better have pressing business indeed, if you intend to break the power of *that* lobby.' Then she turned our way, comprehension evident in her glittering, rather exotic eyes. 'Although I understand that *all* your business, these days, is pressing.' I nodded once, and then Edith clapped her hands loudly. 'All right, my terrible tribe! Now that you've almost certainly woken Archie from his nap, what about washing up for dinner?' (Archie, at two, was the baby of the family; young Quentin, whose death in 1918 would have such a catastrophic effect on Theodore's emotional and physical health, had not yet been born in 1896.) 'And no guests that aren't human tonight,' Edith went on. 'I mean that, Ted. Pompey will be perfectly happy in the kitchen.'

Ted grinned. '*Patsy* won't be, though.'

Reluctantly but without loud protest the children dispersed, while Sara and I followed Theodore into his book-lined study. Works in progress covered several desks and tables in this ample room, along with a plethora of open reference volumes and large maps. Theodore cleared off two chairs near one particularly large and cluttered desk by the window, and then we all sat down. No longer in the children's presence, Roosevelt seemed to take on a subdued air, one that struck me as odd, given events at headquarters in recent days: Mayor Strong had asked one of Theodore's chief enemies on the Board of Commissioners to resign, and though the man had refused to go without a fight, there was a general feeling that Roosevelt was gaining the upper hand in the struggle. I congratulated him on this, but he just waved me off and put a fist to his hip.

'I'm not at all sure how much it will amount to, John, in the end,' he said gloomily. 'There are times when I feel that the job we have undertaken is not one that can be addressed at the metropolitan level alone. Corruption in this city is like the mythical beast, only instead of seven heads it springs a thousand for every one that is cut off. I don't know that this administration has the power to effect truly meaningful change.' Such wasn't the kind of mood that Roosevelt would tolerate for long, however. He picked up a book, slammed it down on his desk, and then looked at us through his pince-nez engagingly. 'However, that's none of your affair. Tell me – what news?'

It didn't prove quite so easy to get our news out, however; and once Sara and I finally had, Theodore slowly sank into his chair and leaned back, as though his melancholy mood had just been validated.

'I've been worried about what Kreizler's reaction to this outrage would be,' he said quietly. 'But I confess I didn't think that he'd abandon the effort.'

At that point I decided to tell Theodore the entire story of Kreizler's and Mary Palmer's relationship in an attempt to make him understand just how crushing an effect Mary's death had had on Laszlo. Remembering that Theodore had also endured the tragic and early loss of someone very dear to him – his first wife – I expected him to react with sympathy, which he did; but a crease of doubt nonetheless remained lodged in his forehead.

'And you're saying that you wish to go on without him?' he asked. 'You believe you can see it through?'

'We know enough,' Sara answered quickly. 'That is, we *will* know enough, by the time the killer strikes again.'

Theodore looked surprised. 'And when will that be?'

'Eighteen days,' Sara answered. 'The twenty-first of June.'

Folding his hands behind his head, Roosevelt began to rock back and forth slowly as he studied Sara. Then he turned to me. 'It's not just grief that's caused him to withdraw, is it?'

I shook my head. 'No. He's full of doubts about his own judgment and abilities. I never really understood before how much he's tortured by that – self-doubt. It's hidden most of the time, but it goes back . . .'

'Yes,' Roosevelt said, nodding and rocking. 'His father.' Sara and I glanced at each other quickly, both of us shaking our heads to indicate that we had not divulged the story. Theodore smiled gently. 'You remember my bout with Kreizler in the Hemenway Gymnasium, Moore? And the night we had afterwards? At one point he and I were rearguing the question of free will – quite congenially, mind you – and he asked me when I'd learned to box. I told him how my dear father had built me a small gym when I was a boy and taught me that vigorous exercise represented my best chance of overcoming illness and asthma. Kreizler asked if, as an experiment, I thought I could force myself to live a sedate life – to which I replied that everything I'd ever learned and held dear required me to be a man of action. I didn't realize it right away, but I'd proved his point. Then, out of curiosity, I asked him about his own father, whom I'd often heard mention of in New York. His aspect changed – drastically. I'll never forget it. He glanced away, and for the first time he seemed afraid to look me in the face – and then he grabbed at that bad arm of his. There was something so instinctive in the way he did it, at the merest mention of his father's name, that I began to suspect the truth. Needless to say, I was utterly aghast at the thought of what his life had been like. And yet I was fascinated, too – fascinated by how different that life had been from my own. How does the world look, I often found myself wondering, to a young man whose father is his enemy?'

Neither Sara nor I could offer any answer to the question. For several minutes the three of us just sat in silence; and then, from outside, we heard Alice shout vehemently:

'I don't care if he *is* a *Strix varia varia*, Theodore Roosevelt, Junior! He's not going to eat my snake!'

The Alienist

That brought quiet laughter from those of us in the study, and got us back to the business at hand.

'So,' Theodore said, with another pound of another book on his desk. 'The investigation. Tell me this – now that we have a name and an approximate description, why not make it a standard manhunt and let my men turn the city upside down?'

'And do what when they find him?' Sara replied. 'Make an arrest? With what evidence?'

'He's been a lot smarter than that,' I agreed. 'We've got no witnesses, and no evidence that would be admissible in court. Speculations, fingerprints, an unsigned note—'

'Which shows at least several signs of deceptive script,' Sara threw in.

'And God knows what he'll do if he's captured and then released,' I went on. 'No, the Isaacsons have said from the beginning that this is going to have to be a *flagrante delicto* case – we'll have to catch him at it.'

Theodore accepted all this with several slow nods. 'Well,' he eventually said, 'I fear that presents us with a new set of challenges. Kreizler's departure from the investigation, you may be surprised to learn, won't make things any easier for me. Mayor Strong has learned of the vigor with which I've been searching for Connor, and why. He views that search as another way in which this department might be connected to Kreizler, and has asked that I not jeopardize my position by letting my personal relationship with the doctor make me overly aggressive. He's also heard rumors that the Isaacson brothers are pursuing an independent investigation of the boy-whore murders, and he's ordered me not only to stop them, if the rumors are true, but to proceed with great caution regarding the case generally. You probably haven't heard about the trouble last night.'

'Last night?' I said.

Roosevelt nodded. 'There was some sort of a gathering in the Eleventh Ward, supposedly to protest the handling of the murders. The organizers were a group of Germans, and they claimed it was a political event – but there was enough whiskey in evidence to float a small ship.'

'Kelly?' Sara asked.

'Perhaps,' Roosevelt answered. 'What's certain is that they were on their way to getting well out of hand before they were broken up. The political implications of this case are growing more serious every day – and Mayor Strong has, I fear, reached that deplorable state where concern over the consequences of action leads to paralysis. He wants no precipitate steps taken in this matter.' Theodore paused to give Sara a small, only half-serious frown. 'He's also heard rumors, Sara, that you've been working with the Isaacsons – and as you know, there are many who will protest vehemently if they find out that a woman is actively involved in a murder investigation.'

'Then I'll redouble my efforts,' Sara answered with a coy smile, 'to conceal that involvement.'

'Hmm, yes,' Theodore noised dubiously. He studied us for a few seconds more, then nodded. 'Here's what I'll offer you – take the next eighteen days. Find out all you can. But when the twenty-first comes around, I want you to tell me everything you know, so that I can post officers I trust at every potential murder site and avenue of escape.' Roosevelt pounded one beefy fist into his other hand. 'I will not have another of these butcheries.'

I turned to Sara, who gave the deal quick consideration and then nodded certainly.

'We can keep the detective sergeants?' I asked.

'Of course,' Roosevelt answered.

'Done.' I put my hand forward and Theodore shook it, taking his pince-nez from his nose.

'I only hope you all *have* learned enough,' Roosevelt said, as he turned to shake Sara's hand. 'The idea of leaving my post without solving this case is not one that I relish.'

'You planning to quit, Roosevelt?' I jibed. 'Has Platt finally made things too warm for you?'

'Nothing of the sort,' he replied gruffly. Then it was his turn to coyly reveal his legion of teeth. 'But the conventions are coming up, Moore, and then the election. McKinley will be our party's man, unless I'm mistaken, while the Democrats look as though they'll actually be foolish enough to nominate Bryan – victory will be ours this fall.'

I nodded. 'Going to campaign, are you?'

Theodore shrugged modestly. 'I've been told that I can be of some use – in both New York and the western states.'

'And if McKinley should prove grateful for your help . . .'

'Now, John,' Sara chided sarcastically. 'You know how the commissioner feels about such speculation.'

Roosevelt's eyes went round. '*You*, young lady, have spent too much time away from headquarters – dashed impudence!' Then he relaxed and waved us toward the door. 'Go on, get out. I've got a pile of official papers to sort through tonight – being as someone seems to have stolen my secretary.'

It was nearly eight o'clock by the time Sara and I got back out onto Madison Avenue; but between the exhilaration of having been allowed to continue our investigation and the warmth of the clear spring night, neither of us felt much like going home. Nor were we in any mood to lock ourselves back up in our headquarters and wait for the Isaacsons to show up, although we were anxious to talk to them as soon as they got back. As we began to stroll downtown a happy compromise occurred to me: we could dine at one of the outdoor tables in front of the St. Denis Hotel, across the avenue from Number 808. Thus positioned, we'd be sure to spot the detective sergeants on their return. This idea suited Sara thoroughly; and as we continued our march down the avenue, she became more thoroughly delighted than I'd ever seen her. There was little of the usual edgy intensity in her manner, though her mind was quite focused and her thoughts were consistently sharp and relevant. The explanation for all this, when it came to me during dinner, wasn't particularly complicated: despite what Theodore had said about the possible official and public reaction to her involvement in the investigation, Sara was, for the moment, her own woman, a professional detective – in fact if not in name. In the days to come we would face many trials and frustrations, and I would have much cause to be grateful for Sara's increasingly good spirits – for it was she more than anyone else who became the driving force behind the continuation of our work.

My consumption of wine that night was such that by the

time dinner was over, the hedges that separated our table outside the St. Denis from the sidewalk were proving insufficient to contain my ardent attentions to the many lovely women who were innocently drawn to the still-bright windows of McCreery's store. Sara became quite impatient with my behavior and was on the verge of leaving me to my fate when she caught sight of something across the street. Following her indication I turned around to see a cab pulling up in front of Number 808, from which Marcus and Lucius Isaacson stepped rather wearily. Perhaps it was the wine, or the events of recent days, or even the weather; but I was absolutely overjoyed at the sight of them, and, leaping over the hedges, I dashed across Broadway to offer profuse greetings. Sara followed at a more rational pace. Both Lucius and Marcus had apparently seen a good amount of the sun during their sojourn on the high plains, for their skins had darkened considerably, giving them a warm, healthy look. They seemed very glad to be back, though I wasn't sure they'd stay that way once they heard about Kreizler's resignation.

'It's amazing country out there,' Marcus said, as he pulled their bags off of the hansom. 'Puts an entirely different perspective on life in this city, I can tell you that.' He sniffed at the air. 'Smells a lot better, too.'

'We were shot at on one train ride,' Lucius added. 'A bullet went right through my hat!' He showed us the hole by poking a finger through it. 'Marcus says that it wasn't Indians—'

'It wasn't Indians,' Marcus said.

'He says that it wasn't Indians, but I'm not so sure, and Captain Miller at Fort Yates said—'

'Captain Miller was just being polite,' Marcus interrupted again.

'Well, that may be,' Lucius answered. 'But he did say—'

'What did he say about Beecham?' Sara asked.

'—he did say that, although most of the larger bands of Indians have been defeated—'

Sara grabbed him. 'Lucius. What did he say about Beecham?'

'About Beecham?' Lucius repeated. 'Oh. Well. A great deal, actually.'

'A great deal that comes down to one thing,' Marcus said, looking at Sara. He paused, his large brown eyes full of meaning and purpose. 'He's our man – he's got to be.'

Chapter 38

Tipsy as I was, the Isaacsons' news, related as we got them some food at the St. Denis, sobered me up in a hurry:

Apparently Captain Frederick Miller, now in his early forties, had been assigned to the headquarters of the Army of the West in Chicago as a promising young lieutenant in the late 1870s. He had chafed under the boring strictures of staff life, however, and asked to be sent farther west, where he hoped to see active service. This request was granted and Miller was dispatched to the Dakotas, where he was twice wounded, the second time losing an arm. He returned to Chicago but declined to take up his staff duties again, electing instead to command part of the reserve forces that were kept on hand for civil emergencies. It was in this capacity that, in 1881, he'd first come across a young trooper named John Beecham.

Beecham had told his recruiting officer in New York that he was eighteen at the time of his enlistment, though Miller doubted that this was true – even when the still-green trooper had arrived in Chicago, six months later, he seemed younger than that. However, boys often lie about their age in order to enter the military, and Miller had thought little of it, for Beecham had shown himself to be a good soldier – well disciplined, attentive to detail, and efficient enough to have made corporal within two years. True, his persistent requests to be sent farther west to do some Indian fighting had annoyed Beecham's superiors in

Chicago, who weren't particularly anxious to have their better noncommissioned officers lost to the frontier; but overall, Lieutenant Miller had been given little reason to be anything but satisfied with the young corporal's performance until 1885.

In that year, however, a series of incidents in several of Chicago's poorer sections had exposed a disturbing facet of Beecham's personality. Never a man with many friends, Beecham had taken to going into immigrant neighborhoods during his off-duty hours and offering his services to charitable organizations that dealt with children, particularly orphans. At first this had seemed an admirable way for a soldier to make use of his time – far better than the usual drinking and fighting with local residents – and Lieutenant Miller had not concerned himself with it. After several months, however, he'd noticed a change in Beecham's mood, a decided shift toward the sullen. When Miller asked the corporal about it he received no satisfactory explanation; but soon thereafter the head of one of the charities showed up at the post wanting to talk to an officer. Miller listened as the man asked that Corporal Beecham be prohibited from coming near his orphanage again; when asked why he was making such a request, the man declined to say any more than that Beecham had 'upset' several of the children. Miller immediately confronted Beecham, who initially became angry and indignant, declaring that the man from the orphanage was only jealous because the children liked and trusted Beecham more than they did him. Lieutenant Miller, however, could see there was more to the story than that, and pressed Beecham harder; the corporal finally became immensely agitated and blamed Miller and the rest of his superiors for whatever it was that had happened. (Miller never did find out the exact nature of the incidents.) All such trouble could have been avoided, Beecham said, if those officers had complied with his requests to be sent west. Miller found Beecham's manner during this conversation alarming enough to warrant sending him on a long leave. Beecham spent that leave mountaineering in Tennessee, Kentucky, and West Virginia.

When he returned to his unit, at the beginning of 1886, Beecham seemed much improved. He was once again the obedient, efficient soldier Miller had first known. This image

Caleb Carr

proved an illusion, however; and it was shattered during the violence that followed the Haymarket Riots in the Chicago area during the first week of May. Sara and I already knew that Beecham had been sent to St. Elizabeth's Hospital after Miller had found him 'stabbing' (as the doctors put it) the corpse of a dead striker during the May 5th melee in the northern suburbs; we now learned from the Isaacsons that this 'stabbing' had borne a chilling resemblance to the mutilations of both Japheth Dury's parents and the dead children in New York. Revolted and horrified at finding the blood-drenched Beecham standing over a carved-up corpse whose eyes had been gouged out with an enormous knife, Miller had not hesitated to relieve the corporal of duty. Though the lieutenant had seen men driven to acts of blood lust in the West, such behavior was uniformly predicated upon years of savagely violent encounters with the Indian tribes. Beecham, on the other hand, had no such history, and no such rationalization for his actions. When the regimental surgeon examined Beecham after the affair, he quickly pronounced him unfit for service; and Miller added his heavy concurrence to this report, prompting Beecham's immediate dispatch to Washington.

Thus ended the tale that the Isaacsons brought back from the Dakotas. Having told it without pause, the two brothers had also been unable to eat, and now addressed their food voraciously as Sara and I informed them of all we'd learned in their absence. Then it was time for the hard news about Kreizler and Mary Palmer. Fortunately, Marcus and Lucius had by then both gotten most of their dinner down – the story destroyed what was left of their appetites. Both men were obviously apprehensive about the idea of continuing the investigation without Laszlo; but Sara stepped in with an even stronger sales pitch than the one she'd given me and within twenty minutes had convinced the detective sergeants that we had no other option than to press on. The story they'd brought back only gave her more ammunition with which to prosecute her campaign – for there was now little doubt in any of our minds that we knew the identity and history of our murderer. The question was, could we devise and execute a method of finding him?

By the time we left the little restaurant, at close to three o'clock that morning, we'd managed to convince ourselves that we could. The task was still a daunting one, however, and not to be undertaken until we'd all gotten some sleep. We made directly for our respective domiciles, relishing the prospect of that rest; yet by ten o'clock Thursday morning we were back at Number 808 Broadway and ready to map out a strategy.

'If no one else has a particular starting point in mind,' Lucius announced, reacquainting himself with the materials on his desk, 'I'd like to suggest one.' The rest of us mumbled general assent, and then Lucius pointed to the right-hand side of the chalkboard, specifically to the word ROOFTOPS. 'Do you remember, John, what you said about the killer after you and Marcus went to the Golden Rule that first time?'

I shuffled through my memories of the visit. 'Control,' I said.

'Yes. So I would suggest that the way to find out what he's doing with his life *now* is to follow the trail of what makes him feel secure, instead of the trail of his nightmares. He's hunting and killing on the rooftops, and his victims are children – all of which suggests that having control over situations is the most vital thing in his life. We know where the obsession with children comes from. We know about the hunting and trapping. But the rooftops? As of 1886, he hadn't spent much if any time in a major city – yet now he's thoroughly mastered them, so much so that he even trapped *us*. That kind of familiarity would take some time to develop.'

'Wait,' Sara said, nodding slowly. 'I'm beginning to see your point, Lucius. He leaves St. Elizabeth's and wants to go to a place where he can be fairly anonymous – New York is a likely choice. But when he gets here he finds that he's completely unfamiliar with how life works on the streets – the crowds, the noise, the agitation. It's all very strange, perhaps even intimidating. Then he discovers the rooftops. It's a completely different world up there – quieter, slower, fewer people. It's much more what he's used to. And he finds out that there's a lot of jobs that require spending a great deal of time on those rooftops – he barely needs to come back down to the streets at all.'

'Except at night,' Lucius added quickly, again holding up a

Caleb Carr

finger, 'when the city's much less crowded, and he can familiarize himself with it at his own pace. Remember – he hasn't yet killed during the day. He understands the nighttime rhythms thoroughly, but during the day – during the day I'm willing to bet he's up there almost all the time.' Lucius's forehead continued to sweat as he quickly went back to his desk and grabbed some notes. 'We talked about the idea of a daytime job that keeps him on the rooftops after the Ali ibn-Ghazi murder, but we never did much with it. I've been going back over everything, though, and it seems to me to be the best way to track him at this point.'

I groaned once with purpose. 'Oh, God, Lucius – do you understand what you're suggesting? We'll have to canvass every charity and mission society, every company that uses salesmen, every newspaper, or medical service. There's got to be a way to narrow it down.'

'There is,' Marcus said, his tone only slightly more enthusiastic than mine. 'But it's still going to involve one hell of a lot of footwork.' He got up and crossed over to the large map of Manhattan Island, pointing at the pins that had been stuck into the thing to mark abduction and murder sites. 'None of his activities have taken place above Fourteenth Street, which suggests that he's most familiar with the Lower East Side and Greenwich Village. He probably lives as well as works in one of the two areas – our theory that he doesn't have much money fits in with that. So we can confine our search to people who do business in those neighborhoods.'

'Right,' Lucius said, indicating the chalkboard again. 'And let's not forget all the work we've done. If we're right – if the killer did start out his life as Japheth Dury and later become John Beecham – then he wouldn't apply for just *any* kind of job. Given his character and background, some things would be far more attractive than others. For instance, you mention companies that use salesmen, John – but do you really think the man we've been studying would make much of a salesman, or would even try to get a job like that?'

I was about to argue that anything was possible, but then something suddenly told me that Lucius was right. We'd spent months putting details of personality and behavior to our killer's vague image, and 'anything' was most distinctly *not* possible. With a rather strange pang of dread and excitement I realized that I now knew this man well enough to say that he wouldn't have sought a job that would have required him to either curry favor with immigrant tenement dwellers or hawk the shoddy wares of manufacturers and store managers, whom he would almost certainly consider less intelligent than himself.

'All right,' I said to Lucius, 'but that still leaves a wide range of people – church workers, charity and settlement people, reporters, medical services . . .'

'You can narrow *them* down, too, John,' Lucius urged, 'if you just keep thinking. Take the reporters who cover the tenements – you know most of them yourself. Do you really think Beecham's a member of that group? As for the medical services – with Beecham's background? When did he get the training?'

I considered all this, and then shrugged. 'Well, all right. So the odds are he's involved with mission or charity work of some kind.'

'It *would* be easy for him,' Sara said. 'He'd have gotten all the religious grounding and terminology from his parents – his father was a powerful orator, after all.'

'Fine,' I said. 'But even if we narrow it down that far, we'll have a hard time checking them all by June 21st – Marcus and I took a week and only got through a fraction. It's completely impractical!'

Impractical it may have been, but there was no way around it. We spent the rest of that day amassing a list of all the charitable and religious organizations that did business in the Lower East Side and Greenwich Village, then divided the list up into four regional groups. Each of us took one of these sub-listings and headed out the next morning, it no longer being practical to travel in pairs if we hoped to check the dozens of organizations on our rosters. In the first few places I visited that Friday I received a somewhat less than warm reception; and though I hadn't expected anything different, the experience nonetheless filled me with a dread of the days and perhaps weeks to come. Repeated reminders to myself that tedious footwork is often the detective's lot did little good.

Caleb Carr

One aspect of this latest search did, however, give me cause for optimism: it didn't appear that I was being followed. Nor did I find, when I returned to our headquarters at the end of the day, that any of the others had noticed any disreputable types dogging their steps. We couldn't be certain, of course, but the logical explanation seemed to be that our enemies simply didn't believe we could succeed without Kreizler. Throughout the weekend we saw no trace of Connor or his accomplices, or of anyone else that looked as though they might be working for Byrnes or Comstock. If one had to pursue a tedious yet nerve-racking task, it was certainly preferable to do so without having to look over one's shoulder; although I don't think that any of us ever really stopped taking those looks.

Though we were hopeful that John Beecham had worked for one of the charitable organizations on our list at some point during the last ten years, we didn't think that he'd necessarily visited any of the disorderly houses involved in the killings in an official capacity. It was far more likely, to our way of thinking, that he'd become acquainted with said places as a customer. Thus, though my assignment included those organizations that targeted the poor and wayward on the West Side between Houston and Fourteenth streets, I didn't make any inquiries at the boy-pandering brothels in that neighborhood. I did, however, stop in at the Golden Rule just long enough to pass the new information we'd gathered concerning the killer along to my young friend Joseph. There was an awkward moment, when I arrived, being as I'd never before seen the boy actually practicing his trade. When Joseph caught sight of me he quickly vanished into a vacant room, and for a moment I thought he might not come back out; but finally he did, having taken the time to wipe the paint from his face. He smiled and waved cheerfully, then listened with a great show of attentiveness as I related my news and asked him to pass it along to his friends.

Every conceivable vice, it seemed, had a society in New York dedicated to its prevention. Some of these were general in their approach, such as the Society for the Prevention of Crime, or the various mission societies, Catholic, Presbyterian, Baptist, and others. Some, like the All Night Mission, chose to make their continuous accessibility the focus of speeches and leaflets delivered by their roaming agents in the ghettos; others, such as the Bowery Mission, were simply regional in their approach. A few, like the Horse Aid Society and the Society for the Prevention of Cruelty to Animals, didn't concern themselves with human beings at all. Then there were the seemingly infinite number and variety of orphanages, all of which employed roving zealots who were constantly on the look out for abandoned waifs. Each of these institutions had to be checked especially carefully, given the predilection for such places that John Beecham had exhibited in Chicago.

It was the kind of work that quickly absorbed hours and then days, without producing any profound sense of satisfaction or reassurance that we were doing everything we could to stave off another killing, the possibility of which came inexorably closer as the clock ticked down toward the feast of St John the Baptist. How many archly sanctimonious churchmen and churchwomen, not to mention their civilian counterparts, did Sara, the Isaacsons, and I have to interview, and for how many tedious hours? It would be impossible to say, nor would there be much point to revealing the numbers even if I knew them – for we learned nothing. All through the following week, each of us forced ourselves again and again through a similar procedure: we'd go to the offices or headquarters of some charitable service, where the simple question of whether a John Beecham, or anyone of similar appearance and manner, had ever worked there would be answered by long, pious statements about the organization's laudable employees and goals. Only then would the files be checked and a firmly negative reply given, at which the unlucky member of our team might finally escape the place.

If I seem either hostile or cynical in recalling this particular phase of our work, perhaps it's because of a realization that came to me as we reached the end of that second week in June: that the only group of outcasts in the city that didn't seem to have several privately funded and nobly titled societies dedicated to its care and reform was the very one that was currently in such grave danger – child prostitutes. As this lack became more and more apparent to me, I couldn't help but think back to Jake Riis – a man lionized in New York's philanthropic circles – and to his blind refusal to admit or report the facts of Georgio Santorelli's murder. Riis's deliberate myopia was shared by every official I spoke to, a fact that caused me more irritation every time I encountered it. By the time I came lumbering into Number 808 Broadway late Monday afternoon I was so sick of the fatuous hypocrites who made up New York's charitable community that I was spewing a steady stream of rather violent curses. Having thought our headquarters empty when I came in, I spun round in shock when I heard Sara's voice:

'That's lovely language, John. Though I must say it fairly well describes *my* mood at this point.' She was smoking a cigarette and staring alternately at the map of Manhattan and the chalkboard. 'We're on the wrong track,' she decided in disgust, throwing the stub of her cigarette out an open window.

I collapsed onto the divan with a moan. 'You're the one who wants to be a detective,' I said. 'You ought to know that we could go on like this for months before we get a break.'

'We don't have months,' Sara answered. 'We have until *Sunday.*' She continued to stare and shake her head at the map and the board. 'And it's not just the monotony that's giving me this feeling.' She cocked her head, trying to nail down whatever was flitting through her mind. 'Has it occurred to you, John, that none of these organizations seems to *know* very much about the people they're trying to help?'

I propped myself up on an elbow. 'What do you mean?'

'I'm not sure,' Sara answered. 'They just don't seem … knowledgeable. It doesn't match.'

'Match what?'

'Him. Beecham. Look at what he does. He insinuates himself into these boys' lives, and convinces them to trust him – and these are some fairly suspicious and skeptical children, mind you.'

I thought quickly of Joseph. 'On the outside, maybe,' I said. 'Inside they're praying for a real friend.'

'All right,' Sara answered, conceding the point. 'And Beecham goes through just the motions required to establish that friendship. As if he knows what they need. These charity people have none of that quality. I tell you, we're on the wrong track.'

'Sara, be realistic,' I said, getting up and joining her. 'What kind of door-to-door organization that deals with large numbers of people takes the time to find out that kind of personal informa—'

And then I froze. Really froze. The simple fact of the matter, I remembered in a numbing rush, was that there was one organization that did take the time to find out just the kind of personal information that Sara was describing. An organization whose headquarters I'd passed every day for the past week without ever making a connection – and an organization whose hundreds of employees were well known for traveling neighborhood rooftops.

'Hell's bloody bells,' I mumbled.

'What?' Sara asked urgently, seeing that I was onto something. 'John, what've you got?'

My eyes darted to the right side of the chalkboard, specifically to the names BENJAMIN AND SOFIA ZWEIG. 'Of course . . .' I whispered. 'Eighteen ninety-two might be a little late – but he might have met them in '90. Or he could've gone back during the revisions, the whole thing was so royally botched—'

'John, damn it, *what* are you talking about?'

I grabbed Sara's hand. 'What time is it?'

'Nearly six. Why?'

'Someone may still be there – come on!'

I pulled Sara toward the door without further explanation. She continued to bellow questions and protests, but I refused to answer any of them as we descended to the street in the elevator and then dashed down Broadway to Eighth Street. Wheeling left, I led Sara to Number 135. Pulling at the door to a staircase that led up to the building's second and third floors, I breathed a sigh of relief on finding that it was still open. I turned back to Sara to find her staring with a smile at a small brass plaque that was screwed to the façade of the building, just next to the doorway:

UNITED STATES BUREAU OF CENSUS

CHARLES H. MURRAY, SUPERINTENDENT

Chapter 39

$\mathbf{W}$e entered a world of files.

Both of the floors occupied by the Census Bureau were lined with wooden filing cabinets that ran right up to the ceiling and blocked every window. Mobile ladders ran on tracks around the walls of each floor's four rooms, and a desk sat in the center of every chamber. Harsh electrical lights with metal shades were suspended from the ceilings, throwing their glare onto floors composed of bare wood. It was a place without feeling or personality of any kind – a worthy home, in short, for bare, inhuman statistics.

The first occupied desk that Sara and I found was on the third floor. At it sat a fairly young man who wore a banker's visor and an inexpensive but particularly well-pressed suit, the jacket of which was slung over his plain, straight-backed chair. Cuff protectors covered the lower portions of the man's white, starched shirtsleeves, and the thin, sallow hands protruding from them attacked a folder full of forms.

'Excuse me?' I said, approaching the desk slowly.

The man looked up sourly. 'Official hours are over.'

'Of course,' I answered quickly, recognizing an incorrigible bureaucrat when I saw one. 'Had this been official business, I would have come at a more appropriate hour.'

The man eyed me up and down, then glanced at Sara. 'Well?'

'We're with the press,' I answered. 'The *Times* actually. My name is Moore, and this is Miss Howard. I wonder if Mr. Murray is still in?'

'Mr Murray never leaves the office before six-thirty.'

'Ah. Then he's still here.'

'He may not want to see you,' the young man said. 'The members of the press weren't exactly helpful last time around.'

I considered the statement, then asked, 'You mean in 1890?'

'Of course,' the man answered, as if every organization in the world operated on a ten-year schedule. 'Even the *Times* made ridiculous allegations. After all, we can't be responsible for every bribe and falsified report, can we?'

'Naturally not,' I said. 'Mr. Murray would be—'

'Superintendent Porter, the national chief, actually had to resign in '93,' the man went on, still glowering at me with an injured, accusing look. 'Did you know that?'

'Actually,' I answered, 'I'm a police reporter.'

The man removed his cuff protectors. 'I only mention it,' he continued, eyes burning at the center of the shadow thrown on his face by the banker's visor, 'to show that the main problems were in Washington, not here. No one in this office had to resign, Mr Moore.'

'I'm sorry,' I said, forbearance becoming an ever more difficult task, 'but we're in a bit of a hurry, so if you could just point me toward Mr. Murray . . .'

'I'm Charles Murray,' the man answered flatly.

Sara and I glanced at each other quickly, and then I let out a perhaps impolitic sigh, realizing what we were up against with this fellow. 'I see. Well, Mr. Murray, I wonder if you might be able to check your employment records for the name of a man we've been trying to find.'

Murray eyed me from under the visor. 'Identification?' I handed him some and he leveled it just a few inches from his face, as if he were checking a piece of counterfeit currency. 'Hmm,' he noised. 'I suppose it's all right. Can't be too careful, though. Anyone might come in here and claim to be a newspaperman.' He handed it back to me, and then turned to Sara. 'Miss Howard?'

Sara's face went blank as she scrambled for an answer. 'I'm

afraid I have no credentials, Mr. Murray. I serve in a secretarial capacity.'

Murray didn't look entirely satisfied with that, but he nodded once and turned back to me. 'Well?'

'The man we're looking for,' I said, 'is called John Beecham.' The name brought no change at all in Murray's impassive expression. 'He's just over six feet tall, with thinning hair and a bit of a facial tic.'

'A bit of one?' Murray said evenly. 'If he's got a bit of a facial tic, Mr. Moore, I wouldn't like to see an *entire* one.'

Again I had that feeling that had swept into me in Adam Dury's barn: the coursing, exultant burn that accompanied the twin realizations that we were on the trail and the trail was still warm. I gave Sara a quick glance, noting that her first experience of that feeling was proving as difficult to control as mine had been.

'Then you know Beecham?' I asked, my voice quavering a bit.

Murray nodded once. 'Or rather I *did* know him.'

Cold disappointment poured over my hot sensation of triumph for an instant. 'He doesn't work for you?'

'He did,' Murray answered. 'I dismissed him. Last December.'

Hope surged again. 'Ah. And how long had he been here?'

'Is he in some sort of trouble?' Murray asked.

'No, no,' I said quickly, realizing that I hadn't bothered, in my enthusiasm, to work out a plausible cover story for my questions. 'I – that is, it's his brother. He may be involved in a – a – land speculation scandal. I thought Mr. Beecham might be able to help us find him, or would at least care to make a statement.'

'Brother?' Murray queried. 'He never mentioned a brother.' I was about to reply to this remark with another fabrication, when Murray went on: 'Not that *that*'s any indication. Not a talkative man, John Beecham. I never knew much about him – certainly nothing about his private affairs. Always a very proper, respectable person. Which was why I found it remarkable ...' Murray's voice trailed off and he tapped a long, bony finger on his chair for a few seconds as he examined first me and then Sara again. Finally he stood up, went to one of the rolling ladders, and sent it down its track to the far end of the room with a sudden, hard shove. 'He was hired in the spring of 1890,' Murray called, as he followed and then mounted the ladder. Pulling out one wooden drawer near the ceiling, he ran through it for a file. 'Beecham applied for a job as an enumerator.'

'I beg your pardon?'

'An enumerator,' Murray answered, coming back down the ladder with a large envelope in one hand. 'The men who do the actual counting and interviewing for the census. I hired nine hundred such men in June and July of 1890. Two weeks' work, twenty-five dollars a week. Each man was required to fill out an application.' Opening the envelope, Murray pulled out a folded paper and handed it to me. 'Beecham's,' he said.

Trying to disguise my eagerness, I scanned the document as Murray summarized it: 'He was quite qualified – just the sort of man we look for, actually. University education, unmarried, good references – all powerful recommendations.'

And so they would have been, I thought as I studied the document, had they been even remotely legitimate. The information before my eyes represented a litany of lies and an impressive set of forgeries; provided, of course, that there weren't two John Beechams with chronic facial spasms roaming around the United States. (I wondered for a moment how high Alphonse Bertillon's system of anthropometry would have put *those* odds.) Sara was looking over my shoulder at the application, and when I turned to her she nodded as if to acknowledge that she, too, had drawn the obvious conclusion from it: that in 1890, as before and after that year, Beecham was sharpening his talent for elaborate deception.

'You'll see his address at the head of the form,' Murray continued. 'At the time I dismissed him, he was still living in the same rooms.'

At the top of the sheet was written, in a hand that I recognized from the note we'd studied weeks earlier, '23 Bank Street' – near the center of Greenwich Village. 'Yes,' I said slowly. 'Yes, I see. Thank you.'

Looking somewhat perturbed by Sara's and my continued

interest in the application, Murray plucked the thing out of my hands and slipped it back into the large envelope. 'Anything else?' he asked.

'Else?' I answered. 'Oh, no, I don't think so. You've been very helpful, Mr. Murray.'

'Good evening, then,' he said, sitting back down and pulling on his cuff protectors.

Sara and I moved to the door. 'Oh,' I said, doing my best to feign an afterthought. 'You say you dismissed Beecham, Mr. Murray. Might I inquire why, if he was so well qualified?'

'I don't trade in gossip, Mr. Moore,' Murray answered coldly. 'Besides, your business is with his brother, is it not?'

I tried another tack: 'I trust he didn't do anything untoward while he was working in the Thirteenth Ward?'

Murray grunted once. 'If he had, I hardly would have promoted him from enumerator to office clerk and kept him on for another five years—' Murray caught himself and jerked his head up. 'Just a minute. How did you know he was assigned to the Thirteenth Ward?'

I smiled. 'It's of no consequence. Thank you, Mr. Murray, and good evening.'

Grabbing Sara by the wrist, I started back down the stairs quickly. I could hear Murray's chair backing up, and then he appeared at the stairway door.

'Mr. Moore!' he called angrily. 'Stop, sir! I demand to know how you knew that information! Mr. Moore, do you hear—'

But we were already out the door. I kept a firm grip on Sara's wrist as we headed west, though it wasn't necessary for me to pull her along – she was moving at a quick, exuberant pace, and by the time we reached Fifth Avenue she had started to laugh out loud. As we came to a halt and waited for a gap in the evening traffic on the avenue to appear, Sara suddenly threw her arms around my neck.

'John!' she said breathlessly. 'He's *real*, he's *here* – my God, we know where he *lives*!'

I returned her embrace, though there was caution in my voice: 'We know where he *lived*. It's June now – he was dismissed in December. Six months without a job may have changed a lot of things – his ability to pay rent in a decent neighborhood, for one.'

'But he could've gotten another job,' Sara said, her jubilation fading a bit.

'Let's hope so,' I answered, as the traffic in front of us thinned. 'Come on.'

'But how?' Sara called as we stepped into the avenue. 'How did you think of it? And what was all that about the Thirteenth Ward?'

As we kept marching farther west toward Bank Street, I explained my line of reasoning to Sara. The 1890 census, I'd remembered hearing from friends of mine who'd reported on it, had indeed been the cause of a great scandal in New York (and the nation generally) when it was conducted during the summer and fall of that year. The chief causes of said scandal had been, not surprisingly, the city's political bosses, whose power stood to be affected by the results of the count and who had tried to influence every stage of the proceedings. Many of the nine hundred men who'd shown up at Charles Murray's Eighth Street offices to apply for positions as enumerators in July of 1890 had been agents of either Tammany Hall or Boss Platt, and they had been instructed by their superiors to tailor their returns so as to ensure that congressional districts loyal to their respective political parties weren't redrawn in a way that would cause them to lose power in state and national affairs. Sometimes this had meant inflating the count of a given district, a job that entailed manufacturing the vital statistics and backgrounds of non-existent citizens. For enumerators, apparently, were far more than simple numbers men: their work entailed careful interviews with a cross section of their subjects, the purpose being to determine not only how many citizens the nation had but also what sorts of lives they led. These interviews included personal questions that might, as one of my colleagues at the *Times* had put it in an article, 'under other circumstances have seemed quite impertinent.'

Enumerators had received their assignments according to congressional districts, which in New York had been subdivided according to wards. My question to Murray about Beecham and the Thirteenth Ward had, I told Sara, been a guess: I knew that

Benjamin and Sofia Zweig had lived in that ward, and I was going on the theory that Beecham had met them while working in the area, perhaps even while interviewing their family for the census. Fortunately, my guess had paid off, though we were still in the dark as to exactly why Murray had dismissed our man.

'It doesn't seem likely that Beecham was involved in falsifying returns,' Sara said, as we hustled up Greenwich Avenue toward Bank Street. 'He's not the type to get involved in politics – and besides, the census was already completed. But if not that, then what?'

'We can send the Isaacsons back to find out tomorrow,' I answered. 'Murray seems like the kind of man who'll respond to a badge. Though if you asked me to post odds right now I'd give you twelve to one that it's got something to do with children. Maybe someone finally came forward with a complaint – not necessarily anything violent, but something seamy, all the same.'

'It does seem likely,' Sara said. 'You remember the remark Murray made when he was discussing how respectable Beecham seemed? And how that made him find whatever it was so "remarkable"?'

'Exactly,' I answered. 'There's an unpleasant little tale in there somewhere.'

We'd reached Bank Street and turned left. A typical series of Greenwich Village blocks opened up before us, tree- and town house-lined until they closed in on the Hudson River, where trucking stations and warehouses took over. The stoops and cornices of the townhouses were a picture of quaint monotony, and as we passed by each residence we could see into the relatively low-standing parlors of the comfortable middle-class families who inhabited the neighborhood. Number 23 Bank Street was only a block and a half from Greenwich Avenue, but as we covered that distance Sara's and my hopes had time to rise high nonetheless. When we reached the building, however, disappointment crashed down hard.

In one corner of the parlor window was a small, very tasteful sign: ROOM TO LET. Sara and I exchanged sobered looks, then made our way up the steps of the building to the narrow front door. There was a small brass bell handle on the right side of the frame, and I pulled it. Silently, Sara and I stood and waited for several minutes; then we finally heard shuffling footsteps and an old woman's voice:

'No, no, no. Get away – go on, now.'

It was difficult to tell whether or not the order was being directed at us; but when several bolts on the door were noisily thrown, I began to suspect that it was not. The door finally opened, and we were faced by a small, white-haired crone in a faded blue dress of a style dating back to the seventies. She was missing several teeth, and there were wiry white hairs protruding from her jaw at several points. Her eyes were lively, though they did not bespeak a particularly clear mind. She was about to say something to us when a small orange cat appeared at her feet. She kicked the creature lightly back into the house.

'No, I said!' the old woman scolded. 'These people have nothing to say to you – any of you!' At that point I became aware of some rather loud mewing coming from inside – by my reckoning, the work of at least half a dozen cats. The woman looked up at me brightly. 'Yes? Did you want to inquire about the room?'

The question put me at a momentary loss; fortunately, Sara stepped into the breach by introducing first herself and then me. 'The room, ma'am?' Sara continued, following the introductions. 'Not precisely – rather, about its former occupant. Mr. Beecham has, I believe, moved?'

'Oh, yes,' the woman answered, as another cat appeared at the door. This one, a gray-striped thing, managed to get to the top of the stoop. 'Here!' the woman said. 'Peter! Oh, do catch him, will you, Mr. Moore?' I bent down, snatched the cat up, and then gave him a little scratch under the chin before returning him to the woman. 'Cats!' she said. 'You wouldn't think that they'd be so anxious to disappear!'

Sara cleared her throat. 'Yes, indeed, Mrs . . . Mrs . . .?'

'Piedmont,' the woman answered. 'And it's only the eight that I actually let into the house – the other fifteen are required to stay in the yard, or I become very cross with them.'

'Of course, Mrs. Piedmont,' Sara said. 'Only the eight – a

perfectly reasonable number.' Mrs. Piedmont nodded in satisfaction, and Sara asked, 'As for Mr. Beecham . . .?'

'Mr. Beecham?' the woman answered. 'Yes. Very polite. Very prompt. And never drank. Not a favorite of the cats, of course – not much of a man for animals at all, really, but—'

'Did he leave a forwarding address, by any chance?' Sara cut in.

'He couldn't,' Mrs. Piedmont answered. 'He had no idea where he was going. He thought perhaps Mexico, or South America. He said there were opportunities for men of initiative there.' The woman caught herself, and then opened the door a bit wider. 'I am sorry,' she said, 'you must forgive me. Please do come in.'

With a slight roll of my eyes I followed Sara through the door, knowing that every nugget of hard information we might get out of the charming Mrs. Piedmont was likely to be accompanied by five or ten minutes of useless babbling. My enthusiasm was further dampened when she led us into her very primly furnished but aged and dusty parlor. Everything in the room, from chairs and settees to a large collection of Victorian knick knacks, seemed on the verge of disintegrating quietly into dust. In addition, the unmistakable odor of cat urine and feces permeated the entire house.

'Cats,' Mrs. Piedmont said merrily as she sat down in a high-armed chair. 'Wonderful companions, but they will run off. Quite disappear, without so much as a word!'

'Mrs. Piedmont,' Sara said indulgently, 'we really are most anxious to find Mr. Beecham. We're – old friends of his, you see—'

'Oh, but you can't be,' Mrs. Piedmont said, her face scowling a bit. 'Mr. Beecham had no friends. He said so. He always said so. "He travels swiftest who travels alone, Mrs. Piedmont," he would tell me in the morning, and then it was off to the shipping office.'

'Shipping office?' I said. 'But surely—'

Sara touched my hand to silence me, then smiled as several cats wandered into the room from the hallway. 'Of course,' she said. 'The shipping office. A very enterprising man.'

'Indeed,' Mrs. Piedmont answered. 'Oh, and there's Lysander,' she went on, pointing to one of the cats, who was mewing profusely. 'I haven't seen him since Saturday. Cats! They do disappear . . .'

'Mrs. Piedmont,' Sara said, still showing remarkable patience, 'how long did Mr. Beecham live with you?'

'How long?' The old girl began to chew at a finger as she cogitated. 'Why, nearly three years, all in all. Never a complaint, always on time with his rent.' She frowned. 'But a somber sort of man, really. And he never ate! Never ate that I saw, that is. Always working, day and night – though I suppose he must've eaten *sometime*, mustn't he?'

Sara smiled again and nodded. 'And do you know why he left?'

'Well,' Mrs. Piedmont said simply. 'The *failure*.'

'Failure?' I said, hoping for a clue.

'His shipping line,' came the reply. 'The great tempest off the China coast. Oh, those poor seamen. Mr. Beecham gave all the money he had left to their families, you know.' A bony hand went up confidentially. 'If you see a small calico lady come through, Miss Howard, do tell me. She didn't come down for breakfast, and they *will* disappear.'

Mean as it may sound, I was about ready to wring Mrs. Piedmont's neck, along with those of her blasted cats; but Sara stayed the course, inquiring congenially, 'Did you ask Mr. Beecham to leave, then?'

'I should say not,' Mrs. Piedmont answered. 'He went of his own accord. He told me he had no money to pay his rent, and he didn't intend to stay where he couldn't pay his way. I offered to give him a few weeks' grace but he wouldn't have it. I remember that day very well – a week before Christmas. It was about the time that little Jib disappeared.'

I groaned quietly as Sara asked, 'Jib? A cat?'

'Yes,' Mrs. Piedmont answered dreamily. 'Just – disappeared. Never a word. They have their own affairs to attend to, cats.'

As my eyes wandered to the floor, I noticed that several more of Mrs. Piedmont's charges had noiselessly entered the room, and that one of them was attending to its own affairs in a shadowy corner. I nudged Sara, indicating the upstairs impatiently.

'Do you think we might have a look at the room?' Sara asked.

Mrs. Piedmont came back from her daydream with a smile, and

looked at us as though we'd only just entered. 'Then it's the room you're interested in?'

'We may be.'

That set off a new round of chatter as we headed out of the parlor and up the staircase, the ancient green wallpaper of which was peeling and torn. The room that Beecham had rented was on the third floor, which, climbing at Mrs. Piedmont's pace, seemed to take an eternity to reach. By the time we finally did, all eight of the house cats had already collected around the door, and were mewing away. Mrs. Piedmont unlocked the room and then we entered.

The first thing that struck me was that the cats didn't follow us in. As soon as the door opened their mewing stopped, and then they sat at the threshold, looking momentarily concerned before they shot off down the stairs. With their departure I turned to survey the chamber, and quickly caught a trace of something in the air: the smell of decay. It was nothing like the stench of feline waste, nor did it match the familiar aromas of old age and antiques that marked the parlor. This was more pungent. A dead mouse, or some such, I finally decided, and when Sara wrinkled her nose sourly I knew that she'd caught it, too. Thinking nothing more of it for the moment, I finally fixed my attention on the room.

I needn't have bothered. It was a spare, empty chamber, with a window that looked out over Bank Street. There were no furnishings other than an old four-poster bed, an equally aged wardrobe, and a plain set of drawers. A washbasin sat on a large doily atop the drawers, along with a matching pitcher; other than that, the room was absolutely empty.

'Just as he found it, is how he left it,' Mrs. Piedmont said. 'He was that way, Mr. Beecham.'

Under the guise of deciding whether or not we wanted to rent the room, Sara and I went through the wardrobe and the chest of drawers, without finding any trace of human activity. There was simply nothing in the ten-by-twenty-foot confines of that chamber that would have made you believe that it had ever been inhabited by anyone, much less by a tortured soul whom we suspected of having done away with at least half a dozen children in a bizarre and brutal fashion. The lingering scent of decay in the air only reinforced this conclusion. Eventually Sara and I told Mrs. Piedmont that, though it was indeed a lovely little room, it was nonetheless too small for our purposes. Then we turned to go back downstairs.

Sara and our hostess, who once again began blathering about her cats, had already reached the staircase when I caught sight of something just inside the door of Beecham's room: a few small stains on the bland, striped wallpaper. They were of a brownish hue, and in a pattern that indicated that whatever the substance was – and it could easily have been blood – it had hit the wall in a hard splatter. Following the path of the stain, I arrived at the bed; and, seeing as Mrs. Piedmont was now out of sight, I pulled the mattress up to have a look.

A stench hit me, suddenly and hard. It was identical to that which I'd detected on entering the room, only of an increased strength that immediately made me close my eyes, cover my mouth, and want to retch. I was about to drop the mattress again when my eyes opened long enough to catch sight of a small skeleton. A furry hide was stretched over the bones, though in some spots the hide had rotted away, revealing the dried remains of inner organs. Old, rotting string was wound around the four legs of the skeleton at the feet, and next to the rear legs lay several sections of jointed bone, almost like tiny vertebrae – a tail, I realized, that'd been cut into pieces. The creature's skull, barely covered by a few small patches of skin and fur, lay some eight inches from the rest of the skeleton. Both the mattress and the spring beneath it bore broad stains of a color that matched the splotches on the wall.

I finally let go of the mattress, then jumped out into the hall and took out a handkerchief, dabbing at my face. Resisting one more urge to vomit, I took a few deep breaths and stood at the top of the stairs, trying to determine if I felt sound enough to navigate them.

'John?' I heard Sara call from downstairs. 'Are you coming?'

The first flight of stairs was a bit tricky, but by the second I was doing much better; and when I reached the front door of the house, where Mrs. Piedmont was standing in the midst of her mewing cats, holding Sara's hand, I even managed to arrange a smile. I thanked Mrs. Piedmont quickly and then stepped out into the cloudless night, the air of which seemed especially clean given what I'd been breathing inside.

Sara followed me, still talking to Mrs. Piedmont, and then the same gray-striped cat bounded out onto the stoop. 'Peter!' Mrs. Piedmont cried. 'Miss Howard, could you . . .?' Sara already had the animal in her arms, and she handed it to Mrs. Piedmont with a smile. 'Cats!' Mrs. Piedmont said one more time, and then she called more goodbyes and closed the door.

Sara came down the steps and joined me, her smile shrinking as she studied my face. 'John?' she said. 'You've gone pale, what is it?' She stood still and then grabbed my arm. 'You found something up there – what was it?'

'Jib,' I answered, wiping my face again with my handkerchief.

Sara's face screwed up. 'Jib? The *cat*? What in the world are you talking about?'

'Let me put it this way,' I said, taking her arm and starting the walk back toward Broadway. 'Regardless of what Mrs. Piedmont may say, cats do *not* just disappear.'

Chapter 40

Sara and I got back to Number 808 Broadway just a few minutes ahead of the Isaacsons, whose mood on entering was little better than ours had been several hours earlier. In a flurry we told the detective sergeants of our adventures that evening, as Sara wrote the details of the encounters up on the chalkboard. Both Lucius and Marcus were profoundly encouraged at our having been able to trace at least some of John Beecham's movements, even though the trips to the Census Bureau and Mrs. Piedmont's house had – to my way of thinking, at any rate – left us in effectively the same position we'd been in that morning: with no idea where Beecham was now living or what he was now doing.

'True, John,' Lucius said, 'but we do know much more about what he's *not* doing. Our idea that he might've been inclined to make use of the knowledge he got from having a minister for a father appears to have been wrong – and there's probably a reason for that.'

'Maybe the bitterness is just too powerful,' Marcus said, considering the question. 'Maybe he can't so much as pay lip service to what his father stood for, even for the purposes of finding a job.'

'Because of the hypocrisy within his family?' Sara asked, still scratching away at the board.

'That's right,' Marcus answered. 'The whole notion of church and missionary work may just make him instinctively too violent

448

– he can't pursue it, because he wouldn't be able to trust himself to keep up appearances.'

'Good,' Lucius said, bobbing his head. 'So he takes the job at the Census Bureau, which doesn't seem to put him in any danger of revealing himself, accidentally or otherwise. After all, a lot of the men who got jobs as enumerators lied on their applications, without anyone discovering it.'

'The job also satisfies a big craving for him,' I added. 'It gets him into people's houses, and close to their children, whom he can learn about without seeming to be interested – which eventually poses a problem for him.'

Marcus took over: 'Because after a while he starts having urges that he can't control. But what about the boys? He didn't meet them at their homes – they didn't live with their families, and he'd already been fired, anyway.'

'True,' I said. 'That's an open question. But wherever he went after the Census Bureau, he'd want to have continued access to people's private affairs – and hopefully go on visiting families in their homes – in order to do research on his victims. That way, even though the boys are living in the disorderly houses, he'd be able to sympathize and commiserate with their specific situations – which would be a very effective way of getting them to trust him.'

'And which is also the element that's been missing from the charity workers we've interviewed,' Sara said, standing away from the chalkboard.

'Exactly,' I said, opening windows to let the evening air into our slightly stuffy headquarters.

'I'm still not sure, though,' Marcus said, 'how this helps us figure out where he is *now*. I don't want to sound anxious, friends, but we're *six days* away from the next attack.'

That prompted a few minutes of silence, during which all our eyes wandered toward the pile of photographs that sat on Marcus's desk. That pile would grow, each of us knew, if we failed now. Eventually, Lucius spoke up in a grimly determined voice:

'We've got to stay with what got us here – follow his confident, aggressive side. He didn't show fear or panic, in his dealings with the Census Bureau and Mrs. Piedmont. He made up elaborate lies and lived within them for extended periods of time without losing control. Whether he'd been killing steadily throughout that time, or whether getting fired from his job brought on a new wave of violence, we don't know. But I'll bet he hasn't run out of confidence yet, even if part of him does want to get caught. Let's assume that, anyway. Let's assume he's been able to find another job that gives him what he wants – use of the rooftops, and a way to move among the tenement population without having to try to help or appeal to them. Any ideas?'

It was hard to watch a streak of creative thinking and good luck die, but die ours did at just that moment. Perhaps we all needed to distance ourselves from the problem for a few hours, or perhaps we'd been overly intimidated by the reminder that we were less than a week away from our literal deadline; whatever the case, our minds and mouths ground to a collective halt. True, we still had one more card to play at the Census Bureau: Marcus and Lucius would visit Charles Murray the following morning, and try to get a better idea of what had prompted Beecham's dismissal in December. Other than that, however, our next steps were difficult to discern; and it was in a mood of extreme uncertainty that we finally let the long day end at about ten o'clock.

During their interview with Murray on Tuesday, the Isaacsons did indeed discover (as they told Sara and me when they returned to Number 808 in the evening) that Beecham had been fired for paying excessive and disturbing attention to a child: a young girl named Ellie Leshka, who lived in a tenement on Orchard Street just above Canal. The address was within the Thirteenth Ward, and not far from where the Zweig children had lived; none of which changed the fact that stalking a young girl who wasn't a prostitute (if such was indeed what Beecham had been doing with Ellie Leshka) was an activity he hadn't engaged in since killing Sofia Zweig, to the best of our knowledge. Marcus and Lucius had hoped to shed further light on this subject by way of a visit to young Ellie and her parents, but as luck would have it the family had recently left New York – for, of all places, Chicago.

According to Murray, the Leshkas had never mentioned anything about violence when they made their complaint about Beecham. Apparently he'd never menaced Ellie – in fact, he'd

Caleb Carr

been kind to her. But the girl had recently turned twelve, and her father and mother had developed perfectly understandable concerns about their daughter spending a lot of time with an unknown, solitary man at such an age. Charles Murray told the Isaacsons that he wouldn't necessarily have fired Beecham, except that the latter had gained access to the Leshkas' home by saying he was on official Census Bureau business, when the family had not, in fact, been scheduled for an interview. Murray's experiences had been such that he was determined to avoid anything that even smelled like scandal.

Sara noted that, in addition to Ellie Leshka's being a girl of good reputation, there was another unusual aspect to her case: she'd survived her association with Beecham. Given these circumstances, Sara thought it possible that Beecham never intended to kill her. Perhaps this was an example of a genuine attempt on his part to form an attachment to another human being; if so, it was the first in his adult life that we'd heard anything about, save for his shadowy behavior in the Chicago orphanages. Perhaps, too, the Leshkas' insistence that he did not approach their daughter, coupled with the family's departure from the city, had contributed to Beecham's rage; again, we had to remember that the recent boy-whore killings had begun soon after the events of December.

Such, however, was about all the information and speculation we could wring out of the Census Bureau connection. We completed that process at close to five-thirty on Tuesday, and then Sara and I presented the Isaacsons with the results of our own day's work: a short list of occupations that we thought Beecham might have moved on to after his dismissal. Taking all the factors that we considered reliable into account – Beecham's resentment of immigrants, his apparent inability to get close to people (or at least to adults), his need to be on the rooftops, and his hostility toward religious organizations of any kind – Sara and I had narrowed down our initial collection of possibilities to two basic areas of employment: bill collecting and process serving. Both were secular pursuits that not only would have kept Beecham on the rooftops (front doors often being barred to such unwanted characters), but would also have provided him with a certain sense of power – and control. At the same time, such jobs would have given him continued access to personal information concerning a broad range of people, as well as a rationale for approaching them in their homes. Finally, Sara had remembered something late in the afternoon that we felt further confirmed our speculation: when Beecham had been admitted to St. Elizabeth's Hospital, he had spoken of society's need for laws, and for men to enforce them. Debtors and those involved in illegal activities (even if only tangentially) would certainly have aroused his scorn, and the prospect of harassing them would probably have been attractive.

Marcus and Lucius agreed with our reasoning, even though they knew, as Sara and I did, that it meant a new round of footwork. However, we had reason to be hopeful: the list of government bureaus and collection agencies that employed agents of the type we'd described was far more manageable than the long roster of charity organizations that we'd already tackled. Knowing that police secretaries such as Sara and reporters such as me would never get any information out of the city marshal's office or any other government entity, the Isaacsons took on the task of assaulting those bureaucracies. Sara and I, meanwhile, split a list of independent collection agencies, again focusing on those that operated in the Lower East Side and Greenwich Village generally, and in the Thirteenth Ward in particular. By early Wednesday morning we were all on the streets again.

If canvassing the city's charities had been a morally infuriating task, going up against the heads of collection agencies proved a physically intimidating one. Generally run out of small, dirty upper-story offices, those agencies were most often headed by men who'd had unhappy experiences in some vaguely related field – police and legal work, confidence games, even, in one case, bounty hunting. They were not a breed that relinquished information easily, and only the promise of reward would even start their jaws moving. Too often, of course, such 'rewards' were demanded in advance, and were repaid by information that was either blatantly false or of a usefulness to our work that only the author himself could possibly have divined.

Once again, tedious drudgery ate up hours (and by Thursday

morning looked as though it would consume whole days) without producing results. The city did indeed keep careful records of those men it employed as process servers, the Isaacsons learned, but no John Beecham appeared in any of the files that they examined in the first twenty-four hours. Sara's initial day and a half of work in the collection agencies resulted in nothing but vulgar propositions; and as for myself, Thursday afternoon found me back at our headquarters, finished with the list of agencies I'd been assigned to cover and at a loss as to what I should do next. Alone and staring out the windows of Number 808 toward the Hudson River, I was again consumed by that familiar sense of dread which said that we weren't going to be ready. Sunday night would come, and Beecham, now aware that we would probably be watching those disorderly houses that dealt in boy-whores, would pick a victim from a new locale, make off with him to some unknown place, and again perform his loathsome ritual. All we needed, I kept thinking over and over, was an address, an occupation, anything that would let *us* get the drop on *him*, so that at the crucial moment we could step in to end his barbarity and his misery, the relentless torment that was driving him on. It was odd, after all I'd seen and been through, to think of *his* torment; odder still to realize that I had some sort of vague sympathy for the man. Yet the sentiment was in me, and it was understanding the context of his life that had put it there: of the many goals that Kreizler had outlined at the beginning of the investigation, we had at least achieved that one . . .

I was jolted back to the business at hand by the sound of the telephone. Picking it up, I heard Sara's voice.

'John? What are you doing?'

'Nothing. I've finished my list and gotten nowhere.'

'Then come up to Number 967 Broadway. Second floor. Quickly.'

'Nine-sixty-seven – that's above Twentieth Street.'

'Very good. Between Twenty-second and Twenty-third, actually.'

'But that's outside your assigned area.'

'Yes. I sometimes don't say my prayers at night, either.' She sighed once. 'We've been stupid about this – it should've been obvious. Now *get moving*!'

Before I could reply she had rung off. I found my jacket and threw it on, then wrote a note for the Isaacsons, in case they returned before we did. I was about to go out the door when the telephone rang again. I snatched it up, and heard Joseph's voice:

'Mr. Moore? Is that you?'

'Joseph?' I said. 'What's going on?'

'Oh, well, nothing, except that—' His tone was rather perplexed. 'Are you sure about the things you told me? About the man you're looking for, I mean.'

'As sure as I can be about anything in this business. Why?'

'Well, it's just that I saw a friend of mine last night – he's a street cruiser, doesn't work any house – and he said something that reminded me of what you said.'

Rushed as I was, I took the time to sit down and grab a pencil and paper. 'Go on, Joseph.'

'He said a man had promised to – well, what you said, take him away, and all that. Said he was going to live in a big – I don't know – castle or something, where he'd be able to see the whole city, and laugh at everybody who ever did him a wrong turn. So it reminded me of what you said, and I asked him if the man had anything wrong with his face. But he said no. You sure about that thing with the face?'

'Yes,' I answered. 'At this point I'm—'

'Uh-oh,' Joseph interrupted. 'Scotch Ann's yelling, it looks like I've got a customer. Gotta go.'

'Wait, Joseph. Just tell me—'

'Sorry – can't talk. Could we meet? Later tonight, maybe?'

I wanted to press him for more information, but knowing his situation I let it go. 'All right. The same place. Ten o'clock?'

'Okay.' He sounded happy. 'See you then.'

I replaced the earpiece of the phone and shot out of our headquarters.

Grabbing onto the back of a Broadway streetcar after leaving Number 808, I made the trip to Twenty-second Street in a matter of minutes. After jumping back down to the cobblestone pavement that bordered the tracks along that stretch of the avenue, I looked across the way at a triangular group of buildings that were covered with enormous signs advertising everything from painless dentistry to eyeglasses to steamship tickets. Tucked in among these notices, painted on the windows of the second story of Number 967, were a tasteful (and therefore distinct) group of golden letters: MITCHELL HARPER, ACCOUNTS SETTLED. After waiting for a break in the traffic, I crossed over and headed into the building.

I found Sara locked in private conversation with Mr. Harper in his small office. Neither the man nor the room matched the pleasant gold-leaf lettering on the windows. If Mr. Harper employed a cleaning service, you couldn't tell it from the soot that coated the few pieces of furniture in his office, while the roughness of his clothing and large cigar were exceeded only by that of his unshaven face and jaggedly cut hair. Sara introduced us, but Harper didn't offer his hand.

'I've read a great deal about medicine, Mr. Moore,' he explained in a coarse voice, locking his thumbs into his stained vest. 'Microbes, sir! Microbes are responsible for disease, and they pass through the touch!'

For an instant I thought of telling the man that bathing might give those microbes something to worry about; but then I just nodded and turned to Sara, my face asking why in the world she'd forced me to come to this place.

'We should have thought of it right away,' she whispered, before saying out loud: 'Mr. Harper was engaged by Mr. Lanford Stern of Washington Street in February, to attend to some outstanding debts.' Recognizing that this didn't jog my memory one bit, Sara added confidentially, 'Mr. Stern, you will recall, owns a number of buildings in the Washington Market area. One of his tenants is a Mr. Ghazi.'

'Oh,' I said simply. 'Oh, of course. Why didn't you just say that—'

Sara stopped me with a touch, obviously not wanting Harper to learn the real nature of our business. 'I saw Mr. Stern this morning,' she said pointedly, and finally I realized why we should have thought of going back to Mr. Stern at the beginning of this phase of our search: the elder Ghazi had been months behind in his rent at the time of his son's death. 'I told him,' Sara continued, 'about the man we're anxious to find – the man who we believed worked as a collector, and whose brother has died, leaving him a great deal of money?'

I nodded and smiled, recognizing that Sara was developing her own talent for impromptu falsehoods. 'Oh, yes,' I said quickly.

'Mr. Stern said that he referred all his back rent accounts to Mr. Harper,' Sara continued. 'And—'

'And as I told Miss Moore, here,' Harper cut in, 'if there's estate money to be had, I want to know what my cut'll be before I reveal anything.'

I nodded and faced the man fully – this was going to be child's play. 'Mr. Harper,' I said, with a broad flourish, 'I feel confident in saying that if you can provide us with the whereabouts of Mr. Beecham, you can expect a very generous percentage. A finder's fee, as it were. Say, five percent?'

Harper's saliva-soaked cigar almost fell out of his mouth. 'Five per – why, that *is* generous, sir. Generous, indeed! Five percent!'

'Five percent of all there is,' I repeated. 'You have my word. But tell me – *do* you know Mr. Beecham's whereabouts?'

The man looked momentarily unsure of himself. 'Well – that is, I know them *approximately*, Mr. Moore. I know of where he's *likely* to be, anyway – at least when he gets thirsty.' I gave the man a hard stare. 'I can take you there, myself, honest to God! It's a little stale-beer dive down in the Mulberry Bend, that's where I first met him. I would tell you to wait for him here, but – the fact is that about two weeks ago I had to let him go.'

'Let him go?' I queried. 'Why?'

'I'm a respectable man,' Harper answered. 'And this is a respectable business. But – well, sir, the fact is you occasionally have to use a little muscle. Do some convincing. Who's going to pay their bills without a little convincing? I originally hired Beecham because he was a big man, and strong. Said he could handle himself in a fight. So what does he do? Talks to them. Chats it up, that's what he does. Well, shit, sir – oh. My apologies, Miss. But you're not going to get any money out of anybody by talking to them. Especially not the immigrants. Hell, you give them the chance, they'll talk you into the grave! That Ghazi

Caleb Carr

character was a good example – I sent Beecham to his place three times and he never got one nickel out of the man.'

Harper had more he wanted to tell us, but we didn't need to hear it. After asking him to write down the address of the stale-beer dive he'd mentioned, Sara and I told him that we were going to check his lead out that very night, and that if it led to Beecham he could expect his money very soon. Ironically, this avaricious little man had given us the first piece of free information we'd had in two days – and the only one that was destined to amount to anything.

Chapter 41

As we came out of Harper's building we ran headlong into the Isaacsons, who had found my note. Immediately repairing to Brübacher's Wine Garden, the four of us went over what the account settler had said. Then we devised a plan for the evening. Our options were fairly straightforward: if we should locate Beecham we wouldn't confront him, but rather telephone Theodore and have him send down several detectives – men whose faces would be unknown to Beecham – whom we'd set to work shadowing the man. Alternately, if we were able to find out where Beecham lived, but if he wasn't in, we'd quickly search his place for evidence that might permit an immediate arrest. That much settled, we all drained our glasses and, at about eight-thirty, boarded a streetcar and began our expedition into Five Points.

The effect of that storied neighborhood has always been difficult to describe to the uninitiated. Even on a pleasant spring night like the one we moved through that Thursday, the place exuded a deep sense of mortal threat; yet that threat was not always or even usually exhibited in loud or aggressive ways, such as was the case in some other shady parts of the city. Indeed, I think the most disconcerting thing about the area around Mulberry Bend was the surprisingly low level of outward activity. The residents of the neighborhood spent most of their time crammed into the miserable shanties and tenements that lined the streets, or, more often, packed into the dives that occupied the ground and first floors of a remarkably large number of those squalid buildings. Death and despair did their work without fanfare in the Bend, and they did a lot of it: just walking down those lonely, decrepit streets was enough to make the sunniest of souls wonder about the ultimate value of human life.

I could see that Lucius was doing just that as we reached the address Harper had given us, Number 119 Baxter Street. A few dirt- and urine-covered stone stairs next to the building's entrance led down to a doorway that, to judge by the laughs and groans floating out of it, was the entrance to the dive we'd been told Beecham frequented. I turned to Lucius, and found him anxiously scanning the dark streets around us.

'Lucius – you and Sara stay here,' I said. 'We'll need you to keep watch.'

He nodded once, producing a handkerchief and wiping his forehead. 'Good,' he said. 'Fine, I mean.'

'And if there's any trouble do *not* show your badge,' I added. 'It's just an invitation to murder, down here.' As Marcus and I made for the steps, I eyed Lucius once more and then murmured into Sara's ear, 'Look after him, will you?' She smiled once at that, and though I could tell that she, too, was apprehensive, I knew that her aim would remain steady through whatever followed. Marcus and I went inside.

I don't know precisely what the caves looked like that prehistoric men are said to have inhabited, but the average Five Points dive cannot have represented any great advancement – and the one we entered that night was nothing if not average. The ceiling was only eight feet or so from the dirt floor, since the space had originally been designed as a cellar for the storefront above. There were no windows: light was provided by four filthy kerosene lamps that hung above a like number of long, low tables arranged in two rows. At these tables sat and slept the customers, their differences of age, sex, and dress more than outweighed by their common air of drunken dementia. There were about twenty people in the place that night, though only three – a pair of men and a woman, the last groaning and cackling at the incomprehensible statements of the other two – showed any real signs of life. They examined us with looks of glassy hatred, and Marcus inclined his head toward me.

'I suppose,' he whispered, 'that the key in here is to move slowly.'

I nodded, and then we wandered to the 'bar' – a plank resting on two ash barrels at the far end of the room. Immediately, two glasses of the substance from which such places took their name were placed in front of us. Stale beer was a flat, repellant mixture of the dregs that were collected from dozens of kegs in slightly more reputable houses – I paid for the drinks but made no move to touch mine, and Marcus pushed his glass aside.

The bartender who stood before us was about five and a half feet tall, with tawny hair, a matching mustache, and a typical look of slightly crazed resentment on his face.

'Don' wan' the drinks?' he asked.

I shook my head. 'Information. About a customer.'

'Fuck,' the man snorted. 'Ge' out.'

I produced more money. 'Just one or two questions.'

The man looked around anxiously and, seeing that the trio of relatively *compos mentis* customers were no longer watching us, slipped the money into his pocket. 'Well?'

I shot the name Beecham over the bartender's bow, producing no reaction; but when I went on to describe a tall man with a facial twitch, I could see by the heightened glimmer in the fellow's sickly bright eyes that our friend Mitchell Harper had played straight with us.

'A block up,' the bartender mumbled. 'Number 155. Top floor, inna back.'

Marcus looked at me dubiously, and the bartender caught it. 'Seen it myself!' he insisted. 'You frumma girl's fam'ly?'

'Girl?' I said.

The bartender nodded. 'Too' a girl up there. Mother thought she'd been 'napped. Didn' hurt her, though – but did near kill a man that mentioned it in here.'

I weighed that. 'He drinks a lot?'

'Didn' used to. Never unnerstood what he was doin' here when he first showed up. Lately more, though.'

I looked to Marcus, who gave me a quick nod. After dumping some more money on the bar we turned to go, but the bartender

Caleb Carr

grabbed my arm. 'You heard nuthin' from me,' he said urgently. 'Tha's no man to cross.' He bared several yellow and gray teeth. 'Iss quite a pick he carries.'

Marcus and I started away again, leaving the bartender to drain the two glasses of stale beer he'd poured for us. Once more we exercised great care in walking by the near-dead bodies at the tables, and though one man by the door did turn and begin to urinate unconsciously on the floor as we passed, there didn't seem anything personal in the act.

As Marcus stepped over the puddle of urine he murmured to me, 'So Beecham's drinking.'

'Yes,' I answered, opening the front door. 'I remember Kreizler saying once that our man might be entering a final, self-destructive phase. Anybody who drinks in a joint like this has certainly done that.'

We got back outside to find Sara and Lucius looking just as anxious as we'd left them. 'Come on,' I said quickly, leading the way north. 'We've got an address.'

Number 155 Baxter Street was an unremarkable New York tenement, though in any other neighborhood the women and children who were hanging out its windows on that seasonable night would have been laughing or singing or at least screaming at one another. Here they simply sat with their heads in their hands, the youngest of them looking as worldly and tired as the oldest, and none of them exhibiting any interest in what occurred on the street. A man who I placed at about thirty was seated on the stoop, swinging a nightstick that looked to be authentic police issue. It wasn't difficult to judge, after getting a glimpse of the man's blow-twisted features and surly grin, just how he'd laid hands on the trophy. I mounted the stoop, and the end of the nightstick poked my chest just hard enough to stop me from going further.

'Business?' the crooked-faced man said, his breath reeking of camphor-laced liquor.

'We're here to see a resident,' I answered.

The man laughed. 'Don't git gay wit me, swell. Business?'

I paused before answering. 'Who are you supposed to be?'

The laugh died. 'I'm *supposed* to be da mug what watches dis building – for da landlord. So don't git gay wit me, boy, les youse wanna taste dis sap.' He was speaking in the Bowery slang long since immortalized by the city's toughs, a language that was always a little difficult to take seriously; still, I didn't like the look of the nightstick, and went for my billfold once again.

'Top floor,' I said, holding some money out. 'In the back. Anybody home?'

The man's grin returned. 'Oh!' he said, taking the cash. 'Youse mean old—' He suddenly began to blink, and then to comically contort his right jaw, cheek, and eye. Apparently unsatisfied with the results of this performance, he heightened its effect by tugging at his head with his hands. Pleased with this additional effort, he began to laugh loud. 'Nah, he ain't dere,' he finally said. 'Never dere, not nights. During da day, sometimes, but not nights. You can check da roof, mebbe he's up dere. Likes it up dere, does dat boid.'

'What about his flat?' I said. 'Maybe we'd like to wait for him there.'

'Mebbe it's locked,' the fellow answered with another grin. I held out still more money. 'Den agin, mebbe it isn't.' The man started into the building. 'Ain't cops, is youse?'

'I'm not paying you to ask questions,' I answered.

The man gave my words something that approached consideration, then nodded. 'Okay. Come on wit me – but keep it quiet, right?'

We all nodded and followed the man inside. The building's long, darkened staircase was redolent with the usual stenches of rotting refuse and human waste, and at its foot I paused to let Sara get in front of me.

'A world away from Mrs. Piedmont's,' she whispered as she passed.

We got up the six flights of stairs without incident, and then our guide knocked on one of four doors that branched off a small landing. After getting no reply, he held up a finger. 'Wait here a minute,' he said, and then he loped up the final flight of stairs to the roof. In seconds he was back, looking more relaxed. 'All clear,' he announced, taking a large ring of keys from his hip pocket and unlocking the door he'd knocked on. 'Hadda make

Caleb Carr

sure he weren't around. He's a touchy one, old—' Instead of saying a name, the man began to contort his face again, which gave him another laugh. Finally, we entered the flat.

A kerosene lamp sat on a shelf by the door, and I lit it. The space that slowly became visible was essentially one narrow hallway, perhaps thirty feet in overall length, in the middle of which had been built a small partition and a doorway with a transom over it. Two recently cut chinks in the side walls were the flat's only connections to the outside world, offering limited, bleak views across narrow airshafts in similar gaps in the walls of neighboring flats. A small stove was set up against the partition, though there were apparently no sanitary facilities, other than a rusted bucket. Only a few pieces of furniture could be seen from the front door: a plain old desk and chair on the near side of the partition, and beyond it the foot of a bed. Coats of thick, cheap paint had chipped and peeled away from the walls, revealing one another and creating the overall impression of a brown stain such as one might find at the bottom of a commode.

In this place lived the being who had once been Japheth Dury and was now the murderer John Beecham; and within this spare little hole there had to be clues, difficult as they might be to see. Without speaking, I indicated the far end of the flat to the Isaacsons; they each nodded, then proceeded past the partition and into that area. Sara and I took a few tentative steps toward the old desk, while our guide remained alertly at the front door.

Our entire search could not have taken more than five minutes, so small and sparsely furnished was the place. The old desk had three drawers that Sara began to check in the near-darkness, putting her hands in each to make sure she missed nothing. Above the desk, tacked to the crumbling wall, was some sort of a map. Leaning over to study it, I noticed a peculiar feeling under my hands: picking them up, I discovered that the top of the desk had been deeply carved into a monotonous series of unembellished grooves. Putting my hands back down I looked at the map again: I was able to recognize the outline of Manhattan, but the marks that had been drawn over that outline were strange to me: a series of straight, intersecting lines with arcane numbers and symbols scribbled in at various points. I was about to put my head closer when I heard Sara say:

'Here. John.'

Looking down I saw her remove a small wooden box from the bottom drawer. She placed it on the grooved desktop rather fearfully, then stood away.

Affixed to the lid of the box was an old daguerreotype, very similar in style and composition to the Civil War work of the eminent photographer Mathew Brady. Based on the picture's aged and battered condition I judged it to be of about the same vintage as Brady's work. The image displayed was that of a dead white man: scalped, eviscerated, and emasculated, with arrows protruding from his arms and legs. His eyes were missing. There were no identifying marks on the picture, but it was obviously one of the Reverend Victor Dury's creations.

The box on which the daguerreotype was mounted was closed tightly, but there seemed to be an aroma emanating from it – the same sort of aroma that'd been present in Beecham's room at Mrs. Piedmont's: rotting animal flesh. My heart sank as I laid hold of the thing, although before I could open it I heard Marcus's voice:

'Oh, no. God, *how* . . .'

Then there were bustling sounds, and Marcus stumbled out to where Sara and I were standing. Even in the lamplight I could see that he was pale – a surprising condition, given that I'd watched the man calmly photograph scenes that would've turned most people's stomachs. In a few seconds Lucius followed him in, bearing something in his arms.

'John!' Lucius called in quiet urgency. 'John, it – it's evidence! Good lord, I think we've got a straight murder investigation now!'

'Aw, shit,' said our man at the door. 'Then youse *is* cops?'

Without answering I struck a match and held it high as I approached Lucius. Just as I focused in on the object in his arms, Sara let out a short cry and then clamped a hand over her mouth, spinning away.

Lucius was holding an enormous glass jar. Inside it, preserved in a substance that I could only suppose to be formaldehyde, were human eyes. Some still trailed their ganglia of optic nerves, and some were smoothly round; some were fresh, others milky and obviously aged; some were blue in color, some were brown, and others were hazel, gray, and green. But it was not the discovery or the condition of the eyes, I now understood, that had stunned Marcus – it was their number. For these were not the ten eyes of our five murdered boys, nor even the fourteen eyes of the boys plus the Zweig children; these were the dozens – the *dozens* – of eyes of more than a score of victims. And all of them were gaping through the curved glass in what seemed silent accusation, pathetically begging to know what had taken us so very long . . .

In a moment my own eyes wandered back to the small box that Sara had found, which I now opened slowly. The stench of decay that wafted up was not so strong as I expected, allowing me to study the receptacle's strange contents without difficulty. But I could make no sense of what I saw: A small, red-black piece of what looked like desiccated rubber.

'Lucius?' I said softly, holding it out toward him.

Setting the large jar down on the desk, Lucius took the box over by the front door and held it under the kerosene lamp. Our guide looked over his shoulder as the detective sergeant studied the contents.

'Shit?' the man with the nightstick said. 'Sure enough *smells* like shit.'

'No,' Lucius answered evenly, eyes ever on the box. 'It is, I believe, the preserved remnants of a human heart.'

That was enough to give even a Five Points thug pause, and our guide turned away and into the hall with a look of utter consternation on his face. 'Who da hell *are* you people?' he breathed.

I kept my eyes on Lucius. 'A heart? Is it the Lohmann boy's?'

He shook his head. 'Too old. This has been in here for a very long time. It looks as though it may even have been coated with something, a varnish of some kind.'

I turned to Sara, who was taking deep breaths and standing with her arms wrapped around her midsection. Touching her shoulder I said, 'All right?'

She nodded once quickly. 'Yes. Fine.'

My eyes went to Marcus. 'You?'

'I think so. Will be, at any rate.'

'Lucius—' I waved the shorter Isaacson over. 'Someone's got to check that stove. Can you manage it?'

Lucius bobbed his head certainly: though he'd been apprehensive on the street, he was all business in this situation. 'Let me borrow a match.' I gave him the little box from my pocket.

The rest of us listened as he went to the grimy black chunk of iron that stood against the partition. A few pieces of firewood were in a bin next to the thing, and a greasy roasting pan sat on top of it. Someone had apparently been cooking. Lucius struck a match, took a preparatory but calm breath, then pulled the door of the oven cavity open. I closed my eyes as he held the match inside; in another fifteen seconds, I heard the thing bang closed again.

'Nothing,' Lucius announced. 'Grease, a charred potato – nothing else.'

I let out a lot of air and tapped Marcus's shoulder. 'What do you make of this?' I said, pointing to the map of Manhattan on the wall.

Marcus studied it carefully. 'Manhattan,' he said quickly. Then, after a few more seconds: 'Look's like a surveyor's map of some kind.' He poked at the spots where the map had been tacked to the wall, then pulled the tacks out. 'Plaster hasn't discolored. It was put up fairly recently, I'd say.'

Lucius rejoined us, and then we all stood in a tight circle away from the box and the jar that sat on the desk.

'That's all that was in the back?' I asked the Isaacsons.

'That's all,' Marcus said. 'No clothes, nothing. If you ask me, he's gone.'

'Gone?' Sara echoed.

Marcus nodded in disappointment. 'Could be he knew we were closing in. But it certainly doesn't look like he's coming back.'

'But why would he leave,' Sara asked, 'without taking all that – *evidence*?'

Marcus shook his head. 'Maybe he doesn't think it *is* evidence.

Or maybe he was in a hurry. Or maybe . . .'

'Or maybe,' I said, voicing what we all were thinking, 'he wanted us to find it.'

As we stood absorbing that idea, I noticed our guide straining to get a look at the jar on the desk, and moved to block his view with my body. Then Lucius spoke up: 'That may be true, but we've still got to watch this place, in case he does come back. We should tell the commissioner to send other men down – because, like I say, we can treat this as a straight murder investigation now.'

'Do you think there's enough evidence to make a charge stick?' Sara asked softly. 'I know this sounds awful, but those aren't necessarily the eyes of our victims.'

'No,' Lucius answered. 'But unless he's got one hell of an explanation for whose they *are*, I think any jury in the city will convict – especially if we fill in the background with what we know.'

'All right, then,' I said. 'Sara and I will get up to Mulberry Street and tell Roosevelt to assign men to watch this building day and night. Lucius, you and Marcus will have to stay here until that relief comes. What have you got for weapons?' Marcus just shook his head, but Lucius produced the same service revolver that I'd seen him with at Castle Garden. 'Fine,' I said. 'While you're waiting, Marcus, see what kind of sense you can make of that map. And remember one thing—' I ran my voice down to a whisper. 'No badges. Not until you've got some support. It wasn't too long ago that cops wouldn't even come into this neighborhood, their chances of getting out were so bad.'

The Isaacsons both nodded, and then Sara and I went out into the hallway, stopping when the man with the nightstick stepped in front of us. 'Now suppose youse tell me what's all dis about an investigation? Is you cops or ain't you?'

'This is a – private matter,' I answered. 'My friends are staying – to wait for the resident.' I automatically went for my billfold and produced ten dollars. 'You can just act like you never saw them.'

'For ten bucks?' the man said with a nod. 'For ten bucks I'd forget me own muddah's face.' He cackled once. 'Not dat I remember it, ta begin wit!'

Sara and I got outside quickly, and started to walk quietly north and then west, hoping to catch a streetcar at Broadway without any trouble. This would be the trickiest part of our journey, though I didn't want to tell her as much: there were only two of us now, and one of those two was a woman. In the sixties or seventies any Five Points gang worth its salt would have laid me out and had their way with Sara before we'd gotten a block from Baxter Street. I was just praying that, with dissipation having replaced violence as the neighborhood's chief pastime in recent years, we'd be able to sneak out unnoticed.

Remarkably, we did. By nine forty-five we were on our way up Broadway, and just a few minutes later our streetcar crossed Houston Street and we jumped off. Unconcerned, now, with whether or not we were spotted together at headquarters, Sara and I rushed into the building as soon as we reached it, then bulled our way up and into Theodore's office, which was empty. A detective told us that the president had gone home for dinner but was expected back soon – the half-hour wait that followed was maddening. When Theodore did arrive he was a bit alarmed to find us present, but on hearing our news he came alive and began barking orders throughout the second-floor hallway. As he did, a thought occurred to me, and I motioned to Sara, indicating the staircase.

'The note,' I explained, as we went downstairs and toward the front door. 'The letter to Mrs. Santorelli – if we can confront Beecham with that, it may help break him down.'

Sara liked the idea, and once outside we grabbed a hansom and made for Number 808 Broadway. I wouldn't call our mood exactly ebullient as we dashed north, but we were quietly alive to the real possibilities of the moment, enough so that our cab ride seemed to take an eternity.

When we entered Number 808 I was moving so fast that I failed to notice, and nearly tripped over, a rather large gunnysack that someone had left in the vestibule. Crouching down I saw a tag attached to the closed top of the bag: NR. 808 B'WAY – 6TH FLOOR. I glanced up at Sara and saw that she, too, was examining the sack and the tag.

'You haven't been ordering produce, have you, John?' she asked, a bit wryly.

'Don't be ridiculous,' I answered. 'Must be something for Marcus and Lucius.'

I studied the sack for a few more seconds, then shrugged and reached down to undo the twine that bound its mouth. The cord was twisted into a complex knot, however, so I pulled out a penknife and slit the thick fabric of the bag from top to bottom.

Out onto the floor, like so much meat, fell Joseph. There were no obvious marks on his body, but the pallor of his skin made it instantly clear that he was dead.

Chapter 42

It took the coroner at the Bellevue morgue better than six hours to determine that Joseph's life had ended when someone jammed either a thin knife, such as a stiletto, or a large needle up under the base of his skull and into his brain. A night spent smoking cigarettes and pacing the hallways of the morgue did nothing for my ability to make sense of this information, when it finally came: I thought briefly of Biff Ellison, and of the quiet, efficient way he settled scores with a similar weapon; yet even in my shocked grief I couldn't picture Ellison being responsible. Joseph wasn't one of his boys, and even if Biff had some new ax to grind with our investigation, such a murderous move would almost certainly have been preceded by an emphatic warning. So unless Byrnes and Connor had coerced Ellison into helping them (a possibility so unlikely as to be impossible), I could think of no explanation and no culprit, save one: Beecham. Somehow, he'd found a way to get close to the boy, despite all my warnings.

My warnings. As Joseph's little body was wheeled out of one of the morgue's autopsy rooms, it occurred to me for what must have been the thousandth time that it was meeting me that had brought the boy to such an unhappy end. I had tried to prepare him for every possible danger – but how could I have foreseen that the greatest of those dangers would be to speak to me in the first place? And now here I was at the morgue, telling the coroner that I'd arranged for a funeral and that everything was to be taken care of properly, as if it mattered whether the boy's body was buried in a nice patch of Brooklyn ground or thrown into the tidal currents of the East River and pulled out to sea. Vanity, arrogance, irresponsibility – all through the night my mind had been pulled back to what Kreizler had said after Mary Palmer's murder: that in our dash to defeat evil, we had only given it a wider field in which to run its own wretched course.

Lost in thoughts of Kreizler as I wandered out of the morgue and into the dawn, I was perhaps less surprised than I might otherwise have been to see my old friend sitting in his uncovered calash. Cyrus Montrose was in the driver's seat, and he offered a small, sympathetic inclination of his head when he saw me. Laszlo smiled and stepped down from the rig as I stumbled over.

'Joseph . . .' I said, my voice cracking from the cigarettes and brooding silence of the night.

'I know,' Laszlo said. 'Sara called. I thought you might need some breakfast.'

I nodded weakly and got into the carriage with him. Cyrus urged the horse Frederick forward with a quiet click of his tongue.

After several minutes I leaned back and rested my head on the folded cover of the calash, sighing heavily and staring at the half-lit, cloudy sky. 'It had to be Beecham,' I mumbled.

'Yes,' Laszlo answered quietly.

I turned my head toward him without picking it up. 'But there was no mutilation. I couldn't even see how he'd been killed, there was so little blood. Nothing but a small hole at the base of the skull.'

Laszlo's eyes went thin. 'Quick and clean,' he said. 'This wasn't one of his rituals. This was pragmatic. He killed the boy to protect himself – and to send a message.'

'To me?' I asked.

Kreizler nodded. 'Desperate as he is, he won't go easily.'

I began to shake my head slowly. 'But how – *how*? I *told* Joseph, told him everything we'd learned. He *knew* how to identify Beecham. Hell, he called me yesterday afternoon, to double-check on the details.'

Kreizler's right eyebrow arched. 'Really? Why?'

'I don't know,' I said in disgust, pulling out yet another cigarette. 'Some friend of his had been approached by a man who wanted to take him away. To a – castle above the city, he said. Something like that. It did sound like it might've been Beecham, but the man had no facial spasms.'

Laszlo turned away, and spoke carefully. 'Ah. Then you didn't remember?'

'Remember?'

'Adam Dury. He told us that when Japheth was hunting, his spasms went away. I suspect that when he stalks these boys—' Seeing the effect his words were having on me, Kreizler cut his explanation short. 'I'm sorry, John.'

I threw my unlit cigarette into the street and clutched my head with both hands. Of course he was right. Hunting, stalking, trapping, killing – they all calmed Beecham's spirit, and that calm was reflected in his face. Whoever the boy, the street cruiser, that Joseph had referred to was, he might in fact have been accosted by our man. Joseph himself certainly had been. All because I had forgotten a detail . . .

Kreizler put a hand on my shoulder as the calash rolled on, and when I next looked up we'd come to a stop outside Delmonico's. I knew that the restaurant wouldn't be open for another hour or two, but I also knew that if any man could arrange an off-hours meal, it was Kreizler. Cyrus got down from the driver's seat and helped me out of the carriage, saying softly, 'There you go, Mr. Moore – get a little food in you.' I found my walking legs and followed Laszlo to the front door, which was opened by Charlie Delmonico. Something about the look in his enormous eyes told me that he knew all the details.

'Good morning, Doctor,' he said, in about the only tone of voice that I could've stood to have heard at just that instant. 'Mr. Moore,' he went on, as we came inside. 'I hope you will make yourselves entirely comfortable, gentlemen. If there is anything at all I can do . . .'

'Thank you, Charles,' Kreizler answered.

I touched the man's elbow and managed to whisper, 'Thanks, Charlie,' before we entered the dining room.

With unfailing psychological insight, Kreizler had selected for

Caleb Carr

our breakfast the only place in New York where I might have been able to either collect myself or eat anything at all. Alone in the silent main dining room at Del's, with the light that came through the windows soft enough to allow my shattered nerves to begin to heal, I actually managed to consume several bites of cucumber fillets, Creole eggs, and broiled squab. But even more important, I found that I was able to talk.

'Do you know,' I murmured, soon after we'd sat down, 'that I was actually thinking – was it yesterday? – that I could still feel sympathy for the man, despite all he'd done. Because of the context of his life. I thought that I finally knew him.'

Kreizler shook his head. 'You can't, John. Not that well. You can come close, perhaps, close enough to anticipate him, but in the end neither you nor I nor anyone else will be able to see *just* what he sees when he looks at those children, or feel *precisely* the emotion that makes him take up the knife. The only way to learn of such things would be . . .' Kreizler turned to the window with a faraway look. 'Would be to ask him.'

I nodded weakly. 'We found his flat.'

'Sara told me,' Laszlo said, shaking himself a bit. 'You've done brilliantly, John. All of you.'

I scoffed at that. 'Brilliantly . . . Marcus doesn't think Beecham will come back to the place. And I've got to say that I agree now. The bloodthirsty bastard's been a step ahead of us all the way.'

Kreizler shrugged. 'Perhaps.'

'Did Sara tell you about the map?'

'Yes,' Laszlo said, as a waiter brought us two glasses of fresh tomato juice. 'And Marcus has identified it – it's a chart of the city's water supply system. Apparently the entire network's been refurbished over the last ten years. Beecham probably stole the map from the Public Records Office.'

I had a sip of juice. 'The water supply system? What the hell does *that* point to?'

'Sara and Marcus have ideas,' Kreizler answered, taking some sauteed potatoes with artichoke hearts and truffles from a small platter. 'I'm sure they'll tell you.'

I looked right into those black eyes. 'Then you're not coming back?'

Kreizler glanced away quickly, evasively. 'It isn't possible, John. Not yet.' He tried to brighten as the Creole eggs arrived. 'You've set your plan for Sunday – the Feast of the Baptist.'

'Yes.'

'It will be an important night for him.'

'I suppose.'

'The fact that he's left his – his *trophies* behind indicates a crisis of some sort. By the way, the heart in the box? His mother's, I suspect.' I only shrugged. 'You realize, of course,' Laszlo went on, 'that Sunday is the night of the benefit for Abbey and Grau at the Metropolitan?'

My jaw fell open and my eyes strained in disbelief. '*What*?'

'The benefit,' Kreizler said, almost cheerfully. 'The bankruptcy has destroyed Abbey's health, poor fellow. For that if for no other reason we must attend.'

'*We*?' I squeaked. 'Kreizler, we're going to be hunting a murderer, for God's sake!'

'Yes, yes,' Laszlo answered, 'but later. Beecham hasn't struck before midnight thus far. There's no reason to think he will on Sunday. So why not make the wait as pleasant as possible, and help Abbey and Grau at the same time?'

I dropped my fork. 'I know – *I'm* losing my mind. *You're* not actually saying any of this, you can't be—'

'Maurel will be singing Giovanni,' Kreizler said enticingly, shoving some squab and eggs into his face. 'Edouard de Reszke will be Leporello, and I hardly dare tell you who's scheduled for Zerlina . . .'

I huffed once indignantly, but then asked, 'Frances Saville?'

'She of the legs,' Kreizler answered with a nod. 'Anton Seidl conducts. Oh, and Nordica sings Donna Anna.'

There was no doubt about it – he'd just described a truly memorable night of opera, and I was momentarily distracted by the prospect. But then a stabbing sensation hit my gut as a picture of Joseph came into my head, wiping out all fantasies about pleasant evenings. 'Kreizler,' I said coldly, 'I don't know what's happened that lets you sit here and talk so casually about the opera, as if people we *both* know hadn't been—'

'There's nothing *casual* in what I'm saying, Moore.' The black

474   Caleb Carr

eyes went dead, and a cool but ferocious sort of determination hardened the voice: 'I'll make a deal with you – come with me to *Giovanni*, and I'll rejoin the investigation. And we *will* end this affair.'

'You'll rejoin?' I said, surprised. 'But when?'

'Not before the opera,' Laszlo answered. I was about to protest, but he held up a firm hand. 'I can't be any more specific than that, John, so don't ask me to. Just tell me – do you accept?'

Well, of course I *did* accept – what else was I going to do? Despite everything the Isaacsons, Sara, and I had achieved in recent weeks, Joseph's murder had left me feeling profoundly doubtful about our ability to see the investigation through. The thought of Kreizler coming back was an enormous incentive to keep going, one that allowed me to get through an entire squab before we finally left Del's and headed downtown. He was being mysterious, all right – but Laszlo wasn't capricious about such things, and my money said that he had a good reason for shrouding his intentions. And so I promised to get my opera clothes cleaned, and then shook hands on the deal; though when I said how much I was looking forward to telling the others about the arrangement on my return to Number 808 Broadway, Kreizler requested that I not do so. Above all, I was to say nothing to Roosevelt.

'I don't ask that out of bitterness,' Laszlo explained, as I got out of the calash at the northern end of Union Square. 'Theodore has been decent and kind in recent days, and diligent in his search for Connor.'

'There's still no sign of the man, however,' I said, having heard as much from Roosevelt.

Laszlo stared off, seemingly oddly detached. 'He'll turn up, I suspect. And in the meantime' – he closed the small carriage door – 'there are other things to attend to. All right, Cyrus.'

The calash rolled away, and I walked downtown.

When I arrived at our headquarters I found a note from Sara and the Isaacsons on my desk, saying that they'd gone home to get a few hours' sleep, after which they planned to join the team of detectives that Theodore had assigned to watch Beecham's building. I took advantage of their absence to stretch out on the divan and try to get some much-needed rest of my own, though the state I subsequently fell into could hardly have been called a sound sleep. Still, by noon I was feeling improved enough to go back to Washington Square, bathe, and change my clothes. Then I telephoned Sara. She informed me that the rendezvous at 155 Baxter Street was set for sundown, and that Roosevelt himself intended to log a few hours on watch. She said she'd pick me up in a cab, and then we both tried to get a little more rest.

As it turned out, Marcus was quite right about Beecham: by three A.M. Saturday morning there'd still been no sign of the man, and we all began to realize that he almost certainly wasn't going to return to the flat. I told the others about what Kreizler had said concerning Beecham's 'trophies' – that if he'd left them behind it indicated some sort of climax to his murderous career was fast approaching – and this notion underlined for us all the importance of devising an ironclad plan for Sunday night. As per our agreement of several weeks earlier, Roosevelt was included in these deliberations, which we undertook Saturday afternoon at Number 808.

Roosevelt had never actually been to our headquarters before, and watching him take in all its intellectual and decorative oddities reminded me strongly of the morning I'd first woken up in the place. As always with Theodore, curiosity soon became dominant over perplexity: He began to ask so many detailed questions about every object – from the big chalkboard to our small kitchen stove – that we didn't get down to work for almost an hour after his arrival. The session was much like any of the dozens that had preceded it: we all threw out ideas, to be weighed and (usually) rejected, all the while trying to assemble solid hypotheses out of airy speculations. Yet this time I found myself watching the process through Roosevelt's initially bewildered and later fascinated eyes, and thus seeing it from a very fresh perspective. And when he started to pound his fists on the arms of one of the Marchese Carcano's chairs and let out exclamations of approval every time we satisfied ourselves that some bit of reasoning was sound, I gained a new appreciation for the work our team had done and was doing.

We were all agreed on one essential point: that Beecham's map

Caleb Carr

of the New York City water supply system bore some kind of relevance not to his past killings but to his upcoming one. While waiting for Theodore's detectives on the night that we'd first discovered Beecham's flat, Marcus had confirmed his initial theory that the map had been tacked on the wall only recently by making comparative analyses of the wall plaster in different parts of the place. Taking such elements as heat, moisture, and soot into account, Marcus had satisfied himself completely that the map had not been on the wall even as recently as the night of Ernst Lohmann's murder.

'Splendid!' Theodore judged, giving Marcus a salute. 'Precisely why I brought you boys onto the force – modern methods!'

Marcus's conclusion was further backed up by several other factors. First, it was difficult to see what connection any of the murder sites to date might have had to the city's water system. In addition, the overall notion of such a system, one of the primary purposes of which was to facilitate bathing, might easily have been metaphorically connected in Beecham's mind to the figure of John the Baptist. Add to all this the fact that Beecham seemed to have been both taunting and pleading with us by leaving the map behind, and we felt confident in saying that the thing was somehow conceptually tied to the next killing. These details were accordingly entered on the chalkboard by Lucius.

'Bully,' Theodore pronounced as Lucius scribbled. 'Bully! This is what I like – a scientific approach!'

None of us had the heart to tell the man that this particular part of our approach was a good deal less scientific than it might have appeared; instead, we took out any and all books we had that related to public works and buildings in Manhattan and embarked on a tour of the island's water supply system.

Each of Beecham's 1896 murders had occurred on the banks of a river, from which we had already deduced that the sight of a large body of water had become a vital emotional component of his murderous rituals. It was therefore important to focus our attention on those elements of the water system that were positioned close to the waterfronts. This didn't leave us with many choices. In fact, it left us, we felt, with only one: the High

Bridge Aqueduct and Tower, whose ten-foot pipes had brought clear upstate New York water across the East River and into Manhattan since the 1840s. True, if Beecham had selected High Bridge it would mean his first murder north of Houston Street; yet the simple fact that he had confined his slaughter to Lower Manhattan did not necessarily mean that he was completely unacquainted with the northern end of the island. And it was always possible that Beecham in fact intended to visit some less imposing site on his map – a water main juncture or the like – and was just hoping that we would jump at the more obvious and dramatic High Bridge interpretation.

'But what about the boy's story?' Theodore asked, deeply frustrated that he could not be more involved in the speculative process. 'The "castle that overlooks the city," and what not? Doesn't that confirm your hypothesis?'

Sara pointed out that, while it might indeed confirm the hypothesis (for the High Bridge Tower, built to equalize water pressure in Manhattan's inland reservoirs, did indeed resemble a tall castle turret), such confirmation did not necessarily mean that Beecham intended to take his victim there. We were dealing with an excessively perverse and devious mentality, Sara explained to Theodore, one who was well aware of our activities and who would get great pleasure from doing all he could to lead us down a false trail. Nonetheless, it was doubtful that Beecham was aware of our understanding of his need to be near water – indeed, he might not be aware of it himself, and High Bridge Tower therefore stood as the most promising location.

Roosevelt absorbed this information with keen interest, nodding and rubbing his jowl and finally clapping his hands together rather thunderously. 'Well done, Sara!' he said. 'I don't know what your family would say if they could hear such talk, but by thunder, I'm proud of you!' So full of genuine affection and admiration were Theodore's words that Sara forgave their slightly patronizing air and turned away with a satisfied smile.

Roosevelt became more intimately involved in the discussion when the time came to plan the actual disposition of police forces for Sunday night. He wanted to handpick the men who would watch the High Bridge Tower, he said, recognizing that it was a

Caleb Carr

job requiring enormous tact – any sign of police activity, we all knew, and Beecham was likely to bolt. In addition to the High Bridge surveillance, Roosevelt intended to have all bridges and ferry stations closely scrutinized, and extra roundsmen would patrol the waterfronts on both the east and west sides at regular intervals. Finally, detective units would be assigned to all the same disorderly houses that we'd watched on the night of the Lohmann boy's death, even though we had good reason to believe Beecham would be abducting his victim from another locale.

All that remained was to decide what part Sara, the Isaacsons, and I would play in the drama. The obvious choice was for us to join the surveillance group at the High Bridge Tower, at which point it became necessary for me to announce that I wouldn't be able to do so until a late hour, as it was my intention to attend the opera with Kreizler. This brought instant expressions of incredulity to my teammates' faces; but since I'd agreed not to reveal the exact terms of the bargain I'd struck with Laszlo, I could offer no plausible explanation for my behavior. Fortunately, before Sara and the Isaacsons could get a full head of baffled steam going, I got help from an unexpected source: Theodore, who, it turned out, was also planning to attend the benefit performance. Roosevelt explained that it was very unlikely that Mayor Strong would sanction calling out a large part of the police force to put in a night's work on the boy-whore murders. But if Roosevelt were seen at a highly publicized society event, which would also be attended by the mayor and one or two of the other members of the Board of Commissioners, it would help to ensure that the night's activities did not become a focus of attention. Theodore supported the idea of my going to the opera as well, saying it could only heighten such a misdirection of official scrutiny; besides, he said, repeating Kreizler's logic, Beecham had never struck before midnight, and there was no reason to think he'd start now. Roosevelt and I could easily join the hunt once the opera was over.

Faced with this attitude on the part of their highest departmental superior, the Isaacsons reluctantly acquiesced. Sara, on the other hand, eyed me suspiciously, and pulled me aside when the others began to discuss further details of the police deployment.

'Is he up to something, John?' she asked, in a tone that indicated she'd brook no nonsense at this stage of the game.

'Who, Kreizler?' I said, hoping it sounded better than it felt. 'No, I don't think so. We made the plan some time ago.' Then a ruse: 'If you really do think it's a bad idea, Sara, I can easily tell him that—'

'No,' she answered quickly, but without looking convinced. 'What Theodore says makes sense. And we'll all be at the tower, anyway, I can't think why you'd be needed as well.' I bridled a bit at that, but discretion demanded I not show it. 'Still,' Sara went on, 'after three weeks without a word it seems odd that he'd choose tomorrow night to reappear.' Her eyes roamed around the room as her mind ran through possibilities. 'Just let us know if it looks like he's got a scheme.'

'Of course.' She scrutinized me skeptically again, and my eyes went wide. 'Sara, why *wouldn't* I tell you?'

She couldn't answer that; *I* couldn't answer that. Only one person knew the full set of reasons for my secrecy – and he wasn't prepared to reveal them.

Important as it was that we all be well rested for Sunday's undertakings, I felt it even more imperative that we return to the streets one more time Saturday night, in order to make at least a minimal effort to locate the young street cruiser that Joseph had mentioned to me. The odds of finding such a boy without either a name or a description were, admittedly, fairly long; and they only got longer as the night wore on. And by midnight we had to accept it – if we were going to find the boy, we were going to find him with Beecham, hopefully before he'd been killed.

That thought was sobering enough to send us all on our respective ways home. It was now quite apparent that there was something very different about this latest prospect of facing Beecham, and it wasn't simply the fact that we knew his name and a great deal about his history: it was the inescapable feeling that the confrontation that was almost upon us – and which had largely been arranged, even if unconsciously, by Beecham himself – might be far more dangerous for us than we'd ever suspected. True, we'd assumed since the beginning that a strong desire to be

Caleb Carr

stopped was evident in Beecham's behavior; but we now under-stood that that desire had a cataclysmic, even apocalyptic, side to it, and that his being 'stopped' could very well entail great violence to those who performed the service. Yes, we would be armed, and together with our official auxiliaries we would outnumber him by tens and perhaps hundreds to one; yet in many ways this man had faced greater odds throughout his nightmarish life, and – simply by surviving – had beaten them. Then, too, the line on any race is not determined by the statistical record alone; it takes into account the intangibles of breeding and training as well. If one entered such factors into our current undertaking, the outlook changed dramatically, even given our side's superior numbers and armaments – in fact, I was not at all sure that, thus calculated, the odds were not decidedly in Beecham's favor.

Chapter 43

It is never easier to understand the mind of a bomb-wielding anarchist than when standing amid a crush of those ladies and gentlemen who have the money and the temerity to style themselves 'New York Society.' Suited, gowned, bejeweled, and perfumed, the fabled Four Hundred top families in the city, along with their various relations and hangers-on, can shove, snipe, gossip, and gorge with an abandon that the amused onlooker might find fascinating but the unfortunate interloper will deem nothing short of deplorable. I was one such interloper on Sunday evening, the twenty-first of June. Kreizler had asked me (strangely, it seemed even then) to meet him not at Seventeenth Street but in his box at the Metropolitan before the benefit performance, making it necessary for me to take a cab to the 'yellow brewery' and then fight my way up the house's narrow staircases alone. Absolutely nothing brings out the killer instinct in the upper crust of New York Society like a charity function; and as I squeezed and pushed through the vestibule, trying to coax movement out of *grandes dames* whose clothing and physical proportions were suited only to stationary pursuits, I occasionally ran into people I'd known during my childhood, friends of my parents who now turned away quickly when they caught my eye, or simply bowed in a minimal way that declared unmistakably, 'Please, spare me the embarrassment of actually having to speak with you.' All of which was fine as far as I was concerned, except that they generally wouldn't then step aside and allow me to get by. By the time I reached the building's second tier my nerves, along with my clothes, had been thrown into disarray, while my ears were ringing with the din of several thousand perfectly idiotic conversations. Remedy was at hand, however: I sliced my way through to one of the pocket bars under a staircase, downed a quick glass of champagne, grabbed hold of two more, and then made directly and determinedly for Kreizler's box.

I found Laszlo already in it, studying the evening's program as he sat in one of the rear seats. 'My God!' I said, falling into a chair next to him without spilling a drop of my champagne. He put his program aside and rubbed his hands together, continuing to look much happier and healthier than he had during our last several encounters. He eyed my champagne. 'You appear to be well prepared for an evening among the wolves.'

'Yes, they're all out tonight, aren't they?' I said, scanning the Diamond Horseshoe. I started to move to a forward seat, but Kreizler held me back.

'If you wouldn't mind, Moore, I'd prefer that we sat in the back, tonight.' To my questioning look he answered, 'I'm in no mood to be scrutinized this evening.'

I shrugged and resettled myself next to him, then continued to investigate the audience, turning soon to box 35. 'Ah, I see Morgan's brought his wife. Some poor actress will be out a diamond bracelet or two tonight, I suspect.' I looked down at the sea of bobbing heads below us. 'Where in hell are they going to put all the people who are still outside – the orchestra seats are already full.'

'It'll be a miracle if we can even hear the performance,' Kreizler said, with a laugh that puzzled me – it wasn't the sort of thing he would usually have found amusing. 'The Astor box is so overloaded it looks as though it'll collapse, and the Rutherford boys were already too drunk to stand at seven-thirty!'

I'd taken out my folding glasses and was scrutinizing the other side of the horseshoe. 'Quite a gaggle of girls in the Clews' box,' I said. 'They don't look *precisely* like they came to hear Maurel. High-stakes husband-hunting, would be my guess.'

'The guardians of the social order,' Kreizler said, holding his right hand out toward the house with a sigh. 'On parade, and don't they make a sight!'

After giving Kreizler a baffled glance I said, 'You're in a rather bizarre mood – not drunk yourself, are you?'

'As sober as a judge,' Laszlo answered. 'Not that any of the judges *here* are sober. And let me hasten to add, Moore, in reply to that very concerned look on your face, that I have not taken leave of my senses, either. Ah, there's Roosevelt.' Kreizler held up his arm to wave, then winced a bit.

'Still giving you trouble?' I asked.

'Only occasionally,' he answered. 'It really wasn't much of a shot. I shall have to take that up with the man—' Kreizler seemed to catch himself as he glanced at me, and then he brightened deliberately. 'Someday. Now, tell me, John – where are the other members of the team at this moment?'

I could feel that the 'very concerned' look was still on my face, but at this last question I finally shrugged and let it go. 'They've gone up to High Bridge with the detectives,' I said. 'To get in position early.'

'High Bridge?' Kreizler repeated eagerly. 'Then they're expecting it to be High Bridge Tower?'

I nodded. 'That was our interpretation.'

Kreizler's eyes, quick and electric to that point, became positively brilliant with excitement. 'Yes,' he murmured. 'Yes, of course. It was the only other intelligent choice.'

'Other?' I said.

Shaking his head quickly he replied, 'Nothing of importance. You didn't tell them about our arrangement?'

'I told them where I was going,' I answered, a bit defensively. 'But I didn't tell them exactly why.'

'Excellent.' Kreizler sat back, looking deeply pleased. 'Then there's no way Roosevelt can know . . .'

'Know what?' I asked, starting to get that old familiar feeling that I'd walked into the wrong theater during the middle of a performance.

'Hmm?' Kreizler noised, as if barely conscious of my presence. 'Oh. I'll explain it later.' He pointed suddenly to the orchestra pit. 'Splendid – here's Seidl.'

484   Caleb Carr

Out to the podium strode the nobly profiled, long-haired Anton Seidl, once Richard Wagner's private secretary and now the finest orchestra leader in New York. His Roman nose graced by a pair of pince-nez that somehow managed to stay on their perch throughout the vigorous exertions that characterized his conducting style, Seidl commanded instant respect in the pit; and when he turned his stern glare on the audience many of the chattering society types also grew hushed and fearful for several minutes. But then the houselights went down and Seidl slashed into the powerful overture of *Don Giovanni*, at which the noise in the boxes began to grow again. Soon they were at a more annoying level than ever; Kreizler, however, continued to sit with a look of utter serenity on his face.

Indeed, for two and a half acts Laszlo endured that boorish audience's ignorance of the musical miracle that was taking place onstage with confounding equanimity. Maurel's singing and acting were as brilliant as ever, and his supporting cast – particularly Edouard de Reszke as Leporello – were superb; their only thanks, however, was the very occasional round of applause and ever more distracting talk and bustle in the house. Frances Saville's Zerlina was a thorough delight, though her singing talents did not stop the besotted Rutherford boys from cheering in a way that indicated that she was indistinguishable in their minds from the average Bowery concert hall dancer. During the intermissions the crowd behaved largely as it had before the performance – like a great herd of glittering jungle beasts – and by the time Vittorio Arimondi, playing the dead Commendatore, began to pound on Don Giovanni's door I was utterly sick of the general atmosphere and utterly bewildered as to why Kreizler had asked me to come.

I soon had the beginnings of an answer. Just as Arimondi swept onstage and held a statuesque finger out toward Maurel, with Seidl whipping the orchestra into a crescendo such as I have rarely heard, even at the Metropolitan, Laszlo calmly stood up, took a deep, satisfied breath, and touched my shoulder.

'All right, Moore,' he whispered. 'Let's go, shall we?'

'Go?' I said, getting up and stepping with him to the darkest recesses of the box. 'Go where? I'm supposed to meet Roosevelt after the performance.'

Kreizler didn't answer, but calmly opened the door to the saloon, out of which stepped Cyrus Montrose and Stevie Taggert. They were dressed in clothes that closely resembled Kreizler's and mine. I was surprised and very happy to see them both, especially Stevie. The boy looked quite recovered from the beating he'd taken at Connor's hands, though he was obviously uncomfortable in such attire, and not very happy to be at the opera.

'Don't worry, Stevie,' I said, taking a swipe at his shoulder. 'It's never been known to actually kill anyone.'

Stevie stuck a finger in his collar and tried to loosen the thing with a few tugs. 'What I wouldn't give for a cigarette,' he mumbled under his breath. 'Don't have one, do you, Mr. Moore?'

'Now, now, Stevie,' Kreizler said sternly, gathering up his cloak. 'We've discussed that.' He turned to Cyrus. 'You're clear on what to do?'

'Yes, sir,' Cyrus answered evenly. 'At the end of the performance Mr. Roosevelt will want to know where you've gone. I'll tell him I don't know. Then we're to bring the rig to the place you spoke of.'

'Taking—?' Kreizler asked leadingly.

'Taking an indirect route, in case we're followed.'

Laszlo nodded. 'Good. All right, Moore.'

As Kreizler slipped into the saloon, I looked back into the house and realized that no other members of the audience would have been able to see this exchange taking place – such was obviously why Laszlo had asked that we sit in the back of the box. Then, glancing at Stevie as he continued to suffer under the yolk of evening clothes, I had another realization: these two were supposed, by supplying vaguely similar silhouettes, to give the impression that Kreizler and I were still in the theater. But for what purpose? Where was Kreizler rushing off to? Questions continued to proliferate in my head, but the man with the answers was already on his way out of the building; and so, with Don Giovanni bellowing in horror as he descended into the

Caleb Carr

inferno, I followed Kreizler to the Broadway doors of the Metropolitan.

His mood, when I caught up to him, was one of exhilarated determination. 'We'll walk,' he said to the doorman outside, who then waved off a group of anxious cab drivers.

'Kreizler, damn it,' I said in exasperation, as I followed him to the corner of Broadway. 'You might at least tell me where we're going!'

'I should've thought you would have determined that by now,' he answered, waving me on. 'We're going to find Beecham.'

The words hit me rather hard, making it necessary for Laszlo to grab me by my lapel and pull me along. As I stumbled with him to the curb and then waited for the traffic to let us cross, Laszlo chuckled once. 'Don't worry, John,' he said, 'it's only a few blocks, but that should give us enough time to attend to all your questions.'

'A few blocks?' I said, trying to shake off my daze as we wound through horse manure and rolling carriages and finally got across Broadway. 'To High Bridge Tower? It's *miles* away!'

'I'm afraid Beecham won't be *at* High Bridge Tower tonight, Moore,' Kreizler answered. 'Our friends are destined for a rather frustrating vigil.'

As we proceeded down Thirty-ninth Street, the noise of Broadway faded behind us and our voices began to echo off the darkened row of houses that stretched on toward Sixth Avenue. 'And where the hell is he going to be, then?'

'You can determine that for yourself,' Kreizler answered, his stride picking up ever more speed. 'Remember what he left behind in his flat!'

'Laszlo,' I said angrily, grabbing his arm. 'I'm not out here to play games! You've got me abandoning people I've been working with for months, not to mention leaving Roosevelt fairly well in the lurch – so just stand still and tell me what the hell is going on!'

For a moment he managed to trade his enthusiasm for compassion. 'I'm sorry about the others, John – truly I am. If I could have thought of another way . . . But there isn't one. Please understand, if the police are at all involved in this it will result in

Beecham's death – I'm as certain of that as I am of anything. Oh, I don't mean that Roosevelt himself would play a part, but during the trip to the Tombs, or while he's in his cell, there will be an incident of some kind. A detective, or a guard, or some other prisoner, perhaps – probably claiming self-defense – will most assuredly put an end to the rather large set of problems that you and I have come to know as John Beecham.'

'But Sara,' I protested. 'And the Isaacsons. Surely they deserve—'

'I couldn't take that chance!' Kreizler declared, continuing east with insistent steps. 'They work for Roosevelt, they all owe their positions to him. I couldn't take the chance that they wouldn't tell him what I was planning. I couldn't even tell *you* all of it, because I knew you'd pledged to share everything you knew with Theodore – and you're not a man to break your word.'

That mollified me a bit, I must admit; but as I hustled to keep up with him, I continued to press hard for details. 'But what *are* you planning? And how the hell long have you been planning it?'

'Since the morning after Mary was killed,' he answered, with just a trace of bitterness. We came to another halt at the corner of Sixth Avenue, and Kreizler turned to me, the black eyes still gleaming. 'My initial withdrawal from the investigation was a purely emotional reaction, one that I probably would have reconsidered, in time. But on that morning I realized something – since *I* had become the main focus of our antagonists' attention, my withdrawal was likely to give the rest of you a free hand.'

I paused to consider that. 'And it did,' I judged after a few seconds. 'We never saw any of Byrnes's men again.'

'*I* did, however,' Kreizler answered. 'And still do. I've had quite a time, leading them around the city. It was absurd, really, but I stayed with it, trusting that the rest of you would be able to find a set of clues that would make a definite prediction of Beecham's next move possible.' As we started through the Sixth Avenue traffic, Laszlo held up his right hand, counting off considerations: 'I'd already made the same assumptions you had about the twenty-first of June – Saint John the Baptist's Day. That left the determination of victim and location in your hands.

I had great hopes that your young friend Joseph would give us help with the first of those questions—'

'He very nearly did,' I said, a now familiar pang of guilt and pain tugging at me. 'As it was, he gave us an idea of who the victim *wouldn't* be – we knew he didn't come from one of the disorderly houses, that he was a street cruiser.'

'Yes,' Laszlo said, as we got to the east side of the avenue. 'The boy did great service, and his death was a tragedy.' He hissed once, in deep remorse. 'There are moments when this entire case, when everything and everyone that comes into any kind of contact with the life of John Beecham seem destined for a tragic end . . .' His determination came suddenly bounding back: 'At any rate, what Joseph said about a "castle," from which the intended victim would be able to view the entire city, was an unqualified help – that is, when considered in conjunction with what you found at Beecham's flat. That really was a superb piece of work, by the way – your finding the place, I mean.'

I only nodded and smiled in appreciation, having by now abandoned any further attempt to question the course of action that Kreizler had evidently settled on for the evening. If such comparatively speedy acquiescence seems surprising, it must be remembered that for weeks I had worked without the benefit of Laszlo's friendship and guidance, and had often felt their absence keenly. To be once again walking purposefully by his side, to hear him dissecting the case in such a deliberate and confident manner, and, above all, to know that Sara, the Isaacsons, and I, along with the investigation itself, had been in his thoughts throughout the time we'd spent apart, all gave me a great deal of joy and relief. I knew that he was now working somewhat at cross-purposes with the rest of our team; and it was easy to see that his wild-eyed enthusiasm contained an unpredictable and perhaps uncontrollable element; but such considerations seemed to count for little as we made our way down Thirty-ninth Street. We were on the correct trail, I was certain of that much, and my own excitement soon made short work of the small, prudent voice in the back of my mind that said that we were only two, rushing in to perform a task that had originally been planned for scores.

I gave Kreizler a conspiratorial glance. 'When Roosevelt finds that we've left the opera,' I said, 'he'll tear the city apart looking for us.'

Laszlo shrugged. 'He'd be better off using his head. He has the clues he needs to determine our whereabouts.'

'The clues? You mean the things in Beecham's flat?' I grew puzzled yet again. 'But it was what we found there that led us to decide on High Bridge Tower – that and the business about a castle.'

'No, John,' Kreizler answered, his hands moving again as he spoke. 'It was *part* of what you found at Beecham's flat that led you to such a conclusion. Think again. What did he leave behind?'

I went over it in my mind. 'The collection of eyes . . . the map . . . and the box with the daguerreotype on it.'

'Correct. Now think what conscious or unconscious considerations caused him to leave only those things. The eyes tell you unmistakably that you have the right man. The map gives you a general idea of where he'll strike next. And the box—'

'The box tells us the same thing,' I interjected quickly. 'The daguerreotype lets us know that we've found Japheth Dury.'

'True,' Kreizler said emphatically, 'but what about the thing that's *in* the box?'

I wasn't following him. 'The heart?' I mumbled in confusion. 'It was an old, dried-up heart – you think it was his mother's.'

'Yes. Now, put the map and the contents of the box together.'

'The city water system . . . and the heart . . .'

'Now add what Joseph said.'

'A castle or a fort,' I answered, still not getting it. 'A place from which you can see the whole city.'

'*And* . . .?' Kreizler urged.

As we turned and began to walk up Fifth Avenue, the answer hit me like a cartload of bricks. Stretching away for two blocks to the north and one block to the west, its walls as high as the buildings around them and as prodigious as those of the fabled city of Troy, was the Croton Reservoir. Built in the Egyptian mausoleum style, it was indeed a castle-like fortress, on whose ramparts New Yorkers often strolled, enjoying the splendid,

Caleb Carr

panoramic views of the city (as well as of the man-made lake within) that the structure afforded. In addition, the Croton was the main distributing reservoir for all of New York; it was, quite simply, the *heart* of the city's water system, the center to which all aqueducts fed and from which all mains and arteries drew their supply. Astounded, I turned to Kreizler.

'Yes, John,' he said, smiling as we approached the thing. '*Here*.' Then he pulled me in close under the walls of the reservoir, which were deserted at that late hour, and lowered his voice. 'The rest of you no doubt discussed the possibility that Beecham *knows* our first move would be to watch the waterfronts – but in the absence of a suitable alternative, you remained focused on those areas.' Laszlo looked up and, for the first time that night, displayed some little bit of apprehension. 'If my guess is correct, he's up there now.'

'This early?' I asked. 'I thought you said—'

'Tonight is very different,' Kreizler answered quickly. 'Tonight he has set his table early, the better to be ready for his guests.' Reaching inside his cloak, Kreizler produced a Colt revolver. 'Take this, will you, Moore? But do *not* use it, unless you must. There is much I want to ask this man.'

Kreizler started to move toward the massive main gate and staircase of the reservoir, which strongly resembled the entrance-way to an Egyptian temple of the dead. Given our purpose that night, the similarity caused a strong shiver to rattle my bones. I stopped Laszlo as we neared the portal.

'One thing,' I whispered to him. 'You say Byrnes's men have been following you – how do you know they're not watching us now?'

There was something about the blank way in which he looked back at me that was deeply unsettling: like a man who has divined his fate and has no intention of trying to avoid it.

'Oh, I don't know that they're not,' he answered, quietly and simply. 'In fact, I'm counting on the fact that they are.'

With that, Laszlo entered the gate and took to the broad, dark stairs that wound up through the massive wall to the promenade. I shrugged helplessly at his cryptic words and was about to follow him, when a faint glimmer of brass somewhere on the other side of Fifth Avenue suddenly caught my eye. I stopped short and tried to locate the source.

On Forty-first Street, beneath one broad-boughed tree whose leaves provided an effective refuge from the glow of the arc streetlamps on the avenue, was an elegant black brougham, whose lanterns were glittering ever so slightly. Both horse and driver appeared to be asleep. For a moment the sense of dread that I felt about climbing the reservoir walls heightened dramatically; but then I shook it off and moved to catch up to Kreizler, telling myself that there had to be a great many people in New York besides Paul Kelly who owned elegant black broughams.

Chapter 44

As soon as we reached the top of the reservoir's walls I realized the potentially disastrous error I'd made in allowing Kreizler to talk me into coming to this place alone with him. The eight-foot-wide promenade atop the walls, ringed on either side by four-foot iron fences, was some six stories from the ground, and when I looked down I saw the streets from an angle that instantly recalled all the rooftop work we'd done in recent months. That reminder was forbidding enough on its own. But when I looked straight out and around me I saw the tar surfaces and multitudinous chimneys of the buildings that surrounded the reservoir, all of which made it even more plain that while we might not be standing on a rooftop *per se*, we had nonetheless reentered the lofty realm over which John Beecham was acknowledged master. We were in *his* world once again, only this time we'd arrived by way of a perverse invitation; and as we strode silently down toward the Fortieth Street side of the walls, the waters of the reservoir stretching out to our right and reflecting a bright moon that had suddenly appeared and was still ascendant in the clear night sky, it became apparent that our status as hunters was in very serious jeopardy: we were on the verge of becoming prey.

Familiar yet still troubling images began to flicker in my head like the projected films I'd seen at Koster and Bial's theater with

Mary Palmer: each of the dead boys, trussed and cut to pieces; the long, terrible knife that had done that cutting; the remains of the butchered cat at Mrs. Piedmont's; Beecham's bleak flat in Five Points, and the oven in which he claimed to have cooked the 'tender ass' of Georgio Santorelli; Joseph's lifeless body; and finally a picture of the killer himself, formed out of all the clues and theories we'd collected during our investigation, yet still, for all our work, no more than a vague silhouette. The infinite black sky and innumerable stars above the reservoir offered no comfort or refuge from these horrific visions, and civilization, as I once again glanced down toward the streets of the city, seemed terribly far away. Each of our careful footsteps tapped home the message that we had come to a lawless place of death, a place where the hopeful intervention of fearful man that I clutched in my hand would likely prove a feeble defense, and where the answers to greater mysteries than those we'd spent the last dozen weeks trying to unravel would be made plain with brutal finality. Despite all these anxious thoughts, however, I never once considered turning back. Perhaps Laszlo's conviction that we were going to end this business on those walls that night was infectious; whatever the reason, I didn't leave his side, even though I knew, as certainly as I've ever known anything, that we stood an excellent chance of never returning to the streets below.

We heard the sobbing before we saw the boy. There were no lights on the promenade, only the moon to guide us, and as we turned onto the Fortieth Street side of the pathway a one-story stone structure that had been built atop the walls to house the reservoir's control mechanisms loomed up spectrally in the distance. The sobs – high-pitched, desperate, and yet somehow muffled – seemed to be coming from somewhere near it. When we'd gotten to a point some forty-five feet from the structure, I caught a vague glimpse of human flesh glowing in the moonlight. We took a few steps closer, and then I made out plainly the figure of a naked young boy on his knees. His hands had been bound behind his back, causing his head to rest on the stone surface of the promenade, and his feet were similarly tied. A gag had been wrapped around his head, holding his

Caleb Carr

painted mouth open at a painful angle. His face was glistening with tears; but he was alive, and, just as surprisingly, he was alone.

Reflexively, I took a quick step forward, intending to help the unfortunate youth. Kreizler grabbed my arm and held me back, whispering urgently, 'No, John! That is exactly what he intends for you to do.'

'What?' I whispered back. 'But how do you know he's—'

Kreizler nodded, his eyes directing me toward the top of the control house.

Rising just above the roof of the thing and reflecting the soft light of the moon was the same balding head that I'd seen above Stephenson's Black and Tan the night that Cyrus was attacked. I felt my heart jump, but quickly sucked in air and tried to stay calm.

'Does he see us?' I whispered to Kreizler.

Laszlo's eyes had gone thin, but he betrayed no other reaction to the scene. 'Undoubtedly. The question is, does he know *we've* seen *him*?'

An answer came immediately: the head disappeared, the way an animal in the wild will do – completely and with astonishing speed. By now the bound boy had caught sight of us, and his stifled sobbing had changed to more emphatic sounds that, though incomprehensible as words, were plainly appeals for help. Another picture of Joseph appeared in my head, doubling my already driving desire to go and help this next intended victim. But Kreizler kept his grip on my arm.

'Wait, John,' he whispered. 'Wait.' There was a small doorway leading from the promenade into the control house, and Kreizler pointed at it. 'I was here this morning. There are only two ways out of that structure – back onto the promenade or down a flight of stairs to the street. If he doesn't appear . . .'

Another full minute went by with no sign of life either in the doorway or on the roof of the control house. Kreizler looked very puzzled. 'Is it possible he's run?'

'Maybe the risk of actually getting caught was too much for him,' I answered.

Kreizler weighed that, then studied the still-pleading boy. 'All right,' he finally decided. 'We'll approach, but very slowly. And keep that revolver handy.'

The first few steps we took down that stretch of the promenade were stiff and difficult, as if our bodies knew and were rejecting the danger that our minds had decided to accept. But after we'd covered ten feet or so without catching a glimpse of our antagonist we began to move more freely, and I became more convinced that Beecham had, in fact, been more intimidated by the prospect of capture than he had expected to be and fled to the street. I felt a sudden, powerful feeling of joy at the thought that we were actually going to prevent a killing, and allowed myself a small smile –

Hubris, as they say. Just as self-congratulation allowed my grip on the revolver to weaken ever so slightly, a dark form vaulted over the iron fence on the outer side of the promenade and laid a stunning blow across my jaw. I heard a thunderous crunching sound, which I now realize was made by the bones in my neck as my head snapped around, and then all was darkness.

I couldn't have been unconscious for very long, since the shadows thrown by the moon had not advanced significantly when I woke up; nonetheless, my head felt groggier than if I'd been asleep for days. As my vision cleared I became aware of several pains, some sharp and some dull, but all acute. There was my jaw, of course, and my neck. My wrists were burning, and my shoulders ached mightily; but the single most piercing discomfort came from under my tongue. I groaned as I tried to dislodge something from that area, then spat at the ground, producing one of my canine teeth, along with what seemed a quart of blood and saliva. My head felt like a solid block of Pittsburgh steel, and I couldn't lift it more than a few inches. Eventually I realized that this was due to more than the blow I'd received: my wrists were tied behind me to the top of the iron fence on the inner side of the promenade, and my ankles were similarly bound to the bottom of the iron divider, causing my head and upper body to hang out painfully over the stone pathway. Lying beneath my face on that surface was the Colt revolver I'd been holding.

I groaned again and kept trying to lift my head, finally

succeeding just enough to be able to turn and catch sight of Kreizler. He was similarly bound, though he seemed quite conscious and unharmed. He gave me a smile.

'Are you back, John?' he said.

'Uhhh,' was all I was able to say in response. 'Where's . . .'

With effort Kreizler nodded toward the control house.

The bound boy lay where we'd first seen him, though by now his urgent cries had reverted to fearful whimpers. Before him stood an enormous figure clad in unremarkable black clothing, whose back was to Kreizler and me. The man was slowly removing his garments and placing them neatly to one side of the promenade. In a few minutes he was entirely naked, revealing more than six feet of powerful muscles. He stepped forward to the boy – who, judging by the adult lines that were just beginning to show in the face and body, must've been about twelve – and picked his painted head up by the hair.

'Crying?' the man said, in a low, emotionless voice. 'A boy like you *ought* to cry . . .'

The man released the boy's head and then turned to face Kreizler and me. His anterior musculature was as fully developed as his posterior – from the shoulders down he was a remarkable physical specimen. I strained my neck to look up at his face, furrowing my brow as I did. I don't know precisely what I was expecting, but I certainly wasn't prepared for the banality of those features. There was something of Adam Dury in the way the skin was pulled tightly over the man's skull, as well as in the thinness of his hair. The eyes, too, were like his brother's, too small for the big, bony head in which they sat. The right side of the face drooped a bit, though it wasn't at that moment spasming, and the big jaw was set firmly; but all in all it was a common sort of face, one that exhibited no hint of the terrible turmoil that boiled without respite deep within the large head. He looked rather as though the construction of this horrendous scene was not altogether different from counting heads for the census.

That fact, I suddenly realized, was the most frightening thing I'd yet learned about John Beecham. In a very businesslike manner he bent down and took his enormous knife from out of his clothes, then walked over to where Kreizler and I were hanging. His chiseled body bore very little hair, allowing it to reflect the light of the moon brightly. He stood in a wide stance and leaned down to look first Kreizler and then me in the face.

'Only two,' he said, shaking his head. 'That was stupid – *stupid*.' He lifted the knife, which closely resembled the one that Lucius had shown us at Delmonico's, and pressed the flat of its blade against Laszlo's right cheek, letting it play languorously around the lines of my friend's face.

Laszlo watched Beecham's hand move, and then said cautiously, 'Japheth—'

Beecham growled viciously and then brought the back of his left hand hard across Laszlo's head. 'Don't you say that name!' He seethed violently. The knife went back under one of Laszlo's eyes, and Beecham pressed it firmly enough to bring a bead of blood from Laszlo's cheek. 'Don't you say that name ...' Beecham drew himself up and took a deep breath, as if he felt his outburst had been somewhat undignified.

'You've been looking for me,' he said – and then, for the first time, he smiled, showing huge, yellowing teeth. 'You've been trying to watch me, but I've been watching you.' The smile vanished as quickly as it had appeared. 'You want to watch?' He indicated the boy with his knife. 'Then watch. He dies first. *Cleanly*. Not you, though. You're stupid and worthless – you couldn't even stop me. Stupid, worthless animals – you I'll dress *alive*.'

As he strode back to the boy I whispered to Kreizler. 'What's he going to do?'

Laszlo was still shaking off the effects of the blow he'd taken. 'I believe,' he answered, 'that he intends to kill that boy. And I believe he intends for us to observe it. After which ...'

I saw that a small stream of blood was running down Kreizler's cheek and jaw. 'You all right?' I asked.

'Ah,' Laszlo noised in reply, showing remarkably little concern over our prospective fates, 'it's the stupidity that hurts the most. We chase a man who's an expert mountaineer, and then we're surprised when he negotiates a simple masonry wall to get behind us . . .'

Beecham was by now crouching over the bound boy. 'Why did he take off his clothes?' I asked.

Laszlo studied our attacker for a moment. 'The blood,' he said at length. 'He wants to keep it off his clothes.'

Having put his knife aside for a moment, Beecham began to run his hands over the young, writhing body before him.

'But is that, in fact, the only reason?' Laszlo went on, some surprise showing in his voice.

Beecham's face continued to betray no sign of anger or lust or any other feeling. He probed the boy's torso and limbs as an anatomy instructor might have done, pausing only when he laid hands on the young genitals. After fondling them for a few minutes he stood and stepped behind the boy, stroking the up-turned buttocks with one hand and his own member with the other.

I grew sickened at the thought of what I believed must come next, and turned away. 'But I thought—' My quiet mumble was almost a protest. 'I thought he didn't rape them.'

Laszlo continued to observe. 'That may not mean that he hasn't tried to,' he judged. 'This is a complex moment, John. He claimed in his note that he didn't "soil" the boys. But did he try?'

I picked my head back up to see Beecham still stroking the boy and himself, failing to produce an erection in his own organ. 'Well,' I said in disgust, 'if he wants to do it why—'

'Because he *doesn't*, in fact, want to,' Kreizler replied, his already strained neck straining further to nod his head as he began to fully comprehend what was happening. 'He feels an obsessive force pushing him toward it, as toward the killing – but it isn't desire. And while he can force himself to kill, he can't force himself to rape.'

As if in response to Laszlo's analysis of the scene, Beecham suddenly howled in deep-seated frustration, raising his thick arms to the heavens and shaking throughout his body. Then he looked down again, stepped quickly around to the boy's front end once more, and slipped his long-fingered hands around the young throat.

'No!' Kreizler suddenly called. 'No, Japheth, for God's sake, it isn't what you want to—'

'*Don't say that name!*' Beecham shouted again, as the boy squealed and twisted madly in his grip. 'I'll kill you, you filthy—'

Suddenly, from my left, a somehow familiar voice came out of the darkness:

'You ain't killing anybody, you miserable bastard.'

Sore as my neck was, it turned quickly to catch sight of Connor, walking down the promenade and holding an impressive Webley .445 revolver. Behind him came two figures who had by now taken on the status of old acquaintances: the same thugs who'd come after Sara and me in the Santorellis' tenement, who'd dogged Laszlo's and my steps during our trip to visit Adam Dury, and whom I'd unceremoniously ejected from the Boston–New York train.

Connor's shifty eyes went thin as he stepped toward Beecham. 'You hear me? Get the hell away from that kid.'

Very slowly, Beecham released his grip on the boy. His face became an absolute blank, and then it changed dramatically: for the first time an emotion – terrible fear – became apparent in the widening of the eyes. Just when it seemed that those organs could open no further, they began to blink, rapidly and uncontrollably.

'Connor!' I said, finally overcoming my astonishment. Turning to Laszlo for an explanation, I saw him eyeing our apparent rescuer with a look of both hatred and satisfaction.

'Yes,' Laszlo said evenly. 'Connor . . .'

'Get those two down,' Connor said to one of his men, as he leaned over to pick up Kreizler's Colt. He kept the Webley trained on Beecham as the man to his right moved somewhat grudgingly to free first Laszlo and then me. 'And you,' Connor said to the cowering murderer. 'Get your fucking clothes on, you blasted sodomite.'

But Beecham made no move to comply. His expression became more fearful, he huddled closer to the wall – and then the spasming began. Initially it was slow, involving only the blinking of the eyes and a tug at the right corner of the mouth; but soon the entire right side of the face was contracting

Caleb Carr

violently and at a quick clip, producing a pathetic effect that I must admit would have seemed, under other circumstances, cruelly laughable.

As he watched this transformation take place, a look of blatant disgust came into Connor's bearded face. 'My God,' he said. 'You sick, miserable bastard . . .' He turned to the man on his left. 'Mike – cover him up, for God's sake.' The man went over, picked up Beecham's clothes and threw them at him. Beecham grabbed the garments and held them close, but didn't try to dress himself.

Once Laszlo and I were back standing on the promenade we both spent a few seconds trying to loosen up our painfully cramped arms and shoulders, while Connor's thugs went over to stand behind their chief again.

'Aren't you going to untie the boy?' Laszlo said, his voice still marked by harsh bitterness.

Connor shook his head. 'Let's get a few things straight, first, Doctor,' he said, as if, despite the Webley, he was afraid of what Kreizler might do. 'Our business is with this one here' – he indicated Beecham – 'and only with him. You get on out of here and there'll be nothing more to it. The whole business ends tonight.'

'Indeed it does,' Laszlo replied. 'But not in the way that you anticipate, I'm afraid.'

'Meaning?' Connor asked.

'Meaning that our leaving is out of the question,' Kreizler answered. 'You made it so when you fouled my home with your murderous presence.'

Connor shook his head quickly. 'Now, just you wait, Doctor – I wanted none of that! I was doing my job, following the orders I'd been given, and that little bitch—' Kreizler's face betrayed open rage and he took half a step forward. Connor gripped the Webley tighter. 'Don't do it, Doctor – don't give me a reason. Like I say, we're only here to do this one, but you know full well I'd be happy to make it the three of you. That might not please my bosses – but if you give me cause, so help me, I'll shoot you down.'

For the first time, Beecham seemed to fix his attention on what was happening around him. His face still spasming, he turned to look at Connor and his thugs; then, in a sudden flurry, he scurried over near Laszlo's legs.

'They—' he said tremulously. 'They're going – going to kill me.'

Connor chuckled once gruffly. 'Yes, it's dead you'll be when they take you off this wall, you damned fool butcher. All of this trouble over you, and what are you? A poor excuse for a man, with your whining and crawling.' Connor began to swagger a bit in front of his cohorts. 'Hard to believe, ain't it, fellas? That – *thing* there is what this has all been about. Just because his idea of fun is to fuck little boys and then cut them up.'

'*Liar!*' Beecham suddenly bellowed, balling his fists but staying in a crouching stance. 'You filthy liar!'

At that, Connor and his men began to laugh, exacerbating Beecham's emotional turmoil. As the mocking howls went on, I walked over to stand by Beecham without knowing why, then gave the three laughing fools in front of me a disapproving scowl that produced no effect. Turning to Kreizler in hope of getting some guidance, I saw that he was staring down the promenade past Connor and his men, his face a picture of anticipation. His mouth fell open, and for no reason that I could divine he suddenly shouted:

'*Now!*'

And then all hell broke loose. With the speed and precision that only years of professional training can breed, an ape of a man leapt up and over the inner promenade fence and crushed Connor's gun-wielding hand with a stout section of lead pipe. Before the other two thugs could react several lightning combinations of blows from two enormous fists laid them both out on the promenade. The howling Connor soon shared the same fate. Then, just for good measure, the newcomer – his face hidden under a miner's cap – leaned over each man's head in succession and delivered a series of resounding blows with the lead pipe. It was a clinic in violence that was awesome to behold – but my joy at the attack faded considerably when the performer stood up and finally revealed himself.

Caleb Carr

It was Eat-'Em-Up Jack McManus, former prizefighter and current enforcer of decorum at Paul Kelly's New Brighton Dance Hall. Tucking his piece of pipe into his pants, McManus picked up both the Colt and the Webley and then stepped toward me. I braced myself, reasonably calculating that Laszlo and I would be the next victims of his pugilistic artistry; instead, McManus straightened his shabby jacket, spat hard into the waters of the reservoir, and handed me the guns. I trained the Colt on Beecham as Jack slowly walked up to Kreizler, raised a hand, and touched the brim of his cap respectfully.

'Well done, Jack,' Laszlo said, at which I almost hit the pathway beneath me in a dead faint. 'Bind them, if you would, and gag the two bigger men. The one in the middle I'll want to talk to when he comes around.' Laszlo studied Connor's body, evidently impressed by McManus's work. 'Or perhaps I should say, *if* he comes around . . .'

McManus touched his cap again, crossed back in front of me, then produced several lengths of rope and two handkerchiefs and carried out Laszlo's instructions like a patient, laboring ox. Kreizler, in the meantime, went quickly to the bound boy, and began to free his mouth, hands, and feet.

'It's all right,' Laszlo said soothingly, as the youth continued to sob and whimper uncontrollably. 'It's all right, you're quite safe now.'

The boy looked up at Laszlo, eyes wide with terror. 'He was going to . . .'

'What he was going to do is no longer important,' Laszlo answered with a small smile, producing a handkerchief and wiping the boy's face. 'What *is* important is that you're safe. Here—' Laszlo retrieved his somewhat mangled opera cloak from the promenade and wrapped it around the shaking young man.

With everything under control, at least for the moment, I satisfied my curiosity by approaching the fence on the street side of the promenade and taking a quick look over it. A few feet below, strung before our arrival and held in place by climbing pitons much like the one that Marcus had found at Castle Garden, was a length of stout rope. As Kreizler had suspected, getting around and behind us had been no great job for an experienced climber like Beecham. I turned back around and looked at our now beaten foe, shaking my head at the sudden, baffling way in which the tide had turned.

Jack McManus had finished the job of binding Connor's men, and he looked to Kreizler expectantly. 'Well, Jack,' Laszlo said. 'All secure? Good. We won't be needing you further. But again – my thanks.'

McManus touched his cap one last time, then turned and strode back down the dark promenade without saying a word.

Kreizler turned to the boy again. 'Let's get you inside, shall we? Moore, I'm just going to put our young friend here in the control house.'

I nodded, keeping the Colt leveled at Beecham's head as Laszlo and the boy disappeared inside. Still huddling and spasming, Beecham had begun to let out a quick, guttural little whimper of his own. It didn't appear that he'd give me any trouble, but I wasn't taking any chances. Quickly scanning the area, I saw his knife lying on the pathway, and moved to pick it up and tuck it into the back of my own pants. Glancing at the unconscious Connor, I noticed that he had a pair of manacles clipped to his belt. I retrieved them and tossed them to Beecham.

'Here,' I said. 'Get these on.'

Slowly and absentmindedly, Beecham fit the manacles around his wrists, closing first one and then the other with some difficulty. I searched Connor's pockets and found the key to the restraints, after which I noticed that there was a small bloodstain on Connor's shirt. Unbuttoning the dirty garment and then pulling it aside, all the while keeping my gun on Beecham, I saw that Connor had a long, half-healed wound in his side, which had apparently been torn back open by Jack McManus. It was the injury, I realized, that Mary Palmer had inflicted before Connor had flung her down Kreizler's stairs.

'Good for you, Mary,' I said softly, standing away from Connor.

Kreizler came back out of the control house, running a hand through his hair and surveying the scene before him with

Caleb Carr

evident, if rather amazed, satisfaction. Then he looked my way self-consciously, as if he knew what was coming.

'You,' I said, evenly but very firmly, 'are going to tell me what in hell is going on around here!'

Chapter 45

Laszlo had just opened his mouth to reply when the sound of a sharp whistle echoed up from Fortieth Street. Kreizler ran to peer over the street-side fence of the promenade, and I quickly joined him, looking down to see Cyrus and Stevie in the calash.

'I fear that explanations will have to wait, Moore,' Kreizler said, turning toward Beecham again. 'Cyrus and Stevie's arrival means that the opera has been over for at least three-quarters of an hour. By now Roosevelt's suspicions have been thoroughly aroused. He'll have checked with the others at High Bridge Tower, and when they learn of our disappearance ...'

'But what do you plan to do?' I asked.

Kreizler scratched his head and smiled a bit. 'I'm not terribly sure. My plans didn't quite provide for this situation – I wasn't entirely certain that I'd still be alive, even given our friend McManus.'

That stung me, and I didn't mind showing it: 'Oh,' I huffed, 'and I suppose I would have been dead, too!'

'Please, Moore,' Kreizler said, waving his hand impatiently. 'There simply isn't time.'

'But what about Connor?' I demanded, pointing to the former detective's prostrate form.

'We shall hold Connor for Roosevelt,' Laszlo replied sharply, crossing over to where Beecham sat huddled. 'Though he deserves far worse!' Crouching down to stare Beecham in the face, Laszlo drew a deep breath to calm himself, then held a hand in front of our prisoner's eyes and moved it back and forth. Beecham seemed utterly oblivious.

'The boy has come down from the mountains,' Kreizler mused at length. 'Or so it would seem.' I took his point: if the man we'd first encountered on the walls that night had been the evolved version of the cool, sadistic young trapper who'd once roamed the Shawangunks, then the terrified creature now before us was the inheritor of all the terror and self-loathing that Japheth Dury had felt at every other moment of his life. Evidently aware that there was little to fear from the man so long as he was in this mental state, Laszlo took Beecham's jacket from him and draped it around the man's huge, bare shoulders. 'Listen to me, Japheth Dury,' Kreizler said, in an ominous tone that got Beecham to finally stop swaying and moaning. 'You've a great deal of blood on your hands. That of your parents, not least of all. Should your crimes become known, your brother, Adam – who is still alive and still attempting to carry on an honest, decent life – will most certainly be privately destroyed and publicly hounded. For that if for no other reason, the part of you that is still human must pay close attention to me.'

Though Beecham's eyes remained quite glassy, he nodded slowly. 'Good,' Laszlo said. 'The police will be here soon. They may or may not find you waiting when they arrive, depending on just how honest you are with me. I'm going to ask you just a few questions now to determine your ability, as well as your willingness, to cooperate. Answer these questions truly and we may be able to arrange a less severe fate than that which the people of this city will demand. Do you understand?' Beecham nodded again, and Kreizler produced his ubiquitous little notebook and a pen. 'All right, then. The basic facts . . .'

Laszlo then launched into a fast, condensed, yet calmly worded review of Beecham's life, beginning with his childhood as Japheth Dury and going into some detail concerning the murder of his parents. As Beecham answered these queries, all the while confirming more and more of the hypotheses that we'd formulated during our investigation, his tone became increasingly weak and helpless, as if in the presence of this man who somehow knew him as well as he knew himself there was no choice other than complete submission. For his part, Kreizler became ever more satisfied by Beecham's earnest attempts to cooperate with his inquisition, finding in them proof positive that a hidden yet still strong part of the murderer's mind had indeed craved this moment.

I suppose that I, too, should have been deeply gratified at the results of this initial interview; yet as I watched Beecham answer Laszlo's questions – his voice growing ever more compliant and even childish, with none of the threatening, arrogant tone he'd used when we were his prisoners – I became powerfully irritated, disturbed at the very core of my spirit. This irritation soon became outrage, as if this man had no right to exhibit any pitiable human qualities in light of all he'd done. Who was this enormous grotesque, I thought, to sit there confessing and sniveling like one of the children he'd slaughtered? Where was all the violence, cruelty, arrogance, and unstoppability that he'd displayed on other nights? As these and similar questions shot through my head, my anger mounted rapidly, until suddenly, unable to contain the feeling any longer, I stood up straight and bellowed:

'Shut up! Shut the hell up, you miserable coward!'

Both Beecham and Laszlo immediately grew silent and looked up at me in shock. Beecham's facial spasms intensified dramatically as he eyed the Colt in my hand, while Laszlo's attitude soon changed from one of stunned surprise to chastising comprehension.

'All right, Moore,' he said, not asking for an explanation. 'Go and wait inside with the boy, then.'

'And leave you with him?' I said, my voice still trembling with anger and passion. 'Are you insane? Look at him, Kreizler, – this is *him*, this is the man who's responsible for all the blood we've seen! And you sit here letting him convince you that he's some kind of—'

'John!' Kreizler said, stopping me. '*All right*. Go and wait for me inside.'

I looked past Kreizler at Beecham. 'Well? What *are* you trying to convince him of?' I leaned down, keeping the Colt pointed at

Beecham's head. 'Figure you can still get out of it, don't you?'

'Damn it, Moore!' Kreizler said, grabbing my wrist but unable to make me move the gun away. 'Stop!'

I drew closer to Beecham's spasming face. 'My friend thinks that if you aren't afraid to die it's proof that you're crazy,' I seethed. With Laszlo still trying to disarm me, I shoved the barrel of the revolver up against Beecham's throat. 'Are you afraid to die – *are you*? To die, like the boys you—'

'Moore!' Kreizler shouted again.

But I was far past listening. Struggling to get my thumb on the hammer of the Colt, I pulled it back in a jerk, causing Beecham to let out a desperate little cry and then pull back from me like a trapped animal. 'No,' I seethed at him. 'No, you're not crazy – you *are* afraid to die!'

With stunning suddenness, the air all around us was consumed by a gunshot. A resonant, slapping sort of impact sounded from somewhere just under my hand, and then Beecham rocked backward in a jerk, revealing a crimson-black hole in the left side of his chest that wheezed with the sound of escaping air. Fixing his small, straining eyes on me Beecham let his manacled hands fall and then slumped over, his jacket falling from his shoulders as he did.

I've killed him, I thought clearly. There was neither joy nor guilt in the realization, just a simple acknowledgment of fact – but then, after Beecham had crumpled to the stone pathway, my gaze fell on the hammer of my Colt: it was still cocked. Before I could get my confused brain to make any sense of this sight, Laszlo had jumped over to Beecham and made a cursory examination of the bullet wound. Shaking his head as the unpleasant sound of gushing air and blood continued to come out of Beecham's chest, Laszlo made a fist and looked up furiously. His glare, however, was directed past me; and following it, I turned around slowly.

Connor had somehow slipped his bonds, and was standing in the center of the promenade. His back was bent with dizziness and pain, and he was clutching his bleeding side with his left hand as he held a small, crude twin-barreled pistol with the other. A twisted smile came into his bleeding mouth, and then he staggered forward a step or two.

'It ends tonight,' he said, holding the gun higher and pointing it at us. 'Drop it, Moore.'

I complied, slowly and carefully; but just as the Colt touched the pathway another gunshot cut through the air – this one from farther off – and then Connor jerked forward as if he'd been struck hard in the back. He fell on his face with a small grunt, revealing a hole in his jacket out of which blood began to pump immediately. The powder smoke from the shot Connor had fired at Beecham had not even cleared when a new figure stepped forward on the dark promenade and became visible in the moonlight.

It was Sara, pearl-gripped revolver in hand. She stared down at Connor for an instant without betraying any emotion, then looked up at Kreizler and me.

'I thought of this place just after we'd gotten into position at High Bridge Tower,' she said tightly, as the Isaacsons appeared in the darkness behind her. 'When Theodore said you'd left the opera, I knew . . .'

I let out an enormous breath. 'And thank God you did,' I said, wiping my brow with my hand and then picking up the Colt.

Laszlo stayed in a crouch by Beecham, but looked up at Sara. 'And where is the commissioner?'

'Out searching,' Sara said. 'We didn't tell him.'

Laszlo nodded. 'Thank you, Sara. You had little reason for such consideration.'

Sara's expression remained impassive. 'You're right.'

Beecham suddenly let out with a bloody, choking cough, and Kreizler got an arm under his neck, bringing the large head up. 'Detective Sergeant?' Laszlo said, at which Lucius rushed over to assist him.

Taking a quick look at Beecham's chest, Lucius shook his head definitively. 'It's no good, Doctor.'

'Yes, yes, I know,' Kreizler snapped. 'I just need – rub his hands, will you? Moore, get those blasted manacles off. I just need a few minutes.' As I freed the dying man's hands Laszlo reached into his pocket, brought out a small vial of ammonia salts, and wafted them under Beecham's nose. Lucius began to

Caleb Carr

slap and rub at Beecham's palms, while Laszlo's aspect became steadily more concerned and his movements steadily more agitated, until they reached a level of near desperation. 'Japheth,' he began to murmur, softly but pleadingly. 'Japheth Dury, can you hear me?'

Beecham's eyelids fluttered for an instant and then opened, the dulling orbs beneath them rolling helplessly about in his head. Finally he fixed them on the face that was very close to his own. He wasn't spasming, now, and his expression was that of a terrified child who looks to a stranger for help that he somehow knows he isn't going to get.

'I—' he gasped, coughing up a little more blood. 'I'm – going to die . . .'

'Listen to me, Japheth,' Laszlo said, wiping blood from the man's mouth and face as he continued to cradle the head. 'You must listen to me – what did you see, Japheth? What did you see when you looked at the children? What made you kill them?'

Beecham's head began to shake from side to side quickly, and then a shudder went through his body. He turned his terrified gaze to the heavens and opened his jaw wider, revealing the big teeth, which were now coated with blood.

'Japheth!' Laszlo repeated, sensing that the man was slipping away. '*What did you see?*'

As his head continued to shake, Beecham's eyes shifted back to Laszlo's pleading face. 'I – have never known—' he gasped, the tone both apologetic and pleading. 'I – have never – known! I – didn't – they—'

The shaking in his face spread throughout his body for an instant, and then he grabbed Laszlo by the shirt. Face still full of mortal fear, John Beecham spasmed one final time, spat some blood mixed with vomit out one side of his mouth, and grew still. His head rolled away from Kreizler, the eyes finally losing their expression of terror.

'Japheth!' Kreizler said once more; but he knew it was too late. Lucius reached up and closed Beecham's eyes, at which Kreizler finally lowered the dead man's head back down to the cold stone beneath it.

No one spoke for a minute or two, and then there was a sound:

The Alienist

another whistle from below. I stood up, moved to the outer promenade fence, and looked down to Cyrus and Stevie, who were pointing toward the West Side urgently. I waved to them in acknowledgment and then went to Kreizler.

'Laszlo,' I said carefully, 'offhand I'd say Roosevelt's on his way. You'd better get ready to explain—'

'No.' Though Kreizler did not lift his head, his voice was firm. 'I won't be here.' When he finally sat up straight and looked around, I could see that his eyes were red and moist. He looked from me to Sara, then at Marcus, and finally to Lucius, nodding as he did. 'You have all given me your help and your friendship – perhaps more of each than I've been entitled to. But I must ask that you continue to do so for just a little while longer.' Standing up, Kreizler spoke to Lucius and Marcus. 'Detective Sergeants? I'll need your assistance in removing Beecham's body. You say Roosevelt's coming by way of Fortieth Street, John?'

'I'd say so,' I answered, 'based on the way those two are carrying on down there.'

'Very well, then,' Kreizler went on. 'When he arrives, Cyrus will direct him up here. The detective sergeants and I will take the body out through the Fifth Avenue gate' – Laszlo walked to the street-side fence and issued a command by waving one hand – 'where Stevie will be waiting.' He stepped over to Sara and took her by the shoulders. 'I wouldn't blame you if you refused to be any part of this, Sara.'

She looked for a moment as if she were about to erupt with a spiteful indictment – but then she simply shrugged and put her pistol away in a fold of her dress. 'You haven't been honest with us about this part of it, Doctor,' she said. Her hard look softened. 'But if it hadn't been for you we never would have had the chance in the first place. I'm prepared to call it even.'

Laszlo pulled her close and embraced her. 'Thank you for that,' he murmured, and then stepped back. 'Now, then – in the control house you will find a rather terrified boy wrapped in a fairly decent cloak of mine. Go to him, would you, and see to it that Roosevelt asks him no questions before we've had time to get downtown.'

'Downtown?' I said, as Sara moved toward the control house

Caleb Carr

doorway. 'Wait a minute, Kreizler—'

'There's no *time*, John,' Laszlo said, moving toward Marcus and speaking to both him and Lucius. 'Detective Sergeants? The commissioner is your superior, and I will understand if—'

'You don't have to ask, Doctor,' Lucius answered before Laszlo could finish. 'I think I know what you've got in mind. I'll be curious to see how it turns out.'

'You shall see for yourself,' Kreizler answered. 'I intend that you shall assist me.' He turned to the taller Isaacson. 'Marcus? If you wish to exempt yourself, I shall more than understand.'

Marcus weighed Kreizler's words for a moment. 'It's really the only riddle left to solve, isn't it, Doctor?' he asked.

Kreizler nodded. 'Perhaps the most important.'

Marcus took a moment more, then gave a nod of his own. 'All right. What's a little departmental subordination against the interests of science?'

Laszlo clasped his shoulder. 'Good man.' Returning to Beecham's body, Kreizler grabbed one of the dead arms. 'All right, then – let's proceed, and quickly.'

Marcus got hold of Beecham's feet, and Lucius draped some of the dead man's clothes over the torso before taking hold of the remaining limb. Then they lifted the body, Kreizler wincing in some pain as he did, and started down the promenade toward Fifth Avenue.

The prospect of being left up on those walls with no one but two unconscious thugs and Connor's body to keep me company put new life into my movements and my mouth. 'Wait a minute,' I said, following the others. 'Wait just a goddamned minute! Kreizler! I know what you're up to! But you can't leave me here and expect me to—'

'No time, John!' Kreizler answered, as he and the labouring Isaacsons picked up speed. 'I'll need six hours or so – all will become clear then!'

'But I—'

'You are a true stalwart, Moore!' Kreizler called.

At that I stopped, watching them fade into the deep blue of the promenade and then vanish into the blackness of the Fifth Avenue staircase. 'Stalwart,' I mumbled, kicking at the ground and turning back around. '*Stalwarts* don't get left behind to explain this kind of mess—'

I ceased my little monologue when I heard a commotion inside the control house: Sara's voice, followed by Theodore's. They exchanged a few heated words, and then Roosevelt burst out onto the promenade, followed by Sara and several men in uniform.

'So!' Theodore boomed when he caught sight of me. He began to approach, holding up a thick, accusatory finger. 'This is my payment for entering into an agreement with what I mistakenly took to be gentlemen! By thunder, I ought to—'

He stopped suddenly when he saw the two bound thugs and the one corpse. Glancing from the ground to me twice in bewilderment, Theodore directed his finger downward. 'Is that *Connor*?'

I nodded and approached, quickly putting my anger with Kreizler aside and then feigning great anxiety. 'Yes, and you're just in time, Roosevelt. We came here looking for Beecham—'

Righteous indignation came back into Theodore for a moment. 'Yes, I know,' he bellowed, 'and if a pair of my best men hadn't followed Kreizler's servants—'

'But Beecham never showed,' I went on. 'It was a trap, set by Connor. He was out to – to kill Stevie, actually.'

'*Stevie?*' Roosevelt echoed incredulously. 'Kreizler's boy?'

I looked at him with deep earnestness. 'Roosevelt, Stevie was the only witness to Connor's murder of Mary Palmer.'

Theodore's face opened up with comprehension, his eyes going wide behind the spectacles. 'Ah!' he noised, now pointing his finger upward. 'Of course!' The brow wrinkled again. 'But what happened?'

'Fortunately, Commissioner,' Sara said, having correctly perceived that my powers of invention were weakening, 'the detective sergeants and I arrived in time.' She indicated the body with more confidence and certainty than I knew she felt. 'That's a bullet of mine you'll find in Connor's back.'

'*Yours*, Sara?' Theodore said incredulously. 'But I don't understand.'

'Neither did we,' Sara said, 'until you brought us wind of what

Caleb Carr

John and the doctor were up to. Although by the time we figured out where they were likely to be, you'd already left High Bridge Tower. But if I were you, Commissioner, I'd get back up there – the rest of your detectives are still on watch, and the killer hasn't struck yet.'

'Yes,' Theodore said, considering it all. 'Yes, I suppose you're right about—' He suddenly stood up straight, smelling the ruse. 'Just a moment. I see what we have here. If all that's true, then kindly tell me this – who is that boy in there?' He pointed his finger at the control house.

'Honestly, Roosevelt,' I insisted, 'you'd better—'

'And where are the rest of them – Kreizler and the Isaacsons?'

'Commissioner,' Sara said, 'I can tell you—'

'Oh, yes,' Roosevelt answered, waving us off. 'I can see what sort of thing's happening here. Conspiracy, is it? That'll be fine! I'm delighted to oblige! Sergeant!' One of the men in uniform snapped to and approached. 'Have one of your men take charge of that boy in there – and then place both of these people under arrest! I want them taken to Mulberry Street immediately!' Before Sara and I could say anything in response, Theodore brought the finger around once more and wagged it in our faces. 'I'm going to give you two a very unpleasant reminder of just who's in charge of the Police Department in this city!'

Chapter 46

It was all so much hot air, of course. Oh, Roosevelt dragged us down to Mulberry Street, all right, and locked us up for a few hours in his office, where we got one hell of a lecture about honor and trust and living up to one's word; but eventually I told him the truth about what had happened that night, although not until I was fairly sure that Kreizler and the Isaacsons had had enough time to get where they were going. I explained to Theodore that I hadn't really lied to him, since I myself hadn't known what was going on before I showed up at the opera; indeed, I said, I *still* didn't have explanations for many of the things that had happened up on the reservoir walls, although I intended to get them. And I promised that as soon as I did, I'd come straight to Mulberry Street and share the information. Roosevelt calmed down considerably as I was saying all this; and when Sara pointed out that the important thing, about which there could be no doubt, was that Beecham was dead, Theodore's mood began to brighten considerably. As he'd told us several weeks earlier, the successful conclusion of the case meant a great deal to him personally (although, given the affair's many complexities, he'd never be able to make much hay out of it professionally); and by the time Sara and I finally got up to leave his office, at about four o'clock, Theodore had traded criticism of some of that night's developments for characteristically effusive praise of our team's work as a whole.

'Unconventional, without doubt,' he clicked, putting a hand on each of our shoulders as he walked us out, 'but, all in all, a magnificent effort. Magnificent. Think of it – a man with no connection to his victims, a man who could have been anyone in this city, identified and stopped.' He shook his head with an appreciative sigh. 'No one would ever believe it. And to get Connor in the bargain!' I saw Sara wince just a bit at that; but she worked hard to conceal the reaction. 'Yes, I will very much enjoy hearing just how our friend Kreizler cooked up that last part of his scheme.' Theodore rubbed his jowl and stared at the floor for a few seconds, then looked up at us again. 'Well, then – what will you all do now?'

It was a simple question, yet one whose implications were, I suddenly discovered, thoroughly unpleasant. 'What will we—?' I echoed. 'Well, we – that is – I don't really know. There are – details to tie up.'

'Of course,' Roosevelt answered. 'But, I mean to say, the case is over – you've won!' He turned to Sara, as if expecting agreement.

She nodded slowly, looking as confused and uncomfortable as I felt. 'Yes,' she finally managed to say, in the face of Theodore's expectant expression.

There followed a long, peculiar pause, during which the vague but unsettling emotion that had been produced by the thought of the case being over took a stronger hold on each of us. In an attempt to banish it, Theodore changed the subject deliberately.

'At any rate,' he said, with a slap of his hands to his chest, 'a fortunate and intriguing end. Timely, as well. I leave tomorrow for Saint Louis.'

'Ah, yes,' I said, happy to talk about something else. 'The convention. It'll be McKinley, I take it?'

'On the first ballot,' Theodore replied with mounting gusto. 'The convention is merely a formality.'

I gave him a needling smile. 'Picked out a house in Washington yet?'

As always, Theodore grew stormy at any suggestion that he indulged in ambitious maneuvering; but then, remembering that I was an old friend who would never have questioned his basic motives, he let the storm pass. 'Not quite. By thunder, though, what possibilities! Perhaps the Navy Department will—'

Sara let out a sudden, uncontrollable laugh, then covered her mouth quickly. 'Oh,' she said. 'I am sorry, Commissioner. It's just that — well, I never would have thought of you as a *Navy* man.'

'Yes, Roosevelt,' I added, 'when you come right down to it, what in the world do you know about naval matters?'

'Why,' he answered indignantly, 'I wrote a book on the naval war of 1812 – it was very well received!'

'Ah, well,' I answered, nodding, 'that does make all the difference.'

Theodore's smile returned. 'Yes, Navy's the place to be. From there we can start planning for a reckoning with those blasted Spaniards! Why—'

'Please,' I cut in, holding up a hand. 'I don't want to know.'

Sara and I moved to the staircase while Theodore stood in the doorway of his office with his hands on his hips. As always his energy seemed not in the least diminished by a long night of activity, and his beacon of a smile was still visible when we reached the end of the dark hall.

'Don't want to know?' Theodore shouted after us merrily as we started down the stairs. 'But you could come along! Why, with the work you people have done, the Spanish empire shouldn't represent any great challenge! Come to think of it, there's an idea in that – the psychology of the king of Spain! Yes, bring your chalkboard to Washington and we'll decide just the right way to thrash him!'

His voice finally became inaudible as we left the building.

Sara and I walked the short block over to Lafayette Place, still in a kind of shock that prevented our going back over the conclusion of the case in any detail. Not that we didn't want to clarify many of the things that had happened at the reservoir; but we both knew that we didn't possess enough information to do so on our own. And the hard knowledge that we *did* possess was going to take time and wisdom to come to grips with. Of nothing was this more true than the fact that Sara had put an end to a man's life that night.

Caleb Carr

'I suppose one of us was destined to do it,' she said wearily, after we'd turned onto Lafayette Place and begun to walk north. Her eyes stared blankly at the sidewalk. 'Although I never would have thought that it would be me . . .'

'If anyone ever had it coming, Connor did,' I said, trying to be reassuring without committing the deadly sin (to Sara's way of thinking) of mollycoddling.

'Oh, I know that, John,' she answered simply. 'Honestly I do. Still . . .' Her voice trailed off, and then she stopped and took a deep breath, looking at the quiet street around her. Her eyes continued to wander from darkened building to darkened building, and finally came to rest on mine – then, in a quick motion that surprised me, she put her arms around me and laid her head on my chest. 'It's really over now, isn't it, John?'

'You sound sorry,' I said, touching her hair.

'A little,' Sara answered. 'Not for anything that's happened – but I've never had an experience like this. And I wonder how many more I'll be allowed.'

I lifted her head by the chin and looked deep into her green gaze. 'Somehow, I get the feeling you're done with people *allowing* you to do things. Not that you were ever very good at it, to start with.'

She smiled at that, then walked over to the curb. 'Perhaps you're right.' She turned when she heard a horse's hooves. 'Oh, there's good luck – a hansom.'

Holding her right hand up to her face, Sara extended her index finger and thumb and, to my consternation, put them in her mouth. She then drew breath and blew hard, producing a whistle that almost split my head open. I clapped my hands to my ears and looked at her in shock, getting another big smile in return.

'I've been practicing that,' she said, as the cab clattered over and stopped next to her. 'Stevie taught me. It's fairly good, don't you think?' She climbed up into the hansom, still smiling. 'Good night, John. And thank you.' Rapping on the roof of the cab, she called out 'Gramercy Park, driver!' and was gone.

Alone for the first time that night, I took a moment to try to decide just where I was going. I was bone-weary, to be sure, but sleep was somehow out of the question. Strolling through the still streets was definitely called for; not, as I say, to make sense of all that had happened, but simply to absorb the fact that it had. John Beecham was dead: the focus of my life, however gruesome, had been removed, and with a sudden ache of dread I realized that come Monday morning I'd have to decide whether or not I was going to report for duty back at the *Times*. The thought, brief and passing though it was, seemed nothing short of horrible.

Without intending to, I'd come to a stop at the corner of Great Jones Street. Looking down the block, I saw that the lights of the New Brighton Dance Hall were still burning bright. Perhaps explanations were not so far off after all, I thought; and then, before I'd consciously decided to go, my feet were carrying me toward the place.

I was still several doors away when I started to hear loud music echoing out of the New Brighton (Paul Kelly employed a much larger and more professional band than the usual three-piece noise gang found in concert halls). Soon raucous laughter, a few drunken screams, and finally the resonant rattle of glasses and bottles joined the din. Not relishing the prospect of actually going inside, I was much relieved to see Kelly emerge from the joint's frosted glass doors just as I arrived. With him was a police sergeant – in uniform – who was laughing and counting a wad of money. Kelly glanced over, caught sight of me, and then elbowed the cop, telling him with a nod of his head to get lost. The sergeant obliged, scurrying obediently away in the general direction of Mulberry Street.

'Well, Moore!' Kelly said, pulling a small snuffbox out of his silk vest and grinning in his handsome way. 'You can forget you saw that,' he said, inclining his head toward the vanishing cop.

'Don't worry, Kelly,' I answered, drawing up to him. 'I figure I may owe you one.'

'*Me?*' Kelly chuckled. 'Not likely, newshound. I see that you're in one piece, though. From the rumors that're floating around town, I'd say you're damned lucky.'

'Come on, Kelly,' I said. 'I saw your rig tonight – and your man McManus saved our necks.'

'Jack?' Kelly opened the snuffbox, revealing a mound of finely ground cocaine. 'Why, he didn't tell me. Doesn't *sound* like Jack,

Caleb Carr

though, to go around doing good deeds.' Kelly put a little cocaine on one knuckle and snorted it hard, then held the box out to me. 'Care for some? I wouldn't myself, but these late nights—'

'No,' I said. 'Thanks. Listen, the best I can figure is that you made some kind of a deal with Kreizler.'

'Deal?' Kelly echoed again, his affected ignorance starting to make me testy. He took a little more cocaine, then stepped aside when a large, well-dressed man came stumbling out of the New Brighton with two homely, garishly dressed women in tow. Kelly called good-night to the man amiably, then turned back to me. 'Why in the world would I cut a deal with the good doctor?'

'That's what I don't know!' I replied, exasperated. 'The only explanation I can think of is that you once said you had a lot of respect for him. That day in your carriage – you said you'd even read a monograph of his.'

Kelly chuckled again. 'That's not likely to make me go against my own interests, Moore. I'm a practical man, after all. Just like your friend Mr. Morgan.' I looked at him blankly, and his smile widened. 'Oh, sure. I know all about your meeting with the Nose.'

I thought to ask him *how* in hell he knew, but it really was useless – he obviously wasn't in a cooperative mood, and I was just giving him sport. 'All right,' I announced, taking a few steps away. 'I've been through entirely too much tonight to stand out here playing who-knows-what with you, Kelly. Tell Jack he's got a favor coming.'

At that I stormed off, or tried my best to, anyway; but I'd only gotten half the distance to the corner when I heard Kelly's voice again:

'Say, Moore.' I turned around, and saw him still grinning. 'It sounds like you people had a hell of a time.' Putting his snuffbox back in his vest, he cocked his head playfully. 'I'm not saying I know anything about it, of course. But ask yourself this when you get a free minute – of all the people who were up there tonight, who do you think is really the most dangerous to the boys uptown?'

I stood there, staring dumbly at Kelly and then at the ground, trying to make sense out of his question. After half a minute, an answer started to form in my overworked brain, and my jaw dropped open a little bit. I glanced back up with a grin and was about to state my reply – but Kelly was nowhere to be seen. I had an idea to go inside after him, but quickly abandoned it: there was no point. I knew what he meant, and understood what he'd done. Paul Kelly, gangland chief, inveterate gambler and amateur philosopher and social critic, was playing a hunch; and though none of us would likely live long enough to see the ultimate outcome of the game, I suspected that his hunch was correct.

Strangely encouraged, I turned back around and jumped into a hansom that was sitting outside Kelly's place, fairly well screaming at the driver to take me down to East Broadway in a hurry. As my driver whipped his horse down Lafayette Place and then east on Worth Street I began to chuckle and even hum a bit. 'The final riddle,' I sang, echoing Marcus's words from earlier in the evening: I wanted to be there when they solved it.

My cab pulled up at the Kreizler Institute at just past four-thirty and parked behind Laszlo's calash. The only sound on the street was that of a baby crying, coming from an open window in one of the tenements opposite Kreizler's two buildings. As I paid off my cabbie and stepped to the street, I caught sight of Marcus, who was sitting on the iron steps of the Institute, smoking a cigarette and running a hand through his hair. He acknowledged me with a nervous wave, and then I went over to peer inside the calash. Stevie was lying on the seat smoking, and when he looked over and saw me he saluted with his cigarette.

'Mr. Moore,' he said amiably. 'Not bad, these what the detective sergeant smokes. You oughta try one.'

'Thanks,' I said, turning around. 'I think I will. Where's Cyrus?'

'Inside,' the boy replied, lying back down. 'Making 'em some coffee. They been at it for hours.' He took a deep pull on the cigarette and then held it to the sky. 'You know, Mr. Moore, you wouldn't figure a stinkhole like this city to have so many stars over it. Seems like the *smell'd* be enough to drive 'em away . . .'

I smiled and walked away from the calash. 'True enough, Stevie,' I said, looking beyond Marcus to the ground-floor windows of the Institute: They were brightly lit.

I sat down next to the taller Isaacson. 'You're not inside?'

He shook his head quickly, blowing smoke out of his long, handsome nose. 'I was. Thought I'd be able to stand it, but—'

'You don't have to tell me,' I said, accepting a cigarette from him and lighting it. '*I'm* not going in.'

The front door of the Institute opened a crack, and I turned around to see Cyrus poking his head out. 'Mr. Moore, sir?' he said. 'Would you care for a cup of coffee?'

'If it's *your* coffee, Cyrus,' I answered, 'most certainly.'

He tilted his head and shrugged slightly. 'I'm not guaranteeing anything,' he said. 'I haven't tried my hand since I got knocked on the head.'

'I'll take a chance,' I answered. 'How are they doing in there?'

'Getting on toward the end, I believe,' Cyrus answered. 'Getting on toward the end . . .'

But it was another three quarters of an hour before there was any sign of things being wrapped up in Kreizler's operating theater. During that time Marcus and I smoked, drank coffee, and tried, in some roundabout way, to accustom ourselves to the conclusion of our quest and the coming disbandment of our team. Whatever answers Kreizler and Lucius were uncovering in the operating theater wouldn't change the fact that Beecham was dead. As the night wore on into morning, I realized just how much this one circumstance was becoming the conditioning force of all our lives.

Finally, at almost five-thirty, the ground-floor door opened and Lucius appeared. He was wearing a leather apron that was stained with many odorous fluids, bodily and other, and he looked utterly exhausted.

'Well,' he said, wiping his hands on a bloodstained towel, 'that's that, I suppose.' Collapsing onto the steps beside us, he produced a handkerchief and mopped at his forehead, as Cyrus came down from the front door behind him.

'That's that?' Marcus asked, a little annoyed. 'What do you mean, that's that? What's what, what did you find?'

'Nothing,' Lucius said, shaking his head and closing his eyes. 'To all appearances, everything was perfectly normal. Dr.

Kreizler's checking a few last details, but . . .'

I stood up, tossing the stub of my cigarette into the street. 'Then he was right,' I said quietly, as a chill ran up my back.

Lucius hunched his shoulders. 'He was right so far as medicine can determine that he was right.'

Marcus continued to study his brother. 'Are you *trying* to spoil this?' he said. 'If he was right, he was right, don't bring medicine into it.'

Lucius was about to point out the less than stellar reasoning underlying that statement, but elected instead to sigh and nod. 'Yes,' he breathed, 'he was right.' Lucius stood up, removed his apron, and handed it to Cyrus. 'And I,' he continued, 'am going home. He wants us all at Delmonico's tonight. Eleven-thirty. Maybe by then I'll be able to eat.' He started to wander off.

'Wait a minute,' Marcus said, as his brother stumbled away. 'You're not leaving *me* to walk home alone – you've got the gun, remember. Goodbye, John. See you tonight.'

'Tonight,' I said with a nod. 'Good work, Lucius!'

The shorter Isaacson turned, rolling one hand perfunctorily. 'Oh. Yes, thanks, John. You, too. And Sara, and – well, I'll see you later.'

They strolled away down the street, chattering and arguing until they were out of sight.

The ground-floor door of the Institute opened again and Kreizler emerged, putting on his jacket. He looked even worse than Lucius: his face was pale and there were enormous circles under his eyes. It seemed to take him a moment to identify me.

'Ah, Moore,' he finally said. 'I didn't expect you. Though I am, of course, pleased.' Then, to Cyrus: 'We're finished, Cyrus. You know what to do?'

'Yes, sir. The driver with the van should be here in just a few minutes.'

'He'll take care not to be seen?' Kreizler asked.

'He's a very reliable man, Doctor,' Cyrus replied.

'Good. Then you can ride with him as far as Seventeenth Street. I'll drop Moore off at Washington Square.'

Kreizler and I climbed into his rig and roused the slumbering Stevie, who turned the horse Frederick around and urged him gently forward. I didn't press Laszlo for information, knowing that he would provide it when he'd had a few minutes to collect himself.

'Lucius told you that we found nothing?' he finally asked as we moved at an easy pace back up Broadway.

'Yes,' I answered.

'No evidence of either congenital abnormality or physical trauma,' Laszlo went on quietly. 'Nor of any of the other physical peculiarities that might indicate mental disease or defect. In every way, a perfectly normal, healthy brain.' Kreizler leaned back, letting his head rest against the calash's folded cover.

'You're not disappointed, are you?' I asked, a bit confused by his tone. 'After all, it proves that you were right – he wasn't crazy.'

'It *indicates* that I was right,' Kreizler answered evenly. 'We know so little about the brain, Moore . . .' He sighed, but then tried to rouse himself. 'However, yes, to the best of our present psychological and medical knowledge, John Beecham was not insane.'

'Well,' I said, reluctantly recognizing that it was going to be difficult for Kreizler to take any satisfaction from the achievement. 'Sane or not, he's no longer a danger. And that matters more than anything.'

Laszlo turned to me as Stevie took a left turn onto Prince Street in order to avoid the intersection of Houston and Broadway. 'You really didn't feel much pity for him by the end, did you, Moore?' Laszlo asked.

'Ah,' I noised uncomfortably. 'To be honest, I felt more than I wanted to. *You* certainly seemed shaken up by his death.'

'Not so very much by his death,' Kreizler answered, producing his silver cigarette case. 'By his life. The evil stupidity that created him. And the fact that he died before we could truly study him. The entire thing seems so wretchedly futile . . .'

'If you wanted him alive,' I asked, as Laszlo lit a cigarette, 'then why did you say that you were hoping Connor would follow us? You must have known he'd try to kill Beecham.'

'Connor,' Laszlo said, coughing a bit. 'There, I must confess, is something I don't regret about this night.'

'Well,' – I tried to be judicious – 'I mean, he's dead, after all. And he did save our lives.'

'Nothing of the kind,' Kreizler replied. 'McManus would have stepped in before Beecham could have done any real harm – he was watching the entire time.'

'What? Then why did he wait so long? I lost a tooth, for God's sake!'

'Yes,' Kreizler answered uneasily, touching the small incision on his face, 'he did make rather a close thing of it. But I'd told him not to interfere until he was certain the danger was mortal, because I wanted to observe as much of Beecham's behavior as I could. As for Connor, all I was hoping for from his appearance was that we'd apprehend him. That, or . . .'

There was a terrible finality and loneliness in Laszlo's voice as he said this, and I knew that I'd better change the subject if I wanted to keep him talking:

'I saw Kelly tonight. I take it you went to him because you had no other option.' Kreizler nodded, still staring off with bitterness in his black eyes. 'He told me why he agreed to help you. Or rather, he hinted at it. He thinks you're quite a danger to the *status quo* in this society.'

Laszlo grunted. 'Perhaps he and Mr. Comstock should compare notes. Although if I'm a danger to society, such men as they will be the death of it. Particularly Comstock.'

We took a right turn on MacDougal Street, wending our way past small, dark restaurants and Italian cafés toward Washington Square. 'Laszlo,' I said, after he'd grown silent again, 'what did you mean when you told Beecham that you might be able to arrange a less severe fate for him? You wouldn't have argued that he was mad, just to keep him alive for study?'

'No,' Kreizler answered. 'But I intended to remove him from immediate danger, and then to plead for a life sentence rather than the electric chair or the gallows. It had occurred to me some time ago that his observation of our efforts, his letter, even his murder of the boy Joseph, all indicated a desire to communicate with us. And when he began to answer my questions tonight, I knew that I'd found something I'd never really come across before – a man who murdered apparent strangers and was willing

Caleb Carr

to talk about his crimes.' Kreizler sighed again and held up his hands weakly. 'We've lost a tremendous opportunity. Such men will seldom do that, you see – discuss their behavior. They're reluctant to admit their deeds after capture, and even if they do, they won't discuss the intimate details. They don't seem to know how. Look at Beecham's last words – he'd never been able to say just what it was that made him kill. But I believe I could have helped him find words for it, in time.'

I studied my friend carefully. 'You know that they wouldn't have let you.' Kreizler shrugged obstinately, unwilling to concede the point. 'With the political dimension this thing was assuming?' I went on. 'He'd have had one of the fastest trials in recent memory, and been strung up in a matter of weeks.'

'Perhaps,' Kreizler said. 'We'll never know, now. Ah, Moore – there are so *many* things that we'll never know, now . . .'

'Will you at least allow yourself credit for finding the man? That's a fairly amazing feat on its own, damn it all.'

Laszlo shrugged again. 'Is it? I wonder. How long would he have stayed hidden from us, John?'

'How long? Well, a good long time, I suppose – hell, he'd been at it for years.'

'Yes,' Kreizler answered, 'but how much *longer*? The crisis was inevitable – he couldn't go forever without society being aware of him. He wanted that, wanted it desperately. If the average person were to describe John Beecham in light of his murders, he'd say he was a social outcast, but nothing could be more superficial, or more untrue. Beecham could never have turned his back on human society, nor society on him, and why? Because he was – perversely, perhaps, but utterly – tied to that society. He was its offspring, its sick conscience – a living reminder of all the hidden crimes we commit when we close ranks to live among each other. He craved human society, craved the chance to show people what their "society" had done to him. And the odd thing is, society craved him, too.'

'Craved him?' I said, as we passed along the quiet perimeter of Washington Square Park. 'How do you mean? They'd have shot him through with electricity if they'd had the chance.'

'Yes, but not before holding him up to the world,' Kreizler

answered. 'We revel in men like Beecham, Moore – they are the easy repositories of all that is dark in our very *social* world. But the things that helped make Beecham what he was? Those, we tolerate. Those, we even enjoy...'

As Kreizler's gaze drifted away again, the calash rolled to a slow stop outside my grandmother's house. The sky was only beginning to glow in the east, but there was already a light on in the upper floors of Number 19 Washington Square. As Kreizler turned his head to take in the streets around him, he caught sight of that light, and it brought the first small smile of the morning to his face.

'How has your grandmother felt about your involvement in a murder case, Moore?' he asked. 'She always took a lively interest in the macabre.'

'I haven't told her,' I answered. 'She simply thinks that my gambling habit has gotten worse. And, all things considered, I'm going to let her keep thinking that.' I got to the sidewalk with a stiff little jump, 'So – we're to be at Del's tonight, I understand?'

Kreizler nodded once. 'It seems appropriate, eh?'

'Absolutely,' I said. 'I'm going to call Charlie – have him tell Ranhofer to lay something really exceptional on. We deserve that much, anyway.'

Kreizler's smile widened just a bit. 'Indeed, Moore,' he said, closing the calash door and offering his hand. I shook it, and then Laszlo faced front with a small groan. 'All right, Stevie.'

The boy turned and saluted to me, and then the carriage kept rolling on toward Fifth Avenue.

Chapter 47

Almost twenty-four hours later, as I was stumbling home after a meal at Delmonico's that would have slowed down a regiment of cavalry *and* their horses, I stopped at the Fifth Avenue Hotel to buy an early edition of the Tuesday *Times*. Walking on down the avenue as I scanned the paper, I found myself once more under the watchful eye of Colonel Waring's helmeted young street cleaners, who were just waiting for me to drop some shred of newsprint. I ignored them, however, and continued my search, finally locating what I was looking for in the bottom right-hand corner of the front page.

That morning the custodian at the Bellevue morgue had made a gruesome discovery. Wrapped in a tarp and deposited near the back door of the building was the body of a muscular adult male who in life had stood over six feet tall. Because the body was not clothed, there were no identifying documents to be found. A single bullet wound to the chest was the apparent cause of death; but the body had sustained further damage, as well. Specifically, the top of the skull had been removed and the brain apparently dissected in a way that, the morgue staff said, indicated an expert hand. A brief note had been found pinned to the tarp, claiming that this was the body of the man responsible for the boy-whore murders – or, as the *Times* put it, 'the deaths of the several forlorn young boys known to have been in the employ of houses too sordid to be mentioned in these pages.' Inquiries made of

Commissioner Roosevelt had confirmed that the murderer had indeed been killed while trying to continue his horrifying work. For various important but unexplained reasons, the commissioner said, he was not at liberty to reveal either the killer's name or any details of his death; but the public should know that members of the Division of Detectives had been involved, and that the case was most decidedly closed.

On finishing the story I looked around the avenue and gave out with a long, satisfying holler.

I can still feel that sense of relish as I look back across almost twenty-three years. Kreizler and I are old men now, and New York is a very different place – as J.P. Morgan told us the night we visited him in his Black Library, the city, like the country generally, was on the verge of a tumultuous metamorphosis in 1896. Thanks to Theodore and many of his political allies, we have been transformed into a great power, and New York is more than ever the crossroads of the world. The crime and corruption that are still the firm foundations of city life have taken on ever more businesslike trappings – Paul Kelly, for example, has gone on to become an important leader of organized labor. True, children still die at the hands of depraved adults while plying the skin trade, and unidentified bodies are occasionally found in peculiar places; but to the best of my knowledge, a menace of John Beecham's stripe has not been seen again in this city. It is my abiding hope that such creatures do not appear very often; Kreizler, of course, suspects that such faith is utterly self-deluding.

I've seen a great deal of Lucius and Marcus Isaacson during the last twenty-three years, and even more of Sara; all of them have pursued their careers in criminal detection with single-minded devotion and brilliant results. There have even been occasions when we've had cause to investigate some little matter together, experiences that collectively form the chain of my most memorable experiences. But nothing, I suppose, will ever be quite like the hunt for Beecham. Perhaps with Roosevelt's passing, that achievement will finally gain public appreciation; if nothing else, it serves as a singular reminder that, beneath all his theatrical bluster, Theodore possessed a heart and a mind expansive

Caleb Carr

enough to have made such an unprecedented undertaking possible.

Oh, and a note to those who may be curious about the fates of Cyrus Montrose and Stevie Taggert: Cyrus eventually married, and brought his wife to work for Kreizler. The couple have several children, one of whom is currently enrolled at the Harvard Medical School. As for young Stevie, on attaining adulthood he borrowed some money from Kreizler and opened a tobacconist's shop across the street from the Fifth Avenue Hotel, in the new Flatiron Building. He's done well, and in the past fifteen years I don't think I've ever seen him without a cigarette in his mouth.

Just three years after the Beecham case, the Croton Reservoir – having been outmoded by a new water system constructed after Boss Platt consummated his Greater New York scheme – was demolished to make room for the main headquarters of that most marvelous of all philanthropical endeavors, the New York Public Library. Having seen a notice in the *Times* announcing the demolition, I went over to take a look at the work during my lunch hour one day. The task of tearing the reservoir down had begun at the southern wall, on top of which we had faced the final challenge of our investigation, and which was now being knocked away to expose an enormous man-made crater one block wide and two blocks long. The structure didn't look like much, all laid open to view that way; it was hard to believe that it had ever been strong enough to withstand the fantastic pressure exerted by millions of gallons of water.

Acknowledgments

While doing the preliminary research for this book, it occurred to me that the phenomenon we now call serial killing has been with us for as long as humans have gathered together into societies. This amateur opinion was confirmed, and paths of deeper research were indicated, by Dr. David Abrahamsen, one of America's foremost experts on violence in general and serial killing in particular. I wish to thank him for taking the time to discuss the project.

The staffs of the Harvard Archives, the New York Public Library, the New-York Historical Society, the American Museum of Natural History, and the New York Society Library all lent invaluable assistance.

John Coston suggested several important avenues of research early on, and took the time to trade ideas. I am grateful.

Many authors contributed unknowingly to this story through their nonfiction accounts of serial killing and killers, and out of these many I cannot fail to offer thanks to: Colin Wilson, for his encyclopedic histories of crime; Janet Colaizzi, for her brilliant study of homicidal insanity since 1800; Harold Schechter, for his examination of the infamous Albert Fish (whose notorious note to Grace Budd's mother inspired John Beecham's similar document); Joel Norris, for his justly famous treatise on serial killers; Robert K. Ressler, for his memoir of a life spent chasing such characters; and again, Dr. Abrahamsen, for his unparalleled

533

studies of David Berkowitz and Jack the Ripper.

Tim Haldeman gave the manuscript the benefit of his seasoned eye. I have valued his incisive comments almost as much as his friendship.

As always, Suzanne Gluck and Ann Godoff guided me from wild idea to completed project with grace, skill, and affection. All writers should have such agents and editors. Susan Jensen's skill, speed, and good humor often helped keep the wolf from the door, and I thank her.

Irene Webb oversaw the fate of this story on another coast with consummate charm and expertise, and I am in her debt.

For his early and dramatic expression of faith, I would like to thank Scott Rudin.

Through his own psychological insight, Tom Pivinski helped turn nightmares into prose. He has been a rock.

James Chace, David Fromkin, and Rob Cowley all provided the friendship and advice so necessary to such a project. I am proud to call them comrades.

Special gratitude goes to my fellow members of the Core Four at La Tourette: Martin Signore, Debbie Deuble, and Yong Yoon.

Finally, I would like to thank my family, in particular my cousins, Maria and William von Hartz.

Warner now offers an exciting range of quality titles by both established and new authors. All of the books in this series are available from:
Little, Brown and Company (UK),
P.O. Box 11,
Falmouth,
Cornwall TR10 9EN.

Alternatively you may fax your order to the above address. Fax No. 0326 376423.

Payments can be made as follows: Cheque, postal order (payable to Little, Brown and Company) or by credit cards, Visa/Access. Do not send cash or currency. UK customers: and B.F.P.O.: please send a cheque or postal order (no currency) and allow £1.00 for postage and packing for the first book, plus 50p for the second book, plus 30p for each additional book up to a maximum charge of £3.00 (7 books plus).

Overseas customers including Ireland, please allow £2.00 for postage and packing for the first book, plus £1.00 for the second book, plus 50p for each additional book.

NAME (Block Letters) ....

ADDRESS..

....

☐ I enclose my remittance for _____

☐ I wish to pay by Access/Visa Card

Number ☐☐☐☐☐☐☐☐☐☐☐☐☐☐☐☐☐☐

Card Expiry Date ☐☐☐☐

THE HALF-LIFE OF HANN

Nick Alexander grew up in the seaside town of Margate, UK. He has travelled widely and lived in the UK, the USA and France, where he resides today.

Nick's first five novels – the *Fifty Reasons* series – were self-published from 2004 onwards and went on to become some of the UK's best-selling gay literature.

His crossover titles, *The Case of the Missing Boyfriend* and its sequel, *The French House*, each reached #1 in Amazon's UK chart.

The Half-Life of Hannah, Nick's ninth novel, has sold more than 260,000 copies to date and a hotly anticipated sequel entitled *Other Halves* is due out at the beginning of 2014.

For more information please visit the author's website on www.nick-alexander.com.

Available now

OTHER HALVES

the sequel to *The Half-Life of Hannah*

ebook (ISBN 978 1 84502 767 4)
available for download now

print (ISBN 978 1 84502 764 3)
available April 2014

THE HALF-LIFE OF HANNAH

Nick Alexander

BLACK & WHITE PUBLISHING

First published 2014
by Black & White Publishing Ltd
29 Ocean Drive, Edinburgh EH6 6JL

1 3 5 7 9 10 8 6 4 2   14 15 16

ISBN: 978 1 84502 719 3

ALBA | CHRUTHACHAIL

A CIP catalogue record for this book is available from the British Library.

Typeset by Iolaire Typesetting, Newtonmore
Printed and bound by Grafica Veneta S. p. A., Italy

ACKNOWLEDGEMENTS

Thanks to Rosemary – without your constant encouragement nothing would ever never get finished, and without your friendship this planet would be a much darker place. Thanks to Allan for his eagle-eyed copy-editing skills and to Jerôme for his help with the French text. Thanks to my family for being there, and to all my readers for sticking with me and showing so much enthusiasm about every new project – you make it all worthwhile. Finally, thanks to Black & White Publishing for making this physical book a reality.

ONE

"I'm sorry," Hannah says, aware that she doesn't sound very sorry at all, "but that's what it says. It says to go straight down this track."

The Mégane slithers to a halt on the gravel. Cliff sighs. "How can it be up there?" he asks. "I mean, seriously, how?"

They have spent fourteen hours in the car since they left Farnham, of which seven already today. Tempers are getting frayed. Hannah peers along the gravelly farm track to where it vanishes into the trees. "Maybe it's at the end of the track," she offers, both unconvinced and unconvincing. "Maybe it's in the middle of the forest."

Cliff pulls on the handbrake and wrenches the GPS from her grasp. "Only it isn't. And we've still got seven miles to go," he says. "It can't be seven miles down a track, can it?"

Hannah rubs the bridge of her nose and turns to look out of the side window at the rolling fields, at the pine forests in the distance. It's stunning scenery, but she can't enjoy it. Not yet. She discreetly takes a deep breath. She doesn't want Cliff to think it's a confrontational sigh. Not at a time like this.

"That is what it says, though," Cliff admits, jabbing at the screen. "I don't know what you've done to it."

"Cliff, I haven't done anything to it," Hannah says quietly, struggling, now, to hide the exasperation in her voice.

"If we had just left it where it was, stuck to the windscreen, I could have followed it myself," Cliff says.

"If you were able to look at a GPS without veering onto the wrong side of the road every time, that would be a good idea," Hannah points out, forcing a false laugh into her voice to mask her rising anger. "But you can't. And anyway, we *have* followed it. Right up this track."

"Veering onto the *right* side of the road," Cliff corrects her. "Not the wrong one."

"The *left* side, not the right side," Luke offers from the rear seat, laughing at his own wit.

"Well, the *correct* side then," Cliff admits. "You know what I mean. And anyway, it's not my fault if the frogs all drive on the wrong side of the road."

Luke undoes his seatbelt and leans forward. "We're the ones who drive on the wrong side, Dad," he says. "The English swapped sides so that they could stab people better with their swords." He demonstrates this by wielding his phone – Cliff's old iPhone – with a flourish.

Aware that in some way, Luke, by contradicting Cliff, has sided with her, Hannah feels a bubble of warmth for him. She reaches back to ruffle his hair. "Is that true, sweetheart?"

"Yes," he says. "I saw it on the telly-box." The term 'telly-box' came from his uncle Tristan, and because it's cute, they all use it now.

"Well, if you saw it on the telly-box!" Cliff says drily, still stabbing at the buttons on the GPS.

"It was on *QI*," Luke tells him.

"That's all very interesting, I'm sure," Cliff says. "But it doesn't much help us here."

Stephen Fry is revered in the Parker household as the font

of all knowledge. So Luke has won. Even Cliff isn't going to argue with The Fry.

"But what do we do?" Cliff continues. "Do we carry on up here until we get stuck, or . . ."

"I'm hungry," Luke says.

"Have one of those biscuits," Hannah tells him a little abruptly – her tone a coded warning – then to Cliff, "It does look a bit muddy."

"So I turn back," Cliff says. "That's what you're saying now?"

Hannah shrugs, still angry about the implication that this is somehow her fault. "We should have bought a map," she says. "I said we needed to buy a map back in that petrol-station."

"This *is* a map," Cliff replies, tapping the top of the GPS. "It has a map of every bloody road in France."

"I'll tell you what then, darling," Hannah says in her special faux-kind voice. "Why don't you look at your map of *every-bloody-road-in-France*, and work out how to get there?"

Cliff fiddles with the box for another minute or so and then sighs. "I don't know how," he admits. "It keeps coming back with the same bloody route."

"You just have to go back to the main road and drive," Luke offers. "It will recalculate a new route."

"Will it?" Cliff asks. "Or will it just keep telling us to turn around?"

"It will for a bit, but then it will recalculate," Luke says. "That's what happens in *Drive Apocalypse* anyway."

"Only this isn't a game. We're not in *Drive Apocalypse*," Cliff says.

"Well, we kind of *are*," Hannah points out, wittily, she thinks, not that anyone notices.

Luke's phone makes a honking noise. He checks the screen. "Jill and Tristan have arrived," he says. "So it must be possible."

"Maybe they have *a map*," Hannah suggests. "Maybe they have a proper actual map printed on a bit of dead tree."

"Dead tree! You're funny, Mum!" Luke says, laughing at her wit, and she loves him even more.

"Are you *sure* that isn't costing a fortune, sweetheart?" Hannah asks him. "I saw *Watchdog* and they said that you have to be really careful about . . ."

"Not to receive," Luke says, interrupting. "It costs to send. But they were on about Internet anyway and I've switched it off. Can I send a text back saying we're lost? Maybe Tristan can come and find us. It's only fifty pee to send an SMS."

"No! There's no point," Cliff replies gruffly, imagining the shame of having to be saved by a gay guy. "We'll be there in a minute anyway."

"In a day, more like," Luke says, sarcastically.

Hannah shoots him a warning glance, and he sinks back into his seat and pulls the biscuits from the seat pocket.

"So we turn around?" Cliff asks, then, after a pause, "Anyone?"

Hannah shrugs. She's no longer in the mood to be helpful. "You're the one with maps of the whole of France, darling," she says. Because she feels bad for repeating that same dig twice, however, she adds, "But yes. You're right. We probably should, shouldn't we?"

Cliff sighs deeply and hands the GPS not back to Hannah, but over his shoulder to Luke. She grinds her teeth at the betrayal.

"OK, I'm gonna reverse back and then turn around. In the meantime, see if *you* can work it out, son, OK?"

"If anyone can solve it, Luke can," Hannah says with apparent generosity, yet praying secretly that Luke, too, will fuck it up.

TWO

Cliff

I met Cliff when I was twenty. I was a late-starter, romance wise, so Cliff was only my second boyfriend.

I got back from that oh-so disastrous holiday in Amsterdam with anarchist boyfriend Ben, and met Cliff on my second night back.

I was in a wine bar with my friend Shelley telling her all about splitting up with Ben when Cliff sent us both drinks. It seemed old-fashioned and chivalrous, and after three weeks of Ben's selfishness, exactly what the doctor ordered.

Cliff was three years older than I and already working as an accountant. He was well dressed and polite and an almost mirror opposite of dope-smoking, unpredictable Ben. He seemed much older than I, much older than Ben, and I found that maturity attractive.

I often think that if I hadn't been rebounding from Ben, I never would have given Cliff a second glance. That's not to say that Cliff was unattractive – he wasn't. He was a tall, well-built young man who played squash and tennis and had two-weekly appointments at the barber's to keep his new-romantic mop in shape. It's just that I had been more attracted by the goths and the bikers up until that point.

But glance, I did, and by the time he had bought both Shelley and me a couple of rounds of rum and Coke, given us a lift home in his Ford Sierra and had treated us to chips and curry-sauce on the way, he had pretty much snared me.

Shelley declared him 'boring' even back then, and I suppose that if there was one criticism that could be levelled at Cliff, boring would be it. But excitement, I reckon, is overrated. Kindness and generosity, an ability to provide, a stable temperament . . . I think these qualities are underrated in these days of unbridled individualism.

So, though I suppose life hasn't exactly been a roller-coaster with Cliff, it has been fine. It has been perfectly *fine*. And I know plenty of women my age – my sister included – who would give their right arms for a bit of 'perfectly fine'.

THREE

When they get to the villa, there are no signs of Tristan's car at all.

"Are you *sure* this is the place?" Cliff asks, apparently, *inexplicably*, directing his question at Hannah.

She shrugs. "Luke has the GPS," she reminds him.

"This is *it*," Luke says, demonstrating his conviction by climbing down from the car and pushing open the heavy forged-steel gate.

"But what if it isn't?" Hannah says, releasing her own seatbelt. "What if there's a guard-dog?" She opens the car door and extracts herself from the seat, noting, as she does so, that after an eight-hour car journey, this isn't as easy as it would have been even ten years before. "Luke!" she calls out, nervously heading past the gate. "Wait!"

"Helloooo!" A voice to her right. "Sweetie!" Hannah spins to find Jill's head peeping over the edge of an orange cotton hammock suspended between two trees.

"See!" Luke declares gleefully as he runs over to his aunt. "I told you."

"Hi Luke," Jill says brightly.

"I told them this was the right place but they didn't believe me," Luke tells her.

Hannah spins and beckons towards the Mégane, then, nodding exaggeratedly at Cliff's questions, silently mimed

8

behind the windscreen, she shouts, "Yes. Yes! This is it! They're *here*! I don't *know* where Tristan's parked, but Jill's here."

"Tristan and Aïsha have gone food shopping," Jill tells her, waving what looks suspiciously like a joint in the air.

As the car crunches up the driveway, Hannah crosses the lawn and ruffles Luke's hair. "Can you go help your dad?" she asks.

"Sure," Luke says, then, already distracted from this idea, "Hey, where's the pool? They said there was a pool."

"It's around the other side," Jill says, her joint leaving a fragrant trail in the air as she gestures. "It's . . ." But Luke is already out of earshot.

"It's empty," she tells her sister more quietly, reaching out now with her left hand to take Hannah's fingers between her own.

"Empty? What, dry?"

Jill nods and pulls a despondent face. "'Fraid so," she says. "How are you, Sis'? How was the drive?"

"Is that a joint?" Hannah asks her.

Jill smiles and shrugs as if she sees no reason for embarrassment. "You want some?" she asks, proffering the joint.

Hannah pulls her hand away and frowns at her. "I do hope you didn't bring that with you through customs," she says. "Not with Aïsha in the car."

"Of course," Jill says. "We put it in Aï's teddy bear."

Hannah opens her lips to express fury, but Luke has returned. "The pool's empty," he says breathlessly. "It's got a dead bird in it. A pigeon I think."

"Well, don't touch it," Hannah tells him. "They have all sorts of diseases."

9

"I can't *touch* it, Mum!" Luke says, now starting to rock Jill's hammock. "It's at the bottom of the pool."

"I'm sure Dad'll get the pool sorted," Hannah tells him. "Now go help him, will you?"

Once Luke has run off, she nods at Jill's joint again. "You're out of control, Jill," she says quietly. "You and I will have words about this later when the kids are in bed."

Jill grins at her and shrugs. "I don't doubt it," she says.

The Mégane parked, Cliff climbs out and places one hand in the small of his back. "Jees!" he says.

"Long drive?" Jill asks him.

"Endless," Hannah says quietly, so that only Jill will hear her. "Absolutely bloody endless. I came close to ramming the bloody GPS down his throat."

Cliff crosses the scrubby lawn to join the women. "Nice place," he says, and Hannah realises that she hasn't properly looked yet. She looks around now, taking in the pink stucco villa, the olive orchard, the hammock, the shady patio, the wooden pergola, the sound of cicadas. She takes a deep breath of the baked, earthy air. "It is," she says. "It's gorgeous."

Jill attempts to extract herself from the hammock, then reaches out again for her sister's hand. "Help me," she says, then, "It's lovely."

Once she has been pulled upright, she keeps her sister's hand and tugs her towards the villa. "The inside is pretty funky too. Come see," she says.

The interior of the villa is dark, and cool. It feels, in fact, almost cold after the scorching Mediterranean sunshine outside. The tiled floor shines and the rooms smell rich and waxy from furniture polish. As Luke runs echoing from room to room, Jill leads them on a guided tour, announcing, as if it weren't obvious – as if this were *her* villa – that *this is the bathroom*, and *this is the kitchen*.

Cliff is struggling to restrain himself from commenting, "*Really? So that's a kitchen, huh?*" He finds Hannah's sister endlessly annoying – unreasonably so. And rarely do they spend time together without some flashpoint being reached. Generally it's a conflict between Cliff's cartesian logic and Jill's random new-wave spirituality that's at the origin of the disaccord. But he has promised himself (and Hannah) that she will not get to him on this trip. He's determined to be nice to her. He will rise above it all.

"So where's Tristan?" he asks her, mainly to stop her listing things – cupboards, shower, washbasin – that they can all see, and identify, perfectly well for themselves.

"They've gone to get food," Hannah informs him.

"He's a shopaholic," Jill says. "He got excited when he spotted the hypermarket on the way in."

"Well, we do need food," Cliff points out.

"Yes, but you know what he's like," Jill says. "He'll come back with one each of every most expensive food item on sale. It's an absolute obsession with him."

"Yum," Hannah says. "I love Tristan's food."

"Well, he is a chef," Cliff says as Jill opens another door revealing a blue bedroom. "My room," she declares, then, "and it's got nothing to do with his being a chef. He's the same whatever kind of shop it is. Clothes, food, gadgets, men . . . It's just consumerism with Tris. It's just *more, more, more.*"

Cliff thinks it's unfair to criticise the guy for going to buy food for them all, but Hannah catches his eye and shoots him her doe-eyed look – a plea – so he asks instead, "So where's our room?"

When the bags have been carried in, Hannah heads for a shower, Jill returns to the hammock and another joint, and Cliff and Luke head off to search, in vain, for the filler valve for the pool.

By the time Tristan returns, techno blaring, his red Wrangler Jeep slithering to a halt on the gravel, they are all installed on the patio drinking – for want of anything else – glasses of tap water.

The silence when Tristan cuts the engine, and with it the music, is total. Even the cicadas have been stunned into silence.

They all stand and move towards the car. Luke runs straight to the passenger door. "Hi Aï'!" he says enthusiastically as his cousin climbs out. "The pool's empty, did you see?"

"Yeah," Aïsha replies. "There's a dead bird in it too. I put a photo on Facebook."

Of course you have, Hannah thinks, checking out her niece's black Dr Marten boots, her black fingernails, her purple lip-gloss.

Luke frowns. "Mum says Internet's too expensive in France," he says, to which Aïsha just shrugs. Aïsha's Mum doesn't worry about such things, and Aïsha wouldn't care if she did.

Cliff watches as Tristan hugs Hannah, and then holds a hand out in front of him to preclude any idea that he and Tristan might do the same thing. It's not that he doesn't like Tristan (though he's never quite sure that he does) nor the fact that Tristan is gay (though he has confused feelings about that too). It's just that Cliff doesn't hug men. Ever.

The two men shake hands. "So we have food!" Cliff says, glancing at the bags piled on the back seat of the Jeep. "Well done."

12

"We do," Tristan replies, starting to lift the bags from the car and to hand them out.

"We have wine, more to the point!" Jill laughs, swiping a bottle of rosé from a passing bag, and heading off towards the kitchen with it, without, Hannah notices, carrying anything else.

"Cool car, Tris," Luke says, taking two bags from his adopted uncle.

"Thanks, Luke," Tristan replies. He's genuinely pleased that someone noticed. "It's brand new. Only three-thousand miles on the clock. Actually not even that. Lovely to drive."

Hannah takes two bags to carry in and notes that Aïsha is already slinking behind the villa. She thinks, *Like mother, like daughter.* She feels a little jolt of pain for her little boy who, though only two years younger than his cousin, won't, she knows, understand that this growing chasm between them has nothing to do with him and everything to do with the fact of Aïsha's adolescence. For the next five years, being cool will trump everything else for Aïsha, whether it be love, friendship or even fun. As a parent, you just have to pray they get over it. Because Hannah has known a few people who got stuck that way, and they were unbearable.

By the time the bags have reached the kitchen, Jill has a glass of wine in her hand.

"You might like to offer everyone else a drink, too," Tristan tells her – his voice polite, without judgement. Both Hannah and Cliff are thankful that it was he, not them, that said it.

Between sips of her own, Jill has served everyone with drinks. The kids have Cokes, and the adults have dewy glasses of fragrant rosé with ice-cubes that clink against the sides of the glass every time they gesture.

Tristan appears with a plate of salmon toasts. "Wow," Hannah says.

"Those look gorgeous," Jill agrees.

"I spreaded the cheese," Luke tells them.

"He's a very good spreader," Tristan says, smiling. "Very precise. No corners were missed."

"Cheese?" Hannah questions, taking a slice and lifting one corner of the salmon.

"Yes. There's cream cheese underneath," Tristan tells her. "Saint Moret."

"And this is rocket, right?" Jill asks.

"Yep."

"Love rocket," she says.

There's something cloying in everyone's tone that vaguely irritates Cliff. He thinks that everyone is making just a little bit too much fuss. They are, after all, just slices of toast with salmon on. But he's glad that Tristan is cooking. Hannah only has about five recipes which she rotates so religiously that you can pretty safely bet what you'll be eating each day based on what came the day before. Salmon toasts make a change.

"This is the life," Hannah says, nibbling at a slice, and then sipping at her wine. "I thought we'd never get here at one point, I swear."

"If it had been up to her, we wouldn't have," Cliff says.

Hannah shoots him a glare. The argument is on the tip of her tongue. But she can't quite decide whether to put it out there and get it over with or say nothing and hope to forget.

Thankfully, Cliff gets it. "Only joking, sweetheart," he says, putting down his glass so that he can squeeze her knee.

"We had some trouble with the GPS," Hannah explains. "It directed us up a farm track."

"We got that too, didn't we?" Jill says, addressing first Aïsha, who shrugs, perhaps because she doesn't remember, or perhaps because with her earphones in she can't hear what anyone's saying. Jill turns to Tristan instead.

"We had to use Google maps instead," he says.

Hannah nods discreetly at Cliff in a *you see?* manner.

"Anyway, just relax now," Tristan says. "We're all here safe and sound, and I'm gonna fix dinner for you all tonight, so . . ."

"What are you making?" Aïsha asks, revealing that she *can* hear even with the earbuds in.

"A hot Niçoise salad," Tristan says. "Any objections?"

Aïsha shrugs.

"A hot salad?" Cliff asks, his tone dubious.

"It's not really a salad. As long as you're OK with tuna it'll be fine," Tristan says.

"I like tuna," Luke volunteers.

"Yes," Hannah confirms. "We all like tuna. That sounds lovely." She catches Jill rolling her eyes. "What?" she asks.

Jill just smiles and shakes her head. "Sounds lovely," she repeats, and Hannah isn't sure if she's agreeing with her or somehow mocking her.

Just as Tristan has left the table, a stranger appears from the rear of the house. Hannah jumps when she sees him and Jill sits up very straight and flicks her hair back. Cliff sees Jill do this and moves his chair so that he can study the man. He is tall and muscular with closely cropped hair, olive skin and thick, dark stubble. He's wearing muddy dungarees (with no shirt underneath) and mustard builder's boots.

"Bonsoir," he says. "Vous deviez arriver demain, non ?"

At the foreign sounds, Aïsha and Luke turn wide-eyed to

15

their parents in faith that they will somehow understand. The three adults glance at each other.

"Pardon ?" Hannah says, one of only ten French words in her vocabulary.

"Vous deviez arriver demain," the man says, again. "Mais ce n'est pas grave. Je l'ai mis à remplir." He nods at the table, and adds, "Bon appétit."

"Bon appétit," Hannah repeats. She knows, at least, what that means.

The guy frowns at her as if her words have confused him, then nods, says, "Merci !" and returns the way he came.

"Who was *that*?" Cliff asks.

"How should I know?" Hannah says. "I didn't understand a word."

"He's hot," Jill says. "We should have called Tristan."

"Really? Do you think he's gay?" Hannah asks.

"No! Tris' speaks French, silly," Jill replies, laughing.

"Oh. Of course. Luke, go watch where he goes. Discreetly."

Luke stands uncertainly. "What, like spy on him?"

"Yes. You can be our secret agent," Hannah says, smiling and giving him a little push.

"I wonder what he wanted," Cliff says.

"As far as I'm concerned, he can have *anything* he wants," Jill says lasciviously, and Aïsha, for the first time today, smiles – a smile that quickly morphs into a blush. She lowers her head and stares at the screen of her phone.

"Yeah, I guess he was quite pretty," Hannah agrees. "If you like a bit of rough."

"You know I do," Jill says.

Cliff watches this exchange and feels a pique of jealousy. Because, of course, he never looked like that, not even in his youth. And he has always wondered what it would feel like, how easy life would be, if one did. He wonders what it must be like to walk into any room and see desire on the faces of all of the women (and a few of the men). Because you can go to college and get first-class degrees, you can build a business and be an expert in investments and tax schedules worldwide, you can provide generously for your family and your ageing parents, and be well off enough to help any member of the extended family that might happen to need it . . . But the women will always want the guy with the muscles, the guy with the stubble, the guy with dirty dungarees and the buttocks. And quite honestly he would have swapped all of his achievements to look like that if he had had the choice. He shuffles in his seat, and then takes a hefty swig of wine.

"He climbed over the fence," Luke declares when he returns.

Hannah glances at the height of the fence. "Really?" she asks.

Luke nods. "There's a low bit around the back. With a big brick on the ground. He climbed over there and went off down the track."

"A neighbour maybe?" Hannah suggests.

"The owner perhaps?" Jill ventures.

"Gardener more like," Cliff says.

"There's a hosepipe filling the pool up," Luke says. "And the dead bird is gone too, so I reckon he's the pool guy."

"Well, *Goodbye Old Guy*, and *Hello Pool Guy*," Jill says, and Hannah rolls her eyes.

"What *did* happen with whatsisname?" Hannah asks and Cliff, despite his best efforts, rubs an eyebrow as if to presage the headache the conversation will give him.

Jill sighs deeply. "Saïd?" she says. "Well . . ."

FOUR

Jill

I love Jill. Of course I do – she's my sister. When you have a single sibling there's really no other choice. But is she annoying? Of course she is.

I'm perfectly aware how irritating poor Cliff finds her, and I empathise entirely. But she's my sister. She comes with the terrain. And Cliff, thank God, understands this.

I'm pretty much immune to it all, myself. My little sister's capricious nature has been washing over me since age two, after all.

Jill is selfish and contradictory, hypocritical and sometimes arrogant. She changes her beliefs so often that you'd need an encyclopaedia of spiritual movements to keep up (if you wanted to – I don't.) And she gets through men so fast that it's *impossible* to keep up. I sometimes wonder if she's addicted to men, or if she hates them. It's a surprisingly fine line.

But Jill has another side too, of course. And as her sister, I suppose that I just try to concentrate more on that.

As is often the case, so much of Jill's brittle exterior is bravado. I've seen her cry over every breakup. I know that there have been times when, if it were not for her daughter, she might have killed herself through sheer loneliness. And I know that, just as I am always there for her, she would, if push came to shove, always be there for me. And let's face it, there aren't that many people in a life that you can say that about.

Luke loves her – kids will always gravitate towards adults with the most relaxed parenting techniques.

I worry about her smoking dope in front of the kids, and I worry about her talking about rave-parties and sex in front of them. But in a way, I'm also glad that Luke sees – through Jill – this side of life too. There's a big, bad, exciting world out there, and I wouldn't want Luke to grow up thinking, like so many mollycoddled kids, that life ends where *EastEnders* begins.

I suppose, if I'm being honest, that I'm grateful for the excitement – albeit second hand – that Jill brings to my own life, too. I complain and tut, and purse my lips, but I love to hear about Jill's adventures, her trips to ashrams, her parties on 'e', and her forays into sadomasochism. It's like having your own personal Madonna.

Am I jealous of Jill? Certainly. Would I swap any part of my life for any part of hers? Never.

I know, too, that, obtusely, Jill is jealous of me. She craves love and stability and reassurance, but, being incapable of acting in a manner that might bring those things to the table, she will always crave them.

We have never fallen out for more than a day or so, both because I'm very easy-going (Jill calls me Little Miss Sunshine behind my back) but also because ours being one of only three stable relationships in her life – her daughter, Tristan, and myself – Jill simply can't do without me.

Tristan isn't the easiest person to get on with either. He is so similar to Jill in so many ways that the slightest argument between them generally reaches epic proportions within minutes. When they do fall out – and it happens frequently

– Jill is not only heartbroken, but, I think, *scared*. She is too competitive to get on with other women, and too predatory to get on with men. Thus gay Tristan is pretty much her only hope. So for all of these reasons (and because he supplies her with drugs) she will compromise in any way, will jump through any philosophical hoop to make up with him.

If only she applied the same determination to her romantic entanglements she would, I think, have a much happier life. But then, perhaps, I of all people understand that if she did, it wouldn't be such an exciting one either.

FIVE

Tristan appears, three plates of food balanced on his right arm, just as Jill is finishing her whinge-fest about Saïd.

"Saïd again?" he asks as he moves precisely around the table. "I'm glad I missed that one."

"Hey, she asked, OK?" Jill says.

"I did," Hannah admits. "He doesn't sound like a very nice character. Did you meet him?"

"Sure," Tristan says, placing her plate before her and giving it a quarter turn, presumably for aesthetic effect. "He was nice enough to me. Which from an observant Muslim is as much as any gay man can ask."

"This looks amazing," Hannah says. "Luke, go fetch Aïsha, will you?" But Aïsha appears at that exact moment.

"Oh, there you are. Come and sit down," Jill tells her daughter, tapping the seat beside her.

Instead, or probably in reaction to this, Aïsha chooses to take Tristan's seat at the table instead. Jill simply reaches over and swaps Tristan's wine-glass with Aïsha's Coke.

"I'm always amazed when I see you do that," Jill says as Tristan returns with the second batch of plates on one arm.

"Once a waiter, always a waiter," he says, placing the dishes before them with renewed flourish. "It's pretty easy once you learn how."

"So is this a dish you serve at your restaurant?" Cliff asks,

21

slicing into the tuna steak and noting the raw red colour of the interior. He likes his tuna *cooked* personally, but you'd have to be a braver man than Cliff to criticise Tristan's handiwork.

"Yes," Tristan says. "Yes, this is on the lunchtime menu at Rez." He glances at Cliff, who attempts but fails to manifest an expression of blank contentment.

"That's how it's eaten," he tells Cliff, nodding at the tuna. "It's blue-fin, the same as they use in sushi. The same as they use *raw* in sushi."

"Dad hates sushi, don't you?" Luke says.

"No," Cliff says. "Not at all. I don't *hate* it."

"Aren't blue-fin almost extinct or something?" Jill asks. "I think I saw a programme."

"No. This is Atlantic blue-fin, not southern," Tristan tells her, slicing into his own and forking a mouthful. "Southern blue-fin is hundreds of pounds a kilo. You'd *never* cook it."

Cliff forks some vegetables, and to avoid eating the fish – just yet – he asks, "So this is what, spinach?"

"Yep. All the other ingredients are the same as a Niçoise salad," Tristan tells him. "Only cooked."

"*Mine's* not cooked," Luke says, and everyone else at the table is secretly grateful for his innocence. "There's blood oozing out of it," he continues.

"It's supposed to be like that," Hannah tells him, even though she's having the same drama. "Just eat up, otherwise it won't be a hot Niçoise salad at all."

"It'll be a cold one, won't it," Luke says.

Tristan puts down his fork, sits back in his chair, and then sips his wine. He looks around the table. He looks bemused.

Everyone freezes.

Tristan slips into a grin, laughs, says, "OK!" and jumps

22

back up. Before anyone can even ask why, he is whizzing around the table whisking people's plates from before them.

"Tris!" Jill protests, but it's too late. Her plate is already in the kitchen.

When he returns for the second three dishes, Tristan says, "Your faces! Unbearable! I shall cook the fuckers to death. And you had better eat them."

Once he has gone, Hannah glances at Jill who raises one eyebrow, then at Cliff who winks at her.

"The pool isn't filling very quick," Luke says whilst they wait. "Will it be full by tomorrow?"

"Quickly," Hannah corrects him. "It isn't filling very quick-*lee*."

"No, it won't be full by tomorrow," Cliff, who the question was directed at, replies.

Jill tuts. "Of course it will," she says.

Cliff shrugs. "I think you're underestimating the amount of water needed to fill a pool like that," he tells her. "It holds thousands of gallons."

"And you, the power of positive thought," Jill says. "If we all believe it will, then it will. Belief becomes reality. Don't be so negative."

Cliff pinches the bridge of his nose as he considers whether to discuss the likely effects of positive thought on the flow-rate from a tap. Or not. Luckily he is saved by the return of Tristan, who plonks, far less elegantly this time, his plate in front of him. "Thanks, Tristan," he says. "I know it's wrong of me, but I've always struggled a bit with raw fish."

"You didn't spit in them, did you?" Jill asks, feigning real concern.

"*Jill*," Aïsha protests.

"It's OK," Tristan explains. "It's an 'in' joke. And no, I didn't."

"'Tris' reckons you should never send food back. The chefs spit on it," Jill says.

"Not always," Tristan laughs. "It's not unknown. But I don't. And didn't."

"This is gorgeous now," Cliff says, honestly. "Thanks." He frowns at the thought that the phrase would have been better without the word *now* but it's too late.

"It *was* a bit on the raw side," Tristan offers. "It's how I like it, but well, I can't expect everyone to have exactly the same tastes as me. Can I, Cliff?"

Cliff notices that Tristan is staring at him, specifically, as he says this last sentence. He looks down at his plate, pierces the poached egg with his fork, and watches as the yellow of the yolk floods out over the surrounding area. He hates it when Tristan does that cute stuff.

After dinner they sit around the cosy glow of the oil lamps and sip glasses of Cognac.

Aïsha and Luke are in the hammock together battling each other on the Nintendo.

"They're doing well," Hannah points out. "It's a good sign."

"Don't worry," Jill tells her. "It won't last."

"What happened to the power of positive thought?" Cliff asks.

"Oh you know what they're like," Jill says. "They always argue. It's because he's Libra and Aïsha's Aries. They're fundamentally incompatible."

Tristan produces a tobacco tin from his jacket pocket and starts to roll a joint.

Hannah tops up her Cognac and then says, addressing her sister, "You know I never say anything about you smoking around them."

"Oh, here we go," Jill says.

"But when you told me about the teddy bear."

Tristan snorts, blowing tobacco over the table. "Look what you made me do," he says.

"It's not funny," Hannah says. "I'm sorry, but it isn't."

"What's this about?" Tristan asks, grinning.

"I told Hannah about how we smuggled our half a kilo of dope through customs in Aï's old teddy bear," Jill says.

"Oh," Tristan says, grinning broadly. "*That*."

Cliff runs his tongue across his teeth and represses a frown. The exaggerated quantity has, for him at least, given the game away.

"I can't believe that you all think this is funny," Hannah says, a wave of indignation rising within her. "It's totally irresponsible. She could have ended up in prison. You all could have."

"Better her than me," Jill says with a shrug.

Hannah, wide-eyed, turns to Cliff for support. He reaches over and lays his hand upon hers, but she snatches it away, angry at his expression, a smirk.

"They're winding you up," he tells her quietly.

Hannah looks from one lamp-lit face to another, her mood quivering on a knife-edge between anger and embarrassment. "Is that true?" she asks.

"Not at all," Jill says, sounding aggressive now. "How else were we supposed to get it here?"

But Tristan, like Cliff, can sense that Hannah is on the verge of a serious upset. He glances at Jill and wonders if she doesn't realise this, or simply doesn't care. "Actually I picked it up from a mate in Lyon," he tells Hannah. "We spent last night at my friend Pierre's place."

"Oh," Hannah says. "Well . . ."

"And it wasn't half a kilo. It was this," he says, holding up a small brown lump the size of a toffee. "They don't even arrest you for this anymore. They don't even fine you."

Hannah doubts this, but she isn't sure enough to argue the point. She shakes her head and squints at Jill. "You're horrible to me," she says, half joking, half not. "You always were."

Jill shrugs. "You're so gullible, it's irresistible," she laughs. "As if Aï' would bring a teddy bear!"

SIX

Luke – in a deckchair – has fallen asleep, so Cliff carries him to his room. It takes half an hour before Hannah realises that Cliff isn't coming back either, that the *fell asleep with Luke* thing, which they both use to escape, when they need to, has happened.

Aïsha is off somewhere doing her thing, and all three remaining adults are tipsy on wine and then Cognac and now wine again. Tristan and Jill, in addition, are stoned.

The conversation is taking on the random nature it always does when marijuana is thrown into the mix. Avenues are explored then abandoned simply because two out of the three people here can't remember what they were talking about.

Hannah remembers, but she doesn't mind. She won't go to bed yet. She's enjoying sitting outside in this balmy Mediterranean evening, frogs croaking somewhere to the right, a thousand stars silent above their heads, clouds of exhaled smoke drifting above them.

"So are you seeing anyone at the moment?" she asks Tristan.

Jill finds this funny and snorts. Red wine drips from her nose.

Tristan, after a short delay, starts to laugh as well, and Hannah can't work out whether he's laughing at the wine dripping from Jill's nose or her question.

"What?" she asks, amused, but confused, by their reaction. "What did I say?"

Jill blows her nose on a napkin and says, "God, that hurts. Do not snort wine. Jesus!"

"It's not you, Hannah," Tristan says. "It's just, well, as they say on Facebook, *it's complicated.*"

"I don't use Facebook," Hannah says. "Sorry."

"He's seeing three guys at once," Jill tells her. "It is *just* the three, right?"

Tristan nods. "It's not as bad as it sounds," he tells Hannah.

"It *is,*" Jill laughs.

"OK, it is then," Tristan says. "But it's not as *frenetic* as it sounds then. Wolfgang – he's the main one . . ."

"The *main* one!" Jill repeats, sniggering.

"Well, he *is!*" Tristan says. "But he lives in Berlin. So I only see him about once a month."

"Right," Hannah says, nodding knowingly.

"And Pete and Matt live in Staffordshire, so . . ."

"Both of them?"

"They're a couple," Tristan explains. "So . . ."

"Of course," Hannah says as if this is the most natural thing in the world. Which she doesn't think it is, of course. But she isn't shocked either.

OK, maybe she *is* shocked a bit, but she isn't *surprised* that she's shocked. Tristan's love life has always been devilishly complicated, which is precisely why she asked him the question. It's another world, really, nothing to do with her world, but interesting all the same. She enjoys these windows into other worlds the same way she enjoys a good novel.

"Hannah thinks *I'm* a slag," Jill says, then, pointing one finger at Tristan, "but *you,* are *sommat* else."

Hannah smiles at her sister. "I have *never* said such a thing," she says.

"You've thought it."

"I haven't."

Jill shrugs. "I don't care anyway."

"So don't any of you get jealous?" Hannah asks, turning back to Tristan. "I would have thought jealousy would be the main worry."

"What? Generally? Or in bed?" Tristan asks.

"Either. Both," Hannah says.

"Wolfie doesn't know about the other two," Jill says. "Tristan hasn't told him."

"No," Tristan admits. "No, well, there would be no point, would there."

"I see," Hannah says, nodding and thinking about this. "And the couple? Presumably they're immune to jealousy issues."

"Yeah, pretty much," Tristan says, lighting a fresh joint. "I mean, in bed, it gets dodgy sometimes. Obviously. You have to make an effort to make sure no one gets left out."

"But someone always *is* left out," Jill says. "That's my experience, anyway."

Hannah turns and narrows her eyes at her little sister in a comical fashion.

"I *told* you already," Jill says. "When I was with Barry."

"Oh, the swingers' club."

"Yeah."

"I didn't know you actually . . . you know . . ."

Hannah is interrupted by Tristan coughing, exhaling smoke and waving the joint randomly in Jill's direction as he does so.

"What?" she asks, taking it from his grasp.

"S–" Tristan splutters, and Hannah realises that he is, in fact, laughing – doubled up with laughter in fact. "S– Sw– swingers."

29

Jill, starting to laugh as well, asks again, "What, Tris'?"

Hannah tries to force a smile. She can sense that it's an unconvincing smile, and this realisation makes her feel unexpectedly old, unexpectedly out of it, like a parent trying to ingratiate herself to her kid's friends.

"S . . . Swingers!" Tristan gurgles, tears in his eyes now. "It's just . . . It's just such a weird word for it. God."

"Swingers!" Jill repeats. She is laughing as well now.

Hannah shakes her head and pushes her chair back. "Right," she says. "That's enough for me."

"Oh don't go, Han'," Jill says. "We weren't laughing at you."

"No," Tristan agrees, struggling to contain himself. "I didn't mean. It's not you. It's just, sometimes, you suddenly realise how funny a word is, right? And swing—" He cracks up laughing again.

Hannah smiles demurely, circles the table, kisses her sister on the back of the head, runs a hand over Tristan's shoulders as she passes him, and says, "I know. But it's almost one. I'm shattered. Good night, kids."

It isn't true though. She isn't tired at all.

It's just that with dope, as apparently with threesomes, unless you participate, you at some point realise that you are just sitting on the sidelines.

Hannah checks on Luke. He's snuggled up with his head squashed into a teddy-bear. He looks beautiful and angelic still. Hannah ineffectually repositions the quilt around him and wonders how much longer this can last. How long do they have before he becomes like Aïsha?

In their bedroom, Cliff is asleep, snoring lightly. She undresses and eases herself into the bed gently so as not to wake him. There have been times in the past when she has

30

done the exact opposite in the very hope of waking him. But it's been a few years if the truth be told.

She slides one hand down beneath the covers and caresses her inner thigh gently. It's not a sexual caress, but it isn't quite asexual either. From outside she can hear fresh peals of laughter.

She tries to imagine what it must be like alternating between three different lovers. She supposes that she could have done that. She supposes that she could have made different choices and been the kind of girl who had three different lovers. Or could she? Perhaps that stuff is pre-destined.

She wonders if they all kiss differently, if they all have different identifiable smells, different dick sizes, different shaped bums. She wonders if Tristan prefers making love to one of them over the others.

She wonders who, out of Tristan, Pete and, Mike? Was it Mike? Or Matt? – she wonders who does what to whom. She wonders if they all sleep together in the same bed afterwards, like some Mediaeval family snuggled together for warmth. That would feel nice, she reckons. Arms and legs everywhere. Lovely in winter. Maybe unbearably hot in summer.

She wonders if they snuggle up, or curl away, wonders who sleeps in the middle, or whether they take it in turns, or draw straws.

As she hovers on the edge of sleep she wonders if they have a big bed, a king-sized bed, or a round bed, or a bed the size of a room, or a bed the size of the moon . . .

And then suddenly it is morning, and Luke is standing in the doorway, saying, "Mum? Mum? Are you awake? Mum?"

SEVEN

Luke

To want your child to remain innocent whilst toughening up enough to survive *This Life* is entirely contradictory, but, as far as I can tell, an almost universal parental desire.

It's a widely held belief that the reasons we parents mollycoddle our children are fundamentally selfish. But it's not true. It's not because we want them to stay infants, as playthings for ourselves – it's because they're so happy rollicking around in the Garden of Eden, we can't bear for it to end. As adults, we know that life, once the apple of knowledge is bitten into, becomes so much more complicated, so much more fraught.

There's something so simplistic, almost autistic, about Luke's outlook still, about his lack of philosophical angst. It's a wonderful thing to behold.

Perhaps this comes from Cliff. He certainly doesn't seem too worried about the big questions of our time: ecology, politics, the planet . . . Nor does he seem overly concerned about the big questions of our lives: where do we come from, why are we here, what is the point . . . Perhaps it's a fundamental difference between men and women.

Tristan doesn't seem overly angst-ridden either as he hops from bed to bed. Like Cliff, his solutions to unhappiness all involve action verbs: buying something, going places, shagging more . . . We women spend so much time in our heads, passively thinking, worrying, hoping.

So perhaps Luke, like his father, will continue to leap out of bed of a morning, full of beans, will continue to fall asleep the second his head hits the pillow. I certainly pray (there's another passive verb) that he'll be happy, contented.

That maternal bond, of hope and fear, of love and terror is aching in intensity – it knows no equal. It's a cliché, perhaps, but there is nothing I wouldn't give for Luke to be happy, nothing I wouldn't sacrifice to keep him safe.

Is that normal? Do all mothers feel the same? I have no idea, though I would guess so. Perhaps my bond with Luke is a bit stronger than "normal" because of what he represented in my own life.

My first pregnancy failed in the third month. She (it was a girl) would have been born in the midst of so much misery that, even at the time, it seemed a logical if heartbreaking outcome.

If she had lived, would I look at her today as I look at Luke? Or would I have forever seen her as the reason my life got stuck? I'm really not sure.

At the time I thought that it was my desire to break free, my resentment, specifically, at being held back, that had killed her.

By the time Luke came along I understood that there was nothing else to run to anyway, nowhere better to go.

Like a mirage at the end of a hot day, James had faded, leaving only Cliff and myself and a child-sized gap in our lives. So Luke felt like a second chance. Another chance at motherhood. Another chance for my marriage. Another chance to forget everything that had happened.

EIGHT

The pool hasn't filled up. This is the important news flash for which Luke has woken her.

Hannah blinks to remove the sleep from her eyes and finally manages to focus on her son, standing in the doorway.

"It's only up to here," he says, pointing just below his knee.

"It's filling though, is it?" Hannah asks.

"Yes, it's *filling*. But I can't swim in it."

"It's a good job we're here for two weeks then, isn't it," Hannah says, becoming aware only now that the bed beside her is cold, that Cliff is already up.

"I wanted to swim today," Luke says. "Dad says it's gonna be really hot."

"Well, you'll just have to wait," Hannah says. "Now go outside and play with Aïsha and let me wake up properly."

By the time she has dozed off, woken up a second time, and dragged herself out to the patio, everyone is in the midst of breakfast. The sky is pure unadulterated blue, the light blinding, and already heat is radiating from the terracotta floor tiles.

"Hey, sleepy head," Cliff says, smiling at her from across the table.

"What time is it?" Hannah asks, sitting down and reaching for the carton of orange juice. "I feel like I have been drugged or something."

"I slipped some Rohypnol into your wine last night," Tristan says.

"Um?" Hannah replies in a tone that expresses that though she doesn't understand what he has said, she *has* understood that it was a throwaway line of no importance and requires no further explanation.

"Tristan's taking us swimming," Luke says.

Hannah sips her juice and nods at Tristan. "Really? That's nice of you," she tells him. She turns to Aïsha. "Are you going too?"

Aïsha nods, shrugs and rolls her eyes simultaneously. Heaven forbid that someone might catch her looking enthusiastic.

"It's just that the pool's still empty," Tristan explains, "So I thought . . ."

"It'll take days," Cliff says. "I told you."

"I'm saying nothing," Jill says, and Hannah sees Cliff shoot a tiny glare at her. She could work out what that's about if she concentrated upon it. She knows it's within her grasp to remember, but she chooses not to.

"We can all go if you want," Tristan says. "It's only about an hour to the coast."

Hannah vaguely raises one hand. "No," she says. "No, it'll be a few days before I'll be willing to get in a car again."

"That's what I said," Cliff agrees.

Hannah glances at Jill, busy picking the dried fruit out of her bowl of muesli – she says it contains sulphites or something – and wonders if she's going with them or staying. But she doesn't ask her yet, because how she phrases that question could influence Jill's decision. So does she want Jill to go and leave her here alone with Cliff, or doesn't she?

It might be nice. It happens so rarely these days. They would probably end up having sex. In fact they would definitely end up having sex. And therein lies the problem. Because it wouldn't be *two-bodies-passionately-drawn-together* sex or even *hey-babe-fancy-a-quicky* sex. It would be *this-is-what-we-do*; it would be *this-is-what-we-do-when-we-find-ourselves-alone* sex.

It's not that Hannah dislikes sex with Cliff. It varies on a scale between feeling mundane but OK to (occasionally) really rather nice. It's just the predictability of everything that suffocates her, that inevitable unfolding of where it will happen and when it will happen and how it will happen. If Jill leaves with the others, Cliff will stand and round the table. He will nuzzle her hair, and then nuzzle her neck. And then he will slide one hand across her shoulder, down over her breast, and reach for her hand. He will say, "Come," and she'll smile and stand and follow him to the bedroom. Every move has been choreographed over the years. Nothing is left to chance. There are no surprises.

Jill, who Hannah now realises she has been staring at, says, "Well, I'm with you guys. I'm not moving a muscle today," and Cliff catches Hannah's eye and shrugs.

Even now, Hannah can't decide if she feels disappointed or relieved.

Once the Jeep has gone, yesterday's techno picking up exactly where it left off, the two sisters clear the breakfast table.

Jill makes an effort to contribute, but in that special way of hers which is more of a hindrance than a help. Jill's ability to perform even the most mundane tasks in the least efficient way possible never ceases to astound Hannah. She often wonders how Jill has managed to raise her daughter at all. But manage, she has.

When Hannah has finished removing the unstable tower of dishes that Jill has piled up in the sink, she starts to empty and re-stack the dishwasher as Jill washes and dries, very slowly, a single mug.

"The culture gap was just too vast to be bridged, really," Jill is saying – Saïd again. "They expect you to do everything, Muslims. Shopping, cleaning. He liked his dinner to be on the table when he got in, d'you know what I'm saying? It was crazy."

Hannah knows she's a bit old-school, but she doesn't consider that crazy at all. Cliff, after all, is right now ensconced in his crime novel while the women present clear the breakfast table. Hannah doesn't consider that macho. She considers it fair. Cliff's long days at the practice pay, after all, for all of this for all of them.

"He was working, though, wasn't he?" she asks.

"Yeah. I told you. At Stansted."

"Yes. Really long hours you said." Hannah doesn't really know why she bothers to scatter pointers this way. Jill has never seemed able to spot them.

"Yeah. It was a drag," Jill says. "Sometimes he didn't get home till ten."

"I think I'd want my dinner ready if I got home from work at ten."

"All the same. I mean, we're not in the fifties anymore, are we? Just because he's the breadwinner doesn't give him the right to meals on wheels and sex on demand."

"You've never been one to complain about sex on demand," Hannah says, straightening from the dishwasher and smiling at her sister, who, she sees, is still drying the same mug in slow, circular movements.

"Well, no," Jill says. "That was the upside really. He was *very* pushy in bed."

"Pushy?"

"Yeah, you know. Do this, do that. Suck this. Roll over. And lord knows I like a man who knows what he wants in the bedroom."

And *there*, Hannah thinks, is Jill's problem. She *likes* pushy men. She needs to feel that the man in her life is running the show, is attracted, in a nutshell, to arrogant bastards. They *excite* her. Of course she splits up with them, every time, for exactly the same reasons. It's a tiny psychological conundrum, an insoluble riddle so simple you could describe it in its entirety on the back of a postcard. But it's sufficient to wreak havoc throughout Jill's life.

Back in the conversation, Jill is still talking. ". . . he actually bought me a dog collar. Can you imagine? He used to put it on me and then I knew we were gonna have a really good session. I mean, I wasn't complaining. I like a bit of kink, as you know. But it's pretty revealing, you've got to admit. It's pretty revealing about how the guy sees women."

"But you liked it," Hannah says, throwing her sister another pointless pointer.

"Yes. Well, yes and no," Jill says.

Hannah turns back to the sink so that Jill doesn't see her roll her eyes.

NINE

They are trying to read. Theoretically, all three adults are trying to read, only Jill can't concentrate, which means, of course, that no one can concentrate.

"The guy in this book reminds me too much of Saïd," she says. She's reading – theoretically – *Wuthering Heights*. All roads, it seems, no matter how unlikely, lead to Saïd. From past experience Cliff, listening despite himself, would place money on the fact that they'll get back together.

"Have you read it?" Jill asks.

"Of course," Hannah says. "Years ago though. Heathcliff is the archetypal bastard."

"At the beginning of May," Jill says, "we went to Margate for a weekend. Saïd found this really good hotel deal, so we just went for it. It was a four-star hotel and everything, but really cheap. I thought it was a great idea until we got there. What a dump! Margate that is, not the hotel. Do you know the shops in the high street were boarded up there? I mean talk about recession. Anyway . . ."

Hannah closes her book. She does this gently so that Jill won't think (or rather realise) that the gesture is a reproach for her blathering. She sits and listens as each of the standard elements of a Jill story are revealed: the disappointing surroundings, the determination to have a good time despite it all, a soupçon of rude service wittily put down, an evening of alcohol, rough (but good) sex, and finally, of course, The Argument.

"We didn't speak to each other the whole way home," Jill says, concluding her story.

It was rather a good story actually. They generally are. But Hannah wants to read. "No, well," she says, faking a yawn. "I'm still sleepy. I might go have another snooze."

Cliff peers over the top of his novel and winks at her, and Hannah, realising that Jill must be driving poor Cliff insane already, raises one eyebrow conspiratorially.

No sooner has Hannah lain down and re-opened her book than Cliff enters the bedroom, locking the door behind him.

Hannah realises that he has misinterpreted her complicit eyebrow wiggle and thinks, *Oh well, we might as well get it over with*. She chides herself immediately for the thought, unsure even as to why she is so uncharitable. In truth, she acknowledges, she wants this. In truth, she needs this.

Sex has always been complicated for her. In fact, pleasure, in general, has always been something slightly alien to her. She has always felt a requirement to accept it under duress rather than throw herself into it. She really doesn't know where that comes from.

"Lord, your sister can talk," Cliff says, shucking his shorts and shirt.

"She can," Hannah agrees, wriggling out of her dress without standing. Cliff yanks off his underpants as she removes her bra. There was a time, at the beginning, when they found undressing embarrassing. For almost a decade, she undressed in the dark or in the bathroom, then sprinted beneath the covers. This easy familiarity is so much easier, yet so much less exciting.

"So are we reading, or . . ." Cliff says, now naked and crawling up the bed towards her, tiger-style.

"'Or . . .' I reckon, don't you?" Hannah says.

The sex follows the dots and squiggles they have laid down over the years – he kisses her like this, she slides a hand there and pulls him in . . . and though predictable, Hannah decides that it's none the worse for that. No one complains that the *Four Seasons* sounds the same every time, do they? Things don't have to be original and unique to be satisfying. They just have to be faithfully performed.

When it's over, they fall into a surprisingly deep slumber and wake two hours later, sweaty and hungry and groggy from too much sleep.

"Half three," Cliff says, answering an unspoken question.

"Wow."

"I'm starving," Cliff says. "I wonder when Master Chef gets back."

"I'll make a sandwich," Hannah says. "We have cheese, and ham. Smoked salmon . . . Gosh, I'm hungry too."

"Is that allowed?" Cliff asks, sitting on the side of the bed and rubbing his face in his hands.

"What, is anyone except Tristan allowed to prepare food?" Hannah asks, laughter in her voice.

"I guess we don't have to tell him," Cliff says. "But if you use up some vital ingredient he'll go crazy."

"He will not," Hannah says.

"Anyway, they're back," Cliff tells her, cocking one ear.

Hannah holds her breath and hears the slamming of doors and Luke's bouncing voice. "They are," she agrees. "God, I feel so woozy!"

"It's the heat," Cliff says. "We're not used to it. Maybe we need to drink more. Water I mean."

By the time they have showered and reached the patio, Tristan is seated, gutting fish. Aïsha is taking photographs of the removed fish innards.

"Ew, you're brave," Hannah comments.

Tristan shrugs.

"We bought fish from the fisherman," Luke tells them. He is, for no apparent reason, wearing a diving mask.

"What's with the mask?" Hannah asks.

"Tris' bought it," he explains.

"He was chatting up all the fishermen," Aïsha says. "It was awful. Embarrassing."

"Not *all* of them," Tristan says.

"Just the hunky one," Luke says, and both Hannah and Cliff bristle at some subconscious discomfort.

"You don't even know what hunky means," Tristan laughs. "But, yeah, he was. He was gorgeous. I was powerless to resist."

"I saw fish in the sea," Luke says, thankfully moving on. "Like, this big," he says, holding his hands apart to demonstrate an unfeasibly large fish.

"Did you see any fish, Aï?" Hannah asks.

She shakes her head.

"Missy forgot her cossie," Tristan explains. "We tried to buy one but she didn't like any of them."

"They only had these lame Paris Hilton things," Aïsha says,

and Hannah thinks she can read between those particular lines.

"You could have swum in shorts and a T-shirt," she tells her. "Like the Australians do."

Aïsha shrugs – her standard response – but then she belies her indifference by asking, "Do they really?"

Hannah nods. "I saw it on TV. The sun's really strong there so they get lots of skin cancers and stuff."

"It's the hole in the ozone layer," Jill says. "From aerosols."

"So they swim in T-shirts to protect themselves from the sun," Hannah continues. "They have a TV campaign. Slip, slop and slap or something."

Egged on by the fact that Aïsha looks, for once, genuinely interested, Hannah explains. "I think it stands for *slip on a T-shirt, slop on some sun-cream, and slap on a sun-hat.* Something like that anyway."

Aïsha wrinkles her nose. "But they *swim* like that?" she asks.

"They do," Hannah says with a serious nod. "They think it's cool."

"I'm gonna check on the pool," Luke says, standing.

"So tell me about the spunky fisherman," Jill says.

Aïsha groans and heads off after Luke.

Tristan looks up from his gutting. "He was beautiful," he says. "He looked like Jean-Marc Barr in *The Big Blue.* D'you ever see that?"

Jill shakes her head. Hannah shrugs.

"I did, I think," Cliff says, surprising them all. "French film, right?"

Tristan raises his eyebrows and nods to show that he's impressed. "Well, he looked like the diver guy from that."

43

"The younger one, presumably," Cliff says.

"Yeah, not Jean Reno," Tristan laughs. "Though he's hot too. If you're into older guys. But no, this one was all muscles and five o'clock stubble. I was in heaven."

Cliff catches Hannah staring at him, staring though him. "It was on Film 4," he tells her. "You went to bed to read, so I watched it. It's about competition divers."

"There's a guy like that here," Jill says. "Something to do with this place. He came by yesterday to fill the pool when you were cooking. He'd be right up your street. He'd be right up *my* street."

"We have a hot pool guy and you didn't come tell me!" Tristan protests.

"Sorry," Cliff says and then, suddenly embarrassed yet unsure why, he dips his head and stares at his book.

TEN

Tristan

Tristan came to us through Jill. They met in Ibiza as I recall, during one of the summers when Aïsha and Luke were over at our place. (In theory the kids spend alternate summers at Jill's, but as this rule is suspended any time Jill meets someone new or anytime Jill splits up with someone, they're more often than not at ours . . .)

I honestly didn't expect her friendship with Tristan to last so long. As I explained, Jill doesn't really do stable relationships, whether they be friends or romances. And Tristan Wilde (his real name is Brian Smith or something – he changed it) seemed highly strung enough that I assumed he wouldn't put up with Jill for long. But eight years on he's still here, and we've more or less got used to him. He's a pretty good friend to her, and I'm grateful for that. It takes some of the pressure off me at least.

I felt pretty uncomfortable around him at first, it has to be said. Of course I have known gay guys before, but I've never been privy to quite so much detail about their personal lives. Tristan is a chronic over-sharer and it's hard not to be shocked by some of what he gets up to. But you get used to being shocked by people. You get to appreciate it even. Difference is good. Difference is interesting. That's what Tristan taught me.

He has some great qualities as well. He's a brilliant chef

(Rez, his first restaurant, has Michelin stars) and he loves to cook even when he's on holiday, which suits me just fine. He's always bouncy, always 'on' and even when he isn't – because Tristan clearly has his share of heartache, perhaps *more* than his share – he has a unique ability to turn disaster into amusing fiction. If you see him regularly you can witness him telling the same story over and over, and each time it becomes a little funnier, a little more ridiculous, and a little less painful.

As I say, the over-sharing made me nervous at the beginning, especially because he does it in front of the kids. Of course I didn't *actually* think that Tristan talking about his boyfriends would make Luke into a gay, but, well, as a mother, you wonder, don't you. You have to wonder if it's healthy.

Tristan must never find this out – I'd be mortified – but I asked the psychologist at the first school where I worked what he thought about it.

He said, with reassuring certainty, that there was nothing to worry about, that if Luke is going to be heterosexual then he'll be heterosexual, and that if he's going to be a homosexual, he'll be one, whatever goes on around him. He said that the only effect having a gay 'uncle' would be likely to have would be to make Luke feel comfortable around gay men no matter which way he turns out.

I had a drunken conversation with Tristan once about Luke, too. He asked me how I would feel if Luke turned out gay (his own father threw him out) and I said, quite honestly, that I'd be OK about it. I'd be worried that he'd be lonely of course, but then plenty of heterosexuals manage that. I'd be worried about Aids, and I suppose I'd be disappointed not to have grandchildren too. So it's hardly my ideal. But I'd be OK about it. And I remember I asked Tristan how I would know if

Luke was going to be gay, and what I should do, what I should say. Tristan made me laugh so much. He said, "Honey, he likes insects, football, video games and guns. If you catch him playing with your jewellery then call me, but until that day, relax." And the very next time I looked at Luke I realised that I knew already. I realised that I don't have anything to worry about. Or not on that score, at least.

ELEVEN

After a lunch of tomato and buffalo mozzarella salad (the tomatoes actually taste like tomatoes here) followed by the fish, snapper, *en papillotte* with asparagus and wild mushroom risotto – a lunch that lasts so long it merges into dinner – Cliff proposes that they go for a walk, and Tristan suggests a bar he has spotted as an ideal destination.

As the sun sinks lower, throwing ever-longer shadows across the garden, they lock up the house and start, en masse, to crunch their way along the lane.

Each property is set within an acre or so of land, so they walk for five minutes chatting quietly, and then pause to peer over a gate or through a hedge, commenting, "*Nice pool,*" or, "*Grass could do with a cut,*" or, "*Someone's a hoarder.*"

"Most of these look empty," Cliff says.

"Holiday homes, I guess," Hannah says, taking his arm.

"But it's July," Cliff says. "Shouldn't people be *in* their holiday homes?"

"It's weird," Tristan agrees. "I thought that as well."

Hannah watches Luke and Aïsha walking in front. Luke's gait is still boyish and sprightly. Aïsha has picked up a stick and is whacking the plants at the side of the road mercilessly as she walks.

"Must be amazing to live somewhere like this," Jill says. "I mean somewhere where it's hot all summer long. It must be heavenly to wake up in the morning and just *know* it's gonna be sunny."

"Maybe you should move," Hannah says. "I wouldn't mind visiting."

"I would," Jill says. "If I met a bloke who lived somewhere like this, I'd move in a second."

"You'd never put up with the French," Tristan says.

"Really?" Hannah asks, a little shocked. "They can't be that different, can they? Surely people are people wherever you go."

"Tris' is just being racist," Jill says.

"Not racist," Tristan says. "Xenophobic. Anyway, I did my training in Paris. I think I know what I'm talking about."

Aïsha turns around. She looks vaguely panicked at the tenure of the conversation. "Jill, we are *so* not moving to France," she says.

"Wouldn't you like that, sweetie?" Jill asks, her tone mocking.

"No," Aïsha tells her. "It's well boring."

Once Aïsha has returned her attention to whacking the bushes, Hannah murmurs, "Well, that told you."

Jill sighs. "That's what they're like at that age. You'll see soon enough. Everything's boring, or . . ."

"Or?"

"Aïsha? What's that word you use for anything that's rubbish? She uses it all the time, only I can't remember."

Aïsha looks back at them and shrugs. "Gay?" she says.

"Hum, not too keen on that one," Tristan says.

"It doesn't mean *gay*," Aïsha tells him. "It just means lame."

"Lame! That's the one," Jill says. "Yep, everything's boring or lame. Once in a blue moon something is awesome, but it really is once in a blue moon."

"It's all very American," Hannah says. "Lame. Awesome . . ."

"Still not keen on the whole gay equals rubbish analogy," Tristan says.

"She doesn't mean anything by it," Jill says.

"I know," Tristan says, "but all the same . . ."

The bar, when they reach it, is tiny. It comprises a single room (Formica and strip-lights) and a small roadside terrace covered with a vine-woven trellis.

There are three clients in the bar, without exception ageing alcoholics with pickled eyes and red noses. As there is no sign of a barman or owner, they return to the terrace and brush leaves from the seats.

"This is nice," Hannah says looking around.

Jill snorts.

"What?" Hannah asks, determined to deal with this head-on this time.

"Well," Jill says. "This is nice . . ."

"It *is*," Hannah tells her. "I *love* places like this. Look at that." She nods at a painted advert, a badly faded wall-sized mural advertising Ricard. "It's so . . . It's just so French."

"Can we go and explore?" Luke asks.

"Of course," Cliff tells him. "Just don't get lost. Do you want a drink?"

Luke looks puzzled. "Do they have Coke in France?"

Everyone grins. Luke shrugs and looks embarrassed.

"They do," Hannah tells him, gently. "They have Coke pretty much everywhere in fact."

"Coke then," Luke says, doubtfully.

"Actually, there's a French drink if you want something different," Tristan suggests.

Luke looks doubtful.

"It tastes like Sprite."

"Sprite's OK," Luke says. "But I prefer Coke."

"The thing about the French version is that it's quite fun to ask for," Tristan tells him.

Luke frowns.

"It's called Pschitt!" Tristan explains.

"Shit?"

"Pschitt! With a P. P-S-C-H-I-T-T. It's supposed to be the sound you get when you open the bottle. *Pschitt!* See?"

Luke wrinkles his nose. "I think I'll just have Coke," he says.

Tristan shrugs. "I always quite enjoyed saying, 'I'll have a Pschitt!' myself."

"Tristan!" Hannah protests.

"Hey!" Tristan says. "I didn't invent the stuff. It's been around for years."

Luke smirks. "Maybe I will have a Pshitt," he says, reddening with restrained giggles. He looks at Hannah. "Can I?"

Hannah grins and nods. "But you have to ask for it yourself. I'm not saying it."

"Aï'?" Cliff asks.

"Coke," she replies, pulling a face.

"You're sure you don't want a Pschitt as well?" he asks.

"Totally," she says. "Sounds gross."

"Vous voulez quelque chose ?" A voice, behind them. They all turn to see the barman. He's a good-looking guy in his twenties with a vaguely old-fashioned-looking mop of hair drifting over one eye and an open shirt revealing a hairless chest and a gold crucifix.

"Sorry, but . . . Vous parlez anglais ?" Hannah asks him.

"I speak French," Tristan volunteers, then, "Je parle français."

51

"Is OK," the barman tells them. "I can speak English. A little."

"Great. So it's a beer for me," Cliff says.

"I'll have a Pastis," Tristan says.

"A glass of dry white wine," Hannah says.

"Me too."

"And . . . what was it you wanted, Luke?" Tristan prompts.

Luke looks about to burst with excitement at the idea of being able to order his drink. He looks at his mother, barely able to believe that he's allowed to say it.

"Go on then," Hannah prompts, smiling broadly.

"Can I have a Pschitt please?" Luke asks.

The barman nods. "Deux vins blancs, une biere, un pastis, et un Pschitt, c'est ça ?"

"Oui," Tristan confirms.

"You liked that, didn't you?" Hannah laughs, once the barman has gone.

Luke nods. "I think I'm going to have a Pschitt every time," he says.

"Well, you haven't tasted it yet."

Luke shrugs, says, "Pshitt," once more, then runs off, closely followed by Aïsha.

"Well, I like the barman, anyway!" Tristan comments.

"I was waiting for that," Jill laughs.

"Definitely dances my side of the fence, that one," Tristan says.

"You reckon?" Jill asks. "I can't tell with the Frenchies. They *all* look a bit gay to me."

"How can you tell?" Cliff asks, genuinely intrigued.

Tristan shrugs. "Gaydar," he says.

The barman returns with a tray of drinks, a dish of olives, another of peanuts, and a third with tiny squares of pizza.

"I love the way they do that," Hannah says. "I love the way you get a mini meal with your drinks."

"It's nice," Cliff agrees, taking a square of pizza. "Do they always do that in France?"

"No," Tristan says. "No it's more of an Italian thing. But we're not so far from the border here, so . . ."

"So are you liking France?" Hannah asks, patting Cliff's hand on the table. He hadn't been keen on the idea of this holiday. He said he couldn't see any reason to change from the usual place in Dorset.

"It's OK so far," he says, then, forcing a smile, "Yes, it's fine actually."

Luke reappears at the table. "We found a ping-pong table," he says. "We found a ball in the bushes too, but there's no bats."

"They probably keep them behind the bar," Tristan says.

Luke turns his bottle around so that he can read the label. "Pschitt!" he says. He points it at Hannah.

"Yes, I saw," she laughs. "So, go on. Taste it."

Luke sips at his drink.

"Well?" she prompts.

"It's lemonade," Luke says.

"Yes, pretty much," Tristan says. "Do you like it?"

Luke shrugs. "It's OK," he says. He bumps his dad with his hip.

"What?" Cliff asks.

"Can you find out?" he says.

"What about?"

"About the bats for the ping-pong."

Cliff laughs. "I don't even know what the word for ping-pong is in French."

"It's ping-pong," Tristan tells him, looking up from his phone. "It's le ping-pong."

Cliff nods in his direction. "There you go, Luke. Tris' will sort it for you," he says.

"Tris'?" Luke prompts doubtfully.

"I'll do better than that," Tristan says. "Just let me finish . . ." He types something on his phone, then slips it into his pocket. "There," he says. "Now, what did you want?"

"Bats," Luke says. "For the ping-pong."

Tristan presses his fingers to his forehead in a faux-mystic manner, rolls his eyes and says, "There. I just ordered them. Telepathically."

Luke raises an eyebrow, then slides into a seat and sips noisily at his Pschitt.

Everyone is watching Tristan. He strokes his chin. "Patience," he says.

Luke tuts. "Can't you just ask them?" he says. "Please, Tris'."

Aïsha returns from the other side of the building, kicking gravel as she zigzags towards them, then slides into a chair and swigs at her drink. "Well?" she asks, looking around at the adults, and frowning.

"Tris' is doing magic," Luke says.

"Right," Aïsha says. "Of course he is."

The door to the bar opens and the young barman appears, grinning broadly and carrying bats and a pack of balls. "C'est ceci que vous voulez ?" he asks.

"Oui," Tristan says. "Oui, c'est parfait, merci."

The barman proffers the bats and Luke seizes them, says, "Thanks, Tris'," and apparently both untroubled and unimpressed by the magic, runs back to where the ping-pong table is.

Once Aïsha has followed on, Cliff asks, "So?"

"So what?"

"So how did you do it?" Jill asks.

Tristan sips his drink and smiles smugly. "If you can guess I'll buy you a drink," he says.

"You texted him," Jill says.

"Hum. But I don't have his number."

"You texted that number," Cliff says, nodding at the sign above the door.

Tristan shakes his head. "It's a landline," he says. "You can't text a landline."

"You phoned them," Hannah offers.

Tristan pouts and shakes his head. "You saw me. I didn't move. And I didn't phone them."

"You did a mime when we were looking the other way?"

"I reckon the barman just saw the kids around the table," Cliff says.

"Nope," Tristan says, then in false French accent, "*Zats not eeet.*"

"It's definitely something to do with the phone," Jill says. "You were fiddling with your phone."

"Warmer."

"So you did send him a message?" she says.

"Yes. But how?"

They sit in silence for a few seconds, then Jill says, "Oh, I know. He's on Grindr, isn't he. I bet he's on Grindr."

"Clever girl."

Neither Cliff nor Hannah know what being "on Grindr" means, so Tristan passes his phone around so that they can see. The display shows rows of little thumbnail photos of men in the area, and shows how far they are from this spot. The top one is a reasonably clear photo of the barman. It says, "- 10m."

"That means that he's less than ten metres away," Tristan explains.

When the phone gets to Cliff, he stares at the screen and frowns.

"You look worried, Cliff," Tristan says.

"No," Cliff replies. "I just don't . . . I mean . . . How does it know?"

"Where people are?" Tristan says. "By GPS."

"Sure, but how does it know that they're *gay*?" Cliff asks. "Or aren't these guys necessarily gay?"

"They are," Tristan says. "But the phone doesn't know. It just shows other people who are running Grindr. And seeing as it's a gay hook-up app, it's a pretty safe bet."

Cliff nods, but continues to study the screen. "Some of these are just black squares," he says.

"They haven't put photos up," Tristan explains. "They don't want anyone to know who they are."

"Doesn't that kind of defeat the purpose?" Cliff asks.

Tristan nods. "A bit. Probably married guys cheating on their wives. But they'd send a photo if I asked. Well, they'd probably send a photo of *something* . . ."

"I see," Cliff says, handing back the phone. "Technology! Amazing really."

"There's a straight version too," Jill says.

"There is," Tristan agrees. "It's called Blendr."

"Brenda?!" Hannah asks, pulling a face.

56

Tristan laughs. "Not Brenda. Blendr."

"Oh. I thought it sounded a bit silly. Then again, so does Blendr."

"And that's for what, guys who want to meet girls?" Cliff asks.

Tristan nods.

"Don't tell him any more," Hannah says. "You'll give him ideas."

"I don't think it ever really caught on," Tristan says. "A friend tells me there are loads of guys and no women on it."

"Hum," Jill says, sipping her wine. "Now that's giving *me* ideas."

It's just after midnight by the time they leave the bar.

Luke is tired and, Hannah guesses, on the verge of becoming fractious. With Aïsha it's harder to tell. Fractious is pretty much her average state of being these days.

"I wish we'd brought the car," Aïsha says.

"We all wish that," her mother agrees.

"Next time you can forego alcohol and *you-know-what* and drive us all then," Cliff suggests.

"I rather like it," Hannah says. "It's a lovely evening, and it's not that far. But I wouldn't want to be Tristan walking home alone."

All the adults are a bit drunk, but Tristan, who has stayed behind to talk to the barman, is particularly so.

"What makes you think he'll be walking home alone?" Jill asks, amusement in her voice.

"Yes, I suppose that barman chappy might give him a lift," Cliff says, pretending to miss Jill's point.

"It's a lovely clear night," Hannah says as they enter another

57

pool of yellow light beneath a street lamp. A cloud of insects is frenetically buzzing around and banging into the glass cylinder as they hurl themselves at the brightness.

"Look," Jill says, pointing at the sky, her finger describing a figure of eight. "Is that a bird, or a bat?"

They all pause to stare into the blackness but can see nothing. Then as they start to move again the animal – very clearly a bat – swoops back into the light.

"Yuck," Aïsha says. "I hope it's not a vampire bat."

"It's not," Hannah says. "They don't even live here, do they, Cliff?"

"No," Cliff agrees, even though he hasn't the foggiest idea where vampire bats live. But he felt the way Hannah gripped his hand when the bat appeared, so he knows that she's trying to reassure the others. Not passing on their own irrational fears to the children is something they agree on. "No, that's just a normal bat. They're attracted to the light because they eat the insects," he says.

As they move farther away from the village the gaps between the street lamps get wider. The trees and bushes make strange, unnerving shapes against the blackness of the sky. At times they can barely see the ground beneath their feet.

"It's creepy out here," Aïsha says, running to catch up with the others and taking, unusually, her mother's hand.

"It is a bit," Hannah agrees as Luke squashes himself between her and Cliff. "But I'm sure there's nothing to be afraid of. It's just that there's no moon tonight."

"If Tris' is going to have a holiday fling with that barman, I hope the pool guy comes back," Jill says, off, as so often, on her own train of thought. "I don't want to end up being the raspberry of the holiday."

"Gooseberry," Hannah corrects, suppressing a smile.

"Yeah, sorry. Gooseberry. That's what I meant," Jill says.

Luke licks the back of his hand and makes a farting noise by blowing against it, one of his specialities. "*That's* a raspberry," he says.

"Yes," Hannah says. "Thanks for that, Luke."

"It's really dark up there," Aïsha says, nodding forwards and sounding vaguely excited but also genuinely distressed.

They all peer out at the blackness ahead. "It's because there's a bend," Hannah says. "I remember it. There was the green gate with the noisy frogs and then a bend."

"How can that make it darker?" Aïsha asks, her tone dismissive.

"No, Hannah's right," Cliff says. "It's because you can't see the next street lamp, that's all. It's around the corner. We should have brought the torch."

"Have we got one?"

"Sure. There's one in the boot of the car."

As they leave the final edge of the pool of light and head towards the void, Luke pulls his phone out and switches it on. It only casts the vaguest beam of bluish light a few feet in front of him, but it's better than nothing.

"Good idea, Luke," Cliff says, and both he and Aïsha do likewise. But even with the light from three phones, the lane ahead is pitch black.

"The corner must be here somewhere," Hannah says.

"Yes, I think that's it," Cliff says pointing at what he thinks might be the grey curve of the tarmac.

As they reach the blackest section of the bend the next streetlight comes into view, a pin-point of light in the distance. Hannah pauses and pulls Cliff and Luke to a halt with her.

"Look at the stars," she says. "Gosh, I've never seen so many stars."

They crane their necks and look at the sky, and as their eyes adjust, small stars appear between the bright ones, and then even smaller ones between those.

"Aeroplane," Cliff says, pointing at a flashing light to the east.

"There's two," Luke says.

"Yes, I can see two," Hannah agrees.

"Gosh that's the Milky Way, isn't it?" Cliff says. "I don't think I've ever seen that before. Not in real life."

"What is?" Luke asks, and Cliff crouches down behind him so that he can point and explain. "See those swirly clouds," he says. "That's millions of tiny stars. That's the Milky Way."

"I wish we had a telescope," Luke says.

"Yes, that would be good," Cliff agrees.

"Can we get one?"

"No, I think they're a bit expensive. And I don't think there are a lot of telescope shops around here."

"There are so many stars," Jill says. "It makes you feel quite alone in the middle of it all."

"It's cold here," Aïsha says. "Can we go?"

Hannah shivers and realises that this is true, but also that Aïsha sounds scared. "There's a river or something," she tells her. "It's damp here, that's why."

"I don't like it," Aïsha says, her tone more urgent now. "Can we go?"

"Sure," Hannah says.

"There's nothing to be scared of though," Cliff tells her. "It's just nature." A mere second after he has spoken these words, an unseen creature in the darkness, not ten metres away, grunts loudly.

Luke makes a short sharp, "Uh!" sound and Aïsha shrieks. The shock of each person jumping is transmitted, through held hands, to their neighbours, somehow amplifying the fear.

They start, as a group, to walk quickly towards the distant street lamp, but when the creature, farther behind them now, grunts again, first Aïsha and then Luke break free, sprinting ahead, squealing. Soon they are laughing hysterically.

At the next oasis of light everyone regroups. "What the fuck was that?" Jill asks.

"It was a monster," Luke says, and Hannah can see from the children's excited faces that this is already the best thing that has happened on the holiday so far.

"I think it was a pig," Cliff says. "A wild pig maybe."

"It sounded like a pig," Hannah agrees, her own heart still racing. "But here? Do you think?"

"Do pigs bite?" Luke asks. "Can they jump up and rip your throat out?"

Aïsha pulls a stick from the undergrowth, presumably to defend herself with, and Luke follows suit.

"No," Cliff says, thinking that he would quite like a stick himself, but that it might look a bit wimpy. "No, pigs don't bite, do they, Hannah?"

"Of course not," Hannah agrees, even though she has absolutely no idea.

"What if there are more?" Jill asks.

"What if there's a pack of them?" Luke asks. "What if they surround us, like wolves?"

"*Luke*," Aïsha whines.

"Yes, stop it, Luke. You'll give yourself nightmares," Hannah says. "They don't like noise. Wild animals never like noise. So just talk loudly or sing a song or something and you'll be fine."

"Wooh wooh wooh!" Luke shouts, brandishing his stick.

"You don't have to wake up the whole neighbourhood," Cliff admonishes.

He shrugs and starts to sing his favourite song from *The Lion King* instead – *I just can't wait to be king*.

"Don't sing *that*, Luke, that's lame," Aïsha says. But as they head into the next patch of darkness even she joins in.

When half a mile down the road the street lamps become more regular and they all start to relax, Hannah moves to Jill's side. "She can sing!" she murmurs. "Aïsha can sing."

"I know," Jill says. "It's amazing, isn't it?"

"It is. She's got a great voice."

"Luke can't," Jill says, and Hannah laughs.

"No! No, he gets that from his mother, unfortunately," she says.

TWELVE

The next morning Hannah is first up – even Luke is having a lie-in.

She quietly makes herself a cup of coffee and sits nursing it as she watches the shortening shadows of the olive trees.

She feels a little tired still, and vaguely hung-over too, but contented also. She likes the calm before the day begins, this sensation that everyone she loves is sleeping nearby. It's so much easier to love them when they're asleep, after all.

When she has finished her coffee she wanders around the garden, looping the house and listening to the morning sounds of Provence: the buzz of insects around the lavender, snoring from Tristan's shutters (a smile), a distant moped buzzing up a hill, water falling from the hosepipe into the now half-filled pool.

When she reaches the front of the house she sees an extra car parked behind Tristan's Jeep, a turquoise Twingo. Its two-tone paintwork shimmers in the morning light. *So Tristan got more than a lift home*, she thinks.

The house continues to sleep, dark and heavy, so, careful not to disturb anyone (for her own benefit, not theirs) she fixes herself some toast and another cup of coffee, and takes them, along with her novel, back to the patio. She reads for a whole hour, uninterrupted – a rarity.

"Morning!"

Hannah jumps and turns to see Jill hanging from the doorway. She's wearing men's pyjamas.

"Is everyone else still in bed?" Jill asks.

Hannah nods. She doesn't want to speak yet. Her head is still stuck in her novel, and she likes it there.

"I think I'll go back to bed for a bit then," Jill says. "I just got up for a glass of water."

Hannah nods again, winks at her sister and flutters her fingers in a goodbye wave.

Another hour passes by before Cliff appears in the same doorway. "How long have you been up?" he asks.

"Since eight," Hannah says quietly. She stretches and stifles a yawn and realises that the day is hotting up – that she's sweating.

"Couldn't sleep?"

Hannah shrugs. "Just reading," she tells him, now reluctantly closing her book.

Cliff's booming voice could wake the dead, and, sure enough, within a minute first Luke then Aïsha appear, requiring breakfast. They are closely followed by Jill and Tristan.

Hannah is the only person who isn't surprised when the barman appears behind him, his floppy hair now a dishevelled bed-head wonder.

"You all know Jean-Jacques," Tristan says by way of introduction. "Now, I'm gonna make pancakes if anyone wants them."

"I'll help," Luke says, jumping up and following Tristan into the house.

The easy morning chat that had prevailed up to that point vanishes the second Jean-Jacques takes a seat at the table.

Hannah looks at him and forces a smile. She nods at him in a friendly way and he smiles weakly.

"So," Hannah says.

Jean-Jacques clears his throat.

"So Tristan got you to drive him home last night?" she says.

Jean-Jacques nods.

Aïsha gets her iPhone out and puts her earbuds in. Hannah wishes she could do the same.

"He's lucky," Hannah says.

"Thank you," Jean-Jacques says, averting his gaze and blushing deeply.

"I meant . . . I just meant that the road was very dark," Hannah explains, flushing with heat herself. She catches Jill's eye and gives her an exaggerated stare and a vague shrug – a plea for help.

"There were wild beasts," Jill says. "On the road. We were scared."

Jean-Jacques frowns. "Beast?" he says.

"Yes, animals," Jill says, miming a four-legged creature on the table-top with one hand.

"Ah. Un daim? Un sanglier ?" Jean-Jacques asks.

Everyone stares at him blankly. They have no idea what he is saying.

"It's a nice bar," Cliff says. "It must be nice working there."

Jean-Jacques shrugs. "C'est tranquille," he says. "It's just a job for summer."

"Of course," Cliff says. "So what do you do the rest of the time?"

"Station de ski," Jean-Jacques says, then, "Ski station. I am teaching the snowboard."

"Snowboard? Cool," Aïsha says, almost immediately looking surprised at her own utterance.

Luke, thankfully, appears with the first plate of pancakes. Everyone is grateful for the distraction.

"That was quick," Hannah says.

"Tris' made the gloopy stuff yesterday," Luke says. "More coming!"

Once everyone is served, Tristan returns with his own plate and sits. "So what have you people been talking about?" he asks.

"Oh this and that," Hannah tells him. "Jean-Paul here is a snowboard instructor."

"Jean-Jacques," Jean-Jacques corrects her.

"Sorry, of course," Hannah says. "Sorry."

"Is there much call for that? Here, I mean?" Tristan asks, looking around the garden as if in search of snow.

"The ski stations is two hour away," Jean-Jacques says. "Is OK."

"I see," Hannah says. "How amazing."

A silence falls over the table again. Cutlery clinks against plates. People chew on pancake.

"So where do you go out around here?" Jill asks.

"Pardon ?"

"I mean, it must be a bit boring being gay in a tiny place like this," Jill says. She sees that Tristan is bristling, but whatever the problem is, it's too late now. "So I just wondered where you go when you want to have some fun."

Jean-Jacques furrows his brow, then swallows and turns his attention to his plate. His hair falls forward, almost completely hiding his face.

"Jean-Jacques here isn't gay," Tristan says, his tone a strange mixture of crisp over-emphasis and amusement.

66

"Oh, sorry," Jill says. "Sorry, I . . . I just assumed."

"Yeas," Tristan says, sounding quite camp now. "Yeas, so did I. But no! So you see. Life still has fresh surprises to throw at us."

Jean-Jacques pushes his plate – which still contains half a pancake – away from him and stands. "So, I 'ave to go," he says. "Sorry. But many things today. Thank you for your hospitalité."

As he leaves, awkwardly, he knocks his chair over, stoops to pick it up, and then, combing his hair with his fingers, vanishes from view.

"What on earth was all that about?" Jill asks once they hear the car driving away.

"Don't ask," Tristan says. "Really. Don't ask."

"No," Jill whines. "Tell me."

Hannah shoots Tristan a warning glance, then seeing that it's a lost cause, turns to Luke.

"Why don't you go off and play for a bit?" she suggests. "You too, Aïsha."

Aïsha pulls a face. Luke mimics her expression and says, "Play? What at?"

"The pool is full enough to swim in I think," Hannah says.

"Really? Is it?" Luke is already standing, already trying to remember where the diving mask is. He had forgotten there was a pool.

"It's over half-full," Hannah tells him. "But don't dive in yet. You don't want to hit your head on the bottom."

"Help me blow up the air beds?" Luke asks Aïsha, and she forks a final mouthful of pancake, stands and, feigning reluctance, follows him.

"So?" Jill prompts, once they have gone.

Tristan pulls a face. "Oh God," he says. "Well . . ."

Cliff stands. "I'll clear the breakfast things," he says, gathering some cups together.

"I can do it in a bit," Hannah offers.

"It's fine," Cliff tells her. "You three have a natter." He always feels a little uncomfortable with these intimate conversations. He never quite seems to be able to strike the correct balance between showing polite interest and sounding as if he's showing too much interest in something that he believes should ultimately remain private.

"Is he really not gay?" Jill asks.

Tristan laughs. "He drives a Twingo," he says. "What do you think?"

Aïsha, who has for some reason returned, asks, "Is a Twingo really gay or something?"

Tristan laughs. "Let me see: a little car with rounded edges in two-tone turquoise-slash-purple no doubt selected personally by Victoria Beckham."

Aïsha shrugs. She looks confused. "OK . . . What about a Jeep then?" she asks.

"A Jeep's far, far worse," Tristan replies. "Especially if it's red."

"I thought you were helping Luke," Hannah reminds her.

"We can't find the pump," Aïsha says. "And I'm not blowing them up. It makes me dizzy."

"It's in the car," Cliff, who is still lingering, says. "Come. I'll get it for you. It's still in the boot."

"So yes, of course he's gay," Tristan says as they head off. "But he can't admit it yet. Not even in bed. Classic Catholic angst."

"He is quite young I suppose," Hannah says.

"Yes, how old is he anyway?" Jill asks.

"Twenty-three I think," Tristan answers.

"Yum," Jill says. "Lucky you."

Hannah frowns at her sister. "Really?" she asks.

"Uh-huh! They're up all the time at that age. You only have to say the word sex and they're ready for action."

"I'm afraid I can't even imagine it," Hannah says after a couple of seconds of trying to do just that. "As far as I'm concerned, if they're young enough to be your offspring then they're too young. That's my theory anyway. No offence, Tristan, it's just me, I guess."

"No offence taken, you're probably right as it happens," he says. "Youth is much overrated."

"Really?" Jill sounds disappointed.

"Totally frigid. Didn't move a muscle."

"Not even . . . you know . . . that muscle?"

Tristan laughs. "That," he says, "isn't a muscle. But yes, that worked. It's just that nothing else did. He got a hard-on, but spent the whole time on his back like this." Tristan links his hands behind his head to demonstrate. "Handy if you need an ironing board, but he really doesn't win any prizes as the world's greatest lover."

"Gosh," Hannah says, thinking about how much she moves when she makes love with Cliff. She doesn't fold her hands behind her head, but all the same . . . She would have to admit that she puts less effort into it these days than she once did. Perhaps she needs to watch that.

"He told me he was straight too," Tristan continues. "Once he had come he asked if I wanted him to leave, and I said, no, he could stay. And he said, 'OK, but I'm not gay. Just so you know.' Can you believe that?"

"Lord," Jill says. "What did you say?"

"I just said, 'Non, chéri, bien sûr.'"

"Meaning?"

"Meaning, 'No dear. Of course you aren't.'"

"The pool guy's back," Cliff says, returning from the car and sliding back into his seat. Then, visibly remembering that he had been in the process of clearing the table, he stands to continue where he left off.

Jill sits up straight, suddenly alert. "He's here? What, round there?" she asks, gesturing towards the other side of the house.

"Yes. He's putting chemicals in the pool. It looks quite complicated."

Hannah has to strain to look up at Cliff, now standing behind her with a pile of plates. "Chemicals?" she asks. 'Chemicals' sounds worrying.

"Chlorine and stuff, I guess," Cliff says. "To keep the water safe."

"Of course."

Jill stands and flicks back her hair.

Hannah laughs. "Where are you going?" she asks. "You don't even speak French."

"I do," Tristan says, smiling and starting to stand as well.

"I'm going for a swim," Jill says. "I'm allowed, aren't I? I just hope I can find my bikini, otherwise I may have to skinny-dip."

Tristan follows Jill inside the house and Cliff catches Hannah's eye – a moment of complicity.

They can hear Tristan and Jill arguing light-heartedly inside the house and then, less than a minute later, they burst from the interior in their swimming costumes, laughing and jostling for position like teenagers.

"Stay back!" Jill is saying as she whacks at Tristan. "Stay back I tell you! You've had yours." They sprint across the lawn and then vanish from view.

"Do they make you feel terribly old?" Cliff asks.

Hannah nods and snorts. "A bit," she says. "You'd certainly never guess that she's only two years younger, would you?" She pushes her chair back. "But I think I need to see this. Are you coming?"

"No," Cliff says. "No, I'll clear this stuff away."

By the time Hannah has found her shoes and rounded the house, Jill is lounging along one edge of the filling pool and Tristan is using the foot-pump to inflate Luke's air-bed, rather absurdly pulling in his perfectly toned stomach.

"God, you're pale, Jill," Hannah says. "I don't think I've ever seen you so white."

"I know," Jill says. "I stopped going to the tanning place. Pale-and-wan is the new brown-and-sexy or something."

"Well, be careful you don't burn."

The pool guy, in the same dungarees as yesterday, is holding a test tube of pink liquid up against a colour chart and saying something in French.

"He says it's fine to swim in, but he'll have to come back tomorrow to add more acid or something," Tristan translates.

"Très bien," Jill says smoothly. She sits up and stretches so that her toe just touches the surface of the water. "It's freezing," she says. "I mean, like, Arctic freezing. Can you ask him how long it takes to warm up?"

Tristan translates Jill's question to French and the man replies, pointing at a duct in the pool wall as he does so.

"He says he can't switch the heater thingy on until the water

71

reaches that tube," Tristan says. "But after that it will be ready in forty-eight hours."

"So it's heated then. That's good," Hannah says.

"Apparently so."

"Do you speak any English?" Jill asks the man, squashing herself back against the pool edge in order to enter his line of vision.

"Ma copine veut savoir si vous parlez anglais," Tristan translates when he shrugs.

"Alors, pas de tout !" the man replies.

"Sorry dear," Tristan says smugly. "He says not one word. Sucks to be you, huh?"

Jill licks her lips. "We'll see," she says.

"Stop, Tris, you'll pop it," Luke says, tapping Tristan's leg with one hand to grab his attention.

Tristan glances down to see that the air-bed is more than amply inflated. He crouches down to disconnect the pump and plug the filler valve. "There you go. Now yours, Aï' – bring it over."

The pool guy starts to collect his various tubes and boxes of kit together, placing them in a bucket, and then straightens and takes the handle of this in one hand and the huge container of chlorine in the other.

Hannah watches Jill surveilling his departure. She looks, Hannah thinks, like a lioness about to pounce.

"Au revoir," he says vaguely, to all of them. "À demain."

As he turns away, Jill sits upright, hesitant. And then, a decision taken, she jumps to her feet and runs across the grass to catch up with him. Joining him halfway across the lawn, she puts one hand next to his on the handle of the bucket and says, "Let me help you with that."

The guy pauses, looking alarmed, as if perhaps he suspects that she's trying to steal his bucket. But then he smiles, looks bashful, lowers his head, and continues to walk, linked now, to Jill, via the bucket.

As they vanish from view behind the house, he starts to talk to her in French.

Hannah stares wide-eyed at the mid-distance where they no longer stand, then refocuses on Tristan and shakes her head.

"Unbelievable," Tristan, who has momentarily ceased foot-pumping says. He grins broadly. "Absolutely un-be-lie-va-ble."

Hannah nods. "My little sister, eh?" she says. "Never ceases to amaze, that one."

She turns to glance at Aïsha to see how she's reacting to this, but she has her headphones on and is tapping her hand in time with the music. She seems totally oblivious.

Hannah turns to leave. "Call me when the pool's warm," she says.

Cliff takes Stieg Larsson to the hammock with him but immediately falls asleep, the novel spread across his chest.

Hannah offers to help Tristan prepare lunch, and Tristan, ever the chef, tasks Hannah with salad-washing duties whilst he fries potatoes and beats eggs for a Spanish tortilla.

From behind the house, Hannah can hear the shrieks of Luke and Aïsha splashing around in the pool. A sound of summer – a sound of childhood momentarily restored. She smiles to herself, is pleased with herself, even, for having insisted on this destination. "Don't you ever get fed up with cooking?" she asks Tristan after a moment's silence.

"I don't cook so much these days," he replies. "Since we

opened the fourth restaurant in Hoxton, I spend more time just managing the business really. Choosing menus, replacing staff, accounts . . . It's pretty hectic."

"Of course," Hannah says.

"So I quite like it really."

"Yes. Yes, I suppose so."

"And anyway, this is hardly what I'd call cooking," Tristan adds.

Hannah pulls a face at this. A mixed salad, fresh salsa, homemade vinaigrette and a twelve-egg Spanish tortilla is about as challenging as her cooking ever gets.

"Jill's back," Tristan says, and Hannah looks up from the sink and sees that this is so.

Jill, beyond the open kitchen window, turns to face them, then pushing chairs out of her way makes her way towards them. Finally she leans on the windowsill, peering in at them and looking despondent.

"That was quick," Hannah says.

"Even for you," Tristan adds cheekily.

"Excruciating," Jill declares. "Why didn't you just stop me?"

Tristan lays down his egg beater and crosses to join Hannah at the sink. Hannah can smell his aftershave – a warm vanilla-honey smell. She wonders if it would be impolite to ask him what it is so that she can buy it for Cliff. "What happened?" he asks.

"I followed him down the track. He was rabbiting away in French. Of course it might as well be Chinese for all the good it did me."

"And?"

"Their place is about a hundred yards away behind those big trees. It's not much more than a shack. A big shed really."

74

"They?" Hannah asks.

"Well, he lives with his mother, doesn't he? I think he lives there anyway. She certainly does. She's about a hundred. No teeth." Jill pulls her lips down and mimes having no teeth just in case there was some doubt.

"His mother!" Tristan says. He claps his hands. "Love it!"

"So I ended up with them both rabbiting on at me in French. It was just . . . it was embarrassing really. And all a bit Hitchcock, to be honest."

"But did you get a bit of slap and tickle?" Tristan asks.

"Nothing. Not even a kiss. Well, I got to kiss the old dear. Which was lovely, of course. She made us coffee, that Turkish stuff where they boil it for hours and then serve you the dregs."

"Nice."

"I still have the bits caught in my teeth. The cups were dirty too," Jill pulls a face. "Honestly, it was awful."

"And then?"

"And then . . . Wonder Boy climbed into his little Fiat rust bucket and drove off. To do someone else's pool I think. He took the stuff with him anyway."

Hannah breaks into a broad grin. "He left you with the mother? How funny."

"He left me with the mother," Jill confirms. "I still didn't know what she was banging on about. In the end, I just waved at her and left. She was still yakking as I walked away."

"It could only happen to you, Jill," Tristan says, returning to the stove.

Aïsha appears behind Jill. She's wearing shorts and a black T-shirt. Water is pooling around her feet. "What could only happen to you?" she asks.

"You're soaked!" Jill says, turning to appraise her daughter and reaching out to take the hem of the T-shirt between finger and thumb. "Why are your clothes soaked? You'll catch your death!"

"We're swimming," Aïsha says. "The water's freezing but if you stay on the lilo and don't move, it's all right. You just drift around."

"Why are you wearing this when you have a perfectly good swimming costume?" Jill asks.

Aïsha shrugs. "This is fine," she says. "But can you get me a towel? I want to go to the loo and I'm dripping."

"It's not fine," Jill says. "I'll get you a towel but . . ."

Hannah hands a towel through the window.

"Oh, thanks, Han'," she says, passing it on to her daughter. "Here. Dry yourself off and then go and put your bikini on."

"I don't know where it is," Aïsha says.

"It's in your suitcase. Where else would it be?"

Hannah leans across the sink and reaches through the window to gently touch Jill's shoulder. "Jill," she says, quietly.

"Hang on," Jill says, gesturing behind her. "Aïsha. Aïsha!" she shouts as her daughter disappears inside the house.

"Jill!" Hannah says again.

Jill glances back at her. "Hang on, Han'," she says. "Just let me deal with this and . . ."

"She doesn't want to wear the bikini," Hannah says forcefully but quiet enough that Aïsha won't hear her.

"I don't care what she wants," Jill says. "She chose it. She can wear it. I'm not made of money."

"She's embarrassed, Jill," Hannah says.

Jill freezes. She pulls a face. "Embarrassed? How can she be embarrassed? She chose it."

"She's embarrassed about her body. Give her a break."

76

Jill wrinkles her nose. "She's got nothing to be embarrassed about. I mean she's packing a few extra pounds, but it's just puppy fat. That will go soon enough."

Hannah sighs deeply. "You don't get it, do you, Jill? Just stop and think. Remember when you were thirteen."

Jill pauses. "I don't remember last night, babe, let alone when I was thirteen."

"I remember," Hannah says. "I remember you putting masking tape around your boobs because you didn't want to tell Mum you needed a bra."

"You didn't!" Tristan exclaims, looking up from his frying pan.

"Just . . . cook, Tris'," Jill says, making a little shooing gesture, then to Hannah, "OK," she says. "Point taken."

"She's getting breasts," Hannah whispers. "It's a shock."

"Yes, yes, I get it," Jill says. She shakes her head. "God, am I a terrible mother do you think?"

Hannah shakes her head. "No," she says. "No, you're fine. You're just a bit too close to be able to see sometimes. We all are."

Jill nods, then she laughs. "I'll tell you what," she says. "It didn't half hurt when you pulled off the tape. I remember that."

After lunch, Hannah, persuaded by Luke, lowers herself onto one of the air-beds. Initially the icy water lapping over the edges makes this excruciating, but, as Aïsha explained, by lying totally still the pain ceases. The water already around her warms up, and the cold water of the pool remains at bay.

As the bed drifts in a seemingly random fashion she watches a single cloud in the blue sky skirting away to the east, now circling above her as the bed spins. She senses invisible waves of air moving across her body. She wonders if this is what a water-bed feels like, and decides that she must ask Jill. She's pretty sure that Jill must have come across a water-bed at some point. Or Tristan. Tristan might even have one at home. She can hear a bird tweeting somewhere, and the rustle of the wind in the leaves and then . . .

Hannah gasps in shock and sits up, causing more icy water to flood around her waist. A fresh jet of spray hits her face and she rolls for protection from the bed and into the pool, gasping at the temperature shock as her sun-baked body is enveloped by the water.

"Luke!" she shrieks, now finding her feet and wading as fast as she can towards the ladder.

Luke, her assailant with a hosepipe, is radiant with glee. "Yes!" he declares, still pointing the jet at her back.

"You cheeky little bugger!" Hannah shouts. "I was asleep. I was fast-a-bloody-sleep and having a lovely dream." She climbs the ladder and starts to run around the pool towards her son, who drops the hosepipe and flees, giggling maniacally.

Hannah chases him barefoot around the back of the house and on towards the patio, in truth enjoying the chase. She feels for the first time as if she's on holiday. She feels young and exhilarated and awake. It's only in these fleeting moments of wakefulness that she realises that she spends most of her life asleep.

Catching sight of Jill climbing back over the fence at the rear of the garden, and making a mental note to question her later, she runs on. "You wait until I catch you, boy," she shouts.

Luke, looking behind him to check on her progress, runs

straight into Cliff, who unsure as to whether Hannah's pursuit is in anger or jest, grabs Luke by the waist.

"Let me go!" he shouts, writhing and kicking at Cliff's shins.

"Hey!" Cliff says, holding him at arm's length and laughing.

"Hold onto him," Hannah says. "The cheeky monkey squirted me!"

By the time she reaches them she is out of breath. "I was fast asleep and he squirted me with the hosepipe!" she explains, trying but failing to grab Luke's flailing feet.

Aïsha, drawn by the noise, has now joined them. She grabs one of Luke's feet, and Hannah manages to seize the remaining one.

"That's not fair," Luke whines, now hesitating between throwing a genuine temper tantrum and allowing this to remain something he calls fun.

"Well nor is squirting your mother with a hosepipe when she's asleep," Hannah laughs, as the three of them manhandle him back to the pool.

"We're gonna throw you in," Aïsha chants, and Hannah, always hypersensitive to Luke's moods, notes that he caves in, sees that he has decided to go along with this, and knows that she doesn't therefore have to cave in herself.

"One, Two, Three!" Cliff shouts and they drop him, ever so gently, into the pool.

"I'll get you back," Luke says, now surfaced and hanging onto the side of an air-bed, apparently oblivious to the cold.

"I think you already did, Luke," Hannah says. "Thanks," she says, smiling at Aïsha and Cliff as they walk back to the house.

"Any time," Aïsha says, restraining a smile.

"Actually, it's good he woke you," Cliff tells Hannah. "You've gone a bit pink."

"God, have I?" she says, touching her arm and sensing the heat of her skin. "I forgot to put any cream on."

"You're not burnt, but I think you've had enough," Cliff tells her.

That evening, Tristan leaves them to their own devices. He has "stuff to do", he declares mysteriously.

Hannah knows, from the fact that Jill doesn't question him, that he must have told her where he is going, but as the Jeep crunches out of the driveway, she denies this. "I've really no idea," she says. "He's probably just bored. You know how high-maintenance he is. He's probably gone off to find a club or something."

"You'd go with him if that was it," Hannah points out.

Jill shrugs. "Maybe it's not the kind of club I'm allowed in," she says.

Hannah looks around, and seeing that both Aïsha and Luke are absent, she asks, "Anyway, where were you earlier on?"

Jill frowns.

"I saw you climbing back over the fence."

"Oh, that," Jill says. "There's a track going down the hill. A hiking trail. I went to see where it goes. There's a little river down there. I'll show you later if you want."

"Right," Hannah says, somehow unconvinced despite Jill's Oscar-worthy performance.

"So the chef's taken the night off, huh?" Cliff is looking out at them through the kitchen window.

"He has," Hannah says.

"So are we staying here or going out for dinner?" he asks. "Because if we're staying I'm opening this." He brandishes a bottle of white wine to demonstrate what this refers to. "But if I have to drive, I'll hold off."

"If we're staying, it's just pasta with pesto sauce," Hannah says. "But if you'd rather go find a pizzeria that's fine with me."

"I'm OK with pasta," Cliff says. "Jill?"

"Sure. Pasta's fine."

"I thought we might take them to the water park tomorrow," Cliff says quietly, confidentially. "Luke's been on and on about it. It's near Antibes, so if we stay in tonight, we could have lunch out tomorrow and then take them to the water-slide place."

Hannah nods. "Sure," she says. "That sounds good." She turns to Jill. "Do you think Aïsha will be up for it or is that too babyish for her now?"

"Um . . . no, she'll be fine. She won't be enthusiastic, but she'll be fine. She'll enjoy it once she gets there. Just don't say anything about how much fun it will be. Over-expectation freaks her out."

"Good. So that's settled then," Hannah says. "Pasta it is. I'll go cook."

"I'll come, too," Jill says.

"To the water park?"

"No. Not my scene. I meant I'll help you cook."

Hannah shakes her head. "I'm boiling pasta and pouring on the sauce," she says. "I'll be fine."

Hannah sleeps badly that night. For some reason the pasta and white wine keep repeating on her. Cliff, as ever, snores soundly at her side.

Shortly after she finally does manage to fall asleep, she is awakened by the sound of Tristan's Jeep returning. The alarm clock reads 03:08.

What seems like a few seconds later, she is awakened by another sound, this time the crunch of feet on gravel. She checks the clock again and is surprised to see that it is almost five.

She silently climbs from the bed and crosses to the window. Frogs are croaking loudly somewhere in the distance; cicadas are clicketing lazily. As she peers through the slats of the shutters she sees someone start to move again, heading now towards the rear of the house. With only the tiniest hint of moonlight it's impossible to see who it is, but judging from his sure-footed plod, she's pretty sure that it's the pool guy. She wonders if he has been visiting someone. Surely he wouldn't be checking on the pool at five a.m., would he?

As she climbs back into bed, she wonders who he has been visiting. As sleep takes over again she wonders if, had she left their shutters open, the pool guy would have visited her. That would have been a shock for Cliff. She laughs at the thought in her sleep.

THIRTEEN

The drive to Antibes takes just over an hour. Luke spends the journey pointlessly naming everything he sees, as if an Esso petrol station or a McDonald's becomes a point of interest simply for being situated in France. Aïsha, for her part, is listening to music on her phone. Hannah knows, from experience, that not only is it not likely to be something they would all want to listen to – she favours a genre called glam-metal, awful – but that even a suggestion that they might want to try would be an embarrassment for poor Aïsha.

"Someone was creeping around in the garden last night," she tells Cliff once they are safely installed on an unchallenging stretch of main road.

"Really?" he says. "I didn't hear anything."

"Of course you didn't. You were fast asleep," Hannah says.

"Was it Tristan coming back?"

"No, this was later. About five a.m."

"The gardener maybe?"

"That's what I thought, but what would he be doing nosing around at dawn?"

"Maybe he's just an early bird," Cliff says. "Maybe he came over to switch the pool filter on or something. But next time, wake me up if you're worried."

Hannah smiles to herself at this suggestion. She has, on

occasion, attempted this in the past. Cliff invariably groans and rolls over without even a pause in the rhythm of his snoring.

They find Antibes without drama – heading to the coast is simply a case of following the signposts. They leave the Mégane in a big sea-front car park and head into the tiny streets of the old town. The day is already heating up and Hannah can sense that the kids won't tolerate wandering around for long. They are already onto the next thing, already anticipating the water slides.

Hannah and Cliff walk through the shady streets peering into shop windows, sniffing at kitsch lavender cushions and listening to the sounds of water falling from fountains whilst Luke and Aïsha drag their feet ten yards behind them, talking constantly about what features may or may not reside in the park.

Hannah would love to be able to explain to her son that though the water slide may represent a ten on his personal preference chart, a walk through a beautiful, sunlit, foreign town whilst licking a velvety Italian ice-cream should be at least a nine. She would love to be able to convey the concept that the present is all that you ever have in life, and that these moments of magic are too precious to be ignored because you're too busy thinking about the next thing. But there are no words, of course, to express this to an eleven-year-old.

"Just enjoy your ice-cream and shut up about the park for a minute, can't you?" is as close as she gets. If she can't fix Luke's present, she can at least try to stop him wrecking hers.

"He's OK," Cliff says, rubbing her shoulder. "He's just excited."

And Hannah knows that he's right. She's just suffering from lack of sleep.

When they reach the edge of the historic town centre, they sit and have an outrageously expensive round of Cokes, then climb up onto the ramparts and circle the town in the other direction.

"The sea is so blue!" Hannah says.

"Well, of *course* it's blue," Luke says.

"Don't be rude, Luke," Hannah reproaches him. "It's not always *that* blue. It's not always azure blue." These flashes of cheekiness scare her a little. They warn her that she needs to prepare herself for a time when Luke will become like Aïsha. It's happening already; these bursts of insolence are creeping in. For the moment, it's only an occasional burst, but she suspects that soon enough it will become a twenty-four-seven feature of their lives.

On the harbour wall, Cliff takes their photo standing inside a huge iron sculpture of a head made out of a latticework of apparently random words, and then the parents cave in to the kids' demands and rather than choosing a nice relaxing restaurant somewhere, they buy sandwiches that can be eaten en route to the water park. "It wouldn't be any fun anyway," Cliff points out. "Not with these two champing at the bit."

This turns out to be a wise decision, because when they reach the location Tristan put into Cliff's GPS, they find not a water park but a vast bill-board advertisement for a water park in a place called Fréjus. The GPS informs them that though the route to Fréjus does begin in the direction the yellow arrow on the signpost indicates, it is, in reality, an entirely different town an hour and a half's drive away.

"So we drive to Fréjus, I guess," Hannah says.

"There's no turning back now," Cliff agrees. "We'd never hear the end of it if we did. Let's just hope that it's worth it."

The sun is dipping behind the olive trees by the time they get back to the Villa.

Hannah finds Tristan and Jill drinking rosé and smoking on the patio. They look up lazily to greet the returned travellers.

"Wow! Someone's caught the sun," Jill says.

"I know," Hannah replies. "I kept smothering myself in that factor fifty stuff, but after yesterday's fry-up . . ."

Tristan glances at Jill. He raises an eyebrow and Hannah pauses, thinking that he's silently prompting Jill to say something, something they have previously discussed – an agreed announcement perhaps.

After an almost-imperceptible head-shake on Jill's part, Tristan turns back to Hannah. "So how was it?" he asks. "Fun?"

Hannah glances behind her to check that she's still alone – the others are emptying the car – before whispering, "Awful. A million screaming children. And loads of chavvy adults barging their way into the queues. Those two *loved* it though."

"I didn't know they had chavs in France," Jill says.

"Nor did I," Hannah says, "until we got to Aquasplash."

"Poor you," Jill says. "Was Aïsha OK?"

"Honestly, Jill, she had such a good time. She was like a little girl all over again. It was a joy to see."

Aïsha, Luke and Cliff appear laden with towels and bags and booty, which they dump on a free chair.

"Good?" Tristan asks again.

"Awesome," Luke says. "Look!" He rounds the table and thrusts a fridge magnet under Tristan's nose. It contains a photo of him and Aïsha on an inflatable tyre in white-water rapids.

"They have a machine that makes these," Luke says, waving the magnet. "It was ten euros."

"Wow, that does look like fun," Tristan says.

"Show me?" Jill holds out her hand and then studying the photo, continues, "Gosh, yes. That does look good."

"Mum went down it too," Luke says, "but she fell off and hurt her ear."

"It's true," Hannah says, nodding shamefully. "It kept bouncing off the sides and eventually it threw me off completely. I thought the whole thing was pretty dangerous to be honest."

"Do we have a photo of that?" Tristan asks.

Hannah shakes her head. "It's automatic so it took a photo of my rubber ring, but I was drowning some way behind."

"And there were those tubes you slide down," Luke says. "And a thing like a helter-skelter but with water in it. And there were these ropes that you hold on to and they pull you really fast across the pool."

"Wow," Jill says. "All of that, huh?" She reaches out to touch her daughter's arm. "And you. Did you have fun?"

Aïsha shrugs. "It was OK I suppose," she says.

A wave of anger rises up in Hannah. She could almost slap Aïsha for that. They have driven a hundred miles today. They have spent almost two hundred euros. And Aïsha spent the four hours in the water park grinning like a five-year-old on Christmas morning. Her response is disingenuous to say the least. She opens her mouth to say something, but then catches Jill's eye, and Jill winks. Jill gets it, which means that it doesn't really matter. So Hannah just licks her lips and exhales instead.

"The pool here is full now," Tristan says. "The heater is on too. It's almost bearable. I reckon it'll be nice and warm by tomorrow."

Luke and Aïsha head immediately to the pool and in less than a minute can be heard splashing and shrieking again.

"She had such a good time," Hannah says. "I don't know why she can't just say so."

Cliff returns from the kitchen with two extra glasses. He sits down and slops wine into both of them. "A really good time," he confirms. "They both did. But it wasn't at all where you said it was, Tris'."

Tristan frowns. "What d'you mean? We drove past it. It's just outside Antibes."

Cliff and Hannah shake their heads in unison.

"You drove past the *sign*," Cliff explains. "It's actually just an advertisement. The park is in Fréjus – an hour up the motorway."

"God, sorry," Tristan says. "I was driving, you know? I was in traffic, so I didn't read the small print."

"It's fine," Hannah says. "The extra drive was just a bit of a surprise, that's all."

Everyone reaches for their glasses at the same time and a silence falls over the table. Hannah suspects that she's picking up a vibe. Tristan seems still to keep glancing at Jill. He looks nervous. They both do.

"So what have you two been up to?" Hannah asks, determined to pierce this particular mystery.

"Nothing," Tristan says, a little too quickly.

"Nothing," Jill repeats, and there it is again: that nervous glance between them.

"It was just a normal lazy day, wasn't it, Jill?" Tristan says.

"Yep," Jill says.

Jill never says 'Yep'.

"We just lazed around," she adds. "Nothing really happened."

"Right," Hannah says. She doesn't believe them one bit.

FOURTEEN

After dinner – a goat's cheese and artichoke salad which
Tristan prepared earlier, served with fresh crispy chunks of
baguette – Hannah leaves everyone at the table and starts
to tidy the kitchen. Tristan is a good cook, but a messy one.
But she doesn't mind; something in the atmosphere outside
has been unsettling her, and she'd rather just escape it to be
honest. She's too tired to spend the evening trying to decode
something if no one wants to tell her.

She is stacking the dishwasher – specifically scraping the
contents of Aïsha and Luke's plates into the bin – when Jill
enters the room.

She crosses to the window, tosses a, "Sorry, mosquitos," to
those beyond it, and closes both sides firmly. She then returns
to the kitchen door and closes that too.

"I knew there was something going on," Hannah says,
straightening.

"I need a word," Jill says, looking nervously beyond the
window to check that everyone has remained seated.

"That sounds ominous," Hannah says. "You haven't had a
row with . . ."

The kitchen door bursts open and Aïsha peers in. "Can I
make some toast?" she asks.

"No," Jill says, uncharacteristically. "No you can't."

"But I'm still h—"

"You should have eaten your salad."

"It was rank," Aïsha says.

"It wasn't *rank*. It was absolutely gorgeous. As you would have found out if you had tried it instead of wrinkling your nose and pushing it around the plate."

"*Jill*," Aïsha whines. "I'm starving."

"Tristan went to a lot of trouble to make that, so, you know, just wait a bit. If you're still hungry later then I'll let you make some toast, but doing it right after dinner is just plain rude."

"Luke says he's hungry too," Aïsha says. "Anyway, it was Tristan who told me to come and make toast in the first place. Can I? Can I?"

"Oh for Christ's sake," Jill spits, grabbing Aïsha's arm and yanking her into the kitchen. "Just do what you want. You always do anyway."

She then pushes Aïsha – who looks as if she might cry – towards the toaster, and grabs Hannah's arm and pulls her *out* of the kitchen before starting to bustle her down the hallway towards the bedrooms.

"Jill," Hannah protests. "Whatever is the mat—"

Jill pushes Hannah into the blue room and then closes and locks the bedroom door behind her. She then crosses and closes the bedroom window as well – the shutters are already closed.

"Jill, you're scaring me now," Hannah says, drying her wet hands on the back of her jeans.

"Come," Jill says more softly now, sitting side-saddle on the bed and holding out both hands.

Hannah twists her mouth sideways but places her fingers in Jill's hands and sits.

"There was a phone call while you were out," Jill says.

91

"A phone call."

"Yes."

"Oh God!" Hannah says. "It's not Mister Mittens, is it?" Mister Mittens is Luke's cat. A neighbour is feeding him while they're away. Luke loves Mister Mittens more than life itself.

"No," Jill says, smiling briefly at this. "No, it's not Mister Mittens."

"Thank God for that," Hannah says. "But what then?"

"It's . . . Look . . . It was James," Jill says. "James phoned."

Hannah looks at her blankly. She doesn't know anyone called James. Or rather she doesn't know anyone *alive* called James. She wracks her brain, but no, the only James she ever knew belongs to the past, belonged, in fact, to a different century. "James?" she repeats.

"James," Jill says, nodding as if encouraging her to guess a quiz question.

Hannah mentally lists Jill's boyfriends in case she has missed one. Then she starts on Tristan's many partners. "I'm sorry, Jill," she says. "I don't know who you mean."

"God!" Jill exclaims, glancing at the ceiling for inspiration. "James!" she says again, with added panache, as if this might somehow help. "Cliff's brother."

Hannah freezes. She holds her breath and stares into her sister's eyes. She can see the reflection of the lampshade in them, two little orange squares stretched across the spherical surface of her eyes. She can sense the blood draining from her face. She shakes her head. "But that's impossible," she says. "James is dead. You know he is."

Jill grips her hands tightly and peers into her eyes. "Only he isn't, Han'," she says. "That's what I'm trying to tell you. He phoned this afternoon to get the address. He's on his way here."

Hannah sighs and frowns deeply, then slowly she shakes her head. "No," she says, matter-of-factly.

Jill nods, visually contradicting her.

"God, I get it. You're high, aren't you," Hannah says, starting to breathe again as the absurdity of Jill's proposition sinks in.

"I knew this was going to be hard for you," Jill says.

"Jill!" Hannah says, her voice shrill now. "It's not *hard* for me. James *died*. He had a bike accident in India years ago. You know that, I know that, we all know that."

"Only he didn't," Jill says, struggling, but failing to keep hold of Hannah's hands as she pulls them away. "I spoke to him, today."

"This is ridiculous," Hannah says. "Why are you doing this? Why are you lying to me?"

"Hannah . . ."

"Even if he were alive – which we both know he isn't – he couldn't possibly know we're down here. Is this supposed to be funny? Are you so stoned that you think this is funny?"

"He went to the house. To *your* house. Marjorie told him."

"Marjorie."

"Your neighbour."

"You see! Lies!" Hannah laughs sourly. "Marjorie doesn't even have the address. What on earth has got into you?"

"I *know*," Jill says. "That's why he *phoned*. To get the address. Marjorie gave him the number here – you must have left it with her – and he phoned and I gave him the address."

Hannah stands. "This is rubbish, Jill," she says. "I don't know what you think you're playing at, but this is bullshit. And I'm not playing."

"Hannah?" Jill says. She is still seated on the bed. "*Hannah!*"

she shouts as Hannah fumbles with the lock and then bursts from the bedroom.

Hannah collides with Cliff, who is at that second stepping out of the bathroom. "Oh!" he says, in shock, then, registering her expression he asks, "What's wrong? Whatever's happened?"

Hannah opens her mouth to reply, but nothing comes out. Cliff glances past her and sees Jill standing in the doorway. "Jill?"

Hannah shakes her head. "She's lost it, Cliff," she says. "This time, she has really lost it."

Jill is advancing nervously towards them. "Han'," she says. "Wait. Let me . . ."

"Just . . . just keep her away from me, Cliff," Hannah says. "I can't be doing with it."

Hannah pushes past Cliff and strides to the front door, out past Tristan and the kids – all gaping – then rounds the house and leans back against the wall. It's still hot from the sun, almost too hot to bear.

She stares at the shimmering water of the pool and she tries to catch her breath. Moths, attracted by the underwater lights, are fluttering against the surface of the water.

"Will you please just tell me what is going on?" – Cliff's voice. He's walking towards her looking almost angry. "Jill won't tell me."

"You shouldn't get involved in this," Hannah says. "It would just . . . it would be . . . You wouldn't . . . God. Look, there's no need for you to get involved. Just leave me alone and . . ."

"I think there's every reason for me to get involved," Cliff says. "Look at you. You're shaking. Jill's upset. You're freaking Luke out. What just happened here, Hannah?"

"It's her," Hannah says, nodding vaguely into the distance. "She's high on drugs or something."

"And this is news, because . . . ?" Cliff says.

Hannah shrugs. She wonders if she can tell Cliff what Jill has said. She tries to calculate how much hurt that might cause him. She tries to work out if there's any way to *avoid* telling him.

"Look, one minute we're having dinner and everything's fine, and the next . . ." Cliff is saying.

"I'm sorry," Hannah says. "But I suppose you'll have to know. Jill claims that James phoned."

"James," Cliff says flatly.

"Yes. She's been trying to tell me that James phoned. Here. While we were out. She reckons he's been miraculously raised from the dead and he's on his way here."

"My brother James?" Cliff says.

"Yes."

"And he's coming *here*?" Cliff exclaims, his eyes widening. "Why would he be coming here?"

Hannah shrugs. "That's what my crazy doped-up sister . . ." Her voice fades. Cliff's response has belatedly struck her. "Cliff?" she asks.

Cliff stares back at her. He looks anxious. He looks like a rabbit in the headlights.

"Oh, *Cliff*! Oh God, no."

"I . . ." Cliff says.

"You . . . you know, don't you?" Hannah says.

"I . . ." he says again.

"Jesus Christ!" Hannah says, feeling faint now. "He isn't dead at all, is he?"

"I . . . I'm sorry," Cliff says, reaching out to touch her arm.

Hannah uses her right hand to push him away, and her left to cover her mouth. "Oh, Cliff," she says. "Oh, how could you?"

Cliff only approaches Hannah one more time that evening. She is lying in the hammock with a blanket, staring at the night sky. He approaches and says, "Hannah, we need to . . ."

"Stay away from me, Cliff!" she says. It came out too loudly, and the whole household probably heard. But she doesn't care. It will keep them away.

And she needs them to stay away. She needs the time and space to remember, time and space to rewrite the narrative of fifteen years of married life.

FIFTEEN

James

James meant nothing to me to start with. He was Cliff's younger brother. That was it. It was the fifteenth of June, and it was raining.

I was three months pregnant, a pregnancy that was neither planned, nor a shock, nor even much of a surprise: though we hadn't been trying to have a child, we hadn't been trying very hard not to have one either. We both wanted kids. It was fine.

It had been raining for days, endlessly, relentlessly. It was so dark outside that I had the lights on. I remember thinking that if one more person said, "I hope it clears up by next Saturday," I would scream. No one wants to get married in the rain. Well, maybe someone somewhere in Africa does, but we certainly didn't.

Everything was ready. We're both good organisers and we were back then too. There was no real stress to focus on other than the weather, which I suppose is why everyone kept banging on about it. Neither Cliff nor I were religious so it was to be a simple registry office service, and neither were we flamboyant, so the reception we had booked was a simple catered affair in a country pub. We had been living together for two years by then anyway and Cliff's mother, our only remaining parent, had died the year before – there was no point making a fuss.

Was I disappointed already by the lack of lustre? Perhaps, a little.

There had been a time, just a few years earlier, when I had wobbled on a knife-edge between gothic flamboyancy and being ordinary. It really could have gone either way.

At the beginning of my fling with Ben I had fantasised about marrying him, and that fantasy had involved Blur playing a concert at our wedding (Ben claimed to know Graham Coxon, the guitarist, though I never saw any proof of that while I was dating him), and inevitably a Harley Davidson to whisk us away to our honeymoon (Ben was a biker).

It's not that this image matched who I was any more than the cliché of becoming a Surrey housewife did; it's just that I was young – I was still a blank canvas ready to take whatever life wanted to throw at me.

When Ben's ego turned out to be impossible to live with, Cliff's calm middle-England approach seemed like the obvious alternative.

So it was raining. Hard. Cliff was upstairs painting a bedroom in neutral green (we didn't know what sex the baby was yet) and I was watching the TV and listening out for James' arrival. He had just finished a degree course in Edinburgh and was driving down with a carload of stuff. I had spent half the week clearing enough storage space in our shed so that James could stack his things there whilst he went travelling. I had fixed up the spare room for him as well. As I say, we were both good organisers.

I had met James only once before, in a London pub. He had been drunk and loud, and I had been bored – it was my turn to drive. We said hello, gave him his birthday gift – a camera, I think – and James vanished to the bar for a round of drinks. He took so long that by the time he came back I had convinced Cliff to leave. It didn't take much – they had never been close.

So I had met James already and I had found him unremarkable; there was no sense of expectation that Saturday in June. I was more concerned about what was on the television. A bomb had gone off in the centre of Manchester. A big one.

Cliff appeared in the doorway.

"You've got paint on your nose," I told him.

He dabbed at it with a finger. "Oh yeah," he said, then, "Still no sign of Wonder Boy then?"

I shook my head, then nodded at the images of carnage on the television screen. "They say hundreds of people have been injured. And at least two deaths."

"The IRA?"

"They don't know yet."

"But it probably is."

"Yes, that's what they think. There's no reason James would stop off in Manchester is there?"

Cliff shook his head. "No. His car's full of stuff. He'll drive straight down. I suppose I might as well go start the skirting boards then."

"OK," I said, waving at him mockingly and turning back to the television. I didn't feel guilty. I had spent three days sanding the buggers down and had been officially exempted from painting because the fumes made me retch.

A car pulled up outside, and I tore my eyes away from the screen to check that it wasn't James. It was one of those big four-by-fours – everyone seemed to be getting them back then. A woman and kids got out – they all had matching umbrellas. Funny the things you remember. I wondered if they would move on before James arrived. It would make it easier to carry his stuff in if he could park outside, I reckoned. But that's as much thought as I gave it. He was just Cliff's younger brother, after all.

John Major came on the television talking about terrorism and I think I turned the sound off. I had never liked John Major. There was always something about his sweaty top lip that made me feel a bit queasy.

By two o'clock there were four people dead in Manchester and James still hadn't arrived. We needed bread for lunch, so I shouted up to Cliff that I was nipping out.

"Get white spirit if they have any," he said.

I opened my own umbrella and headed up to the Spar, where I bought bread and some extra cheddar (they didn't have any DIY materials) before heading home. 'The Day Before You Came' was playing in the shop, and I had it stuck in my head as I walked home. A premonition almost.

When I got to our house a faded orange Volvo estate had replaced the four-by-four. The windows were all steamed up.

As I reached the car, the passenger window opened and James' face appeared, peering up at me. "Can you tell me which house number twenty-two is?" he asked.

"James!" I said.

"Hannah! God, sorry!" James laughed. "Get in!"

"Get in?"

"Yes." He leaned across and part-opened the door.

"Don't be silly," I said, opening it just wide enough to look inside. "Come indoors."

"I will," James said. "But get in first. I want to ask you something."

I folded the umbrella and climbed into the car. The rain was

100

drumming so hard on the roof you had to talk loudly just to make yourself heard. "Why are you sitting out here?" I asked, turning myself as far in the seat as I could.

"I only just parked," he told me. His eyes were the most astounding blue, the exact same blue as his T-shirt. In the dark interior of the pub where I had met him previously, I hadn't noticed. Cliff's are green.

"I just wanted to check with you," he said, "you know, honestly."

"Yes?"

"Are you OK about all of this? About me staying? About me leaving all this shit at your place?" He gestured over his shoulder, and I glanced behind at the mixture of boxes and bin-bags and tatty furnishings.

"Of course," I said. "You must have spoken to Cliff about it."

James smiled at me, and as he did so, he reached across and touched, ever so lightly, my shoulder. I was fully clothed; I was wearing a mac – there was nothing intimate about the gesture. "Oh, you know what Cliff's like," he said. "He always says the right thing, always *does* the right thing. But you never know what he's really thinking, do you?"

"No," I said. It was so true. And it was something I had realised subconsciously but had never really thought about until now.

Because it seemed disingenuous somehow to gang up on him I simply said, "Yes, anyway, as far as I know he's absolutely fine about it. We've been looking forward to you coming all week."

"Have you?" James asked. He was peering into my eyes, a strange air of concern upon his brow, as if it were suddenly terribly important that this were true.

"Yes," I said, unexpectedly flustered. "Now let's get inside. It's crazy sitting out here."

"Sure," James said. "You go in. I'll be there in a second."

When I got indoors, I hung up my mac. I stared at the wall for a second, then snapped myself out of it and shouted up to Cliff, "James is here, he's just parking."

"I'll be down in a minute," Cliff called back. "I just have to finish this stretch."

I went into the lounge and crossed my arms and watched the Volvo and waited for James to reappear. And I wondered why my heart was pounding so.

SIXTEEN

London – 19th June 1996

Dear H.

Just a note to wish you the best on your wedding day.

As you know(!) I'm unable to be there, but I hope it is wonderful and that everything turns out just the way you want and all your wishes come true.

I'm so sorry about the precipitous departure, but, needs must ...

For my part, I have postponed my departure for Thailand. I have been feeling pretty shaken up since I left last Tuesday, and there would simply be no point traveling when I feel this miserable.

Plus, I keep hoping you'll appear outside my door (my address is above) though of course, I know that you won't (will you?).

I can't seem to get you out of my mind, but I expect that's because I don't yet want to.

Anyway, I hope you are happy, and that Cliff is well. I hope above all that he realises just what a lucky bloke he is. Forgive me for everything.

J.

SEVENTEEN

"Are you OK?"

Hannah rolls her head to see Jill crouching at her side. She barely remembers moving from the hammock to the sofa.

She stares at her sister, only now realising that she has been asleep, that she had finally fallen asleep.

"I've been worried about you," Jill says. "Are you OK?"

'OK.' The two letters sound alien and strange, the way any word can if you think about it long enough. OK. Is she OK?

She doesn't know what time it is, but it's barely light, and she has barely slept. She has lain awake half the night thinking about the same things over and over and over again. That James isn't dead. That her husband has been lying to her for fifteen years. That she perhaps didn't have to choose the life she chose at all. That she didn't actually choose this life either, that it just happened, because it seemed, because of the lie, that there was no choice. But James isn't dead. James is alive. James is on his way here.

"Hannah," Jill says. "How are you feeling?"

She feels excited. Which is absurd, ridiculous even. Would it be shameful to admit that? "I'm fine," she says. "I'm just tired. And shocked."

"I've hardly slept," Jill says. "I've been so worried I did the wrong thing."

Hannah frowns as she tries to drag herself from her own

thoughts enough to be able to converse with her sister. "Why, what did you do?" she asks.

Jill looks confused. "Well, I was the one who gave him the address," she says. "I told him to come."

"You told him to come?"

"No . . . No, I didn't *tell* him to come. But I didn't tell him he couldn't come either, did I?" Jill says.

Hannah nods. Given the scope of the drama in which they are all embroiled, giving James the address is pretty insignificant in the scheme of things.

"He just seemed so nice," Jill says, taking Hannah's silence as reproach and trying to justify herself. "He sounded really rounded and friendly. He has a really lovely voice. But then I always think Aussie accents sound lovely."

Hannah moves to a sitting position and runs a hand across her face. "God. You're an outrage, Jill," she says.

Jill stands and then moves to sit next to her sister. "Oh, that came out wrong," she says as she slides one arm around Hannah's shoulders. "I thought you'd want to see him, too."

"Too?" Hannah repeats.

"I thought you'd want to see him," Jill says. "That's why I gave him the address. I mean, he asked for it. So I had to choose. And he sounded nice."

"Yes," Hannah says. "You said."

"But imagine if I hadn't. Imagine if I hadn't and he never phoned again," Jill says. "I didn't think about the effect it would have on Cliff, I admit. But I knew you'd want to see him again. You do, don't you?"

Hannah flops her head onto her sister's shoulder. She knows the way Jill's mind works, and she is almost certain that Jill didn't think about her at all. A nice-sounding guy phoned and offered to add extra spice to Jill's holiday. That's the only thought that Jill will have had. But there's enough drama in this situation without falling out with her sister on top of everything else.

"So did Cliff think he was dead?" Jill asks. "That's what I can't work out. Or was that a—"

"A lie," Hannah says. "Yes, it was a big, bold, fifteen-year lie."

"God," Jill says. "But why would he do that?"

"Jealousy, I think," Hannah says. "I guess he thought I hadn't forgotten James."

"But you hadn't, had you?"

"No," Hannah admits. "No, I never forgot James. When is he coming? When's he arriving?"

Hannah feels Jill shrug beside her. "He didn't say," she says. "In a couple of days, I think. That's what it sounded like. He said he was going to look at flights and cars and things."

"So it's not definite?"

"I think it was. He sounded pretty sure."

Hannah nods, sits up straight again and tries to force one complete breath of air into her lungs. They feel as if they are compressed, as if she has a weight compressing her chest that won't let her breathe. "Don't tell Tristan or Aïsha, will you?" she asks.

Jill doesn't answer, so Hannah turns to look at her.

"Tris' already knows," Jill says. "He was here when James called, so . . ."

"I know," Hannah says, blinking slowly. "That's fine. I mean just don't tell him the back story. That stuff is private."

Jill licks her lips.

"Oh, Jill!" Hannah says.

"I'm sorry," Jill says. Her sister suddenly reminds her of their mother. When disappointed she had exactly the same expression. "I was stoned, Han'," she says. "You know what I'm like when I'm stoned. I can't keep anything secret."

Hannah shrugs Jill's arm from her shoulder. "You're . . . Honestly . . . You're impossible."

"Look, I'm sorry," Jill says.

"Sure," Hannah says. "Anyway, just, you know . . . don't tell Aïsha. I don't want her filling Luke with a load of confused ideas, OK?"

"OK," Jill says.

Hannah dozes on until the rest of the house starts to awaken, then folds and stores the blanket. She doesn't want Luke to realise that she has slept here.

Breakfast is negotiated through forced smiles – a sterling rendition of normality. But once everyone has eaten, Cliff says, "Can you kids clear the breakfast stuff away? Hannah and I want to go for a stroll together."

"Do we?" Hannah asks.

"Yes," Cliff says flatly. "Yes, we do."

Jill nods encouragingly at her, and reckoning that she is too tired to judge what is best, Hannah capitulates.

Once she has showered and changed her clothes, she goes in search of Cliff, finally finding him sitting in the car listening to classical music. "You can play that in the house you know," she says, as she opens the door.

"I know," Cliff replies. "I just needed the space."

Once they have closed the gate behind them Cliff reaches for Hannah's hand.

She snatches it away, unable to believe that he is able to

misread her mood so severely. "I don't think so, Cliff," is all she says.

They walk for a few minutes in silence, each lost in their own thoughts.

"It's a lot less scary by day," Cliff eventually comments.

"Yes. Look. Why are we out here?" Hannah asks, her tone terse. The last thing she feels like is a summer stroll. "If you have something to say to me, please just get on and say it."

"I'm sorry," Cliff says.

"It's fine, but just, you know, whatever you want to say . . ."

"No. I meant, that's what I wanted to say," Cliff says. "I'm sorry."

"Oh, right."

They walk on for another minute before Cliff says, "So are we OK then?"

Hannah exhales sharply, a barely contained snort of derision. "You're joking, right?" she says.

"I . . . I don't really know what else to say."

"You lied to me for fifteen years," Hannah spits. "Or have I got that wrong?"

"Well, yes. I mean no. No, you haven't."

"So, sorry doesn't really cover it, does it?"

"No," Cliff says. "No, I suppose not."

Hannah stops walking and turns to face her husband. "How could you, Cliff?" she says. "How could you? He's your brother. Can't you see how . . . disturbed . . . that is?" Disturbed isn't really the right word, but she can't think of a better one.

Cliff shrugs. "I thought it was better," he says.

"Better? To pretend that your brother is dead?"

"I thought it was better for *us*," Cliff says. He drops his regard to the ground and kicks at a stone. "I thought it was better for you, for me, for Luke."

Hannah gasps. "Don't you dare try to make this about Luke," she says. "Luke wasn't even born when this started. This is *me* you're talking to. I remember. I remember everything. It was years before Luke was born."

"I'm not . . . I wasn't . . . I just get confused with the dates," Cliff stammers. "Really I do."

"The letter arrived the summer we got back from Scotland," Hannah says. "Which was . . . God!" A wave of shock washes over her. Because beyond the lie itself are the constituent acts of deceit. Layer upon layer of lies required to maintain that first fictional creation. "That letter . . ." she says. "The letter about James' accident. You wrote it yourself. It was a fake."

Cliff chews at the inside of his mouth, then swallows and nods dolefully. "I'm sorry, Hannah," he says. "I didn't know what else to do."

A car, one of those new Beetles, rounds the corner heading towards them, and they are forced to separate momentarily to let it pass. At the last minute, Hannah glances in to see who the driver is. Her heart flutters strangely when she sees that it is not James (would she even recognise him now?) but a woman.

The car past, they begin to walk again.

"I know you're angry," Cliff says, "but . . ."

"Angry?" Hannah laughs derisively.

"But I'm not the only one who . . . I mean, it's not all . . ." Cliff coughs. "Look, what I'm saying is that this isn't only about me," he finally manages.

"But to say he was *dead*," Hannah says.

"I didn't think we'd ever get over it. That was the thing.

I didn't think we would ever be able to forget what had happened. Not unless you could forget about James."

"So you killed him," Hannah says.

"I didn't actually . . ."

"Well, clearly not! On paper, I mean. You killed him on paper."

"I knew he wasn't coming back anyway. So . . ."

"How?" Hannah asks. "How could you possibly know that?"

Cliff licks his lips, opens his mouth to speak, but then closes it again and turns away.

"Oh Jesus," Hannah says, pulling a pained expression. "He's been in contact then? Of course he has."

"Yes, he wrote," Cliff admits. "Just a postcard. To say that he was taking Australian nationality."

"Australian?" Hannah says, her mind's eye attempting to fill in all the missing years with the collage of random images she has seen of Australia. "Of course, Jill said that, yes."

"Jill said what?"

"That he has an accent, an Australian accent."

They reach the bend in the road which was so terrifying in the dark last night. "There is a street lamp," Cliff says pointing. "It must just not work."

"Yes," Hannah says. "Yes, there is. They need to fix it."

When they reach the apex of the bend, it seems obvious to both of them that this is the right point to turn back, so without having to discuss it, they do so.

Cliff's mind is occupied performing a cost–benefit analysis, wondering how many of these dissimulations he should now own up to. He's wondering if James will help him out, whether he can get to him first and ask him to keep at least part of this

110

story under wraps. He hardly has any reason to. He owes Cliff nothing. But perhaps he'll do it for them. Perhaps he'll do it for Hannah.

Hannah is realising that, in his own twisted way, Cliff is right. That James' "death" did mark the point when she gave up imagining parallel lives, did mark the point when she gave in, did, indeed, mark the moment in time when she abandoned herself to a certain kind of happiness – a rather ordinary, passion-less contentment, but a certain kind of happiness all the same.

"Australia," she says again, that single word somehow encapsulating the one thing that she had always sensed. That James' life would be exciting.

"I loved you. I *still* love you, Hannah," Cliff says. "And I didn't want to lose you. You do understand that, don't you? You do get why I had to . . . ?"

Rather absurdly, a song pops into Hannah's head. It's 'If you love somebody, set them free'.

"I couldn't let James just steal you from me," Cliff says.

"Yes," she says. "Yes, I see your logic." It's the best she can manage.

Lunch passes in an ambiance of uneasy truce. Hannah's and Cliff's acting isn't fooling anyone, of course, but they have had arguments before and they know how to do this – no one gets to be married for thirteen years without getting good at playing happy families in front of the kids.

So though everyone, including Luke, can tell that something's not right, everyone is reassured that they're at least behaving in a known, if incomprehensible, manner.

By the time they have finished lunch – prawn and jerusalem

artichoke salad with rice-and-tuna-stuffed peppers – the pool, now in full sunshine, has reached twenty-six degrees. As the day is the hottest yet, the pool becomes the centre of attention, pulling not only Luke and Aïsha from the front of the house, but Tristan and Jill too. This leaves enough room for Hannah and Cliff to perfectly avoid each other.

Hannah nabs the hammock before the table has even been cleared. It's the one place in the garden where – unless you're prepared to share the hammock itself, which she isn't – no one is likely to disturb you.

Cliff is on the far side of the porch pretending to read his novel. He can't concentrate. His eyes keep skimming the page, and after a few failed attempts at starting a new chapter he gives in and does the same thing as Hannah. He remembers the past.

EIGHTEEN

James II

I didn't speak much over lunch. I made cheddar sandwiches and mugs of tea and watched my paint-splattered husband struggle to be civil to his brother. I watched the two men interact and tried to work out what it was about James that annoyed Cliff so. And what it was about him that I found so appealing.

He was very quick-witted. That is the first thing that anyone would have noticed about James. He was daft and silly but fast enough to run semantic circles around most people, including Cliff.

That's not to say that Cliff is, or was, stupid – far from it. But intelligence takes many forms, and Cliff simply never had the fast-footed sarcasm that James so excelled at. In a bear-baiting kind of way it was pretty entertaining to watch.

Because there appeared to be a lull in the rain, and because we were all a little stir-crazy – Cliff and I from being trapped indoors, and James due to the drive from Edinburgh – we decided to go for a walk. Cliff drove us to Puttenham and we walked to Hog's Back. It was cool and misty, but lovely to be outside again.

The rain didn't start again until we were on the ridge, at the farthest point from the car.

As Cliff was wearing his walking anorak, he was the only

person with a hood. And so it was that James and I were forced to huddle underneath my umbrella.

The drizzle soon turned to rain proper, and so as Cliff strode ahead – he had generously volunteered to bring the car as close as possible – James and I sheltered ourselves beneath a tree and then, as the rain intensified, underneath my umbrella, beneath the tree. When it became clear that the rain wasn't going to fade, that it was, in fact, getting worse, we relaunched ourselves into the downpour.

In the interests of reducing our exposure at the edges of the umbrella, James and I linked arms, and then as the downpour intensified we started to run, and James started to laugh.

I remember intentionally splashing through a puddle – we were so wet it didn't seem to make much difference – and as we ran, James turned to glance at me. His face was shiny from the rain, but lit up with mirth – glowing with joy. It was fun; I couldn't help but laugh too, and it struck me that it had been a while since I had laughed like that. I was only twenty-three but already it had been a while since I had felt that light-footed, that carefree. And that was the first time I wanted to kiss him, the first time that desire had crossed my mind.

By the time we got home, reason had prevailed, and I was steering well clear. I didn't know quite what these feelings were, but I sensed that they were dangerous. And so I stayed as far from James as I could, busying myself with as many unlikely tasks as possible to avoid having to share the sofa with him. Cliff, as ever, had taken the armchair.

On Sunday I launched myself, with exceptional enthusiasm, at the task of producing a full Sunday roast. The idea was to be busy. The idea was, again, to stay out of James' way.

Cliff decided to apply a second coat of gloss paint upstairs, and James volunteered to help me peel the potatoes for lunch so we ended up in the kitchen together. I was hyper aware the whole time, of his body there beside me, of his arm occasionally brushing against me as we worked at the sink. And though I tried to be stern and unamused, I couldn't help it. James knew how to make me laugh, and he took relish in doing so.

I can't remember the exact conversations, but I remember he regaled me with funny, self-deprecating stories of student life. I had been a student too, of course, but I had been living at home. I had been living at home with Jill – who was already a handful – and our sick father: my college years had been far from effervescent.

James, on the other hand, had spent four years in a shared house in Edinburgh. He had taken drugs and gone to rave parties and had protested against the poll tax. There really was no comparison. Even then I could see how exciting he was, how much *more* exciting he was. James was like my ex-boyfriend Ben, only without the crazed ego. It was a combination I hadn't known could exist.

"You two are having fun." It was Cliff, standing in the doorway. His tone was condescending, and like naughty schoolchildren who had been caught out, we did our best to wipe the smirks from our faces.

Once Cliff had finished washing his brushes and left the kitchen we looked at each other. James pulled a face and said, in a silly, stern, mocking voice, "You two seem to be having fun," and we both cracked up laughing all over again. Cooking Sunday lunch had never been so much fun.

NINETEEN

Bombay – 10th December 1999

Dear H.

I'm sorry I haven't written for so long. I mentioned you yesterday to my new friend and confidant Suga. He thought me literally wicked for not writing, so here we are: I'm writing.

How are you? How is your kid? What did you have, a boy or a girl?

I have been living in this weird country for nearly two years now. I think I was wanting to lose myself somewhere. India seemed perfect. It is full of lost hippies, lost businessmen, just about every European you meet seems somehow lost here.

I am living in a very strange little cottage which used to be the guard house to a rich Englishman's estate way back. Now it is an out of place, draughty cottage surrounded by half finished concrete hi-rises.

I am working as a satellite dish installer. Whoever would have thought it? In India!

This is an amazing country, so many people, so many extremes. The streets are teeming with the poor and the rich. The strange thing in India is that the poor are mostly happy whilst the rich seem mostly unhappy – a strange state of affairs. Suga, my very close friend here, who is part-time teacher, part-time philosopher, considers this to be perfectly normal. In fact he doesn't believe my view that in England the rich are happier than the poor. I wonder if it is true after all.

Bombay is a very shocking place. Even after all this time, I see at least one sight a day which takes my breath away. The colours, the people, the mix of religions and cultures, the smells and the tastes, it's really quite indescribable.

I work most days, installing these satellite dishes on schools and community centres and banks so that all of the categories of people who go to these places can see images, beamed in from space, of other parts of the world which mean nothing to them.

In the evenings Suga and I sit beneath the stars and play chess, and sometimes as we play he tells me about some philosophy or religion he's been reading about. Last night it was Taoism, which apparently comes from China. The only thing I understood about it was that it was unexplainable, like India perhaps.

Sometimes, now, as I talk to Suga, as I tell him about my adventures they seem like different lives, unrelated to each other. I think, am I the same person who grew up with Cliff in Reading? Do you really exist or did I just read about you in a book somewhere? I sometimes wonder.

God I wish you were here to see all this.
HAPPY CHRISTMAS!
J.

TWENTY

That night Hannah returns to the bedroom. She waits until she thinks Cliff is asleep before she does this, and Cliff obliges by fabricating vague snoring noises. Though he has never heard himself sleep he's surprisingly accurate – accurate enough, in fact, to fool Hannah.

Hannah herself lies awake again. She can't sleep either. She needs to sleep but her mind won't stop churning. She can't stop wondering when James will come, *if* James will come, what will happen if he does, how she will feel seeing him again. It's utterly ridiculous to be this upset, this obsessive, this *excited* about someone she last saw when she was twenty-three. Isn't it?

She glances at the clock. It's almost half-past one and still sleep evades her. She's not sure she can cope with another sleepless night. She's a wreck as it is. She should have asked Jill for a sleeping pill. Jill always has sleeping pills.

Hannah slides silently from the bed and creeps through the sleeping house to the bathroom. She rummages in Jill's wash-bag and finds a pack of Introvate – which she knows are birth control pills – and a blister pack of Triazolam, which for some reason sounds like a sleeping tablet. But she isn't sure, and she doesn't know the dosage, so she decides to wake Jill. She'll forgive her, just this once.

Her hand barely caresses the handle to Jill's room before

she snatches it back. Beyond the door she can hear voices. She stands there a moment in silence. It doesn't sound so much like conversation in fact. It sounds more like two people making out.

In shock, she heads back to the kitchen where, with a fatalistic shrug, she downs one of the pills with a glass of water.

She sits at the small kitchen table until she starts to feel drowsy – that special kind of heavy-headedness washing over her in waves – and then reassured that it was, indeed, a sleeping pill, she makes her way back to bed.

She is just drifting off when a voice says, "He wouldn't have been any good for you, you know." The voice sounds like Cliff, but at the same time not-like-Cliff. Hannah wonders if she is dreaming.

"No?" she asks, unsure if she is talking to Cliff or her own subconscious or perhaps some angel of truth.

"James was always all sparkle and no substance," the voice says.

Hannah forces her drugged head to turn so that she can look at Cliff. He has his back turned to her. His breath sounds slow and steady. There is nothing to demonstrate that he is awake.

It's gone ten by the time Hannah wakes up from her drug-induced slumber, and it's gone eleven by the time she manages to roll from the bed.

There is no one on the patio, so she pours a cold cup of coffee from the pot (breakfast things still strewn across the table, wasps buzzing around the empty orange-juice carton) and then walks, intrigued by the silence, to the corner of the house.

Tristan and Jill are sunbathing on towels next to the pool. Cliff is reading in a pink deckchair she has never seen before with his back to her and Luke is draped sideways over an air-bed with his head underwater. Were it not for the hollow rasp of his breathing through the snorkel, one could think that he had drowned.

"Where's Aïsha?" Hannah asks, and Luke surfaces with a splash, Tristan looks up at her, Jill props herself up on her elbows, and Cliff leans around the side of his deckchair and slips off his sunglasses. It's as if a pause button has been released.

"Morning, drug thief," Jill says.

"Sorry, Jill. I just really needed to sleep. You know how it is sometimes."

"Yes, I guessed," Jill says. "I found the packet in the kitchen. Did you take a whole one? They're really strong, those are."

Hannah nods. "Yes," she says. "I noticed. You don't mind, do you?"

Jill blinks, pushes her lips out, and shakes her head.

"Can I make you some breakfast?" Cliff asks.

"No," Hannah says. "No, I'm fine. So where *is* Aïsha?"

"She went down to the river," Jill says.

"On her own?"

Jill shrugs. "Apparently so."

"And is that OK?" Hannah asks.

Jill shrugs again. "Apparently so," she says. "She is thirteen, Han'."

At the sound of a car coming along the track, everyone pauses. Hannah, the only person in a position to see, turns to watch as a yellow postal van comes into view beyond the gate.

"Just the post," she says, realising as she returns her attention to the others, that she sounded disappointed.

"S'il vous plaît?"

Hannah looks back to see the post-lady leaning over the gate waving a letter. "Tris', can you come talk to her?" she asks. "I can't . . . you know . . . speak the lingo."

"Sure," Tristan says, jumping up.

Hannah returns to the patio, where she swipes at wasps and picks at the breakfast leftovers. The shock of James' potential visit is in danger of ruining her whole holiday, she realises. It's in the process, in fact, of ruining *everybody's* holiday. She needs to get a grip. "*If he comes, he'll come,*" she murmurs. "*If he doesn't, he doesn't.*"

She looks up to see Tristan standing on the far side of the table, waving an envelope, and realises, with embarrassment, that he has heard her talking to herself. She nods at the letter, a mimed question mark.

"Recorded delivery. I signed for it," Tristan says.

Hannah sits up straight. Maybe James has written. She didn't even think of that possibility. "Is it from . . . ? I mean, who's it for?" she asks.

"A Monsieur Hoff," Tristan says.

"Oh. That's the owner," Hannah says, slumping back into her chair.

"That's what I thought; I'll just . . ." Tristan steps inside the doorway and then returns. "I just left it on the table next to the phone," he says with a shrug.

Hannah nods.

"Are you OK?" he asks, sliding into a seat opposite her.

Hannah laughs sourly.

"I'll take that as a 'no' then."

Hannah gestures vaguely with her open hand. "Look, I'm fine, Tris'," she says. "I just need to pull myself together."

"You must try to have a good holiday all the same," Tristan says. "I know it's difficult, but . . ."

What do you know? Hannah thinks, and as if to answer that thought, Tristan continues, "Jill told me, you know . . . a bit about what happened."

Hannah takes a deep breath and blinks slowly. "Yes, I know she did," she says.

"I had a thing a bit like that once," Tristan says.

"A thing?"

Tristan glances over his shoulder to check that they are alone before continuing, "A guy I was in love with. From way back," he says. "Tom. He became a real obsession. I bumped into him in the gym. In Bath of all places. It was such a shock."

Hannah nods. Her brain is a little sozzled still from the drug. She can't for the life of her work out what this has to do with her and James.

"I had really, you know, idealised him over the years," Tristan continues. "But he was pretty ordinary when it came to it. It was quite a disappointment."

Hannah frowns. "I don't really . . ." she says.

"I guess I just mean, you know, don't get your hopes up," Tristan says. "He may not be as much as you remember. It may not be such a big deal after all."

Hannah laughs unconvincingly. "I don't know what Jill told you," she says, "but I was never in love with James."

"Oh," says Tristan. "Oh, sorry . . . I must have got the wrong end of the stick."

"It's OK," Hannah says. "Now, if you'll excuse me, I really need to shower if I'm ever going to wake up properly."

She collects fresh clothes from the bedroom and takes a long, hot shower. The water pressure in the villa is amazing and by the time she has finished, the bathroom is full of steam and she feels as if she has taken a sauna – she feels revitalised. She feels ready to pick up the holiday where she left off.

She opens the tiny bathroom window to let out the steam and as she does so she hears a snatch of conversation between Luke and Aïsha who are walking around the back of the house. ". . . being so weird?" Luke is saying.

"It's 'cos of that James bloke," Aïsha replies.

"I know," Luke says, "but so what?"

"Everyone thought he was dead," Aïsha says, "only he ain't. And he's, like, your mum's old boyfriend. And he's your uncle. I s'pose he might even be your dad."

Trailer trash, Hannah thinks. She makes us sound like trailer trash. She clasps one hand over her mouth and stands on tip-toe to better hear Luke's reply.

Thankfully, Luke just laughs. "Don't be stupid," he says. "Dad's my dad. So are we going to the river then?"

Once she has dressed, Hannah heads back outside and returns to the corner of the house. With the exception of Luke – who is presumably at the river with Aïsha – the configuration is exactly as before.

Hannah waves to get Jill's attention, but it is Tristan who spots her and sits up, so she points at Jill beside him and beckons.

"Jill," Tristan says quietly, nudging his neighbour gently.

Jill lifts her sunglasses and sits up. "Yes?" she says, causing Cliff to turn and peer back at her as well.

"Is everything OK?" Cliff asks.

"Fine," Hannah says. "I just need Jill for a minute."

Jill yawns, stretches and then stands. "Oh dear," she asks jokingly as she crosses the lawn. "What have I done now?"

Once they have reached the patio, Hannah leans back against the wall of the house. "It's about Aïsha," she says.

"It's a tiny river," Jill says, misunderstanding the reason that Hannah has summoned her. "It's about three feet deep. They're perfectly safe."

"Oh. Good," Hannah says. "Look, I need to know what you've told Aïsha."

"Oh," Jill says, pulling a face. "Why, what has she said?"

"Nothing to me. But I overheard her talking to Luke. She was telling him that James is my old boyfriend."

"Oh God," Jill says. "God, I'm sorry, Han', I told her not to say anything. I specifically said . . ."

"You shouldn't have told her, Jill," Hannah says. Her voice sounds a little more edgy than she intends it to be, a little more quivery. She clears her throat before continuing. "I specifically asked you not to say anything."

Jill sighs and gently grasps her sister's elbow. "I already had. When he phoned. That's the thing. So I just told her to keep her mouth shut. I didn't think . . ."

"She told Luke that James might be his father as well," Hannah says. "I mean, honestly!"

"No! Really?"

"That didn't come from you, did it?"

Jill shakes her head sharply. "Of course not," she says. "He isn't though, is he?"

Hannah cups her hands across her nose, closes her eyes and murmurs, "Oh God!" before continuing, "Of course he isn't! How could he be? For Christ's sake."

Jill shrugs. "I don't know," she says. "Stranger things have happened."

"Luke was born two years after James . . . after James *supposedly* died," Hannah says.

"Right," Jill says. "Of course. Sorry. So what? Shall I have another word with her?"

Hannah shakes her head slowly. "I don't know," she says. "I mean, I don't want Luke thinking that James is my ex, but . . ."

"Even though he kind of is," Jill says.

Hannah rolls her eyes skywards. "For God's sake, Jill. It's bad enough as it is, without everyone embroidering the situation."

"But you two did . . . you know . . . Didn't you?"

"No. We didn't. We didn't do anything. I just . . . I just had a crush on the guy I suppose. That's all it was. That's all that happened."

"Oh, I assumed, you know . . . What with all the fuss and everything."

Hannah sighs deeply.

"Hey, it's not my fault if you don't tell me anything," Jill says, relaxing her grip on Hannah's elbow and gently stroking her arm instead.

"There wasn't anything *to* tell," Hannah says. "Anyway, isn't there something *you* want to tell *me*?"

Jill shrugs, all innocence.

"I came to your room last night," Hannah says. "You had someone in there with you."

"Oh," Jill says. "That."

"Yes, that."

"It was just Pascal."

"Pascal."

"Yes."

"Pascal being . . . ? The pool guy?"

Jill licks her lips and attempts to restrain a smirk. She nods and flashes the whites of her eyes at her sister. "He is such a good shag, Han', you have no idea."

"That's outrageous," Hannah says.

"Why?" Jill laughs. "I'm single. I'm on holiday. What's so outrageous about it?"

"But . . ." Hannah shrugs. "I don't know. You can't even talk to each other, can you?"

Jill snorts – a genuine out-loud laugh. "You're so funny, Hannah," she says.

"Why? Why am I funny?"

"Well, I don't *want* to *talk* to him."

"Jill! Jesus!"

Jill looks so pleased with herself, Hannah becomes confused about whether she herself should feel angry or amused. "Anyway, how did you even *book* your midnight rendezvous? Was it when you were over there? When you had coffee with his mother?"

"We pointed at the clock," Jill says, as if this is evident. "And his mother wasn't *really* there. You realised that, right?"

Hannah looks confused. "Well, no; no, I didn't."

"The mother was a decoy. I just didn't want to announce it front of everyone," Jill says. "Even I like to keep some mystery."

"You didn't want to announce what?"

"Well, that I'd had a quick shag against the wall of the shed," Jill says. "It doesn't sound very classy, does it? Even I know that. I do have some standards, Han'."

"Of course you do. The highest standards."

"So again. Do you want me to talk to Aïsha about the James business or not?"

Hannah tips her head back and rubs the back of her head against the cool stone of the wall. "No," she says. "No, I don't think so. Luke seemed to just laugh it off. I'd rather let sleeping dogs lie. And anyway, there's nothing really to tell. But if he says anything . . ."

"Sure," Jill says. "If he says anything, I'll let you know."

TWENTY-ONE

James III

On the Monday, Cliff had to work. I was still trying to avoid James, not out of any logical thought process, but from an instinctive feeling that he was dangerous. I was pregnant with Cliff's child after all. Perhaps the mother in me felt threatened, perhaps even the baby did.

To avoid James, I told him that I had shopping to do, errands to run. I needed some food from Waitrose, and I had to pick up Cliff's suit from Moss Brothers and my dress from the seamstress. It was a plain little white dress but expensive and hand-made for the simple reason that I hadn't been able to find anything straight-forward enough for my tastes anywhere else.

The rain had stopped and James declared himself in need of exercise, so my escape plan failed miserably. We would end up spending most of the day side-by-side.

On the way into town we stopped at Costa and had toasted tea-cakes and mugs of frothy cappuccino. I remember that because James aped around by putting a blob of froth on his nose and going up to the counter to ask for sugar. He wanted to see if the barista would tell him about his nose – she didn't say a word.

In Waitrose he continued his one-man show by hiding behind the bread-shelf I was looking at and hanging onto the other side of the loaf I selected. It will all sound a bit childish now, I suppose, but it wasn't. It was charming and funny. We were still so young I suppose.

And then we went to the dress shop . . .

The assistant assumed that he was my fiancé and James played along magnificently. When I stepped out of the changing rooms, James clapped his hands and said, "Wow! Stunning," and I sensed from his regard that it was true, and felt good about myself.

The woman smiled at me and nodded her approval, then said to James, "You shouldn't really be seeing this, you know. People say it's bad luck."

"We don't believe in luck, do we, Han'?" James said. "We're going to make our own luck."

I felt myself blushing. Because I had momentarily wished that it were true. I had momentarily imagined that it was funny, grinning, blue-eyed James that I was going to marry in less than a week and not Cliff. As I changed back into my jeans, I felt disgusted at myself for even having had the thought.

After the dress shop, James convinced me to go for lunch in a pub we were passing. It was late and I was hungry and my nerves were all jangled from trying the dress on – in short, I felt in need of a drink.

Lunch was nothing special really. I had a not-very-nice burger and James had fish and chips. I downed two glasses of white and James two pints of beer. But the alcohol helped me relax. It stilled my racing heart.

The sun finally came out while we were inside. The rays shone through the dirty pub window and lit up the back of James' head. He looked freaky really, like some Christian icon. He was talking constantly, being funny still. And then he suddenly changed tack and asked me what it was I loved about Cliff.

I told him I was exhausted thinking about Cliff and the wedding and that I'd rather hear more of his stories. But that wasn't true. It was simply that I couldn't, when put on the spot, think *what* it was I loved about Cliff. Or rather it was that the things that I would have listed, that Cliff was level-headed, and good-humoured, and reliable, suddenly didn't sound like love at all. I kept thinking of a song lyric – the Smiths perhaps – that asked how you would know what love looked like if you had never seen it. And I remember thinking, that the more important point was, how would you know what love *wasn't* if you had never seen it. My definitions of what love was and wasn't seemed suddenly to be shifting, and I wasn't sure how I felt about that. I wasn't sure how I felt about that at all.

James was eating chips and rabbiting on about something or other in that animated manner of his and I saw that he had a spot of mayonnaise on the corner of his mouth.

Without thinking, I reached out and smudged it away, and then I flinched, knowing instantly that some taboo had been breached by my doing so.

In a fluster of false excuses about the food defrosting at our feet – food which had been forgotten until that point – I stood and clumsily knocked over James' empty glass and announced that we had to leave; that we had to leave right now.

We walked home in near silence. I was carrying the dress and a carrier bag, and James was carrying Cliff's suit and the second bag of shopping. It crossed my mind that James and Cliff were about the same size and I wondered what he would look like in the suit. The silence between us became quite uncomfortable. I think we were both aware that something had happened.

When we got inside, I went straight to the freezer. I could tell from the soggy packaging that things were melting. As I turned from stacking the freezer, I bumped into James – he was standing right behind me. He was just inches away, with an expectant look on his face.

I laughed falsely, and said, "What on earth are you . . . ?" And that's when he kissed me.

TWENTY-TWO

Brisbane – 15th December 2001

Dear Hannah,
So I finally managed to get my shit together and drag myself from India. I made it to Australia. The other side of the world. If I go any farther, I'll be coming back.

This is an amazing place, so English and yet so different.

It is summer here, Christmas will be mid-summer, imagine! The houses are English, the people are English, and yet they're not. They're tougher and more friendly, more solid, like country people in England maybe. When you leave the city, amazing animals are everywhere, kangaroos and parrots and crocodiles. It really is like living in a kid's pop-up book.

I am boarding in a hotel on the edges of Brisbane, a friendly, clean, basic place over a pub. (They call all the pubs hotels here.) I am working for an outfit installing electric fences in the outback. It is not technically breathtaking, and it's not that well paid either, but my money ran out, so ...

I want to tell you about Australia, but I can't work out what to tell, it is such a strange place, so much is different and so much the same.

I still haven't found anyone to replace you. I look at this country and I wish you were here to see it with me. Is that crazy after all these years?

I'm still not sure I will be happy here, though, but perhaps one never really ever is. Perhaps they all just pretend.

I hope you are all well, I wonder if you get my letters? A reply would be cool, just to let me know that you're OK.

And HAPPY CHRISTMAS!

All my love as always. J.

TWENTY-THREE

After a second night on Triazolam, Hannah wakes up feeling floaty and relaxed. The whole James thing has taken on a surreal, dreamlike quality. She is even starting to doubt that he will come at all.

When, after breakfast, further interrogation of her sister regarding the exact nature of her conversation with James provides nothing further of substance, nothing but further reasons to doubt, she decides, unilaterally, that he *isn't* coming. She's surprised at herself that this leap of faith is not only possible, but relatively easy.

Re-centred in the here and now for the first time in two days, Hannah notices that Luke and Aïsha are becoming bored and argumentative. Tristan, too, is spending more time tapping messages into his phone than interacting with anyone else.

It's at the moment Hannah suggests that they drive somewhere for dinner that she realises why no one has suggested leaving the villa for the last two days. No one wants to be elsewhere if and when James should finally arrive. No one wants to miss the action.

But her suggestion is seized upon by Luke and Aïsha – who immediately specify that the restaurant must serve pizza – and from that point there is no going back.

Just after four, as they are leaving, Cliff offers to stay behind so that everyone can fit into Tristan's Jeep.

Hannah is having none of it. There is no way she is letting Cliff head James off at the pass. "Just get in the car," she says with a sharpness that surprises even her. Cliff, bless him, buckles.

Hannah, Luke and Aïsha climb into Tristan's Jeep whilst Cliff and Jill follow on in the Mégane. Hannah glances back occasionally and sees that they are engrossed in a very serious-looking conversation. She wonders what they're talking about.

When Tristan hits the open road and accelerates, the present momentarily overwhelms her. She had forgotten that she was in France. She's in France and it's hot, and they're out of the house, and the sensations of driving with the top down and her hair whipping crazily around her head are ecstatic. She's tapping her hand to Tristan's crazy electronic music and the kids, in the rear seats, are grinning again. She's overcome by a surprise wave of the joy of now, so powerful it moves her to tears. She's tired, she rationalises. She's tired and drugged – no wonder she's emotional.

She glances across at Tristan, and he smiles back briefly before his expression changes to concern. "It's too windy for you," he shouts. "Your eyes are watering. Do you want the top up?"

"No," Hannah says, smiling back at him and reaching out to touch his shoulder. "No, it's fine. It's better than fine. It's brilliant, Tris'. I love it."

They end up in a beautiful little pizzeria in a hilltop town called Cabris. The tables are covered with red and white checked tablecloths, and the cutlery glimmers with the light from the oil lamps placed on each table.

Luke and Aïsha leave the table almost the second the pizzas

are served, returning only occasionally for another mouthful before running off again to explore the tiny streets.

Hannah cuts into her calzone and watches as raw egg-white oozes out. "Ooh. Look. This egg's not cooked," she says. "D'you think that's OK, Tris?"

Tristan shrugs. "It's impossible to fully cook the egg inside a calzone," he says. "If you send it back they'll just cremate it."

"But it's OK to eat?"

"Sure," he says. "Why wouldn't it be?"

Hannah nods and starts to cut into the other end of the calzone. "Look how all the French kids just sit there," she says, looking around the terrace. There are three French families eating here tonight, and their kids, ranging from about five to fifteen, are without exception sitting elegantly, engaged in polite conversation with the adults.

"Oh, they're fine," Cliff says, meaning Luke and Aïsha. "They've just been cooped up a bit. It'll do them good to run around."

"Anyway," Jill says. "You wouldn't want Luke to behave like that, would you?"

Hannah discovers that by tipping each slice of calzone sideways the raw egg simply runs off. "Maybe," she says, forking a mouthful.

Jill scans the terrace again and then pulls a face. "They look like they've been drugged to me," she says. "They look like they've been given tranquillisers."

Hannah and Tristan laugh. "It's true," Tristan says.

"They do," Hannah agrees.

"Maybe there's a special kid's pizza with Valium. You should have asked."

"I'd rather Aïsha grows up stroppy and rebellious," Jill says.

"I'd far rather she grabbed life by the balls than became some placid L'Oréal queen."

Hannah nods. "I suppose," she says. And there it is again, she thinks. How best to live a life? Respectably? Politely? Or as a stroppy rebel?

"Talking of which, I need to be back at midnight by the way," Jill says. "We will be back by midnight, won't we?"

"I would think so, but why?" Cliff asks. "You gonna turn into a pumpkin?"

Hannah glances at Tristan and she can tell from his restrained smile that Jill has told him and that he approves.

"Jill has a regular midnight visitor," Hannah explains.

"Really?" Cliff asks. "Who?"

TWENTY-FOUR

James IV

His lips grazed mine, and, at first, I kept my mouth firmly shut. But even then, even like that, that kiss felt like no kiss I had ever had. And yes, I know how ridiculous that sounds, but it happens to be true.

I had only ever had sex with Ben before Cliff, remember. And I had only kissed a handful of boys before Ben.

So though I had known good kissers and bad kissers (Cliff was actually one of the better ones) I had never experienced such heart-stopping desire. I *wanted* James. The second our lips touched, I felt as if I had been drugged, as if I had been injected and heroin or something was suddenly rushing through my veins. It was as much as I could do to remain standing. I had never experienced that before, and if you've never experienced something before, how could you possibly know what you're missing?

I slowly started to open my lips (I was melting, my defences were vanishing) but then a noise, the slamming of a car door, jerked me back to the here and now of who I was and where I was and, above all, who James was. My heart beating crazily, I pushed him away and ducked under his outstretched arm and ran to the front door, grabbing my coat as I passed it in the hallway. I don't think he even attempted to follow, but I don't know. I didn't look back.

I walked to the park and wandered around until I came to a bench. I sat and stared at the still wet grass and felt numb. I watched as the sun dipped in the sky, finally disappearing behind a purple bank of cloud.

I waited until I knew that Cliff would be home before I returned to the house. I half expected that James would be missing, that he would, in shame, have vanished.

Cliff was drinking a can of beer and watching the news. "Hi love. Where have you been?" he asked, in an unsuspicious tone.

James, from the sofa, was eyeing me warily.

"I went to see Shelley," I lied, realising as I did so that it was the first time I had ever lied to Cliff.

"Ah, I said you'd gone shopping," James said. "I thought that's what you said, sorry."

"I intended to, but you know what I'm like when I get together with Shelley," I said. "I'll have to go tomorrow now."

"I'm pretty hungry," Cliff said. "I know it's early, but . . . Do you want me to get a takeaway? I can go and get fish and chips if you want."

"No, it's fine," I replied, remembering the dob of mayonnaise on James' lip. "I have stuff for tea. I'll get it going."

I had just dropped the spaghetti into the pan when James entered the kitchen. "I'm sorry about before," he said. He was standing too close to me for comfort. He had his arms folded. He looked uncomfortable.

"It's fine," I said, "Just, you know . . ." I made a shooing gesture, and he took a step further back.

"The thing is, Hannah," he said.

I was stirring the bolognese sauce around the pan, and then squishing the spaghetti into the boiling water. Only once it was submerged did I look up. "Yes?" I asked.

James glanced behind him and then said, "The thing is, I think I'm falling . . ."

I stepped forward and placed my fingertips on his lips, effectively silencing him. "For fuck's sake, James," I whispered, glancing towards the lounge.

"But I need to . . ." he said.

I tutted sharply and yanked him out of the back door.

"You just can't do this, James," I said once we were outside. "It's not fair."

"But I'm in love with you," he said. "You know I am."

"I don't know anything," I said, but then he slipped one arm behind me and kissed me, and I felt myself melt against him all over again.

We kissed for a few seconds before I turned my head sideways. I rested it on his shoulder. "God, James," I said quietly. "You're just so . . ."

I had been about to say, "*sexy*", but it suddenly struck me as the sort of thing Jill might say. It sounded slutty.

"You're amazing, Hannah," he said, and he kissed me again, and I let it happen – it was wonderful, and the last of my defences collapsed and I allowed myself to fall into him. His tongue slipped into my mouth and I shivered and wanted more of him, all of him. I wanted every bit of him deep inside me, I wanted, somehow, to merge with him. *Oh God*, I thought, simply.

And then, as if from nowhere, the absurdity of the whole situation hit me again and I started to laugh.

James pulled away. He looked hurt. "What?" he asked.

"Well!" I said. "Can't you see how ridiculous this is?"

"I don't see why."

"I'm *pregnant*," I said. "I'm getting married on Saturday. To your *brother*."

"But what if you didn't," he said, his eyes looking a little crazed. "What if you came away with me instead."

"Away?"

"Yes, travelling. To India, and Thailand. We'd have such a great time you and me. I know we would."

"You're crazy, James," I said. "You know that, right?"

James shrugged and broke into a broad smile, and I looked into his eyes, and just for a second, I glimpsed that, despite everything, this madness was a possibility, and I started to grin stupidly too.

"This sauce is burning!" It was Cliff, calling from the kitchen.

I broke from James' grasp and ran back inside to snatch the spatula that Cliff was ineffectually using to stir the still-burning sauce. I pulled the pan from the heat. "Sorry about that," I said. ". . . got distracted. Don't worry. I have another jar."

"I just smelt it burning," Cliff said. "What were you doing out in the g—"

At that instant, James stepped back through the door. He smiled at Cliff, and there was something aggressive, something challenging about his stance.

"Oh," Cliff said. "Right." And then he turned and left the kitchen. "Let me know when dinner's ready," he said, flatly.

James watched him walk to the lounge and then whispered, "Hannah, I . . ."

I turned to face him, furious now. I raised the palm of my

141

hand. "Stop!" I hissed. "Just stop it." And then I added, quite loudly, "Please get out from under my feet, James. Please just go and watch television or something." And that's what he did.

Everything seemed normal enough that evening. I think we were all pretty good at playing normal, even back then. I served dinner, and we watched some TV, and then I went to bed followed, after half an hour, by Cliff.

I couldn't sleep for ages. I stared at the ceiling and calculated possible lives. I tried to imagine getting up the next morning and announcing that I wouldn't be marrying Cliff, that I was leaving with James. I imagined announcing nothing at all, simply eloping with James in the old-fashioned way – the way they did in films. I pictured going downstairs and telling James that he should leave, expelling him from the house so that Cliff and I could get married in peace. But all of the options seemed as unlikely as parallel universes. I couldn't imagine myself doing any of them.

So I stared at the ceiling and listened to Cliff snoring and wondered, as if there were a script to all of this, as if there were no such thing as free will, what would happen next.

And in a way, I was right. There *were* no choices to be made.

Because what happened next was that I finally fell asleep. And by the time I woke up in the morning James had gone.

TWENTY-FIVE

Brisbane – 3rd July 2003

Dear H.

I am writing to tell you that I'm gonna get hitched.

Her name is Judy, and she is an amazingly strong woman – the daughter of farmers – very lively, very organised. She keeps my life in good order, keeps us busy and well kept. I sometimes wonder if my heart isn't still a bit broken, and Judy does too. She calls me the ice-man, but swears she will melt me. Please wish her luck.

We met over a year ago and have decided that it's time (now she's pregnant!) that I made an honest woman of her.

I haven't sent you an invitation, as it's not a practical proposition for you to attend, but the date of the wedding is 2nd August, so if you don't hate me too much you could toast us on that date.

Deepest apologies for any hurt I ever caused you two.

Much love, J.

PS: The above is our new address. I have enclosed a photo so that you can see how we live over here. Through the big window you can just see the amazing Glasshouse Mountains. It was summer though, when the photograph was taken, it's winter now, and a cold, windy one at that.

TWENTY-SIX

"Where's your mum?" Hannah asks.

They are seated on the patio awaiting Cliff's return. He and Luke have bravely ventured into Frenchy-land in search of fresh bread and croissants.

Aïsha shrugs. "The door's locked," she says. "She locks it when she wants a lie-in."

At the sight of the Mégane returning, Hannah heads indoors to fetch the coffee. She crosses paths with Tristan coming out of the bathroom, a towel wrapped around him, his hair still wet.

"Morning," she says, and he nods, and returns the greeting before turning and heading towards his room. Hannah, despite herself, steals a glance at his muscular back as he walks away.

She then carries the pot of coffee outside before walking around the back of the house to peer through Jill's shutters. Sensing that they aren't locked, she pulls on them gently and looks into the room – into the empty room.

Back at the table, Tristan, now in shorts and a T-shirt, is taking a seat.

The croissants – still warm – are a buttery marvel, and combined with the thick dark coffee they make a perfect, if not particularly healthy, breakfast.

"Are we doing something today?" Luke asks.

The adults glance at each other. "I suppose we could go

somewhere this afternoon," Cliff says. "We could maybe go to Cannes or something."

"What's in Cannes?" Luke says.

"It's a seaside town. Beach, shops, cafés . . ." Hannah says. "Why, are you bored?"

"A bit," Luke admits.

Aïsha, who has been jabbing at the screen of her phone, sighs and slaps it down on the table.

"Careful, Aï"," Tristan says. "You'll break it."

"It doesn't work anyway," she says.

"Internet?" Tristan asks. "Or the whole thing?"

"Facebook."

Tristan holds his hand out. "Show me," he says.

Aïsha stares at him. She looks alarmed.

"I'm not gonna look at your stuff," Tristan says. "I just want to check the settings for you."

"Promise?" Aïsha asks, dragging her phone towards her, and then rounding the table to Tristan's side.

"I promise," Tristan says. As he starts to fiddle with the phone he mumbles, "Now, it might be your network settings . . . and those are in here . . ."

"I didn't do anything," Aïsha says. "I was on Facebook talking to Jess and then it stopped."

"How is Jess?" Hannah asks. Jess is Aïsha's best friend.

"She's OK," Aïsha says. "Her mum's pregnant again."

"Ah!" Tristan says. "Eureka! You've reached the limit, haven't you."

"What's eureka?" Aïsha asks. She doesn't know what Tristan is talking about.

"There's a fifty-euro limit," Tristan explains. "That's what this text you got says."

"What's fifty euros?" Jill has reappeared, standing in the doorway.

"Oh, you're back," Hannah says, smiling falsely at her sister. "Sorry, I mean 'up' of course. You're *up*!"

"Yes," Jill says, shooting her a knowing glance, and then, returning her attention to Aïsha, "So what's this about fifty euros?"

"She's reached the data limit," Tristan says. "There's an EU limit. Fifty euros. After that it stops working unless you phone them and get the limit removed."

"I only used Facebook," Aïsha says defensively.

Jill takes her seat at the table. "Croissants," she says. "Yum."

"Me and Dad got them," Luke explains. "Those square ones have chocolate in them. The man was French and we didn't know what he was saying and Dad made me pay."

Jill takes a bite and then speaking through a mouthful of croissant, says, "Ooh, these are good. So have you really spent fifty euros on Facebook? That's crazy. We've only been here four days."

Hannah sits and stares at her sister, ever a mystery. Jill never has a penny, and yet when her daughter spends fifty euros on Facebook, she only sounds vaguely surprised, and certainly not angry.

"Can we phone them?" Aïsha asks. "Can we phone them and do the thing so it works again?"

Jill laughs. "No, we can't," she says, and Hannah thinks, *Well, thanks be for small mercies.*

Aïsha frowns at Tristan. "So when will it work again?" she asks.

"When you get home," he says, handing the phone back.

"You're joking me," Aïsha says.

Tristan shakes his head. "Sorry, babe."

146

"Does yours still work?" she asks.

He nods. "Mine's for work though. I need my emails. So I have to pay for it."

"I *need* my Facebook," Aïsha says.

"It'll do you good to have a break," Hannah says. "You're on there all the time."

Aïsha shakes her head in disgust. "That's so lame," she says, turning and walking away from the table. "I hate France," she adds – her parting shot.

"Fifty euros!" Jill says, once she has gone.

"How much is fifty euros?" Luke asks, sipping his orange juice. "In pounds I mean."

"About forty," Cliff tells him.

"Wow. I'd be in trouble for that, wouldn't I?" Luke says.

"You would," Hannah agrees.

"I better not switch it on then," Luke says.

"No," Cliff says. "No, you had better not."

"Facebook's boring anyway," Luke says, and all the adults smile, because they understand that Luke doesn't think Facebook is boring at all; Luke just knows that it's a cool thing to say to the oldies.

Breakfast over, Hannah manages, for the first time in days, to read her novel. James is still occupying half of her mind and occasionally – whenever a car comes along the lane – all of it. But the rest of the time she is managing to abstract herself from thoughts of James as one might manage to ignore the rhythm of a washing machine.

When Jill appears at her side and asks, "Han', d'you know where the kids are?" she realises that she has been lost in her book for the last five chapters.

"Um?" she says. "Um, no. I thought they were with you at the pool."

"My guess is that they're down at the river," Jill says. "Tris' is making lunch, so I'm going to see if I can find them."

"I'll come with you," Hannah says, folding her book and jumping up. "I haven't been down there yet."

Hannah pulls on her sandals and then the two women climb over the fence at the rear of the property and start, in single file, along the track.

"You have to keep your eyes open for snakes," Jill calls back.

"You've seen snakes?"

"No," Jill says. "But Pascal said to watch out."

Hannah frowns at this. "How?" she asks. "How did he warn you?"

"What d'you mean?"

"In what language?"

Jill stops in her tracks. She points at her eye, then at the track, then makes a slithering motion with her hand. "Sssssss!" she says.

Hannah laughs and gives her sister a push. "Get on with you," she says.

"It's true," Jill insists. "Keep your eyes peeled."

Hannah starts to pay attention. The grass either side of the track is elbow-high and humming with insect-life and, no doubt, silent, lurking, snakes. She wishes she hadn't worn sandals.

As they turn onto a wider path heading down the hill, Hannah spots a wooden chalet farther down the first track. "Is that where he lives?" she asks.

"Yeah," Jill says. "Well, it's where his mother lives in summer. It's quite pretty isn't it?"

"It looks nice," Hannah says. "Presumably they have their own access? I take it they don't have to trip along that track every time?"

"No, there's a road the other side."

"Anyway, I thought you made the mother up. Or am I getting confused?" Hannah asks.

Jill laughs. "*Intentionally* confused," she says.

Hannah tuts. "Can you please just tell me," she says. "I'm getting bored with all these confused versions of your stories."

"I'm sorry," Jill says genuinely. "I don't mean anything by it. It's just habit."

And Hannah knows it's true. Jill has been weaving multiple contradictory realities around her since she was fourteen. Because fourteen was when Jill started having sex. And the only way to dissimulate what she was really up to was to keep her father and older sister permanently guessing by alternately exaggerating or denying her sins. Poor Hannah has been in a state of confusion as to what really goes on in Jill's life ever since.

"So how *do* you manage to communicate with him?" she asks.

"Like I said," Jill says, making the snake gesture again. "Sign language, mime, drawings . . . it's quite fun really."

They reach a set of steps cut into the hillside and have to revert to single file. As they enter the shade of the canopy of trees that have grown up along the line of the stream, Hannah says, "Ooh, it's lovely and cool down here."

"I know," Jill says. "Mozzies though."

"Yes," Hannah says, swiping at her arm. "Yes, I just found that out."

The "river" is in reality no more than a tiny stream, a

trickling brook, but with the speckled patterns of sun and shade from the trees above, the water sparkles and dances magically.

Hannah shouts Luke's name twice, then Aïsha's. Her voice echoes vaguely from the rocks on the other side of the brook but there's no sign of the kids.

"It's lovely down here," she says again, sitting now on a large stone.

"Isn't it?" Jill says, squeezing in beside her.

"So tell me about Pascal," Hannah says. "Tell me the truth."

"Pascal?" Jill says. "Well . . . He's quite nice really. I mean, as far as I can tell. We do have some comms issues as I said."

"And you're sleeping together?"

"We are now," Jill says. "But only the last two nights."

"So you *didn't* do anything when you went off with him that first time?"

Jill wrinkles her nose and shakes her head.

"You are such a wind-up merchant," Hannah says.

"His mum lives there. And she really did make horrible Turkish coffee."

"And then?"

"He came back the next day. To do the pool."

Hannah pulls a face as she struggles to remember when this might have happened, so Jill explains, "You were at the water-park place."

"Oh, of course."

"And Tristan was here, so he translated. We were able to talk a bit. And it turned out he was nice."

"Right," Hannah says, nodding thoughtfully.

"What?"

"Well, that was the bit I couldn't fathom," Hannah says.

"How you got from holding his bucket to . . . you know."

"Holding his bucket sounds like a euphemism," Jill says.

"It does rather."

"But, no, it was all quite sweet and innocent to be honest. Coffee with mum. He spent the afternoon with me and Tristan. I showed him my room but he didn't take the bait. Only he did give me a peck when he left."

"And then?"

"He was outside my shutters the night before last. Said he couldn't sleep. So we came down here. Had a kiss and stuff. And he came back to the house with me and . . ."

"OK, OK," Hannah laughs. "I can imagine the rest."

"You are strange," Jill says. "I mean, you want to know, and then you don't want to know."

"I don't want to know the sordid details, that's all," Hannah says.

"It's not sordid," Jill says. "That's your whole problem."

Hannah laughs. "It's just a figure of speech. But you may be right."

"So what about you?" Jill asks.

"Me?"

"Yes, how are you feeling about the whole James thing now?"

Hannah takes a deep breath and exhales loudly. "I don't know really," she says. "I've been kind of blocking it out. I've been pretending he isn't really coming. After all, we're not exactly sure that he is, are we?"

"No, I suppose not. I still think he will, but . . . So *were* you in love with him?"

"I don't know, Jill," Hannah admits. "That's the truth. It was fifteen years ago. I don't really remember."

"I think you remember pretty well," Jill says.

"Well, of course I do. I had a mad crazy crush on a guy called James. I'm just not sure I trust my memories. I mean, we only kissed a couple of times. We never even . . . you know, slept together. We kissed, and I spent half the night wondering what to do in the morning, but by then he was gone."

"What to do?"

Hannah swipes at a mosquito on her arm. "Why do they always go for me?" she asks.

"My sun cream has insect repellent in it," Jill says. "So you're the bait."

"Ahh," Hannah says.

"So you were saying?" Jill prompts. "You were wondering what to do . . ."

"I was supposed to be marrying Cliff, wasn't I?"

"Oh God, yeah. The first time around. I forgot about that." Jill slides her arm around Hannah's waist and gives her a squeeze. "That was horrible," she says. "I can't believe I forgot."

"That's probably no bad thing," Hannah says. "I wish *I* could forget."

"So when you say you were worrying what to do, you mean you were thinking of calling the wedding off? Even then? Even before . . ."

Hannah nods. "Maybe," she says. "I'm not sure."

"But that means it was a bit more than a crush," Jill says.

"Maybe," Hannah says again.

"Oh, sweetie," Jill says, giving her another squeeze before releasing her. "So what does Cliff say about it all?"

Hannah picks up a small stone and throws it into the water. "Nothing," she says.

"Nothing?"

"We don't really talk about stuff like that. We don't really know how to. Does that make any sense?"

Jill nods. "Most men don't," she says. "That's why finding one who doesn't speak a word of English is something of a relief. No expectations, you see."

"But it's not just Cliff," Hannah says. "It's both of us. Neither of us could ever talk about feelings really."

"You talk to me," Jill points out.

"Well, that's different, isn't it," Hannah says. "You're my sister."

Jill laughs. "I suppose," she says. "I don't really tell anyone else my secrets either."

"You do, you tell Tristan."

"That's true actually," Jill says. "But you're the only two. Talking of Tris', I suppose we should get back. Lunch will be ready."

"Yes," Hannah replies, scratching at her leg. "Yes, I'm getting bitten to death here as well. Luke? LUKE! Aïsha?"

TWENTY-SEVEN

At the house, Luke and Aïsha are already seated: lunch has been served.

"Wow, that looks good," Hannah says. "Quiche?"

"Yep. Well, a tart really – salmon, asparagus and goat's cheese," Tristan says. "I stole it from Hugh Fearnley-Whittingstall."

"It looks gorgeous."

"You put asparagus in everything, don't you?" Jill comments.

"Well, it's such a lovely summery flavour, isn't it?" Tristan replies.

Hannah turns to Luke next to her. He is slumped, uncharacteristically, in his chair. "Are you OK?" she asks. "You look a bit peaky."

Luke nods.

"We went looking for you down by the river," she tells him. "Where were you?"

Luke shrugs. "Here," he says.

Hannah glances at Aïsha, who is looking equally glum, and wonders if her moods are finally rubbing off on her usually buoyant son. Heaven forbid that these two weeks together should be the final straw that nudges Luke into adolescence.

"You all right, champ?" Cliff, returning from the kitchen with a salad bowl, asks.

Luke nods again, but wrinkles his nose and shrugs at the

same time. It's one of Aïsha's favourite combinations of gestures.

"Cliff made the salad," Tristan says as he takes a seat, reaches for the salad bowl and passes it to Jill. "Dig in, folks."

"I don't think I've ever seen you cook," Jill says, serving herself and passing the bowl on to Hannah.

"Cook!" Cliff laughs. "I'd hardly call washing a few leaves and peeling a few avocados cooking." But he looks, and feels, quite proud. He enjoyed making the salad and mixing dressing with Tristan. He has today made a decision to get more involved in the kitchen from now on. Against all expectation, food preparation is relaxing.

"Do you want some of this?" Hannah asks.

Luke shakes his head.

"But you like avocado," she says.

Luke shakes his head again and says, "I'm not hungry."

Hannah cuts a sliver of quiche and puts it on his plate. "Well, just eat this then," she says. "You have to eat something."

"So you went down to the river?" Cliff asks.

"It's lovely," Hannah tells him. "Beautiful. Put insect repellent on first though. There are loads of mosquitos."

"It is really nice," Jill agrees. "It's shady and cool."

"We're lucky we don't have them up here really," Hannah says. "The mosquitos, I mean."

"I've been bitten here," Cliff says.

"Me too," says Tristan.

"Luke, eat something," Hannah says. "Sit up straight and eat something."

"I'm not hungry," he says again.

Hannah puts down her fork and touches her son's forehead. "You do look pale," she says. "Please try to eat something."

With visible effort, Luke sits up and forks a mouthful of quiche.

"So are we going to Cannes this evening?" Cliff asks.

"I thought after lunch," Jill says. "I want to get out and about. I feel the need to move."

"Hum. I'm getting quite used to having a siesta after lunch," Cliff says. "Plus I may have had a couple of glasses of wine whilst we were cooking."

"We could take two cars," Tristan offers. "Meet up in Cannes."

"We have to take two cars anyway," Jill points out.

"Sure," Tristan says. "You know what I mean."

"*Luke!*" Aïsha whines. She sounds disgusted.

Everyone turns to look at Luke who is bent over his plate, spitting out the mouthful of masticated tart.

Hannah shoots Aïsha a questioning glance and then peers in at Luke. "You're not OK at all, are you?" she says, and Luke, at that instant, confirms her diagnosis by vomiting onto his own lap.

"Jesus," Cliff says, jumping up and joining Hannah, now crouched at Luke's side.

Luke retches again, so Hannah stands, grabs his arm and pulls him upright, then tugs him towards the bathroom. "You had better come inside," she says.

"It's her fault," Luke mumbles as she drags him into the house. He is pointing at Aïsha's seat, now, mysteriously, empty.

Once Luke is in bed with a bucket by his side, Hannah returns to the dinner table.

"Where is she?" she asks. "Where's bloody Aïsha gone?" Her voice has the staccato rhythm of a machine gun.

Tristan shakes his head. "We don't know," he says.

"That'll teach them not to dip into our stash at any rate," Jill says. She sounds amused.

Hannah turns so that she can aim the full force of her anger at her sister, but can't, for a second, find the right words to express herself.

Jill pulls a face. "Hey, it's not my fault," she says.

Hannah gasps. "How?" she says. "How is this not your fault? You spend your entire life taking drugs in front of Aïsha . . ."

"It's only dope," Jill says.

"Jesus! You spend your entire life taking drugs in front of your kid," Hannah repeats. "You bring the stuff on holiday. You leave it lying around."

"It's actually mine," Tristan volunteers.

"Shut up, Tristan," Hannah tells him. "This is between Jill and me."

"O-K!" Tristan says, pedantically. He stands, gathers a few plates, and heads into the house.

"I didn't make your son smoke dope," Jill says. "So, just chillax, OK?"

"No, Jill, I will not *chillax*. And you're right, you didn't make Luke smoke dope. Your daughter did."

"So Luke says," Jill snipes.

"Yes, so Luke says. But you never told Aïsha not to do *anything*, did you? Ever? That's the problem here. You smoke around them all the time, you don't teach her right and wrong, you . . . You shrug off all responsibility and your daughter is out of control and as a result my son is stoned and crying and vomiting."

Jill laughs bitterly. "For fuck's sake, calm down, Hannah," she says. "It was just a bit of dope."

Hannah lets out an exasperated gasp. "Cliff!" she says, turning to her up-till-now silent husband. "Backup please."

Cliff opens his palms skywards and exhales loudly. "It's pretty irresponsible leaving the stuff around," he says. "You have to admit."

Jill pulls a face and points at Tristan, who has returned to gather the dirty glasses and cutlery. "Tell him," she says.

Cliff turns to Tristan. "Tris'?"

"Sure. Whatever. But it wasn't lying around," Tristan says. "It was in my room in my jacket pocket. Aïsha must have gone into my room and gone through my pockets."

"Or Luke," Jill says.

"Oh, come on!" Hannah says. "You know who's behind this."

"Yes," Cliff says. "It's far more Aïsha's style than Luke's."

"Whoever it was," Jill says, "it still wasn't me, was it?"

"Aïsha's your daughter," Cliff says.

"Which makes it my fault?"

"Well, yes, of course it does."

"I don't see *you* taking any responsibility for the fact that your son has been smoking dope," Jill spits.

"*We* didn't *bring* the stuff here!" Hannah says. "You did!"

"Oh, I don't have to sit here and listen to this," Jill says, pushing her chair back and standing. "Aïsha may be out of order but your precious son is the one who's bloody gone and got himself stoned."

Hannah watches Jill enter the house, then turns to Cliff. "Unbelievable!" she says.

Cliff opens his palms at the sky again. "It's just Jill," he says.

Hannah rubs her brow. "How long does it last?" she asks, after a moment's pause. "Do you remember?"

Cliff shakes his head. "I only ever took it twice, I think. And then I threw up like Luke. Never cared for the stuff."

"I used to smoke Jill's," Hannah says. "When we were at college."

"It's the same thing," Cliff says. "Don't worry too much. It's just one of those rites of passage. He'll be fine in a couple of hours."

"He's eleven, Cliff."

Cliff nods. "Sure," he says.

"Wait till I get my hands on Aïsha," Hannah says, then, "And where the *hell* do you think you're going?" Jill and Tristan are leaving the house. Tristan is jangling his car keys and looking embarrassed.

"We're off to Cannes," Jill says.

"You're *what?*"

"We're off to Cannes," she repeats belligerently.

"And your daughter?"

"I'm sure she'll reappear," Jill says. "And I'm sure you'll have a go at her too. You're good at that."

They start to walk towards the Jeep, so Hannah stands and runs after them. "Jill," she says. "Jill!"

As Jill reaches the passenger door of the Jeep, Hannah reaches them and grabs her sister's sleeve.

Jill shakes Hannah off, then raises her palm in a stop sign. "Just . . . just step away from me, Hannah," she says. "You're making me seriously angry now, so just, you know . . . back off!"

Hannah glances at Tristan, now starting the engine. He shrugs and mouths "sorry" at her, and there's nothing that Hannah can do except stand, fuming and forlorn, as she watches Jill climb aboard and the car reverse urgently out of the gate.

159

Cliff meets Hannah at the corner of the house. "Come here," he says, opening his arms.

"She's just . . ." Hannah says.

Cliff hugs her tight. "I know," he says. "The most shocking thing is that you're still surprised by it after all these years."

Over Cliff's shoulder, Hannah sees Aïsha, sidling towards them across the garden, her hands in the pockets of her shorts. She breaks free from Cliff's hug and strides across the gravel. "Aïsha!" she shouts. "Aïsha! I am so bloody angry with you . . ."

But as soon as she reaches her, her anger melts.

Because Aïsha is crying. "Where's Mum gone?" she asks. "I don't feel well."

TWENTY-EIGHT

By five, both Luke and Aïsha are up again, both well enough, in theory, to go to Cannes. But Hannah feels that rewarding their bad behaviour with a treat would be a parenting faux pas of massive proportions. So when Aïsha finally plucks up the courage to ask the question she says, "No, Aïsha. We *aren't* going to Cannes. I'm furious with both of you, so you had better just stay out of my way today."

Both Luke and Aïsha immediately make themselves scarce.

"The trouble with that of course is that we get punished too," Cliff comments.

"I know," Hannah says, nodding sadly. "But the truth is that if I bumped into Jill living it up in Cannes, I might just punch her, so it's probably just as well."

Hannah is changing for bed that night when she hears a car pull up. She thinks that it's the sound of the Jeep, but she can't be sure, so she pulls her clothes back on and heads outside, crossing paths with Cliff heading for bed.

"Tristan and Jill?" she asks.

Cliff nods. "I wouldn't bother though, Han'," he says.

"Don't tell me what to do, Cliff," Hannah says, immediately regretting having sounded so sharp. "I'm sorry. I just mean, well, she is my sister," she adds as she advances down the corridor. "This is kind of between me and her."

When she gets to the patio, however, she sees what Cliff was trying to say. Jill is standing in the doorway smoking a joint, and swaying, gently, from side to side.

"Are you pissed now, on top of everything else?" Hannah asks.

Jill wobblingly turns to look at her. The remains of her joint slips from her fingers and spins to the floor. She attempts to stub it out with her toe but misses and grinds the floor just to the left of the smouldering butt instead.

"Oh, *fuck off*, Hannah," she says as she unsteadily passes her, supporting herself against the wall, and then, more falling than walking, she vanishes through the door of her bedroom.

Hannah steps outside to recover the still-glowing butt, and finds Tristan sitting. He's pouring the dregs of their bottle of wine into a glass.

"She's drunk then," Hannah says when he looks up.

"You noticed," Tristan says.

"I'm fuming," Hannah says as she squashes the stub out in the ashtray.

"I'm sure," Tristan replies. "Is there any more of this?" he asks, tapping the neck of the empty bottle. "I haven't had a drink all night because I was driving. I've had to put up with your sister sober. Can you imagine?"

Hannah makes a trip to the refrigerator and returns with a fresh bottle of rosé and a corkscrew.

"So are you angry with me too?" Tristan asks as he opens the bottle with professional flourish.

Hannah sighs and perches on the edge of a chair. "I guess not," she says. "It's just Jill. But even beyond the whole Aïsha getting Luke stoned affair . . ."

"So that is what happened then?" Tristan asks.

162

"Yes. But even beyond that, the fact that she then pissed off and left me nursing both children . . ."

"Aïsha was sick as well?"

Hannah nods. "She was worse than Luke. Jill should have stayed. It's not right. It's not fair."

Tristan pours himself a glass of wine and then points the bottle vaguely at Hannah. She shrugs and pushes a nearby glass across the table. "Oh, just a drop," she says, pulling her chair up and settling into it more permanently.

"Jill can't cope with conflict," Tristan says as he pours the wine. "So if you shout at her, *ever*, well, she'll just run a mile. You must know that by now, right?"

Hannah frowns at him and sips her drink. Though she has obviously noticed this on many occasions, she has never heard it put into words. "You're right," she says. "That's true actually."

"She says she feels physically afraid," Tristan says. "She feels like she's in danger. As soon as anyone starts shouting, she has to run. It's instinctual."

Hannah laughs bitterly. "Well, that's just ridiculous," she says. "I have never hit Jill. I have never hit anyone, and she knows it."

"She knows it's stupid," he says. "But it's something to do with her childhood. When people start shouting she feels scared. She reckons your dad used to slap her."

"He did. It's true. He slapped both of us plenty."

Tristan shrugs. "Well, there you go," he says.

"But she was uncontrollable. You have no idea, Tris'."

"All the same," Tristan says.

Hannah nods. "It was a different generation, wasn't it. That's what people did then."

"But that doesn't make it right."

"No, I suppose not."

"You never hit Luke, I bet."

Hannah creases her brow as she tries to remember. "I think I slapped his legs once. He ran into the road. He was about six. And I slapped his legs. But that was more in fear than in anger. And I felt terrible afterwards."

Tristan nods. "My dad used to take his belt off to me."

"God."

"But anyway. Just give her some space and she'll come apologise. That's what I reckon."

Hannah runs her finger around the rim of the glass. It sings briefly but then stops, and she can't get it to do it again. "Well, that would be a first," she says. "Jill never apologises."

"It's not easy being Jill, you know," Tristan says. "I'm not sure you really get that."

Hannah pulls a face. "You're right!" she says. "I don't."

"She's a single parent. She's broke. She's lonely . . ."

"But that's all her fault, Tristan."

"Fault," he repeats flatly.

"Well, it is. She could learn to compromise. She could learn to apologise. She could stick in a relationship. She could get a bloody job."

Tristan shrugs. "Maybe that's not all her fault though," he says.

"I don't see who else . . ."

"Maybe it's not entirely her fault if she's not very good at those things. At compromising. At relationships . . . We all have different skill-sets."

Hannah rolls her eyes. "If you go down that road, then maybe it isn't the serial killer's fault that he's a serial killer."

"Well, maybe it isn't," Tristan says. "We're all damaged. We're all damaged in different ways."

Hannah sighs deeply and takes another sip of wine. A tiny gust of air moves across the patio, making her shiver. "It's cooler tonight," she says.

"It is. Storms tomorrow."

"Really?"

"So says the weather forecast."

"That's a bit hard to believe," Hannah says.

"It is," Tristan agrees. "But going back to Jill, you know she's jealous of you, right?"

"Jill? Jealous? Now that *is* ridiculous."

Tristan nods exaggeratedly. "It's true. She sees you as this perfect grown-up who has everything sorted while she's wallowing around in the mud like an adolescent. Those were her actual words."

"She should just stop wallowing," Hannah says. "And she really was drunk if that's what she told you. I'm nothing to be jealous of, and Jill knows it."

"You have a stable relationship with someone you love. You have a great house, a job you enjoy . . ."

"It's only a few hours at the school."

"Even better," Tristan says. "A part-time job that you enjoy."

"But Jill could get all of that, Tristan, that's the point," Hannah says. "But she's never known how to . . . how to *forego* anything so that she can reach a further goal. Do you know what I mean? She's never known how to compromise."

"I know," Tristan says, now rolling a cigarette. "She has certain . . . limitations. We all do. But that's not necessarily her fault. And it doesn't mean that she isn't jealous."

165

"I suppose," Hannah says, unconvinced.

Tristan pops the cigarette into the tobacco tin and stands. "Well, I'm shattered," he says. "Are you coming to bed or . . ." He laughs. "Sorry, that sounded weird. I meant . . ."

"It's OK, Tris'," Hannah says. "I know what you meant. And no, I think I'll sit here for a bit. It's nice and quiet. You don't have a cigarette for me, do you?"

Tristan turns back from the doorway. "For you?" he asks, shocked. "I've never seen you smoke. Ever."

"I know," Hannah says. "I gave up when I met Cliff. So it was a very long time ago. But I just fancy one for some reason."

Tristan pulls his tobacco tin back out of his pocket and proffers it.

"Could you roll me one, do you think?" Hannah asks. "I never was very good at rollies."

"There's one in there," Tristan says, shaking the tin at her. "It's just a cigarette though. That is what you want, right?"

Hannah nods. "Thanks, Tristan," she says, taking the tin. "Goodnight."

"Night."

Hannah lights the cigarette, and though it makes her feel a little dizzy, it does exactly what she had hoped. The taste, the smell, the sensation of smoking takes her back to when she was twenty-one, to before she met Cliff, to a time when a million different life trajectories seemed possible.

And now here she is. At thirty-eight she could easily be halfway through her life. Her mother died at sixty, so she could very well be more than halfway through. What a terrifying thought.

She thinks a bit about the concept of Jill's being jealous

and figures that if you could somehow add Jill's life to her own it would make up one complete whole instead of the two half-lives that each of them are making do with. But there's no way to do that, is there? Choose romance and adventure and excitement and crazy sex adventures and you exclude, by definition, security, safety, comfort and calm.

Yes, she thinks, as she smokes her cigarette. *Yes, you can have whichever half you want, but you can't have both.*

Jill, surprisingly, is up before Hannah the next morning. She finds her sitting in the cool shadow of the lounge, nursing a pint of water.

"What are you doing in here?" Hannah asks, wondering at the change of routine. It is only after she has said it that the full horror of yesterday comes back to her. She realises that her first words should perhaps have been angrier.

"It's a bit bright out there first thing," Jill says.

"Ah," Hannah says. "Hangover then?"

Jill nods.

"Good," Hannah says. "I'm glad."

She makes herself a mug of instant coffee – she can't be bothered with the machine this morning – and walks back past Jill and out onto the patio. The sun, still low enough in the sky to pass beneath the eaves, is blinding but she turns her chair to face it and closes her eyes. The warmth on her eyelids feels wonderful.

"Look, I'm sorry, OK?" Jill says. Her voice, coming from the doorway behind her, makes Hannah jump.

Hannah doesn't move. She doesn't open her eyes. She simply shrugs.

"So you're still angry, huh?" Jill says.

Hannah snorts in derision. "Even when you apologise you sound belligerent," she says.

Jill doesn't say anything for half a minute. "It's because I'm embarrassed," she says.

"Embarrassed," Hannah repeats.

She hears Jill move to her left and take a seat at the table. She casts her a glare and then turns to look back out at the garden. "Aïsha was sick too," Hannah says. "Just in case you wanted to know."

"Aïsha? Really?"

"Yes, I had both kids vomiting while you were swanning around having fun in Cannes."

"I didn't have fun," Jill says. "For what it's worth."

"Aw, poor Jill."

"I was crying if you must know," Jill says. "I was crying by the time we got to the end of the road."

"That must have been really awful for you," Hannah says.

"God, you're harsh sometimes."

"Jill, you told me to fuck off last night," Hannah says. "So don't talk to me about harsh."

"Did I really?"

"Yep."

"Oh."

"Yes, 'Oh.'"

"I don't remember that."

"No," Hannah says. "Well, just to make sure you haven't missed any of the other joys of yesterday, your daughter stole Tristan's dope. She and Luke got stoned and vomited all over the shop. You went out and left me to deal with it alone. And then came back drunk and told me to fuck off. So if I sound a little harsh this morning, that'll be why."

168

"I'm sorry, Hannah," Jill says. "Really I am."

Hannah shrugs again and throws another brief glare at her sister. "What's new?" she says.

"So James didn't come?" Jill asks.

The attempt at changing the subject is so transparent that Hannah just laughs.

"I still think he will," Jill says. "If it's meant to be."

"Just . . . *don't*, Jill, OK?"

"I'm sorry."

"And stop saying you're sorry. It isn't any use to me. It isn't any use to anyone."

They sit in silence for a few more minutes before Jill says, "It *is* a bit hard to know what to say to you when you're like this."

Hannah chews the inside of her mouth before replying. "It's not about saying anything, is it, Jill?" she finally says. "It's about being. It's about doing."

"Yes," Jill says.

"What would be really lovely, for example," Hannah continues, "would be if just for a bit, say, just to the end of the holiday, you could behave like a responsible adult instead of some chavvy teenage lush." She glances over at Jill, who has flushed red as if she has been slapped. Hannah fully expects Jill to now stomp off, probably throwing some random insult over her shoulder as she leaves. Such is the ritual between the sisters.

Instead, Jill says, "Yes, I get that."

It's such a surprise that Hannah has to check Jill's face to see if she is mocking her.

"Really," Jill says, nodding. "I get it."

"Well, good," Hannah says, disarmed by the unexpected

departure from their script. From the interior, she can hear the echo of doors opening and closing. "Sounds like people are stirring," Hannah says. "I had better get this table cleared and breakfast on the go."

Jill stands and touches Hannah's shoulder. "I'll do it this morning," she says, starting already, to gather last night's glasses from the table. "You have a break. I owe you."

Hannah sits back and watches Jill clear the table. At the sound of cupboard doors and the opening and closing of the refrigerator drifting from the kitchen, Hannah pushes her lips out and nods thoughtfully. "That's new," she says quietly.

The window to the kitchen opens, and Jill leans out. "Where's the coffee?" she asks. "I can't find it anywhere."

"It's in the freezer," Hannah says. "Tristan says it keeps better."

"Oh, of course," Jill says.

Hannah listens to the sounds of the freezer opening and closing, then the clatter of random cupboard doors.

"And the tea?" Jill shouts.

"In the tea-caddie on the counter."

"Oh, right. Cheers."

Hannah rolls her eyes.

"Are we using these baguettes from yesterday, or the sliced stuff?" Jill asks.

"*Not* so new then," Hannah murmurs, as she stands and heads into the kitchen.

TWENTY-NINE

After breakfast, Hannah takes to the hammock, where she dozes for another hour. She has a strange dream where Cliff gets into the Jeep and drives away, leaving her stranded with Tristan (who for some reason has James' face) and Jill (who looks like their mother).

She's awakened, shockingly, by Aïsha grabbing her arm. "Hannah!" Aïsha is shouting. "Hannah! Hannah! Hannah!"

Hannah drags herself from the dream and focusses on Aïsha's panicked features, then, powered by a surge of adrenalin, she rolls from the hammock (her leg has gone to sleep) and then starts with difficulty to run after the girl. "What is it? What's happened?" she calls.

As she reaches the gravel of the car park, she hears the sound of Luke's wailing and switches from a run to a sprint.

Luke's voice turns to a piercing scream as his mother rounds the corner. She reaches the poolside, already scanning the scene for indicators of what might have happened here. Luke's mask is lying shattered on the floor. A mixture of blood, water and tears are running down his face in long, pinkish streaks.

"Jesus, Luke!" she says as she reaches her son and crouches down before him. "What's happened here?"

Luke is crying almost hysterically now, so Hannah glances at Aïsha for answers. "Well?"

"It was an accident," she says. "We were just playing."

Hannah tips Luke's face towards the light. He has multiple cuts around his closed eye and blood is running thick and fast around and into it and perhaps from it.

"*Jesus!*" Hannah exclaims. "Get Cliff! Now!"

"I got him out of the pool," Aïsha says.

"Yes. Get Cliff."

"I think he's asleep," Aïsha says, on the edge of tears herself.

"Then *wake* him! Quickly. Go!"

"Is he gonna be OK?" Aïsha asks.

"Go!" Hannah shrieks.

Aïsha runs off, and Hannah lifts Luke and carries him over to the garden tap, where she tips his head downwards and washes around his eye in the hope of removing any remaining broken glass.

"It hurts," Luke wails.

"I know, baby," Hannah says, her voice trembling. "But you're gonna be fine."

Cliff – still in his underpants – and Tristan and Jill all arrive together in a confusing medley of "What's happened?" and "Is he all right?" and "Oh my God!"

"His mask smashed," Hannah says, sidestepping the question of cause for the moment for expediency's sake. "He's got glass all around his eye. Maybe in it too."

Cliff crouches down next to them and peers in at Luke's face. "Can you open your eye, Luke?" he asks. "Can you see out of it?"

"I can't," Luke sobs. "It hurts."

"It's bad, isn't it?" Hannah says, her own eyes watering in sympathy. "I think it's really bad."

"I don't know," Cliff says. Looking between Jill and

Tristan's faces, he asks, "Do either of you know how to call an ambulance here?"

Jill shakes her head. Tristan too.

"Cliff?" Hannah says, her voice pleading.

Cliff shrugs. "I don't know," he says. "Isn't there an international number or something?"

"Cliff. We need to do something," Hannah says. "Maybe go get a neighbour."

Tristan pulls out his phone. "Wait," he says. "I've got this."

"What can I do?" Cliff asks.

"I don't know," Hannah says. "Who are you calling, Tris'?"

But Tristan is talking in French. He raises one hand to tell them to let him do whatever he is doing.

"So how did this happen, Aï?" Jill asks. Aïsha is clinging to her leg looking pale.

"It was an accident," Aïsha says. "But I helped him out of the pool. I thought he was gonna drown."

"Just leave the hows and whys for now, Jill," Hannah interrupts. "Please. We just need to work out what to do."

Tristan hangs up. "The nearest hospital's in Grasse," he says, urgently. "It's fifteen minutes max. I know where it is. I think it's quicker to take him to A and E than to wait for an ambulance."

"Really?" Hannah says.

"That's what Jean-Jacques says," Tristan tells her. "And he is local. He says the pompiers take ages. It's eighteen – the phone number's eighteen – but he says it's best to go to the hospital."

"OK, we'll do that then," Hannah says.

"I'll get the keys," Tristan says, sprinting off.

"Can you get his clothes, Cliff?" Hannah asks. "And a towel."

Hannah lifts Luke – whose crying is reaching a new crescendo – and carries him to the front of the house, where she meets Cliff coming the other way with a random assortment of the boy's clothes.

Together they dry and dress him, then Cliff picks him up and they run to the Jeep.

"In the back," Hannah directs. "I'll get in the back too."

"I'll get dressed and follow on," Cliff says as he lifts Luke into the car and buckles his belt for him. "You go. I'll be there as soon as I can."

"Daad!" Luke wails as he realises that Cliff is stepping away from the car.

"I'm coming," Hannah says, climbing next to him. "I'm with you. You're gonna be fine."

Fresh blood is still running down Luke's face. "Give me the towel too," Hannah says, and Jill runs back, scoops it from the floor and hands it to her.

"I'll call you," Tristan tells them, already starting the engine. "I'll call you as soon as we get there."

The traffic is light, and it takes them less than ten minutes to reach the hospital.

During the journey, Hannah holds Luke in her arms and strokes his hair, and perhaps because of this or perhaps because he's simply exhausted, his wailing fades to a series of quiet, whiny sobs.

In Grasse, Tristan drives to the entrance to the Accident and Emergency dock and parks next to a red pompier's truck. Someone berates them – in French – for parking where they have, but Tristan says, with irony, "I didn't understand a word of that, did you?" and they push on into the emergency ward.

The rows of plastic chairs inside contain only two other people: a single Arab man with his arm in a sling and an old grey-haired woman who looks like she may have been living, for some years, under a bridge.

The receptionist takes one look at Luke and uses the tannoy system to call for a nurse. The nurse, in turn, takes one look at Luke and trots off in search of a doctor. The rapid escalation confirms what Hannah thought – that this is serious. Her heart starts to race.

Tristan, in fact, is reassured by their rapidity. "It certainly beats England," he says. "When I broke my finger in London, I had to wait two hours before anyone even spoke to me."

"But this isn't a broken finger, is it?" Hannah says.

"No," Tristan agrees. "But you get my point."

"I do."

"Do you want me to phone Cliff?" Tristan asks. "I didn't even give him the address yet."

Hannah shakes her head. "There's no point yet. Wait till they tell us something." It seems to her, at this instant, that adding another stressed adult to the mix would be more of a hindrance than a help.

In just over a minute, the nurse reappears with a young doctor in tow. He crouches down in front of Luke and points a torch into his eye whilst attempting to lift his eyelid. Luke shrieks and begins to cry again.

"OK," the doctor says. "Emmène-le directement en ophtalmologie."

"I'm sorry," Hannah says, "but do you speak English?"

"We must take you upstairs," the nurse says. "Come."

She leads them to a lift and on up to the third floor. "You

175

have very good chance," she tells them in the lift. "The Doctor Graffin is 'ere today. Surgeon. He is very good. Really."

The word 'surgeon' makes all of the hairs on Hannah's neck stand on end, which is the exact opposite of what the nurse intended.

When the lift doors open, she leads them along a seemingly endless corridor and through multiple sets of double doors, and finally into a small room where the surgeon is standing with his back to them talking on the phone.

Hannah places Luke on one of the two chairs in the room and places her palm at the base of her back and stretches. One more year and she won't be able to carry him at all.

The doctor ends his conversation quickly and turns to face them. He is over six feet tall with olive skin and deep-brown almost black irises. An imposing presence, he shakes Hannah's and Luke's hands, and then crouches down in front of Luke.

"Ils sont anglais," the nurse tells him.

"English, huh?" the surgeon says, his accent a mixture of American and French.

"Yes."

"So we 'ave a little accident, huh?"

"Yes."

"How this 'appen? You tell me, please?"

"A diving mask," Tristan says. He is met with blank looks from both the doctor and the nurse. Lacking essential vocabulary, notably the words for mask and diving, Tristan performs a rather impressive charade involving putting on a mask and diving into a pool, swimming, and whacking himself in the face. Were the circumstances not so dire, it would be pretty funny.

"I understand," Doctor Graffin says, restraining a smirk

176

and reaching into his desk drawer to pull out a pair of powered magnifying goggles, which he clips across his eyes.

"Superpower goggles," Tristan says. "What do you think of those, Luke?"

Luke, apparently paralysed by fear, remains silent.

The surgeon then grasps Luke's head with one hand and pulls back his eyelid with the other, provoking a quivering round of sobs.

"He needs to look and see what's wrong," Hannah whispers. "Try to be still for him. You're being amazingly brave, Luke."

The doctor straightens almost immediately. "OK, my little friend," he says. "You have glass in your eye. We will 'ave to take that out and very quick is better. How long this 'appen?"

"About half an hour now," Tristan says, checking the time on his phone. "Maybe forty-five minutes."

"It's good. You are very quick."

"Is that difficult?" Hannah asks, "to get the glass out, I mean. Will he be OK?"

The doctor gives her a Gallic shrug. "It's a little operation. 'E should be. But you know, the eye is a delicate *organe*. You are the mother, yes?"

Hannah nods. She feels a wave of shame, as if this question is in fact some accusation of responsibility. And she fears that the accusation is reasonable. She should have been watching them.

"Good," he says. "The nurse will get the form. I 'ope we can do it right now." He glances at his watch. "You are lucky. Is quiet today. Very quiet. Is strange."

He rattles off some French at the nurse, who leaves, then says, "I return. Please, stay," and follows her through the door.

177

"He sent her to get consent forms," Tristan says. "And something or other financial forms."

"I need to get Cliff to bring that card thing in," Hannah says.

"The E111? Have you got one of those?"

"They don't exist anymore. It's a European Health Card or something now," Hannah says. "But yes. We got one before we left. Didn't you?"

Tristan shrugs. "Didn't cross my mind."

"I'm not even sure what it covers," Hannah says, "But to be honest, I don't care. When he says operation, that's not with a general anaesthetic, though, is it? They're not going to put him to sleep?"

"I don't want a general anaesthetic," Luke says. "Don't let them put me to sleep."

Hannah realises that the only time Luke has ever heard the term 'put to sleep' was in reference to their previous cat. She regrets the turn of phrase immediately.

"A general anaesthetic is just when they give you something to make you snooze for half an hour," Hannah says. "So they can fix things without it hurting while you're asleep. But it's not always necessa—"

At that moment the nurse reappears with a wad of paperwork on a clipboard.

"Can you ask her, Tris'?" Hannah says.

"I don't know what general anaesthetic is in French," Tristan says.

"Anaesthesie generale," the nurse says.

"And will Luke need one?" Hannah asks.

"Yes," the nurse says. "Yes for the kids, with the eyes, always. Otherwise they are moving too much."

"I won't move," Luke says. "I promise."

"Is it really necessary?" Hannah asks.

The nurse nods. "Yes," she says. "Is necessary."

"It's better really, Luke," Tristan says. "If I had the choice, I'd have one too. Have a nice little snooze in a comfy bed and when you wake up we'll be next to you watching over you and it will all be fixed."

With the nurse and Tristan working together, they translate and answer almost fifty questions about Luke's medical past, his allergies, drug histories and blood type, and then the nurse leaves Hannah to read and sign the other forms: an admissions request, a financial resources form and a consent form.

"I can't translate half of this," Tristan tells her, studying the first page.

"It doesn't really matter, does it?" Hannah says as she puts her initials on each page. "There isn't really any choice, so . . . But call Cliff for me, would you?"

When she has finished the forms, Tristan dials Cliff's number and hands Hannah the phone.

She tells him that they are going to operate, and that she is randomly signing anything that they put in front of her. She asks him to agree that this is the right thing for her to be doing.

"I guess so," Cliff says. "Unless you want me to phone Europe Assistance and see what they say."

"What could they possibly say?" Hannah asks.

"I don't know. They might tell us if it's a good hospital or not, or if it's better to fly him home, or . . ."

"There's no time, Cliff," Hannah says. "They said it's urgent that they get the glass out. And it is a good hospital. I can tell."

179

"*How* can you tell?"

"I just . . . I don't know. I just can. It's clean and friendly and we've been here less than an hour and we've already seen the surgeon."

"Well, just go with the flow then," Cliff says. "You know best. Give me the address and I'll come and join you. And I will phone Europe Assistance just in case."

"Oh, the nurse is here. We have to go. Don't come now. I'll . . . I'll phone you when we've stopped rushing around." Hannah hands Tristan's phone back. "Thanks," she says.

The nurse leads them to a pre-op ward, where they lay Luke fully clothed on a gurney, take a blood sample to confirm his blood type, and inject him with a sedative.

"You're being so brave," Hannah tells him. "I'm so proud of you."

"It didn't really hurt," Luke says of the injection.

"This *is* amazing service," Tristan comments. "I mean, we've only been here an hour, and they're prepping him for s—"

Hannah raises her hand, silencing him. "Scary word," she mouths.

Tristan nods. "Sorry," he says.

"How are you doing there?" Hannah asks Luke.

"Sleepy," he says, his head already lolling.

Yet another nurse appears, checks over Hannah's paperwork, and then she and Hannah wrestle Luke's floppy body from his clothes and into a hospital gown.

"OK, je le prends," she says, kicking off the brakes on the trolley. "À tout à l'heure."

"She says she can take it from here," Tristan translates.

"Sure," Hannah says, reaching out to grasp the rail of the

trolley as a wave of panic sweeps over her. "I can go with him, right? Tell me I can go with him?"

Tristan translates Hannah's question, but the nurse's reply is clear enough. "Non."

"But he's eleven," Hannah says. She's breaking out in a sweat at the idea of abandoning her son to these strangers.

"I think it's normal, Han'," Tristan says. "It's an operating theatre."

"S'il vous plaît," the nurse says, nodding at Hannah's whitened knuckles, and so she slowly releases her grip.

"How long, Tristan? Ask her how long it will be," Hannah says as the nurse pulls the trolley from her, expertly spins it, and then begins to push it towards the double doors.

"One hour." The nurse casts the words over her shoulder as she pushes through the doors. "Maybe one hour and half. You wait here, and I come get you for wake up." She points at the waiting room, and then she and Luke vanish beyond the closing doors.

In the small, empty waiting room, Hannah sits, then stands and paces to the window, then walks back and sits and sighs before standing up all over again. "I just don't know what to do with myself," she says.

"I know," Tristan says, chewing a fingernail. "It's horrible."

"He'll be OK, won't he?" Hannah asks.

Tristan's honest reaction would be to shrug, but he suppresses this and nods. "Of course he will," he says. "They said it was good that we got him here so quickly. And the nurse said that the surgeon is a good one."

"But she would say that, wouldn't she?"

"I'm not sure," Tristan says. "I have known a few nurses in my time – of the male variety of course – and they rarely had a good word to say about the doctors. So I think that it's a good sign."

"This is my fault," Hannah says. "So stupid of me leaving them in the pool unattended. Anything could have happened. Anything *has* happened."

"If it's anyone's fault, it's mine," Tristan says. "I should never have bought him that mask."

"You couldn't possibly know that this would happen," Hannah says.

"No, well . . . Nor could you."

"I think Aïsha smashed it," Hannah says. "She seemed guilty. That girl so needs some discipline."

"But she got him out of the water," Tristan points out. "That can't have been easy. Luke's almost as big as her now."

"Yes," Hannah says with a sigh. "Yes, I suppose so."

A series of images of Luke with a missing eye spontaneously manifest on the projection screen of Hannah's mind – an empty eye socket, a sewn-up eyelid, a glass eye pointing the wrong way – and the weight of tears that have been building since the day's drama began suddenly overwhelms her. She sinks into the nearest chair and puts her head in her hands and lets the tears roll down her face. Her body shudders.

Tristan crosses the room and sits next to her and drapes one arm around her shoulders.

"God, I hope he's OK," Hannah says through snuffles. "I love that boy so much. I just couldn't bear . . ."

"I'm sure he will be," Tristan says again. "Do you want me to call Cliff?" he asks, unsure as to how best to deal with Hannah's tears. He doesn't really know her *that* well.

Hannah nods, but then as Tristan pulls his phone from his pocket, she snatches it from him, says, "Actually don't," and then hands it back. They sit in silence for a moment as both Hannah and Tristan wonder why she just did this.

"Is everything OK between you and . . ." Tristan starts.

But Hannah interrupts him, saying simply, "Bathroom, sorry."

In the women's toilets she stares at herself in the mirror for a moment. Her mascara has run. She looks a mess. *What is happening here*? she thinks numbly. And then she shakes her head, lowers her face to the sink, and washes away the tears.

When she returns, Tristan looks up at her expectantly. "Cliff phoned," he says.

"Is he coming?"

"I told him to come in an hour," Tristan says. "At twelve."

Hannah glances at the clock. "Right," she says.

"I said that was best."

"Right."

"Is that OK?" Tristan asks.

Hannah nods.

"Aïsha can't stop crying apparently."

"No, well . . ." Hannah says.

For fifteen minutes they sit in silence interrupted only by an occasional set of heels clip-clopping along the corridor. And then, out of the blue, the culmination of some private thought process, Tristan says, "It must be amazing to have a child. To know that he's your own flesh and blood."

"It is," she says. "And at times, like today, it's really painful. It's hard to describe."

"Yes," Tristan says. "Yes, I'm sure."

"It's like his pain is your own. Only worse. Because you can't do anything about it."

"Yes," Tristan says. "I get that."

"Did you ever think about children of your own?" Hannah asks.

Tristan tuts. "It's not really an option, is it?" he says.

"I suppose. Though people do manage it, don't they? Like the gay couple on that TV show, *Modern Family*."

"Sure," Tristan says. "There are ways. If you're determined enough. But I've never been able to keep a boyfriend for more than a week, so . . ."

"A week?" Hannah says. "Really?"

"No," Tristan replies. "*Not* really."

"Oh."

"You know that anyway. You know I was with Paul for two years."

"Yes. I'm sorry. My mind's, you know . . . elsewhere."

"Understandable."

"So what happened with Paul?" Hannah asks. "I don't think I ever really knew. He just vanished one day. And you were with . . . Mark? Mike?"

"Matt. But it's OK," Tristan says. "We don't have to talk about me."

"No, it's good," Hannah says. "I swear that clock moved a whole minute when you were talking."

"It's the world's slowest clock, isn't it?" Tristan says.

"Torture," Hannah agrees.

"Well, Paul was lovely," Tristan says. "Kind, thoughtful, generous . . ."

"Yes, I liked him, I must say."

"But kind of boring."

"Really?" Hannah says. "I thought he was pretty funny."

"Oh, he was funny. But I missed all the stuff I did before, I guess. Going out, clubbing, drinking, dancing. Even dating.

I actually missed all the cruising and chatting people up online and the wondering if . . ."

"The excitement of the chase," Hannah says.

"Exactly. We'd be in of an evening, and you'd just know that all that was going to happen was *Corrie* and a glass of wine."

"*Corrie?*"

"*Coronation Street*. He's from Manchester, so . . ."

"Of course."

"And though, in a way, it was all I ever wanted – you know, someone to snuggle with on the sofa – I just kept feeling this *is this it* kind of feeling. I don't suppose that makes any sense to you."

"It does," Hannah says. "More than you can imagine. But you can't have both, can you? That's the point."

"Both?"

"Yes. I mean, you can't have the excitement *and* the stability. It's life's great dilemma. That every choice excludes something else."

Tristan nods thoughtfully. "After Paul, I thought I wanted to be single forever more, but then I got bored with that too, so I thought maybe I needed someone really adventurous. An extreme sports enthusiast or a mountaineer or something mad like that."

"Right," Hannah says. "And?"

"Well, it's a bit of a tall order, isn't it?" Tristan says. "I mean, I can't even find someone who wants a relationship most of the time. It's never really going to happen."

"No."

"So I went out with Matt. But Matt was just a butterfly. You know, flitting from one thing to the next. So he flitted on elsewhere. And now I think that I should have stayed with

Paul really. I think that leaving Paul was my greatest error probably."

"And is he still . . . I mean, couldn't you get back with him?"

"Nah, he's married now. Well, civil partnered. To a really nice guy. A bit boring too. They watch *Coronation Street* together and eat too many doughnuts. It probably wouldn't have suited me anyway."

"Life's complicated," Hannah says.

"And there's no instruction manual, is there?"

"No. I guess you always regret the choices you didn't make, because you imagine that they would have been better choices, that's the thing. But in the end, you just have to choose something and get on with it. Because if you hedge your bets forever, well, you end up with nothing, don't you?"

"Like me?" Tristan says.

"No, I was thinking of Jill to be perfectly honest."

"Yes. We're very similar that way, Jill and me," Tristan says. "Never satisfied. I often think that people all have different genes or skill-sets or whatever and, you know, perhaps, I just didn't get the one called '*making a relationship work*'. Maybe that's just bad luck for me. But maybe I can't really do anything about it."

"I suppose," Hannah says.

"You don't sound convinced."

"I'm not sure it's a skill," Hannah says. "Or a gene. And I'm not sure it comes down to luck either. I tend to think it's a choice. I tend to think most things are a choice."

Tristan chews his lip as he thinks about this.

"God, it's only twenty past," Hannah says, nodding at the clock.

"I know."

"I saw a drinks machine down the hall," Hannah says. "Have you got any change? I haven't got a penny. Or a centime or whatever."

Tristan stands and jingles his pocket. "Sure," he says. "I'll go. What do you want?"

"Coke I think," Hannah says. "I could do with some caffeine."

"Diet, or . . ."

"Normal. I think I need some sugar too."

When Tristan returns, he hands Hannah her bottle of Coke. "Open it carefully. The machine shook them up a bit during delivery," he says, lifting his half-empty bottle to show her. "Mine went all over the place and I had to get someone to mop it up."

"I hate that," Hannah says. "It happened to me in a super-market once."

They stand side by side at the window and sip their drinks. "Crazy to build the whole town on the hill like that," Hannah comments.

"I suppose it was so they could see the enemy coming or something," Tristan says.

"Yeah," Hannah says vaguely – she's thinking about something else. "Last night you said that Jill is jealous of me," she says.

"Did I?"

"Yes. You did. Is she really?"

Tristan nods. "Yes," he says. "Yes, she is a bit."

"It's funny," Hannah says. "I was thinking about that last night after you went to bed. We're all jealous of what we haven't got, aren't we?"

"Well, except those of us who have got it all," Tristan says, nudging Hannah vaguely with his hip.

"Me?" Hannah says. "You have to be joking."

"A husband, a son, a house . . ."

"A dishwasher. Three bedrooms. A Dyson," Hannah continues.

"Exactly. So what's missing from your life?"

Hannah shrugs. "I don't know," she says. "I guess a proper career, a daughter, passion, excitement, adventure, travel."

"We're in France. Doesn't that count?"

"If you knew how hard I had to twist Cliff's arm . . . But you can always find something to feel dissatisfied about I suppose. It's like you say, maybe none of us can help wondering if this is really all there is. If this is really *it*."

"There's Cliff," Tristan says.

"Yes, Cliff . . ." Hannah says. "I'm not sure what I . . ."

Hannah belatedly realises that Tristan isn't *discussing* Cliff, he's pointing at him in the square below. "Oh! Yes!" she says.

They watch him cross the pavement and then attempt to pull a door open before realising that it opens the other way, then he enters the building and vanishes from sight.

"I'll go down and meet him," Tristan says. "I wonder where he p—. Shit!"

Hannah turns and she and Tristan stare into each other's eyes, and then, in unison, they say, "The car!"

Despite Tristan's directions, it takes fifteen minutes for Cliff to find the opthalmology waiting room. He crosses the floor and hugs Hannah, and notices, but doesn't comment on, the brevity of the embrace. "Any news?" he asks.

Hannah shakes her head. "Nothing new yet. Only what I told you on the phone. He's still in there."

"Tristan's car got towed," Cliff announces. "Apparently he left it right in front of the ambulance bay."

"I know, I was there."

"Daft bugger."

"Well, we were kind of in a hurry."

"Sorry, I know that. I just meant . . ." Cliff's voice fades out.

"Poor Tris'," Hannah says.

"He's gone to get it from the pound – is it called a pound? Anyway it's walking distance, so . . ." Cliff says.

"We must give him money to pay the fine or whatever," Hannah says. "I don't know what I would have done without him."

Cliff vaguely resents what he perceives as the implication that Tristan succeeded where he himself has failed. "I don't think Tristan is short of a few bob," he says.

"Neither are we," Hannah says.

"No."

"Well then."

"I could kill Tristan for giving him that shitty mask," Cliff says.

"Don't, Cliff," Hannah says. "He feels terrible about it already. Personally, I could kill Aïsha for smashing it."

"Yes, she did too."

"So do we know what actually happened? How, I mean."

"She dive-bombed him in the pool – put her foot through it."

"Stupid little bitch."

"Quite. She cut her ankle too. Nothing major. She didn't even notice till later. But, yes, proof if any were needed."

"That girl needs some proper discipline," Hannah says.

"She does," Cliff agrees. He crosses to where Hannah is standing and looks out at the window. "That's a view," he says.

"It is."

"Did they give you any prognosis whatsoever?"

Hannah sighs. "I *told* you all this, Cliff," she says.

"I know, I'm sorry. It's just been difficult, not being here. I keep feeling like I'm missing some vital piece of information."

"I know, I'm sorry," Hannah says. "They vaguely said that he should be fine. But in that bland way hospital staff always do."

"Under-promise, over-deliver," Cliff says.

"Well, hopefully."

"I contacted the assistance people. They said they'll pay part of the cost."

"And the Euro-thingie covers the rest?"

"Part of it," Cliff says. "They were a bit vague about that. I'm not sure they knew to be honest. They said that we might have to pay it all and claim it back. It could run to thousands, they said. They wanted to know if I had the funds."

"And you do."

"Of course."

"Thank God for that," Hannah says.

Cliff slides one arm around her and says, "See, I am good for something."

Hannah shrugs him off. There's something unsavoury about the comment that she can't quite put her finger on, but something about it displeases her profoundly.

"We will be OK, won't we?" Cliff asks.

"What do you mean?" Hannah asks, mainly to gain extra thinking time.

"I mean with Luke and Aïsha and all this hassle and James maybe arriving."

"Yes? And?"

"Well, you won't let it . . . you won't let it wreck everything?" Cliff says. "You won't let it wreck *us*. Not when Luke needs us? Not when he's depending on us?"

Hannah's feelings about Cliff, which have been a maelstrom of confusion for the last few days, solidify at that second into hatred. She has never liked it when people attempt to manipulate her feelings – no doubt because her mother was such an expert – but such blatant use of their injured son strikes her as beyond the pale.

"Of course I won't," she says sharply.

"You promise?" Cliff asks.

"Of course I promise," Hannah says. But childish or not, she has her fingers crossed behind her back.

Just as Cliff starts to lurch towards her for another attempt at a hug she is saved by the appearance of a short, black female nurse pushing through the double doors. She continues along the corridor past them and then suddenly doubles back. "Monsieur et Madame Parker ?" she asks.

"Yes," Hannah says. "Oui."

"Il est sorti," the nurse says. "Il est en salle de réveil. Tout va bien. Il . . ."

"Sorry, do you speak English?" Hannah asks, interrupting her.

"Est-ce que je parle anglais ?" the nurse says. "Non. Je suis désolée – vous êtes en France. Nous parlons français ici."

Hannah shrugs. "I'm sorry," she says. "We don't speak French."

The nurse rolls her eyes, pushes her lips out, makes a short sharp "pff" noise by blowing through her lips, and then spins on one heel and returns from whence she came.

"She seemed stroppy," Hannah says.

"What was all that about?" Cliff asks.

"I don't know," Hannah says. "I don't, as you know, speak French."

"I expect she's gone to get someone else," Cliff says.

"Do you think Luke's OK?" Hannah asks. "She didn't look happy."

"She didn't look like anyone's died either," Cliff says.

"Don't!" Hannah says, genuinely shocked.

"I didn't mean . . . I only meant . . ."

Hannah starts to pace the floor anew. At one point she approaches the double doors and peers through, but there is nothing but another stretch of endless corridor on the far side.

After ten minutes of this, and specifically when Hannah says, "God, I wish Tristan were here," Cliff – despite the bilingual *Staff Only* sign – pushes through the doors, but within seconds the same black nurse as before appears to march him back to the waiting room.

"Can you please find someone who speaks English?" Cliff asks. "We need to know how our son is."

"Non, non, non !" is all the nurse says.

It's another half an hour – half an hour that stretches like a day – before another nurse, a man this time, comes to speak to them.

"Vous ne parlez pas français ?" he asks.

"Sorry," Hannah says.

"Luke is waked up," he says. "He ask for you. Why you 'ere? Come!"

"No one told us," Hannah says as they follow him back down the long corridor again. "Is he OK?"

The nurse doesn't answer their question, but leads them back to the lift, up one floor, and then down an identical corridor to an individual room which Hannah guesses must be almost exactly above where they were standing before.

Inside the room, Luke is lying in bed, his eye bandaged. "Is he awake yet?" Hannah asks.

"Mum?"

"I'm here, baby," Hannah says, running around the bed so that Luke can see her with his good eye.

"I didn't know where you were," Luke slurs, his pronunciation that of someone who has just left a dentist's chair.

"I'm sorry, baby," Hannah says, pulling up a chair and taking his hand. "They didn't tell us you were awake. We came as soon as we knew. We're here now. Is he going to . . .?" Hannah begins to ask, but as she looks up she sees that the nurse has already gone.

Reassured that his parents are there, Luke ceases fighting the anaesthetic and falls asleep again. While Hannah strokes his hand, Cliff makes repeated sorties in an attempt at getting some information about the success, or otherwise, of Luke's operation, but succeeds only in annoying the staff nurse so seriously that, reminding him that he's outside visiting times, she threatens him with eviction. Returning to the room, his tail between his legs, he tells Hannah, "I think we had better just shut up and wait or they'll kick us out."

"He woke up again," Hannah says. "Just for a few seconds."

"Any pain?" Cliff asks.

"No, I don't think so," Hannah says. "I just hope that behind that bandage . . ." She pulls a face.

"I know," Cliff says.

It's not until Tristan returns at four-fifteen that they are able to get fresh information.

"We don't know anything," Hannah tells him, her voice panicky. "Can you do something, Tris'?"

"Sure," Tristan says, "I'll go give them hell."

"I tried," Cliff says. "But they won't know anything until the surgeon does his rounds."

When Tristan returns less than a minute later with a perfectly informed, English-speaking male nurse, only Cliff's solace at getting some information counteracts his desire to punch Tristan.

"Is good," the nurse tells them, and Hannah gasps with relief.

"He have three little glass in his eye, but is OK now. All gone."

He fumbles in his pocket and pulls out a tiny plastic jar. "Glass," he says.

"God," Cliff says, taking it from his grasp, shaking it, then holding it to the light. He tries to hand it back, but the nurse says, "You can keep. But not for the boy. Is dangerous."

"Sure," Cliff says.

"So he'll be OK?" Hannah says, slightly frustrated by all this boyish gloating over the fragments of glass.

"Perfect," the nurse says.

"And his sight?" Cliff asks. "Will that be affected?"

"Perfect," the nurse says. "La rétine . . . retina?"

"Yes, retina."

"The retina was not affected. Nor the . . ." he points vaguely to his eye. "The *lentile*," he says. "So it's good."

"Oh thank you," Hannah says, sensing fresh tears forming. "And the eye-patch?"

"I'm sorry?"

"This?" she says, pointing.

"Ah, quarante-huit heures."

"Forty-eight hours," Tristan translates.

"And before we can go home?"

"Non. This . . ." the guy mimes an eye-patch. "Is for forty hours. Two day."

"So we can go home when? Now?"

"Non !" he laughs. He checks his watch. "Twenty hours."

"In twenty hours?" Hannah asks, trying to calculate what time that will be.

"I think he means at eight o'clock," Tristan says.

"Yes at eight clock. I'm sorry, my English is not so good," the nurse says.

"No, it's very good," Hannah says. "Thank you!"

"So now I go get you some *ordonnance* for antibiotics . . ."

"Yes."

"And someone must come with me for . . ." He makes a money gesture.

"Right, that'll be me," Cliff says, eager for an opportunity to prove his worth in all of this.

"Sorry, do we need to come back for a check-up?" Hannah asks.

"Checkap? What is checkap?"

"Must we come back here? In a day, a week? To see the doctor?" Hannah paraphrases.

The nurse shakes his head. "No. It's not *néccessaire* . . ." he says. "OK." He turns towards the door, but then hesitates. "I'm sorry, but only one person in the room," he says. He looks at Hannah. "Maybe you are staying?"

"Yes," Hannah confirms. "I'll stay."

"I'll come with you," Tristan tells Cliff. He turns to Hannah and adds, "Just in case he needs help with the forms or *something*," and winks.

"So I can't come back here when I've paid?" Cliff asks.

"No, I'm sorry. Only one person in this room."

"It's fine. Go home. Have a rest. I'll meet you downstairs at eight," Hannah says.

"At the reception? In A and E?"

"Yes."

"I'll be there," Cliff says. "And if there's some delay, don't worry, I'll wait."

"Thanks."

"You don't have a phone, do you?" Tristan asks Hannah.

"No," Hannah says. She left her battered Nokia in England.

"Here, have mine," Tristan says, proffering his iPhone.

"It's better if I take Cliff's, isn't it?"

"No," Cliff says. "Take Tristan's. My battery is nearly dead."

Tristan hands his phone over. "The code is two-four-six-four," Tristan says.

"Two-four-six-four," Hannah repeats. "Got it."

"And don't go chatting the boys up on Grindr."

"No . . . no, well, I wouldn't even know how."

Tristan flashes the whites of his eyes at her, and then the three men file from the room.

Hannah sits for a moment thinking about Tristan's strange glance. What did it mean? And then she realises, and shakes

196

her head at the fact that even here, even in the midst of this mayhem, Tristan has spotted a cute male nurse.

She peers in at Luke. He is still sleeping. She strokes his forehead gently, then kisses it and pulls her chair a little closer so that she can lay her head next to his body.

A single final tear of relief slides down her cheek, and then against all expectation she falls asleep.

THIRTY

Luke, still vaguely under sedation, falls asleep in the car.

"He has been amazing," Hannah says, glancing back at him.

"Yes," Cliff agrees. "Yes, I'm so proud. Can you imagine what Aïsha would have been like?"

"No," Hannah says. "No, I can't. Tristan said she couldn't stop crying as it is."

"This morning? Yes. It's true."

"Is her heel OK?"

"I think so. It was nothing really – just a scratch. They've gone," Cliff says. "You know that, right?"

"Gone?"

"Uh-huh. Tristan took them to the station when we got back. I think there were too many bad vibrations for her or something. That's what Tris' said."

Like boiling milk, Hannah's anger froths, rises and overflows. "What a cow," she says. "She didn't even wait to see if Luke was OK!" Hannah hesitates, then asks, "When you say, *gone*, you mean . . . ?"

"Oh, just for one night. They went to Nice. Change of scene, she said."

"Oh, right," Hannah says, swallowing, and trying to force herself to calm down. "God, I thought you meant that she'd gone completely. As in gone home."

"All the same, she could have phoned," Cliff says. "She might have shown a little concern."

Hannah shakes her head and sighs. "I think I'm getting to the point where . . ." she says.

"Yes?"

She shrugs. There's no point feeding Cliff's Jill-phobia. "Oh, nothing. It's just Jill, isn't it. So they've gone to Nice, huh?"

"Yes."

"A nice little treat for Aïsha to reward her for all her good behaviour."

"Well, quite."

They drive in silence for a moment until an advertisement for new-build apartments with a price displayed in euros prompts Hannah to ask, "So, how much did it cost? Are we broke?"

Cliff laughs. "The hospital? No, it was fine actually. I had to pay the, what is it they call it? The, you know, patient's contribution."

"The co-pay."

"Yes, that's it. It was twenty per cent. And apparently we can even try to claim that back."

"And how much was that then?"

"Three hundred-ish. Out of one thousand two hundred and sixty or something."

"That's pretty reasonable," Hannah says.

"Quite interesting seeing the bill – I'll show you later. The anaesthetist was almost half of it. It's a good job you got the Euro-card before we left. Otherwise we would have had to pay the whole lot."

"Good old Europe," Hannah says.

"Yes, for once," Cliff agrees.

As Hannah climbs out, the sudden movement makes her feel so dizzy that she has to lean against the car to steady herself. "God, I just realised. I haven't eaten all day," she says.

"I'll carry Luke in," Cliff says.

But Luke is awake. "I'm fine," he says, already emerging from the car.

Tristan comes to greet them. "Hey, kids," he says. "Everything OK?"

Hannah, still leaning against the car, looks at him and smiles weakly. "I think my blood sugar's low," she says. "I forgot to have lunch. Could you make me a quick sandwich or something?"

"I can do that," Cliff says. "What do you want? Ham? Cheese? Tuna?"

"There's no need, Cliff," Tristan says. "I . . ."

"Just let me make my wife a sandwich, will you?" Cliff says.

Hannah notes, but chooses to ignore, the tension between the two men. She simply doesn't have the energy to care right now.

When they reach the patio however, it's clear why sandwiches aren't needed. The table is covered with food.

"Oh, Tris'," Hannah says. "You didn't have to do all of this." The truth is that she would rather have had a quick sandwich and gone to bed.

"If you'd rather just have a sandwich, I'll make you one," Cliff offers, and Hannah wonders briefly if he has read her mind.

"No, it's fine," Hannah says. "This is lovely."

"I thought you'd be hungry," Tristan says.

"Yes, well, I am, I'm starving."

"I'm hungry too," Luke says.

"So tell me what happened?" Hannah says, once they are all served and seated. "I still don't really know."

"Aïsha dive-bombed me," Luke says.

"So it is Aïsha's fault entirely, or . . . ?"

Luke shrugs. "Well, I kind of dive-bombed her first," he admits.

"Right."

"She was asleep on the air bed like you was when I squirted you."

"Like you *were*," Hannah says.

"Yeah."

"So you sort of started it, did you?" Hannah asks.

Luke shrugs again. "Yeah," he says. "I suppose so."

Dinner over, Luke, unusually, admits that he is tired, so Hannah takes him to bed. "You were so, so brave today," she tells him as she undresses him.

"I wish we took photos," Luke says. "For school. Stephen Hill had his appendix out, but this is way cooler."

"I didn't think. I'm sorry," she says, arranging the bedclothes over him.

Luke yawns. "It's weird having only one eye though," he says.

"Well, it won't be for long," Hannah tells him. "You're lucky it's not for life."

Hannah sits for thirty seconds watching him breathe, then says, "I was so proud of you, you know. You were so brave."

But Luke is already asleep.

"Wow, that was quick, even for you," she says quietly.

She sits and watches her son sleeping for five minutes, and then, without undressing, or even brushing her teeth, she climbs onto the bed beside him. He's almost too old for her to do this now. Indeed, if he were awake, it's fifty–fifty these days whether he would snuggle against her or tell her to leave. But today counts as special circumstances. She loves him so much she simply can't bring herself to go.

When Hannah wakes up the next morning, Luke is gone. She drags herself from his bed and staggers to the bathroom. She feels as if she has been sedated herself.

In the mirror she examines her face: she has a deep imprint from the seam of the pillow right across her left cheek. "Foxy," she murmurs with irony. She runs a finger along the indent before bending over the sink and washing her face vigorously.

Outside on the patio, she finds Cliff, Luke and Tristan having breakfast.

"You're up before me," she says, kissing Luke's head as she passes behind him. "How is my little soldier this morning?"

"Tired," Luke says.

"That will be the anaesthetic," Hannah says.

"No, it's your fault. You took all the bed. I had to sleep with Dad. And he snores."

"Oops," Hannah says. "Sorry. I meant to move but I fell asleep."

"That's what you always say," Luke says. "I couldn't even wake you up."

"Sorry," Hannah says, pulling a guilty face.

"Tris' says I look like a pirate," Luke says proudly.

Hannah laughs. "He's right. You do."

"So do you a bit," Tristan says.

Hannah runs a finger across her cheek. "What this?"

Tristan nods.

"I know," she says. "It's awful, isn't it."

"I went to the pharmacy," Tristan tells her, pushing a paper bag across the table towards her.

"I was perfectly happy to go," Cliff says. "But Tristan wouldn't let me."

"Well, you don't speak French," Tristan points out.

"I would have managed."

"I doubt that. I had a ten-minute argument to get these," Tristan says.

"Really?" Hannah asks, peering inside the bag. "Why?"

"Lack of ID," Tristan says. "My name didn't match with the prescription or something. But I used my famous powers of persuasion on them. No one can resist."

"My ID would have matched, wouldn't it?" Cliff says. "I wouldn't have had that problem."

Hannah yawns and rubs her brow. She looks between Tristan and Cliff's faces and wonders why they are being so competitive this morning and vaguely recalls some bitchiness last night.

"I'd like to have seen you try," Tristan is saying.

"Boys. Boys!" Hannah interrupts. "It really doesn't matter who got them, does it?" She fishes in the bag and pulls out a box of blister-packed pills, then a bottle of eye-wash, another of eye drops and a package of fresh eye-patches.

"The pills are two at breakfast today," Tristan says. "He's already taken those . . ."

"Antibiotics?"

"Yes. And then one every morning. You have to do the eye drops and change the dressing three times a day."

"Will that hurt?" Luke asks.

"No, I don't think it will hurt at all," Hannah says. "And anyway, it's only today and tomorrow, right, Tris'?"

"Right. Just two days the guy at the hospital said."

"He did," Cliff agrees. "I remember. I was there too."

After breakfast, Cliff carries a batch of plates in and begins to unload and then stack the dishwasher. Tristan continues to carry the rest of the breakfast things back indoors.

"So what's going on with you two?" Hannah asks him quietly when he returns. The kitchen window is closed and Hannah's pretty sure that Cliff cannot hear them.

"Who?" Tristan says, pausing with a jar of marmalade in one hand.

"You and Cliff."

"Nothing," Tristan says. "Why?"

"Nothing," Hannah says.

"Nothing!" Tristan repeats more definitively. "Anyway, why ask me? Ask Cliff."

Hannah sighs. Until that last phrase, she had been prepared to believe him. Now she knows something's wrong. "Luke! Where are you going?" she shouts. Luke is heading off in the direction of the pool. He's wearing swimming shorts.

"The pool," he says. "I won't wear the mask."

"Well, you can't, can you?" Hannah says. "It's broken and binned."

"So is it OK?"

Hannah stands. "Come with me and let me change that

dressing. And then you can as long as you don't get it wet. You'll have to keep your head out of the water, OK?" She ushers Luke back indoors.

As they pass the kitchen, Cliff looks up from the dishwasher and asks, "Is everything OK?"

"Fine," Hannah replies. "I'm just going to change Luke's dressing."

"I can do that if you want," Cliff says.

"No thanks. We're fine," Hannah says, pulling a puzzled face as they continue down the corridor.

Luke's bedroom is already too hot – the sunshine is streaming in. She pulls the shutters closed with a *clack* and then sits him on the bed and gently starts to pull back the dressing.

"Ouch," Luke protests.

"I'm sorry, it's a bit stuck," Hannah tells him.

"Owww!" Luke says in a voice that confirms to her that it doesn't really hurt at all.

"There, that's it. How's that?"

Luke shrugs.

"Well, open your eye," she prompts.

Luke opens his injured eye and closes the good one. "It's all blurry," he says.

"Yes, it's a bit gunky," Hannah tells him, fiddling in the paper bag. "That's why we have this to clean it."

She opens the bottle of eye-wash and fills the plastic eye-bath with the solution. "So tip your head forward onto . . . that's right," she says. "And now tip your head back. That's it. And now open your eyes and hold this in place . . . that's right."

"Do I open both of them?"

"Yes."

"It's cold," Luke says.

"Yes."

"Like swimming underwater."

"Yes. It doesn't hurt though, does it?"

"Only here," Luke says, using the hand that was supposed to be holding the eye-bath in place to point to his eyebrow and spilling the solution down his chest.

Hannah and Luke both laugh. "Sorry," Luke says.

"It doesn't matter," Hannah tells him, scooping a dirty T-shirt from the floor and using it to dry Luke's chest. "So how's that now? Can you see better?"

"Yeah. It's OK," Luke says.

"OK, *OK*?" Hannah asks. "Or OK, perfect?"

"OK perfect. Like normal."

"Good."

"So do I still have to have the patch?"

"You do, I'm afraid. But only until tomorrow night."

"That's OK," Luke says. "I don't mind."

Hannah opens the box containing the eye-drops. "Now, tip your head back and keep it there," she says, fiddling with the plastic seal around the bottle.

At the sound of a car door, followed by their gate opening and closing, Hannah stands, and, still fiddling with the packaging, she crosses the room and peers out through the slats.

She sees a grey hatchback parked beyond the gate and a man closing the gate behind him. He turns and looks straight at her, but she can tell from his blank expression that he can't see her.

He has gone grey. That is the first thing that she notices. She could have deduced as much had she thought about it.

After all, Cliff has been grey for years. He has grown a little goatee beard as well. It suits him.

Beyond the shutters, Hannah watches as James crosses his arms behind his head and stretches. He's wearing what looks like hiking gear. Walking boots, lightweight shorts with lots of pockets, a sleeveless checkered shirt. He looks fit and rugged and to her eyes – in a *Brokeback Mountain* kind of way – a little bit gay.

"Mum?" Luke says.

Without averting her gaze, Hannah raises one hand behind her and says, her voice distant, "Yes. Just wait a minute, sweetheart. I can't get this open."

She watches James as he peers inside the Mégane, no doubt looking for clues to confirm that he's in the right place. He must see something which reassures him, because he then crosses the gravel until he's standing just feet away from her – she actually sniffs the air in case she might catch the scent of him.

He cross-links his hands, stretches again, purses his lips, exhales slowly, and then, starting to walk towards the front of the house, calls out, with theatrical bravado, "Hello? Hello? Anybody home?"

"Mum!" Luke says again.

Hannah turns back to see Luke with his head still tilted back.

"Sorry," she says, returning to the bed and finally wrestling the cap from the bottle of eye-drops. "So open your eye and look up at the ceiling . . . There."

"Yuck," Luke says. "I can taste it."

"Yes, that's funny, isn't it," Hannah says.

"It's stingy."

"Yes, just a bit. But it will be OK in a minute."

"Who was that?"

"Who was who?"

"I heard someone outside."

"I'm not sure," Hannah lies. "Let's get this dressing on and then we can go and see. How does that sound?"

Luke's eye re-bandaged, Hannah says, "OK, Luke. Off you go. I'll just put these things away and I'll be out. And don't get it wet, OK?"

Luke runs off and Hannah sits back down on the bed and rests her temple against her fingertips. She sits and stares at her feet. She wiggles her toes.

From the other side of the house she can hear the men's voices but not their words.

She takes a series of long deep breaths, and then, on an exhalation she breathes, "OK!" and stands.

Out on the patio, Cliff, Tristan and Luke are standing with their backs to her, almost as if to prevent James, opposite, from entering. It looks like some kind of rugby defence.

James, facing her, is the first to see her arrive, and she sees him look past Cliff; she sees his eyes wrinkle as he smiles.

". . . that you found it," Cliff is saying.

"I just used the GPS," James replies. "Brought me straight here."

James nods at Hannah and grins, and Cliff turns to see her. "Ah, there she is!" he says, stepping to one side to make room.

Hannah moves forward so that she is between Cliff and Tristan and bristles a little at the implied possession when Cliff lays an arm around her shoulders and says, "My wonderful wife."

"Hi James," Hannah says. "You're looking very . . ."

"Yes?"

"Very *alive* actually."

James laughs. "Why thank you?" he says. "You're looking very *alive* too?"

"Gosh, you *do* sound Australian," Hannah says.

"Well, it has been ten years?" James replies. "More than ten years?" His voice goes up at the end of each sentence as if, perhaps, he's unsure of what he's saying, as if it's a question.

"Yes," Hannah says. "Yes, I know. Well, *now* I know."

Why am I being so bitchy? she thinks. "Would you like something? Tea? Coffee? Juice?"

"Keep going?" James says/asks.

"Beer, wine?" Hannah offers.

James nods. "Sure, a beer would be great?"

Hannah heads to the kitchen and pulls a single beer from the chill-box at the bottom.

She pauses and watches through the window, now ajar, as the men discuss the pros and cons of GPS. *Men,* she thinks. *Fifteen years apart and they're discussing GPS.* She studies James' face as he talks animatedly, notices again the incredible blue of his eyes, and then he glances indoors and sees her watching and, slightly flustered, she returns outside and hands him the beer.

"You aren't expecting me to drink alone?" James says.

Cliff glances at his watch. "It's a bit early for me," he says.

"For me too," Tristan agrees.

"I'm still on Ozzie time," James says. "Hannah! Have a beer with me so I don't feel so lonely?"

"Hannah never drinks beer," Cliff says.

"Actually," she says, "I will." She heads back to the kitchen and returns with a second can.

"I can't even remember the last time I saw you drink beer," Cliff says once she has reappeared, the can in her hand.

"No," Hannah agrees as she pulls the ring-pull and chinks her can against James'. "I'm glad I still have the power to surprise. Cheers, James. Welcome back. Welcome back from the dead."

THIRTY-ONE

Tristan makes a fresh pot of coffee for Cliff and himself and the adults settle around the large table on the patio. Luke, intrigued by the newcomer, soon joins them as well, saying, "The pool's kind of boring on your own. When's Aïsha coming back?"

"Should be today," Cliff says. "Maybe even this morning."

"Is it more interesting when Aïsha's dive-bombing you?" Tristan asks.

"No, not really," Luke replies, with a sheepish grin.

"So what happened to your eye, Bud?" James asks.

"I smashed my mask and got glass in it," Luke explains.

"We had a day of drama yesterday at the hospital," Hannah tells him. "You missed all the fun. He had a general anaesthetic – the works."

"That's a quick recovery then," James says.

"It is," Hannah agrees, stroking Luke's head.

"So how did you get down here?" Tristan asks James. "Did you drive all the way, or . . . ?"

"No, I flew to Nice with some low-cost outfit," James says. "EasyJet?"

"Yep. That's the one. It wasn't very low cost at all, in fact."

"Well, you have to book in advance," Tristan says. "If you buy your ticket three or even six months beforehand, it can be very cheap. Otherwise it's pretty much the same price as everyone else. More sometimes."

"I'm not really a six-months-in-advance kinda guy," James says.

"No," Tristan agrees. "I know what you mean. Nor am I. And the car is a hire car then?"

James nods. "A rental. Yes. I picked it up at the airport. I guess I should bring it inside," he says, standing. "It's still parked out on the road."

When he returns, he changes seats so that he is directly opposite Hannah and Luke. "So where's your sister, Luke?" he asks.

"My sister?" Luke says.

"Aïsha, is it?" James says. "She must be, what, fifteen?"

Luke shakes his head. "She's not my *sister*," Luke says, with what sounds like disgust.

Cliff frowns and catches Hannah's eye.

"Aïsha's Jill's daughter," Hannah explains. "My sister's daughter. They're here with us on holiday, but they've gone off to Nice. They should be back soon."

"Oh," James says, looking confused. "So how old are you, Luke?"

"Eleven," Luke says. "Aïsha's thirteen."

"Oh," James says. "OK."

Hannah can see him counting, calculating. She can see him trying to understand. "They're like brother and sister really," she says, trying to head off any more embarrassing questions. "Which is nice for them, being only children."

"Sure," James says, nodding thoughtfully.

"So you live in Australia?" Hannah asks, attempting to change the subject. "That must be nice."

"Yes," James says. "Yes, I'm Australian now. I took the nationality."

"Why did you do that?" Cliff asks.

James shrugs, and swigs at his beer. "I had my reasons," he says.

Tristan nods at James' hand. "So is that a wedding ring?" he asks. "Did you find yourself an Australian beauty?"

Hannah's stomach lurches. Which is absurd. She can't work out how she managed to not notice the ring.

"This?" James says, using his other hand to turn the ring. "Yes. I was married. Not now though. I just . . . I can't really imagine taking this off," he says.

"Any children?" Hannah asks.

James physically winces at the question. They all see it. "I . . ." he says. He closes his eyes for a second, and then reopens them and adds, "Hey, let's not talk about me. Tell me what you guys have been up to all these years."

"Is he gay, do you think?" Tristan murmurs when he catches Hannah alone in the kitchen.

"I haven't the foggiest, Tristan," she says, only barely hiding her irritation at the frivolous nature of the question. "He wasn't fifteen years ago, but who knows. Why don't you ask him?"

Luke runs into the kitchen at that moment and announces, "Jill's here. She wants to know if you've got any money."

"Money?" Hannah asks, drying her hands on a tea-towel.

"To pay the taxi guy."

"I've got fifty euros, I think," Hannah says, heading to her room for her purse.

"I've got some cash too if you need it," Tristan calls after them.

Out at the gate, she finds Jill standing next to the open

213

cab-driver's window, a circle of expensive-looking shopping bags at her feet.

"Hi Han'," she says. "Can you please pay this guy for me? He doesn't take credit cards."

"Where's Aïsha?" Hannah asks.

"She went inside," Jill says, nodding towards the back of the house.

"I've got fifty," Hannah tells her. "Is that enough?"

"It's ninety-seven," Jill says. "I haven't got any cash left at all."

"Ninety-seven?!" Hannah exclaims, turning back to the house. "I'll see what Cliff has."

The taxi paid, Jill heads to her room to shower and change. When she returns, she makes a bee-line for the new arrival. "So you must be James," she says, interrupting a conversation between James and Tristan.

"Yes," James says, holding out his hand.

"I'm Jill," she says, grabbing it and pulling him in for an embrace. "We spoke on the phone."

"Right," James says. "So that was you."

"So you found it OK?" Jill asks. "My directions were spot-on then?"

"You gave me the address," James says. "That was spot-on."

"Yes, of course," Jill says, wondering why she even said that. "So is everyone looking after you?"

"They are."

Jill nods. James' expression is a mixture of wry amusement and confusion. It's a very attractive look, she decides. "Anything you need?" Jill asks.

"Another stubby would be good," James says.

"A what?"

"Sorry, a beer," James explains.

"Coming right up," Jill says.

Hannah, who has been watching this exchange from the doorway, follows Jill into the kitchen. "Please don't flirt with him," she says as her sister stoops to pull a beer from the fridge.

"Why?" Jill asks. "Do you want him for yourself?"

"No," Hannah says.

"Well then! Anyway, I wasn't flirting with him. I was just being hospitable."

Hannah raises one eyebrow and sighs. "I just think that the dynamics around here have been complicated enough the last few days, don't you? It would be nice to have a normal, relaxing time for a bit."

"I'm just being friendly," Jill says.

"Sure," Hannah says, then, "I still can't believe you spent nearly a hundred euros on a taxi."

"Well, if you choose not to invest in your own environment-wrecking, carbon-pumping box of metal then sometimes a taxi is your only choice," Jill says.

"I just meant that if you had phoned, one of us would have come and got you."

"You'll get your money back," Jill says.

"I'm not worried about the money," Hannah says.

"In which case you *won't* get it back," Jill laughs.

"I knew I wouldn't anyway," Hannah says. "You never honour your debts."

Jill puts one hand on her hip. "Oh, come on, Han'," she says. "Lighten up, will you? This is supposed to be a holiday."

"It's been a stressful couple of days, Jill," Hannah says. "I don't feel very *light*."

"I know. I was here. Remember?"

"You were here until you decided to swan off to Nice for a little shopping trip," Hannah says, pointedly.

"Ah, *now* we're getting to the point."

"Honestly, Jill. I'm in the hospital wondering whether my son is going to lose an eye, and you take your daughter – who caused all the trouble in the first place – off on a shopping spree to Nice? Did you even wonder how Luke was doing? Did you even care?"

"That's so unfair!" Jill protests, her voice louder now. "And you know it."

"I don't think that's unfair at all."

"We knew Luke was fine before we left."

"Did you? How?"

"Tristan told us when he got back. He said everything was fine and that you'd be home in a few hours."

"Oh. I got confused. I thought you left before then, but of course you didn't."

"And we had been worried sick all morning. Aïsha couldn't stop . . ."

"Crying, yes, I heard," Hannah says.

"So when we found out everything was OK I decided it would be better for us, and for you, if we all had a bit of space."

"OK," Hannah concedes. "I still don't think rewarding Aïsha by taking her shopping was—"

"And it wasn't a reward. I wanted some time alone so that I could talk to her. And I did. We stayed in a horrible little hotel, if you must know, and we had a good long talk about the dope and the mask and how serious it could have been and I made her fully aware that she was out of order and that she had better buck her ideas up."

"Right," Hannah says. "And then you took her shopping."

Jill shakes her head. "I hate you sometimes, Hannah," she says.

Hannah blinks slowly. "I know," she says. "It's fairly mutual, actually."

"The shopping was Aïsha's idea . . ."

"I'll bet it was."

"Those are gifts. For you. We bought holiday gifts for all of you. We thought it would be *nice*."

Hannah swallows with difficulty.

"So . . ." Jill says, tiling her head sideways momentarily.

"I see," Hannah says.

"You see, do you?"

Hannah shrugs.

"This is where *you* say sorry," Jill tells her.

"OK, I'm sorry," Hannah says. "Look, I *am*. It's just all this . . ." she says, gesturing vaguely around her. "But you see how it looked, right? We got back from the hospital and you'd gone off on a jolly to Nice. Then you reappear with a pile of shopping bags and ask me to pay for the taxi."

"God, are we back to that again?" Jill asks, wide-eyeing her sister. "Shall I go and get some cash out now?" she asks, pointing. "Is that what you want me to do? I could get Tristan to drive me to a bank and be back within an hour if that's what's required here."

"No," Hannah says. "No, really. That's not what I'm saying. I'm just trying to explain how it *looked*."

"Right," Jill says. She looks down at the countertop for a moment, takes a deep breath, and then says, "OK, I get that. And I get that you're stressed out by . . . you know who . . . and I'm sorry Aïsha got Luke stoned, and I'm sorry she smashed

217

his mask. And I'm even sorry the taxi driver didn't take credit cards, OK?"

"OK."

"So can we now, please, just, move on?"

Hannah nods gently and smiles sadly. "It's me," she says flatly. "I'm just so stressed out at the moment."

"So don't be," Jill says. "Have a beer and chillax."

"I hate that word," Hannah says.

"Actually, so do I," Jill agrees. "So, have a beer and *relax*."

"I had one this morning already," Hannah says.

"You devil you," Jill laughs. "Have another." She proffers the beer and Hannah laughs and takes it from her grasp.

"I do love you," Hannah says. "You do know that, right?"

"Of course," Jill says.

"You annoy the hell out of me, but I love you."

"That feeling's mutual too."

James pokes his head around the door. "I guess I shouldn't count on that being for me," he says, nodding at the beer can.

"This?" Hannah says. "No, this one's mine. Get your own."

"I'm sorry, sweetheart," Jill says, turning to face James and sticking her hip out. "Hannah's need was greater than yours." She wrenches open the door to the refrigerator. "I'll get you another," she says. "There's plenty more where that came from."

Because James' presence flusters her in a way she can't quite put her finger on, Hannah chooses to help Tristan prepare lunch rather than remain on the patio.

They are running low on provisions – someone needs to go shopping – so they end up serving a trio of salads: potato and chives; tomato, cucumber and goat's cheese; and last night's

218

pasta salad – recycled. (Tristan replaces the slices of tomato in it with fresh, a "dodgy restaurant trick" he says.)

At one point during the preparations when he's standing right next to Hannah at the sink, Tristan says, "He's nice."

Hannah looks up and sees James talking to Jill while she swings Aïsha in the hammock.

"Yes," Hannah says. "He is, isn't he?"

"So what do you think happened to the wife?" Tristan asks.

"I really don't know," Hannah says. "But I'm sure we'll find out before the holiday is out. I expect you're hoping that he left her because he decided he was gay, aren't you?"

"Something like that," Tristan laughs. "Cheeky! Just dump those chives on the potatoes and then pour the dressing over, OK?"

"Don't you want me to cut them up?"

"Well, of course," Tristan says.

Over dinner, James regales them with tales of his travels: his trip to Thailand, his time in India, his summer in Bali, and finally his arrival in Australia.

"How did you finance all of this?" Hannah asks. "I mean, if it's not an impolite question . . ."

"We got our inheritance," James says. "When Mum died."

"Of course you did," Hannah says.

"Cliff was sensible with his half."

"I bought our house," Cliff reminds her. "Best investment we ever made."

"Exactly. Whereas I blew mine."

"All of it?" Cliff asks.

James nods. "Pretty much," he says. "But it was worth it."

"So how did you end up owning a farm?" Cliff asks.

"Farm?" Hannah says. She has no recollection of anyone mentioning a farm.

"Yes, um, James here, was, um, telling me he has a farm," Cliff stammers.

"Yes," James says, looking confused. "Well, I sort of inherited that too. It was in my wife's family. It was falling apart when we took it over. But as I say, that's a long story."

"We have all night," Jill says. "We have all week for that matter."

"Maybe another time," James says.

"So how long *are* you staying?" Jill asks.

"Where are you staying, more to the point?" Cliff comments.

James shrugs. "I haven't really got that far yet," he says.

"You must stay here," Hannah says automatically, unsure once she has said it if she regrets it or not.

"That would be great," Cliff says, "obviously. But I can't really see where. What about that little auberge place down the road?"

"Rubbish," Hannah says. "There's plenty of room here."

"I could double up with Mum," Aïsha offers, clearly on her best behaviour.

"Well, there you go," Hannah says. "You can have Aïsha's room. And if she gets fed up with it, we can all take turns on the sofa bed."

"I'm totes happy with the sofa bed," James says.

"There's no need," Jill says. Then suddenly wondering if she will still be able to sneak out to see Pascal, she adds, "Not for tonight anyway. Aïsha says she's happy in with me."

"So what kind of farm is it?" Tristan asks. "Is it livestock? Are you a cowboy?"

James laughs. "It's a bit of everything. It's the only way

to survive these days. We grow sugar cane and wheat and sorghum."

"Sorghum?"

"Hay to you. So not really a cowboy, no."

"Is it big?" Hannah asks.

"Not really," James says. "Thirty acres, so not huge. But it's pretty beautiful. We have palm trees out front, and a view of the Glasshouse Mountains out back. The sunsets are pretty cool."

"Sounds lovely," Hannah says.

"It is."

Hannah sits and listens to James' smooth baritone voice, so similar to Cliff's, but now, because of the accent, so much more exotic. Tristan keeps topping up her glass, which means that she drinks more than she intended, but she feels that it's doing her good. It's helping her relax.

It's a funny thing, because though it is all new to her, nothing James says actually surprises her. He has led exactly the kind of life she thought he would have all those years ago, a life filled with changes and challenges and achievements and exciting adventures and warmly described friendships. It's such a big life, she can't help but compare it with her own fifteen years living in the same house in Surrey, working at a local school. She feels a bit like she has failed in some fundamental way.

As James tells them about his bionic leg (he was trampled by horses and has metal pins in it that caused him much hassle going through airport security) and about the killer spiders and crocs and snakes of Queensland (Luke and Aïsha are, for once, both gripped), lunch merges into afternoon tea, which merges, as the sun sets, into high tea.

Tristan, throughout, manages to continue rustling up snacks,

221

seemingly from nowhere, and at one point James tells him, "You'd make someone a great wife, Tristan, has anyone ever told you that?"

"Do you know, no one ever has?" Tristan laughs. "Though *I* have been trying to tell everyone that for years."

"He has," Jill says. "He even has it printed on a T-shirt."

"Tristan's a chef," Hannah explains. "Which is why the food's so good."

"Ah, I guessed as much," James says.

"Come to my room later, and I'll show you just how well I fulfil my other wifely duties," Tristan comments. He has had a bit too much to drink as well.

Hannah fears that the comment might be a little too much for an Australian farmer, and says, "You'll have to excuse Tristan. He likes to shock."

James, though, appears to already have Tristan's measure. "I'm afraid I don't bat on your side of the fence, mate," he tells him. "But I'm one happy guy as long as the food keeps coming."

"You know what they say," Tristan says. "If you like it, try it. If you don't like it, try it, you might like it. My room's the one at the end of the corridor on the left."

Everyone laughs.

"Anyway," Tristan says. "Who wants a slice of dessert? I knocked up a little raspberry charlotte earlier on."

"You did?" Hannah asks. "When?"

Tristan sends Hannah a theatrical glare. "OK, *evil* one," he says, putting one hand on his hip and camping it up. "So it's frozen, OK? It still looks pretty tasty though."

"Can we do the thing after?" Aïsha asks.

"The thing?" Cliff asks.

"Yes," Jill says. "Yes, we have little surprises for everyone. Go get them. They're in my room."

That night, in bed, lying plank-like, side by side, Cliff says, "That was nice of Jill to buy us all gifts, wasn't it?"

"Yes," Hannah says. "Yes, they were nice gestures."

"Not sure I'm ever going to wear skimpy orange Speedos, but it's the thought that counts."

"Yes."

"And James is a nice guy, isn't he?"

"He is," Hannah agrees. After everything that has happened, there's something not right about discussing James with Cliff in a polite manner, so she adds, "I'm glad he's not dead."

After a minute's silence, during which Cliff considers rising to that particular challenge but decides against it, he continues, "You maybe shouldn't ask him about his wife though."

"Why not?" Hannah asks. "Do you know something?"

"No," Cliff says. "I just get the feeling he doesn't want to talk about it. I don't think it's a very happy story."

"Yes, I picked that up for myself," Hannah says.

For ten minutes Hannah lies thinking about James sleeping next door in Aïsha's bed, about Australia, about farms, and horses, and crocodiles and combine harvesters, and about how alien the life he leads is, compared with their own suburban existence.

She's assuming that Cliff is asleep, but he suddenly says, "So how do you feel about him? Seeing him after all these years, I mean."

She waits a full three minutes before she makes what she considers to be a pretty convincing snoring, snuffling sound and rolls onto her side. But Cliff isn't fooled one bit.

THIRTY-TWO

It's five a.m. To be precise, it's five *thirteen a.m.* Hannah has been awake for forty-two minutes.

She had hoped that, by lying very still and concentrating on her breath, she would be able to get back to sleep, but now her back is aching and she feels hungry and thirsty – too hungry and thirsty to stay in bed.

In the kitchen, she finds James eating a cheese sandwich. "James," she says quietly. "Gosh, you're up early." She closes the kitchen door behind her. Should she kiss him good morning? Of course not. The British don't kiss each other. Why did she even think that?

"I have jet-lag," he says wearily. "What's your excuse?"

Hannah fills the kettle and plugs it in, aware that James is watching her as she moves around the room. "I don't know really," she says. "I just woke up feeling hungry. It happens sometimes."

"D'you want a sandwich?" James asks. "This cheese is really good."

Hannah shakes her head. "No, I'll stick to muesli thanks." Once she has made two cups of tea and filled her bowl with cereal, she adds, "I'm going to take this outside. It's lovely out there first thing."

"I'll join you," James says. "Unless you want to be alone with your thoughts."

"No, please feel free."

Outside the air is still cool and vaguely misty. The grass is covered with dew and the low sun is cutting atmospherically through the trees.

"So how has life been?" James asks once they are seated.

Hannah smiles and shrugs. "Oh, it's been fine," she says. "Just normal life really. You know how it is."

James nods.

"I think yours has been more exciting by the sound of it," Hannah says.

James copies her shrug. "Well it's been a mixed bag," James says. "Plenty of joy and a shed load of sadness." He has to clear his throat before he can continue. "It's good to be away," he says. "It's good to be elsewhere frankly."

Hannah nods, detecting something in his voice, yet understanding nothing.

She eats in silence with only a pair of warring birds in one of the olive trees for accompaniment.

"So how long before the rest of the mob wake up?" James asks once Hannah has finished her cereal.

She leans back in her seat in an attempt at checking the kitchen clock, but the reflection of the sun on the window makes this impossible. "I'm not sure what time it is now," she says, "but they generally wake up between eight and nine at the moment. Luke's usually first, but after yesterday, well, it wouldn't surprise me if he sleeps in. Why?"

"I thought we might have time for a walk," James says.

Hannah stares at him. "Yes," she says. "Yes, we do. I'll show you the stream if you want."

"We have a stream?"

"We do. It's lovely down there."

Once they have sprayed each other with insect repellant, Hannah leads James past the pool to the back of the house and over the fence. "You have to beware of snakes apparently," she tells him.

"Venomous snakes?" James asks.

"I don't know really," Hannah admits. "Just keep your eyes open."

As they walk single file along the track, the sun is warm on her face and contrasted against the cool, damp morning air, it feels quite special.

After the intersection of the two paths, they are able to walk side by side once more.

Hannah is hyper aware of James' hand swinging mere inches from her own as they walk, but rationalises that the desire to take it is as absurd as her desire to embrace him at breakfast. She's amazed though to discover that the attraction between their two bodies is still here after all these years.

"So you must really like Australia," Hannah says.

"Must I?" James laughs.

"Well, you took Australian nationality," Hannah says. "And you never came back."

"Yes, I guess so," James says.

"So why now?"

"I don't know," James replies. "I think I needed to touch base with my roots, if that makes any sense."

"Maybe," Hannah says.

"I had a bad few years. I think sometimes you need to remember who you were before. Remind yourself that you even *existed* before, so maybe you can survive now, on your own again . . ." James' voice fades.

"Are you talking about your divorce?" Hannah asks.

"There was no divorce," James says as they reach the climb down to the riverbank.

As they file down the steps Hannah thinks about James' words, about the fact that if there has been no divorce then she is about to be cast in the role of confidante. She promises that she will be generous. She promises to herself that she will help James and his wife get over whatever their problems are. She is not Jill. She does not see every man as a potential conquest.

Once they reach the riverbank, they start to walk slowly downstream. The babble of the brook combined with the screeches of the birds makes the place sound like a tropical rainforest this morning.

"Marriage is tough," Hannah says. "There are always problems. You always have to fight for it if you want it to survive."

"Yes," James says. "Yes, I suppose so."

"So what happened, James?" Hannah asks, eventually.

"A car accident," James says, and Hannah's heart lurches in two directions at once. "They were both killed outright."

Hannah stops walking, and turns to face him. "Both of them?" she says.

James closes his eyes briefly and nods his head. He swallows and licks his lips. "A truck driver . . . he was texting," he says. "She had broken down and he . . ." he shrugs. "He just drove into them. He didn't brake at all apparently."

Hannah takes James' forearms in her hands. She shakes her head. "I'm so sorry, James," she says. "I . . . I don't know what to say."

"There's not much *to* say," James says.

"No."

"But I needed to remember, you know? I needed to remember who I was before."

"Yes, that makes perfect sense."

"She . . ." James pauses and looks up at the sky. When he returns his gaze to Hannah his eyes are watering. "She was six . . ." he says, his face screwing up. "Hannah, she was only six."

Hannah's eyes are watering too now. She leans in and takes James in her arms and hugs him tight. "I'm so sorry," she says again.

It is James who ends the embrace. He pushes Hannah to arm's length, and smiles sadly. "Let's walk," he says, swiping at a tear on his cheek. "I'm tired of blubbing. Honest I am."

Beyond the bend, the path is blocked by a fallen tree, so James climbs on top and pulls Hannah up and then lowers her down the other side.

"When was it, James?" Hannah asks. "How long ago did this happen?"

"Two years last February," he says.

They continue to walk and then after a while, Hannah says, "Losing a child is the worst thing of all."

James nods. "You can just never get your mind around that one really."

"No."

"Is that what happened to you as well?" James asks.

"Kind of," Hannah says.

"I did wonder," he says.

"Because I was pregnant?"

"Yes. It looks like this is it," he adds, nodding at the way the riverbank they have been walking vanishes just ahead.

"There's a path up there," Hannah says, pointing higher up the bank.

"Let's do that then," James says.

"So how old was yours when . . ." James says once they have scrambled to the higher path.

"It was before she was born," Hannah says. "It was a miscarriage."

"God," James says. "I'm sorry. I didn't know."

"Well, no," Hannah says. She shrugs. "It was a long time ago now," she adds.

"Sure."

"It was the day after you left," Hannah tells him.

"Really?"

Hannah nods.

"It wasn't . . . you know . . . the stress of . . . all of that?"

Hannah shakes her head. "No," she says. "No that wasn't it. It was just one of those things, I think."

THIRTY-THREE

James V

I waited for Cliff to leave for work before I got up. As soon as I heard his car drive away, I dressed and went downstairs. My stomach was fluttering weirdly as I made two cups of tea and carried the one I had made for James upstairs.

I hesitated outside his bedroom for a moment – I had no idea what was going to happen but a compressed sensation of excitement seemed to fill me. Life seemed full of possibilities, both terrifying and exciting. I felt as though I was reading a novel and couldn't wait to see what would happen next. I knew we needed to talk about what had happened. I suspected that we might end up kissing again, and that with Cliff out we might even end up sleeping together. But I also knew that it might all simply be imaginary. James would perhaps apologise for his behaviour and I might feel nothing more than silly and the whole story could end right there and then. I was convinced that the second I saw him I would know, that the instant our eyes met, everything would be clear one way or another. There was only one possibility that I hadn't imagined.

I opened the door and was surprised to see that the room was lit – the curtains were still open.

I threw the door wide open and saw that James' bag was no longer on the floor. The bed had not been slept in.

I put the mug down on the dresser and ran downstairs, still hoping that I might find James in the lounge, watching TV and smiling up at me. When he wasn't, I walked nervously to the window and looked out. The Volvo was gone.

I sat on the sofa and tried to imagine a reasonable scenario in which James would have had to leave so early but I couldn't come up with one at all.

I went back upstairs to the bathroom where the lack of James' toothbrush finally convinced me that he had really gone, that he had left in the night.

I waited a full hour before I phoned Cliff at work. In a rehearsed voice, feigning casual interest, I said, "James seems to be missing this morning. Any idea where he is?"

"James has gone," Cliff replied, and I wasn't sure if he was repeating my phrase in surprise or confirming it.

"Do you know *where* he has gone, Cliff?"

"No, I have no idea," Cliff said.

"So do you know when he'll be back?"

"No," Cliff said.

"I just need to know how many people I'm catering for," I told him.

"Two by the sounds of it," Cliff said. "You and your fiancé."

"OK. See you this evening."

The house was entirely silent. I sat on the sofa and stared at the wall until a postman pushed something through the letterbox, making me jump. And then I started to cry.

I don't think I did anything that day. I made a sandwich at lunchtime and ate it and drank tea and stared into the middle distance. Occasionally I would look out at the street and hope and pray that the orange Volvo would reappear.

Dinner was not ready when Cliff got home that night. He was pretending that everything was normal, that everything was fine, but I could sense that he was lying – I could tell that he was angry.

He spoke about his day at work and I pretended to listen, and then he asked what was for dinner, and I silently went through to the kitchen where I boiled potatoes and sliced carrots and fried pork chops. I felt like a robot performing to a script. I felt as if the part of my brain that controlled emotion had been surgically removed.

I was just serving up when Cliff came into the kitchen. "Is that going to be long?" he asked. "I'm starving."

"It's ready," I said, moving my body so that he could witness that I was in the process of serving up.

"Good."

"So do you have *any* idea where James went?" I asked without looking up from the plates.

"None," Cliff said.

"But why would he leave like that?" I asked.

"I think you know the answer to that," Cliff said.

He picked his plate up and carried it through to the dining room and I followed.

We sat in silence, and began to eat.

"Presumably he'll be back," I said, aware that this was dangerous, but unable to stop myself. "I mean, our shed is full of all of his stuff."

Cliff put his knife and fork down. As he stared at me he started to redden. His head seemed to swell, and for a second, I became worried about him – I wondered if he was having a heart attack or a seizure or something. And then his arm twitched violently to the right, and his plate slid across the

232

table like an ice-hockey puck and flew into the wall. Without a word, he stood and left the room.

I sat for fifteen minutes looking at the stain on the wall before I got up, picked up the broken plate and the food and went through to the kitchen for a sponge.

Outside in the fading light of the garden I could see that Cliff was lighting a bonfire.

I finished cleaning the stain from the wall and then I took my coat and left the house. I went to the park, where I sat on a bench until the sky was dark. I still felt entirely numb.

When I got home, the bonfire was still burning. Cliff was sitting on a fold-up chair swigging at a can of beer, his face lit by the flames.

I brushed my teeth and went to bed, and pretended, an hour later when Cliff arrived, that I was asleep.

He undressed, got into bed, and then reached over to pull me towards him. "Kiss me," he said.

I told him that I wasn't in the mood.

"Kiss me," he said again, more insistently.

"No, Cliff. I'm tired," I said. "I just want to sleep."

Then he pulled me towards him and rolled on top of me. He did a lot of sports in those days – he was strong. And I don't think I fought either. I don't remember actually fighting.

But I did say "no". I did turn my head away. I did say, "Please, don't."

"You're my fiancée," he said, forcing his legs between mine. "You're *my fucking* fiancée."

And as he started to fuck me, I began to cry.

As soon as it was over – and because I was crying, he gave up quite quickly – I went to the spare room. Cliff didn't follow or try to stop me.

I locked the door behind me and crawled into the single bed. And there, in sheets that still smelt of James, the ceiling still flickering from the flames that outside were slowly consuming his every possession, I cried myself to sleep.

The next morning I awoke at dawn to find that the sheets were cold and clammy – there was blood on them. I lifted the covers and saw that there was blood everywhere, pints and pints of it, and knew that the worst thing possible was happening.

Paralysed by fear – I was convinced that if I moved it would make things worse – I screamed and then screamed again, specifically screaming for Cliff to come.

He had to kick in the door to reach me.

THIRTY-FOUR

Brisbane, 7th February 2010

Dear Cliff and Hannah,
Whatever shall I do now?
James.

HORROR ON THE BRISBANE
VALLEY HIGHWAY

Two victims were dragged yesterday (Tuesday) evening from the wreckage of a Holden Commodore on the Brisbane Valley Highway just north of Ipswich.

Judy Parker (32) of Brisbane was trying to push the car to the roadside after apparent engine troubles when the accident happened.

Witnesses, who had stopped just after the junction and were returning to help, watched horrified as a petrol tanker appeared over the brow of the hill and without braking ploughed into the Holden.

Judy Parker died on impact, Hannah Parker (6 years old) died later in Brisbane Central Intensive care.

The driver of the truck and the two witnesses, currently unidentified, are all currently being treated for shock.

Police and ambulance services were on the scene of the accident within twenty minutes, which Chief Constable Dower of the Brisbane police pointed out was extremely fast considering the location. "We have launched a full investigation into the cause of this horrific accident," he said.

The Brisbane Times sends its condolences to James Parker, husband and father of the deceased.

THIRTY-FIVE

By the time James and Hannah return, everyone except Jill is up. Luke and Aïsha are sitting on the edge of the pool with their feet in the water.

"Hannah, can you tell Luke the new mask we got is OK?" Aïsha asks as Hannah passes. "He won't use it."

"It is OK, because it's plastic," Hannah confirms. "So it can't smash. But you can't use it until the dressing comes off anyway. Did Dad change it yet this morning?"

Luke nods. "And I took my pill," he says.

"Good," Hannah says.

James crouches down beside the children and tests the water with one hand. "It's warm!" he says.

"It's heated," Aïsha tells him.

"I might go for a swim later, then," James says.

Hannah continues to the front of the house, leaving him talking to the children. As she reaches the front door she hears echoey voices drifting from within. Angry-sounding voices.

She pauses and holds her breath. ". . . tell her." Tristan is saying.

"It's none of your fucking business," Cliff replies.

"Fine!" Tristan says, and then a door somewhere slams.

Hannah does her best to fix a neutral expression and then heads indoors.

"Morning," Cliff says when she reaches the kitchen. "Where were you?"

"I couldn't sleep; I showed James the river."

"Nice," Cliff says, and she's not sure from his voice if he's being genuine or facetious. "How long's he staying anyway?" Cliff continues.

"I don't know," Hannah says. "Don't you like him being here?"

"I'd just rather we got back to normal."

"Normal," Hannah repeats. "Yes."

"Meaning?"

"Meaning nothing, Cliff. Anyway, what was all that about?"

"All what?" Cliff asks. His voice sounds neutral but Hannah notices that he averts his gaze. She sees that he busies himself with the coffee machine. It's hard to dissimulate after fifteen years of living together.

"You were arguing with Tristan," Hannah says.

"Oh *that*," Cliff says. "That was nothing."

"It didn't sound like nothing."

"Just politics," Cliff says. "You know what he's like."

Hannah stares at her husband's back and frowns. Because yes, she knows what Tristan's like, and she knows what Cliff is like, and two less political animals would be hard to find. "OK," she says quietly, then, "Well, I'm going to shower."

At breakfast Hannah sips her coffee and watches everyone eating. She tries to decode the multiple tensions within the household and is surprised to note that the hub seems to be Cliff, who is prickly with not only James but with Tristan as well. Even Jill, when she arrives, gets greeted with, "So you finally deigned to join us, huh?"

Jill just laughs this off. "I didn't know there was a schedule we had to stick to," she says.

By the time breakfast has been cleared it becomes apparent that the early morning mist is not clearing but intensifying. "Are they still predicting storms on the forecast?" Hannah asks Tristan.

He nods. "But they've been saying it for days," he says.

"Can we go somewhere today?" Luke asks. "Can we go to Nice like what Aïsha and Jill did?"

Hannah rolls her eyes. "When you can phrase that question correctly I might think about answering it," she says.

"Could we please go to Nice in the same way as what Aïsha and Jill have done yesterday?" Luke says, and everyone laughs at his convoluted attempt at correct grammar.

"Cliff?" Hannah says.

Cliff shrugs. "Why not?" he says. "I wouldn't mind a dip in the sea."

"How about we do it tomorrow?" Hannah says. "Then Luke can swim without worrying about the eye-patch."

"Sure," Cliff says.

"But what about today?" Luke says. "I'm bored."

"Why don't you get one of the board games out?" Hannah suggests.

Luke pulls a face.

"I could put the badminton net up," Cliff offers. "How would that be?"

Luke glances at Aïsha, who shrugs. He turns back to Cliff. "OK," he says.

★

Cliff ties the net between two trees and Hannah watches from the hammock as he thrashes first Luke, then Jill, and then Tristan and Aïsha at badminton.

She tries to imagine, for the first time, Cliff's feelings in all of this. He still assumes, she knows, that she and James slept together all those years ago. He has never said as much, but it was the only explanation she ever came up with for his overflowing anger at the time. Anger, which, judging from his badminton performance, is still very much alive today.

She thinks about the fact that they have never discussed those events, initially because she was so angry herself that she was happy for him to think the worst, and then later because it had become such a dangerous taboo that no one ever dared mention it again.

But watching Cliff swing angrily at the shuttlecock as he hammers James at badminton, she wonders if the time hasn't come to release the pressure from that particular boil. But how to have that conversation now?

By twelve, the sun has vanished entirely behind a dark bank of cloud. It still feels hot; in fact the oppressive nature of the weather makes it seem even hotter. Even the flies seem angry.

With Cliff now forcibly removed from the badminton tournament – no one wants to play him – Aïsha and Luke are playing doubles against Jill. Cliff is reading on the porch, James is floating in the pool and Tristan has gone to his room. Hannah levers herself from the hammock and heads indoors determined to interrogate him.

As she passes Cliff, he looks up from his novel and asks her if she would like him to perform Luke's midday change of eye-patch.

"No," she says. "It's fine. I'll do it."

"Luke!" she calls out. "Dressing!"

Luke – provoking protests from his badminton partner – drops his racket and runs to Hannah's side. "You're keen," she says.

"It's the last one, isn't it?" Luke says.

"You're right," Hannah confirms. "When you go to bed tonight, it's all over."

She leads Luke through to his bedroom, sits him on the bed and pulls back the dressing. "How's that now?" she asks.

Luke blinks repeatedly and then looks around the room. "Fine," he says.

"Your eyebrow has healed too," Hannah says, tracing it gently with her fingertip.

"I hope I get a scar," Luke says.

"I hope you don't," Hannah counters.

"So where's Tristan going?" Luke asks as Hannah fills the eye-bath with solution.

"I'm sorry?" Hannah asks, applying the plastic cup to his eye and tipping his head back.

"Tristan," Luke says, pointing behind her. "He looks like he's going out."

Hannah puts Luke's hand on the eye-bath to hold it in place and turns to look out of the window. Beyond it she can see Tristan loading suitcases into the boot of the Jeep. She stands and crosses to the window, then opens it and shouts, "Tristan!"

Tristan turns and smiles at her. He looks a little sad.

"Where are you going?"

He shrugs and mimes driving.

"OK, that's enough, Luke," Hannah says. "Just . . . just hang on a minute. I'll be back to finish it."

Hannah bursts from Luke's room and runs to the patio, past Cliff, and around to the front of the house, where she finds Tristan in the driver's seat of the Jeep, already fastening his seatbelt.

"Tris'!" she says breathlessly. "Wait!"

She grips the edge of his door and Tristan, whose hand had been on the ignition key, relaxes his grip and drops his hand to his lap. "I thought I'd managed the perfect getaway," he says.

"Where are you going?" Hannah asks.

"Sitges."

"In Spain?"

Tristan nods.

"For good?"

"For good?" Tristan repeats, looking puzzled.

"I mean, are you coming back here?"

Tristan shrugs. "Maybe. To pick Jill and Aïsha up. We haven't worked out the details yet."

"But why?" Hannah asks. "Has something happened?"

Tristan shakes his head. "Nah," he says. "Not really. You know what I'm like around hetties."

Hannah tuts. "I thought you were getting bored," she says. "I'm sorry it hasn't been too exciting."

"It's all a bit *too* exciting to be honest," Tristan says. "It's all getting a bit tense for me."

"The James thing?" Hannah says.

"Amongst other things."

"Have you fallen out with Jill?"

"No," Tristan laughs. "No, not at all. But she's busy with Aïsha, and when she isn't, she's busy with Pascal."

"Is that still going on?" Hannah asks.

"I'm just feeling a bit superfluous to requirements."

"And Cliff?" Hannah asks.

She sees a hint of a shadow cross Tristan's features before he masters them and morphs his expression to one of benign indifference. "Cliff?" he says.

"You were arguing about something," Hannah says. "I heard you. You're not leaving because of something Cliff said?"

He shakes his head. "Not at all," he says.

"OK," Hannah says, unconvinced. "So how is Jill getting home?"

"As I say, we haven't got that far yet. She's going to look at flights. But I might swing by and get them on my way home."

"OK," Hannah says, twisting her mouth sideways to express disappointment. "Well, I'm sorry to see you go."

"Sorry, babe," Tristan says. "I might be back in a few days. But I just need some time with my own people."

"Sure. Well, drive carefully," Hannah says, leaning in to kiss him on the cheek. "You're important to me, you know? So look after yourself." As she says it, she realises that this is true and feels strangely tearful at his departure.

Tristan blinks slowly. "Thanks," he says.

Hannah releases the door and steps back. She watches as Tristan starts the engine and performs a three-point turn on the driveway.

As he edges towards the gate, Hannah follows the car with the intention of closing the gate behind him, but then the car stops. "Hannah?" Tristan calls back.

When Hannah catches up with him, she leans in the passenger window. "Yes?"

"I think James is a really great guy," he says.

"Yes?"

"Yes. Just so you know."

Hannah frowns. "He's not gay, Tristan," she says. "I would put in a good word for you but . . ."

"I don't mean for me," Tristan says. "I mean for *you.*"

Hannah inhales sharply. She stares into Tristan's eyes, which seem to be filled with meaning, only she isn't sure exactly what that meaning is.

"I *care* about you," Tristan says, "that's all. And you deserve to be happy."

"OK," Hannah says, her brow creasing. "Thanks. I *think.*"

"James is a great guy. And he likes you a lot."

Hannah laughs lightly. "Thanks," she says, "but so is Cliff."

"Is he?" Tristan says.

Hannah laughs again. "Well, yes."

"Do you know that?"

"After fifteen years . . ." Hannah says, "yes, I think I know that."

"OK," Tristan says. "Well . . ."

Hannah turns to see Cliff rounding the corner of the house and heading towards them.

Tristan follows her gaze and says, "OK, well, I've said enough. See you in a few days maybe."

And then just as Cliff reaches her side, he engages first gear and, spitting gravel, drives away.

"Everything OK?" Cliff asks. "I had to finish Luke's dressing."

"Of course," Hannah says, patting his arm briefly, then turning towards the house. "Tristan's gone away for a few days, that's all."

"Right," Cliff says flatly.

They jointly close the gates and then Hannah heads to the pool, currently unoccupied. She removes her sandals and lowers her feet into the water. She reruns the conversation with Tristan through her mind over and over as she tries to decode any hidden meaning. It is, she decides, truly one of the strangest conversations she has ever had.

Less than five minutes later, Aïsha appears at her side. "It's Tris'," she says, brandishing her phone. "He wants to talk to you."

"Really?" Hannah asks, taking the phone.

"Don't drop it in the pool, will you," Aïsha shouts back as she runs away.

"No," Hannah tells her. "No, I won't."

She raises the phone to her ear. "Tris'?" she says.

"Yes."

"I'm glad you phoned, I've been trying to work out—"

"Listen, Hannah," he interrupts.

"Yes?"

"I shouldn't really say this, but . . ."

"Yes?"

"But I like you, so . . ."

"Right. Well I like you too, Tris'."

"So check his phone, OK?"

"Whose phone?"

"Cliff's."

"Check it?"

"Yes."

"Check it for what exactly?"

"Just check it," Tristan says. "Discreetly."

"Why? What's wrong with . . ." Hannah starts, but Tristan interrupts her.

"OK, gotta go," he says. "There's a police car and I'm driving."

The line goes dead, and so Hannah lowers the phone from her ear and stares at the screen until it turns black, and then she sits and stares at her own face reflected in it.

After a few minutes, she stands and returns to the patio, where Aïsha reclaims her property. "Has Tristan gone?" she asks.

"Yes," Hannah tells her. "Yes, he has."

"Bummer," Aïsha says.

"Yes," Hannah agrees. "It is a bummer. Where's Jill?"

"She's gone to shower. We got all sweaty playing badminton."

"Thanks," Hannah says, heading indoors.

Hannah goes to Jill's bedroom, where she sits and waits. The room feels cooler. Is it cooler, or is it just because it's painted blue?

"Ugh!" Jill exclaims as she steps into the room. "God, you gave me a fright."

"Sorry," Hannah says.

Jill pulls the towel around her middle a little tighter and skirts around the bed until she is out of Hannah's line of sight. "Don't turn around," she says, when Hannah starts to turn her head.

"I think I've seen what you look like before," Hannah laughs.

"Of course you have," Jill says. "But not for a few years."

Hannah raises one eyebrow and turns to face the dresser, where she realises she can watch Jill in the mirror just as well. "So what happened with Tris'?" she asks.

Jill drops the towel and finishes drying herself. "I don't think anything happened, did it? You know what he's like. He got bored. He's gone to Sitges to get some man-love."

"Why didn't you tell me?"

246

"Tell you what?" Jill says, stepping into a sexy pair of panties.

"That he was leaving."

"I thought he told you. Didn't he tell you? Didn't he say goodbye?"

"Yes, but . . ."

"Well then."

"But only because I caught him sneaking off," Hannah says.

Jill pulls on a pair of shorts and walks back around the bed. "There," she says.

"So you stopped waxing," Hannah says.

"You peeped."

"Erm, big mirror Jill," Hannah says, nodding at the dresser.

Jill rolls her eyes, and pulls a halter top from the drawer. "Yes, I stopped waxing."

"You used to have such a go at me about that," Hannah says.

"Well, we were young then," Jill says. "It was the fashion. Whereas letting it grow wild is all the rage now."

"Is it?"

Jill shrugs. "Apparently so. Shaven is the new unshaven or something. I mean, unshaven is, oh you know what I mean."

"So Tristan," Hannah prompts.

Jill starts to dry her hair with the towel. "What about him?"

"I still don't get why he left so suddenly."

"I told you," Jill says.

"He was bored then, that's it?"

Jill pauses and peeps out through the towel at Hannah. "I think so," she says. "He's always been like that."

"Like what?"

"I don't know. Independent," she says, starting to rub her hair again. "A free sprit. He does what he wants."

Hannah nods and glances out of the window. "I think it might actually rain today," she says after a moment.

"I think that might be a good thing," Jill says, now sitting down in front of the mirror. "This heat is horrible."

"I heard them arguing, you know," Hannah says. "Tris' and Cliff."

Jill fumbles in a drawer and retrieves her lipstick. "Really?" she asks, taking a seat at the dressing table and looking back at Hannah via the mirror. "What about?"

"I don't know," Hannah tells her. "I was hoping you'd be able to enlighten me."

"Sorry, babe," Jill says, stretching her lips, and swiping the lipstick expertly across them. "When was this?"

"This morning. Before you were up."

"I doubt that," Jill says. "I was up at four."

"Really?"

"Uh-huh. I went over to see Pascal."

Hannah nods. "So that's still current then?"

Jill shrugs. "Yeah, it's nice," she says. "I think it's just a holiday fling, but it's nice."

"But Aïsha's in with you. In here, I mean."

"Yes."

"So she knows."

"Well, of course she knows. She's not blind."

"And she doesn't mind?"

"Why would she mind?"

Hannah shrugs, but then realises that Jill isn't looking at her – she's applying mascara. "I don't know," she says.

"She quite likes him I think. Well, as much as anyone can like anyone who speaks a foreign language."

"When did they even meet?"

"When we went to Nice. We had dinner together," Jill says.

"Oh. He didn't stay with you though? In the hotel?"

"Of course he did," Jill says. "We all slept in the same bed."

"You said you weren't going to do that anymore," Hannah says. "You said you were going to stop trying to confuse me."

Jill looks back at her and rolls her eyes. "Of course he didn't. What do *you* think?"

Hannah frowns confusedly.

"What now?" Jill asks.

"I'm just trying to imagine dinner for three when one of you doesn't even speak English," Hannah says.

"We got an app for Aïsha's iPhone," Jill says. "It's really good. You type in a phrase and it translates it to French."

"So you spent the meal passing the phone back and forth."

"Something like that," Jill says. "But really. Aï's fine about it."

"She's actually been amazing since . . . you know . . . the accident. I don't know what you said to her, but it worked."

"She has," Jill says. "But you know it won't last. So just make the most of it."

"I will," Hannah says. "So have you *really* no idea what Tris' and Cliff were arguing about?"

Jill massages her brow with one finger, rubs her lips together, and then turns to face her sister. "Nope," she says. "So how do I look?"

"Hot," Hannah says.

"What shiny, sweaty hot?" Jill asks, turning back to the mirror.

"No. Hot as in sexy. Have you got a date or something?"

Jill shakes her head. "Not really," she says. "But we are going shopping."

"Again?"

"Food shopping," Jill says. "He's taking us to some big supermarket. Says it's cheaper."

"How domesticated."

"Isn't it?"

"So you really have absolutely no idea?" Hannah asks again.

"About Tris' and Cliff?" Jill says. "None. I can phone him if you want."

Hannah wrinkles her nose. "No," she says. "No, I just wanted to know if he'd said anything."

"I would guess it was about James if it was about anything," Jill offers.

"James?"

"Well, Cliff hasn't exactly been being nice to him, has he?"

"Hasn't he?"

"Well, no," Jill says. "I mean, there's not much brotherly love going on there, is there?"

"No," Hannah agrees with a sigh. "No, I suppose not."

"Still, I expect he's a bit jealous," Jill says. "Don't you think?"

Hannah laughs sourly. "God, they don't call you Sherlock for nothing, do they?"

"I wasn't aware they did," Jill says, spraying on perfume.

"It's a figure of speech."

"Yes," Jill says, "I got that."

"Do you know what aftershave Tris' uses? I really like it."

Jill shrugs. "Not sure. Ungaro something or other, I think."

"It's lovely. I thought I might get some for Cliff."

"Not sure he'd appreciate being made to smell like Tristan," Jill laughs.

"No," Hannah says. "Maybe not."

"So how *do* you feel about James this time around?"

"How do I *feel*?"

"Yes. I mean, he's pretty hunky, isn't he?"

Hannah laughs sadly. "Hunky," she repeats.

"Well, he is."

Hannah nods and fingers at the hem of her shorts. "You're right, of course," she admits. "He's very hunky. And he's friendly, and sweet and rather lovely."

"But . . ."

Hannah shrugs.

"He's still married?" Jill asks. "Is that it?"

"He's widowed," Hannah says. "His wife and child were killed in a car accident two years ago."

Jill pauses brushing her hair, then flashes the whites of her eyes at her sister. "God, that's awful," she says.

"I know."

"And you're not even a bit tempted to, you know . . ."

Hannah pulls a face indicating incomprehension.

"To . . . *console* him?" Jill says.

Hannah laughs. "I know you don't really get the whole concept of monogamy, Jill, but I'm *married*."

"So you are then?" Jill says, poker faced. "Tempted, that is."

"I'm married to Cliff," Hannah says pedantically.

"Yes, to *Cliff*," Jill says, pulling a face.

"God, you're terrible," Hannah says. "You're like . . . like some kind of little devil sitting on my shoulder."

Jill smiles wickedly. "I know," she says. "I can't help it."

When Jill and Hannah step outside, they find Pascal sitting with Cliff, waiting, silently. He is wearing normal clothes – white shorts and a blue short-sleeved shirt – and looks relaxed and boyish. "Bonjour," he says, rising to embrace both Jill and Hannah.

"Tout va bien avec la maison ? Avec la piscine ?" he asks.

"I'm sorry," Hannah says. "I don't speak any French."

"I think he wants to know if the house and pool are OK," Aïsha says.

Hannah raises one eyebrow and shoots an astonished look at her.

"He's told me some words," she says. "Piscine is pool and maison is house."

"Very impressive," Hannah says. "Oui. Bien. Merci," she answers. "I'm afraid that's about the limit of my French."

THIRTY-SIX

Once they have cobbled together a shopping list and Hannah has given Jill the code for her Visa card, Jill and Pascal climb into the little red Fiat and drive away.

With James in the bathroom and Luke and Aïsha arguing about points through the badminton net, Hannah finds herself alone on the patio with Cliff, seemingly for the first time in days.

"She seems happy," Hannah says.

"Jill? Or Aïsha?"

"Both. Aïsha's being amazing at the moment. Long may it last. But I meant Jill. I think she really likes that Pascal guy."

"Aïsha's probably up to something, and Jill likes anything in trousers," Cliff says.

"A little unfair," Hannah says. "He seems OK."

"Sorry. Yes. He seems nice enough."

"Not that we'd know really."

Cliff shrugs. "He's smiley. He's taking her shopping . . ."

"It's a shame the kids couldn't go with them. But we're taking them to Nice tomorrow, right?"

"That's what we said. I hope the weather will be OK."

"It looks stormy over there," Hannah says, pointing at the horizon, where the sky is an even darker shade of grey.

"And it's coming this way," Cliff says. "Anyway, they could have taken the kids, couldn't they? I expect they just didn't fancy going shopping."

"No, they wanted to go," Hannah explains, "but the Fiat only has two seats. It's a commercial vehicle."

"Oh," Cliff says. "I didn't know. They should have taken ours. It's insured for any driver."

"Well . . ." Hannah says. "They seem happy enough playing badminton for now. Well, arguing about badminton. I wish Tristan had stayed though."

"No more haute cuisine," Cliff says.

"No," Hannah agrees. "No, we're back to Hannah-cuisine now."

"I didn't mean . . ." Cliff says. "That's not what I meant."

"I know. But you're right. I prefer it when Tristan's cooking too." Hannah clears her throat, and then adopting a casual tone of voice, asks, "So what did you two argue about?"

"With Tristan?"

"Yes."

"Nothing."

"Nothing?"

"It's of no importance," Cliff says, picking up his novel from the table and opening it.

"To you maybe. But Tristan has gone."

Cliff sighs and closes the book again. "What did he tell you?"

"Nothing," Hannah says. "But I have eyes to see. And ears to hear. I'm not totally blind to what's going on around me, you know."

Cliff snorts dismissively.

"What?"

"Nothing," he says.

"No, go on, what?"

"Well, you're not the only one," Cliff says.

"The only one who . . . ?" Hannah ends the phrase with a tiny questioning upward nod of the chin.

"The only one with eyes to see," Cliff says.

"OK, that's enough. You've been weird for days. Please stop being cryptic. You know how I hate it."

"I just wish Tris' had taken James with him," Cliff says.

Hannah is momentarily aware that Cliff has dodged the subject of his argument with Tristan by mentioning James, but then her frustration at his relationship with his brother takes over and she forgets. "He's your brother, Cliff," she points out.

"Really? Gosh! Hold the front page," Cliff says.

"You haven't seen him for fifteen years. You could at least try to be nice to him. Try to get to know him."

"I *do* know him," Cliff says. "That's the problem."

"I don't get you two," Hannah says. "You have one brother. You pretend he's dead for fifteen years. And when he turns up . . ."

"When he turns up, he's the same selfish bastard he always was."

"I haven't seen any selfishness. I haven't seen any sign of that at all."

"No, you don't see anything, Hannah," Cliff says. "But James is the same as he always was. This is what he does."

"This?"

"This . . ." Cliff says, gesturing in an all-encompassing manner. "He comes in; he takes over; he spoils everything; and then he fucks off leaving the wreckage behind him."

"What has he taken over? What has he spoilt? You're not making any sense at all."

Cliff snorts again. "I see the way you two look at each other," he says.

So there it is out in the open. Hannah inhales sharply. "And what way is that, Cliff?" she asks.

"You know full well."

"You're being ridiculous," Hannah says, simultaneously angry, guilty and embarrassed.

"You know what's ridiculous?" Cliff says. "What's ridiculous is having your brother come spoil your party even now. It's having your brother *still* trying to steal your stuff at forty-two."

"Your *stuff*?" Hannah says in disgust. "Your *stuff*?"

"It's a figure of speech," Cliff says.

"When you say *your stuff*, do you mean me?" Hannah asks, wiping her forehead, now damp with perspiration.

"No, it's just what he always did," Cliff says, "when we were kids."

"I am not your *stuff*," Hannah says. "How dare you!"

"That's not what I meant, Hannah, and you know it."

"It's exactly what you meant. *And I know it*. How dare you! I'm your wife, Cliff. Your *wife*. Do you know what that means? It mea—"

"It clearly doesn't mean much to James," Cliff interrupts.

"Is that so?" – a voice from the doorway. They both turn to see James standing in the shadows. He takes an extra step forwards onto the doorstep.

"Oh, just . . . go away, James," Cliff says.

"Go away?"

"Yes, just *fuck off*, will you," Cliff says.

"Oh, fuck off, is it?" James repeats, laughter in his voice. "Nice."

"Yes," Cliff says. "Fuck off back to Australia or wherever it is you hide out when you're not trying to steal my wife."

James stares at Cliff, his amusement fading and being replaced by an expression of eyebrow-raised shock. "Maybe I will," he says, quietly. "Maybe that's the best thing here."

As he heads back into the house, Hannah stands. "Really, Cliff! For God's sake, what is wrong with you?"

Hannah heads inside in pursuit of James. "James? James!" She finds him in Aïsha's room stuffing clothes into his rucksack.

"You don't have to leave, James," she says. "Don't listen to him."

James looks up. His face has turned pink.

"He's just . . ." Hannah says.

"An asshole?" James offers.

"No, don't say that."

"Well, he's *what*, Hannah?"

"I don't know. He's jealous," Hannah says.

James laughs bitterly.

"Don't leave."

James sighs and releases the handle of his bag. "I don't know, Hannah," he says. "What's the point?"

"The point?"

"I just seem to be causing a load of shit for everyone. Isn't it better if I go?"

Hannah shakes her head. "No," she says. "No, I don't think it is. If you leave, this will never get sorted out."

James sighs deeply.

"Please?" Hannah says.

James shrugs. "You're sure you don't want me to leave?"

"It's the last thing I want," Hannah says.

James nods, pushes the bag from the bed to the floor and then sits on the edge of the bed. "You need to talk to him then,

Hannah," he says. "You need to calm him down. Because I can't."

"I'll try," Hannah says running a hand through her hair. "Just give us a little space and I'll try."

She heads to the bathroom and washes her face in cold water, then pats it dry and heads back outside. The time has come, she decides. She will tell Cliff that she never did sleep with James. Her failure to do so has been shameful, she now realises. It's been the cause of an unbridgeable gap between her husband and his only surviving family, and it's time to fix it.

She pauses in the kitchen to drink a glass of water, and then, steeling herself for the next round, heads back out to the patio, but Cliff is no longer there.

She walks around the grounds, past the exit to the track, past the pool, past the Mégane, still parked. Finally when she reaches the hammock, she finds Luke and Aïsha lying side by side playing with their phones. "Any idea where Dad is?" she asks Luke.

"He went for a walk, I think."

"Are you two OK?"

"We're on Facebook," Luke says. "I'm letting Aïsha use my phone. But only for a bit."

"That's nice," Hannah says, absent-mindedly. As she carries on back towards the porch, she sees Aïsha nudge Luke sharply but it only barely registers, and she doesn't even stop to wonder why. She has other things on her mind.

Back in the house, she finds James in the kitchen opening a beer. Seeing her arrive, he offers her the can. "Beer?" he says.

Hannah nods and takes the can from his grasp.

"Well?" James asks, opening the door and reaching for another one.

"I don't know where he is," Hannah says. "He's gone for a walk, apparently."

"Right," James says.

Hannah sips at her beer and then rubs the cold can against her forehead. "He still thinks we slept together," she says out of nowhere. "That's the thing."

"I'm sorry?" James says.

"Cliff. He thinks we slept together. Fifteen years ago."

"Oh," James says. "Why does he think that?"

Hannah shrugs. "I never explained. It's my fault. I'm so sorry."

James shakes his head and swigs at his beer. "Can I ask why?" he asks. "Can I ask *why* you didn't explain?"

"I was angry," Hannah says. "It's stupid, I know. But he assumed that we had slept together, and that hurt me. So I let him carry on thinking it. And then he was . . ." She closes her eyes briefly at the almost physical pain the memory still brings, then continues, "He was so awful to me after you left. I really hated him for a while."

"Wow," James says.

"And by the time that was over, well, it seemed better not to mention it. I'm so sorry," Hannah says. "This is all my fault, isn't it?"

James tips his head sideways. "Well, not entirely," he says. "I mean, I guess I did try to steal you. He was right about that at least."

"God, you heard all of that?"

James blinks and nods slowly. "And I'm sorry about that too," he says. "It was wrong of me. It was clearly a mistake."

"What was a mistake?"

"Trying to steal my brother's fiancée," James says.

259

Hannah laughs sourly. "Well, you didn't try very hard," she says.

"I thought I made a pretty good stab at it," James says. "But you were never going to leave Cliff, let's face it."

Hannah shakes her head. "It's weird," she says. "It all feels like it was yesterday."

"It does," James agrees.

For five minutes they stand in silence, each lost in memories, and then Hannah asks, "Why *did* you leave?"

"Why did I leave?" James repeats.

"Yes. Why did you vanish in the middle of the night like that?"

James clenches his teeth and stares into the middle distance, remembering, then replies, "Cliff told me to go, didn't he."

"He *told* you to go."

James nods. "Uh-huh."

Hannah takes a swig of beer. "I still don't understand though," she says. "I mean, you never did what Cliff told you to do before. Why the sudden . . . I don't know . . . obedience?"

"He convinced me, I guess," James says. "He said you weren't gonna leave him and that all I was doing was making everyone crazy. He said he'd kill me if I stayed, and I kind of believed that a bit too. I was a kid. He was my big brother. But mainly, I thought he was right. I didn't reckon I had much choice but to bugger off."

"God, I wish you hadn't," Hannah says, screwing up her face in an attempt at holding back an unexpected batch of tears.

"You wish I hadn't left?"

"Yes."

"What would it have changed if I had stayed?" James asks. "Honestly?"

"Everything. It would have changed everything."

"You were pregnant," James points out. "You told me your-self, remember? You were with Cliff and you were pregnant, and you were about to get married."

"Not by the next day, I wasn't. By the next day I had lost the baby, and I hated Cliff and the marriage was cancelled."

"It was cancelled?"

"We cancelled everything. We had to. I had lost a lot of blood. I was in hospital for a week. I couldn't have got married even if I had wanted to. And I didn't."

"I didn't know," James says. "I'm sorry."

"I kept thinking you'd come back, you know," Hannah says. "For years I thought you'd come back. How stupid is that?"

James pinches his nose as if to prevent a sneeze and then swings his head from side to side to stretch his neck. "So what happened after?" he asks eventually.

"After?"

James nods. "I mean, you got married in the end. Well, I assume you did, anyway."

"We broke up for a while. Three months, I think it was. I stayed with Jill. They had a spare room in her student house, so I camped there. It was miserable. I remember we ate beans and rice every day to save money. And then we got back together. Cliff was pretty tenacious. But even then I thought you'd reappear. For ages, I thought you'd just turn up on the doorstep one day and whisk me away. And then Cliff told me you had died, so . . ."

James' forehead creases. "He *what*?" he whistles.

"He said you were dead. I thought maybe you knew about that."

James shakes his head rapidly from side to side as if to

dislodge this crazy idea. He opens his mouth to speak, but then gives up trying to find the right words and closes it again.

"A motorbike accident, he said. In India," Hannah explains.

James raises one eyebrow. "Well, at least it's exotic," he says.

"Yes."

James shakes his head slowly. "I can hardly believe that," he says.

"It's true. So I gave up hope. And things were OK with Cliff by then, so . . ."

"So you got married after all."

"We lived together for a few more years. I had kind of gone off the idea of marriage. But then I got pregnant with Luke. So . . ."

"So?"

"So it seemed the right thing to do."

"I see."

"So who knows what might have happened if you hadn't left. Or if you had come back."

"I did, you know," James says. "Just once. But I did come back."

"God, did you? When?"

"The day after the wedding. Well, the day after the wedding was supposed to be. I sat outside all day watching the house. I just wanted to see you again. I wanted to congratulate you if you'd got married, or . . ."

"Or . . ."

James shrugs. "I didn't know really."

"The day after the wedding, you say? The Sunday then?"

James nods.

"I was still in hospital then."

James nods again. "If only I had known."

"What would you have done if you had known?"

"I don't know," James says. "But I was so in love with you. I was totally sold on you."

"Were you really?" Hannah asks.

"I was."

"Really?" Hannah asks. "Or was it just . . . I don't know . . . infatuation or something?"

"I think so," James says. "I think it was real."

"Yes, I think it was too," Hannah says, and unable to hold the tears back any longer, her face collapses.

"Here," James says, putting down his beer can and crossing the kitchen towards her. "Come here."

Hannah lets him take her in his arms, then lays her head on his shoulder, and cries. Her angst is so powerful that she can hardly breathe. It feels the same as it did the last time James held her in his arms, fifteen years ago. A mixture of misery at the impossibility of the situation, and yet, even here, even now, a stirring of desire.

When she opens her eyes again she sees that Cliff has returned and is standing outside on the patio, just beyond the open window. He is staring at them – his own eyes red and watery.

She pats James' back, then, when he fails to understand, she tries to push him away. "Let me go," she whispers. "Cliff's back."

"I'm sorry?" James says, pushing back so that he can see her face.

"She said to let her go," Cliff says loudly, his voice almost a shout. "She said her husband's back."

By the time they have separated, Cliff is in the kitchen. "Right, that's enough," he says, seizing James' forearm. "Now, you *really* need to go."

"Cliff, please," Hannah says, stepping towards the two men.

Cliff raises his left arm, barring her path, and even pushes her away with it.

"Cliff!" Hannah protests. "What's got into you? You've got this all wrong, you know."

James prises Cliff's hand from his arm. "Fuck off, Cliff," James says. "You don't get to tell me what to do."

"Actually, I do," Cliff says. "Hannah's my wife. And you're leaving."

"I'll leave when *Hannah* tells me to leave," James says.

"I swear that if you don't butt out of my life, I will fucking punch you out of it," Cliff says quietly.

Hannah watches her husband in disbelief. She has virtually never heard Cliff swear. She has certainly never seen him threaten anyone with physical violence. "Cliff?" she protests.

"Only you can't, mate, can you!" James says, his tone goading. "That's what I didn't realise last time. You may be my big brother, but you're not so big after all, are you, mate? You couldn't punch out a fucking opossum."

Hannah sees Cliff squaring his shoulders as if preparing to carry out his threat, which, faced with James' stature, would be a terrifying and futile exercise. "Please, STOP THIS!" she cries, managing now to step between the two men. "Stop behaving like idiots."

"He has to go," Cliff says, pointing over her shoulder. "Tell him he has to go!"

"No!" Hannah says. "No, I won't. I want you two to sort this out once and for all. But like adults, not like this."

"TELL HIM TO GO!" Cliff says, lunging at James over her shoulder.

"Don't you fucking talk to her like that," James says. "Or I'll bloody punch you out myself."

"People! PEOPLE! STOP!" Jill has returned and is standing in the doorway with one hand on Luke's shoulder. The boy looks pale and terrified. He looks about to burst into tears. "It's OK, Luke," Jill says, then, "Looks like it's a good job I got back, though."

At the sight of Luke, everyone freezes. Hannah steps from between the two men and crouches down in front of him. "We're just having a bit of an argument," Hannah tells him, her voice wobbling strangely. "It's just the same as you do with Aïsha sometimes, sweetheart. But don't worry. It'll all be fine in the end."

"Just don't anybody say a word until I've got these two out of the way," Jill says.

As she leads Luke back outside and indicates through a mixture of mime, English and French that Pascal should take the children down to the river, Cliff and James glower at each other. Hannah pours herself a glass of water and Cliff follows suit.

When she returns, Jill says, "Really! What were you thinking?"

"I'm sorry," Hannah says, touching the bridge of her nose. "Things got a bit out of hand."

"He still needs to fuck off," Cliff says.

"Cliff, just shut up for a minute, will you?" Jill says acidly. "Actually, I'll tell you what. Just go outside for a bit, will you? I need to talk to Hannah."

"Don't tell me what to do," Cliff says.

"Cliff?" Hannah pleads. "Please? Just for a minute."

"This is bullshit," Cliff says, but he obeys all the same.

"You, stay here," Jill says to James. "If you move, I'll slap you myself." Then to Hannah, she says, "Come."

Once she has led Hannah to her bedroom and shut the door, she asks, "So what the hell is happening here, Han'?"

Hannah shakes her head dolefully. "I don't know, Jill," she says.

"It's my fault for inviting him," Jill says. "Shall I tell him to leave? That would be best, wouldn't it?"

Hannah shakes her head. "I don't want him to leave," she says. "I want this all sorted out. This has all gone on for too long anyway."

Jill nods seriously, then sighs. "But that's not all, is it?" she says. "That's not the only reason you don't want him to leave."

"I don't know," Hannah says again.

"OK, well," Jill says, visibly switching into a rarely seen practicality mode. "This place is turning into a war-zone, and it's no good for the kids."

"No. You're right."

"So let me take them to the seaside for the day. We could even stay the night. How does that sound?"

"I guess," Hannah says.

"We might need you to take us to the station or something," Jill says. "Pascal's old banger only has two seats."

"You can take the Renault," Hannah says. "Cliff already said that it's fine. But you will look after them properly, won't you?"

"What do you mean?"

"I mean, no dope. No masks. No . . ."

"Hannah! How many times have I looked after Luke?"

"Lots, I know, but . . ."

"So, he'll be fine. You know he will."

"Sure."

266

"I won't even drink, how's that?"

"Well, if you're driving, you had better not."

"Are you sure it's OK for us to take the Renault?"

"Absolutely."

"OK, well, we'll do that then. That way you'll have the whole place to fight in. And you'll get it sorted by tomorrow, by the time we get back, OK?"

"I will."

"OK, well, we had better get the shopping in before the frozen stuff melts."

"Sure," Hannah says.

"I might need to keep your card," Jill says. "Mine got refused at the supermarket."

"Sure," Hannah says, with a wave of one hand. "Whatever."

When Hannah opens the bedroom door, she can hear that Cliff and James have already resumed hostilities. Followed by Jill, she runs down the corridor to the lounge where Cliff is prodding James with his forefinger.

"Nothing ever changes with you, does it?" he is saying. "That's the fucking problem. That's why I . . ."

Hannah pushes her way between the two men again. "Just STOP THIS!" she shrieks, pushing them apart. "You're like bloody children."

"You're a bloody psycho, mate, that's your problem," James tells Cliff.

"You come with me," Jill says, grabbing James' arm, and dragging him reluctantly outside.

"He has to go, Han'," Cliff says. "You have to tell him to go."

"Listen," Hannah says. "We need to get the shopping in and . . ."

"Shopping? Are you crazy?" Cliff says. "I don't give a shit about the shopping."

"We need to get the shopping in . . ." Hannah repeats. "And then Jill and Pascal are taking the kids off to the beach so that we can sort this out like adults. And maybe at the end of that James will have to leave."

"He will."

"Maybe. But I want to try. I want to at least *try* to get this sorted."

"He *is* leaving," Cliff says.

"Well, maybe he is. But until the kids are out of the way, please, *please*, just stay out of each other's way."

"How?" Cliff says. "How the fuck am I supposed to do that?"

Hannah rolls her eyes. "Please stop behaving like a ten-year-old," she says. "Just go for a walk, or go to the bedroom or read a bloody book for half an hour."

Cliff groans, then heads back towards the bedroom. "I'll tell you how this ends," he says loudly, as he walks away. "This ends with my arse-hole of a brother leaving. And it ends with him never coming back."

THIRTY-SEVEN

Hannah climbs over the fence and then heads down the track. Hearing the sounds of children coming from the valley, she heads down towards the stream, climbs down the staircase, then follows the flowing water to the first bend, whereupon Jill comes into view.

Luke, Aïsha and Pascal are all paddling; Jill is sitting on a large flat rock watching them.

"God, you haven't left them alone, have you?" Jill asks as Hannah approaches. "They'll knock seven shades of shit out of each other, won't they?"

Hannah shrugs and squeezes onto the rock next to her sister. "Let them," she says. "I'm beyond caring."

"You don't mean that," Jill says.

"You're right," Hannah says. "I don't. But I do wish they'd just behave like adults. Anyway . . ."

"Anyway?"

"I thought you were all off to Nice."

"We are in a bit. But it's nice down here, and the kids are having fun. Luke was really upset before, so this is good."

"The water's freezing!" Luke shouts. "Come try."

"No, I'll take your word for it," Hannah calls back.

"I was wondering if we can take Luke's patch off," Jill says. "It's supposed to come off today anyway, right?"

Hannah nods. "I'll do it when we get back."

"Are you sure this is the right thing?" Jill asks. "I don't need to worry about you, do I?"

Hannah shakes her head. "No, you're right. Get the kids out of the way for a bit. It's perfect. I'm quite tempted to come myself. Shall I go back and pack an overnight bag for Luke?"

"I guess," Jill says. "Actually, I'll come with you and do ours."

Aïsha, who has just splashed up to join them, asks, "Where are we going?"

"To Nice," Jill says.

"Again?"

"Yes. But we're taking Luke this time as well."

"We're not staying in that hotel again, are we?"

"No, I think we might try to find somewhere nicer," Jill says.

"There were these really gross insects in the bathroom," Aïsha tells Hannah.

"Cockroaches," Jill informs her. "There were only two, but all the same . . ."

"Yuck," Hannah comments. "Well, definitely don't go there again."

An hour later, the car has been loaded and Cliff's keys handed over. Jill wishes Hannah luck, and drives the loaded Renault away.

Hannah closes the gate slowly. She's in no hurry to return to the drama of the house.

She heads around the back and crouches to dip her fingers in the pool. She watches the ripples emanating from her hand and then, seeing what she thinks is a raindrop, glances up at the leaden grey sky. But though the air feels almost wet with humidity, it's still not raining – it must have been an insect hitting the water, she decides.

She walks to the rear of the house, past the track once again, past the lavender – she picks a sprig – and finally returns to the porch where she expects to find James.

Seeing that he is absent, she heads indoors to Aïsha's room, but when she reaches the door she changes her mind and decides to tackle Cliff first.

When she enters their bedroom, she finds Cliff sitting on the bed. "You're not reading," she says – an attempt at normality.

"I don't want to read," Cliff says.

"No," Hannah says. "No, I'm sure."

She circles the bed and then perches on the edge of it next to her husband. "Look," she says. "I know that this is all difficult still, but there's something you need to know."

Cliff nods. "Go on," he says.

Hannah sighs. "You need to know that I never slept with James," she says.

Cliff scrunches up his features. "What?" he asks.

"We never slept together," Hannah says again. "It never happened."

"Why . . ." Cliff says.

"Why?"

"Yes, why are you even saying that to me?"

"Because I know that you think we did," Hannah says. "But we didn't."

Cliff shakes his head, half in confusion, half in disgust. "I *know* you didn't," he says. "But you wanted to."

"Oh," Hannah says, a little deflated that her great problem-solving revelation has turned out to be entirely ineffective.

"Jesus," Cliff says, rubbing his brow.

"What?"

"If you're not even going to deny it . . ."

"Deny what?"

"That you wanted to," Cliff says.

Hannah laughs falsely, and stands. She crosses to the window and looks outside. "I don't even remember," she lies. "It was so long ago."

"And now?" Cliff says, sliding off the bed and following her to the window.

"Now?" Hannah asks, glancing at him and then returning her gaze to the olive tree outside. It's covered in tiny green fruits. She hadn't noticed before.

"Yes, now," Cliff says sharply.

"I like James," Hannah says. "I like him a lot. But the question of whether I want to sleep with him doesn't even come up because I'm married to you."

Cliff snorts. "So I'll take that as a 'yes', then, shall I?"

Hannah glances at Cliff again. "Oh, take it how you want, Cliff," she says. "I'm getting to the point where . . ."

"I should have let him stay," Cliff says, cutting her off and taking her arm now in an attempt to make her look him in the eye. "I should have let him have what he wanted fifteen years ago."

"Well, thanks," Hannah says, furious at the implication that this was somehow an option within Cliff's control, but unable to find a way to put that specific outrage into words.

"He would have had his fun and thrown you away like a used tissue," Cliff says.

Hannah shakes her head. "How *foul* you are when you want to be."

"That's all he wanted," Cliff says. "It's still all he wants. It's just because you're mine, you know."

"I'm not *yours*," Hannah says even though she realises that

272

it's open to misinterpretation and risky. "And stop squeezing my arm! You're hurting me," she adds, as she attempts to prise his fingers from her.

"That's what you just don't get about James," Cliff says. "You like the idea that James thinks you're special. But he doesn't. James isn't interested in you. The only thing he ever liked about you was that you were mine."

Hannah shakes her head. Some line is being crossed here, and she's beginning to doubt if they will ever find their way back. She turns her body to face Cliff now. "That's enough," she says. "You're just going to end up saying things that you'll regret because you're angry. And get your hands . . . off . . . me." She shakes him free. "And stop talking about me as if I'm one of your things."

"Why don't you go and fuck him now?" Cliff says.

Hannah stares deep into her husband's enraged eyes and doesn't recognise him at all. "God, have you been drinking? Is that it?"

"No, seriously," Cliff continues. "Why don't you just go and get it out of your system?"

"How dare you!" Hannah spits.

She turns and starts to walk towards the bedroom door, but Cliff follows her and grabs her arm again, spinning her around and pushing her back against the door. "Where are you going?" Cliff asks. "To *James*?"

His face is too close to hers now. In this instant, she hates him as much as she ever has – as much as she hated him that night fifteen years ago in fact. *Everything's the same*, she thinks. *We've come full circle, and we're back here again. Everything's exactly the same.*

"What's the matter, Hannah?" Cliff asks, his voice now a

revolting sneer. "Married life getting you down? Think you want a bit of variety? I wonder if he's still interested. You have aged a bit, put on a bit of weight . . . but maybe . . ."

"I can't deal with you when you're like this," Hannah says. "Let me go."

"Why should I?" Cliff says. "You're my wife, aren't you? Surely this is within my marital rights?"

"You're hurting me again," Hannah says, her voice now trembling as the first inklings of physical fear hit her. "Get off me!"

"Let her go, Cliff." James has appeared at the window and is looking in at them.

"And here he is," Cliff says. "The knight in fucking armour to the rescue."

"Let her go," James says again, his voice still calm.

"Fuck off, James," Cliff says. "This is between me and Hannah."

"Fuck off?" James says. He sounds amused. "Again?"

"You're hurting me, Cliff," Hannah says again. "Will you just stop . . ."

"Tell him to leave," Cliff says, "and I'll let you go. Tell him to fuck off."

Hannah thinks about this for a second, then decides that it's worth saying anything right now to end this crazed conflict. "Leave," she says. "Cliff's right. Please, just go."

But it's too late, because James is climbing through the window, and Cliff is already releasing her and lurching towards him.

Hannah watches in horror as Cliff scrambles over the bed and throws a punch at James, who, still off-balance from climbing in, stumbles against the bed, loses his balance, and falls to the ground.

"Stop!" Hannah screams. "Please, Cliff, stop!"

He throws himself on top of James, now sprawled on the floor, and lands a single punch to the side of James' face before his brother manages to seize both of his hands.

"Ha!" James laughs, as he rolls Cliff onto his back and pins him to the ground. He looks totally un-traumatised by the whole thing, thoroughly amused about it all.

"You're a worm, James," Cliff says, dominated yet un-cowed by his brother's physical strength. "You're a fucking worm, and you always were."

"Not so tough now, are we, mate?" James says.

"It was always the same," Cliff spits. "Anything I had, you stole. When we were kids, it was toys. When we were teenagers it was my records. Every fucking thing I ever had . . . Well, you can't have my wife, you cunt."

"Oh, shut the fuck up, Cliff," James says, now managing to pin down both of Cliff's arms with a single hand. "You sound like a fucking three-year-old."

"So, Hannah," James asks, "what do you want me to do with this . . ." His voice trails off as he looks up, because he sees that Hannah has gone. "Hannah!" he shouts. "Hannah? Shit!"

He slaps Cliff hard across the cheek. "That's for being a wimp," he says, and then, a little unsettled by the fact that Cliff now starts to cry, he releases him and stands. "Hannah?" he shouts. "HANNAH!"

THIRTY-EIGHT

Hannah opens the gate, closes it quietly behind her, then runs away from the house as fast as her legs will carry her. She doesn't know where she is going and she doesn't have a plan. Pure instinct is driving her actions – she's scared and she *needs* to escape. If she can just get to the corner, she thinks, glancing back, if she can just get out of sight, then no one will know where she is.

As she reaches the broken street lamp, she notices a track to her left leading into the forest, so with one last glance back at the house, she ducks down it and out of sight.

Doubled up, she pauses to catch her breath. Sweat is dripping into her eyes, making them sting. Her T-shirt is clinging to her chest. The stormy heat of the day is unbearable.

When her heart has slowed, she starts to stride on into the trees, a cloud of flies buzzing irritatingly around her. The stupid men can beat shit out of each other for all she cares. She has had it with them.

As the neighbours' houses vanish into the greenery behind her, her fear turns to anger, and then as this too wanes, tears start to flow instead. After another twenty yards, her vision is so blurred that she is stumbling, so when she reaches a clearing, she pauses and sits on the trunk of a massive fallen tree.

Her thoughts are a swirling mess. She is thinking about

seeing the two brothers together fighting like children. She is thinking about the fact that this fight has – and, in a way, Cliff is right about this – nothing to do with her. It really is all about sibling rivalry. It's all a childhood ritual played out because that's what these two brothers do when they're together.

From feeling special and loved by both men, she has gone, in a day, to feeling unloved by either of them, and to feeling stupid for having been duped in the first place. Cliff's remarks have hurt her so badly she feels – even though experience tells her that she is probably being over-dramatic – that he may never claw his way back from them. And James? As far as James is concerned, she fears that Cliff may be right. The way he sat on him, the way he pinned him to the ground and gloated about it – maybe it *was* all about competition, about domination, about possession. Maybe she has wasted her life dreaming about something that was never entirely real. And maybe, yes, he *would* have used her and tossed her away like a used handkerchief once he had demonstrated his superiority over his brother.

A second wave of tears hits Hannah, and she lets it happen, lets the tears slide unhindered down her cheeks. It feels like release, and there's no one here to see anyway.

She has had this thing stuck deep within her for years, she realises, a doubt, a fear, pushed aside and squashed down, and compressed until it was an almost unnoticeable lump of darkness, a tiny manageable chunk of coal squashed deep within her chest. It began, she remembers, even before James came on the scene. It began because even compared with selfish, impossible Ben, life with Cliff seemed dull, and that made her doubt her choices, that always made her wonder.

James was a brief gust of oxygen that made that coal burn bright, and for a moment, for those few hours he was in the house all those years ago, she had been able to see clearly that she was making a mistake, that she was *living* a mistake, and that this was not how her life was meant to be. And even after James had left, that doubt had stayed, even after he had "died" it was there, ever present, because during those few hours she had spent with him, she had learned that true love really did exist, that passion and almost irresistible sexual attraction were real things, not fiction, and that this being the case, the train she was on – to Surrey, and marriage, and motherhood and a part-time job in a school – was the *wrong* train to the wrong destination.

But she never found the courage to get off. That was her crime. She had never had the courage to face that doubt. Because what she had felt for James had seemed so rare, so unlikely – so *unreasonable* – that she feared that if she chose it, she would end up with nothing. Had he come back for her she would have perhaps had the courage to jump carriages. But he didn't come back, so she squashed it down, became expert at compressing, at containing, at dousing that doubt, and ultimately became so expert that she managed, for the most part, to pretend that it didn't exist at all.

And now, today, it has expanded again. It has exploded and tainted everything, leaving her life suddenly dark and polluted and dirty and wrong.

She thinks of Luke and wishes she had her phone with her. She feels a profound need to hear his voice, to know that he's OK. Wonderful, beautiful, innocent Luke, the diamond in her life. And how can she allow herself to even think that her relationship with Cliff has been a mistake when something so beautiful has come from it? But they say that coal and diamonds are the same thing, don't they? She read that somewhere – that diamonds are just coal compressed even more tightly.

Hearing the crack of a twig, Hannah turns to see James coming along the forest path towards her.

"You're here," he says breathlessly as he reaches her.

"Yes, I'm here," she replies, wiping her eyes on the sleeve of her T-shirt. She's pretty certain that she must look shocking.

"I was worried about you," James says, swiping at the sweat trickling down his own brow. "I didn't know where you were."

"I needed to get away," Hannah replies. "I needed to be alone."

"Should I go?" James asks. "Do you want me to leave you in peace?"

Hannah swallows and turns away. She looks out at the grey skyline beyond the trees and feels ashamed because, even now what she wants, she realises, is for James to hold her. She has just seen him pin her husband to the floor and humiliate him, and still all she wants is a kiss that might prove to her that something important she once felt was real.

At the lack of reply, James sighs and sits down next to her. He lays one arm loosely across her shoulders.

"Did you hurt him?" Hannah asks.

"Cliff?"

"Yes, Cliff."

"No," James says. "No, I didn't hurt him. I gave him a slap because . . ." He shrugs.

"Because?"

"He punched me, Hannah," James says. "He gave me a fuckin' nose-bleed."

Hannah looks up and sees from the drying blood around James' nostrils that this is true. She reaches out to touch it, but then stops herself in time. "I'm sorry," she says.

"He told me not to come," James says. "I guess I should have listened."

Hannah nods.

"But then I wouldn't have seen you, would I?" James says. "I wouldn't have seen my Hannah."

"Is it true?" Hannah asks. "Is it true what Cliff says?"

"That I'm an asshole?" James says. "Probably."

"No, what he said about me. That it was all just to prove a point."

"Of course not," James says.

"It's OK," Hannah tells him. "If that's it, it's OK."

It's OK, but it would break my heart, she thinks.

"I can see how competitive you are," she continues. "But if that's all it ever was, then I'd rather know. I need to know now. It's time."

James takes a deep breath. "What can I say?" he says. "I fell in love with you, Hannah. I fell in love with you the first time we met."

"The second time," Hannah says. "The first time we met you were too drunk to even know who I was."

James shakes his head. "Nope," he says. "Nope, it was the first time, in the pub. I remember it like it was yesterday."

"Really?"

James nods and squeezes her shoulder. "Why do you think I went off and hid at the bar?" he asks. "Why do you think I never came to visit?"

"I didn't realise. I just thought . . . I don't know what I thought really."

"And then, when I came down from Edinburgh . . . God. Do you remember, you sat in the car with me?"

"I do."

"I wanted to drive away there and then, but . . ." Something about Hannah's expression makes him pause. "What is it?" he asks.

"You just said he *warned* you not to come," Hannah says.

"I'm sorry?"

"You said Cliff warned you not to come and you should have listened to him."

"Ah," James says, pulling a face.

"*When* did he warn you?"

"I'm not supposed to . . ." James says.

"Not supposed to what?"

"I'm not supposed to tell you. Cliff made me promise when I arrived."

"You're not making any sense to me, James," Hannah says.

"I don't suppose it makes any difference now," James says. "You might as well know."

"OK. Know what?"

"I wrote to say I was coming," James says.

"You did?"

James nods and licks his lips. "And Cliff emailed me to tell me not to come."

"So he knew you were coming?"

"Uh-huh. Well, to England. Not here, obviously."

"But he knew the dates?" Hannah asks.

"Yes."

"Cliff knew the dates you were coming to England?" Hannah says again.

"Yes," James says again. "Yes, I sent him my flight details."

"Which, of course, is why we're here," Hannah says. James frowns, so she expounds, "Oh, Cliff didn't want to come to France, that's all. But he suddenly changed his mind. And he suddenly wanted to come for two weeks, not one."

"Right," James says. "Well, that figures, I guess."

"God, so you were in contact with him and he didn't tell me. That's unbelievable."

"The thing is, Hannah . . ." James says.

"Yes?"

"I wrote quite a lot, actually."

"You wrote *a lot*?"

"Well, maybe not *a lot*. But I wrote quite a few times, yeah. And I sent a card most Christmases."

"You wrote to us every Christmas?"

"To *you*. I sent you a card most years. You told me you loved Christmas. Do you remember?"

Hannah shakes her head. "I don't remember. I do love Christmas, but I don't remember telling you."

"Well, you did. So I wrote most years."

"And Cliff, what? He stole them?"

"Yes."

"Maybe they got lost. Maybe the address . . ."

"No, he told me, Hannah. He told me he took them."

"He *stole* my letters."

"Yes. He made me promise not to tell you. He said it might upset you. But . . ."

"Upset me?"

"Yes."

"Jesus." Hannah closes her eyes and strokes her eyelids as she rewrites yet another aspect of the last fifteen years. "Did he read them, then?"

James shrugs. "I think so," he says.

"So what did they say?"

"It's kind of embarrassing really," James says.

"Tell me what they said."

"That I missed you. That I loved you. That I couldn't forget you. Stuff like that."

"God," Hannah says.

"I know. I'm sorry. I didn't think he was reading them. I thought you were."

"No wonder he's jealous."

"I wrote other shit too."

"Other shit?"

"You know. About my travels. Where I was at. What I was doing."

"Right."

"And it was more of that as time went on, of course."

"Of course."

"Once I met Judy, obviously I didn't . . . I mean, I wrote more ordinary stuff. I wrote about life on the farm, and about little Hannah. I wrote to tell you about . . ." James clears his throat. "About the accident as well. I really thought you'd reply then. I could have done with a reply back then."

"Hannah?" she repeats, a fresh bout of tears already welling up. "Did you say little Hannah?"

"Yes," James says, his own voice quivering and his eyes glistening. "Yes, I named her after you."

James turns sideways on the log, and the sadness in his eyes makes Hannah melt into fresh tears. He hugs her, and after a few minutes, her sobs fade and she dries her eyes on her sleeve again and stands. "Let's walk for a bit," she says.

They head, in silence, deeper into the forest, and as they do so, the pines become taller and taller, the trunks ever more massive, the air quieter, stiller.

"I love pine trees," Hannah says for no reason other than it feels good to say one normal sentence today.

"Yes," James agrees. "It's always so quiet. Dead almost."

"It is."

"So what happens now, do you think?" James asks.

"I don't know," Hannah says, then after a few seconds silence, she adds, "But I suppose you need to leave. And I need to work out if I can forgive Cliff."

"Forgive him for . . . ?"

"Well, he lied to me about so many things," Hannah says. "He said you were dead. He stole my post. I can still barely believe that. I wonder if he kept them all."

"But you still love him despite it all?"

Hannah can't answer that now. She's not sure right now if she ever loved Cliff, but she's also unsure of her judgement. In the end, she just shrugs and says, "Love . . ."

They walk on a little farther, startling a bird, which screeches in turn startling *them*. As the path narrows, James' hand bumps against hers. The contact is so light, so vague, that it could almost go unnoticed, but it happens again and again, and each time Hannah senses the hairs on the back of her neck prickling. The fifth time, she stops walking and turns to face James. "What are you doing, James?" she asks, her voice flat, almost robotic with constrained emotion.

"I still want to kiss you," he says. "Isn't that crazy?"

Hannah sighs deeply and shakes her head. "No," she says. "That's not crazy at all."

He's going to leave soon, she thinks. *He's going to leave, and I'll*

284

probably never see him again before I die. She glances left and right and leans in.

James half-smiles and then their lips touch and his arms come up to hold her. Momentarily, everything is all right with the world. Just for an instant, she is home.

They kiss delicately and then Hannah opens her lips and lets James' tongue slip inside, exploring her mouth. They start to kiss more passionately, start to grind their bodies together. She becomes aware of James' hands slipping inside her T-shirt, becomes aware of the roughness of his fingers against her shoulders. And then suddenly, James pulls away and rests his head instead on her shoulder. "God, I want you so bad, Hannah," he whispers.

"I know," she replies – her own legs have gone so weak she's struggling to stand.

"Is it too late for us?" James asks, and Hannah, in spite of herself, bursts out laughing.

"Of course it's too late for us," she says. "I've spent half my life with your brother. We have a child."

She senses James' body shudder against her strangely and then he says, "Spend the other half with me, Hannah," and she realises that he is trying not to cry. "Tell that stupid brother of mine to get lost," James says, "and come with me."

Hannah laughs again. She can't help herself. The absurdity of this time-warp they are stuck in strikes her as too ridiculous for words. "I think we both know that's not going to happen, James," she says. "If it was going to happen, it would have happened fifteen years ago."

"But I want you so bad," James says, pulling her tight again, so tight that she's aware of his erection pressing against her through their clothes. She wonders if, just for half an hour, she can be someone else. She wonders if, just here, just now, just for a bit, she can do what Tristan or Jill, or half of the other people on planet Earth would probably do.

She's considering both this and the folly of even considering this when a large, aged Labrador pads up to their feet and starts nuzzling their legs. James breaks free and crouches down. "Hello buddy," he says. "Where have you come from?" and Hannah hates that dog, could kill that dog for destroying the moment.

A few seconds later, the owner, a short man with a vast pot-belly comes into view. "Milou !" he shouts. "Ici !"

Hannah and James smile falsely and nod at the man, and, as he passes, he apologises for the dog. "Désolé," he says, "mais il aime tout le monde."

"He gave me a funny look," Hannah says, once the man has waddled on. "Do I look shocking?"

"Your eye-stuff has gone a bit crazy," James says.

"Panda eyes?"

James nods, then leans in to kiss Hannah again, but this time she turns her head. That moment has passed.

"Hannah?" James asks.

"I think that's enough for now," she says, pushing him gently way.

"For now?" James says.

"For forever probably," Hannah tells him.

"*Probably*," James repeats.

"Just stop it," Hannah says.

"Sorry."

"I think we should go back now," she tells him, suddenly business-like. "And I think you should leave."

James nods sadly and blinks acquiescence.

"This is enough," she says. "This is just . . . *enough*."

"Yes," he says, nodding again.

As they turn to walk back to the house, James reaches for her hand, and she lets him take it.

"We can keep in touch this time though, right?" James says, squeezing her fingers.

"I guess," Hannah says.

"And if, you know . . ." James says, "things change for you."

"Yes," Hannah says. "Yes, if anything changes . . ."

"Do you have email?" James asks.

"I use Cliff's, so, no, not really," Hannah replies.

"Maybe you could get your own?"

"Yes," Hannah says with a sigh. "Yes, that would seem like a good idea, all things considered."

Once they hit the road, they separate and Hannah pauses and asks, "Do you have your keys with you? The car keys?"

"Sure," James says. "But I have to get my stuff from the house."

"Right," Hannah says. "Maybe I can go and get that for you. It might be better if you don't come inside. Just in case it all kicks off again."

"Sure," James says. "I can just wait in the car, if you want. If you think you'll be all right."

"I'll be all right as long as you don't come in," she says, then, swiping at her cheek, "Is it raining?"

"Yes, I just got hit too," James says.

Another drop hits Hannah's forehead and then another her leg, and then suddenly they are running towards the house through a deluge.

When they reach the property they open the gates and

James climbs into his car, calling to Hannah to get in as well.

She jumps into the passenger seat and pulls the door closed behind her. She is already drenched. The rain drumming on the roof gives her a sense of déjà vu that is so powerful it makes her come up in goosebumps.

"God," James says. "Do you remember?"

Hannah nods. "That's exactly what I was just thinking."

"I should have driven away there and then," James says. "I wanted to, you know."

"Yes, you said. But it was a whole lifetime ago now."

"Well, half a lifetime ago," James says.

"Yes. So. I'll go get your bag from your room."

"My wallet's on the side too," James says. "Are you sure you don't want me to . . ."

"Really, no," Hannah insists.

"And you'll be OK. He won't . . . you know . . ." Hannah creases her brow, so James explains, "He was holding you before. He seemed pretty aggressive. Will you be OK?"

"Of course," Hannah says. "He's my husband, James. He's not going to *hurt* me."

"Right. So, my wallet, bag, the phone charger is plugged in next to the bed. My bathroom bag – the grey one. I think that's about it."

"I'll scan around for anything else," Hannah says. "Where will you go?"

James shrugs. "It's getting late," he says. "And this is hardly ideal . . ." he nods at the water cascading down the windscreen.

"There's a bar-hotel place at the end of the road," Hannah tells him. "We went there for drinks the other night."

"This road?"

"Yes. It's half a mile after that bend. Just straight down. You can't miss it."

"I'll go there then," James says, "then head down to the coast tomorrow morning for a few days. My flight back's not until Saturday."

"Right," Hannah says. "So, wish me luck."

"Yes, good luck," James says. "And if you need anything, just shout or something."

"I'll be fine."

She climbs from the car and runs to the house. The raindrops are the biggest she has ever seen, each one almost a puddle of its own.

Inside the house is dark and, with the exception of the white noise of the rain falling outside, completely silent.

She checks the kitchen and then seeing that their own bedroom door is closed, she takes her shoes off and creeps to the bathroom, then to Aïsha's room, where she stuffs James' wallet, phone charger and toiletry bag into the rucksack before heading back to the patio.

Then she heaves the bag over one shoulder, and runs, still barefoot, back across the gravel to the car.

James has the hatchback open, and is standing beneath it, using it for shelter. He takes the bag from her and drops it in the boot.

"Your wallet's in there," Hannah says, aware that the rain is still lashing her legs. "Everything's in there, I think."

"If you find anything else, you know where I am," James says.

"Yes."

"And if you want to see me for any other reason," he says, looking searchingly into her eyes.

Hannah nods and swallows. "Yes," she says. "But I won't. You know I won't."

"If you change your mind . . ."

"Stop it, James. Just leave, will you?"

"Right. Oh! Here," James says, rifling in one of the smaller pockets of his rucksack and producing a business card. "It's a bit formal, but it has my email and stuff on it."

"Thanks," Hannah says, sliding the card into the damp pocket of her shorts. "I'll get an account set up and I'll send you a message – an email."

"Is that a promise?" James asks.

"It is," she says, then, "Right!"

They look into each other's eyes, and then both sigh simultaneously.

"Hannah," James starts, but she interrupts him.

"Don't," she says. "Please, just go, will you?"

James swallows with difficulty, then nods. "Fine," he says. "Right."

He opens his arms, embraces her in a final hug, and then closes the hatch and runs to the driver's door. "Go inside!" he shouts through a gap in the window. "You're soaked."

"I don't care!" Hannah says. "It's warm. It's like a warm shower."

James smiles sadly at her, shakes his head and starts the engine. And then with the tiniest of waves, he is gone.

Hannah closes the gates and leans on them to watch as the Clio shrinks in size, and then finally vanishes around the bend.

In those last twenty seconds before it disappears from view, she considers running after him, she considers screaming, and she considers sinking to her knees to writhe in the mud. But though they all seem like possibilities, she can't imagine herself doing any of them. She is, she realises, a prisoner of her own body, trapped by her genes, or her conditioning, or her upbringing, or expectation or whatever it is that makes Hannah, Hannah.

She's thirty-eight, and if at thirty-eight you're still not Jill and you're still not Tristan, then you might as well get used to it. Because ultimately, that is the greatest revelation of all. That even now, even after all the years of dreaming, of wanting, she is not Tristan, and she is not Jill, and she is not anyone who can recklessly seize unexpected opportunities. She is Hannah. She is Hannah Parker. And standing in the pouring rain once every ten years is about as crazy as it gets.

The water running down her neck makes her shiver. She glances down and sees that her T-shirt is drenched and transparent and is clinging to her breasts.

She looks left and right to check that no one has seen, and then turns and walks briskly back to the house.

THIRTY-NINE

Hannah dries herself in the bathroom. She washes her face and removes her blurred make-up. Not wanting to face Cliff yet, she changes into dry clothes from the laundry basket – the T-shirt and shorts she was wearing yesterday.

She heads through to the lounge, now dark as evening, and sits on the cold leather sofa and watches the rain plummeting from the overflowing guttering beyond the French windows.

For half an hour, she sits like this, and for half an hour she has no thoughts at all.

Eventually, she hears the bedroom door open, then Cliff's footsteps. She doesn't turn around, just continues to sit staring at the rain. She waits for him to speak.

"I take it you were with him," Cliff finally says, still standing behind her.

"Yes," Hannah says, but the word comes out as a croak, so she has to clear her throat and say it again. "Yes."

After a few seconds silence, Cliff asks, "So what are you going to do?"

Knowing that he can't see her face, she allows herself to frown deeply. The question makes no sense to her.

After a while, she hears Cliff head into the kitchen and pull a beer from the refrigerator. As he comes into view he cracks the ring-pull and takes a sip. He sits in the armchair and looks out at the garden. "Rain," he says.

"Yes," Hannah agrees.

"So what are you going to do?" Cliff asks again.

Hannah stares at him blankly. She still doesn't understand the question, but it seems somehow important not to reveal this.

"Are you going to leave me?" Cliff asks.

Still, she stares at him, transfixed. *So that's an option, is it?* she thinks. Presumably if Cliff thinks she might leave him then it's a possibility. "I can't believe how much you lied to me," she says, the first logical sentence that springs to mind.

"He told you then?"

Hannah nods. "Did you keep them?"

"The letters?"

Hannah nods again.

"No," Cliff says. "No, I didn't keep them."

"But you read them?"

"I'm sorry?"

"Did you read my letters, Cliff?"

Cliff shrugs. "He's my brother. I wanted to know he was OK despite everything."

Hannah nods. "I did too," she points out, simply.

Cliff fidgets in his seat.

"And he wasn't OK, was he?"

"Sometimes he was, and sometimes he wasn't."

"You had no right," Hannah tells him. "You had no right to steal my post."

Cliff shrugs. "He had no right to send you letters like that," he says.

"Maybe," Hannah says. "But all the same . . ."

She turns back to watch the rain falling, and sees, from the corner of her eye, that Cliff is doing the same.

"So are you going to leave me?" he asks again. "Are you leaving me for James?"

It strikes Hannah, that every time he says it, it becomes a little more real. That every time he repeats it, the option becomes a little more plausible. She expected him to apologise. She expected him to fight for her. She expected to have no option but to patch things up and carry on, because that, in life, is what generally seems to happen. But instead, he seems almost to be willing her to go. The conversation feels unreal, somehow. Like a bad script from a dodgy TV drama.

"It's weird," Hannah says, "but you don't sound like you care."

Cliff's brow creases. He stands and crosses the room to join her on the sofa. "Of course I care," he says. "I just have this feeling that you want out."

Hannah stares at him beside her. There's something still wrong with the script, something false. But she can't put her finger on it. And she doesn't want him this close. She doesn't want him this close at all.

"Do *you* want out?" she asks, squinting at him as if attempting to peer into his soul. "Is that it?"

"Of course I don't," Cliff says. "We have a son together. I couldn't even imagine . . ."

Hannah nods, vaguely convinced by this.

But then Cliff adds, "But if you're not happy. If you need something that I can't give you . . ." And there it is again. That false note.

As displacement activity, because she simply doesn't know what to say next, and because his physical proximity is somehow embarrassing her, she heads to the bathroom.

She locks the door, lowers the seat, and sits and stares at the door. Beyond the tiny open window, the noise of the rain

294

falling into the pool is impressively loud. The temperature has plummeted since the rain began, and the air drifting from outside is almost cold now.

So, *does* she want something Cliff can't give her? It's almost as if she lacks the circuitry required to work out what she wants, what she needs – as if fifteen years of worrying about other people's needs, of looking after Jill and Luke and Cliff, fifteen years of trying to make sure that everyone else is OK has left her bereft of any sense of what she wants herself, what she herself needs.

And if she *did* want James, rather than Cliff, is that *really* an option? Jill seems to think it is. Tristan thinks so too. James says it is, and now, even Cliff apparently agrees, has virtually offered it up on a plate.

Beside her, on the sink, she sees Cliff's iPhone – forgotten in the bathroom.

She picks it up and plays with it absent-mindedly, but then she remembers Tristan's strange comment. "*Check his phone,*" he said.

She presses the on button and swipes at the screen to unlock it, but sees that, of course, it is protected with a pin code.

She sighs and stares at the screen. One-three-zero-nine, she types – Cliff's birthday. Wrong Password. Two-zero-one-zero – Luke's birthday. Wrong password. Zero-seven-one-two – *her* birthday. Wrong password.

She wonders if there's a limit to the number of attempts. She doesn't want the phone to get somehow stuck, she doesn't want to have to explain that.

And then, suddenly, she's sure she knows what the code is. Two-zero-two-four she types – Cliff's pin number for his Visa card. The phone unlocks with a click.

What to look for though?

She's no iPhone expert – she's not even much of a fan of technology in general, but she manages to find the recent calls list: Tristan, Jill, Aïsha, Luke, Dave (Cliff's business partner), Jenny (his aged secretary), Brian (squash), herself (wife). Nothing to see here.

Next she finds his email account, and decides that that's probably what Tristan meant – he probably knew about Cliff's emails to James. But the phone only holds a few days' messages. There's nothing revealing there either. She finds the contact list and scrolls through it. There are plenty of names she doesn't know there, but they're probably just clients. How would she know?

She sighs and clicks the phone off. She's just about to stand, when it crosses her mind that she can use the phone to call Tristan and ask him. She types in the pin code again and calls him, but it goes straight to voicemail. He's probably driving.

She ends the call and hits the home button. She is debating whether to phone Jill when a little yellow icon catches her eye. Grindr.

She frowns. Wasn't Grindr the gay dating app that Tristan was using the other day in the bar? She clicks on it and the screen fills with the same little thumbnail photos and the phone chirrups to signal that it has new messages. She glances nervously at the toilet door, then switches the phone to silent mode before, with a sick feeling in her stomach, continuing.

Messages are showing from three people. The first is a face-shot of Tristan. She clicks on it.

WILDEMAN: Cliff?
WILDEMAN: Cliff? Is that you?
WILDEMAN: WTF are you doing on Grindr?

She's not sure she understands entirely how the program works, but there don't appear to be any replies.

She returns to the main screen and clicks on the second icon, a balding guy with a full beard.

ACTIF83: SLT. A/P?

She has no idea what that means, but again, she can see no reply.

Finally she clicks on the third conversation. A photo of Jean-Jacques from the bar appears.

HOLIDAYGUY: You speak english?
MECDUSUD: Pics?
HOLIDAYGUY: Sorry, no pics.
MECDUSUD: Why?
HOLIDAYGUY: Married.
MECDUSUD: Tristan? Blageur!
HOLIDAYGUY: Not Tristan. Clive.
MECDUSUD: Sorry. Hello Clive.
HOLIDAYGUY: Hello.
MECDUSUD: Top or bottom?
HOLIDAYGUY: Both. Either. I'm free for one hour, now.
MECDUSUD: Send me a pic and we meet.

Hannah scrolls the screen up and then down, but no further messages appear.

"God," she murmurs. She feels numb.

Perhaps Cliff lent Tristan her phone, she reasons. She had taken Tristan's phone that day at the hospital, hadn't she? But no. That makes no sense. She returns to the previous dialogue. It is clearly Tristan talking to Cliff.

She feels shocked, yet strangely unsurprised, like when

Amy Winehouse died. Someone tells you Amy Winehouse is dead, and you're shocked, but part of you thinks, "Of course she is," as if you already knew. And that's how she feels now. Shocked, but somehow . . . A wave of nausea sweeps over her, so she puts the phone down on the edge of the sink and jumps up. She opens the lid to the toilet bowl and vomits, efficiently, into the pan.

After half an hour of staring at the bathroom tiles, Hannah washes her face, unlocks the door and steps outside.

"I was beginning to think you'd got lost in there," Cliff offers.

Hannah ignores his feeble attempt at humour, and saying, "Here!" she throws him the phone.

"Jesus! Careful!" Cliff exclaims as he scrambles to catch it. "It's made of glass. That cost five hundred pounds."

"Only, I don't care, Cliff," Hannah says, her voice as hard as marble.

"No? Oh, OK."

Hannah walks over to the French windows and looks outside. The rain has slowed now, but the sky is still a deep, devilish grey. "So is there something you want to tell me?" she asks.

"Erm, no," Cliff says. "No, I don't think so."

Hannah laughs bitterly. "Oh, I think there is," she says.

"To do with James?" Cliff asks. "To do with the letters?"

"I know about the letters," Hannah says. "I think we've covered that particular lie." She sounds harsh and bitchy, she knows that, but she can't seem to manage any other tone.

"It's only because I loved you," Cliff says. "Love you."

"What is it they call that?" Hannah asks, turning, briefly to look at him. "A Freudian slip, isn't it?"

"That's not what I mean," Cliff says. "That's not what it was."

"So is there something you want to tell me?" Hannah repeats, in exactly the same hard voice as before.

"No," Cliff says. "Unless, what, do you want me to tell you I lo—"

"Maybe holiday guy has something to tell me then," Hannah says, interrupting that particularly nauseating declaration.

"Holiday guy?"

"Yes, holiday guy," Hannah says.

"I'm sorry, Hannah, but I don't . . ."

"Stop bullshitting me," Hannah says, her voice rising almost to a shout. "I know, Cliff."

"You know what?"

"About Grindr."

Hannah looks back out of the window and waits for Cliff to reply.

When he fails to do so, she turns to look back at him.

He is sitting on the sofa staring at her. His face is pink and his eyes are wide and watery. He looks like a child caught out, a child on the verge of tears.

"So?" Hannah asks.

Cliff shrugs.

"Are you gay, Cliff?" she asks, as gently as she can manage, which sadly isn't very.

He matches her stare, then very slowly shakes his head. "I . . ." he says.

"Yes?"

"I just wanted to look," he says. "When Tristan said about it, I just wanted to look."

"Because?"

"Because . . . I don't know. I just wanted to look."

Hannah holds her hand out for the phone, and because Cliff thinks initially that she is going to delete the app and then, a second later, that she is going to smash the phone – either of which strike him as getting off lightly – he hands it over.

Instead, Hannah returns to the dialogue screen, and reads, "Top or bottom?"

"I'm sorry?"

"Are you top or bottom, Cliff? Or both perhaps. Both apparently."

"It doesn't mean anything," Cliff says.

"I'm free now for one hour," Hannah reads. "How about that, Cliff?" she asks, raising her eyebrows and performing a sharp perfunctory nod. "Doesn't that mean anything either?"

She tosses the phone back to him again, and he stares at the screen, strokes the side of it, and then switches it off. When he glances up at her, his expression is so wretched that she can't bear to look at him.

"When was that anyway?" she asks.

"When was what?"

"*When* were you free for an hour?"

"I wasn't really . . ." Cliff says.

"God, was it when I was at the hospital? Is that it?"

Cliff stands, slips the phone into his pocket, then moves towards her. "Hannah," he says.

"Just . . . just stay away from me, Cliff," she says, slapping away his hand, which was reaching out to touch her arm. "You disgust me."

She pushes past him and walks to the kitchen, but when she gets there, she has no idea why. It feels no better here than the lounge, in fact it's worse. It's a room with only one exit, and Cliff has followed her and is now standing blocking the doorway.

"Hannah, I'm not, you know . . ." he says. "You're getting this all out of proportion."

"You're not what, Cliff?" she asks, turning to look out of the window again, anything to avoid his gaze.

"I'm not, you know, like Tristan," he says.

"You're not like Tristan."

"No. No it was just once or twice. When I was younger. At the beginning. But it all stopped. I promise, it all stopped when we got married."

Hannah spins back to face him now. "When we got married?" she cries.

"Before."

"You were gay, even back then?"

"No," Cliff says, his voice pleading now. "No I stopped, like I said. I'm not gay."

"But you were with other . . . you were with men . . . when we were together?"

"It was when we split up, Hannah. And it never happened again."

"Until now."

"But I didn't do anything," Cliff says. "It was just fantasy. I gave it all up to be with you."

Hannah buries her face in her hands for a moment, takes a deep breath, then lowers them again. "Well, I had fantasies too, Cliff," she says. "And I gave them all up for you. Actually, I didn't even give them up. You took them from me."

Cliff launches himself towards her. "You're getting this all out of proportion, Han'," he says.

"No! Stay away from me, Cliff," Hannah shrieks, raising

her hand. She feels sick. She's scared she's going to vomit again. "You revolt me, Cliff. You disgust me. Just stay away."

As she pushes past him, he pleads, "Don't say that, Hannah. It's not, I'm not . . . it's not like you think. I'm not *gay*."

She pauses and looks back at him. "I don't care what you are, Cliff," she says.

"What do you mean, you don't care?"

"This isn't about you being gay. It's not about that at all. It's about you being a bloody liar. It's about you being a compulsive liar."

She pushes into Aïsha's bedroom and locks the door behind her, then stands with her back against the door, breathing heavily.

After a minute, she hears the front door slam, and then, her strength suddenly exhausted, she slides down to her knees and begins to sob.

Once her tears have subsided, Hannah climbs onto the bed and pulls a pillow to her stomach. Only once she is hugging it does she remember that James has been sleeping in this bed, that James has been using this pillow. She sniffs it but can't find any detectable scent.

For hours, she lies on her side like this, simply staring out of the window, watching as the rain fades, then stops, and then, eventually, the first tentative glimpses of sun appear.

As the weather starts to clear, so do her thoughts. The problem is that *of course* Cliff is gay. Well, perhaps he's not gay per se, perhaps he's bisexual or metrosexual or whatever they call it. He did, after all, manage fifteen years of fairly regular performances with her, and that's not, from what she has been told, something that guys like Tristan can manage.

But her biggest shock today is her lack of surprise at the concept that Cliff isn't entirely heterosexual either. She has never once, not in fifteen years, had that thought before, but now that it's out there, well, *of course!* She has never caught Cliff looking at other women, not once surprised him a little drunk in a party flirting with another woman. One of his greatest qualities has been that she has never once felt jealous or threatened.

But she *has* seen him look at men. She always assumed that these discreet glances were him eyeing up rivals, but as she thinks about it now, she can see him peering over his book at the pool guy or hiding behind the book as he pretends not to listen to Tristan's latest conquests, excusing himself from the table whenever the discussion got too intimate, or worse, involved him in some way. That one can spend half a lifetime trying to do the right thing only to find out that it was entirely the wrong thing for everyone concerned is more irony than she can bear.

Then again, if what Cliff has wanted all of these years is a guy, then why would he have gone to such absurd lengths to keep her away from James?

As the sun regains its full force outside, even this starts to make sense to her. She feels strangely centred, unusually calm, and, a unique experience, suddenly wise. For something about her life, something that has forever escaped her is starting to make sense. From the desire she felt for James to the repetitive and increasingly rare sex she has had with Cliff; from their stiflingly "normal" existence – a perfect cover if ever there was one – to Cliff's exaggerated insensitivity towards her moods, towards anything remotely feminine whether it be film, or book, or television . . . Even his dislike for anything gay-themed, his discomfort around Tristan and, yes, even his desperation to beat his brother for her affections, it has all been cover. It has all been a textbook performance of heterosexuality.

She's just toying with the idea of getting up again, when Cliff knocks on the door.

"Hannah? It's Jill for you. On the phone," he calls.

She climbs from the bed, and opens the door just enough to take the phone from him, then closes and locks it again.

"Jill?"

"Hi. I've been worried sick about you. Is everything OK?"

"Yes," Hannah says. "It's all been pretty dramatic but everything's fine now. How's Luke?"

"He's fine. We just had pizza, and you know how Luke likes pizza. Do you want to talk to him?"

"In a minute, Jill. I need to ask you something first."

"Fire away."

"I need to ask you a huge favour."

"Right."

"Can you look after the kids for a while?"

"Sure. For how long?"

"Until the end of the holiday maybe."

"What? Till next Saturday?!"

"Yes."

There's a pause, during which Hannah hears Jill take a sharp intake of breath. "I don't know, Han'," she says. "They're quite a handful, and what if I . . ."

"Jill!" Hannah interrupts. "How many times have I saved your bacon?"

"I know," Jill says. "It's just . . ."

"Jill! How many times?"

304

"You're right. It's just that . . ."

"And how often have I asked you for a favour? Seriously. How often?"

"Virtually never, I guess."

"So just do this for me, will you?"

Jill tuts. "Where are you going anyway?"

"I don't know. But I need some time alone. If I stay here, I swear I'll explode."

"Are you going away with . . ."

"Not in front of Luke, Jill."

"Sorry. Are you going away with *you know who*? Is he still there?"

"No, he's gone."

"But what if I want to spend some time with Pascal?" Jill says.

"He's there with you now, isn't he?"

"Well, yes, but . . ."

"So."

"Can we come back to the villa tomorrow, or do you want us to stay away?"

"No, you can come back. Cliff's here."

"But that's going to be awkward, isn't it?"

"Not really. You can leave the kids with him while you go off and do whatever you do with Pascal."

"I guess," Jill says. "So you're not going away with James?"

"Jill, not in front of the kids, for God's sake."

"Oops. Sorry. But are you?"

"I have no idea to be honest."

"But you might be."

"Like I said, I have no idea. But I'll phone you tomorrow, OK?"

"OK, I guess. Shall I put Luke on?"

"Sure."

"Luke? It's your Mum . . ."

"Mum?"

"Hi, sweetie, are you OK?"

"Fine. We had pizza. And tomorrow we're going swimming in the sea."

"Good. Well, just be careful, OK?"

"The hotel's all blue."

"Right."

"Are you OK, Mum?"

"Yes, of course I am."

"You're not still arguing with Dad then?"

"No. That's all dealt with now, just like you and Aïsha."

"We're still arguing a bit."

"That's fine too. Just make sure it doesn't go on too long."

"OK."

"When you get back tomorrow, I won't be there, but Dad will."

"OK."

"I'm going to see some tourist things before we go home. Boring things you wouldn't like."

"OK."

"But I'll be back in a few days, OK?"

"Sure."

"Night, Luke."

"Night, Mum."

The conversation over, Hannah sits and stares at the phone. She thinks about Luke, wonders what will happen to him, how he'll react if . . .

But then she stops herself. These what-if equations have kept her life static since adolescence. And if life proves one thing, it's that the best-laid plans don't necessarily lead to the best results. Luke will be fine. Whatever happens, she trusts herself to make sure of it.

She dashes to the bathroom and locks herself in. She showers and fixes her make-up – her eyes are still a bit red, but otherwise she looks OK – then nervously returns to their bedroom. Cliff, thankfully, is elsewhere.

She dresses in clean clothes, throws two further changes of clothes into her smallest bag along with her purse and her passport, then carries the bag out to the lounge.

"Here," she says, and when Cliff looks up she tosses him the phone.

"Jesus, don't do that!" Cliff protests, once he has caught the phone for the third time.

"OK, I won't," Hannah says with meaning.

Cliff notices her bag now. "What's in the bag?" he asks.

"Just some clothes. I'm leaving."

"You're leaving . . ." Cliff repeats.

Hannah dumps the bag on the sofa then crosses the room to her husband.

He stands to meet her, his expression a strange mixture of confusion and fear.

"I don't understand," he says.

Hannah takes his face between her hands and kisses him on the lips, then wraps her arms around him and hugs him tightly. "I love you, Cliff, I do," she says before releasing him. "But life's too short for this. I only just worked that out, but life really is too short for this."

"For what?"

"For all this . . ." Hannah says, gesturing vaguely. "For all this mucking around."

She sighs deeply, then squeezes his arms and releases him. She returns to the sofa and hikes the bag over her shoulder.

"I still don't get it," Cliff says. "Where are you going?"

"I'm off on my holidays," she says.

"Your holidays?"

"Yes, Cliff. For one week I'm going to do whatever the fuck I fancy. I can only suggest that you do the same."

As Hannah turns to the front door, Cliff says, "But I want . . . I mean, I don't want . . . Hannah!"

She pulls the door open and steps out onto the porch.

The storm clouds have moved to the east and the setting sun is streaming out from beneath the band of cloud, making every wet surface shine with its yellowy light. Steam is rising from the terracotta floor-tiles.

As she reaches the gate, Cliff calls out to her, and she pauses and looks back.

"I don't understand where you're going," Cliff says.

"It's OK, Cliff," Hannah tells him. "You don't need to."

"But you can't walk anywhere from here," Cliff says. "You're being stupid."

Hannah wrinkles her nose. "Nah," she says. "Nah, this isn't stupid. The last fifteen years have been stupid, but this isn't. This is fine."

"Well, wait till Jill gets back at least," Cliff says. "Wait until tomorrow, and they can drive you somewhere."

Hannah shakes her head. "Relax, Cliff. It's all going to be OK."

"But what am I going to do here on my own?" Cliff asks.

"I don't know. Do whatever you want to do. Call

Jean-Jacques on your Grindr thing. Knock yourself out. No one cares anymore."

"I'm not gay, Hannah," Cliff says. "I know you think I am, but I'm not."

"Then Jean-Jacques is perfect," she says. "He's not gay either. Enjoy."

And then she closes the gate behind her and starts to walk along the road, steam rising from the puddles around her.

She's imagining James' face when he sees her arrive in the auberge, and that image is, despite all of the trauma, making her smile. She doesn't know quite what will happen when she gets there, but she trusts that instinct will tell her, that instinct for once, unconstrained by conditioning, or genes, or circumstance, will tell her exactly what to do.

Because though she is still Hannah, she feels like an entirely different Hannah right now. She feels as free as the birds that are tweeting so crazily in the wet leaves of the trees; she feels light-footed and wise and centred and reborn.

Whatever happens next, it will be something new, something wonderful. She has, after all, a whole half-life ahead of her.

Find out what happens next in

OTHER HALVES

The hotly anticipated sequel to *The Half-Life of Hannah*
Read on for a sneak preview . . .

ONE

HANNAH

I was in the middle of a family holiday in France when I walked out on my marriage. Some would say that I could have chosen my moment better, but the appearance at our holiday villa of the man I had fallen in love with in my twenties – a man who unfortunately happened to be my fiancé's brother – not only provided the opportunity, but opened the floodgates on a tsunami of revelations that revealed my marriage to be built upon nothing more substantial than a sea of untruths.

My husband, Cliff, had been revealed as a compulsive liar – to keep us apart, he had told me that James had died, when in fact he had simply been living in Australia – and my feelings for James were rekindled with the same intensity as fifteen years earlier.

But though one could explain my walking out of that door in terms of these events – my attraction to James and my betrayal by Cliff – in hindsight, I think that would be somewhat missing the point.

What really happened that day was that my bubble of steely self-control burst. A muscle that I had been exercising, stretched to its limit in order to keep myself centred in the middle of my life, gave way. The desire to break free, to live something new, to change not this, not that, but *everything* about my life became, in an instant, irresistible.

Perhaps it *was* what people call a "midlife crisis". Some buy sports cars, others have affairs, and perhaps it was a similar thing going on here, only in my case, it didn't build slowly enough for me to identify small safety valves that might enable me to get by. In my case, the water suddenly boiled and blew the top right off the pressure cooker.

I blamed Cliff, of course, for making a lie of our marriage, and I thanked James for returning and providing a catalyst and a suitable destination, but the truth is, I think, that both were almost innocent bystanders in a much larger process grounded not in events but in some internal body-clock. I truly believe now that the explosion would have happened anyway; it was just a matter of time.

So, one minute I was sitting on the bed feeling trapped in my marriage and confused about my feelings, and the next I was walking away from the house with a bag over my shoulder – my husband protesting behind me.

I don't know what Cliff was thinking as he watched me walk away, but I expect he thought I had gone mad. Perhaps I had, a little.

As Cliff didn't know that James was staying in the little auberge down the road, it certainly must have seemed crazy of me to head off on foot without any apparent destination.

When I got to the auberge, I asked Jean-Jacques, the barman, if he could put me through to James Parker's room.

"Il est parti," he said, which I somehow managed to understand: James had already left.

I surprised myself by thinking, *"Oh, OK then."*

One part of me watched the other react calmly, and was surprised at the lack of emotion. That was the moment I first suspected that this was bigger than Cliff or James – that this was about escape.

I ordered a glass of wine and, because all the seats outside were wet from the recent rainstorm, I sat in a window seat and watched steam rising from the ground. I thought, "*So, no James.*"

I felt unexpectedly calm and strangely wise. It was such an unusual feeling that I thought, as I sipped my wine, that I might be having some kind of nervous breakdown.

It was a surprise, and I wondered if all the melodrama hadn't perhaps been because I needed to be alone. As a wife and a mother, day after day, you forget to notice just how stifling, how suffocating motherhood and marriage can feel. After the drama of the day, a glass of wine, alone, in an empty bar felt like everything I had ever wanted. It crossed my mind that this might be a momentary need, that perhaps I would want, in an hour or so, to return to the villa to carry on as if nothing had happened.

Jean-Jacques brought me a plate of nibbles and said something that I didn't understand.

"I'm sorry," I reminded him. "I don't speak French."

"Ah . . ." he said. "Will you be stay 'ere? In the 'otel?"

Exactly as he said these words, the door to the hotel lobby opened, James reappeared, and my heart did a little somersault.

At first he didn't see me, and I didn't say a word – I just watched him and thought about my feelings.

Jean-Jacques returned to the desk and retrieved James' room key from a board. Jean-Jacques glanced in my direction and so James turned and saw me sitting with my bag and my glass of wine. He broke into a smile – a lopsided, confused smile – and said, "Hannah?" and my heart fluttered again. So my feelings for him were real, after all.

"Hannah!" he said again, distractedly taking the key that Jean-Jacques was proffering and crossing the room to where I sat. "What are you doing here?" he asked, crouching down beside me.

"I . . ." I stammered.

James raised his eyebrows expectantly.

"I think I've left him."

James nodded. "Wow," he said.

"I thought you'd gone. I thought I'd missed you."

"Nah, I just went to get some food. I didn't think you were coming."

"Yes," I replied. "I know."

"Are you . . . ?"

"Yes?"

"I don't know," James said, looking hopeful and scared at the same time. "Are you . . . here for me? Or just . . ."

"I'm not sure," I said, aware that I was sounding less enthusiastic than I intended. "I think so."

James nodded slowly. "D'you want me to go?"

I shook my head. "God, no!" I said. "I'm just . . . I feel a bit strange. It's all been a bit much."

James glanced at the barman, then back at me. "Do you want to go up to the room?" he asked.

I sipped my wine and stared outside for a moment before I replied, a little robotically, "No, actually, I think I'd like you to take me somewhere else."

James nodded thoughtfully.

"Can we do that? Can we go somewhere away from here?"

I asked, with increasing urgency. "Can we just get out of here and go stay somewhere else?" I suddenly needed to be as far from Cliff as possible.

James nodded. "Sure," he said, standing and offering me a hand. "Sure we can."

The hotel in Antibes was beautiful. It was set on the ramparts behind the old town, overlooking the sea.

We had barely spoken during the drive there, just sitting side by side in a weird, numbed silence, but James seemed OK about this. He seemed to understand that the day had been monumental, and that it was perhaps normal that this hadn't been a passionate falling into each other's arms.

The receptionist asked, "A twin room or a double?" and I replied without thinking, "A double." I think that was the moment both of us realised that this was really going to happen.

The receptionist took our names down and assumed that we were married. I was – stupidly – surprised to find that James and I shared the same surname. It hadn't crossed my mind that his being Cliff's brother would make hotel check-ins that much easier. And then we followed the porter up to the room.

Our room had the most stunning sea view, and the afternoon sun was low enough to be flooding through the windows.

While James tipped the porter, I opened the French doors, then stood on the tiny balcony and sniffed at the air. It seemed like the freshest, purest, most oxygenated air I had ever breathed.

James came and stood behind me, so close that I could feel his breath on my neck, and after a moment, I reached for his hands and pulled his arms around me.

He nuzzled my neck and my spine tingled and he said, "I'm so glad you're here."

And like some other, younger, more confident woman I barely remembered from way back, I said, "Yes, I know," and I turned to kiss him.

My newfound confidence lasted precisely until I had to undress in front of him; after all, it had been fifteen years since I had shown myself to anyone other than Cliff. This time around, I was closer to forty than twenty. Plus I had had a baby in the intervening years.

I had never been that sure how attractive Cliff had found me, and though I now realised that this sense of doubt might not have been entirely of my own making, I still felt incredibly uneasy about my body.

I broke free from James' embrace just long enough to pull the blinds and switch the lights off. Daylight was still filtering around the edges, but it was certainly an improvement. If James did notice my stretch marks or cellulite, it certainly didn't put him off his stride and that reassured me sufficiently that I was able to relax – just enough – to enjoy sleeping with him.

We stayed in that hotel for five nights, eating in little local seafood restaurants, wandering the streets of the old town and making love in the semi-shade of our room.

Though occasionally I would think of Cliff and my vision would tint red with rage or blue with guilt, I mainly managed to push every other aspect of my situation from my mind, and for five days and five nights, I let myself live in the moment. I felt a little crazy, but that craziness felt heavenly.

Jill, my sister, phoned a couple of times from the villa, and I reassured her that I was fine, thanked her for looking after my son, Luke, and headed her off when she tried to tell me anything about Cliff. Whatever it was, I didn't want to hear it. Whatever it was, I couldn't *bear* to hear it.

In Antibes, we visited the Picasso museum, which had beautiful floor tiles but little else of note – "It's a bit shit really, isn't it?" was James' comment – and another day we drove along the coast around the stunning shallows of Cap d'Antibes past the millionaires' residences, on to the golden beaches of Golfe-Juan and then Juan-les-Pins, and then Cannes, where, sitting on a sandy beach with James' arms around me, I wept for the mess that, unexpectedly, my life had become.

"It'll all be OK, Hannah," James said, but I didn't believe him. I couldn't see any way that could possibly be true.

Opposite the beach in Cannes we could see two small islands that looked gorgeous, so the next day we returned and took the small ferry out to the larger of them. Here, we wandered around the island, pausing to kiss, or picnic, or sit on the beach and stare back at the mainland, where everything seemed, from this calm haven, so unreasonably chaotic. Armed with pots of lavender honey bought from the monks, and over a rougher sea – the wind had got up – we travelled back, eating in a gorgeous but outrageously expensive restaurant in Le Suquet, before driving back to Antibes.

James was gorgeous throughout: a little abrupt at times, a little vulgar at others, but thoughtful and kind and, above all, undemanding. I think he understood that for our time together to be anything but horrific, reality had to be suspended. And that required avoiding whole areas of discussion, specifically anything pertaining to the future or the past.

At the end of the holiday, I bought a plane ticket so that I could fly home with James.

The horrid security personnel at the airport confiscated my pots of honey – apparently they were potentially explosive – and, ridiculously, I worried that, as they were the only thing I had bought with James to take home, this was somehow a bad omen.

It wasn't until we were actually seated side by side on that EasyJet flight that James asked me, rather nervously, "So what happens now?"

"I don't know," I told him. I purposely hadn't projected any further than passport control.

"Do you just go back to Cliff?" James asked.

I shook my head. "I don't think I can," I said.

"Do you like me?" he asked.

I laughed. "Can't you tell that?"

James nodded. "Well, I can hang around, or I can head back to Oz," he said, once the safety demonstrations were over.

I nodded. "Then hang around."

"Yes?"

"Definitely."

"Will you go back to the house?"

"Luke's there," I said, simply. "So, yes, initially at least . . . God, James. I don't know . . ."

"I could just find somewhere to stay then. Somewhere not too far from you. I can stay for a while. Ryan, my manager, is running the farm."

I covered my eyes with my palms, trying to think, then dropped them and said, "Yes. Then please stay."

"And then we just, what?" James asked. "See how things pan out?"

I nodded. "I don't know how else to play it," I said. "I'm sorry."

James nodded. "Suits me fine," he said. "I'm cool with that."

It's strange that those are the only words we exchanged on the subject – I think that it all seemed too vast to think about, the links between everything and everything else too criss-crossed and confusing even to be considered.

I had never been a big *let's-sit-and-talk-about-this* kind of person anyway, and I now realised that this part of my relationship with Cliff – the stilted communication that we had always experienced – had probably been more my doing than his, and would probably follow me wherever I went and whoever I was with.

On arriving home, I braced myself all the same for hysterical arguments with Cliff, but they didn't transpire either.

Cliff knew, through Jill, that I had spent the week with James, and by the time I got to the house he had moved to the spare room. It wasn't the first time in fifteen years that he had slept in the spare room, so Luke, though unusually surly, simply assumed, I think, that we were going through a rough patch.

For a few weeks we lived this strange, brittle silence of non-communication, gliding around each other without any unnecessary word being uttered. It was horrible, tense, unbearable, almost . . . but as the days went by it became more and more obvious, to me at least, that there was no going back.

Things with James, though unscheduled, continued in a relatively easy manner. Considering the horrifically stressful circumstances surrounding us, the fact that we never had a single argument struck me as astounding. He was undemanding and easy to get on with – a model partner. When I looked at him, I felt myself melt with desire, and whenever he was elsewhere, I missed him. My feelings for James were growing stronger by the day and my marriage to Cliff was revealed to be a sham. It was over, and I attempted to make Cliff realise this in the only way I knew how: through my actions.

OTHER HALVES

ebook (ISBN 978 1 84502 767 4)
available for download now

print (ISBN 978 1 84502 764 3)
available April 2014

Other fiction titles from Black & White Publishing

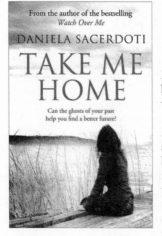

Take Me Home
Daniela Sacerdoti
RRP £7.99 – 978 1 84502 746 9

Heartbreaking and uplifting, *Take Me Home* is a beautiful story of love, loss and never forgetting who you really are.

Inary Monteith's life is at a crossroads. After a stolen night with her close friend Alex, she's just broken his heart by telling him it was all a terrible mistake. Then she has to rush home from London to the Scottish Highlands when her little sister's illness suddenly worsens – and in returning she must confront the painful memories she has been trying so hard to escape.

Back home, things become more complicated than she could ever have imagined. There's her sister's illness, her hostile brother, a smug ex she never wants to see again and her conflicted feelings about Alex in London and a handsome American she meets in Glen Avich. On top of that, she mysteriously loses her voice but regains a strange gift from her childhood – a sixth sense that runs in her family. And when a voice from the past keeps repeating, 'Take me home', she discovers a mystery that she knows she must unlock to set herself free.

Take Me Home is a beautiful story of love, loss, discovering one's true abilities and, above all, never forgetting who you really are.

www.blackandwhitepublishing.com

Watch Over Me
Daniela Sacerdoti
RRP £7.99 – 978 1 84502 528 1

Eilidh Lawson's life has hit crisis point. Years of failed fertility treatments, a cheating husband and an oppressive family have pushed her to the limit. Desperate for relief, Eilidh seeks solace in the only place she's ever felt at home – a small village in the Scottish Highlands. There, Eilidh slowly begins to mend her broken heart but soon learns she is not the only one in the village struggling to recover from a painful past.

Jamie McAnena, Eilidh's childhood friend, is trying to raise his daughter Maisie alone. After Maisie's mother left to pursue a career in London and Jamie's own mother, Elizabeth, passed away, he has resigned himself to being a family of two.

But sometimes there is more to a story than meets the eye. Despite their reluctance, curious circumstances keep bringing Jamie and Eilidh together. For even when it seems all is lost, help can come from the most surprising places.

An ethereal and beautifully written debut novel, *Watch Over Me* is a poignant story about letting go and moving on – with a little bit of help from beyond the grave.

'A fabulous book. A poignant and beautifully crafted story ... impossible to put down.'
NOVELICIOUS

WATCH OVER ME

When all seems lost, help can come from the most extraordinary places.

DANIELA SACERDOTI

www.blackandwhitepublishing.com

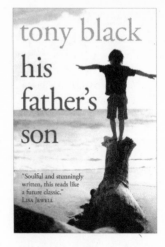

*"Soulful and stunningly
written, this reads like
a future classic."*
LISA JEWELL

His Father's Son
Tony Black
RRP £11.99 – 978 1 84502 636 3

Australia is the Lucky Country, and Joey Driscol
knows it. It's a far cry from his native Ireland, but
he believes this is the place he and his wife can
make a new life and forget the troubles of the past.
And for a time, they do just that. There's a good
life, a new house, regular work and, in time, they
welcome their new son Marti into the world.

But as the years pass, this new life thousands of
miles from the Old Country comes under threat.
Joey's wife has been struggling with demons of her
own, their marriage is on the rocks and suddenly,
Joey's wife disappears and takes Marti with her.
Joey is beside himself, with no clues about where
they are, with both his childhood sweetheart and
his son – his pride and joy – now missing.

Then, when Joey gets word that his wife and son
have returned to Ireland, he knows that he'll now
have to do the same if he ever wants to see his son
again. And he also knows that he'll finally have to
confront the ghosts of his past that he's been running from for years.

His Father's Son is a touching and beautiful story
of a family struggling to come to terms with their
past, their present and an uncertain future.

www.blackandwhitepublishing.com